A Comedy of HEIRS

A Novel by Bunkie Lynn

A Comedy of Heirs

Published by LadyBug Publishing LLC
235 East Main Street #162, Hendersonville TN 37075

Member, Publisher's Marketing Association

ISBN 0-9721301-0-1

Library of Congress Control Number: 2002094413

Printed in the United States of America

The events, places and characters within this novel are purely fictitious; any similarity to actual persons, occurrences or locations is strictly coincidental, not at all intentional, and has been incorrectly inferred by the reader. This novel is a product of my wild imagination, and no liability will be assumed regarding the misinterpretation of its contents, in part or in whole, as fact. Please try to enjoy it anyway. – Bunkie Lynn

Visit the author's website at www.bunkielynn.com

Printed in the United States by Morris Publishing
3212 East Highway 30
Kearney, NE 68847
1-800-650-7888

Acknowledgments

Many people have offered generous support with this effort, and I thank them. This novel represents the fulfillment of a dream that would not die, despite my best attempts.

Specifically, I am indebted to: Nancy Ayers, Carol & Tim Webster, Richard Swan, Paul Frank, Jimmy & Shannon Lane, Teresa Gravelle, Felicia Bennett, Lake & Kelly Lambert, Paul & Mary Schabacker, Betsy Pierpaoli, Bryan Elwood, Cornell denHertog, Kelley Neumann, and Amy Heiman for their friendship, encouragement, and laughter; Cindy Kershner and Jamie Clary for commiserating with me on the drudgery of a writer's life; my son for teaching me about unconditional love; Julie Edwards and Pat Belanger whose loving care of my son made it possible for me to physically put these words to paper; Anne Jordan and Klair Kimmey for their honesty and editing skills; Sam Stricklin and Judy Sinz for keeping me straight; Colonel Russ Baugh for his military expertise; my dad for "you could if you really wanted to,"; my mom for always being there; my brother and sister for "Mark Farkle & Starkle Fahrquart"; my late Uncle Phil who unflaggingly admonished me to be a writer; Frank & Ruth Wessel for their love; authors Cameron Michaels and Kyle Mooty for their time and patience; Andy Kimmey for finding the old photographs of the souls who remain nameless; and to everyone who ever uttered a kind word my way when they discovered I was writing a novel.

Most of all, I wish to thank my husband, Mike; without his complete, absolute confidence, respect and love, I could never have found the strength to finish this task, let alone begin.

Author's Note

As any good American Southerner, I am skeptical of things "Yankee." I'm fortunate and proud to know my Born-and-Bred-Yankee friends, particularly since they finally got smart and relocated. But for me Yankeeland is just too cold, crowded, noisy, dirty and the food's bland. Yankee Shepherd's Pie is great if you like your vegetables boiled until they're tasteless, but I never ate a Shepherd's Pie that would make you want to slap your granny the way a good bowl of gumbo or a cat-head biscuit will.

We Southerners are curious about our neighbors because ever since 1865 it's been mostly Yankees buying up all the good real estate and that would make anybody a little suspicious. Most Southerners will engage you in friendship whether you have a silver spoon in your mouth or if you were born in a rag heap under an old Chevy; you're just another one of God's creatures stifled by the heat and in need of a good cold drink.

But some people just can't get past their roots, and I'm not talking hair, here, but plain old-fashioned snobbery. Recently I learned that King Charlemagne had a girlfriend in every forest, so there are more than two million people in the world unaware that royal blood pumps through their veins. And a guy in England sells official titles like hotcakes. He tells his detractors, "*Hey*! How do you think the original snobs got their titles in the first place? They bought them, fair and square! They paid for the King's war or ignored his Moral Impropriety and *BAM*, Lord of the Big Hill! So shut up and save your money because you know you want one too!"

Which brings me to my point and like any Southerner worth his salt, I like to take my time telling a story so hush. Maybe one percent of the world's population is fully cognizant of who its umpteenth-great ancestor was; the rest of us just thank God we don't look like Great Aunt Sookie who bless her heart married a blind man. America was supposed to be the Land of the Free, where ancestral snobbery would be abolished; *oops*, I guess it didn't take.

Some Seriously Genuine English Snobs flocked to the American South to become Count of Chattanooga and Duke of the Mosquito-Filled Swamp; with them came a few humble folks who just wanted to leave church with their heads still attached. It took a hundred years to teach the first group how to cook, and a Civil War to bash the concept of slavery out of their brains. The second group just went haywire; maybe it was the heat, but they lost their humility, revised their priorities, and told the rest of us we're all gonna burn in hell, when in truth maybe they were just jealous that the first group grabbed all the best land.

So I guess it doesn't matter a hoot about our ancestry, or our beliefs, because under the right circumstances we can all act like two-year olds, myself included. Human nature was the research lab for this novel; pull up a chair, enjoy my work, and then look in the mirror.

This novel is dedicated to anyone
who has ever dreamed the dreams of a better life,
and to those who extend helping hands
to the dreamers in need. We are all God's children,
finding our way in the world, and how joyful our path
when it is sprinkled with friends.

Twenty years from now you will be more disappointed by the things that you didn't do than by the ones you did do. So throw off the bowlines. Sail away from the safe harbor. Catch the trade winds in your sails. Explore. Dream. Discover.

– Mark Twain

CHAPTER ONE – FOUNDING FATHERS

December 28, 1922;
A deserted limestone quarry outside Chestnut Ridge, Tennessee

The skinny child dawdled along the well-worn path. Her coat of heavy scarlet wool with its black rabbit fur collar contrasted with the steely grey of a winter sky. Fluffy red lambswool earmuffs made her thick, coal-black rag curls stand out nearly perpendicular to her head. She was tall; those who did not know better might expect her to be ten or twelve years of age, but she had only recently celebrated her seventh birthday.

The child stooped to pick up an arrowhead she spied among the wet brown leaves a few feet off the path. Granddaddy will really like this one, she decided, noting that it was practically perfect, no cracks, chips or surface scratches. He taught her to be selective, to keep only the arrowheads that were in the best condition. *These hills are fulla Injun stuff, girl, there's no need to bring home every dad-blamed one you see.* Granddaddy built her a display case of the finest burled maple; their arrowhead collection was quickly growing.

Soon as winter's over, girl, I'm gonna build us another cabinet, with two secret compartments, and a big carved Injun chief on the front. Granddaddy was busy in the winter, because he was the only doctor in town, practically in the whole county, unless you counted Daddy, too. He was a doctor but for some reason he didn't work as hard as Granddaddy did and he sure didn't make house calls to poor folks the way Granddaddy did. Granddaddy was 91 years old, in excellent health and he still tended to people at all hours of the day and night. He loved to joke about it with folks who chided him for working a schedule that would weaken a man half his age. *Slow down? I am slowed down! You shoulda seen me back in the War…why, one day at Shiloh, I sawed the arms and legs off a hunnert soldiers! No, I ain't of a mind to slow down…the good Lord saved my neck for a reason, an' I ain't gonna insult His decision-makin' by sittin' around the house!*

A hawk screeched and the girl stopped to watch it circle overhead. Below in the distance Granddaddy's loud voice filtered up through the woods to the path; he was tending to a family of coloreds that lived in a shanty built from the remains of the dilapidated quarry office. She figured she probably had about another half-hour to look for arrowheads; then Granddaddy would call for her and they would ride back to the clinic on his old horse, Jack. People made fun of the fact that every horse Granddaddy ever owned he called Jack; he just laughed and said it was easy to remember. *Three-fourths of my brain's plumb full of War memories that I ain't ever gonna unlock,* he would chuckle, *so I've only got one-fourth for rememberin' stuff like what to call my dad-blamed horse!*

The girl scanned the ground but found no more arrowheads. Ordinarily she would have poked around in the wet leaves, but it was Sunday, she was dressed in her finest and Mama would whip her if she soiled her new red mittens. She looked up and found that she was at the end of the path. Ten yards more and she would be at the edge of the huge quarry pit. She took a deep breath and looked around. Granddaddy said it was so cold he figured the quarry pond was frozen over, that it was probably solid ice. What would it look like, solid ice in the quarry pond? She wondered if it would be huge and glassy and bright white, like the drawings of the iceberg in Grandmama's *Tragedy of the Titanic* picture book. She gingerly dug one toe of her patent leather shoes into the sandy gravel and edged a little closer in the direction of the pond.

Don't you ever go to the edge of that pit, young lady, or I'll whip you with a cane until you have a striped back end! Young girls have no business digging in the dirt for filthy, heathen Indian charms and trinkets! Mama liked to put the Fear of God into her, according to Granddaddy. He said Mama's people all put way too much stock in the Fear of God and if they'd help folks more and talk about 'em less, there'd be nothing to fear in the first place. She glanced at a scrub cedar tree that grew in a lonesome twist halfway between her and the edge of the pit.

I could stand by that tree and probably see into the pit. It's not exactly the edge. Mama's not even here. She won't even know whether I see that ol' iceberg or not. The child inhaled and took a few steps, then froze. She lifted one woolly earmuff and listened. Someone was coming...on the path behind her. She knew it wasn't Granddaddy...she could still hear his gruff, loud voice clanging up from the scrap metal walls of the shanty. Her heart quickened; she ran back into the woods and hid behind a huge oak growing amidst a stand of pines. The footsteps grew louder; something about their rhythm wasn't right...there was no regular pattern. It was as if the person, if it was a person, had a bad leg, or was injured.

The child realized she was breathing too loudly and covered her mouth with a red-mittened hand. Granddaddy'd taught her all the tricks the Injuns used when they wanted to hide in the forest. One time Artemis Gooch teased her and said that the only reason Granddaddy knew all his Injun tricks was because he'd been run out of his doctor business in some place called Baltimore and lived like a savage with the Injuns. Artemis said the Injuns threw him out and then Grandaddy'd hid from the Yankees for six months until he hitched up with the Johnny Rebs. The child wasn't sure about that; everybody knew Artemis Gooch was a twelve-year old cuss and a liar to boot, but when she'd asked Mama, Mama whipped her. All she knew was that she loved Granddaddy so much it hurt and she knew he was the smartest man on earth, no matter what Artemis Gooch or anybody else had to say. *Watch and wait...listen and learn...keep still and silent.*

She heard a branch snap, then a sound like something being dragged across the gravelly ground, followed by a thud and a loud cackle of a man's laughter. She grasped her hands together tightly over her mouth. *Watch and wait...listen and learn...keep still and silent.* She blinked to see a short, stooped old man swaggering up the path in her direction. He carried a brown paper sack in the hip pocket of his ancient, muddy wool coat. He wore no hat or gloves, his ears and nose glared bright red from the cold and his head hung down in a slump. He took a step, then stopped, then wobbled and swung around. He rubbed his face with cracked, bleeding hands.

It's that old man...that bad old drunken man who lives in the boxcar! The child's eyes opened wide as the man's hand floundered and flapped with his coat pocket trying to locate the paper sack. He raised the sack to his mouth, took a deep swig and the child inhaled. *He's drinking Demon Alcohol on a Sunday!* She watched as the man wiped his mouth with the back of one raw, bloody hand. After three attempts he replaced the sack in the pocket of his tattered coat. He put a hand to his temple, then sat down in a wobbly heap on top of a large boulder beside the path. His back was to her, but she could see the clouds of his wheezy breath puffing into the air in front of his face.

The girl panicked; she was no more than fifteen feet from discovery and she knew her scarlet wool coat was not exactly the best Injun-in-the-Woods disguise. *Granddaddy says I'm the fastest runner in three counties...by the time that ol' bad drunk man hears me or sees me run, I can be halfway down the path and hollering so loud Granddaddy'll be sure to come for me.* She slowly removed her hands from her mouth and took three deep, measured breaths. But the old man shifted on his rock, turning to face her. He grinned sourly and his eyes rolled back and forth as he tried to focus. The child realized she had not yet been seen. The old man ran a hand through the few strands of reddish-grey hair that clung to his scalp. He looked up at the sky and pointed a shaky finger toward the clouds.

"What I gotta ask *you* is, what'd I ever do ta deserve this kinda life anyhow? I's a good soldier an' I ain't kilt no more Yankees than I had ta, an' Lord knows I hated ever' minute of it! I'm a good man, *hell,* I had me a good wife an' fam'ly. I worked hard, had me a good bizness...but fer nigh on sixty years now, ever' time I turn 'round...them Grahams er them Lees er them Festrunks is right there ta make sure I fall on my face! I'm the laughin' stock a Chestnut Ridge...I been a laughin' stock alla my life!"

The child's ears pricked at the mention of her family's name and she gasped. She replaced her hands over her mouth but it was too late. The drunken old man turned his head in her direction and glimpsed a scarlet vision behind the pine trees.

"HEY! YOU THERE! Well, now, ain't *you* a purty li'l gal! Mighty fancy red coat ya got...An' looky them earmuffs, an' them fancy mittens...why, I bet yer daddy's done spent haif his paycheck a'payin' fer them nice warm duds, huh? Com'ere, lemme take a good gander at ya, li'l gal! Ya got anythin' in that coat ta eat? Three days a whiskey drinkin'll make a man powerful hungry!"

The child froze in place. She glared at the old man with blazing eyes. She'd heard horrible stories about how he'd deserted his own family, how he did nothing but drink and steal, how he was the reason for every single failure or bad thing that happened in the whole town. He was not to be trusted, or talked to, ever.

"I know who *you* are, mister. You're that old drunk bad man who lives in the boxcar by the freight yard. My daddy says you and all your family are no-good whiskey-drinkin' fools and your whiskey drinkin' was the ruination of this quarry business. He says you almost took the whole town for a ride and thank God they stepped in when they did. And it's too bad my Granddaddy sewed you up, that's what my daddy says."

The old drunk pursed his lips and nodded. "Reckon I done heard alla that afore, young lady. Yer *granddaddy...whuh?* You *Doc's* li'l rascal? Well, ain't that a coincidence! Me sittin' here on this rock, mad at my Maker fer givin' me nothin' but seventy-five years a mis'ry an' the grandbaby a one a my sworn enemies standin' not more'n five yards away!"

The man pointed up at the sky, and laughed. "HEY! Ya see who's a'lecturin' me *now?* This here's the *third* gennyration, a' tellin' me I ain't nothin' but a loser! Well, li'l rascal, I tell you what...this here's my birthday today...that's right...I been on this hell-hole earth fer nigh on seventy-five years, an' I ain't had but a coupl'a good days the whole danged time! *First,* I's a bastard, livin' in the hills with a buncha low-'count, lazy Irishers. An' then my momma died of a cancer when I was off workin' ta pay fer her 'lixirs. My wife an' haif my children's been daid fer forty years...kilt in a fire set by them Grahams an' Lees an' Festrunks...an' the other haif a my brood's worse drunks than me, 'cept they's all young 'nuff they kin still find work ta pay fer their bottles...me, I gotta beg fer my liquor."

The drunk chuckled and slapped his thigh. His head bobbed as he swatted at the paper sack. The child swallowed and decided once more to run, but the old man raised his head and she stood transfixed. His eyes were glazed behind a thick veil of tears; salty trails traced his wind-burned cheeks. He slid off the rock onto the cold ground and let out a keening cry the likes of which the child had never heard. She shivered; the sound of Granddaddy's voice from the shanty below brought to mind the words he told her at least once a week. *Girl, there's a powerful heap o' sufferin' in this world. Ways I see it, you can pitch in an' do your part, or you can turn your back an' hope it ain't never gonna happen to you someday. Me, I pitch in, 'cause us doctors make us a solemn vow to help folks. But you ain't gotta make no promise in fronta some stiff-necked professors to help people, girl. You just do what's right in your heart, you'll be fine, you hear?*

The child shifted back and forth on her feet. *Mama says I can't talk to this bad man. But he looks real sick and if Granddaddy comes up here and finds out I didn't help him, he'll be mad at me...and I'd rather have a passel of whippin's from Mama than have Granddaddy mad at me for one minute.*

She took off a mitten and rooted around in her coat pocket. She pulled out a crisp linen handkerchief and inhaled; frozen air stung her nostrils. She stepped quietly out of her hiding place and walked across the path to the old man. He reeked of whiskey and sour sweat. The child had never seen so much dirt under an adult's fingernails and she noticed that the toes on his left foot poked through the top of his worn shoe. Without a sound she knelt down next to the drunk and handed him her handkerchief. He turned to her in confusion and after a few seconds gingerly took it. He mopped his eyes and the child watched him climb back onto the rock.

"Mister bad drunk man sir, I don't have anything to eat, but if I did, you could have it. I'm sorry you're so sad on your birthday. I just had a birthday ...I turned seven years old. And if I'd known I was gonna run into you today, I might have saved you a piece of my cake."

The old man smiled in spite of himself. "I reckon yer Doc's li'l rascal after all. Doc ain't got the same mean streak in him them others got...he's always tendin' me when things is real bad, 'course in secret, but never did charge me not one red nickel, neither. An' when my missus was hollerin' out in ter'ble agony from them burns after that fire, Doc give her somethin' ta ease her pain 'til she passed. But I still blame him an' them others fer alla them things done ta me my whole life...maybe he warn't the ring leader, an' maybe they done forced him inta cooperatin', but he shore didn't do nothin' ta stop 'em, no how."

The child stared at the old man as he sat on the rock. "Mister, did all those bad things happen to you because you drink the Demon Alcohol?"

The old drunk sighed. "Well, yer as *smart* as the Doc, I give ya that! Yeah, li'l gal, some a my troubles is owed ta my fondness fer whiskey. But it's all I ever knowed...my momma's people, they was all drunks. I had me my first taste a whiskey when I's nigh on six years old. But it ain't all whiskey, I figger. It's due ta what I done seen with my own eyes back in eighteen-an'-sixty-three...an' them Grahams an' Lees an' Festrunks ain't never lemme fergit it, neither, an' I reckon they won't never will 'til they see me daid. Lord knows they done tried ta kilt me off so many times…must be some kinda angels on my back watchin' over me's why I'm still walkin' 'round. I wish them angels'd done leave me be! But I tell ya true, I'm takin' matters inta my own hands, angels er not."

The child frowned. She couldn't imagine anybody drinking whiskey when they were six years old…she was seven years old and wouldn't even dream of it, because Mama and Daddy both would whip her into next week. She didn't see any angels standing on the old man's back, either.

"If somebody's trying to hurt you, mister, you're supposed to tell the sheriff, or a grown-up. That's what my Mama says."

The drunk smiled weakly and daubed his eyes. The child noticed her crisp linen handkerchief was now smeared with mud and blood from the old man's cracked hands. She could tell Mama she lost it, but either way she'd get a whipping.

"Young lady, it ain't workin' like that if yer from my side a the tracks. We gotta look out after ourseves."

The girl shook her head in confusion; why would Mama tell her to call the sheriff if it wasn't true. "Well, I better go now. Granddaddy's down there helping the coloreds…they have the influenza…and he'll be mad at me if I don't come back when I'm supposed to. 'Course, he's the one always tells me to help people. I sure wish I could help you, Mister. You don't look so good."

The old man blinked and stared solemnly at the child in the scarlet coat. She was the spitting image of Doc. He raised a finger.

"Yer a sweet gal. Thanks fer this here snot rag. I'm right sorry I done mussed it up. Looky here…ya really wanna help me? I'll make ya a deal…my time's 'bout over, rascal. In 'bout ten minutes, I'm gonna throw myself inta that quarry pit afore them angels can stop me, 'cause I figger seventy-five years a sufferin's 'nuff fer one man ta handle. But afore I do, it'd be nice ta tell my story ta somebody…somebody nice an' smart like you…somebody who'll listen up real close, get alla them partic'lars right. An' then that somebody's gotta go back, an' tell my story ta the whole town, so's alla them folks is hated me my whole life might reckon they made a bad mistake an' fergive me after I'm gone; ya know, maybe they's finally gonna think kindly on me when I'm daid. Can ya do that fer me, gal?"

The girl hesitated and looked over her shoulder. She could hear Granddaddy laughing below; when he laughed, it meant he was almost finished tending to folks, he was trying to put them in a good mood and make them feel better before it was time for him to leave them all alone with their misery. She bit her lip and looked at the man and saw another tear roll down his cheek.

"Well…I think Granddaddy's almost done down there…'course he always whistles for me when he's ready. I haven't heard a whistle yet, have you?"

The old man smiled and shook his head. "Nope, rascal, I ain't heard me no whistlin'…how 'bout you listen up while I talk real fast…an' when we commence ta hear some whistlin', we'll call it quits. Whaddya say?"

The child nodded and leaned against the rock, upwind of the odors emanating from the drunk. He looked up at the sky and began his tale as if he'd rehearsed it a hundred times.

"It's June eighteen-an'-sixty-three an' I were barely sixteen years old. My momma's up an' died, I ain't got no reason ta stay where I ain't wanted, so I hitch up ta kill Yankees an' Fed'rals. I folla Cap'n du Bois over haif a Virginya, then one day Cap'n says ta me I been transferred an' I gotta ride with Colonel Gray, he's some big-wig goin' inta Tennessee with some fellas is called the Tennessee Riders. I ain't never been ta Tennessee, but Cap'n says this Colonel Gray, he done asked fer me special an' I gotta go. I figgered Cap'n foun' out I been sneakin' his whiskey an' this Colonel Gray's gonna fix me good. But saints preserve us, like my daid momma used ta say, this Colonel Gray feller, he comes ta git me hissef an' durned if he don't hug me hard like a bear! Me, I ain't sayin' nuthin', I's nuthin' but a dirt private an' if'n some high-falutin' off'cer wants ta hug my neck and carry on, reckon I gotta let him. An' fer two days we ride tagether, jus' us two, ta meet up with them Tennessee Rider fellas. An' them whole two days, Colonel Gray he's sharin' his tent an' his whiskey an' his beans with me, an' he tells me ever'thang 'bout his whole life. I mean that ol' feller never stopped fer breath, he's such a talker! I figgered he musta been Cath'lic like me, maybe he needed a good confession er somethin' an' since there warn't no priests, I'd jus' haveta do."

The child shifted and stomped her feet; she was getting cold and she didn't want to listen to a long story about Catholics…Mama said Catholics were just shy of the devil himself. She wasn't exactly sure what a Catholic was, but if Mama didn't like them, they must be bad. The old man took a deep breath and continued.

"So's we meet up with these Rider fellas, they was twenty-seven of 'em, an' we commence ta killin' Yankees at Shiloh, then we ride break-neck all over Tennessee, killin' more Yankees. Somehow, 'bout November, we done ended up in Miss'ippi. An' the whole time, this here Colonel Gray, he treats me better'n anybody in the whole reg'ment. He calls fer me ever' night, has me set in his big ol' tent when the resta the boys is layin' on the cold groun'. He shares his supper with me, lets me take a pull offa his bottle now an' agin, he done give me a new blanket…well, it warn't new, but it was a danged sight newer than no blanket at all! An' course I still ain't figgered it out, but

I ain't so dumb ta look a gift horse in the mouth, so I ain't askin' no questions, jus' enjoyin' mysef best's I can."

The girl blinked and pursed her lips. The drunk ran a stiff hand over his wrinkled forehead.

"I don't gotta tell ya, the resta them boys is gittin' antsy, seein' as how I'm gittin' alla this right special favorin'. Partic'lar the Major an' the Lieuten't...ever' day they tell Sarge McArdle ta give me the worst jobs in the reg'ment on accounta they said I's the Ol' Man's fav'rite an' it warn't fair ta the resta the men. So's I'm in a fix, I am, but I ain't one ta stir up trouble, no sir, an' it jus' keeps on goin'. So one night, Ol' Colonel Gray, he starts askin' me 'bout my momma...an' he's knowin' stuff he ought notta know. Like her name's Maureen...an' she's Irish, from 'cross the sea, ya know, from Irish Land. An' she's got long, red hair...or she did, 'til she done got so sick an' it all turn white an' then it done fell plumb out."

The child touched a mittened hand to her curls; how could a person's hair all fall out? *A woman's hair is her crowning glory,* Mama says...how could a woman not have any hair? Maybe it had to do with being Catholic. The drunken man coughed several deep, tubercular-sounding coughs and wiped his mouth on the muddy handkerchief. He wheezed and looked at the child who stepped back a bit; Granddaddy warned her time and again about breathing other people's coughs.

"Our last two nights in Miss'ippi, we's camped out at some big farm b'longs ta some red-headed widda lady the Ol' Man's been a'knowin' a few years. This here widda lady give us a coupl'a dozen chickens, so we's eatin' pretty good, afore headin' back ta kill more Yankees in Tennessee, in Murfreesboro. The Ol' Man an' me's in his tent pickin' our teeth an' havin' us a chaw. An' the Ol' Man says ta me, he says, '*Boy...Miz Jameson...*that was the farm lady's name...*Miz Jameson, she's up in her boodwar waitin' on me. I been knowin' her a long, long time. She's the spittin' image a yer momma, an' when I'm with her, I dream I'm in Heaven, like when I's a young man in Nashville. We had a bond, yer momma an' me...we's gonna up an' marry, raise you right, but she done run off an' though I looked an' looked she warn't nowheres ta be found. An' the resta my life's been misery, pure an' simple. 'Til I found you.'* An' I reckanize what he's sayin'...see, I done knowed my momma got with child in Nashville an' that child, it was me! It ain't just he knows my momma...he's my *daddy*!"

The child's eyes widened like saucers. No grown-up had ever talked to her about such things; it was fascinating and she didn't want the old man to stop. "Then what, Mister? Then what happened?"

The old drunk slapped his knee. "Well, rascal, I'll tell ya. The Ol' Man, Colonel Gray, he whispers up real good an' says ta me he's got five thousand

Fed'ral gold pieces in his satchel with my name on 'em. He's givin' 'em ta me ta sorta make up fer lost time, git me a new start in life. He tells me he's aimin' ta git me discharged after we git back ta Tennessee an' if'n I'm innerested, then me an' him's gonna ride home ta his plantation in Virginya an' I'm a'goin' ta school, if I'm a mind to. Be a Virginya gennelman like him, I reckon. Live the life a Riley right there with my daddy. Eat me 'bout as much as I kin eat, ever' day, sleep in a real bed, too, all by my lonesome! But it warn't ta be."

The enthralled girl removed her earmuffs to take in every word. "Why not?"

"Ol' Man, he grabs his leather satchel fulla gold, an' thows it 'roun' his neck an' puts on his big wool coat. He tells me Major Graham's a been pokin' 'roun' in his desk an' he thinks he's done seen them Fed'ral coins. Now the Major, ever' man in the Reg'ment hated him, fer he warn't nothin' but a coward an' a liar an' a cheat, on 'count he was a Yankee from Ohio turned Reb, an' maybe even a spy. An' since it warn't usual fer no Confed'rate off'cer ta have him no Fed'ral coins, 'cept in a partic'lar circumstance like gittin' hardtack fer his starvin' men, the Ol' Man figgered the Major'd gonna turn him in, er worse, take them coins an' run off.

"So we traipse inta the big house, an' Colonel Gray, he tells me ta be guardin' the boodwar door whilst he goes in an' sees his lady friend, an' he takes them coins in with him. But soon there's a powerful heapa screamin' comin' outta that boodwar. Seems good Lieuten't Leigh had him a mind ta visit this lady too. Anyhow, I hear alla this screamin' an' carryin' on, an' I reckanize this red-headed widda's been tellin' the Lieuten't 'bout the Ol' Man's gold, an' he's aimin' ta take it fer hissef. But I cain't git in the boodwar seein's how the door's locked. So's I run outside an' high-tail it fer the winda, figgerin' ta climb up somehow an' git the Ol' Man, my daddy, some help. But soon's I put one foot up in the big oak tree outside next ta the house, here comes the Ol' Man a' flyin' out the winda. *SNAP*, he hits the groun', daid as a post. I'm hollerin' an' fellas is runnin' over hollerin', an' then I look up."

The child's eyes widened in horror and fascination. "Which bad man pushed him? Tell me, Mister! Who pushed your daddy out the window?"

"Lord, gal, I ain't sure! I seen the Lieuten't an' this red-haired widda woman a'laughin' an' dancin' 'roun' the room, wavin' the Ol' Man's satchel, an' I'm a'knowin' that gold is mine! Ol' Doc, he come over an' he tried ta help the Colonel, but it warn't enough, he was daid. An' then I seen the Major, now he's inside the boodwar, hollerin' at the Lieuten't an' the red-headed widda woman ta hand over them coins. Doc, he done closed the Colonel's eyes an' covered him up with his coat, an' he looks at me. *'You been in there, boy? What happened?'* an' I says, *'Yessir, Cap'n, Colonel was fixin' ta call on Miz Jameson but the Lieuten't done got there first, I reckon. An' they done shoved the Ol' Man out the winda.'* I ain't sayin' nothin' 'bout that gold until I's asked, I figgered. But Ol' Doc, he says, *'Son, 'smuch time as you been spendin' with the Ol' Man of late, I reckon you know 'bout them gold coins...an' I reckon them gold coins is what pushed the Ol' Man out the winda. Boy, you know why the Ol' Man had alla them Fed'ral gold coins?'"*

The drunk coughed and hacked again while the child fidgeted; her knees were numb with cold and she rubbed them with her mittened hands. She was impatient to hear more.

"So I says, *'Yessir, Cap'n, I do. Them gold coins is fer me! Colonel Gray jus' tole me he's my daddy, an' he done foun' me after all these years an' I'm goin' ta live with him in Virginya.'* Well, Ol' Doc, he sorta laughs quite-like an' shakes his head. *'Yer in shock, Private, so we'll jus' keep this ta ourseves, but it's a good story, I reckon.'* An' then he tells Sarge an' them other fellas ta git back ta their tents, 'course they don't. They was all cryin' an' carryin' on somethin' fierce. Them fellas loved the Ol' Man an' they was all knowin' now Major Graham was in charge, an' there'd be hell ta pay."

The child hugged herself, anxious for more details. "What happened to your poor daddy? Did you bury him? Did the sheriff come and get those bad men?"

"Hell, no...'scuse me, gal. All night long the Major an' the Lieuten't an' the widda woman an' Doc, they's holt up in the parlor a this big house, hollerin'. I sneak 'round the winda an' I hear Doc tell 'em what I done said, how that gold b'longs ta me. You ain't never heard such laughin' an' carryin' on. But they see me through the winda, an' the Major points a gun at my haid an' the Lieuten't runs out an' drags me inside. They slaps me 'roun' a bit, an' the Lieuten't tells me I's nothin' but an Irish bastard lucky ta be 'live. They say we's leavin' in the mornin' fer Tennessee an' the Major's gonna file an o-fishal report 'bout how the Colonel done stole a Fed'ral payroll. But I holler out, *'He ain't stoled no payroll, that war his gold, an' now it's mine 'cause he's my daddy an' you done murdered him an' yer gonna pay!'* Well, gal, that's all I 'member fer a whole week ...Lieuten't done smacked me hard an' Major made Doc pour somethin' pow'rful down my thoat. Sarge tole me later how they done tied me ta my horse. I woke up an' we's in Tennessee, right 'roun' here...they done buried the Ol' Man on Miz Jameson's farm. I didn't even git ta say goodbye ta my daddy, once't we'd done foun' each other."

"What if your daddy didn't get a good Christian burial? Mama says it doesn't count unless you get a good Christian burial."

The old man smiled sadly. "Rascal, I cain't say if he did er not. I like ta think he did, seein' as how all them other fellas loved him so, an' since ol Sarge he's a Cath'lic hissef, like me. I reckon he done 'leastways said a few 'our fathers.' All my life I was gonna git me a good horse an' go see his grave, put flowers on it, tend it up a bit, say a prayer fer his soul. But I ain't never had the chaince."

"Why didn't you call the sheriff? Those men did a bad thing!"

"Gal, they's ain't no sheriffs in war time. We's camped out in the late December cold, waitin' fer orders from Murfreesboro, but then we done heard the battle's over an' plumb near every Reb's dead. Yankees is ever'where. There's so much sufferin' ain't nobody cares 'bout tellin our li'l Reg'ment where ta go 'cept ta hide an' stay put. One night it was so cold we's all of us haif-froze an' I ask Major, *'Why cain't we all sleep inside a that there deserted mill over yonder, ta git outta the wind, 'bout ta cut us in haif like a blade.'*"

The drunk chuckled as the child rubbed her face with her hands. The tip of her nose was numb. "Well I got my answer...Major an' Lieuten't grab me an' stuff me inside that ol' mill. They tie me up tight an' tell me they's headin' fer Richmond ta file that o-fishal report. They say it's ever' man fer hissef, battle's done over, ever'body's free ta go. Well, I knowed fer sure they's a'wantin' me ta run off 'cause they're fixin' ta run off with my gold, I ain't that stupid. *'That money's mine,'* I say, *'an' you killed my daddy an' yer gonna pay!'* An' shore 'nuff Lieuten't gives me that money all right, he hits me on my noggin' with that sacka gold coins. My haid's all bleedin' an' them coins has done fall outta that satchel all over the floor a that mill. Then Doc breaks down the door an' points a gun at the Major an' Lieuten't. *'Leave that boy be an' git outta here afore I shoot you both daid,'* he says. *'Now pick up them coins an' pull yerseves tagether. They's a whole passel a folks headin' over here from 'cross that ridge a chestnut trees. Seems we done camped by a town them Yankees don't even know 'bout an' these folks is a'wantin' us ta git outta plain view seein' as how they still got food an' they ain't too inter'sted in givin' it up ta no Yankee pigs.'* Major an' Lieuten't unloose me an' tell me reckon I best keep my mouth shut or they'll shoot me fer dinner."

The old man stopped for a deep breath and flexed his frozen hands. The child looked up and noticed the sun breaking through the clouds. She edged over toward a patch of sunlight where it met the path next to the boulder. It was downwind of the old man but she was so frozen she didn't care. He continued his tale.

"We come outta that mill, the full moon was jus' a shinin' an' I ain't never seen so many purty girls an' women, ever' one of 'em's got smiles a mile wide. These folks is actin' like we's all out here havin' a haymowin' picnic, 'cept they's all whisperin' an' yellin' at us ta be quite...they's handin' out warm pies an' sausidge an' cider an' biscuits...an' this ol' feller, he's stompin' out our campfire. They's tellin' us ta hush up an' folla them if we want us some more food. Well, you ain't gotta tell no starvin' soldier twice't 'bout food. Our tents was struck an' we's high-tailin' it behin' these folks lickity-split. 'Bout three miles out we come to that ridge over yonder…then we scramble down a hole in the groun'…foun' ourseves in a cave! It's warm, they's a big fire blazin' an' food cookin'…these folks been livin' in a cave ta hide from the Yankees! Nex' mornin' they take us further inta that cave 'bout a haif -mile an' lorda mercy, we come out on the other side a that ridge starin' at a big dry-goods store an' a coupl'a empty buildin's an' some a the purtiest li'l houses you ever seen, all boarded up."

The child knitted her brow and pointed. "You mean that ridge over there? *Chestnut Ridge?* That's where you were? My Daddy says it ought not to be called Chestnut Ridge any more, 'cause the chestnut trees are dead from the blight. Hey, wait a minute…this is just like the story they tell at the Pageant. Mister, you mean you were there with the *Founding Fathers*? The soldiers that rescued all the poor orphans and widows from the Yankees? My Daddy says only the best families in town are Founding Fathers."

She stared skeptically at the old drunk; every year in school there was a Founding Fathers Pageant. And every year the children from the founding father families re-enacted how the brave Confederate soldiers swooped down out of the hills and rescued a handful of widows and orphans from the clutches of Yankee spies, repaired the grist mill, opened a bank, and reinstated commerce to a town they subsequently named Chestnut Ridge. The child knew better than to believe that this stinking old drunk was part of that beautiful tale of chivalry and happiness. The old man pursed his lips in sarcasm.

"You been listenin' ta them uppity Pageant women, ain't ya? It warn't none of it true, gal. Them Yankee maps was all wrong… they ain't had no idee 'bout that cave an' they was all too lazy ta climb up that ridge ta see what's on the other side! They whupped us Rebs at Murfreesboro, they'd done took Nashville, hell, they figgered they got all us Rebs in the area wrapped up nice an' tight, warn't no need ta go scoutin' 'roun' fer more. But these here folks, they ain't got no way a knowin' that, they done took all their vittles an' their firewood an' such an hid it in that big ol' cave. Made it 'pear like the whole town's deserted. No need of it, I reckon, since no Yankees ever found 'em anyhow but they's pretty smart ta think of it. Anyhow mosta these folks is widda women an' children…lotsa young girls too…the men is all dead from the War. Their grist mill's broke, they's 'bout outta flour an' ain't planted no crops fer fear the Yankees'd shoot 'em. But there warn't no heroes savin' nobody from no Yankees, nor any Yankee killin' neither, like I heard tell in that Pageant. I seen that durned Pageant once't, it give me the sour stomach!

"So anyhow, this one ol' man, Mister Gooch, he tells Major an' Lieuten't an' Doc they best stay put awhile, 'til the Yankees clear out. *'We could use us some help fixin' the grist mill,'* he says, *'We'll feed ya right good fer yer labor an' such. Ya'll kin hep us figger out a way ta git some gold an' buy us some more supplies...an' we gotta plant us some corn...you boys oughta think 'bout jus' stayin' put fer good...this here's a right purty li'l acre...any man's haif a mind, they's a prime spot fer a limestone quarry over yonder an' the Yankees is buyin' limestone block like there's no tomorra, fer cash money.'"*

The child pulled off her earmuffs and mittens and raised her face to the sun that now shone fully down around her. The warmth caressed her and she flexed her arms. The old man stood and stretched, rubbing his behind. He shifted in his coat then returned to his perch on the boulder. The child rolled her neck back and forth in the warm sun. She sighed.

"I guess your story's done, 'cause I know how it ends from here, my teacher told me at school. Those soldiers stayed and fixed the mill and started the bank with the money they stole from the Yankees, after they rescued all the poor widows and orphans from the clutches of death."

The old man shook his head in anger. "No, gal, it warn't like that! There warn't no clutches a death! There warn't no stolen Yankee money! That money was stole from *me*! It was the Colonel's gold, meant fer me, that's done stole an' used ta open a bank an' ever'thang else!"

The child tossed her head and her shiny black curls flew about. "You're lying, mister. I liked listenin' to your story and I thought maybe everybody had you pegged wrong, but you're lying, just like they say you do."

"No I ain't, gal. Listen up...all us Riders was fixin' our beds in that ol' cave, happy as larks ta be outta the wind an' bellies fulla hot food. But the Major an' Lieuten't an' Doc come over an' git me an' take me outside. *'Boy, here's the terms.' 'What terms,'* says I. *'The terms a our new bizness 'greement,'* says the Major. *'As a this moment, we's stayin' put. Ain't nobody, Fed'rals er Rebs knowed we's here an' it's gonna stay that way. We got us a rare opp'tun'ty...we got some gold an' we got some willin' patrons. We got a mill need's fixin' an' a quarry ta open an' we got widda women an' orphans ta care fer. But we gotta have resources...Boy...yer our bizness pardner...ya say this money's yers, well it's yer word 'gainst us. If we don't figger ya in on this deal, reckon you'll open yer mouth, so yer in fair an' square. Course we could shoot ya, but Doc ain't havin' none a that. So's we's all gonna haveta be together on this here deal. We gotta use some a this gold ta git staked so's we can make more. Now, see this big book? I'm a' writin' down yer name an' puttin' five thousand dollars aside it. Ever' one a us is gonna sign...this here's an eyeohyou...in a coupl'a years, Boy, when things is up ta snuff, you'll git all yer money back, an' you kin leave, fair an' square, if ya keep yer mouth shut. Now listen up, Boy...yer young an' strong...that quarry's yers fer the takin' if you've a mind ta open it an' make it a go. We's all pardners...we'll help ya, work tagether. But you gotta promise ta keep yer trap shut an' don't say nothin' 'bout the or'gin a this money or nothin' else done happened, you hear? First time ya open yer mouth, this eyeohyou's gonna burn fast an' we'll be tannin' yer sorry hide.'"*

The old man's voice had grown low and sinister. The child's eyes widened in fear.

"Mister…is your story almost over? Granddaddy's gonna be lookin' for me."

The old man smiled a bit and cocked an ear to the wind. "I ain't heard no whistlin', you?"

The child shook her head. Granddaddy was still talking down below; there must be complications, she figured. Complications happened a lot, according to Granddaddy.

"Well, then, let's keep a'goin'. I signed that eyeohyou with them others…the Major, the Lieuten't. Doc, he fin'lly signed it, but said he don't want no part of it. Hell, I ain't had no t'other chaince, did I? If'n I run, Yankees is gonna hang my sorry hide if the Major don't shoot me first. Ain't nobody gonna b'lieve no Irish bastard what cain't read er write, when his soopir'r off'cers is all a'tellin' their story an' it ain't the story I'm a tellin'. Nope, I figgered if Colonel Gray's givin' me that gold ta git me a new start in life, it don't make me no never mind if it's in Virginya on a plantation, er in Tennessee in a limestone quarry. An' fer a few years, ever' thang war sweet as pie. We done fixed the mill an' all them li'l houses, Major started a bank an' I worked like a dog openin' this here quarry. I's sellin' limestone block ta the Yankees like no tomorra. I married me the purtiest li'l gal…Fredericka… my Freddie…we had us ten children, we did. Ever' one had red hair, too! An' the onliest swigga whiskey I had that whole durn time was at the birth a each a them young'uns."

The girl put on her mittens once more. "That's not what my Daddy says. My Daddy says you stayed drunk and you drank up all the profits and stole from your partners until they had to close you down."

The old man snarled a lip in the child's direction. She rared back, but then realized he must be angry at a forgotten memory, not at her.

"Well, gal, yer daddy's lyin'. I was sober as a judge, an' after 'bout ten years 'bout as rich as one too. But then the trouble done started. The Major an' the Lieuten't, they ain't happy 'bout all the money I'm a makin' off that quarry, even though I done worked my hind end off six, sometimes seven days a week. They seen me gittin' rich an' successful-like, better'n them. 'Coupl'a times they done tried ta buy that quarry out from under me, hire me on as the foreman but I tole 'em no, it's my bizness jus' like we 'greed to an' since't I been kept my trap shut, they ain't had no right ta take it from me at any price. The last time, my man Hosea Ransom had ta back me up with a shotgun an' git 'em off my prop'ty. That shore didn't set too well."

The drunk took a raspy breath and bowed his head. "One day, I had me the idee ta go down Miss'ippi an' git my daddy buried proper, git him a nice marker an' all. I went ta the Major, sittin' in his big fine bank. Now I ain't needin' no money, but I'm figgerin' my daddy'd want me ta set things straight an' get that five thousand back, honorin' his mem'ry, like they promised me we was gonna do when we all signed that big book. An' I says, *'I reckon how yer doin' so well, an' Lee's doin' so well at playactin' he's a lawyer, an' the good Doc's got hissef a clinic, it's 'bout time we settle up that eyeohyou.'* But the Major, he says, *'Fine. Jus' pay me the five thousand you owe us an' yer free ta go.'* I'm cold as a stone, I am. I cain't breathe. *'I ain't owin' you no money...yer the ones that's owin' me!'* I says. *'Boy, you oughta learn ta read an' write afore you make yer mark on somethin'!'* An' the Major, he pulls out that big book what had the eyeohyou in it. Then in comes the Lieuten't, jus' hap-p'nin' ta be payin' a call. "He an' the Major start laughin'. *'Boy,'* says the Lieuten't, *'we got us pure ev'dence you made yer mark right here...right where it says you r'linquish all claims ta any money an' you owe me an' the Major five thousand dollars fer stakin' you in the quarry bizness!'"*

The old man jumped off the boulder, picked up a stick and broke it in half in anger. "Here they done stole my five thousand but they's tricked me inta signin' somethin' sayin' I gotta pay 'em back 'nother five! Then the Major, he says, *'Boy, you jus' sign right here this piece a paper an' give us that quarry an' we'll us fergit 'bout yer debt.'* No sir, says I, an' I rush outta there an' head home, ta git my money box. See, I warn't so stupid ta keep my own money over ta the Major's bank...an' I'm a'countin' money, pilin' it all up, my missus, she's frettin', an' I'm sayin,' *'Hush, we got plenty a money an' I got contracts fer more limestone I can ever d'liver! I'm gonna pay 'em an' be done with it an' then I'm gonna sell this here quarry an' we's leavin' town.'* But then I hear hollerin' an' bells a clangin' an' horses thunderin' on the main road. *'The quarry foreman's murderous daid! He's done drowned in the pit!'* Well I run outta the house, hands fulla money an' who do I see but the sheriff. An' he's lookin' at me with a buncha cash in my hands an' sweat on my brow. He says ta me, *'The Major an' the Lieuten't say you jus' sold yer bizness to 'em an' you was mad on accounta they ain't keepin' you 'roun' as foreman. They say they seen you shove their new foreman Hosea Ransom inta the quarry pit an' now he's daid. An' now it seems yer fixin' ta maybe leave town with all yer money...you best come with me.'"*

The drunk sighed and wiped tears from his eyes. He sobbed as he spoke. "They thew me in the jailhouse, no trial, no nothin'. All the law was beholdin' ta the Major, he done owned purt' near ever'body in town. That night when my Freddie an' my babies was a'sleepin' they burnt down my sweet li'l home. Five a my babies was burnt ta death an' Freddie died the next mornin', warn't nothin' Doc could do. Major comes inta the jailhouse five minutes after Doc tole me 'bout the deaths a my fam'ly. He says, *'I'm real sorry ta tell ya this but I'm callin' yer loan. I cain't be lendin' money on no burnt-out house an' you in the pokey fer Lord knows how long.' 'All my money's done burnt up in the fire,'* I says. *'Oh, that's too bad, that's ter'ble. But how 'bout this...how 'bout you jus' sign this piece a paper, handin' me that quarry fair an' square? It's yer lucky day! An' 'cause I'm a' feelin' sorry fer ya, I'll waive them five thousand dollars too...if ya ever git outta this cell, you kin jus' walk right outta town, scot-free a yer burdens. You ain't gotta worry 'bout them other young'uns...they's all been sent ta the orph'nage in Murfreesboro. An' oh yeah, I saved that Ol' Man's pearl brooch from the fire...it'll look right nice on my wife.'"*

He threw his head back. "That pearl brooch was the one my daddy the Colonel give ta my momma when he'd asked fer her hand...she give it ta me when I went off ta git her med'cine that last time...it war the onliest thing a hers I'd ever had an' I sewed it in my shirt an' kept it with me ever' day."

He wept uncontrollably. The child wrung her hands in confusion; she'd never seen a grown-up man cry so much. She patted his hand. "It's ok, Mister. Please don't cry. It's okay. Please stop crying."

The old drunk rubbed the sleeve of his coat across his face and inhaled a few breaths. "Fifty years gone an' it still hurts me raw. All right, gal, listen up, I'm comin' ta the end. They kept me in that cell fer two years. When I got out, warn't nobody in town could look me in the face. Stories was runnin' 'roun' 'bout how I stole money outta the quarry b'longed ta my pardners, pardners I ain't never even had an' how I kilt my own foreman. Said I set my own house afire, too. Warn't nobody believed my side a the story no matter how much I tole it. I hid out in that ol' cave under the ridge, livin' like a dog fer years, tryin' ta earn some money ta git my survivin' babies back. But it warn't no use. Only job I could git was runnin' the sluice over ta the quarry...the quarry I opened with my own hands, now b'longin' ta the Major. Then the Major up an' decides ta close it down an' I ain't got no job. Warn't nobody in town gimme the time a day, let 'lone a day's pay. I figger ta git myself over ta Nashville an' tell a fed'ral marshal my whole story, but I got me the croup so bad I cain't walk but haif a mile afore I plumb give out. I started stealin' jus' ta eat.

"My babies what lived, they ran off from the orph'nage, but they cain't stand ta look at me, thinkin' I done fired up their mama an' brothers an' sisters. Ol' Buzzy over ta the tavern, he's the onliest person what looks out fer me, hands me a bottle once't a week. 'Bout ten years ago, I's standin' outside the tavern talkin' ta a fella passin' thew town. I seen he's a Texas Ranger an'

I commenced ta tellin' him my tale. He's might inter'sted, he's been knowin' Colonel Gray's brother, an' knowin' the Ol' Man had him a bastard son, an' he starts takin' notes, says he'll check it out. That night I wake up in my cave starin' at the barrel of a pistol, an' at the other end's the Major an' the Lieuten't. If Doc hadn't come 'roun' the next day ta bring me my croup 'lixir, I'd a been daid as a post fer sure. He sewed me up but it ain't ever healed right. That warn't 'nuf, they done dynamited my cave plumb in. I been a'livin' in that boxcar ever since. Guess it's better'n 'at cave...not as far a piece ta walk ta the tavern ever' week. An' sometimes folks is take pity on me an' leaves me stale bread er a messa cabbidge."

He leaned his head back against the boulder and closed his eyes against the winter sunlight. "I'm pow'rful tired, gal. Seventy-five years a mis'ry done took their toll, I reckon. See here, now. I'm gonna jump inta that pit an' meet my Maker. But you promise me good yer gonna go back an' tell ever'-body what I done said here today true, okay? You tell ever'body how Colonel Gray a Virginya done give me five thousand in gold coins that was robbed from me by a buncha cheats an' liars. Colonel Gray was my daddy an' they took his money an' kilt him, right in fronta my own eyes, an' then they kilt my Freddie an' my babies an' they danged near kilt me more an' once't."

The child breathed deeply and nodded. She wasn't sure that the old man's story was completely true, but it was obvious to her that he had suffered a lot and was in need of help.

"Mister, nobody's going to believe me and I'll probably just get a whippin' for talking to you and for being up here without my Granddaddy. But I feel bad about your wife and your dead babies...I promise I'll tell everybody somehow. I'm real sorry you've had such a bad life. But Mister...didn't you ever say your prayers and ask God to help you?"

The drunk blinked and stared up at the breaking clouds. "God don't help no Irish Cath'lics, gal, you heard that, I reckon from yer Sundy school. Some folks say them Irish kilt in the 'tata famine was nothin' more 'an God tellin' ever'body *'looky here what happens when ya'll don't try ta better yerseves with the two hands I give ya.'* Ever'body knows them Irish is lazy an' all drunks. Leastways, that's the 'scuse they gimme when I used ta ask fer jobs."

There was a sudden rustle on the path behind them. The child looked up to see her Granddaddy standing next to a large black man with a shotgun, but before she could move, the old drunk leaped from his rock and grabbed her around the waist, dragging her toward the edge of the quarry pit. She screamed and hit him repeatedly but he pinned her arms and stood her at the mouth of the pit. She looked down. There was no big, beautiful iceberg after all; only a very long drop to a pond with a frozen surface that shone like glass in the pale winter sun. Granddaddy and the black man froze in place. Granddaddy calmly called her name and winked at her, then carefully raised a hand and said in a measured voice,

"Private! You turn loose of that girl now, you hear? That's my granddaughter there an' you've got no bone to pick with her. If you don't turn her loose right now, Russell's gonna pump you full of lead. And if he don't, I will."

The child thrashed but the old man's grip was surprisingly strong. His eyes were wild. His breaths rattled loudly in his chest. The child thought she would gag from the stench of his clothes. Granddaddy took a step forward.

"Private, now you're real sick, an' you know I'm the only person around here who's ever helped you. You owe me a favor or two...who was it brought you medicine for your croup...who was it sewed up your bullet hole...who was it tended your wife when she....when she..."

"WHEN SHE WAS A'DYIN' FROM HER BURNS? IN THE FIRE YOU AN' THEM OTHERS SET? Doc, I ain't owin' you NOTHIN'! I've had seventy-five years a livin' hell an' today's the day I'm callin' it quits! You got no right ta ask me fer nothin', you hear Doc? *You hear?* Now you gotta fine li'l rascal here an' she's done promised she's gonna set the story straight fer me...tell ever'body the truth 'bout my daddy an' that five thousand dollars was stole from me when the Colonel was pushed outta that winda."

Doc surreptitiously glanced down to note that Russell had cocked the shotgun trigger. He sighed. "You beat all, you know that? Still tellin' that same old story...you oughta be ashamed, Private an' let the Ol' Man's memory rest in peace. Now I'll say it like I've said it a thousand times since eighteen-and-sixty-three...I don't doubt the Major and the Lieutenant stole some money from the Colonel. But you ain't never been able to tell me how it is the Colonel could ever possibly be your daddy, when he was a blue-blooded Virginia gentleman, related to General Washington himself, and you are an Irish drunk from up in the hills who can't even read and write. I want to believe you, Private, truly I do. You've had a hard life, I know. But I just can't figure it out. You got no evidence, man! How can I believe you with no evidence, without proof? Now just come over here an' lemme see 'bout that cough, an' turn loose of my girl."

The old man slightly eased his grip on the child; she peered once again into the pit and then shut her eyes tight. She was a strong swimmer, Granddaddy said, but she'd never been swimming in ice. Doc's brow broke into a sweat and he hoped she couldn't see the beads trickling down his temples. The old drunk started to sob loudly and he covered his eyes with his hands. Doc dashed over and swung the child to Russell. She screamed and reached for Granddaddy; but caught only his blue cashmere scarf, pulling it to her chest. Doc turned to coax the old man away from the edge of the pit, but as he heard the child scream he looked back and slipped on the wet gravel, falling flat on his back with a loud *snap*. He lay motionless and cried out in agony. The drunk looked up from his sobs and fumed. He kicked Doc in the kidneys as the child screamed for Russell to shoot. The drunk man became hysterical.

"I cain't even kill mysef 'out the likes a you interferin'! Would that you was the Major er the Lieuten't, but they's already daid, so I reckon yer the onliest one left ta *pay*!"

He grabbed Doc's ankles and dragged him toward the edge of the pit. Doc grunted and moaned in pain, helpless. The child screamed and tried to run to Doc but Russell threw down his gun and gripped her tightly with both arms. He wanted to shoot the drunk white bastard so bad he could taste it, but he and Doc both knew what would happen if a black man shot a white man, whether or not it was called for. The drunk stood at the edge of the pit, one foot on Doc's chest, waving his arms and muttering gibberish at the sky. Doc called out between gritted teeth, "Girl, you're all right now, you hear? Hush up an' listen to me while I can still talk!"

Tears streamed down the child's face in salty ribbons. She was obediently silenced and clung to Russell's shoulder, staring at Granddaddy.

"I love you like I ain't ever loved anybody, you hear, girl? You an' me are kindred souls, child, an' you did the right thing. I'm right proud of you for helping this man out here today! He's in a heap of pain an' like I always told you, you gotta help folks 'cause it may be you next that needs helpin'! *Always help folks*, you hear me, girl? Tell me you hear me! An' you tell the Private's story like you promised, you hear?"

The child sputtered, "I hear you Granddaddy...I hear you...please, Mister, please don't hurt my Granddaddy! I'll tell your story! I will! Just please don't hurt my Granddaddy!"

Russell looked over the child clinging to his shoulder and spotted his gun on the ground; he slowly bent down to reach it with one hand, but as he did the old drunk caugh sight of his efforts and grabbed Granddaddy's arm. He jumped over the edge of the pit and dragged Granddaddy with him. The child screamed in terror. She heard her Granddaddy yell, *"TELL HIS STORY!"* Then there was a horrible thud, and a splash, and then only frozen silence.

Russell fired five shots and held the child tightly as she sobbed. He screamed down to the shanty for his oldest son to run get the law. After an unbearable time the sheriff and his deputies arrived on horses frothy with break-neck foam. Sheriff McArdle, a beefy man, held the devastated child on his knee while Russell informed the lawmen that after Doc tended his family he'd followed Doc up the path to find his granddaughter and see how many arrowheads she'd found. Instead they'd seen her with the old drunk that lived in the boxcar. The drunk had grabbed the child and threatened to throw her over the edge, but Doc intervened and sacrificed himself. The sheriff frowned and looked at the child.

"Honey, is that what happened? Is that exactly what happened up here? Did this big nigger try to hurt you? Did he push your Granddaddy into that pit?"

The girl stared in horror at the sheriff. "*No, sir,* he's a *friend* of my Granddaddy's! It's just like he already told you! Granddaddy and I came up here to help his family. I took a walk to look for arrowheads. That old bad drunk man that lives in the boxcar was up here and he was real sick. He wasn't right in the head, somehow. It's just like Mister Russell told you, I swear. But somebody needs to go down into that pit and get my Granddaddy! He needs help!"

The sheriff looked up warily at Russell. Other than being a black man, Russell had never caused any trouble in town and the sheriff had no reason not to believe him. He'd seen the drunk hanging around the quarry road that morning but he never dreamed the old fool would jump into the pit and take the town's most beloved citizen with him.

The sheriff passed a hand over his rough beard and nodded at Russell once more. "All right, boy, get on back home."

Russell touched the child on her shoulder and she saw huge tears spill from the big black man's eyes. "Chile, I'm right sorry 'bout wha's happened. Now, you'd best be tellin' the sheriff what ol' Doc he say 'fore he fell over inta that big pit...go on, now, tell him. Promise like that's gotta be kept, girl, ol' Doc, he a great man an' you done made him a death promise. Go on."

The sheriff looked from the child to Russell. "What you talkin' 'bout, Boy? You leave this girl be. Honey, what's this big nigger talkin' about?"

The child sniffed and wiped her nose on a red mitten. She set her jaw and said nothing, staring at Russell with black eyes. Russell prodded her on the shoulder, then concerned that the sheriff would accuse him of foul play, he shuffled his feet.

"Sheriff, ol' Doc he tole this here young'un to tell somethin' 'bout that ol' drunk bastard. He make her promise an' she done say she would. It were his last words, I swear!"

The sheriff eased the child off his knee and stood, eyes fixed on Russell. He pulled the black man away, then he approached the child tenderly. "Honey, it's okay. Sometimes terrible things happen and we don't reckon we know why. Now tell me 'bout this promise you made ol' Doc...what are you s'posed to tell me, huh? I know you're real upset, but you gotta tell me what's goin' on, young lady!"

The child burst into tears. "You've got to send your men down into that pit right now, get a rope and go get my Granddaddy right now! He's going to be all right! I know it! He can't leave me! And you've got to put that bad drunk man in jail! Or hang him! Hang him right here for what he did!"

The sheriff rubbed his jaw. "Girl, listen up. I wish more than anything that I could help yer Granddaddy. But he's dead, child, that water's so cold I just hope he died quick. Now me and my men, we'll get some ropes so we can get his... well, it'll have to wait 'til the weather warms up and that pit pond thaws out. I'm real sorry. Now you gotta get on home to yer Mama."

The child sobbed through closed eyes as the sheriff handed her to a deputy mounted on horseback. The deputy wrapped a wool blanket around her and the sheriff patted her knee.

"Honey, you'll be goin' home now and I'll come around in a spell to talk to yer Mama and Daddy. You sure there's nothin' else you wanna tell me? I can't understand why that old drunk would wanna shove your granddaddy off a cliff...Doc was the only fool in town ever did help that bastard...you swear there ain't nothin' else you need to say, maybe tell me when I come 'round later on? We'll have us a little talk, ok? You *promise*?"

The child's jaw set and she opened her eyes. She stared straight ahead in the silent defiance of a young girl whose blissful childhood died in the frozen waters of a quarry pit. *I promise all right, I promise I'm not telling anybody, never, no matter what I said! I hope that old bad drunk man burns in hell for killing Granddaddy! I hope crows peck his eyes out and fire and brimstone scorches his skin and worms eat his insides! I hope the Devil himself and all the Catholics too pour kerosene over his head and laugh while he burns! I'll never tell his story, never! He was nothing but a crazy old man and he took my Granddaddy away from me and left me all alone...I'll never tell another living soul a single word about this day, as long as I live, ever.*

CHAPTER TWO – IMPOSSIBLE DREAMS

December 28, 1998; a cold, dark room in Chestnut Ridge, Tennessee

Granddaddy! It's really you! It's me…it's me! Don't you recognize me? Oh, Granddaddy I missed you so bad there's a hole in my heart! I've prayed you would come and visit me and now you have! I love you so much! Have you been watching me all these years? Are you proud of me, all those folks I've helped? Did you see, your name's on the Clinic…right up front…you always did like green, and there's no speck of red paint anywhere on site; you hated red after the War, I remember.

What did you say? Do my job? I've been doing my job, Granddaddy… I've been a nurse for sixty years…I've been running your Clinic and helping people just like you said…I never even married or had babies…I sacrificed everything so I could help folks and make you proud. You're proud of me, aren't you, Granddaddy?

Granddaddy…what's the matter? Why are you shaking your head? Why are you pointing your finger at me? Granddaddy…don't walk away! Please come back…I want to throw my arms around you and smell lye soap and hair tonic and your starched cotton shirt. I want to kiss your hard cheek and sit in your lap and listen to my heartbeat with your stethoscope. I want to stick my hand in your shirt pocket and find a piece of stale wintergreen candy and pop it into your mouth. Oh, Granddaddy…wait…please come back! Where are you going? Who is that man? His clothes are filthy… Granddaddy! That's the bad old drunk man who killed you! Why are you smiling at him when he's the one that pulled you into that pit? He killed you and I was left all alone! I was so alone I couldn't even talk about it…Mama tried to whip the Fear of God into me for days but I couldn't open my mouth to say one word…I wouldn't talk to anybody…never did…never did…

The old woman woke with a start; her heart skipped between shallow breaths as she adjusted her eyes to the darkness. She sat up in her rocker and clutched a tattered, faded blue cashmere scarf, kissing it tenderly as a tear traced her left cheek. She stood and walked to the bedroom window and looked up at the stars in the clear, cold sky. Every year on this day she willed herself to dream about Granddaddy, hoping that the dream would bring him back to her so she could wrap herself in his love just once more in her stark life. It had never come; no image of Granddaddy ever filled her sleep, but somehow even the effort always left her with a little warmth when she awoke, if only for the fleetest of moments.

But today it had happened. Granddaddy was right there in her dream in all his tall, skinny glory, with a wily grin on his face, his shirtsleeves rolled up to his elbows and a piece of wintergreen candy rolling around on his tongue. He'd winked at her and for a few seconds she was again a seven-year-old child, innocent and loved and carefree. But why was that murdering drunk with Granddaddy? Why did they walk away together like they were best friends? Why had Granddaddy turned his back to her, pointed at her in disappointment?

She sighed and stood up easily from her rocker; she had Granddaddy's agility yet in her recently-celebrated eighty-third year. She wrapped the scarf around her shoulders and put her face to a cold window pane. For three winters she had prayed to God to take her. Medicine had changed; it was no longer a simple question of helping folks. There were too many demands by the Board that she step down and retire, too many regulations and too much talk about potential lawsuits and codes and too many days her body ached despite the shame she felt when she remembered that Granddaddy had worked without complaint and would have kept on working if it hadn't been for that terrible day. If she'd never talked to that bad man.

It's just not your time to go yet. There's still something that God needs you to do in this town. It made her sick to think about her sappy sixty-eight-year-old baby sister's sunny dismissal of her death wish. It was absolutely nobody's business. *She has no idea of the sacrifices I've made. I've sheltered her all her life. I've done things no woman could have done alone but I did them anyway. I've done it all for God and Granddaddy...it's all I've done, I'm tired of doing it and there's nothing left to do! I'm ready to quit!*

A twinge of guilt streaked across her soul like a shooting star in the winter sky. No matter how terrible her life became after Granddaddy died, she knew that he never quit, and he died doing exactly what he wanted to do...he was trying to help someone in pain. She stiffened. *I've never turned anyone away, never refused to help. I've done everything everybody's ever asked me to do...and done it better than anyone ever could have, too. But I'm so very, very weary. Bone-cold tired.* The old woman staggered away from the window and the scarf fell to the floor. She sank down into the rocker and let out a deep breath.

Do your job, he'd said in the dream, pointing a hard, knotted finger directly at her chest. *Do your job.* Tears filled the old woman's eyes and spilled down her face. Her stomach knotted and icy fingers gripped her chest as seventy-six years of memories were swept away, leaving only one unanswered promise standing tall and defiant in her conscience.

I can't do it, Granddaddy. I can't tell that man's story after all these years! He killed you! Nobody will believe me now! I'm so old and they're trying to run me off from the Clinic! What good would it do...there's nobody left to care anymore, those things happened over a hundred and thirty-five years ago...they'd surely know I was crazy…nobody's even alive to…what difference would it make now…nobody's alive still…

The old woman gasped, walked briskly to the dark kitchen and flipped on the light. She rummaged through a deep drawer in an antique pie safe and pulled out a telephone directory. Her fingers skimmed the names printed on the pages. She held a finger under one name in particular and read it over and over again; her throat sank to her gut and she leaned against the cool metal door of the thirty-year-old refrigerator. She swallowed hard. Although she recognized the name and could put a face to it, for sixty years she'd been utterly wrapped up in her work. Saving people was her mission, but befriending them threatened her focus. She had no time for socializing with the perfectly healthy.

Which one of his drunken children lived to have more, she wondered. *Or is this one a bastard too, like his…what would it be…great-grandfather…great-great-grandfather? This man certainly has the same bad luck, if what everybody says is true. They say he's a loser, a lazy bum…but I wonder… what would have happened to him, to his family, if I'd told that story, if he'd had a better childhood…*

She stiffened as a vision stole across her memory; an alley behind the Clinic, where a dirty, crying child sat in a mud puddle. A red-headed, thin child with dark circles under his eyes. Then a frail young woman scooped up the child. *"I'm hungry mama!" "Hush, now, we'll find somethin' ta eat real soon, I promise!" And what did I do? Nothing. Ignored them. Went back inside to check on patients, to help people, people who were in need…*

The old woman's head ached and her temples pounded. She padded to the cupboard and took out a jelly jar, then unlocked the liquor cabinet and poured herself two fingers of whiskey like Granddaddy had done on so many evenings so long ago. She drained the jelly jar of its contents, then returned to her rocker in the darkness.

She clutched the worn arms of the rocker and slowly eased back into the silence. A whiff of wintergreen caressed her nose and she inhaled deeply. A single tear dropped from one eye onto her wrinkled cheek. *There's no turning back now. Granddaddy was very specific then and he was very specific in my dream, no getting around it. Sister's right, God's not done with me just yet, thanks to Granddaddy. I've gotta do this before I can die in peace. After everything I've done to honor him and yet he's so unhappy with me…I can't disappoint Granddaddy ever again…Lord have mercy…what in Heaven and earth should I do?*

CHAPTER THREE – AMELIORATION

December 29, 1998; Chestnut Ridge, Tennessee

Henry Bailey rolled out of bed and rubbed his behind. He started toward the kitchen, but remembered his wife's admonition that trotting around in his skivvies was fine when he was a wild divorced bachelor, but would he please respect her presence and cover himself with the chenille bathrobe she'd bought him as God intended. As Henry donned the ill-fitting robe he smiled to himself; there'd been no wild divorced bachelor life, primarily because he'd had no funds or friends to be wild with, and when a man's living in his car he doesn't exactly have much use for bathrobes. He scuffed to the tiny kitchen and poured himself a cup of black coffee; he walked four steps, poked his head into the bathroom and kissed his wife on the cheek that wasn't covered with cold cream.

"Mornin', babe. You workin' an eight-ta-five today?"

Euladean nodded. "Yep, darlin' and then I got me that church meetin' tonight, don't forgit! And don't you eat that chicken salad in the fridge, that's for my meetin'! Whatcha got lined up today, Henry? You think you can move any cars? It's been a long while since we had us a sale, hon…"

Henry winced and edged out of the bathroom, heading back toward the kitchen. "Um hmm. I'm doin' my best, babe, but it's like I tol' ya… them Christmas holidays wreck *hammock* on a car salesman's livelihood…you ain't realization it, but I made more money here'n the last six months than I been makin' in the last six years…an' it's all on a count a you, babe. Now 'fore ya git yer knickers in a wad, hon', it ain't gonna pick up none leastaways 'til after the New Year! But don't you worry, yer my good luck charm!"

Euladean spit into the sink and called out, "Well, this good luck charm's also payin' all the bills, Henry! Now I ain't *complainin'*, but all I'm *sayin'* is that maybe you oughta think 'bout sellin' out and comin' ta work at the Groc'ry, take that job as produce manager Corny offered…we could work together and you'd be makin' good money, that's all I'm *sayin'*."

Henry shuddered; working with his wife under the direction of his brother-in-law Corny at the Poe family-owned grocery store was more terrifying than a mild-mannered used car salesman could stomach on a post-Christmas-sales-slump-weekday. He loved his wife but a man had his limits. His mind wandered back to how Euladean had rescued him; it was impolite to be ungrateful, but a job at the grocery would be nothing short of hell on earth. Henry sighed as he listened to Euladean gargle.

Euladean Poe was an extremely plain woman of forty-five with a big heart, and her big heart had all but broken one day as she walked home from

Brother Culpepper's Tuesday Bible Study Class at the First United Assembly of God's Children. She'd heard the most miserable crying and carrying on emanating from a 1965 Mustang parked on Henry Bailey's Used Car Lot. Euladean was amazed to see Henry Bailey himself sobbing uncontrollably amidst a carful of crumpled Quigley Quick-Steak bags and dirty clothes, and she astutely realized from the evidence and from the pervasive odor that the Mustang was Henry's permanent residence.

She offered Henry a Kleenex and learned that Fay, his ex-wife of ten years, had hired a shark lawyer and taken Henry back to court to clean him out financially because his business was finally turning a profit, and Fay decided to steer that profit in her direction. After the nasty court battle, the judge ordered Henry to sell all his belongings and every one of the thirty late-model vehicles on the Henry Bailey Used Car Lot at auction. The only thing in the world now left to Henry was the blacktop lot itself and the three scrap-heap automobiles remaining on it.

Euladean was nothing if not a practitioner of Christian charity and she decided right then and there that Henry Bailey could use a hot meal and most definitely a hot shower. She trotted him to her father's home behind the Poe House Grocery where her family had lived for four generations. Euladean washed Henry's clothes, ironed his shirts and hung them on little padded hangers and fed him the best three bowls of chili he'd ever eaten in all his born days. This was accomplished in secret of course, as her father Raleigh Poe was at the grocery helping Corny with the frozen food inventory, and Euladean knew they'd be working late. If her father had been home, Euladean would never have dared bring a no-good Bailey into her father's house, Christian charity or not, especially since everybody knew that not only were the Baileys bad news, they were Catholics. The fact that Henry Bailey had personally not attended church, Catholic or otherwise, in thirty years didn't matter.

Euladean continued to check on Henry Bailey in secret for several months. One Tuesday morning as she delivered freshly washed shirts to him in a Poe House grocery sack (the padded hangers had been a nice touch but the Mustang had no closet) she realized that it must be a special day — the car had been washed, waxed and cleaned of all its previous residential appointments. A beaming Henry blurted out nervously that he'd sold two of the three cars on the lot and he had enough cash to buy an engagement ring, a tiny chip of a diamond which he shakingly proffered; would Miss Euladean Poe do the honor of marrying him and if she said no, would she at least please make him some more chili before they forever parted company?

Euladean, swooning despite an involuntary resolve toward singledom, accepted on the spot and they hopped in the 1965 Mustang, removed the "FOR SALE - GREAT TIRES" sign and drove to the next county, where a judge pronounced them legally bound for all time without needless complications or blood tests. Mr. & Mrs. Henry Bailey couldn't very well take much of a honeymoon, however, as the backseat of the Mustang was quite cramped and particularly as Euladean had to work a four-to-twelve, so they decided to postpone the celebration for a few days. Euladean was Head Checker at the grocery; she earned time and a half on the late shift plus she received a sixty percent discount on all purchases. This fact significantly impressed Henry such that he didn't mind foregoing the usual honeymoon festivities, in trade for newfound grocery discounts and Euladean's home cooking. He drove the Mustang merrily back to Chestnut Ridge in record time, to avoid both a dock in his new wife's pay and any questions regarding her morning whereabouts.

After completing her shift at the grocery that night, Euladean returned to her father's house and packed all her belongings into forty-seven plastic grocery sacks, double-bagged, naturally. She slept in her own twin bed for a few hours and for the last time. At dawn next morning, Euladean wrote her father a note informing him that she had a doctor's appointment and that he should eat breakfast at the Poe House bakery counter. Then she made twenty trips to her ancient Dodge, packing it tight with her grocery bag trousseau; she put the old car in neutral and silently pushed it up the driveway and onto the main road. She drove over to the Henry Bailey Used Car Lot, and after checking on Henry, whose loud snores rocked the Mustang, she parked her car in front of the First National Bank of Chestnut Ridge and waited for it to open, to transfer her life savings into a new joint account as Mrs. Henry Bailey.

Euladean was no fool...she knew there was no way on earth her father or her brother would allow the likes of Henry Bailey to move into the Poe family home. The Baileys had been definitive white trash for over a hundred years. Even though Henry's ancestor Hardy had single-handedly saved Chestnut Ridge from post-Civil War recession by opening a stone quarry, the fact that Hardy murdered his partner and that subsequent generations of Baileys had never repaid their debts was not easily forgotten. As far as Euladean knew, Henry had never actually committed a crime or an injustice, but he was a Bailey and therefore the town scapegoat, in the fine and time-honored Bailey tradition.

Euladean knew full well the risk she'd taken by marrying Henry, but she could see what others could not, and she believed that Henry had a good heart wrapped up in a whole lot of bad luck. She didn't care what anybody said about her, because they gossiped about her just as much before, saying she was too plain to ever get a man. Even so, there would be hell to pay once her father and brother found out about this marriage, so she had to act fast. After completing her banking transactions and swearing the teller to absolute secrecy about her new marital status, Euladean made a quick visit to Roy Quigley at the Quigley Realty. She put down a deposit on the 1973 silver Airstream camper Roy had been trying to unload for months, with the promise that Roy would tow it to the Bailey Used Car Lot after midnight that evening when her four-to-twelve shift was complete. When Roy pressed her about the strange circumstances and why on earth she needed an Airstream camper, and why in God's name she wanted it delivered to Henry Bailey's Used Car Lot, Euladean threatened to call Roy's wife Ruby and inform her that a single pink carnation had consistently and mysteriously appeared on the dashboard of Penni Poe's station wagon every Wednesday for the last six months. Roy was dutifully silenced.

Euladean returned to her father's house and spent the entire afternoon making thirty-four individual servings of Chicken Topsy Turvy, which she promptly labeled and placed in the deep freeze. *If I can't be here to cook for Daddy,* she thought, *at least I can make it easier for him to heat his own supper.* She arrived for her shift just as her brother Corny was leaving; he didn't even acknowledge that she was two minutes late. After that, it was a fairly uneventful evening at the Poe House Grocery, with the exception of one near-tragic incident involving a can of improperly priced peaches.

At midnight Euladean clocked out and drove the Dodge five blocks to the Henry Bailey Used Car Lot, the site of her own personal honeymoon cottage, or honeymoon recreational vehicle, depending upon your point of view. She arrived just in time to supervise the placement of the Airstream in a remote corner of the lot. She thanked the tow driver, who although confused, was excited about the fact that he'd earned double wages for the late-night job. Euladean looked around for Henry, who slept through the miraculous appearance of his new home from his cozy perch in the Mustang.

Awakened by his beaming wife, Henry looked over the steering wheel through his bedroom windshield and gazed upon his new residence in disbelief; he was utterly convinced that Euladean Poe Bailey was his redeemer. Six months, one add-on redwood deck and two lawn chairs later, Euladean and Henry Bailey were the perfect picture of Main Street wedded bliss. There were now five EXCELLENT CONDITION automobiles on the Used Car Lot that doubled as their front yard, a freezer full of delicious chili and Henry had a hunch he'd soon be asked to chair the Sons of Glory Festival Parade Vehicles Committee. His life was in complete and total turnaround status and his aching back was at long-last healed from sleeping in a real bed, instead of in the Mustang.

Henry sipped his coffee and smiled at his wife as she squeezed out of the RV's bathroom and poured herself a glass of orange juice with one hand, removing gigantic pink plastic rollers from her hair with the other.

"That's all I'm *sayin,'* Hon…I mean, your ex cleaned you out somethin' fierce, Henry, an' we gotta make tracks if we're gonna save up so's we can retire to Panama City. I mean, we're no spring chickens an' Corny's offerin' you real good money, that's all I'm *sayin.'* An' he's gonna start us management employees a pension plan in the new year, you'd be comin' in at a good time, that's all I'm *sayin.*"

Henry turned and stared out the small window over the built-in kitchen table of the RV. He noticed an ancient green Pontiac slowing down as it approached the car lot, the driver seemed to be surveying the inventory. He wanted no part of the Poe House, pension plan or no pension plan. Corny Poe was the most self-righteous, nickel-and-dime conservative in town; the only things he respected in the world were the Almighty Dollar and getting his name engraved on some sign at his church. The green Pontiac made a u-turn and slowly passed the car lot once more.

"Babycakes, I was savin' this fer yer New Year's surprise…but I got me a cust'mer comin' in today wantin' ta trade in his ol' green Pontiac…'coupl'a good sales an' we'll be in hog heaven. Spring's the big sales season in the Used Car bizness, I'm tellin' ya. I heard Newt Fentress is gonna be startin' him a taxi service right here in town, an' seein' as how he ain't got nothin' but an' ol' beat-up Dodge with a rust hole big as Texas, I figger he's gotta be plannin' ta buy him a coupl'a good-qual'ty used cars ta carry all them taxi riders in. I'm in like Flint, I tell ya…but you cain't rush a big sale, hon…you jus' gotta trust me!"

Henry winked at Euladean and she smiled and gave Henry a peck on his balding head, then padded down the short hall to the bedroom. He stared out the window and again watched as the green Pontiac approached the lot, slowing down as it drew closer. He squinted into the early morning sun.

Guy must be a real serious buyer. Guess I'd better git dressed…might be a potenshul cust'mer, scopin' out my year-end clearance sale…wait a minute… that's Miz Amelia! Lordy, she's so old her driver's license's prob'ly scratched inta one a them stone tablets God give Moses! Heh! That's a good one, Killer! Stone tablets God give Moses! Killer, you slay me! But maybe she's lookin' ta buy a clean, depend'ble used car…

Henry stood and refilled his coffee cup, then quickly pulled his robe over his belly as Euladean came out of the bedroom. She made a pretty picture in her pink Poe House Grocery uniform. Marriage and a bit of makeup had completely transformed Euladean Poe Bailey. Henry whistled.

"Whew, doggies, ain't you a vision! Come over here an' give Killer a big kiss!"

Euladean blushed like the bride she was and kissed Henry full on the mouth. He swatted her behind and she hooted in protest, then squeezed around Henry to grab her lunch from the counter. Henry helped Euladean put on her red plaid car coat.

"Now, Henry, 'member what I said 'bout that chicken salad…there's some chili in the fridge for your supper while I'm at my meetin' tonight. An' if it's slow today, whyn't ya come on over to the Groc'ry and just talk to Corny 'bout that job? What'd it hurt, huh? You think about it, okay, babe? I love you hon!"

Henry winked and wiped his wife's red lipstick from his lips. "Love you too, babycakes, you have a good day, now, hear?"

Henry stood at the window and waved at his wife as she pulled away. Then he spied the green Pontiac coming in for a third perusal of the Used Car Lot. He sighed and looked at the kitchen clock.

"Shitfire, it's seven-forty-five in the ayem an' this ol' bag's out lookin' at used cars! An' knowin' she's tighter than dick's hat band, she's prob'ly gonna wanna beat me down so's I ain't makin' nothin'…oh, well, Killer…a sale's a sale, an' it beats workin' fer Corny Poe any dad-burned day of the week!"

Henry dressed quickly in black work slacks, a white polyester dress shirt and the new green sweater Euladean gave him for Christmas. He'd nearly ruined Christmas when he'd declared that no real man would be caught dead wearing some sissy sweater, until Euladean pointed out that men who wore sweaters didn't necessarily have to wear neckties. Henry hated wearing ties, so right then and there in front of Euladean and the tabletop Christmas tree he confessed that he was indeed a sweater-wearing sort of man after all, in keeping with his new image as a happily married Used Car Sales success.

At precisely eight o'clock Henry Bailey walked to the front window of the RV and flipped the CLOSED sign to read OPEN. Thus he was officially ready to face another hectic business day in the world of automobile purveyance. He pulled on a light jacket, then checked his look in the bathroom mirror.

"Okay, Killer! Let's go sell us an old car to an old bag!"

He darted out the door of the RV and whistled a tune as he surveyed the five EXCELLENT CONDITION cars on the lot. There was a bit of a chill in the air this time of day, Henry noticed, that typically wasn't a factor by the time he regularly opened for business around ten or eleven. He strode up to a red 1974 Datsun and realized he'd forgotten to implement the special Henry Bailey Bald Tire Remedy on said vehicle. He dashed inside the RV, then returned with a bottle of black shoe polish. Henry knelt down by the left front tire of the Datsun, which was as smooth as the top of his own head, and began the painstaking process of applying the polish to the portion of the tire that was visible. He checked his watch.

"Yep, good an' dry. An' I don't reckon Miz Amelia'd be wantin' no stick-shift Jap car, anyhow."

He stood up stiffly, decided to make another pot of decaf and headed toward the door to the RV. Suddenly a loud honk broke the early morning silence of the car lot and nearly jolted Henry off the front steps to his home office. It was the green Pontiac with Miz Amelia at the wheel and she almost rammed the wreck into his new redwood deck as she screeched to a halt just inches in front of the RV. Henry scratched his head.

"Well, now, mornin', Miz Amelia! That's what I call parkin' on a dime! Uh, merry Christmas to ya an' Happy New Year! What can I do fer ya today? You want some decaf? I's jus' fixin' ta make me a fresh pot."

Amelia Festrunk climbed effortlessly out of her car and closed the door behind her with a rusty creak. She was dressed in a starched white nurse uniform and cap and a heavy white sweater jacket. A white patent leather handbag swung from one wrist and her huge feet sported the largest white orthopedic shoes Henry had ever seen. She was a six-foot-two bleached-white terror approaching Henry with lips pursed, strictly business. She stared over her trifocals and nodded.

"Good morning, Mr. Bailey, is it? I am Amelia Festrunk, as I'm sure you know and I would like to ask you a few questions, if you don't mind."

Henry smiled and nodded his head. "Shore thing, Miz Amelia! You lookin' ta see what I'd give ya fer yer car? If'n ya don't mind me sayin' so, Miz Amelia, no 'fense, but yer ridin' in a classic rust-bucket an' I reckon it's 'bout time you traded up, don't ya think? That carburetor give out on ya yet? Insurance fixin' ta drop ya on 'counta alla them recalls?"

Amelia Festrunk's mouth gaped wide. How did this man know her carburetor was behaving badly, or that her automobile insurer had dropped her just last week? She shivered as Granddaddy's face skipped across her brain, then snapped her mouth shut and recovered. As she was about to speak, Henry piped up.

"See, Miz Amelia, that ol' Pontiac yer drivin's done been recalled purt near 'bout forty times, an' yer prob'ly the onliest person I know in the whole U.S. of A. still drivin' one. HEY! Ya know what PONTIAC stands fer, don't ya? *'Poor ol no-good thinks it's a Cadillac!'* Well, I reckon we can sure fix ya up, don't you worry none. Ya know, back when I's nearly successful, afore Fay cleaned me out, I's fixin' ta open me up a Lemon Museum an' I shore woulda liked ta put this here Pontiac in it...I had me an Edsel fer 'while, too...an' one a them Hugos...well, what's past is past, I reckon. Now come on up here in my sales office an' let's have us a cuppa joe."

Amelia shivered again and stared at Henry Bailey. *Why did I pull into this lot? I only wanted to observe this man from a distance, see how he lives...it's like my car has a mind of its own! And why did I get out? This isn't how I do things... I give the orders, I don't waste time! But it is cold out here... if I go inside for just one cup of coffee, I can look around and maybe get some answers, decide what to do...*

Henry walked down the steps toward Miss Amelia. "Uh, Miz Amelia, you okay? I reckon that stunt drivin' you jus' did maybe done shook ya a trifle. Come on in here, now, an' set a spell. Here, lemme hep you up these here steps...we jus' did us some renovatin' ta our sales office, ya know, added this here redwood Car Lot Observation Deck so's our cust'mers can set up here in open-air comfort an' decide whicha these fine cars they'd like ta buy...come on in, now, have you a seat right here."

Amelia Festrunk climbed the five redwood steps to the deck and stooped as she entered the front door to the RV. Inside was a sink and small kitchen area, a built-in table and two chairs beside a large window and a bank of built-in seats that she presumed could serve as beds. To the left was a tiny hallway that led to a bathroom and bedroom. Next to the front door hung a small television from a hospital-type mount on the wall. She squinted and noticed that the television mount's base sported the initials "FRHBC."

"Mr. Bailey...where on earth did you get *that*? I believe, sir, you are in possession of a piece of property that belongs to the Festrunk Respite Home and Birthing Clinic!"

Henry grinned sheepishly as he helped Miss Amelia into one of the kitchen chairs. Then he dashed over to the coffee maker and poured water into it.

"Oh, no, Miz Amelia, well, *yes an' no*. See, Mister Leonard, yer brother, he pulled up here one day in that hospital truck he's always drivin' an' it was fulla stuff he's fixin' ta take to the dump. An' he done asked me would I like ta have any a that stuff on 'counta he's gonna jus' thow it all away. Miz Amelia, I reckon you know how my fam'ly's always been on the receivin' end a charity in this town, leastaways from a few good folks...we ain't none of us Baileys ever had a dime...but Mister Leonard's always been right good ta me, jus' like he was ta my mama afore me. Anyhow, I seen that there tv holder an' I asked Leonard could he rig it up fer me in here, ta surprise Euladean, that's my wife...an' sure's shootin', he did. He said it warn't no good fer the hospital no more on 'counta it was broke, but after what he done to it, I shore cain't tell, can you?"

Chills traced Amelia's spine. *Her own seventy-five year old simple-minded brother who couldn't read or write but who could repair anything on God's green earth had apparently aided the Bailey family for years right under her nose! Leonard helping the very people she herself should have helped so many years ago...it was unfathomable...*

"Oh, I *see.* Well, I'm happy Leonard could assist you, Mr. Bailey. Pardon me for the accusation."

"Don't sweat it none, Miz Amelia. I git blamed fer stuff all the time, have been alla my life. It jus' rolls right off, don't ya give it no more thought."

Henry placed two dainty china coffee cups and two china saucers on the table in front of Amelia. She noticed that none of the cups and saucers was of the same china pattern. Henry poured coffee into the cups and approached the table, but paused.

"Miz Amelia, you take cream er sugar?"

Amelia nodded *no*, and Henry sat down across from her.

"Mmmm, boy, there ain't nothin' like a hot cuppa joe on a cold day, is there Miz Amelia? Now, let's us talk 'bout yer car sitiation…"

Amelia waved a bony, wrinkled hand in the air. "Let's don't just *yet,* Mr. Bailey, if you don't mind. I have another question I'd like to ask you and it's much more important than the condition of my automobile."

Henry warmed inside but it wasn't from the coffee; the first rule of a good used car salesman was to keep the customer talking about anything but cars. *Make a new friend and the sale's as good as closed,* that's what the articles in *Used Car News* always said. He'd be happy to sit here all day and talk to Amelia Festrunk about any subject on God's green earth, so long as it finally led around to used car buying.

"Shore 'nuff, Miz Amelia. Shoot!"

Amelia sipped her coffee, then carefully replaced the cup on the saucer. "Henry Bailey, are you happy? Has your life been full of love, good memories? Do you look forward to your future?"

Henry was caught off guard and fingers of fear gripped his throat. He expected Miz Amelia to ask him if he would like to become the official Used Car Purveyor for the Festrunk Respite Home and Birthing Clinic, or whether he enjoyed being a newlywed for the second time. He shifted uncomfortably in his chair and toyed with his coffee cup.

"Wow, Miz Amelia, when you *shoot,* you shoot a right big gun, don't ya! Whaddya mean, am I *happy?*"

Amelia Festrunk leaned closer and pointed a finger in Henry's direction. "Exactly what I said, Henry. Are you happy? Do you enjoy your life?"

Henry pulled a powder blue paper napkin from the Lucite napkin holder on the kitchen table and wiped his brow. This kind of question made him nervous; when a man's family is known as white trash and gets blamed for everything bad that ever happens, that man learns to be a little gunshy with respect to personal inquiries about happiness and the future. In Henry's experience, kindness typically wore a cloak of disappointment or shame.

"Miz Amelia, ain't nobody never asked me that afore now. I mean, us Baileys... we's none of us ever had a fair shake. All them stories 'bout murderin' an' baby-burnin' an' thievin' an' livin' in boxcars an' shacks...don't know how much a that's true. All I know is my daddy took off an' left me an' mama when I's five an' we had ta live in our car fer 'while...but that ain't nothin', I've lived in cars since, an' it ain't no big deal. An' then mama got her a good job at the fact'ry, we had us a one-room 'partment all the way up 'til I gradgiated from the high school, on account my mama worked her hiney off an' folks in town was nice ta her even if she'd done married her a Bailey that run off.

"Now I warn't no looker nor had no nice clothes like some a the fellas, but mama tole me I's the first Bailey ta ever gradgiate. That made me happy, I reckon. But when mama died wouldn't nobody give me the time a day. I tried changin' my name, but 'roun' here ever'body knows ever'body else. I thought 'bout leavin', but then I figgered even if I got me the no-good Bailey name, I ain't never done nothin' bad my whole life. This here's my home, an' I ain't done nothin' ta run from! I opened this here car lot an' I was doin' all right, mostly sellin' ta folks seen my sign offa the highway...'til like a fool I married that ol' Fay what divorced me an' took ever'thing I had. It was purty bad 'til Euladean came 'long, she's my good luck charm. Miz Amelia...I reckon I ain't so much happy as I'm less miser'ble...you know what I mean?"

Amelia Festrunk steeled herself against the tear that was forming in her right eye. "Henry, what would make you truly happy? Money? Success?"

Henry grinned and rared back in his chair. "Shoot, no, Miz Amelia! I've had money an' I been broke! 'Course I ain't never been on easy street like you an' yer fam'ly, but I ain't had ta eat outta no trash can like folks said the resta my rel'tives did. No, money ain't ever'thing. I woulda liked ta have kids, but they'd jus' be poked fun of all their lives like me, so it's better I ain't had none. Now I tell ya what'd be a hoot...I'd like ta be the chairman a that Parade Ve-hicles committee they's fixin' up fer that festival. Now that'd be somethin' ta be proud of! But ta be *happy* after so many years a mis'ry...well...I reckon the onliest thing that'd make me happy'd be if the people in this town'd stop kickin' my name an' the names a my ancestrals all over the place an' show me some respect. See, Miz Amelia, way I got it figgered...mosta that stuff they tell 'bout us Baileys is prob'ly hogwash...I heard it say them that wins the wars writes the hist'ry, an' I reckon it's prob'ly the same way 'bout us Baileys, since none of us is left ta argue no more, 'cept me. I'm the last Bailey in town...I guess when I'm gone ever'body'll be thankful they fin'lly got ridda us fer good. But jus' once't I wish I could know what really happened way back then an' let folks know we Baileys ain't so bad, if ya ever git ta know us. We're jus' reg'lar folks like ever'body else."

Amelia swallowed hard and nodded as a wave of discomfort rolled over her. She gulped the hot coffee silently until her cup was drained. She stood to leave. Henry's heart froze; it was time to talk turkey about a new vehicle, not up and take off out of the sales office! Had he said something wrong?

"Miz Amelia, whoa, now, I'm sorry if'n I offended ya by alla my belly-achin'. Here, sit back down now an' let's us talk 'bout yer car some."

Amelia shook her head. "No thank you, Mr. Bailey, you didn't offend me at all. You answered my question most eloquently, in fact. I know I need a new car but I'm afraid I don't have the time to transact any business with you today, I'm late for a meeting at the Clinic. But tell me, Mr. Bailey...what exactly is that old car of mine worth?"

Henry cocked his head in Serious Used Car Sales Manager fashion and performed some quick calculations in the air with his hands. "Tires are good, leather seats could prob'ly be sold...I reckon 'bout two hunnerd'd be the best I could do, Miz Amelia. There jus' ain't no call fer the parts on that ol' car no more. But we got all kinda payment plans here at Henry Bailey Used Cars! An' if ya don't like what ya see out there on the lot, hang tight, 'cause I'm fixin' ta make me a trip over ta Nashville to the auto auction. Jus' tell me what yer lookin' for an' I'll find it, or my name's not Henry Bailey! 'Course folks say my name ain't worth a hoot, but I reckon it's the onliest name I got!"

Amelia pursed her lips in what appeared to be her attempt at a smile. She opened the RV door and tromped down the redwood steps with surprising agility. She turned back and extended her right hand and Henry trotted down the steps to shake it.

"Mr. Bailey...Henry. Thank you for the coffee and thank you for your time. I really enjoyed our talk this morning. And you know ...it will soon be a new year. Perhaps 1999 will bring you the prosperity and respect that you wish for. I will certainly do what I can to help you."

Henry smiled in confusion as Amelia got into her car. *Be cool, Killer...sellin' a good cust'mer takes time...she said she had a nice chat with ya...she'll be back...yeah, an' my daddy's the President, she'll be back.* He turned back towards the door to the RV, but jumped as Miz Amelia honked the horn. She leaned her head out the window and hollered.

"A *Cadillac*! That's what I want Henry, a Cadillac! A late model...not brand new, but solid. And what is it they say? Oh, yes, *loaded!* And I'm partial to the color green. See what you can find Henry, and call me. Good day!"

Amelia Festrunk thrust the rusty Pontiac in reverse and sped backwards out of the car lot onto Main Street, nearly rear-ending an approaching station wagon. She drove off towards the Clinic, oblivious to the accident she'd almost caused. Henry whistled out loud.

"Killer, *you da man*! One loaded green Cadillac fer the bigshot uppity Miz Amelia Festrunk, comin' up! Work at the Poe House Groc'ry be hanged! Henry Bailey, yer ship's done come in!"

He danced a jig and returned to the warmth of the RV. He decided to wait and surprise Euladean with his big news upon her arrival home, mostly because he knew she'd never believe that the famous skinflint Amelia Festrunk was in the market for a late-model Cadillac from none other than Henry Bailey. It would be best not to break that kind of news over the phone. Euladean tended to mis-scan groceries when she was upset.

Amelia Festrunk pulled off Main and turned into the parking lot of the Quigley Quik-Steak, which was closed at this hour. She drove to the back and parked behind the dumpster where no one could see her car. She turned off the ignition and slumped back in the seat, and bawled like a baby for fifteen minutes at the tragedy of the Baileys and her sworn refusal to set their story straight nearly eight decades before. Guilt and shame flooded her entire being as she remembered her decision on that day so many years ago; now she'd come face to face with its effects on the life of what seemed to be a good and decent man. *How many others' lives did I ruin, Granddaddy? I was just a little girl, an innocent child, miserable at the loss of the one person on earth I loved more than anything. I couldn't bear to speak of it, couldn't bear to think about it...how was I to know what to do? How do I know what to do now? Do my job...do my job...tell the story...*

She dried her eyes with a Kleenex and took a few deep breaths. *Tears are not the solution, Amelia,* she remembered Mama's reprimand so well. *I could just give Henry a lot of money...an anonymous gift...he'd be extremely comfortable...I have more money in my trust fund than I can ever spend and no one to share it with...Granddaddy's disappointed face sailed across her mind. But that's not doing my job, is it, Granddaddy? They'd just accuse Henry of stealing ...he'd only have more trouble...and the money wouldn't bring him the respect he wants so much. Poor man...he'll never be elected to serve on that ridiculous Festival committee...I wonder who's in charge of making those appointments...that would be easy enough to insist upon if they want the support of the Clinic...I'll just tell Mayor Gooch if he wants our participation he'll have no choice but to make Henry a part of the Festival. And I really always have dreamed of a Cadillac...it's high time I had one and it will no doubt be profitable for Henry. At least it's a step in the right direction...I'm trying, Granddaddy, I am.*

Amelia cocked the rearview mirror and examined her face. The fatigued visage that looked back at her had definitely aged a decade in the last twenty-four hours. *Now I do look eighty-three...the Board is after me and here I sit, late for a meeting. Oh this is so difficult! Granddaddy, I should just tell him the truth! I know that's what you want me to do...it's what I should have done all those years ago. But it's so hard! That man robbed me! How can I do what he asked me when he dragged you into a frozen pit and ruined my life! I've given up everything to dedicate myself to your memory...He was a murderer, don't you see? Maybe not the way everybody thought he was, but he killed you...I vowed to hate him forever...I thought you'd understand... I promised myself I'd never tell... I'm good at not telling, just ask Leonard...*

Amelia Festrunk stared at the dumpster as her mind raced back to another time, the other veiled era of her life; she saw a beautiful blonde young woman, her best friend. They both wore stylish dresses and silk stockings, rare and cherished in those days of world war. Her best friend's husband was somewhere in the Pacific but the war was over and she decided thirty years of age was too young to sit at home with a baby when there was celebrating to be done, married or not. They'd dragged Leonard along too, nineteen years old and a looker like nobody in town, but too simple-minded to serve his country. For months the three of them had been inseparable and now they twirled together on the dance floor under the sparkling lights. They danced with each other and they danced with total strangers. It didn't matter who your partner was or how often or how deeply you kissed him. The war was over. A soldier came in with three cases of champagne and everybody drank straight out of the bottles. Amelia nearly passed out from the drinking and swirling and twirling and when she looked around, her best friend was gone and Leonard was nowhere to be found.

She needed some air, so she walked home alone under the stars that twinkled just like the lights in the dance hall. The stars made her feel that all would be right with the world. The men would come home and maybe she'd find true love, even though she was an old maid of thirty, maybe she'd find a tall soldier in need of a good nurse's care. She tugged at her bra for a key and unlocked the door to her apartment at the back of the new wing to the Clinic. Twenty new patient rooms with twenty new beds, ready and waiting to help people under the grand green sign that said HOMER FESTRUNK RESPITE HOME AND BIRTHING CLINIC. Twenty new ready rooms she'd financed and built with the money her parents left her after the accident. First Granddaddy, then just last year her own parents, all dead in tragedy. She'd heard folks say they were cursed. But she'd fought to have good come out of it all. She'd built this Clinic despite everybody's naysaying. It would be her livelihood and it would offer a comfortable apartment for her and for her fifteen-year old sister MayBelle, with a small room for Leonard if he wanted it. He preferred sleeping in one of the patient rooms in the old wing of the Clinic, said he'd rather stay out of the girls' way. And since there were plenty of new rooms for the patients, she couldn't very well deny him, she loved him so and he was her right hand.

She needed him close by.

As she unlocked the apartment door, she paused. The sound of a woman giggling floated into the courtyard...it came from the direction of the new patient rooms, from an open window. She re-locked the apartment door, then crossed the courtyard to the back door of the Clinic. The giggling was uncomfortably familiar. It grew louder and was now mixed with a man's voice. Inside the corridor, she removed her shoes and tip-toed down the hall, past each new room. Empty. Empty. Empty. There were no patients yet, the staff was all out celebrating. Louder giggles. Heavy breathing. She stopped with a jerk, her feet glued to the floor.

There in Room Number Nineteen was Leonard. And on top of him was her best friend. They were both naked as the day they were born and most definitely enjoying one another's company. Her best friend alternately sipped on a champagne bottle and Leonard's neck. Leonard smiled sheepishly and nudged his companion, who sat up as if she had every right to be in that room, with that man, without clothes. She tossed a giggle in Amelia's direction and said in a mock whisper, "Uh oh, sug, we've been caught! 'Melie, pick your chin up off the floor and wipe that smirk off your face! I told you I was gonna have some fun tonight! Don't be such a prude! Leonard, you think your sister *ever* lets her hair down and has a good time?"

Amelia braced herself against the door frame, then hung her head; she couldn't face them, but neither could she walk away. "Leonard... how could you? For God's sake, cover up with that sheet! I looked all over the dance hall for both of you ...you left me to walk home alone so you could do this to me? To your husband? You're a married woman! Your husband's on his way home from halfway around the world, where he's been fighting for his life, for God's sake! How could you do this? To all of us?"

"Sug, I'm not doin' it to you...and I'm not doin' it to us...I've been doin' it to Leonard! Hell, we've been doin' it right here under your prudish nose for 'bout six months now...don't fret 'Melie...Leonard's a grown man...he *knows* what he's *doin'*, believe me!"

The woman took another swig from the champagne bottle and made an attempt to pull a sheet over her body. Leonard lit a cigarette and smiled at his sister. "We're in love, 'Melie. I couldn't help myself! We love each other!"

"But she's *married*! What are you gonna do? Leonard...I just can't believe...what were you thinking? Were you just gonna pretend this never happened now that the war's over?"

The blonde took a drag off Leonard's cigarette and exhaled in Amelia's direction. "I'm gonna *pretend* that this baby I'm carryin' is my *husband's*, 'cause I found out today he'll be home tomorrow. And you're gonna deliver that baby, 'Melie, and you're gonna keep that secret for me and Leonard until the day you die…promise me, Amelia. You promise me you won't say anything about this. We were gonna tell you when I found out two weeks ago…I kept hopin' to get a telegram from Uncle Sam so we could get married, but I guess that's not gonna happen now unless the old coot drowns on the boat home…I swear we were gonna talk to you tonight…figure out what to do…but now the war's over…Leonard and I have agreed I'll raise this baby in my own home, with my husband. Leonard wants our child to have every advantage…he's right I guess. But we just had to have tonight, don't you understand? One more blissful night in what will be a lifetime of misery with a man I don't love. Can't you understand that, 'Melie? You are my blood-sworn friend and I love you like a sister, and I'm begging you to keep this secret. This is our secret, the three of us, 'Melie. We all have a love for each other that most folks can't ever have. Say you will, Amelia. Swear you'll never tell anybody about who that baby's father is…swear you'll help me care for this baby…your brother's baby…your best friend's baby…please!"

Amelia blinked and stared out at the red dumpster behind the Quigley Quik-Steak. She reached into her purse for another Kleenex and daubed her eyes. *I kept my word without a flinch because I loved them both so much. I've kept their secret all these years, never asked her for anything. Maybe she can help me now. Maybe she won't hate me when I tell her what I promised Granddaddy. She'll help me figure out what to do, how to make this thing right. Got to talk to her, today. But she's never alone anymore. God, I don't even know if she'll remember who I am, or what I'm even talking about. But she was the decisive one…she'll know what to do, if she's got her wits about her. Give me more time, Granddaddy…please…*

December 30, 1998; Festrunk Respite Home & Birthing Clinic

"*Now Miz 'Melia, Miz MayBelle...*ya'll both know that one little bitty ol'sign ain't gonna hurt *nobody*, an' it'll probly get ya'll more puh-bliss-ty than ya'll have ever *dreamed* of!"

Mayor Barnard "Barney" Gooch tugged slightly at his best polyester tie, the one with the Confederate Battle Flag motif, where it encircled the too-tight neck of his polyester short-sleeved dress shirt. Despite the grey, cold day, Barney Gooch was sweating, because for the past two hours he had diligently followed behind Miss Amelia and Miss MayBelle Festrunk as they made their rounds visiting patients at the Festrunk Respite Home and Birthing Clinic. It was two hours of Pure-D Hell, and Barney Gooch was exhausted.

He had been summoned from home at six-thirty that morning by Miss Amelia who demanded that he make his immediate presence known at the Clinic, holiday week or no holiday week. And since Miss Amelia had rejected every effort he'd made in the past two months to discuss the importance of sponsoring the 136th Annual Chestnut Ridge Sons of Glory Festival, he knew he'd better hit the ground running. Barney intended to review with the Festrunk sisters his detailed Sons of Glory advertising charts and diagrams, the ones he'd designed himself on his home computer. This morning, when Amelia Festrunk informed him that any discussion would only take place as he followed her on rounds, Barney had soldiered up his charts and diagrams and dragged them down every one of the Clinic's corridors. He soon discovered it was too much of a challenge to set up his visual aids across the laps of seriously ill patients, without disrupting their quality of care.

After two hours of watching the Festrunk sisters take countless temperatures, change bedpans, and dress ghastly oozing wounds, Barney Gooch had just about reached his limit with these two old maids, and he was quickly losing his diplomatic mayoral demeanor. He ushered the ladies over to a small lounge area and pointed to the chairs.

"Miz 'Melia, Miz MayBelle, we gotta stop right *here*, right *now* an' ya'll gotta give me *five minutes*, 'cause I'm 'bout ta have a heart attack an' ya'll ain't heard the first word I said!"

Amelia Festrunk looked over her trifocals at Mayor Gooch, then examined the clipboard in her left hand. It was working out just as she'd planned. She straightened to her full six-foot-two inch height and spoke in a gentile but stern voice, "Mayor, I was most forthright with you on the telephone this morning. We are *not* in the Festival-running business here...we have patients whose lives are at stake."

She checked her watch, then pursed her lips at the Mayor. "All right. I suppose we can stop here for five minutes. Begin."

Barney Gooch inhaled with surprise as the sisters each took a seat. "Great! Okay, listen up. The Festival sponsorships is five thousand each an' we're askin' ya'll ta be a sponsor, seein' as how ya'll are one a the town's Foundin' Fam'lies an' ya'll turn a good profit offa all us sick folks. Afore we go any further, is that somethin' ya'll would 'gree ta do?"

This was not the sales pitch he'd planned, but a man had to work within the parameters he'd been given. Amelia turned to MayBelle and nodded.

"Yes, Mayor, although I feel that this Festival is nothing but a supreme waste of taxpayer dollars. A simple pageant such as we've had every year for the last one hundred and thirty-five years is one thing, but a *week* of Festival activities? I think it's utterly ridiculous, just another excuse for a bunch of socialites to traipse around in unflattering evening gowns. Are there opportunities for our young people to learn about the history of the founding of this town?"

Mayor Gooch nodded enthusiastically. "Oh, yes ma'am, fer sure. There's gonna be reenactments a plenty! Lotsa edyacational stuff an' all, 'course that ain't my area...I'm in charge a publissty...so ya'll'll do it? Great, that's great, thank ya'll very much!"

Amelia silently noted that the reenacting would most likely take a different twist once she figured out how to Do My Job and tell the truth. *I'm really going to sock it to them...wonder how many people will want to participate after they learn what really happened?* Mayor Gooch rared back on his heels.

"Now, all ya'll got ta do is 'gree ta post one *'CHESTNUT RIDGE SONS OF GLORY FESTIVAL'* sign in one tiny corner of ya'll's big, spacious, *prime vizbilty* lot by that innerstate highway fer the next year. Ya know, it'll help improve ya'lls imidge, too, sorta hide the fact that this here main buildin' needs a bit a renovatin'. Ya'll jus'tell me where ta stick that sign, an' I'll be outta ya'll's hair like lice after lye soap! Oh, an' I'll need yer check fer the five thou too."

Amelia frowned and crossed her arms. "Mayor Gooch. I am not in the habit of *'sticking'* anything on the grounds of this facility. Our image doesn't require any improving whatsoever, and our building is completely up to Code! May I remind you that my sister and I have dedicated our lives to serving the fine citizens of this fair town, just as our beloved grandfather Captain Homer Festrunk, Medical Officer to the 44th Regiment of the Tennessee Riders, did until the day of his very tragic death in 1922, at the able age of ninety-one?"

"Yes, ma'am, but...."

"And may I *remind* you, Mayor Gooch, speaking now in my official capacity as Chief Operating Officer of the Festrunk Respite Home and Birthing Clinic, that our *sole* function at this facility is to nurture our sick, heal our wounded, and vaccinate our unguarded youth against the many vile medical scourges on this planet which remain yet untamed? Medicine is *war*, Gooch and serious business, and every dollar I spend to *'improve my image,'* as you say, is one less dollar I have to pay my nurses or buy bandages made in the good old U.S. of A.! We must continue our mission, Sons of Glory Festival or no Sons of Glory Festival, do you understand, Mayor? It is here that the real battles and triumphs of life are won!"

"Yes, Miz 'Melia, but I reckon ya'll don't...."

"And I will remind you that we are the medical instruments of God Almighty, and if the citizens of this town don't like our methods or our policies, then they can just drive themselves over to the government charity hospital at Murfreesboro and take their chances with government charity germs!"

Barney Gooch nervously tugged at the tired elastic waistband of his polyester slacks.

"Well, now, Miz 'Melia, there's no need ta..."

"Mayor Gooch, while your frivolous administration spends the hard-earned dollars of the taxpayers, we here at the Festrunk Respite Home and Birthing Clinic will continue to nurse, to bandage, to collect from Medicare. We will strive for better bedpans, improved cholesterol scores and surgery-free breast augmentations through regular chest exercise. No, Mayor Gooch, not for *this* facility the merriment of Chestnut Ridge, because we are sworn to our task, and *someone* must be here when the merry-makers fall from their high-heeled dancing shoes, or from the water tower, whichever comes first. I have never allowed any kind of outside advertisement to touch the sacred grounds of this facility, and I will not start *now*."

Barney Gooch stared at the sisters. Amelia Homeranne Festrunk might be eighty-three years old, but her words were as firm as the grip of her gnarled hands. She waged her own medical war on the diseases of Chestnut Ridge, and through it all she remained the veritable embodiment of the Battle-Axe Nurse. Amelia Festrunk ran a tight ship, but she had deep pockets and a long arm in a working class town. MayBelle, barely five feet tall and plump, was altogether a different breed. Her pink nurse's uniform was supplemented with a long quadruple strand of pink pearls, matching pearl cluster earbobs and bright pink orthopedic pumps. Miss MayBelle was fifteen years younger than Amelia and in her day had been considered the Festrunk family beauty, if there was such a thing. MayBelle Festrunk's warmth, charm and general naiveté starkly contrasted with Amelia's curt tone and savvy business acumen. But the folks of Chestnut Ridge readily accepted their assistance and forgave the Festrunk sisters their occasional eccentricities, particularly as they operated the lone medical facility within a forty-five mile radius. MayBelle winked at Barney.

"Oh, now, 'Melie, dear, don't you just think it would be precious to have one *little itsy bitsy sign* for the Festival? I mean, don't you think Granddaddy and Daddy would be proud that we were doing our fair share?" Miss MayBelle's voice was sweeter than corn syrup. She touched Amelia's arm.

"One little ol' sign in the far corner of the Felicia Festrunk Tuberculosis Recuperatory Garden won't matter a smidge, and besides, if we don't take part, we may lose heads, uh, *beds*, to St. Ignatius the Elder. I guess you heard the latest, Mayor...they've got tv's in every patient room! Those heathen Catholics just have to watch their soap operas, even if they're on their deathbeds!"

Miss MayBelle's face drew into a tight frenzy of flesh as she twisted her hands in Amelia's direction, fearing she may have pushed too far. Amelia Festrunk shot MayBelle a stern look, then drew an exaggerated breath. Her leverage was nearly complete.

"Mr. Mayor, as usual, my sweet baby sister has expressed her deepest desire without first considering the business ramifications of such a foolish whim."

Amelia tapped an ink pen on her clipboard in silence. Barney Gooch smiled sheepishly at Miss MayBelle, who returned his gaze with the worried, confused stare of a small child. He could see it was necessary to give his best Gooch Office Supply Super Sales Pitch on this one. He folded his hands and closed his eyes in mock despair, then he looked pleadingly at Amelia Festrunk and raised one hand over his heart.

"On my honor, I promise, Miz 'Melia, as Mayor a Chestnut Ridge, that we will dig the TEE-*niniest* hole necessary, an' we'll keep that sign painted an' lookin' fine, an' we'll even give ya'll a free haif-page ad in the 'ficial Sons of Glory O-fficial Program! An' look, Miz 'Melia, the Festrunk Clinic's southeast corner was s'lected as the *top*, number one prime location fer this here sign! Now, if ya'll don't 'low us ta put this up in yer lot, we'll miss hunnerds an' thousands a po-tential Festival visitors off I-24! I mean, ya'll got ta think about this here bizness ya'll are runnin'!"

Barney Gooch adjusted his tie once more, held out his hands, and went in for the kill. "*Hell,* oh, 'scuse me, but ya'll just *think*, Miz 'Melia, Miz MayBelle, if just *haif* a them hunnerds an' thousands a folks need medical 'tention during the Festival, ya'll will just 'bout be guaranteed more bizness than ya'll can *handle*! Ya'll'd best be hirin' some more *people* roun'here right quick! I mean, a Festival like this one we're a-plannin' is gonna draw all them hist'ry busts, you know, all them ol' timers who wanna see who's re-lated ta the Great Confed'racy! Them collecters a Civil War paraplegia an' all! There's *big money* in this thing, I'm tellin' ya!"

In the realization that he had seized upon the potential winning point in this debate, Barney Gooch's countenance deepened to a bright burgundy. Sweat poured off his bald brow, and his Confederate flag tie clung to his sweat-soaked shirt. Mayor Barney Gooch was the epitome of the carnival barker gone bad. Yet there was no response from Amelia or MayBelle. Barney took a deep breath.

"Hey, now, I don' tole ya'll, I mean it, this thing's gonna be *BIG*! We're gonna advertise in the Nashville papers, an' on the radio, an' them spectaters is gonna drive out here in *drones*! An' with that there Miss Americana Beauty Contest, well, we cain't even begin ta perdict the crowds, no, sir! Why, they'll pack up Granpappy in about fifteen blankets, an' stuff him in the car, an' drive right there on that highway by *your facil'ty*!"

Barney loosened his tie, planted both legs firmly with bent knees, and stretched one hand out as if he could see the crowds gathering at that very minute.

"But *oh my God*, Granpappy's gittin' too excited 'bout seein' some a this hist'ry stuff, his mem'ry's comin' back, an' some li'l rug rat in the backseat's gonna holler, *'PULL OVER QUICK, DEDDY! Granpappy's a-havin' one a his fits, an' we got ta git him to a HOSPITAL! He's COMATOAST!'*

"An' then the Momma, or the Granny, dependin' on who's ridin' shotgun, will holler, *'HEY, I 'member there's a hospital back there RIGHT ON THE MAIN ROAD!'* An' the sister will shout, *'DEDDY! Don't ya'll 'member that BIG SIGN we saw for the FESTIVAL? OH, MY GOD, THAT'S WHERE THE HOSPITAL IS! DEDDY! GIT THE LEAD OUT!'*"

Barney straightened his posture and his tie, ran a hand over his glistening bald head and said, "I'm tellin' ya'll, them people'll high-tail it right over here an', well, there's yer saved lives an' yer payin' patients. Might even bring in 'nuff fer one a them big Cap Scan Machines, like they got over ta Nashville! Ya'll listen up, I heard thew the grapevine them St. Ignoramus Cath'lics is gonna git one a them Cap Scans in here real soon!"

Miss MayBelle stood up and patted Barney on the back as he drew great, heaving breaths. She handed him her pink lace hankie and whispered, "You're *glowing*, Barney! My stars, you're so very *passionate*!"

Miss Amelia stood and glanced at Mayor Gooch in disgust. She looked at her clipboard, then at the Mayor. She had toyed with Barney Gooch long enough.

"Very well, Mayor. I do not have any more time to waste arguing with you today. You may put *one*... I repeat *one* tasteful sign on our property. And we will take a free *full* page ad in that program and my sister MayBelle shall design it..."

Barney exhaled with relief as MayBelle winked at him. Amelia pointed at the chair she had vacated, motioning for Barney to sit. He did, and she bent her six-foot-two-inch frame over him and stared directly into his face.

"And as we have indeed been blessed in our business endeavors in this town, you may put the Clinic down as a five-thousand dollar sponsor. You may also note that my sister, brother and I will add another five thousand of our own money, for a total of ten thousand dollars."

Barney Gooch's heart fluttered in his barrel chest. This was worth every single second of lost sleep and greater than he'd ever dreamed. MayBelle clapped her hands like a young child, but Amelia wasn't finished.

"Now, Mayor. There is one small thing you must do for *me*, and if you refuse, I shall completely withdraw every sponsorship penny *and* my prime visibility sign-displaying real estate, do I make myself clear?"

Giant beads of perspiration trailed Barney's temples. He nodded.

"You shall appoint Henry Bailey as Official Sons of Glory Festival Parade Vehicles Chairman. There shall be no discussion, no deliberation, no argument now or in the future, and he shall be treated with the utmost respect by you and your entire Festival crew. If I so much as hear the slightest *rumor* that Mister Bailey's abilities, faculties or reputation is in question, I shall not only withdraw my support... I shall come after you with my number twelve scalpel, and you, Mayor, will learn the true meaning of a sucking chest wound. Now I do not wish to speak to you again on this subject. And if there is the slightest problem, the smallest inconvenience..."

"No, ma'am, Miz 'Melia, I will per-son'lly undertake this 'sponsibility, although it don't make no sense..."

"It is not up to you to determine what is sensible and what is not, do I make myself absolutely clear? Now, if we are finished, we must complete our rounds. I expect a full report on Mister Bailey's appointment...you should do it immediately. *Good day!*"

Amelia Homeranne Festrunk clasped the clipboard rigidly at one side as her bony legs escorted their orthopedic-shoed feet down the pink and blue tiled corridor. As she passed from earshot, Barney Gooch hugged Miss MayBelle and kissed her on the cheek. He noticed that she smelled a tad of stale violet water, the kind his grandmother used to wear. He glanced at his watch and realized he was late for his appointment at Leigh-Lee & Sons.

"Oh, Miz MayBelle, thank ya, thank ya, thank ya! Yer a real fine lady, an' I am in yer service, although I ain't so sure yer sister's of a right mind, askin' fer that no-good sumbitch Henry Bailey ta be in charge a the Parade Veh'cles. But hey, money talks an' I'm a'listenin'! Now, I'm runnin' real late, I got ta git over downtown, I got a 'portant meetin', but when can we get tagether for a 'ficial sign review? You just name the day an' the place an' I'll be there with bells on!"

Miss MayBelle smiled demurely, twirling pink pearls across an ample bosom and checked her nurse-cap-coiffure with one hand. Barney's kiss made her cheeks flush, and she felt warm and tingly all over. She giggled loudly, placed one plump hand on her hip and winked.

"Oh, Mayor, you just made a *funny!* You'll be there with *bells on*... my middle name is Belle! Isn't that a *scream*? *With bells on*! Oh, my... Barney... And you bein' the Mayor...I've never had a City Official...you wanna try me on for *size*, honey? I've always thought you were just as cute as a jaybird, and I know you must be overworked and under way too much stress, sweetie, right? I can cure you of that, sugarplum, you *betcha*! You know, just because there's snow on the mountain, doesn't mean there's no *fire* in the valley! I always *knew* you had a thing for me!"

A stunned Barney Gooch raised a hand in protest; Miz MayBelle had it all wrong, completely wrong, *severely* wrong. But she placed a hand over his mouth and ran one plump finger around his ears. Then she whispered into the crook of his neck,

"Oh, now...don't you say one word! You just let li'l ol'Miss MayBelle fix everything! How 'bout Tuesday, say three o'clock? We can meet in an empty patient room in the old sanitorium wing...Melie will be taking her afternoon nap! Oh, this is gonna be *fun*! I just love advertising!"

Barney gulped as Miss MayBelle's finger stroked his cheek.

"And Barney, you listen to me...anything you need for this Festival...and I do mean *anything*...you just let me know...don't you worry about my sister...anything at all!"

Miss MayBelle turned to leave, then blew Mayor Gooch a great big kiss over her shoulder. She twirled her pink pearls in his direction and waved as she sauntered off toward the elevator. As he watched Miss MayBelle stroll lazily down the pink and blue corridor of the Festrunk Respite Home and Birthing Clinic, Barney Gooch realized that being Mayor of Chestnut Ridge during a Festival was far more hazardous to his health than selling office supplies, and that it was gonna be a very long year indeed.

CHAPTER FIVE - GOD LOVES A WINNER

New Year's Day 1999; The Leigh-Lee Mansion, Chestnut Ridge, Tennessee

"Hello, Miss Stella? This is Tiffany Noel Leigh-Lee and...oh, did I wake you up? Well, of course I know it's New Year's Day, but it's also Friday, and it's only three-hundred-and-sixty-four days until the Pageant, and that's really the only thing I can focus on right now! Uh-huh....uh-huh...well, hey, it's not my fault you drank twenty-seven beers at some trashy trailer park New Year's Eve party!

"You won't get any sympathy from me, Miss Stella, 'cause I'm officially in training, and right now I'd give my Little Miss Cotton Picker's tiara just to drink half a beer, but I really don't have time for this, ok? I'm looking for Miss Forrestine....uh-huh...uh-huh...well, isn't she scheduled for her weekly root rub and flaky heel treatment today? So what you're telling me is that you're *CLOSED*? Oh, you're opening up just for Miss Forrestine...at three...yes, Miss Forrestine does always say that *'Beauty never takes a holiday!'* Well, just *please* Miss Stella *please* have Miss Forrestine call me the very second she gets there. And tell her it's a dire emergency!"

Tiffany Noel Leigh-Lee hung the pink princess phone on its cradle and leaned back against frilly pillows piled high on her mother's pink chintz-canopied Louis XIV bed. Tiffany Noel's perfect size 36B breasts moved slightly underneath a tattered Kappa Zeta Mu nightshirt. Her flawless skin was exquisitely tanned, despite Chestnut Ridge's January cold, thanks to the efforts of Mrs. Forrestine Culpepper, Tiffany Noel's personal beauty pageant career manager.

Tiffany Noel's daddy was Chestnut Ridge's most influential and powerful attorney, descended from a long line of town fathers; and when it came to his beautiful daughter, money was no object, which made the fact that he was also on the board of the only bank in town a definite plus. If Tiffany Noel needed a personal career manager to strategize and win a Miss American Beauty Pageant crown, and if Forrestine Culpepper was able and willing to *be* that manager, at an affordable ninety-five dollars per day (plus out of pocket expenses), then by God, Tiffany Noel would get what she needed. The pursuit of national pageant titles was not for the faint-hearted nor for the impoverished.

In the salon-challenged burg of Chestnut Ridge, Forrestine Culpepper's influence at the Quigley Beauty Box was a critical factor for any pageant hopeful. Forrestine secured Tiffany Noel's standing Monday-Wednesday-Friday *"Tan to Your Personal Best"* sessions at reduced rates for the twelve months prior to The Big Day. Forrestine's trademarked, pageant-winning

"Positive Attitude Over Adversity" program required perfect tanning, without tan lines.

And though the Fiftieth Miss American Beauty Pageant was not until January 1, 2000, a full year away, this was war, and not only would Tiffany Noel win, she would win *tanned.* But more importantly, to be eligible for the Miss American Beauty Pageant, Tiffany Noel had to first capture the crown at the 136th Chestnut Ridge Sons of Glory Festival, held during the last full week of December, in the last year before the new millennium. Forrestine Culpepper's entire career in the beauty business was riding on the perfectly proportioned shoulders of Tiffany Noel Leigh-Lee. Her twenty-five-plus years of also-ran anguish from watching hundreds of her young pupils fail to make the cut at the Miss American Beauty Pageant level would soon be turned to triumph. Tiffany Noel Leigh-Lee was Forrestine's all-time trump card, and if God had one merciful atom in His being, her Tiffany Noel would not only win the last beauty pageant of this century, but also the very first one of the new century and the new millennium. Forrestine didn't believe in coincidence; if this wasn't a direct sign from God, well, Forrestine Culpepper didn't know what was.

But it hadn't been easy. Thanks to a constant and beleaguering stream of letters written by Forrestine and her league of pageant-hopeful parents and investors to the Miss American Beauty Pageant organizers, the Fiftieth Anniversary Miss American Beauty Pageant would take place in a location none other than Chestnut Ridge, Tennessee. And it would come on New Year's Day, 2000, the closing day of the 136th Annual Chestnut Ridge Sons of Glory Festival, a wholesome, week-long, all-American event planned to attract thousands upon thousands of Civil War history buffs and end-of-the-millennium thrill seekers, not to mention the hundreds and thousands of Miss American Beauty Pageant spectators from around the world.

Forrestine Culpepper had single-handedly put Chestnut Ridge on the map with this beauty pageant coup; now her neighbors and detractors would be present as they watched her prized candidate, Tiffany Noel, win the 136th Annual Chestnut Ridge Sons of Glory Festival Queen title, and then the very next day, take the Fiftieth Anniversary Miss American Beauty Pageant crown, with its five-hundred-thousand dollar cash prize. A cash prize of which Forrestine Culpepper would earn no less than fifty percent.

There was a great deal more than beauty and poise at stake, however. Forrestine intended to desposit her fair share of that prize money directly into her own bank account, for the glory of God. She had earned a small fortune over the years from discerning parents who paid dearly to expose their Chestnut Ridge hometown belles to everything from charm and party manners to exclusive European fat-reduction regimens. After nearly three decades of molding countless young women into proper, upstanding models of eligible Southern young womanhood, for the purpose of attracting eligible, well-to-do Southern husbands, Forrestine Culpepper was hungry for The Big National Win, and Tiffany Noel was the repast.

Forrestine's sculpted successes graduated to become the *grande dames* of the South, or at least, the *grande dames* of the Chestnut Ridge area, and she knew that no one could refute her expertise, her reputation or her fees, because she was also the dutiful wife of Chestnut Ridge's most popular minister, Reverend Cameron Culpepper, of the First United Assembly of God's Children. She was therefore the church's single largest cash donor. Brother Culpepper was the fifth-generation Culpepper to work in the ministry founded by his ancestor Chester Culpepper, one of Chestnut Ridge's celebrated Confederate heroes and town founders. The Brother and his dutiful wife lived up to extremely high expectations concerning good Christian behavior, and for the most part, their unquestioning flock forgave Forrestine if she occasionally seemed to place more emphasis on skin tone and mascara than she did on studying The Good Book.

If certain members of the Church Ladies Guild chided her lack of concentration during Bible study, or her absence at soup kitchen duty, Forrestine retorted with a smile that she was merely using her God-given talents in makeup application and posture therapy to further His mission on earth. If those no-good gossipers didn't like her career choice, they could just look in Brother Pete Taylor's ledger and see that Sister Culpepper had been a Tither of Meritorious Record for the last twenty years straight! Beauty was an excellent business venture, and The First United Assembly of God's Children proved an even better tax deduction.

Tiffany Noel Leigh-Lee was Forrestine's greatest project. Since her third birthday, upon winning the "Little Miss Southern Sugar" contest under Forrestine's direction, Tiffany Noel's mass of shiny black curls and her robin's egg blue eyes had charmed Chestnut Ridge and twelve surrounding counties for over sixteen years. Tiffany Noel won an endless stream of beauty pageants, twirling competitions and festival queen titles, all supervised and handled of course, by Forrestine Culpepper, at reasonable rates by the hour or by the crown.

And if Tiffany Noel had only stayed with the Forrestine system, if she had truly worked her program, Tiffany Noel could have won Miss American Beauty two years ago, no doubt about it; she could have been the veritable embodiment of Miss American Beauty, because everyone knew that the Pageant prize money was merely a drop in the bucket. Once you cinched the Crown, there were cars and stipends and the lecture circuit, and after about two or three years of that, well, Forrestine would have been sitting right now in some elegant spa in Switzerland, nurturing her pores into retirement instead of laboring tirelessly along the endless beauty trail. But Tiffany Noel's meddling father had insisted that his daughter attend a "real" university, forty-five miles from home, instead of the Chestnut Ridge Community College, despite Forrestine's protests that big city smog and fuel emissions were "certain skin tone death and beauty ruination."

So Forrestine's Miss American Beauty shoe-in left home to meander through the smog and fuel emissions amidst the unchurched and unclean, and meander she did. In just two semesters at Middle Tennessee State University in Murfreesboro, Tiffany Noel earned the distinction of being the cheerleader with the prettiest smile and the lowest grade point average in the history of the school. She partied with the jocks, pulled all-nighters with the Kappa Sigs, chain-smoked cigarettes, drank Jack Daniel's from endless paper cups, and spent her entire four-year college fund on designer clothes during one sorority spring break road trip to Beverly Hills.

But what was worse, in Forrestine's eyes, was that Tiffany Noel totally and completely ignored the strict Forrestine Culpepper No-Fail Beauty Regimen! *Totally*! It was inconceivable to Forrestine that such a results-proven system could be so casually dismissed...it was a wonder that Tiffany Noel had any complexion left whatsoever. Nine months without exfoliation was an unthinkable, unredeemable sin, but now Forrestine Culpepper was once again the conductor of Tiffany Noel's personal beauty train. Forrestine sincerely believed that Tiffany Noel's little trip to co-ed hell and back was a punishment which had been instituted by God, courtesy of some prayerful plea-bargaining on her part.

Every miserable night during Tiffany Noel's college career, as Forrestine wound her long platinum hair onto satin rollers, as she expertly applied twenty-dollar-a-pop Italian mud on her cheeks to prevent the onset of premature age lines, she looked hard into the bathroom mirror, past the *"A DAY WITHOUT MAKEUP IS LIKE A DAY WITHOUT JESUS"* sticker, past the photo of herself winning the 1963 Miss Chestnut Ridge Centennial Queen title…

Forrestine stared right past these daily reminders of beauty duty and swore aloud (while the faucet ran at full tilt so Cameron wouldn't hear) that she would personally donate to the church *every single cent* of all future beauty instruction revenues if only God would answer her One Prayer. Nothing more would she ever ask of her Maker but that He grant her this dream, *please Jesus*, please let Tiffany Noel return to her Beautiful Flock.

And it would really glorify Him as well, she reminded God, because it would prove that the errant ways of the un-beautiful and un-dutiful world bring no salvation. Forrestine Culpepper was prepared to make an example of Miss Tiffany Noel, to save hundreds, perhaps thousands of lives on the

Holy Beauty Highway. And so for nights on end, Forrestine tilted her rollered head back to the Heavens, closed her eyes tightly while the faucet gushed, drew a very large breath, and begged,

"Please-just-please-dear-God-and-Saviour-Merciful-make-Tiffany-Noel-fall-from-grace-flat-on-her-face-and-come-crawling-back-to-Chestnut-Ridge-for-my-help-in-time-to-enter-the-Miss-Chestnut-Ridge-Sons-of-Glory-Queen-crown-so-she-can-apply-for-the-Miss-American-Beauty-Pageant-under-the-auxiliary-regional-title-winner's-clause-section-eight-dash-three-of-the-Miss-American-Beauty-Contest-Inc.-official-rules. PLEASE!"

Night after night she prayed, and finally, after nine prayerful months, just as Forrestine's patience with the Almighty was about to run dry, God Most Merciful in His Infinite Wisdom came through. Of course, He had to drag it out just a *bit* longer than Forrestine would have preferred, and then there was that *test*, that momentary heart failure at the Quigley Beauty Box last May, while Forrestine's roots were being camouflaged.

As Stella Stanley pulled Forrestine's hair through a tight beige spandex cap, she tauntingly informed Forrestine how she'd heard that Tiffany Noel Leigh-Lee had not only been kicked out of school, but that she had also run off and gotten *married* to an MTSU football player; a football player who had himself dropped out and who now planned a promising career selling lawn mowers at his father's hardware store. Her Tiffany Noel! *A lawn mower salesman's wife!* With the voice of a thousand devils, Stella Stanley pointed out to Forrestine that her One True Chance at Beauty Greatness, Tiffany Noel Leigh-Lee, was now no longer a virgin and that she was living in Memphis, that evil, sordid city full of heathen Negro music and pore-clogging humidity! Stella had to throw ice water in Forrestine's face to make her come round.

Forrestine was undaunted, however, and she continued her prayers every night, despite Stella Stanley's bad news, despite the constant flurry of rumors that Tiffany Noel had gained thirty pounds and was living on chocolate doughnuts and macaroni and cheese. Despite an eyewitness account from Sister Bernice Hoover, whose cousin had a third cousin that lived in the same apartment complex as Tiffany, who claimed that Tiffany Noel wore spandex shorts and rubber flip flops, and horror of horrors, she was seen buying outdated, over-the-counter mascara at the Memphis Flea Market. Forrestine had great confidence in her Maker…this was just a momentary setback, and she continued to pray hard at every opportunity. In the interest of time and success, however, she altered her prayer,

"Dear Father, I now know You are testing me in preparation for The One True Test of Every Soul. But I can TAKE IT! You know I can! I know that Tiffany Noel's marriage will not last because I know that YOU want me to supervise her in the Miss American Beauty contest! Because YOU want me to win, so YOU

can win more souls! YES! I know! And I also know that under Section Five of the National Pageant Code, Tiffany Noel can maintain her eligibility if she gets an annulment, not a divorce!

"And because I BELIEVE, I will PROMISE that if you answer this poor, humble pilgrim's plea, I will BUILD for You! I will build the First United Assembly of God's Children Forrestine Culpepper Mission in Your honor! In some poor, undeserving country where they don't even have NAIL FILES! YES, LORD! I'll build You a mission, with tasteful brick and a bell tower and oak... no... mahogany prayer benches, I promise!"

Forrestine Culpepper was very convincing, and after three months of intense begging, at all hours of the day and night, finally God took the hint. One Friday as she departed the Quigley Beauty Box en route to teach her four o-clock *"Party Manners for Pretty Misses"* class, Forrestine looked up from her patent leather handbag and stared at God's Gift Materialized.

The hour of deliverance was at hand. Tiffany Noel, sporting a really bad haircut, zero makeup, a Calvin Klein suit that was at least three seasons *passé*, two sizes too tight, and wrinkled, stood at the edge of the sidewalk. She carried a garment bag in one hand, and *oh my God bless me Jesus*, a *cigarette* in the other. She walked straight up to Forrestine, dropped both bag and cigarette on the ground, wrapped her arms around Forrestine Culpepper, and cried her heart out,

"OHHH, M-M-MISSSS FORRESTINE! I-I-I-M S-S-SO UNHAPPY! I'VE L-L-LEFT M-M-MY HUSBAND AND C-C-COME HOME! W-W-WILL YOU PL-PL-PLEASE HELP M-M-ME?"

Instantly recognizing God's little miracle personified, Forrestine wasted no time. She reached out to Tiffany Noel, "Come, child, we must PRAY!"

Forrestine sharply pulled Tiffany Noel Leigh-Lee down onto her knees in the parking lot of the Quigley Beauty Box, right in front of Stella Stanley and all of Chestnut Ridge Main Street, but most importantly, in front of God. Forrestine was not one to delay God's gratification. There was just way too much at stake. The deal had been done, and the meter was running. So Forrestine deposited her most polished coins.

"OH LORD, FOR BRINGING THIS SWEET LOST CHILD BACK TO HER HOME AND BACK TO HER SENSES, WE GIVE YOU THANKS AND GLORY AND HONOR, AND WE WILL NOT FORGET OUR PROMISE FOR THE GIFT THAT HAS FINALLY BEEN DELIVERED, OH GOD MOST MERCIFUL."

Tiffany Noel suddenly stopped bawling, and as she realized she was kneeling on blacktop in her designer dress, she released her arms from around Forrestine's shoulders and moved to stand, but Forrestine's quick, tight fingers pulled her back to the prayer position.

"AND FOR THE GREAT HEINOUS SINS THAT THIS CHILD HAS COMMITTED DESPITE MY CEASELESS, TIRELESS, CHRISTIAN EFFORTS TO TEACH HER BETTER, WE HUMBLY ASK YOUR FORGIVENESS, AND ASK YOU TO SET TIFFANY NOEL BACK ON TRACK IN HER LIFE OF SERVICE TO THE BEAUTY-CHALLENGED... AND TO YOU, OH LORD."

A small crowd of Main Street onlookers began to gather immediately behind Forrestine's big powder-blue Cadillac Eldorado convertible (not only did it have ample trunk space for carrying makeup cases to pageants, the convertible doubled as a Cost of Goods Sold because pageant contestants could ride in it during parades, waving beautifully while they saved on car rental costs). As Forrestine continued her litany, some of Forrestine's fellow church members knelt down next to Tiffany Noel and joined hands, swaying as Forrestine's strong voice carried her words over the parking lot of the Quigley Beauty Box. As she swooned with the prayerful, Forrestine's platinum beehive hairdo moved perilously from side to side, which caused Stella Stanley to frown from the door of the Quigley Beauty Box and wonder whether that deal on Do-Rite Hairspray was really such a bargain after all. Stella made a mental note to donate the rest of the cans to the Chestnut Ridge Charity Auction next month as Forrestine's private Thanksgiving service grew louder.

"AND ALSO OH LORD WE THANK YOU JESUS FOR THE HURT WHICH YOU HAVE BROUGHT ABOUT IN AN EFFORT TO TEACH THIS YOUNG WOMAN A MUCH-DESERVED LESSON."

Tiffany Noel was now very uncomfortable, as parking lot gravel dug into her knees, as the germy, sweaty hands of total strangers held hers, and with Miss Forrestine about to lecture her in front of the entire town. She turned her tear-streaked face around nervously and saw Stella Stanley sit down on the hood of Forrestine's powder-blue Eldorado. Stella lit a cigarette and eyed Tiffany Noel's ill-fitting designer dress.

"YES, LORD, WE THANK YOU FOR THE HEALING HURT WHICH HAS FINALLY SHOWN THIS ERRANT SERVANT THE WAY HOME TO ME...uh...TO HER FAMILY AND TO YOU, OH GOD."

"AMEN, SISTER CULPEPPER! PRAISE GOD!" The small crowd was now linked together arm in arm to form a prayer circle, which was in actuality more of a prayer obtuse triangle, around and behind the Eldorado. They continued to sway and nod in concern for Sister Tiffany Noel's well-being. It was time for the big finish, the hook. Forrestine jerked Tiffany Noel up from her knees and shouted, eyes closed toward Heaven,

"DEAR LORD, THIS YOUNG SINNER OFFERS YOU A PROMISE AS TESTIMONY TO HER NEWFOUND REDEMPTION! HEAR HER PROMISE, OH LORD!"

Forrestine extended Tiffany Noel's arms toward heaven, and as the prayer obtuse triangle elongated, Forrestine put her own face directly in front of Tiffany Noel's tear-stained one and said calmly,

"Tiffany Noel Leigh-Lee, you must make a pact with God. You must promise to be the best person you can be and never waste another chance in life! Are you prepared to make this pledge, to repay God for the awful mess you've made of your Natural Talents and Gifts?"

Tiffany Noel swallowed hard, looked nervously around at the strangers-turned-prayer-brethren, and longingly eyed her still-burning cigarette on the pavement by the Eldorado's left rear tire.

"Well, Miss *Forrestine*, I mean, you know I believe in *God* and everything, but I don't really go to your *church* or anything, and um, I think God knows what I've been through… I really don't see why I have to re-hash the details right now in front of *everybody* since he's...what is it...oh yeah...he's *omni-impotent* and all that, and I'd really just like to go home and see my Mama. If God wants me, I guess he can just find me there. He should know where I live, I guess."

Tiffany Noel smiled her prettiest smile at Forrestine Culpepper and the gathered flock, reached down to tug at her dress, and started to walk away. Suddenly she was yanked back by Forrestine whose red face glared in disgust at her prized pupil.

"CHILD OF THE DEVIL! OF COURSE YOU'D RATHER JUST GO ON HOME! TAKE THE EASY WAY, THE QUICK WAY!"

"AMEN! AMEN SISTER CULPEPPER! THE DEVIL! AMEN!"

The members of the crowd, torn between their disbelief at Tiffany Noel's flippance and their growing concern for Forrestine's badly leaning hair unit, became inflamed.

"SHE'S STILL A SINNER!!" IT'S A TRICK!!" "THE DEVIL'S SEIZED HER INNARDS!" "SHE MUST HUMBLE HERSELF BEFORE THE LORD!!"

Forrestine quickly shot the crowd a *"This is my little crisis and you keep your mouths shut"* look, and resumed. *"TIFFANY NOEL, YOU MUST DECLARE TO GOD THAT YOU ARE READY TO REPENT, TO REDEEM, TO RESTORE! HOW WILL YOU PLEDGE TO GOD YOUR SINCERITY? WHAT WILL BE YOUR OATH?"*

Tiffany looked as if she would cry but maintained a horrified silence. Forrestine began to sweat profusely, or "glow," as she preferred, and that was a public beauty no-no. Time was running out. She whispered in Tiffany Noel's ear,

"Just say you'll follow a new path of righteousness and service to God, honey! That will be fine! Of course you *believe* in God, you don't have to go to my church, sweetie, if you don't care anything about being *saved*! How *convenient* it is for you Whiskey-pal…*Episcopalians*, with so many masses every week, and all those statues of the V.M. and J.C. to pray to."

Tiffany Noel bit her lip, then cleared her throat, scanned the crowd.

"SISTER TIFFANY! PRAISE GOD!" they shouted, urging her to speak.

"Um… I promise to be a better *person*… and to help *others*… and to take care of little helpless animals if I see them on the *street*…and to donate last season's shoes to the Halfway House…and to…"

"AND TO BE OF TOTAL SERVICE TO YOU, OH LORD, AND FOLLOW MY CHOSEN PATH! AMEN!"

Forrestine intervened in the interest of time, as it was exactly three-fifty-five, her ten-dollar per hour students were waiting, and her hair was now leaning completely over to the right in full-tilt topple position. A whoop went up from the crowd as people hovered around Tiffany Noel, hugging her, kissing her, blessing her with those germy, sweaty hands. Forrestine read the disgust on Tiffany's face, and she broke through exclaiming,

"DO NOT TOUCH THE NEWLY CLEANED ONE!"

She held Tiffany in a bear hug as the faithful wandered slowly back onto Main Street, in awe of yet another miraculous intervention by the wife of the infamous Brother Culpepper. Forrestine worriedly pushed at the leaning lacquer tower that was her hair to silently assess the damage.

"Oh, child! It is *ever* so good to see you! Now I want you to come to my studio at ten sharp tomorrow so we can talk! And I will even ask Juliette Kimball to bake some of your favorite chocolate eclairs as a treat, even though you do look like you've gained between twenty-eight to twenty-nine and three-quarter pounds, I'd say. Ok, precious, I've got to go, but I want you to remember one thing…your misfortune has just ended because next Monday is the final deadline for all contestant entries in the 'Miss Chestnut Ridge Sons of Glory Festival Queen' pageant, and sweetie, you and I will TAKE IT!"

Forrestine surreptitiously placed one hand on her hair tower and continued, "And after I…*we*…after *we* win that little title, honey, LOOKOUT and PRAISE JESUS, because Miss American Beauty, *here we come*! It's the Fiftieth Anniversary, you know…the prize money's unprecedented in the history of the pageant. An excellent investment for your father, dear."

Forrestine kissed the top of Tiffany Noel's cheap-haircut head, and out of the corner of her eye, she saw Stella Stanley quickly scoot off the top of the Eldorado. *HELLFIRE!* Stella's studded leather hot pants probably scratched the paint! Forrestine was elated that God finally granted her the means to achieve her one dream, but she still had to protect her assets.

"Stella, *please* do not sit on my investment! That is *not* merely an automobile! That car is working capital, and those little studded hot pants you're so proud of and wear so often have most likely *ruined* the custom powder-blue paint job I paid good money for! OH MY LORD, I am so *late*!"

As Forrestine frantically cranked the Eldorado, Stella Stanley definitely decided that the Do-Rite hairspray donation idea was a bad one and that Forrestine would just have to suffer until that ol' fifteen-can supply was exhausted. Stella stepped over to Tiffany Noel, who was trying to gather up her belongings, as well as her act.

"Good to see ya, Miss Tiffany. But ya shore look like hell! Who did yer *hair*, honey? I done heard yer marriage broke up...I'm real sorry..."

Stella drew deeply on a cigarette, then offered the pack to Tiffany, who gladly accepted, waiting until Forrestine turned the corner to touch cigarette to lips.

"Hey, Stella... it broke up all right! And I don't even want to *talk* about my hair! My husband Battle had me on a damned *budget*, and I had to get my hair cut at the Barber College! Can you believe? It wasn't so bad being married, I guess. I mean we had a cute little apartment with teak furniture that Battle's daddy bought for us, but I was just so *bored* all day...I mean, I shopped a lot, went to Atlanta a couple of times, but I got so tired of Oprah and Sally Jesse and Geraldo...but boredom wasn't the worst problem."

Tiffany Noel took a long drag on her cigarette, giving Stella ample opportunity to enviously study Tiffany's expensive but now gravel-scuffed spectator pumps and ask, "So what exactly *was* the problem, honey? He hit ya?"

Tiffany Noel exhaled a tired stream of smoke, "Well, Miss Stella, you know how in *school*, when they tell you about the birds and the bees, and you, well, you *sort of* know what they're talking about, but not *really*, and I don't care *what* ya'll have heard about me, I was a *good girl* in high school; and I crossed my legs all through my entire college freshman year, and I told Battle when we started dating before Spring Break that my personal goal was to remain a virgin until I was a married woman! And so I was pretty naive, I guess... I mean... I had some tell-all friends in the Kappas, but until you actually *do* it... well, let me tell *you*, those birds and bees can *have* it! We had sex on our wedding night, and there is no way in hell I will *ever* have sex again as long as I live! On this *earth*!"

Stella Stanley laughed so loud and so hard she almost swallowed her cigarette. *"OH SHIT I BURNED MY LIP!"* Stella pressed a finger to her bottom lip and shook her head in disbelief.

"*Damn*, Tiffany, yer 'bout the silliest gal I think I've ever known! Lotsa gals don't like screwin' at first, 'cept maybe me! But after 'while, ya git used ta it...and ya git ta *use* it, to git what ya need and what ya *want*. An' onc't ya git a li'l older, an' git a li'l more familiar with yer parts an' all, ya know, get 'em all broken in, then's when it's real fun, 'cause ya can hook up with some hot young stud an' have you a great ol' time!"

Stella winked and pulled another cigarette from the pack stashed in her leather vest pocket and gingerly touched her now-swollen lip. Tiffany Noel carefully snuffed out her cigarette on the parking lot pavement with the toe of one spectator pump.

"*Not me.* I swore that I would *die* before I ever have sex again because it is *disgusting* and *degrading* and *slimy*, and I am too young and beautiful to have to put up with anything that *gross*! Besides, what do I need with a husband's hard-ons and household budgets, anyway, when I've got my Daddy to take care of me? See ya, Miss Stella. Soon as my hair grows out."

Tiffany Noel Leigh-Lee shouldered the garment bag, set her size six designer dress as straight as possible over her size twelve figure, and pumped off in the spectators toward Daddy's law firm, two blocks up. Stella dragged on another cigarette, cringing as the effort shot pain through her burned lip. As she watched Tiffany Noel's picture perfect posture cross Main Street, Stella Stanley figured it was gonna be a very hot September, gossip-wise.

And so it was, despite Tiffany Noel's determined efforts to the contrary. After her return, the endless stream of questions, even from complete and total strangers, continued. It seemed to Tiffany Noel that all four-thousand-two-hundred citizens of Chestnut Ridge were abuzz with Tiffany Noel stories. Tiffany tried to remember Forrestine's long-ago advice, that one cannot be the most beautiful girl in a twelve-county region and expect to waltz through life unnoticed and untainted by gossip. But it was so embarrassing, and it seemed everyone in town stared at her and whispered about her weight gain, her bad haircut, her failure at MTSU and her inadequacy as a bride.

Through October, Tiffany Noel managed to hide out in Mama and Daddy's big antique-filled house, reading *People* and *Cosmo*, and talking to the housekeeper. Tiffany Noel's solitary connection to the outside world was her princess telephone, but even that was not much comfort because all her college friends were still in college, studying and going to sorority parties.

At the insistence of her mother, Tiffany applied to the Chestnut Ridge Community College in an effort to improve her grades and hopefully complete at the very least a two-year degree. But even the community college informed her that she would be on probation and ineligible for any extracurricular activities, and, so...well, Tiffany Noel just pitched *that* little letter in the trash.

Even the God-inspired efforts of Forrestine Culpepper couldn't shake Tiffany Noel from the safe haven of her daddy's great house. Tiffany Noel faked a migraine on the day following the fateful Parking Lot Salvation episode, but that definitely didn't stop Miss Forrestine. She'd just packed up the chocolate eclairs and popped on over, and then the two of them joined Mama in the sunroom for what had seemed like an eternity of not-so-pleasant conversation.

That first meeting with Miss Forrestine was horribly stressful, so much so that Tiffany Noel focused all her energies on subtly depleting the delicious supply of eclairs, while Miss Forrestine and Mama talked in hushed tones about things like undue hardships placed on young college women, and how that horrible Battle Sanderson had tormented Tiffany Noel until she married him, just because he needed solace after an NFL rejection, and how he'd expected Tiffany Noel, of all people, to live in a tiny apartment, *with no housekeeper*! Tiffany was so upset, Mama said, that it was impossible for her to even *think* about competing in pageants again! Oh, the world was such an evil place, said Forrestine, but thank God it was still not too late to repair Tiffany Noel's damaged skin tone. Somehow Miss Forrestine always got around to skin tone. And what luck, she'd exclaimed, because the National Pageant Association Rule Number Seventeen had just passed, which meant that Tiffany could qualify for the 136th Chestnut Ridge Sons of Glory Festival Queen title as late as November first! You just get plenty of sleep and exfoliate daily, Miss Forrestine said, and we'll just talk about the Sons of Glory Festival another day.

As Tiffany polished off another eclair, Mama and Miss Forrestine spoke in low voices about Tiffany Noel's impending divorce. Mama informed Miss Forrestine that Daddy had already prepared the papers and that he was getting ready to file them personally the next day at the Stones River County courthouse. Forrestine was prepared to deflect this potential setback.

"Well, of course, I'm no *lawyer*, AnnElise, but as beauty and character advisor to many of our town's finer families, I *hear* things! You remember Camilla DuShay's daughter, Priscilla? Well, when she was just eighteen, she was tricked into marrying a shiftless stockbroker who was determined to get the inside scoop on Dillon DuShay's plastics business... anyway when Dillon found out two months later that his only daughter had run off and gotten married, and that she'd been hiding her husband in the west wing of the DuShay house...you know, they only use that wing during the winter social season... well, let me tell you, Dillon got that thing annulled quick as *that,* from a judge friend of his over in Nashville!"

Forrestine leaned back for effect. "And now her record is *spotless*...it's like she was never *soiled*! And of course, the most important thing, in my opinion, is that Priscilla is still eligible for the Pretty Maids of Murfreesboro Society Debutante Ball this year! I mean, all that work would have gone to absolute *waste*!"

Forrestine took a sip from a dainty antique teacup as she waited for her words to sink into AnnElise Leigh-Lee's ears. Out of the corner of her eye she noticed that Tiffany Noel had now eaten *six* of the ten eclairs she'd brought from Juliette Kimball's bakery. She continued,

"The *"A"-word* would be so much better than the *"D-word"* for this child, my dear! And that devil Battle Sanderson should agree if he's got one brain in his football-bashed head, because then his daddy won't have to pay alimony to Tiffany and your dear, sweet husband won't have to take time away from his busy practice to act on Tiffany's behalf! In fact, if I'm not mistaken, an annulment is completely erased from public record. *Forever.* Why, my stars, AnnElise, you of all people should know, wasn't it the Catholics and Whiskey... *Episcopalians* who invented annulment for those Kennedys?"

AnnElise Leigh-Lee wrung her hands lightly, careful to avoid undue tugging at her porcelain nails. "*Mon Dieu,* I believe you are right! Now if you'll excuse me, I've got to go and call Richard this instant! Whatever would we do without you, Forrestine? Thank you so much for guiding us through this! Do you have Camilla DuShay's number handy?"

After that day and for the next eight weeks, Tiffany Noel's days ran together in a mixture of telephone calls, baked goods, soap operas, annulment papers, and talks with Mama and Delilah. And within exactly two of those eight weeks, Mama and Delilah noticed that Tiffany Noel had "outgrown" her entire post-wedding wardrobe, and that she seemed permanently resigned to wear a perky bluebell-blue Kappa Zeta Mu nightshirt over a pair of tan stretch shorts, day in, day out.

AnnElise Leigh-Lee's one attempt to rationally discuss with her daughter this unacceptable, depressive, blimpish behavior was met with such hysterics from Tiffany Noel that only four slices of Delilah's lemon chiffon cake could calm the storm. Not even Mama's efforts to tempt Tiffany Noel with a shopping trip to the Boaz Outlet Mall could budge Tiffany Noel from her perch. It seemed quite hopeless, until one fateful day, right before Halloween, when Miss Forrestine showed up on the Leigh-Lee veranda, tears streaming down her face, beehive hairdo once again tilting to the right like the Leaning Tower of Pisa.

Forrestine knew it was AnnElise's day to chair the volunteers at the Chestnut Ridge Historical Society; she couldn't waste any more precious time. Delilah asked Miss Forrestine to sit in AnnElise's white wicker rocker in the sunroom while she fetched Tiffany Noel. Then Delilah brought out her special lemonade tonic, and Tiffany Noel sat down on the floor of the sunroom in front of a tearful Miss Forrestine, handing out an endless supply of Kleenex, waiting patiently for Miss Forrestine to pull herself together.

"Oh, Miss Forrestine, do try to stop crying so I can figure out what's wrong! Delilah, can I please have another lemonade tonic?"

Forrestine moaned in anguish, "Tiffany Noel, *please* don't make me cry harder...we say *may I* please have a lemonade, dear! Good Lord, I thought I'd taught you better!"

She daubed at her quickly depleting supply of tears and prepared to drop the decisive bomb. "Tiffany Noel, now you know that one of the most important Culpepper Beauty Principles is to refrain from taking advantage of a friendship, but my stars, child, I am at a total loss, and I simply must put aside my pride and ask you for your assistance. Can you ever forgive me?"

Tiffany Noel pulled another Kleenex from the bright green metallic box and nodded enthusiastically, "Yes, ma'am, anything! Miss Forrestine, are you having a *stroke* or *the change* or something?! Can't you just wait until Mama comes home?"

"Oh, child, you are such a dear! Heavens! I knew I could count on you! You see, for the past several years, I have instituted a new event in the Poise and Party Manners curriculum. I stage a Halloween *tableaux* where all my little participants don appropriate costumes with a specific literary theme, and they present readings on manners and etiquette. Then we break for Pumpkin Cupcakes and bob for complimentary Quigley Beauty Box bath sponges! Isn't that cute?"

Tiffany Noel nodded again, though somewhat less enthusiastically than before.

"Well, each year, I always entreat a Special Guest to present the award to the Best All-Around Beauty. Of course, the Special Guest is *always* a former Forrestine Culpepper Beauty & Pageant Instruction Graduate. This makes an incredible impression on these young, open minds, you know, gets them on the right track at an early age. Well, so anyway..." Forrestine looked Tiffany Noel straight in the eye, "...this year's Special Guest was *supposed* to be Chastity Weatherford."

"*CHASTITY WEATHERFORD*! You don't *mean* it, Miss Forrestine! CHASTITY WEATHERFORD? That *blimp*? I mean, what on earth is so *special* about Chastity Weatherford? Does she still have dark *roots*? And zits on her *back*? She practically SCREWED the entire eighth grade!"

Tiffany Noel stood up and then promptly sat back down on the floor in a fury in front of Miss Forrestine. *CHASTITY WEATHERFORD*! Tiffany Noel's beauty pageant archrival, her most-hated enemy! For sixteen years they competed for titles and crowns and boys and popularity, and Tiffany Noel managed to win every match, no matter how bloody!

"Miss Forrestine, what in hell...I mean what on *earth* would possess you to have Chastity Weatherford as the Halloween Special Guest...special *spook*, more like it! Chastity Weatherford doesn't even *live* in Chestnut Ridge anymore!"

Tiffany Noel crossed her arms tightly over her perfect size 36B breasts and frowned at her Beauty Mentor.

"Tiffany dear, now don't be angry with me, but I had no choice but to ask Chastity Weatherford to be the Special Guest; I've tried every last Forrestine Culpepper Beauty & Pageant Instruction Graduate on my list, except for *you*, and in June, when I made these arrangements, well, you were, how shall I say, *detained due to an unexpected honeymoon."*

Forrestine daubed at her eyes in an exaggerated fashion, "I had no idea whatsoever as to the condition of your health and skin tone, after two semesters of smog and a hasty, ill-advised marriage! Well, it's a moot point, now, I guess, but in any case, Chastity Weatherford's mother just called me this afternoon, and Chastity has to beg off because she has a photo session in Mobile next week with the Miss American Beauty pageant! So I've come here to ask you to help me find an alternate. We'll have to comb the phone books of at *least* three counties to find a replacement!"

Tiffany Noel Leigh-Lee stopped listening as Forrestine's words smacked her cheek like a glove, with exactly their intended sting. Forrestine sat back in the white wicker rocker and sipped her lemonade tonic, as Delilah reappeared, carrying a tray of fresh tonics and homemade gingersnaps.

"CHASTITY WEATHERFORD IS IN THE MISS AMERICAN BEAUTY PAGEANT? IS THERE NO GOD? IS EVERYBODY BLIND? WHO DID SHE PAY? She has no more chance of winning that crown than I do of becoming the Queen of...of...of Canada! *IS THERE JUST NO END TO MY MISERY?"*

Tiffany Noel jumped up, grabbed a fistful of gingersnaps, and crammed the cookies into her mouth two at a time. Forrestine, horrified at Tiffany Noel's total lack of grace or respect for her figure, averted her eyes and turned to Delilah, who sat in the white wicker swing, fanning herself with a pink paper napkin.

"Delilah, this is the absolute *best* lemonade in the whole world! If I didn't know better, I'd just guess there was a little bit of *demon whiskey* in this glass! Can you simply believe how hot it is for late October? My stars, have I left my phone books in the car? I must go and get them so Tiffany Noel and I can start to make Replacement Special Guest calls! Tiffany, dear, are you done with your *little snack*?"

Tiffany stopped stuffing gingersnaps into her mouth and swallowed entire cookies whole. She brushed her hands across her stretch-shorted thighs and stood up.

"Miss Forrestine, we don't need any old damned phone books...oh, excuse me, phone books! *I* will be your Special Guest! I can do it, and I'll be *much* better than any old Chastity Weatherford would EVER be! DELILAH! Where's Mama? We have to go shopping in Boaz *A-SAP*! Miss Forrestine, what should I wear?"

Tiffany Noel paced across the sunroom, stepping past Delilah and Miss Forrestine. Forrestine set a drained tonic glass on Delilah's tray and abruptly stood to leave, hands on her hips, black patent leather pocket book swinging wildly from the crook of one wrist. Her lips were tightly pressed, and a glare shot from her eyes.

"Well, Miss Tiffany Noel. I cannot believe my ears! You think you can just announce to me and the world that *you, 'Miss-Just-Let-Yourself-Go'*, can traipse in here and take over Chastity Weatherford's place like *that*?"

Forrestine snapped her bony fingers and stomped on the floor for emphasis. "We are talking SERIOUS skin tone lapse here, missy! And your weight gain is no small matter, either! Forrestine Culpepper graduates do NOT adopt cookie cramming as a lifestyle! I just don't know if I should expose those innocent little brains to something so sad as this, a former Miss Top Potential, Miss-Could-Have-Been-An-American-Beauty...at least with Chastity, those little girls could look at someone who has a GOAL! Someone who has been *accepted* into the Miss American Beauty pageant!"

Forrestine's face turned bright red, and her icy words caused Tiffany Noel to slink back to the floor, while Delilah continued to fan herself with the pink paper napkin, silently observing that Miss Forrestine Culpepper could sniff out her prey better than one of grandpappy's best bird dogs.

"But Miss Forrestine, you don't know what it's *like* to go through beauty hell and back! Battle wouldn't even let me buy any Oil of Olay unless it was on *sale*! I had to *re-use* my emery boards! You just don't understand the horror of it all! It's not *FAIR*!"

Tiffany Noel's eyes began to swim, and Delilah handed over the gingersnap plate to stem the tide. Tiffany Noel took a tiny bite from the edge of one cookie and looked soulfully at Miss Forrestine through beautiful blinking lashes.

"Miss Forrestine, you always said it was good manners to give people a second chance, like even if a boy talked with his mouth full at the hors d'oeuvres table, it was just proper politeness to dance with him if he asked you because he might have been so smitten with one's beauty he'd forgotten proper etiquette, right? So why can't I have just one tiny little chance to prove to you and to those little girls that there is life after skin tone death?"

Forrestine returned to the white wicker rocker and sighed dramatically as she sat down. Time for the Kill. "Oh, child, I just don't know...just don't know. I mean, put yourself in the mind of a young miss — she is at the dawn of her day, receiving the prize for Best All-Around Beauty from by far the absolute BEST graduate of the Forrestine Culpepper Beauty & Pageant Instruction curriculum, Miss Tiffany Noel, when she stops and thinks...what is Miss Tiffany Noel doing *now*? She doesn't attend college....she is *divorced*...she does not have a promising career...her nails are just a tad bit ragged...and she is *grossly obese*...well, if you're that young impressionable child, you might even say to yourself, why should *I* continue to exfoliate or buff my nails or practice perfect posture because what good will it do me after it's all over and done with? And, *young lady*, that's not even the worst thing that could happen if you were the Special Guest..."

Tiffany looked anxiously at Delilah, who continued to fan herself and closed her eyes, ignoring Tiffany Noel's horrified expression.

"I'M NOT DIVORCED! I'M ANNULLED! AND WHAT? WHAT IS THE WORST THING? TELL ME, MISS FORRESTINE! PLEASE!"

Forrestine pursed her lips, looked at Delilah, then shook her head sadly,

"Well...I don't even like to THINK about it, but it would happen, I just know it. How will you respond when one of those sweet little students says, *'Miss Tiffany Noel, thank you so much for substituting for Miss Chastity, since she had to go have her photograph made for the Miss American Beauty pageant. You used to be beautiful too, so why aren't YOU in the Miss American Beauty pageant?'* and THEN what will you say, Miss Glamour Lapse?"

Forrestine reached for Tiffany's untouched second lemonade tonic and drained it dry. Tiffany Noel stood up once again and stomped her feet on the dark green tile floor of the sunroom.

"Why, I'll tell you what I'd say! I'd say that I *AM* in the Miss American Beauty pageant, and that they are looking at the next *WINNER* of the Miss American Beauty pageant, and that my photo session was delayed, that's all, because I've just recently come out of retirement and *ENTERED* the pageant, because I'm gonna beat the panties off Chastity Weatherford, THAT'S what I'd say!"

Forrestine hung her head in mock despair and stared down at Delilah's left foot, which was encased in a satin slipper in the most interesting shade of lime green Forrestine had ever seen.

"Tiffany, Tiffany, Tiffany Noel. You were once my only hope of ever winning the Miss American Beauty pageant. Of all my girls, you were The One. But your training has been interrupted. You'd have to work double-time to get back on track, and, oh, I just can't think about all the lost days and minutes we'd have to make up! There's no telling how deeply we'd have to cleanse those pores... I've even closed your account after all these months..."

"Oh, pooh, Miss Forrestine, you know Daddy's good for it! He'll give me anything I want, and if I decide to be Miss American Beauty, he'll pay for it! He feels real bad that he forced me to go to MTSU and ruin my entire life!"

Tiffany Noel knelt down in front of Forrestine and clasped her hands tightly in a fervent prayer to the goddess of Beauty and Poise. "Miss Forrestine, what if I promise to work five hours a day..."

"Twelve...." Forrestine interrupted.

"...twelve hours a day from now until the pageant? What if I work hard and lose ten pounds..."

"Thirty..."

"WHAT? Uh, ok...thirty...and follow every single solitary Culpepper Beauty Principle *verbatim*...will you help me? I just HAVE to beat Chastity Weatherford! I know I can do it! And I don't have a silly old *job*, so you won't have to worry about me interrupting my concentration or anything! PLEASE, Miss Forrestine? Can...*may* I *please* have a second chance?"

As Forrestine Culpepper hugged the second chance's shoulders, she turned and smiled sweetly at Delilah, "Delilah, isn't this just a blessing from God, that Miss Tiffany Noel has finally come around to fulfill her one true beauty destiny? My stars, I am swooning! Well...it could be from that lemonade, too much citric acid, but oh, *sweet Jesus*! Delilah, would you be a dear and go fetch my tote bag from the foyer so Miss Tiffany can sign the necessary Miss American Beauty pageant entry papers? It's a good thing I just happened to bring that bag...the one that still has those papers inside, because just yesterday I thought about just throwing that bag *and* those papers in the TRASH! Can you *believe* that?"

From that day forward, Tiffany Noel spent nearly every waking moment under the close personal supervision of Forrestine Culpepper, working overtime on all eight Culpepper Beauty Principles. Tiffany Noel was scrubbed, rubbed, hydrated, aromated, oiled, lotioned, cremed, tweezed, tanned, waxed and wrapped in a regimen that would have taxed even the most ardent European spa patrons and which would have sucked gaping holes in all but the most well-lined pockets.

And with the assistance of AnnElise and Delilah, Tiffany Noel managed to drop twenty-nine pounds by eating "Forrestine's Cuisine" (celery sticks and rice cakes wrapped in colored cellophane with typewritten "Positive Attitude Over Adversity" notes inside) and by drinking lots of apple cider vinegar water.

There were a few serious low spots, however. Christmas was a real downer, and a total food challenge. Tiffany Noel wanted to give her family, even her frumpy lawyer sister Danita Kay, absolutely perfect gifts to remind everyone just how special she was and to help jog their memory as to how glad they all were that she had returned home. But there was so little time away from Forrestine for shopping (Forrestine was concerned Tiffany might be tempted to buy snacks), Tiffany Noel finally decided to give everyone on her list the exact same gift: an eight-by-ten color enlargement of her wedding elopement picture, framed in pink glass, with Battle Sanderson tastefully and entirely cut out of the photograph.

Phil's Photo Stop could only remove a portion of Battle from the photo, however, so Tiffany paid a neighbor's daughter, a promising fifth grade art student, to hack the rest of Battle's body out of each individual print. Tiffany was ecstatic with her gift selection. She could think of no better item to truly symbolize her soon-to-be-triumphant return to the beauty arena. To Tiffany Noel, the rented wedding dress in the photo really didn't look that much different from a ball gown, and since she had worn Battle's mother's diamond pendant as something borrowed, and her own Miss Tri-County Watermelon Festival rhinestone tiara as something old, the photo could just pass for yet another of Tiffany Noel's pageant success stories. A good luck omen, indeed.

In December, Tiffany Noel maintained a relatively low profile, gossip-wise; at the few obligatory holiday functions she did attend, Tiffany Noel stayed close by her mother or drifted off to "powder her nose" if the hors d'oeuvres looked tempting, or if she was asked a question about her suffering at the hands of Battle Sanderson, who was now living in sin in the Bahamas with his father's former secretary.

On New Year's Eve, Tiffany attended a dreadfully boring party at the home of another prominent Chestnut Ridge family, the Grahams. All night Tiffany was hounded by Hoot Graham, just back from some L.A. hippie commune. Hoot followed Tiffany all evening, explaining that he'd sacrificed a huge film career to come back to Chestnut Ridge and document the Sons of Glory Festival's Battle Re-enactment for his sister-in-law, who coincidentally was the Sons of Glory Festival Chairwoman. It was the ultimate filmmaker's opportunity, Hoot told Tiffany, but it was not without sacrifice on his part as he'd been forced to leave his posh L.A. existence for a full year, in order to adequately prepare, get inside the minds of Chestnut Ridgers.

When ancient Mother Nell Graham shouted at Hoot that Tiffany Noel's most recent fall from grace last May would make an excellent documentary, that it was a true trashy story sure to get ratings bigger than any old re-enactment. Hoot promptly proceeded to follow Tiffany Noel around for the rest of the evening, probing about her failed marriage, her dramatic weight gain and framing her face with his hands to *"get the most stunning camera angle possible, darlin', don't look directly into the light!"*

Tiffany was at last nearing the close of the difficult holiday season, and she'd gained only three pounds. Of course, Miss Forrestine's platinum hair would probably pop right off after weigh-in on Friday, and since that was only two days from now, Tiffany Noel's usual plan of extra jump-roping and Rapping It Off would most likely prove futile. At long last, today was New Year's Day, and her sordid past was behind her. She had to focus, Miss Forrestine said, because she had less than a year to perfect her craft and win the Sons of Glory Festival Queen crown, and if she failed, she wouldn't even be allowed into the auditorium to *watch* the Miss American Beauty Pageant, let alone participate for her chance at winning the Big One.

Now, on New Year's Day, from her perch on her mother's pink bed, Tiffany Noel was not at all pleased that a great contingency of Daddy's lawyer and judge friends had descended upon the living room to watch football on Daddy's fifty-seven inch screen tv. How could she focus with all the noise? Tiffany Noel grew furious. She had planned a major final holiday binge today to reward herself for all her hard work. But she'd forgotten it was Delilah's day off, and there was *no way* Tiffany Noel was going to walk through that living room to get to the kitchen with all those men in there, drinking their bourbon and howling like banshees at some silly old football players. She could sure tell *them* a few things about football players! Particularly NFL-rejected football players who expected to have sex every time the wind blew!

DAMN! The pink princess phone still hadn't rung! Where was stupid Miss Forrestine? She should have been with Stella by now! And where was Mama? Tiffany Noel Leigh-Lee, lying in style atop her mother's pink chintz-canopied Louis XIV bed, plopped over on her stomach and gathered more of Mama's beautiful Belgian lace pillows around her. Mama's boudoir was Tiffany's absolute favorite place in the entire world. All pink and lace and softness and so protected, so insulated from stupid people asking stupid questions about why she left school, why she got married, why she got an annulment, hadn't she gained weight, why she cut her hair...did she *really* expect to win the pageant...it never stopped!

If she could just find Mama and pretend to have a migraine, then Mama would at least go and get her some of Delilah's holiday ham and biscuits from the fridge, and maybe some Christmas coconut cake...and a Jack and coke...no, Mama would probably not get her *that*, but, oh, *DAMN*! Where was everybody? Weren't they at all concerned for her holiday wellbeing? She could just starve to death right here in this room and nobody would even care now that Christmas was over and everyone already opened their gifts!

And stupid old Danita Kay down there with all those men in the living room! She thinks just because she works at Daddy's law firm she can hob-nob with all Daddy's lawyer friends! Well, pooh, Danita Kay never even *went* to a football game *ever*! She doesn't even *like* football! All through school, she'd stay home and study, or watch Star Trek, why, she wouldn't even come to the games to see her own baby sister, Chestnut Ridge High's head cheerleader! It was disgusting! Tiffany Noel needed a cigarette. She'd gone so long without one drag of nicotine!

Maybe she could sneak one out of Mama's stash...Mama told everybody she'd quit, but Tiffany Noel knew that some nights when Daddy was down in the library reading his papers and passing out over his bourbon, Mama bolted the door to her boudoir and secretly smoked in the garden tub because she could open the skylight to vent all the evidence. Just as Tiffany Noel leaned over to open Mama's bedside table drawer, Mama herself breezed in.

"*MAMA!*" Tiffany Noel jumped off the high canopied bed and rushed over to her mother's side.

"*Mon Dieu,* Tiffany! It's half past twelve... don't you think it's time you put on some decent clothes and made yourself presentable for Daddy's guests?"

AnnElise Leigh-Lee was a striking figure in a black cashmere sweater dress accented with a gold French-designer silk scarf. Her thick, shiny auburn hair was pulled into a chignon at the nape of her neck, and the cameo at her throat matched the ones on each earlobe. AnnElise looked disapprovingly at Tiffany Noel's New Year's Day wardrobe selection, the ever-present, tattered Kappa Zeta Mu nightshirt and tan stretch shorts.

"Tiffany, is it *necessaire* to wear those rags now that you've nearly regained your competition figure? What did you do with all the clothes we bought in Boaz, *cherie*?"

"Oh, silly Mama, I was just about to change, but I'm doing a treatment on my hair...and pooh, I don't want to see any of those ugly old friends of Daddy's. They're only interested in their football game, not in me!"

AnnElise crossed over to the Louis XIV vanity and sat down on the white and gold brocade bench. She kicked off expensive designer pumps and examined her image in the mirror. Then she selected a gold-encased nail buffer from an assortment of beauty tools laid out in at-ready stance atop the vanity and slowly buffed her nails as she spoke.

"Tiffany, now you know your poor Papa will be heart-broken if you don't go and at least say hello to his guests! It's the proper thing to do, especially since Papa is completely footing the bill for your Miss American Beauty entry! *Vraiment,* Tiffany, you should realize that every single influential man in Chestnut Ridge is in that living room, and most of them have wealthy, eligible sons, all of whom would cross mighty rivers to be *votre beau* at the Masked Ball! It's not considered polite to snub one's family or friends on New Year's Day to say nothing about the bad luck it will bring us!"

AnnElise Marie L'Enfant Leigh-Lee was of French descent, from a very wealthy and influential Charleston family, and she maintained as did all good French Charlestonians, that bad luck was to be avoided at all costs.

"Mama, talk about *bad luck*, we just *have* to take down the Christmas tree *today*! If we don't take it down before midnight, we'll have a run of bad luck that won't stop; I might as well just go back to bed for the rest of the year because I'll be jinxed, with no chance of winning the pageant, and my life on this earth will be over as I know it. At least, that's what Miss Forrestine says."

"Tiffany Noel, *ma cherie*, you are just a *petite peu* too upset about something that has absolutely no bearing on your ability to win those crowns! The Festival is not until next January, one year from now! And, *ma petite chou chou*, you are the only candidate who can claim to have been a combination cheerleader-twirler *continuously* since the age of four; the only young woman in a twelve-county region to have won every beauty and poise honor possible in your age category this side of the Mississippi, and besides, *ma bon bon*, you have absolutely no competition when we take a *serious* look at the field! But of course, dear, as soon as Daddy's men leave, we will immediately remove all traces of our tree from your sight!"

AnnElise buffed her already perfect pink nails until they appeared liquid. She put down the buffer, slid her pedicured size seven feet into pink silk slippers and stood up from the vanity, glancing sideways at the striking, darkly seductive beauty of her face in the great lighted mirror. She walked over and patted Tiffany Noel's chestnut head, which was very difficult to do as it sported hundreds of Quigley Beauty Box Personal Home Salon Protein Intensifier rods. AnnElise whispered into Tiffany's perfect pink ear as Tiffany curled her lip further into serious pout position,

"*Ma belle Tiffane Noël. Tu est numero un avec moi, toujours.*"

"*Mama*! You *know* I can't look good *and* understand French at the same time! Why couldn't our silly old ancestors have come from England, like everybody else who speaks English! What did you say to me? *OH MY GOD! MY HAIR! MAMA! WHAT TIME IS IT?* I left the treatment on too long! I can *not* have frizzy ends at the Contestant Round-Up Tomorrow! Ms. Forrestine says if I don't plan to *'win every little beauty battle'* I might as well go and enter a convent! I've just *got* to beat the pants off that Chastity Weatherford!"

Tiffany Noel scrambled over to the mirror, gingerly lifting the sprawling Beauty Box Personal Home Salon Protein Intensifier Rods from her scalp for inspection. Her mother laughed softly, shook her head, then placed a loving arm on Tiffany Noel's shoulders.

"No, darling, another ten minutes should be just *parfait*! Oh, *ma belle*, you remind me so of myself, when I was about your age, I left our family home on historic Queen Street in Charleston for New York, en route to *L'Ecole du*

Gran Tour in France. I was so full of life, so ready to reach out and grab the world and squeeze the wonder from it, drink it into my very soul! I am so delighted you have pulled yourself up from that nasty little setback!"

AnnElise stared dreamily at the top of her daughter's rod-laden head, while Tiffany Noel rolled her neck from side to side, performing the ritual Forrestine Culpepper Posture Perfect Spine Stretching Exercises for the requisite fifteenth time that day.

"Tiffany, darling, if anyone can win Miss American Beauty, it will be you. But you must stop focusing on all of these extremely trivial details and concentrate! It's like André, my masseuse says...you must give your pain a *name* and see it in your mind. You must visualize that crown on your head, dear!"

Tiffany continued to pout into the flawless glass of the Louis XIV gilt-edged mirror. "No one knows what it's like to have to win two major pageants in one week! I can't focus on anything else! I didn't even get to enjoy Christmas, or New Year's, because I am already *on stage*! Mama, you were always so perfect and so beautiful you *never* had to fight for anything in your life! And your daddy was so rich, and Miss Forrestine says you probably have the best genes God ever granted to a human body. You were so lucky to grow up in Charleston and go to balls and parties with handsome *beaux*, you had a whole houseful of servants; I bet you had *closets* full of designer clothes from Paris! Didn't you just once make a teeny-tiny little mistake *EVER*?"

Tiffany Noel looked up at her darkly beautiful, enchanting mother with eyes full of awe. AnnElise Leigh-Lee spoke directly into the mirror's frank reflection, one arm around her daughter's slouching shoulders.

"Ah, *mon Dieu, c'est ici*, the day I must tell you the absolute truth. Yes, Tiffany darling, I did make a very terrible mistake. I married your father. And in so doing, I made the greatest mistake in the history of the universe!"

January 6, 1999; Downtown Chestnut Ridge, Tennessee.

Caramel swirls of perfectly-aged Kentucky bourbon danced lazily in the bottom of the Waterford crystal highball glass as Richard Napoleon Leigh-Lee IV, Principal Partner, Leigh-Lee & Sons, Attorneys, stared out the window of his fifth-floor office, on the most expensive and prestigious downtown corner of Chestnut Ridge. He yelled in his most noble courtroom voice,

"*Miss Gober! Where is my lunch?*"

Richard Napoleon Leigh-Lee IV never made use of the thirteen thousand dollar intercom system, bestowed on him the day his father retired ten years prior, the day Richard Napoleon Leigh-Lee IV became Chief Executive Officer of the family law firm. He preferred his own booming baritone to the state-of-the-art intercom; he did not like electronic "gadgets," because they interfered with one's innate ability to exude power over human beings, and it was this power which enabled one to control life, and ultimately, the checkbook. And to Richard Napoleon Leigh-Lee IV, fifty-six years old, with an extremely high-maintenance wife, an even higher-maintenance, national beauty queen-title-seeking daughter, and a wealthy lifestyle to uphold, the checkbook meant everything. He bellowed again.

"Miss Gober, god....*gol-durnit,* I am about to faint dead away from hunger and *starvation,* and I would most assuredly appreciate your distinct efforts toward alleviating this dreadful *situation!*"

He drained the highball glass of its contents, slammed it down loudly on his desk, and cocked his grey-blonde head toward the open mahogany door that led to the executive suite's outer office and private reception area. It was obvious after only three days that the new secretary, hired by his wife, did not operate within his personal definition of what should comprise a comfortable executive environment. After one full minute with no response from the outer office whatsoever, Richard Napoleon Leigh-Lee IV sank down in his custom-crafted Corinthian leather chair and surveyed the vast array of books that filled the hand-carved mahogany bookcases.

Perhaps the most recently departed secretary, Ms. Whitaker, had overlooked one small bourbon stash, hidden so cleverly among Dickens, Homer and Poe. Perhaps there was yet a bottle remaining to redeem him from this imminent mid-day crisis. *Damn* that Ms. Whitaker for cracking *every* seal on *every* bottle, in *front* of him, and pouring their contents down his very own gold-plated, executive washroom sink, while she threaded together slurs and slang he himself had never dared to *think,* let alone speak in public! And damned if she didn't look just like an Angel of the Lord, wings outstretched here in this very office the week before Christmas, hurling empty bottles into his brass engraved trash can. Oh, what he wouldn't give to feel those very wings wrap around his back once more...to taste those angelic lips...topped off with a big glass of Chivas....

In the two weeks since Ms. Whitaker had vanished, taking his liquid sustenance, his platinum MasterCard and his new red Cadillac Seville, Richard Napoleon Leigh-Lee IV actually, if very briefly, considered sobriety as a lifestyle. Particularly after AnnElise, his wife, threatened to sell her version of the story to the *Chestnut Ridge Tell-All* just to see him fry. Ah, Ms. Whitaker...beautiful auburn hair, fresh, freckled face, strong legs, and those bosoms... fine little lesson, that one. Too bad his definition of working late on his briefs didn't mesh with hers. He just wanted to enjoy her physical attributes and leave the lawyering to the other partners. But it was not to be. She had too many serious aspirations and alas, he had none.

"MISS GOBER! *DAMMIT!*" Richard Napoleon Leigh-Lee IV rose from the massive chair as Miss Gober primly appeared. Miss Eustacia Gober was one of several personally selected surrender conditions instituted by AnnElise after the Ms. Whitaker episode, but in Miss Gober's case she actually drew breath, whereas AnnElise's other post-Ms. Whitaker requirements merely drew from his bank accounts. Richard Napoleon Leigh-Lee IV looked up in disgust as skinny Miss Gober stepped prissily into his office. He mused to himself that she bore a striking resemblance to the Wicked Witch in the *Wizard of Oz.*

"Mr. Leigh....Lee, *sir,* " Miss Gober's late-fifty-something eyes looked out over the top of her bifocals as she stopped at the edge of the doorway, "As I explained to you clearly on my first day, which was, oh, yes, just *yesterday,* I am a devoted member of the First United Assembly of God's Children; it is *not* in my behavior bag to frequent liquor stores, boss or no boss. Now, sir, if you're quite through with your temper tantrum, I will return to my *official* duties, wherein I perform *tangible, legal* assignments for you and the other partners!

"I must complete these summaries before Miss Danita Kay returns from court, and I should think a man of your social stature would be more discreet, that he would most certainly want to mend his ways now that his own daughter is working by his side, within these very walls! As the Good Book says, *'Teach your children well.'* It's a new year, sir, and I should think a man who can run an entire law firm could quite handily take control of his little *problem.*"

Miss Gober pushed chained bifocals back up her nose and stuck a red pen into the strands of grey-brown hair wrapped tightly in a bun on the back of her neck. She stared with hard disapproval at Richard Napoleon Leigh-Lee IV. He did not respond.

"Really, Mr. Leigh...Lee.... a grown man such as yourself should *easily* be able to defend himself from a life of drink! I am aware that there are those who believe that alcoholism is a sickness, although I *highly* disagree...all God-fearing Christians know that alcoholism is simply a sign of character weakness! That's why you're helpless to stop drinking...you're so weak, you can't even *walk* to the LiquorLand yourself! It's only two blocks! *Weakness!*"

"*My dear Miss Gober...* I am *forbidden* to cross the threshold of that fine establishment! My wife AnnElise threatened the owner of the LiquorLand that she'd buy all her expensive French wines online if they so much as sell me a *Co-Cola*! DAMN! I OWN HALF THIS TOWN AND I CAN'T EVEN DO MY OWN SHOPPING!"

Richard Napoleon Leigh-Lee IV took a deep breath, "That is why I hired *you*, Miss Gober! To assist me in my business affairs, and any purchasing endeavors! Now please sit down!"

Miss Gober smirked, rolled her eyes from behind sliding bifocals, and adjusted a vintage 1950's grey lambswool sweater tighter around her shoulders in a noncommittal manner. She remained standing and waved a bony finger in the air.

"Excuse me, sir, you are most likely delusional...I am quite familiar with the Seven Warning Signs of Chemical Dependence, mind you...and I also know for a *fact* that it was *Missus* Leigh...Lee who hired me, hand-picked from a field of seven candidates sent over by the Perky Personnel Agency in Murfreesboro. And I do *not* recall reading *'maintain demon alcohol supply for employer'* on the job description!"

Richard Napoleon Leigh-Lee IV's red-veined face grew redder, and he waved his hands through the stale early January air of the big office in frustration. Miss Gober's reference to his wife gave her the upper hand, a hand he did not want to play.

"*Fine*, Miss Gober, fine! If that's how you want to play, then I will personally revise your official duties to *exclude* the purveyance of sustenance for your poor, suffering employer! Are you satisfied, Miss Gober? I won't bring it up again, so as to avoid bringing scandal to my lovely wife and my family!"

Miss Gober turned to exit the doorway, but Richard Napoleon Leigh-Lee IV was not properly satisfied that he had pronounced the last word. He cleared his throat, "WAIT, Miss Gober, I will *remind you again* that my name is not 'Leigh...*pause*...Lee," Miss Gober. It's Leigh. Just Leigh. One time. That's it, L-E-I-G-H—L-E-E!"

Miss Gober stopped and peered back sarcastically over her bifocals, "Yes sir, Mr. Leigh...Lee, UH, Leigh, but I do not understand why, if you have only *one* last name, you must write it *twice*?"

As Mr. Leigh-Lee turned to face the window, Miss Gober stiffly crossed both arms across her meager bosom and stepped inside the office once again to lean authoritatively against a mahogany bookcase.

"Ah, yes, Miss Gober. *'The Question.'* And I must pay throughout eternity with the delivery of an answer. *Fine*, Miss Gober, fine. Do please sit down, this will take a few moments of your valuable time, that is, if it's within the confines of your *job description*!"

Richard Napoleon Leigh-Lee IV stepped to face Miss Gober, habitually picked up then ruefully set down the empty Waterford crystal glass and glared at his new secretary, who promptly took a seat in a leather side chair placed just across from her employer's massive desk. Self-same employer now paced slowly back and forth in front of the office window, speaking with measured drama, as if he was about to argue his greatest legal battle in front of a packed courthouse.

"You *see*, Miss Gober, my great-great-grandaddy was one Lieutenant Richard Napoleon Leigh, *L-E-I-G-H*, of the no-good, nobody West Virginia Leighs, but he somehow bribed his way into West Point, cheated his way through and fought for the Great Confederacy in The War Between the States. Then he helped found our proud town here of Chestnut Ridge."

Mr. Leigh-Lee waved a finger in thought. "Actually, Miss Gober, the town was already in existence back in eighteen-sixty-whatever, but my ancestor and several other illustrious Confederate officers supposedly rescued the early inhabitants from certain starvation by repairing the grist mill and devising ways to inspire commercial growth! But I digress. Now, where were we? Oh, yes, Miss Gober, you may recall from your schooldays, in whatever century and one-room prairie venue those took place, that there was another very famous military man, also named Lee, L-E-E, of just plain Virginia proper."

Miss Gober ignored the insult to her age and brightened at the mentioned of the infamous General Robert E. Lee. Her boss, however, took no notice and continued.

"Now we all know about *that* L-E-E, don't we, Miss Gober? Think back all those many years to your schooldays...can you, Miss Gober? Can you remember your teacher, and in your case what was back then most likely a wooden schoolhouse with no electricity, did they have paper then, Miss Gober, or did you write on scrolls? You certainly remember that General Robert E. Lee was a brave, scholarly, respected gentleman? The very man the South would immortalize in statue, song and verse throughout time as the picture of honor, character and virtue? Can you think back that far, Miss Gober?"

Miss Gober pursed her lips and nodded silently.

"*Fine*, Miss Gober, *excellent*! Well, in stark contrast, Miss Gober, my dear, departed ancestor was a severe coward, a thief and a liar; his one great talent was an uncanny ability to connect himself through fanciful tales to the L-E-Es of *'the Virginias'*, and thereby *everyone* in this neck of the woods thought he was, in fact, an *L-E-E* and thus, without question, an honorable man."

Miss Gober, momentarily taken in by the promise of scandal, did not notice her bifocals as they slid down the long ridge of her bony nose. Mr. Leigh-Lee waved one hand.

"Ah... Miss Gober, your glasses. Shall I continue?"

Miss Gober re-adjusted the glasses with a quick touch of one skinny index finger, then nodded. Her employer raised his eyes to the heavens, fanned out his hands and shook his head in an expression of wonderment.

"*Fine*, Miss Gober, superior attention span you have for a woman your age. So, after portraying himself in Chestnut Ridge to be a decorated war hero, my dear great-great-grandfather decided that his own frequent, *personal* escapades and close encounters with law enforcement thereby enabled him to *practice* law, and thus he opened our illustrious firm. And he promptly painted his name in great, gold letters atop our five-story, Main Street building as L-E-E & Sons."

Richard Napoleon Leigh-Lee IV again raised his fingertips to the heavens, as if waiting for some divine inspiration. He breathed deeply and faced his audience of one as if addressing an overflow crowd at the Trial of the Century.

"He opened that law office, *despite*, Miss Gober, *despite* the fact that there were at that time, *no* Sons, *no* connection to the L-E-E-s, and that he had indeed procured *no* actual sanctioned *training* for his chosen career. He practiced under that name, in this very office, for forty years! He argued cases in the most honorable courts of the Great State of Tennessee, he signed legal documents, he even ran successfully for county judge, all of this illustrious activity did he engender as an *L-E-E*, and he remained unchallenged until the day he died."

Richard planted his feet firmly in front of Miss Gober's chair and shook his fist into the air. "The God's *truth*, Miss Gober, is that this illustrious ancestor of mine actually argued most convincingly and *won* all of his legal cases, despite his terrible charade!"

Miss Gober, leaning closer to hear every word, chewed on the silver chain of her bifocals as Mr. Leigh-Lee's voice became softer and sad, full to the brim with courtroom emotion.

"Yes. *Fine*. To continue, Miss Gober, ours being a tight-knit family, my granddaddy inherited the name of L-E-E, and he gave it to my daddy, and

I grew up listening to the enthralling tales of how Richard Napoleon L-E-E the First rode with *'The General'*; how Lighthorse Harry's fighting spirit was in our blood, and oh, my word, all those tales about the ancestral plantation home in *'the Virginias'* and the value of honor and valor! All those stories about my great-great grandfather's endeavors to aid our fair town. My family never once made any reference to the official distinction about West Virginia, or *cowardice,* or *thievery!*"

As his voice boomed, Miss Gober jumped in her seat. Obviously a tad worked up at this point, Richard Napoleon Leigh-Lee IV returned to his own chair, sat down and with a sigh, laid his head back on the Executive Stress-Relief Custom Neckrest Accessory.

"My upstanding, prestigious family just rolled right along under the auspices of our supposedly esteemed ancestral heritage until one day in 1963, Miss Gober, when my mother, after countless years of hard lobbying and politicking, was finally selected to be President of the Chestnut Ridge Centennial Cotillion. And in my mother's infinite grace and wisdom, she declared that as ours was one of the original founding family pillars of Chestnut Ridge, descended from those illustrious Virginia *L-E-Es,* then we had a duty to trace our history back *past* those Virginia L-E-Es to our fundamental European roots, and wouldn't *that* theme make for a winning float in the Centennial Parade? You can just picture it, now can't you, Miss Gober? My beautiful mother, holding the Centennial Cotillion Grand Prize for Best Float?"

Miss Gober's intense listening and leaning caused the bifocals to slip entirely down her nose and rest upon her upper lip, and as she quickly jerked to right them, she knocked her elbow into the lampshade of a great brass floor lamp that stood beside her chair.

"Oh my, yes, OOPS! Mr. Leigh-Lee, how exciting! What a theme! How historic! Please continue, truly fascinating! *Oh, dear!*"

Miss Gober's attempts to straighten the lampshade failed, causing the lamp to topple to the floor.

"Um...be careful, there, Miss Gober...the lamp...uh, *fine,* yes, it just sits right there. So, Miss Gober, my daddy, in his dutiful and unceasing efforts to please my mother and co-exist with her as peaceably as possible, agreed to investigate the official ancestry of the Virginia *L-E-Es* and trace those fellows all the way back to our glorious European forefathers. But on the first day of his task, when he opened up the family lockbox down at the First National Bank of Chestnut Ridge, where he was also a board member, he discovered hidden away in an old, moldy envelope, a Civil War discharge document signed by one Richard Napoleon *L-E-I-G-H.* And after a secretive trip to Richmond to verify his ancestral claim and right this disastrous clerical error, whereupon he was laughed out of town, my poor daddy ended up in the Parkersburg, *West* Virginia courthouse. And it was there he stared back at the microfiched truth."

"*What truth? What happened?* Was someone MURDERED?"

Miss Gober's bifocals fell hard onto her flat bosom, and as she leaned across Mr. Leigh-Lee's desk, mouth open, breathing rapidly, waiting for more, the glasses swung wildly from side to side. Undaunted by Miss Gober's display, Richard Napoleon Leigh-Lee IV leaned back in his chair once again, looked up at the ceiling, made a tent with his extended fingers and continued, immensely pleased with the power he held over his audience.

"No, Miss Gober, murder is most likely the *one* heinous crime my ancestor did not commit! But my daddy, having grown up with all of that *'code of honor and valor'* horse-shit…*oh*, pardon me, Miss Gober, those, how shall I say, *liberties with the truth,* well, he felt it was his duty to set history straight and promptly informed my mother *and* the Stones River County judiciary, of the…shall we say…long string of the Leigh family improprieties! And because so much of Dick the First's assets remained viable, in real estate and trust holdings, in stock at our hometown bank, in dozens of private business, all under the 'legal' name of *L-E-E,* the presiding judge, in *his* infinite wisdom, ruled that henceforth from that fateful day in 1963, everyone in our illustrious family must use BOTH spellings, in hyphenated fashion. A use of only one spelling would legally deny the bearer access to all existing and/or future financial benefits, and let me tell you, Miss Gober, those financial benefits are *substantial*, particularly after over one hundred years of compounded interest!"

Richard Napoleon Leigh-Lee IV closed his eyes and said sorrowfully, "You see, that judge had a bone to pick with my daddy…my daddy won the battle for my mother's hand, back in their college days, and this was his Hizzoner's little jab at our entire clan! We must carry this humiliation forth for generations, lest we do a financial disservice to our heirs...we must wear our embarrassment like a scarlet *'A'* on our veritable chests for posterity… oh, pardon me, Miss Gober.... I do go on so! I don't mean to personally involve you in my little worthless life, particularly after you have offered to serve me so loyally!"

He waved the empty bourbon glass in Miss Gober's direction. Miss Gober frowned and stood up straight, bifocals slung to one side.

"That's *it*? Just a stupid name change? Well, I suppose it's of some comfort to you to know that you come by your dishonest ways of drink legitimately! I guess it's part of your birthright. Hmm…just a stupid name change. *Weakness.*"

Miss Gober's hopes for soap opera spectacle vanished, and crestfallen, she reinstated the bifocals in their rightful place atop her nose.

"*Fine,* Miss Gober, if that is how you care to view this matter, this very personal trauma, this shameful heartache, as a *'stupid name change.'* Yes, I must go through life signing my name as Richard Napoleon L-E-I-G-H-*SLASH*-L-E-E, explaining the situation to countless strangers or lose all claim to my family fortune. And despite *your* personal opinions or experiences with respect to alcohol, it is perfectly acceptable to be a drunk, Miss Gober, as long as one is a wealthy, socially *respectable* drunk! Your temperance lectures are completely wasted on me...the unfortunates without financial resources or privilege are the ones who behave badly and need your help. You see, Miss Gober, as long as I meet my obligations to home, my Maker and my community, then my family and my town are perfectly accepting of my *weakness,* as you call it...it's part of our code. And we do have the good graces not to speak of it in public!"

Mr. Leigh-Lee smiled self-servingly at Miss Gober, who glared at her new employer with disappointment and reproach. Miss Gober stood, readjusted her sweater and the imminently sliding bifocals and started toward the office door.

"Well, I certainly don't understand how this law firm could remain open and so successful after such a shocking episode! Certainly the people of this town can't honestly believe they will receive fair representation from a firm whose principal founder lied to his own clients, and lied in court! How can you show your face in public?"

Richard Napoleon Leigh-Lee IV cleared his throat loudly. "Miss Gober, you are a shrewd little minx, aren't you? And that is an excellent point. However you forget that by the time Dick's transgressions were aired, he was long dead. And every lawyer at this firm has since indeed earned a certifiable law degree and license. And, Miss Gober, when you're the only law firm in the county, and you happen to represent the majority of the industrial movers and shakers in that county, and when you consistently and reliably win every case you take, I would imagine that might clarify one's decision-making process with respect to the selection of a law firm, would it not?"

Miss Gober pursed her lips and shrugged. Richard Leigh-Lee IV waved a hand in the air at his new secretary.

"Now, Miss Gober, that is all I *ever* want to say about this little family matter, if you don't mind. I have enough to worry about right now with my daughter joining the firm. Lord knows, and you will soon discover, I haven't worked around here for a long time, and I've been happily able to live off my L-E-E bankroll, sip my lunch and write checks to cover the infamous shopping escapades of my wife and youngest daughter Tiffany Noel."

He walked slowly past Miss Gober and lingered in the doorframe of the entrance to his office. "But now Danita Kay, my smart one, fresh from Harvard, has joined us...I can see that my entire lifestyle is in jeopardy...my perfectly well-oiled machine stands at the brink of collapse! Danita Kay says she's going to right every wrong in the Chestnut Ridge judicial district! And she'll probably do it, too...which brings me to another little trivial matter, Miss Gober...there may yet be a way in which you can assist me...a manner more suitable to your, shall we say, *missionary* lifestyle."

Mr. Leigh-Lee stood directly in front of a visibly nervous Miss Gober, who fidgeted with her bifocals as she slowly nodded her head, looking anxiously at her boss's large, pot-bellied frame as he blocked her exit from the executive suite's inner office. He continued to speak in a very hushed voice.

"I must protect Danita Kay from the illuminating truth regarding my infamous law practice. Since we're all baring our souls here, Miss Gober, I'll go so far as to tell you that I have never actually set one *foot* in a courtroom, thanks to all the obligatorily hired cousins who have slaved their legal butts off on my behalf, in hopes that I, the official heir, will one day drop dead of cirrhosis! And I'm proud to say that in nearly thirty-five years of association with this firm, I've thus never prepared the first brief, tort or statement for the defense, let alone for the prosecution! Even my poor daddy never had a clue regarding my charade, which I proudly liken to that of my great-great-grandfather Dick the First! So you see, Miss Gober, you are right...I didn't fall too far from the tree, now did I?"

Mr. Leigh-Lee licked his lips in thought, then smiled self-satisfactorily at Miss Gober, whose eyes widened as she stepped backward. "I have been a model senior partner, and for the past few years, a superior CEO! I play golf with the politicos, I grease the appropriate palms, I'm an excellent image man, Miss Gober, you'd really be amazed! I have every state judge in my pocket, every judicial board in my good stead, and I have no intent of expending one ounce of legal energy at this late date of my life!"

Miss Gober's open mouth and wide eyes did nothing to stem the tide of her employer's words. He placed a hand on Miss Gober's nervous shoulder.

"But Danita Kay has taken to heart every single sarcastic word my lovely wife AnnElise has ever sarcastically spoken regarding *'daddy's judicial triumphs,'* and Danita intends to do me proud as a lawyer in her own right! I can fool the best of them, Miss Gober, but I'm not at all up to fooling my own daughter on a turf she's mastered with a vengeance! So, Miss Gober, I believe that in your insistence to preserve my morality and sobriety, and thereby with your refusal to traipse to the LiquorLand, you have unwittingly presented me with another means to serve my needs!"

Miss Gober's eyes widened behind her bifocals, and she nervously wrung her hands in anticipation of her employer's inappropriate suggestions. Richard Leigh-Lee IV grinned like a Cheshire cat.

"You must be an excellent legal secretary...oh, excuse me, legal *assistant*, because my wife always gets the best money can buy! Ahh, I forgot…the Perky Personnel Agency reaped all the reward…you obviously don't make very much, now do you, Miss Gober? Live in a meager little apartment, do you? Bring your lunch every day …God how I hate the smell of warm baloney! Drive an old car, I think? A *Dodge*? You certainly don't spend much on clothes, Miss Gober! Supporting several illegitimate children? Oh, I forgot…immaculate conception happened but once…well Miss Gober, what say you…shall we *negotiate*?"

Richard Napoleon Leigh-Lee IV now smiled what he believed to be his best Southern lawyer smile. He gestured for Miss Gober to sit once more, then he closed his office door and turned the deadbolt. He whistled a tune as he perched once again in his fine executive desk chair. Miss Gober's eyes followed Mr. Leigh-Lee across the room. She gripped the chain of her bifocals tight in anticipation of a sexual approach. She knew what had happened between Mr. Leigh-Lee and his former assistant, and she was not going to be another statistic on this pathetic man's Trek to Hell. She stood her ground. Mr. Leigh-Lee opened a desk drawer.

Swallowing hard, Miss Gober clasped the ever-present can of pepper spray hidden in the pocket folds of her sensible wool skirt, prepared for the worst. *He's probably looking for a rubber! He's probably going to demand intercourse on top of his desk!* Miss Gober tried to remember the sexual abuse prevention tips she'd gleaned from all those Friday nights spent watching *Criminals Among Us*...she was a Potential Perpetrator Identification School Graduate…she would *not* be a victim of sexual abuse…she mentally counted the steps to the door…

Mr. Leigh-Lee retrieved a very large three-ringed checkbook and found the next available blank check as he shook the ink in his expensive Swiss fountain pen, oblivious to the look of terror on Miss Gober's face.

"Yes, Miss Gober. I shall be *happy* to grant you exclusion from the dreaded lunch duty...I'll just have to work harder to procure a spirits courier of my very own and you, Miss Gober, you will of course take the Fifth, no pun intended! Yes, you will, Miss Gober, because you will in turn receive a fifteen-thousand-dollar-a-year raise in pay! Oh, Miss Gober, there is just one other little thing... all *you* have to do is prevent my Danita Kay from learning the terrible truth about her dear daddy's lack of judicial expertise! What do you say to that, Miss Gober? Are you a woman with ambition? Are you a modern career girl? The price of pantyhose is going up, old girl!"

Richard Napoleon Leigh-Lee IV signed a blank check with a flourish, tore it from the checkbook, and waved it in Miss Gober's direction, "What I wish from you, Miss Gober, is to cover my tracks. I want my daughter to continue in the steadfast belief that I have been the judicial wonder of this three-county district. I don't care how you achieve this task, and I don't want to ever speak of it again, because, Miss Gober, I trust you implicitly. What did I hear you say the other day…oh, yes, *'when the Good Lord closes a door, he always opens a window'*…well, God has slammed the door to the LiquorLand in my face, but you, Miss Gober, are my Danita Kay escape hatch, yea, therefore, *I believe.* But more importantly, do *you believe,* Miss Gober? Can you accept a fifteen-thousand dollar offering in exchange for protecting *'our little secret'* for the rest of your natural born life?"

Eustacia Gober sucked in the air of an almost-victim, removed her bifocals, released her tight grip on the hidden pepper spray can and gave Mr. Leigh-Lee a long, cold, silent up-and-down. God in his Infinite Wisdom had just handed her, on a silver platter, the means to take the Millennium Tour of the Holy Land with the Bible Bees next year...she cleared her throat.

"Mr. Leigh-Lee, I am a *professional*! I value my reputation, and unlike the apparent weeds in *your* family garden, my sense of honor is *not* to be tested or reckoned with! You wealthy socialites are all the same...you think you can just buy your way in and out of every situation! I am appalled at your total lack of decorum, of dignity, of respect for yourself and your peers! I had absolutely no idea that I would be expected to behave in any manner other than my upstanding, Christian best!"

Miss Gober drew a deep breath and frowned at her boss, continuing, "Sir, true faith and unbroken vows have a price...every good God-fearing Christian knows that, and practices self-sacrifice on a daily basis! It's what I have been trained to do...I *excel* at suffering!"

Richard Napoleon Leigh-Lee IV stopped writing the check; he was beginning to think that he'd made a grave error in judgment and that he would suffer more pain at the hands of AnnElise when suddenly Miss Gober crossed the room and sat primly on the edge of his desk.

"Now, what you have described is an utter abomination...a request the price of which I can't…well, to be quite honest, sir, I can't even *consider* for less than *twenty-five thousand*, upfront, with a ten percent annual raise for the next five years! I want Friday afternoons off, three weeks paid vacation per year and a one-month sabbatical next March. And thus saith the Good Book, *'He that delivereth, receiveth the benefit.'* Yea, verily, *Amen*!"

Miss Gober shoved her long bony hand at an astonished Mr. Leigh-Lee, and as they shook on their newfound mutual faith and respect for one another, they heard the click-click-click of Danita Kay's sensible shoes on the floor of the executive suite's private reception room. Mr. Leigh-Lee willingly wrote a check for twenty-five thousand dollars, handed it to an exuberant Miss Gober and watched her quickly tuck it where her bosom should have been. He stood with a smile as his daughter entered the room. Danita Kay, extremely near-sighted behind large eyeglasses, didn't see her father and Miss Gober across the room, and she called out to them, as if they were in the hallway.

"Daddy...Miss Gober! Where are those ads I ordered for the Sons of Glory Festival program? Mayor Gooch is finally coming over to pick them up, and I can't find them anywhere, and *oh!* There you are!"

Danita Kay Leigh-Lee's eyes opened wide behind Coke-bottle lenses. Never accused of being a style monger, her grey wool suit appeared rumpled as if she'd slept in it, and one collar point of her stiff white blouse stood straight up in the air. Her ash-blonde hair was pulled into a bun similar to the one sported by Miss Gober, and there was a Mont Blanc pen stuck into the bun. As Danita Kay marched closer, Miss Gober looked on in feigned interest as Richard Napoleon Leigh-Lee IV stood to one side, intently reviewing a sheaf of papers. The papers, however, were upside down and so he just pretended to scan them quickly. Miss Gober clicked into twenty-five thousand dollar overdrive.

"*Good day,* Miss Danita Kay! Your father and I were just reviewing several critical details of *Epperson vs. Hockaday,* and he remarked how well you are handling that case, and said he is not *about* to interfere with the superior judgment and legal leadership you have shown, despite your request for his assistance!"

Richard Napoleon Leigh-Lee IV chuckled to himself, thoroughly satisfied at the miraculous and immediate transformation Miss Gober had just displayed. God did work miracles, indeed. "Yes, Danita Kay, a *fine* piece of work! Just *fine*! I'm damned proud! Oh, sorry, Miss Gober!"

Danita Kay blushed to the roots of her bun. She tugged nervously at her suit jacket. "Thanks, daddy! But I really need to ask you a couple of questions about Section III, Title Two, and how it relates to *Morris vs. Morris* with respect to easement. Do you think we could go to lunch and discuss it?"

Richard Napoleon Leigh-Lee IV's stomach sank to his shoes, but he was promptly rescued by his new loyal assistant, Miss Gober.

"Oh, my, dear, I'm afraid that's not possible! Your father is due at the Club for a board meeting, aren't you, sir?"

"No, Miss Gober, that meeting's not until..."

"*Sir! Remember the meeting was changed?* Let's not *forget* ourselves! Just *whom* is keeping the schedules around here, may I ask, hmmm?"

Richard Napoleon Leigh-Lee IV looked at Miss Gober, then at his wristwatch in mock surprise, "Ah, *yes*, Miss Gober, my goodness, I'm *late*! Danita, honey, take your questions down to cousin Curtis on the third floor...he's one of our best clerks! He's got to earn that salary, you know! No handouts around this firm! Gotta run, *fine job, fine job!* Wonderful woman, that Miss Gober, *excellent!*"

He planted a swift kiss on top of his daughter's head, then dashed out the door, totally unaware of his destination, but thoroughly relieved that he'd been freed of any responsibility. This well-oiled machine might just clack right along after all, in the capable, gold-plated hands of Miss Gober.

Danita Kay sighed, "Well, I guess I'll go find cousin Curtis...where is Mayor Gooch? It's twelve-fifteen, and he was supposed to be here at noon to pick up our ads for the Sons of Glory Festival Program!"

Danita Kay looked at her watch again, raised an ear toward the corridor for any sign of Mayor Gooch's arrival and pursed her lips at Miss Gober.

"Miss Gober, would you mind waiting to go to lunch until Mayor Gooch comes by? And please show him that we have a new logo, I designed it myself, and tell him that we want a four-color ad, not a black-and-white, ok? We've just got to pull this firm out of the Dark Ages! Miss Gober...is something wrong?"

Miss Gober crossed her arms disapprovingly and pursed her lips. "Well, *frankly*, Miss Danita Kay, I don't mean to sound nit-picky, but acting as Advertising Manager for this firm was *not* in the job description posted for this position at the Perky Personnel Agency! I think we need to review all of my duties once again in *explicit* detail...if I am required to do tasks in addition to those as defined by the phrase, 'legal assistant,' then I most definitely must insist on a *raise*!"

Miss Gober waited for her words to land. She was on a roll, orchestrated by God's Holy Travel Planner, and she might as well keep going for all it was worth. A new sport utility wagon could not only deliver more Bible Bee quilts to the needy, it could carry more Bible Bee members, and wouldn't that just make Harriet Trimble green with envy…

Danita Kay nodded in thought. "You're right, Miss Gober. I'd like to add to your responsibilities; after seeing you in action, I'm convinced you can handle far more than this firm has afforded you at present, for a substantial pay increase, of course…could we discuss this over lunch tomorrow at noon?"

Miss Eustacia Gober shook her head. "I'm sorry. I've just spoken to your father about this…my new work schedule will allow me to leave every Friday at noon so I may do the Lord's charity work with the Bible Bees. But I'm quite free on Monday…your *treat*, of course…"

Mid-February 1999; The Graham Mansion, Chestnut Ridge, Tennessee

"You do *realize*, Will darling, that the Festival kick-off is only three hundred and forty days from today? Oh, I told AnnElise that the absolute best evening for our little Festival planning *soireé* would be next Thursday, after we get past next weekend and the Masked Ball. I mean, *really*, none of us can *ever* seem to get organized every year until after the Masked Ball! Now, Will, it is critical that you mingle with all the husbands at the planning soireé and get every single one signed up for the Sons of Glory Charity Golf Scramble...I'm really depending on you, dear, not only as the Sons of Glory Festival Chairwoman, but as your wife. Remember, darling, we are the most influential family in Chestnut Ridge, and it's our duty to uphold proper social tradition!"

Dorothy Graham passed the sterling silver meat platter to her son Horatio, or Horry as he recently requested, and continued to address her husband Will, who was seated at the far end of a gigantic antebellum cherry dining room table. The table itself had been in the Graham family for four generations, and it was now heavily laden with glowing candelabra, two huge floral centerpieces which strained against their silver vases and entirely too much china and crystal for a simple, routine family dinner on a plain, old Monday evening.

"Will...did you hear me? Next *Thursday*? Hester, Horry, you will both also attend, seven-thirty sharp, so we can discuss the Festival Cotillion dinner. Naturally, I want Chéz Horatio to serve as official Festival caterer, and I expect you to honor us with your latest culinary triumphs, since your dear mother is committee chairwoman, and since Chéz Horatio is *the* source for fine dining in Chestnut Ridge!"

Dorothy cut a small sliver of meat, speared it with a fork, brought it to her lips, but stopped short and said, "And Will, don't forget you'll need to take Mother Nell to The Beauty Box that day so she can look as presentable as possible before my meeting...there will be photographers from Nashville there, you know...I'd do it myself, but I will be *very* involved in selecting the floral arrangements. Oh, and Amelia Festrunk keeps calling for you...something about wanting to see Mother Nell."

Dorothy took a minute bite of her supper but stopped chewing as her son Horry tore the cloth napkin from his lap and threw it on the table.

"*Well!* Once again you believe yourself to be the only living soul on the face of the earth! Mommie, dearest, did you maybe think that you should check with us first, to see if we were already engaged next Thursday? I mean,

I'm sorry you have forgotten that your children are extremely overworked in their efforts to run the area's most successful restaurant! Why, of course we'll just drop everything and run right over to your silly little meeting! Would you like me to serve dinner at this shindig, as well? Six, or seven courses? *Hmm*? Why don't we just close the restaurant for the next twelve months, in case you might need us to make coffee for you every morning!"

After his outburst, Horry Graham forced a most gracious, dutiful son smile at his platinum helmet-haired mother, from his place at the long dining room table. Dorothy Graham pretended not to notice her son's sarcasm and continued to nibble at the sparse selection of food on her plate. She had to watch her figure carefully; photo-ops were constant during the Winter Social Season in Chestnut Ridge.

Horry's twin sister, Hester, spoke up quietly from the opposite side of the table, "Oh, Horry, stop it! Mom, you see, Thursday's are bad for us... the Elks banquet…but I think we've got it down pat. Horry, it's really ok, you go to Mom's meeting. It's so exciting! How I wish I could go to the Festival Cotillion again...I know just what I would wear…"

Dorothy Graham glanced approvingly at Hester and opened her red-lined mouth to speak, when Horry cut in, "Really, Mother, what's the big deal? It's just like all the other 'to-die-for' social queen events around here! What is so difficult? The only real decision your old committee has to make is whether they want tuna balls or creamed snails for an appetizer...I'd have to order the snails way in advance...I mean, everybody with an ounce of sense knows you don't just go out and get good snails off the street!"

Satisfied that he had taken the matter well in hand, Horry returned his napkin to his lap and passed a steaming silver bowl of mashed potatoes across the wide table to Hester. He caught his dashing reflection mirrored on the bowl's surface and tugged slightly at the chartreuse silk scarf that ringed his neck. Chartreuse was Horry's signature color; he wore it every day of his life and insisted that every apron, uniform and linen accessory at Chéz Horatio be chartreuse as well. Horry was convinced that regular patrons of fine dining expected such attention to detail.

"DID THAT COOK PUT NUTMEG IN THESE MASHED POTATOES? SHE KNOWS I CAN'T EAT NUTMEG! IT WILL CLOG MY FEMALE ORGANS! I'LL HAVE TO GET A PELVIC EXAM! SHE'S TRYING TO POISON ME! *WILL!* DO YOU HEAR ME?"

Eighty-three-year old Mother Nell Graham pointed a long, blue-veined finger from the folds of her red velvet bathrobe and sat up as best she could in her wheelchair, which was parked at the table next to Hester. Mother Nell was severely hard of hearing, and every word she uttered came out of her mouth at an ear-splitting decibel level.

"Grandma, I'm sure there's no nutmeg in the potatoes. Would you like some beets?"

Hester was the only person in the room who paid the slightest bit of attention to Mother Nell, as everyone else continued to eat. Dorothy, ignoring both Mother Nell and Hester's attempts to calm her, spoke again.

"Now, Horatio, you know that I need your total support to get through all these months of pre-Festival tension; if you're going to be difficult at the very onset, I may as well resign my post *now* and be spared the horrendous shame and humiliation of failure later. Hester, pass the green beans, please...OH, Hester, be careful! Watch what you're doing! Please don't spill anything on my good tablecloth!"

Dorothy Graham had worked countless party crowds, volunteered at too many charity luncheons, and lobbied Chestnut Ridge's most important social butterflies for over five years in pursuit of an appointment as the 136th Annual Chestnut Ridge Sons of Glory Festival Chairwoman. She was not going to allow her children, her husband or her ancient, sickly mother-in-law to ruin the best thing that had happened to her since she was named Chestnut Ridge Homecoming Queen some thirty years before. Her family owed her a great deal and she was simply not asking too much from them. She needed Horry and Hester at that planning meeting, come hell or high water; they owed their mother that.

"Mom, it's ok, we'll work out something, if you insist, then Horry will be there, won't you, Horry? I'll ask Juliette Kimball to help me with the Elks...she's usually available to help serve...those Elks banquets run pretty late, and Horry will probably be back before it's over anyway."

As his twin, Hester Graham should have been the exact replica of her brother Horry. They both sported their mother's light blonde hair, light green eyes and fair freckled skin. But where Mother Nature indulged Horry with the family's good bone structure and thin frame, she had cursed Hester with a lump of a body that plopped along with very little trace of noticeable movement. Every morsel of food Hester ate went straight to her pudgy hips and thighs, and where Horry was outspoken, even theatrical, Hester was the very definition of shyness. Hester's reclusivity and lack of attention to her appearance was a great disappointment to her mother, who had envisioned at her birth that Hester would become the most desirable young woman in town, the belle of Dorothy's proverbial ball.

Not for Hester the ballet lessons, school dances or Prom Queen accomplishments so cherished by Dorothy. She was much more content to remain a homebody and dream the romance novel dreams of a lonely young woman who was too shy to ever think about a relationship with a real man. As manager of the small restaurant she owned with Horry, Chéz Horatio, Hester proved an efficient and dedicated partner. As a single young woman whose mother expected her to find a life of love and social position, however, she was a complete and total failure. She spent every night after the restaurant closed curled up in her loft behind Chéz Horatio, reading a seemingly endless supply of gothic tales and eating chocolate eclairs from Juliette Kimball's bakery next door. Hester was the family peacemaker, and she felt obligated to smooth over the guaranteed fights between her mother and Horry during their Monday night dinners.

"Don't worry, Mom, I've handled the Elks crowd enough now that I almost feel like an honorary member! Wouldn't that be a kick? Me wearing an Elks hat! Maybe that's what I need to do, become the first female Elks member! I mean, what a great way to meet eligible men! I wonder if they'd teach me the secret Elk Moonbeam dance?"

Hester placed a large blob of mashed potatoes into her mouth and looked dreamily at her reflection in the huge silver vase centered on the dining room table. She pictured herself dancing with a tall, seductive Elk member, the tassles on his purple hat tickling her face, as he twirled her across the hardwood floor of Chéz Horatio's private banquet room...

"THOSE ELKS ARE SATAN-WORSHIPERS, AND YOU BETTER WATCH IT, GAL, OR THEY'LL STEAL YOUR MAIDENHEAD!"

Mother Nell's wobbly finger shook at Hester as Hester swallowed mashed potatoes with a start. "THEY BRAINWASHED YOUR GRANDPA AND MADE HIM HAVE SEX WITH THEIR TORRID DEMON WITCHES, AND THAT'S WHY HE DIED AT THE AGE OF FORTY-NINE, BECAUSE HE PISSED OFF GOD! THOSE ELKS ARE IN LEAGUE WITH THE DEVIL!"

Mother Nell failed to notice that during her diatribe against the Elks and her late husband, the sleeve of her red velvet bathrobe had dragged unmercifully through the untouched mashed potatoes on her plate. She inadvertently slung potatoes around the room with every finger-pointing, punctuated shout. Horry threw down his napkin in disgust, rolled his eyes at Mother Nell; he smoothed one fine-boned hand over his pageboy-cut, ash blonde hair.

"No, Hessie, it's *NOT* ok! The Elks are quite demanding and at their last banquet, they were not at all pleased with the lengthy delay between soup and salad! They have rented Chéz Horatio *in toto* for the evening next Thursday, which means they want both Hester and me present to serve their every whim!"

Horry waved one hand in the air toward his mother, "*Mumsie,* dear, Hessie and I have a serious business to operate...this is not some precious hobby we've recently decided to toy with! You must understand we will treat your little Festival as any other paying customer, and you'll just have to follow our standard catering order procedure! I will, of course, be happy to consult with you on menus if you would care to come by the restaurant between the hours of two and four daily. For you, dear Mother, I will even waive my usual and customary consultation fee. But I will *not*, I repeat *not*, come to any silly meetings with ladies who wear Peter Pan collars and serve packaged cookies as refreshment!"

Horry waved his fork in the air with a flourish, then plunged it fiercely into the chicken breast on his plate. Hester stood up next to Mother Nell and attempted to wipe stray potatoes from her grandmother's red robe, blue hair and the dining room wallpaper.

Dorothy pursed her red lips and cocked her head, "*Splendid*...I'll just tell AnnElise Leigh-Lee, who is just dying for me to trip up so she can claim my Presidency, that my own son and daughter, owners of Chéz Horatio, the finest dining and catering establishment in Chestnut Ridge, thank-you-very-much that their father and I financed, were just too busy to attend the most important society planning meeting of the century! A meeting that their very own mother, the woman who labored over *thirty-six hours* to bring them into this world, is chairing... *excellent*! In fact, I'll just go right now and tell AnnElise to call that quaint supper club in Smyrna, what's the name, *The Country Cousin*? Maybe we'd be better off if they catered the Festival Cotillion, and Chéz Horatio can just provide the corn dogs for the carnival!"

Dorothy Graham slammed her fist onto the lace-covered table, splashing mashed potatoes sans gravy (too many pre-Masked Ball fat grams) onto the skirt of her red wool suit. She carefully wiped her perfectly red-lined mouth with one dainty edge of a lace napkin and pretended not to notice the fine trail of potatoes melded to her right thigh. Her face reddened with simmering rage as she sipped wine from an elegant crystal goblet.

"Mom, now don't be angry..." Hester pulled a gigantic blob of mashed potatoes from Mother Nell's hair. "This is all very easy to work out, and you and Horry just need to..."

"Hester, *dear*, it is obvious that your ungrateful brother cannot spare two hours of self-importance to assist the woman who endured great pain and a near-death experience to bring you both into this world, and ..."

Horry pushed his chair two feet back from the expanse of the table, stood up and exclaimed in a screechingly high voice, "*Oh my God*! I just realized I forgot to curtsy to Her Royal Highness when I entered the Throne Room! Oh, really, Mother, aren't we the dramatic one! Give her an Oscar, Katherine Hepburn! Look at the girl emote! I have never seen such passion, such fire! Mother, do go on, encore! *ENCORE*! Have we practiced our acceptance speech? Is the marble monument ready to be unveiled in the backyard? I do hope the eternal flame is ready!"

Horry stood on the gold brocaded cushion of the cherry dining table chair, waved his arms and clapped for more. "*The Country Cousin*! Big Momma's gonna call the Country Cousin and see if they can do, what is it, a high-society dinner for four hundred? Hey, *no prob, babe*, if you want pimiento cheese and banana pudding! Oh, I can see it in the *Tell-All* now '*FOUR HUNDRED PEOPLE ADMITTED EN MASSE TO FESTRUNK CLINIC...POISONED BY THE BOTULISM SPECIAL AT THE COUNTRY COUSIN CAFE!*"

Horry stepped back onto the floor and raced around behind his mother's chair. He removed a gold candle from a candelabra and held it like a microphone, continuing in his best five o'clock newscast voice, *"Doctors report the culprit to be bad mayo in the pimiento cheese sandwiches, and one poor woman found a HAIR in her grits! But the real clincher of the evening was the discovery that the 'imported wine' was brought in especially from ALABAMA! Film at eleven!"*

"THAT BOY IS TAINTED! I THINK THE ELKS HAVE BRAINWASHED HIM, TOO! HAVE YOU DONE THAT SECRET MOONBEAM DANCE, BOY? SPEAK UP! YOU'RE ACTIN' JUST LIKE YOUR GRANDFATHER DID THE NIGHT HE WAS BRAINWASHED! GET MY GUN! THERE'S ONLY ONE WAY TO DEAL WITH THOSE ELKS!"

Mother Nell looked around the dining room, but when it became apparent that her gun was not forthcoming, she reached out a shaky hand for her water glass, which was actually filled with her daily dose of dinnertime vodka, or as she preferred to call it, her stomach tonic.

"*HORRY! MOTHER!* Stop it! You two are acting like children!"

Hester's freckled face turned as red as the untouched beets swimming in their silver serving dish. "Now, quit! There is certainly a solution to this whole thing, and if you'll just give me a minute, we'll figure it out! Daddy, Daddy, can you please ask them both to calm down?"

Will Graham, silent at the other end of the table, momentarily set aside the latest issue of *Cash* magazine and drained the wine glass to his left. "Hmmm...Hessie, dear, what did you say? You want some beets?"

"No, Daddy, Mom and Horry are fighting again, and I want them to stop! Can't we just have one single Monday night family dinner without them fighting?"

Hester broke into tears and ran from the dining room. Dorothy Graham rang the bell for the maid, while Will re-folded his magazine and in a calm, low voice, asked,

"Dorothy darling, what's all the fuss? Horry's right, you should approach his services like any other vendor and make an appointment! We have way too much invested in Chéz Horatio to pit a one-time festival against our regular, paying customers."

Dorothy, amazed that Will had processed even the slightest word during the last twenty minutes, mindlessly pushed her blonde helmet into place and continued to furiously ring the maid's bell to no avail. Will sat back in his chair and raised his hand for silence. Dorothy put down the bell and glared at her husband, who frowned,

"Restaurant business is bitter, I know that for a fact! Why just yesterday, we foreclosed on the Grits 'N Gravy...it'd been two full months since their last payment, and I said to Dan Gastineau, you just watch because Chestnut Ridge's fine eating establishments are dropping like flies! It's painful to come down hard on a place that makes such good biscuits, believe me!"

Will took a bite of cold mashed potatoes and winked at Dorothy. Grey and distinguished, Will Graham sat at the head of the Graham family table every Monday night in suitcoat and tie, *Cash* magazine in hand, monitoring the squabbles of his wife and their two children; and more recently, seeing to the needs of an infirm mother who was thrown out of the only assisted living facility in the county due to her inability to follow the rules.

In December, after flashing a young orderly and ordering him to 'love me like the hellcat I am,' Mother Nell was moved out of the assisted living facility and back into what had once been her own home, her father's and her grandfather's before that. Her only son Will had converted the downstairs parlor into a bedroom for his mother, and the arrangement worked as well as it could, with the exception of Sundays and Mondays when Mother Nell's high-paid private nurse thoroughly enjoyed her days off.

As the chief executive officer and majority shareholder of the First National Bank of Chestnut Ridge founded by his great-great-grandfather Major Jebediah Horatio Graham, Will's sole responsibility in life was to maintain financial status quo in a small town that bordered on the fringe of the mundane. Will was a simple, soft-spoken man whose demanding, social-climbing wife did not care that she had ever given birth to twins; twins who in appearance, mannerisms and temperament bore slight resemblance to anyone else in the Graham family.

Dorothy wanted minimal contact with the children, at least until the day Chéz Horatio opened and received rave reviews from area newspapers, making minor celebrities of Hester and Horry. Now Dorothy reserved public bragging rights on the twins and their fame, particularly when it suited her social aspirations. But for the most part, Dorothy involved herself in endless charity causes, or at least, those charity causes which also featured other "top drawer" society personalities; those charities in which Dorothy was given an office or a title, or some kind of above-average recognition for doing mysterious things like eating finger sandwiches and planning countless details for fundraising events. Dorothy made it plain that she would not be caught dead changing her children's diapers or wiping their runny noses, and she was much too busy in society to cook and keep house. Three days after the birth of the twins, Will Graham hired Bessie Thibodeaux, a Jamaican woman, to protect his wife from the dastardly deeds of motherhood.

Bessie had been a wonder. For twenty years, she'd seemed more of a wifely companion to Will than Dorothy, in a strictly platonic sense, of course, as Will was loyal to Dorothy and would not have dreamed of thinking about any other woman in "that way." Bessie moved in to the three-room suite above the garage and managed not only the children, but also the entire household. She fired the cook, replaced the existing maids with her niece, and set to work, and to Will's great relief and surprise, pleased even Dorothy. Bessie knew how to make the old house a home...she was its warmth, and its soul. Somehow, with Bessie's contagious laughter and the aroma of her delicious Caribbean dishes wafting through all seventeen rooms of the big house that Major Jebediah Horatio Graham built, Hester and Horatio rarely had to face the fact that their own mother was disenchanted with their very existence.

But after nearly twenty happy years, just when Will was really settling down and allowing himself to dream about retirement and passing along the family bank to Horry, Bessie announced that the twins no longer needed her; she had saved enough money to pay cash for a business of her own, a dressmaker's shop in downtown Chestnut Ridge. And on the day Bessie departed, Will's entire world collapsed. Dorothy suddenly had to face hiring a new cook, and a maid, because Bessie's niece left to help run the dress shop. Dorothy was so overwhelmed, she took to her bed with a three-day sick headache and the new Van Cleef & Arpels catalogue, leaving Will and the twins to fend for themselves with tv dinners and Grits 'N Gravy takeout.

After six months of chaos, repeated failed attempts to send the twins to college far from their mother, and too many maids and cooks to keep track of, Will reached bottom. As he stared at the broken remnants of his great-grandmother's crystal vase, which Dorothy lobbed at Horry during a scorcher about whether the shrimp fork goes on the left side or over the plate, Will realized he was ill-fed, highly stressed, and that for the past twenty years, Bessie had been the glue that held his world together. So the next day, Will left his bank office a little early and went over to see Bessie at her dress shop. Bessie was not very sympathetic, and spoke sternly to Will as she hung candy-striped curtains in the window of her newly opened Thibodeaux's Duds.

"Mista Will Graham, you a fool! What dose young folks need is an occupation, *cher*!" You can't 'spect tose two ta know what ta do wit' t'emselves all day, now! Miz Dor't'y ain't gonna have not'ing to do wit' t'em, t'ey ain't in da school, Mista Horry, he don't wanna work at da bank, an' Miz Hessie can't get her nose outta a book long enough ta even t'ink about anyt'ing else! Mista Will, *cher*, if you don't give t'ose two a projec', *quick*, an' git t'em outta Miz Dor't'y's hair, t'ere's gonna be a funeral, an' Bessie ain't gonna go! T'ose kids have smarts, an' if Mista Horry says he wants ta *cook*, den by da Lawd in Heavn', get him a *res-trawnt*! Lawd, Mista Will Graham, have you don' lost your min'? You own t'at *bank*, *cher*! Now git outta here so's I can finish what I got ta do! Here, han' me t'at curtain rod! Mista Will...you know I love t'ose children like my own...but you don' need Bessie ta fix not'ing! You just gots ta be da *mans*!"

So in an effort to remove Horry from Dorothy's daily outrages, and secure a little peace for himself, Will took Bessie's advice, and that very day he went over to Quigley Realty and paid cash for a stone bungalow and its accompanying two guest cottages in Chestnut Ridge's trendy old town section, just a few blocks up from Bessie's new shop.

That evening, prior to the expected nightly tirade at the dinner table, Will presented Hester and Horry with the deed to their new real estate, along with a joint bank account in their names toward renovation expenses. The twins were astonished and thrilled, and they clapped their hands in glee at their newfound opportunities.

"You can turn the bungalow into a restaurant, and there's a cottage for each of you. They're not large, by any means, but it's a great start! It's also a great investment, that part of town's really coming back…consider this your college fund, kids…although I'm still disappointed neither one of you ever earned a degree…but here's your chance to do me and your mother proud! And Dorothy, you may close your mouth, please, because this is one argument I won't even let you begin!"

Chéz Horatio was born. Horry made it plain that he could not be involved in anything so trivial as renovation or dining room design. He jotted down a few decorating preferences such as the exclusive use of chartreuse as a theme, and informed Hester that she was to oversee all of the arrangements, as his full concentration would be devoted to the development of prospective menus. Horry then decided to attend the Cordon Bleu cooking school and become a French chef.

It was a major obstacle, however, that Horry was terrified of flying. As the Cordon Bleu to date had opened no satellite campuses in Chestnut Ridge and offered no correspondence course, Horry then determined that his current study venue, watching countless hours of cooking shows on cable, would serve as an acceptable substitute. He made florid notes in a chartreuse notepad and talked to himself about his restaurant's vision and his signature dishes.

Will, being a successful businessman himself, and out of concern for his investment, graciously offered to send the twins off to a cooking school *together*, in hopes that Horry might actually study cooking with a live person. He also secretly anticipated a more peaceful home life during the cottage renovations, should the twins take him up on his offer, but Horry adamantly refused to attend any instruction in his newly chosen field.

Hester, always willing to please, made Horry's chosen occupation her priority as well. She supplied him with note pads and circled cooking programs for him in the *TV Guide*. She went to the Chestnut Ridge Library and substituted books about the food service industry and business management for her usual diet of gothic romance novels. Juliette Kimball invited Hester to join the Chestnut Ridge Women's Commerce League, and during their weekly meetings Hester successfully networked with the other female business owners in town. She learned how to handle vendors, employees and accountants...all the mysteries of the commercial universe were made known to her, although she did draw the line at participating in the League's "Women's Business March on Main Street," fearing repercussions from her mother.

With her newfound knowledge, Hester completely supervised the transformation of the once-dilapidated bungalow into a health-department-approved dining facility, and the two guest cottages into suitable living quarters. She surprised everyone with her hidden knack for dealing with contractors, interior decorators and restaurant supply salesmen. Privately, Hester fantasized that vendors were in reality well-bred nobles, in tool-belted disguise, come to rescue the lovely Princess Hester of Chestnut Ridge and take her away to some remote and soundly constructed castle in a far corner of the Scottish Highlands. She was growing quite fond of one apprentice painter, Estéfan Rodriguez, who was also becoming a fast friend of Horry's, particularly as Estéfan seemed to have an excellent sense of color.

It was Estéfan who pointed out to the twins that chartreuse was not only charismatic, but was also scientifically proven to encourage wanton restaurant spending. Hester beamed with pride one morning as her favorite knight declined his fifteen-minute break in order to personally review paint swatches with Horry; they shared a package of Ding Dongs and discussed the various virtues of flamingo pink and its ability to add texture. Yes, her Champion was a gentleman...Hester amended her fantasy to substitute the coast of Spain for the Scottish Highlands.

Estéfan was a compact, brown young man with jet-black hair and eyes, and he sported a thin mustache which made him look quite sexy, in Hester's opinion. He was muscular and lean, and occasionally he removed his shirt when the air inside the restaurant lay thick with heat and paint fumes. Hester imagined that her Castilian Champion was in bondage to the Evil Paint Sorcerer, and that one day she would free him from a life of slavery. She lived for his brief moments of undress, and a few times he'd smiled at her when she'd looked up from the paperwork she was reviewing.

Every day, Hester sat at the card table placed in the middle of what was to become Chéz Horatio's dining room, and stared in silence as Estéfan, the gallant Painter-Knight, refilled his supervisor's paint bucket with the exact shade of chartreuse he'd recommended. Her eyes followed his every move as he crossed the room to the turpentine buckets and cleaned the paint brushes. On the final day of painting, when Hester could no longer find anything in the cottage to patch or re-paint, she was faced with the fact that Estéfan would be leaving her for another fair damsel in renovation distress. The Evil Paint Sorcerer was taking her Castilian Knight to unknown lands and days of unspeakable torment. She couldn't bear the thought. She nervously approached Horry, who was standing on the front steps of the restaurant, fussing over an awning catalog.

"Horry...I've been thinking...you know, it's only a few weeks now until we open, and you and I have managed to handle everything ourselves so far...but what are we going to do when you're cooking all day and I'm going over paperwork and ordering and supervising all day...and well, who's going to be our headwaiter? Don't you think we should hire someone to be our right hand?"

Horry threw the awning catalog he was flipping through to the ground in a huff. "It's over, Hessie! The world has totally ignored the significance of chartreuse! There are no chartreuse awnings to be had anywhere! We're *ruined*...that's it...tell the workers to *stop*! Get me a 'FOR SALE' sign! Hessie, have you seen Estéfan?"

"Well, Horry, that's what I wanted to talk to you about! We need to think about hiring some staff people, and a headwaiter! Don't you think Estéfan would make an excellent headwaiter? I mean, he's only been a painter for a few weeks, so it's not like he'd be giving up any significant training or anything. What do you think, Horry? He seems to be very good with details, and you two seem to get along so well..."

Hester wrung her hands in nervous anticipation. She didn't want Horry or anybody else to discover her secret love for the Castilian Champion, but she was desperate.

"My God, Hessie! Headwaiter? Please! It's *maitre d*! How can I be expected to create culinary magnificence amidst such heathens! Of course Estéfan would make an excellent choice...that's why I've hired him for you! I talked to him about it last night...oh, I hope that's ok! But I ran into him at the Poe House Grocery, we were both in the cheese section lamenting over the lack of acceptable Bries in this town, and we went for a drink. Sorry, Hess, I should have told you, but this awning decision thing has just completely drained me!"

Hester's jubilation nearly caused her blood to boil. *Estéfan*! Working right by her side, every day, every night! The Castilian Knight would shed his armor and stay with her! The Evil Paint Sorcerer be damned! OOH, Estéfan would look so good in a tux...

Hester could barely speak. She hugged Horry with all her might, smiled, and shouted, "YIPPEE!" at him as she skipped off the front steps and headed next door to Juliette Kimball's bakery.

And so Chéz Horatio was successful, the grand opening was a dazzling affair; Horry was in culinary heaven, and the Castilian Knight was finally freed from his life of slavery by a fair damsel, a damsel who could show him the true meaning of love and fine dining, and hopefully entice him to her own fair castle made of stone. As the renovation bills trickled in, Will Graham was not at all concerned that Horry's construction tastes were quite costly and that the painting labor invoices were extravagant. All he knew was that Chéz Horatio was a success, and what-ever it cost, it was a bargain and a small price to pay for his sanity.

In fact, he reminded a very vocal Dorothy, who was incensed at such a complete waste of money, that a real college education, at an Ivy League university, for two young people, could easily have approached a higher number. With this line of reasoning, Dorothy was momentarily silenced, particularly after Will offered to send Dorothy and her mother to Aruba for a month. And, as luck would have it, Dorothy returned from her vacation with a young maid who spoke virtually no English, but whose housekeeping and culinary skills rivalled Bessie's, so once again, there was peace in the Graham household.

Two happy years had passed since Chéz Horatio had opened its doors and its kitchen to the fine dining patrons of Chestnut Ridge. Much to Will's amazement, the place was an astounding success, except for one minor incident with a flaming dessert that sent fourteen Elks to the Festrunk Clinic last New Year's Eve.

But all in all, the efforts of Horry and Hester prospered, primarily because no one in Chestnut Ridge had any pre-conceived ideas about what passed as gourmet cuisine, and second because it was the only place in town where a non-country club member could brown bag a drink with a good dinner. Will was proud of his children and their hard work, and they repaid him the renovation costs in full just last month. Everyone seemed truly happy, and best of all, with the exception of their Monday night family dinners at the Graham home (Chéz Horatio was closed on Mondays), Will was able to read his *Cash* magazine in peace and quiet, relatively speaking, of course, if you discounted Mother Nell's occasional vodka-inspired ravings.

Now Will was suddenly roused from his reminiscent dreams by the blonde sting of reality that shouted at him from the other end of the dining room table. Dorothy was saying something, and he noticed that Horry was standing directly behind her, mocking her with his hands.

"Well, Will, as usual, you have taken the children's side over mine! *WILL*! Do you *hear* me?"

Dorothy backed her chair from the table, daubed at the corners of her mouth very deliberately, and turned to Horry behind her.

"Horry, I demand and expect that either you or Hester attend my Festival Cotillion Dinner meeting next Thursday, and if it would not be too much trouble, please bring over a tray of your mini cabbage rolls and a little Dijon sauce, so I may serve them to my guests after we have conducted business. Now, I must go and organize my papers for tomorrow's Parade Committee luncheon, and I do not want to discuss this subject again. Excuse me!"

Dorothy Graham strode off across the hand-tied Persian rug, leaving Will and Horry in awkward silence as Mother Nell loudly slurped vodka from her goblet. Will reopened his magazine and continued to eat forkfuls of cold food.

"Daddy, can you believe her? Isn't she just the cat's meow! She could pop the feathers right off a chicken with that tone!"

Horry snorted, sat down in his chair, and drained his wine glass. Will mindlessly turned the page of the article he was reading.

"Son, now, just hold on, you know your mother's on edge these days, and she's totally committed to supervising a successful festival...it's very important to her. Let's not add insult to injury...it's better to walk a mile in your mother's moccasins, as they say...you know how she can be."

"There aren't enough odor-eaters made for me to walk in her moccasins! That girl is cold! C-O-L-D COLD! Elton John, write her a theme song! Oh, she makes me so mad I have upset my nervous system...*HAY-UMMMM....HAY-UMMM....HAY-UMMM...*"

Horry raised his palms to the heavens, closed his eyes and began to waver back and forth in his chair as he chanted strange words and breathed heavily every few seconds. "*HEE-UMMM....HEE-UMMMM....HEE-UMMM...Release the stress...slow the tension tide.....HEE-UMMMM.....HEE-UMMM...WACKAWACKAWACKA HMMM.* Let the goodness of your soul shine through and slap those bad thoughts right on their *booty*!"

Will Graham peered hard at his son over the magazine. It was often a challenge believing that a creature such as this was actually produced from his own loins.

"Horry. Stop that! *Horry.* I will not listen to that stuff at the dinner table! Stop that! You are going to hyperventilate, son! *Horry!* I have told you before, none of that toga around me!"

"THAT BOY IS A FREAK, I TELL YOU! THE ELKS HAVE BRAINWASHED HIM, THAT'S THEIR SECRET CHANT! YOU WILL BURN IN HELL, YOUNG MAN, FOR THAT DEVIL WORSHIP! THOSE SEX WITCHES WILL COME FOR YOU AND CUT OFF YOUR MANHOOD, IF THEY CAN FIND IT, 'CAUSE YOU SURE AIN'T EVER BEEN ON A DATE WITH A GIRL!"

Mother Nell drained her goblet and with surprising adeptness for a woman of her age and infirmity, wheeled herself from the room. Horry opened one eye at his father and called after his grandmother,

"Oh *pooh-tee-pooh,* grandma, it's not demon worship! I'm trying to relax my turbulent bowels, before I erupt into a frenzy of mashed potatoes and gravy right here on Mother's good lace tablecloth! HA! I would pay good money to see just how that would set the old gal off! *HEE-UMMM...HEE-UMMM...* It's not *toga...*it's *yoga,* and you really should try this, Daddy...it's very beneficial. André, the masseuse at the Beauty Box, learned these methods at a very respectable bath house in the Poconos. *HAY-UMMM...HAY-UMMM.*"

"Daddy, may I see you a minute, in the drawing room, please?" Hester's tear-stained face peeked around the dining room door.

"Sure, punkin. I'll be right there." Will stood up and laid his magazine on the chair. He grabbed one last forkful of cold mashed potatoes and wiped his mouth with a napkin.

"Horry, please ring for Juanita when you've finished hee-hawing. I'm gonna go see to Hessie. Shall I tell her you're about ready to go home?"

"*HEE-UMMM...*sure Daddy, tell her that the last train departs Peyton Place in ten minutes! I've got to review menus for the Elks banquet with Estefan. *HAY-UMMM...HAY-UMMM...*"

As Will passed Horry on the way from the dining room, he noticed for the first time the small diamond stud earring pierced through the topmost portion of Horry's right earlobe; it was partially hidden by the straight hair which usually covered both ears, but which had now fallen back in response to Horry's yoga swoons. When did *THAT* happen, Will wondered? Must be a *chef-thing,* as Horry says. Oh, well, no time to rock the boat now, had to see what Hessie needed. She was so fragile, and Will would do anything to make Hessie feel better.

But why on earth would a chef need an *earring*, for God's sake? Could be a health hazard, fall into the stew or something, and the resulting lawsuit could mean the loss of the entire restaurant. Only one man he'd known wore an earring, except of course for Errol Flynn when he played a pirate in the movies, and that was that Estéfan Rodriguez boy...Will had hired him as a bank teller last summer but had to let him go when Estéfan came to work wearing a *"GOD IS GAY BUT HE STILL LOVES YOUR STRAIGHT ASS"* t-shirt. Although now Estéfan seemed to be doing a good job as headwaiter for Hester and Horry, Will was concerned that Horry was too easily influenced by people with unusual ideas. Estéfan Rodriguez was a little too flamboyant and he liked to stir up trouble, even if Will did tote the note for Estéfan's parents' cleaning business.

His folks are on the up and up, even if they are foreigners. They sure could've caused a mess when Corny Poe painted over their sign, changed it to read 'Spic 'N Span Cleaning Service.' Whew, what a close one! Naw, they're good people, but I wish Horry'd spend less time with Estéfan and more time dating some of the pretty girls of Chestnut Ridge society...he's gotta think about his future, managing the Graham family businesses.

Will figured Estéfan Rodriguez wasn't necessarily a bad young man, he was just *different.* It was perfectly acceptable for a person to have his own opinions, as long as he didn't try to force them on other people, but it seemed to Will that Estéfan Rodriguez was always trying to get a rise out of everybody, like he had something to prove. *Always egging folks on to join his radical causes,* Will remembered, *like last spring when Estéfan bullied Horry into playing ball at the Alternative Lifestyles Softball tournament in Boiling Springs...just to get my dander up since he got fired from the bank...Horry never played ball in his life!*

Need to have a private talk with Horry about that earring, Will mused. *He doesn't realize what people might think about men going around wearing earrings...not good for the image of a wholesome, family restaurant owner. Not good for a man who would someday want to marry and have children of his own. No, sir, not good at all for a man who would someday replace his father as the pillar of the community.*

Late February 1999; First United Assembly of God's Children, Chestnut Ridge, Tennessee

"And I would like to c-c-close this evening by reminding each and every one of you th-th-th-that Saturday is our fair town's annual M-m-masked Ball, that infamous charity event which has in the past twenty years raised c-c-countless thousands of d-d-dollars to benefit the Senior Center!"

Reverend Cameron Culpepper, Pastor of the Chestnut Ridge First United Assembly of God's Children, stood at a massive carved pulpit in the church built by his great-great grandfather Chester. He stared out at the three hundred or so members of his diligent flock who were gathered in the historic church to receive their Wednesday night directions to God's Chosen Path.

Brother Culpepper was an educated man of fifty-eight with a round face and a few whispers of red hair still clinging desperately to his bald scalp. He was a pillar of the community, but unlike so many of his fellow pastors, Cameron Culpepper was not judgmental, critical, or disrespectful of the unchurched in his town. He firmly believed that each person had the right to make his or her own choices with respect to religion, and he staunchly refused to interfere with those choices. It was precisely this belief which now found Brother Culpepper embroiled in a most bitter controversy with several ultra-conservative members of his congregation. Brother Culpepper grasped his great ancestor's leather-bound, well-worn Bible and raised it above his head. Folds of crimson robe fell away from his short arm as he held the Bible aloft for all to see.

"*This.* This is why we meet in this gr-gr-great house. We set an example of faith for this community which endures the test of t-t-time. Service to our Lord which knows no e-e-equal. Our doors are always open, for all, to make their own choices on h-h-how to live!"

Brother Culpepper lowered the Bible, rested one arm on the pulpit and grasped the opposite corner of the pulpit with his free hand. "When my great-great grandfather, the Esteemed Brother Chester Culpepper, founded this humble church in the name of God, he felt an obligation to l-l-lead his flock, the people of this wonderful community, away from s-s-sin. Now, perhaps h-h-he had a little more s-s-sin in his day than he could rightfully deal with on h-h-his own, being a rather timid soul, so he instituted some pretty ha-ha-harsh lifestyle guidelines to help him main-main-maintain civility and duty to God. And for one hundred and thirty-six years, this faithful flock has fo-fo-followed those guidelines to the *letter*, has-has-has crusaded against drink, against dance, against lust, against v-v-vanity, against profanity and excess, and against evil in general!"

The faithful flock, seated for what was now approaching twenty-five minutes, began to stir in uncomfortable church-clothed anticipation of their pastor's continuing discourse. If good Brother Culpepper would just stop *now*, they could still beat the Baptists to the Quigley Quik-Steak for the Wednesday night All-You-Can-Eat-Ribs special. But Brother Culpepper obviously had more on his mind this evening than ribs.

"The times they are a ch-ch-changin'! The good Elders of this church have constructed and approved our new *'Policy on Fast Living,'* a policy which will guide this body of be-be-believers for another hundred and thirty-six years, God willing! Change is not easy! Change is not for the timid! But ch-ch-change is good! Je-Je-Jesus loves it when we change!"

The seated congregation shifted in the hard wooden pews, and many members openly held up their wristwatches in front of their faces, hoping that Brother Culpepper would take the hint and save this diatribe for Sunday. However, the good Brother, aflame with inspiration, burned on.

"I tell you, Brothers and Sisters, I thank God for opening my eyes to our new message of Christian love! Who are we to judge if a man or woman wants to take a dr-dr-drink now and then? Who are we to j-j-judge if a little dancing at a community social event helps to raise money for our el-el-elderly, to give them nutritious, ho-ho-hot meals every day? Did Jesus not drink and dance at the wedding in Cana?"

Brother Culpepper continued, "What right do we have to t-t-turn away a young man who seeks the Lord, just because he lives an alt-alt-alternative lifestyle? Were the Blessed Twelve considered normal in their day? I ask you, Brothers and Sisters, would Je-Je-Jesus have c-c-closed these very doors? *I THINK N-N-NOT*!"

The members of the First United Assembly of God's Children were now becoming visibly restless. The 'Policy on Fast Living' was old news; it had been in effect for exactly six weeks, and it was time to move on and go to supper. No single issue had been more divisive or more eruptive in the church's history. Throughout its one hundred and thirty-six years, a dedicated core of the church's fundamentalists insisted on maintaining an antiquated adherence to a strict lifestyle, a lifestyle which had driven scores of tithing members on to greener, and much more lenient, pastures.

But after enduring budget deficits and the embarrassment of lost members to the Methodists across the street for as long as he could stand it, Brother Culpepper decided it was time to take matters into his own hands, with the help of God, of course. They desperately needed a new roof, an enlarged Family Unity center and a new bus, and Brother Culpepper knew the only way to attract the members with the means to accomplish these holy goals was to lighten up a bit. His proposal to loosen behavioral restrictions and thus increase membership had finally won, but the wounds of the violently-opposed losers were still open, and still quite raw.

Brother Culpepper was determined to make his point to those as-yet dissenting sheep amidst his flock. He had a little over ten months until the 136th Annual Chestnut Ridge Sons of Glory Festival laid all its proposed ceremony, vain pageantry and raucous merrymaking at the feet of his congregation. He saw the Festival as a prime opportunity to seize new financially liquid souls and impress upon the unchurched that they could drink a beer during Festival week, and still gain entrance to Heaven. He had it all planned; *'God loves a cheerful giver, Brother...if an occasional sip of wine cheers your soul and inspires you to show your gratitude, then let it be, just put in a few extra shekels to thank Him for your pleasure.'* This week's Masked Charity Ball was the perfect road test on the recently widened soul-seizing highway.

"I admonish you, members of this good congregation, to be b-b-bold and step up to the plate, in the Big Ballpark of L-L-Life! Take the charity challenge, buy a ticket to the Masked Ball! Wear a co-co-costume! Drink a four-dollar glass of wine! The proceeds go-go-go to your community, and by participating, you not only set an example for your neighbor, you help f-f-feed him! We-we-we will show our fellow citizens that we are no longer judg-judg-judgmental! We will show true-true-true love and allow *God* to be the judge!"

Brother Culpepper instantly bowed his head and raised his hands into the air, to the relief of the hungry parishioners. "Now, let us pray..."

As the reverend prepared to dismiss his hungry fold, Fay Bailey and her escort, Estéfan Rodriguez, stood up from a pew at the very front of the church and walked hurriedly down the center aisle toward the door. Fay, in all her vampish, middle-aged glory, was extremely late for her dinner date with a wealthy widower from Murfreesboro, and since her car was on the fritz again, Estéfan was the lucky man nominated to drive Fay to said social obligation. Fay's bad luck with automobiles was notorious in Chestnut Ridge, but not as notorious as her ability to procure young, handsome drivers to whisk her all over town.

At the sight of curvacious Fay Bailey prissing down the aisle in a red satin, backless dress and matching spiked pumps, all eyes in the First United Assembly of God's Children remained open during Brother Culpepper's Benediction. Each and every God-fearing man seated among the faithful gasped deep for breath as Fay passed by in a scented cloud of wicked perfume. Fay Bailey was among the newest members of Brother Culpepper's flock; her first appearance required the Reverend to quietly admonish the women of the congregation that an open door policy meant an open door for *all*, despite their personal preference for clothing, or the lack thereof.

At the altar, in their pre-pubescent hormonal Fay trance, the two young acolytes bumped into one another and accidentally set fire to the altar cloth, as Brother Culpepper finished his closing prayer, "A-A-Amen! *Oh my Lord, get the fire extinguisher*!"

Brother Culpepper flew from the pulpit in a flurry of crimson robe, yanked the altar cloth to the floor and stomped on it repeatedly, much to the disgust of the Altar League ladies, who had painstakingly sewn new lace trim on it just last week. The exiting congregation buzzed loudly in a post-Fay-fire frenzy.

"Well, I don't care what you say, Nadine, it is not appropriate to wear that color in the Lord's house...well, 'wear'...excuse me, but that dress was *glued* to that hussy! I mean, no self-respectin' man would ever think of marryin' her, because she's givin' out free samples to anybody who's just window shoppin'! Oh, I'll call ya tomorrow 'bout that other thing!"

Penni Poe stood up and adjusted the pink pillbox hat atop her bobbed strawberry blonde hair. She smoothed her pink wool winter suit, smiled at a friend in the next pew and motioned to her children to stand up and follow their father into the aisle. Then she spoke in a low voice to her husband, Cornelius.

"Corny, how can anyone deny that Fay Bailey is *evil*? I mean, first, she leaves poor ol' Henry and takes all his money, so's he has to live in that ol' Mustang on his used car lot! Then she dates both Bill and Bull McArdle at the same time! And how on earth could she bring that gay boy, Estéfan Rod-er-i-guez, into God's House? I hear they're dating! Well...Euladeen's said she's seen them over at The Cow Poke more than once, anyway! Now you answer me, how in the world could any self-respectin' God-fearin' woman date a gay boy? Can you believe? I mean, that just smacks *'God strike me dead'* all over it!"

"Wife, we're still in the house of our Lord, an' I'll ask you to stop thinkin' any more ill thoughts 'bout our neighbors while we're in earshot of the Senior Elders and their wives! That danged Culpepper...I don't know what's gotten inta him, but I don't like it! Not one bit! No Poe has ever, or *will ever*, set one God-fearin' foot inta that Masked Ball, never! But we'll fix him, won't we, hon?"

Cornelius Poe, a balding, forty-ish church Elder, tried to tactfully readjust his creeping boxer shorts without being noticed by the other exiting worshipers. A soft spotlight from high overhead reflected off a stained glass window and wove an intricately colorful design on the top of Corny's scalp. He sighed and began to murmur to himself, *"Oh, no, he just cain't let that Fast Livin' Policy die! He's gotta bring it up ever' week, an' rub our losin' faces in it!*

His great-great-grandaddy's prob'ly turnin' cartwheels in his grave! Go to the Masked Ball! Drink a glass of wine! I'll burn in Hell before I give in to that kind of liberal behavior! It's not what God intended! Penni! Where's Edgar Allen? Edgar Allen Poe, you stop hittin' your sister on the head with that church bulletin, you hear?"

The recent defeat of Cornelius Poe and his steadfastly conservative church faction was a story that set the town of Chestnut Ridge on fire during the typically peaceful days between Thanksgiving and Christmas. As the Elders of the First United Assembly of God's Children hotly debated, week after week, whether to amend the cultural restrictions placed on members over one hundred and thirty-five years ago, the smoke from the local gossip fires lured hundreds to weekly services, in hopes of witnessing a walk-out from either side. When the congregation swelled to capacity the week before Christmas, packed full of nosy onlookers, it resulted in record collection-plate receipts, and the Elders realized there might be a method to Brother Culpepper's madness after all. They promptly voted to place Brother's new 'Policy on Fast Living' into effect January 1. All of the Elders, that is, except Cornelius Poe.

Despite January's new liberalism, Corny continued to attend services at the church his family had belonged to for four generations. Although he maintained his opposition to the changes and their ramifications, he decided that it was ungodly to break ranks with the First United Assembly of God's Children altogether, primarily because he would soon become a Senior Elder, and his name would then be permanently affixed to a bronze plaque just inside the entrance to the church. A plaque which bore the names of his father and his father's father before him. Corny was not going to be the Poe that broke the chain, just because of a major disagreement; that plaque was his birthright, and he'd get his name on it, with or without Brother Culpepper's Policy on Fast Livin'.

In the humiliating week after his defeat at the hands of Brother Culpepper and his band of sinners, Corny consoled himself by mindlessly rearranging produce at the Poe House Grocery, the grocery his family had owned for four generations, and where he was manager. *We'll just quit the church,* he told himself. *We'll go to a different church, a better one, one where God will smite dead on the spot anybody who even utters one small word about Liberalizing! Besides,* he told himself, *that church is gonna burn to the ground with God's wrath! I'm not gonna set one foot in it ever again!* But it was not so easy. There was that bronze Senior Elder plaque...his name preserved for all posterity...next to his ancestors. It loomed large in Corny's mind, consumed his every waking thought. All his life's hard work, piety and good example for nothing.

Then one afternoon as Corny lazily stacked a pile of sweet potatoes to entice impulse buyers, he had the sudden realization that he could go one better than to leave the church...he would Fight the Good Moral Fight without ever entering into a single visible battle. It dawned on him that he was still the leader of the church's Family Unity Encounter Program! He was fully in charge of its content! Nobody else in that church was interested in taking his place, the time commitment was too great; too many weekends involved with retreats, too many pamphlets to distribute...*that's it*! Corny could just modify those program themes a bit, and use them as a forum for God's True Conservative Lifestyle Plan.

And he could write a couple of his *own* little pamphlets about the evils of Liberalism and the Ways of the Devil and stick them right in there with the rest of the retreat materials, and nobody'd ever suspect anything! *And God will help me, as I casually, and in a non-threatening manner, persuade other straying members to see the Light,* Corny mused. *Brother Culpepper won't be able to say anything about my tactics, either...open judgment of others was one thing; subtle coercion was another. I wonder how I'd look in that crimson robe...*

It was a brilliant and subversive plan, in Corny's opinion, and he was prepared to be patient, to wait as long as necessary to slam-dunk Brother Culpepper right out of town in disgrace. *Yeah,* Corny smiled to himself as he waved a sweet potato into the air, *after one or two Family Unity retreats full of his secret propaganda, I bet every one of them no-good, money-hungry Liberals will come crawlin' right back to the way it used to be, the Right Way, the Lord's Way! Without Masked Balls, demon alcohol and the tricks of the devil!*

Corny was so excited at the prospect of regaining his respectability in God's name, he knocked the entire display of tantalizing sweet potatoes to the floor. As he chased the rolling potatoes and re-stacked them haphazardly, he felt something like a Divine Inspiration come over him; slowly, like a warm wave. He stared at the last sweet potato in his hand and blinked his eyes. He gasped. It was the face of Jesus! *On the sweet potato*! Smiling at him! How comforting it was! A miracle! A sign! Corny held the sweet potato to his breast, whispered a prayer of thanks to God, and dashed over to his wife, Penni, who was counting cereal boxes on Aisle Thirteen.

"*Penni! Penni! Come in the back room, right now!*"

Penni looked at her husband in disgust, "Corny, I told you last night, I'm havin' *my time* this week! Go get a fudgesicle or somethin, hon..."

Corny shook his head, "No, Penni! Come here right now! I've had a message from *Jesus*!"

Corny pulled Penni back to the tiny office of the Poe House Grocery. He closed the door, pulled the shade and told her every detail of his Vision, his Plan and his Jesus Sighting. He held out the sweet potato.

"Look! See! Right there, it's Jesus plain as day! See?"

Small tears of ecstasy streamed down Corny's cheeks. Penni bit her lip. It was just an ordinary sweet potato; no face of Jesus, or Moses, or anybody else she recognized, although one lumpy end of the sweet potato did remind her of Fay Bailey's big behind. She stared at Corny. It had happened. Her husband had cracked. All those months of stress over the Policy on Fast Living. She opened her mouth, but thought better of what she was about to say. If this sweet potato was the key that would give Corny something to focus on besides his humiliation at the hands of Brother Culpepper, she wasn't going to tell him otherwise. Maybe if he had something to believe in, their lives could get back to normal...

"I see it, hon! Oh, my God! Sweet Potato! I mean, *Sweet Jesus*! But *Corny*!"

Penni seized Corny's arm in a painful grip, fearful of what her husband might do and the additional humiliation his actions might bring to their family.

"Corny, we can't tell a *soul* about this! Not until we figure out what God wants us to do! I mean, if all them Liberals find out that we've had a Jesus Sightin' on our sweet potato, they'll just say we're crazy! They'll just shake their heads and walk away, and we'll look worse than ever! *No*! We got to stay *calm* and open our hearts to God's message! Now, hon, I got to get back and count them cornflakes, but you just sit here for a minute and catch your breath, and we'll talk about this later, at *home, in private*, ok? You *promise* me? Promise, Corny? God doesn't just go handin' out miracles to everybody, hon! We got to keep quiet 'bout this, and pray!"

Corny nodded and wiped his eyes. He had never been more proud of his wife Penni than at this very moment. He kissed her, and then he kissed the sweet potato, thankfully, Penni noted, in that order. "Ok, hon, I may just go on home...I'm too eat up with the Holy Fire to do anything else..."

Penni nodded, "I think that's a *real* good idea, Corny. Why don't you go on home and take a rest; and take this Sweet Potato with you, here, put it in this paper sack. Your daddy'n me'll close up. Supper's already in the oven, and I'll be 'long directly."

Penni untied Corny's grocer's apron, handed him the car keys and sent him packing with his sweet potato. That was two weeks ago, and fortunately, Penni had prevailed in keeping the Sweet Jesus Sweet Potato a secret. Corny insisted on hiding the sacred relic in his nightstand drawer, right on top of the family Bible. He took it out every morning and night and held it as he said his prayers. When little Edgar Allen asked one evening at the dinner table why his daddy was talking to a sweet potato, Penni piped up that it was a new herbal cure for the arthritis, and that Corny's doctor had prescribed that he talk to it twice a day for maximum relief.

True to Penni's hopes, Corny's preoccupation with the Jesus Sightin' and his subtle counter-attack at the church liberals had been just the thing to rejuvenate her husband. The first Family Unity Encounter of the year was just around the corner; the pamphlets were ready. And now that Brother Culpepper's endless Wednesday night diatribe had finally ended, as the Altar League Ladies rushed to inspect the charred altar cloth damaged by the distasteful attire of Fay Bailey, Penni and Corny stepped out into the crisp night air with the other church members who were heading for their cars in a hungry frenzy. But Penni and Corny turned in the direction of the Family Unity Center. Edgar Allen looked at his parents in frustration. "You're going the wrong way, Mommy! I'm hungry!"

Penni Poe bent close to her four-year old son. "I know, sweetie, but your daddy has to get the key to the Family Unity Center for Saturday night's retreat! He'll just be a minute, ok?"

Penni stood up and smoothed her pink wool backside and blushed to see Roy Quigley standing in the foyer of the church and smiling a little too lustfully at her rear end. Roy's wife Ruby waddled over, which caused Roy to quickly avert his eyes. The Quigleys, noted Chestnut Ridge entrepreneurs, were dressed in matching blue plaid polyester blazers, made by Ruby herself, on the Bernina 2000 Roy gave her for their twentieth wedding anniversary. Ruby waved her church bulletin at Penni.

"Penni Poe, Penni Poe! I'm so glad I caught ya! You an' Corny need ta come over Friday night! Ya know, because a this new 'Policy on Fast Livin,' well, I's able ta get myself ta be the Chairwoman a the Masked Ball Decoratin' Committee! Well, ok, I ain't really *Chairwoman*, but I'm the one who came up with the idea fer the decorations anyhow! Did ya *ever*? Well, we're gonna put the finishin' touches on them centerpieces, ya know, the ones we saved all them three-liter co-cola bottles for? An' then we gotta fill all them little crinkly paper nut cups fer the punch table, an' we'd just love it if ya'll could come over an' help! You know my Roy always says, *'Lotsa hands make light work!'* Now, 'course, we'll have Roy's famous drunk weenies an' my chunky cheese sticks, and Roy's gonna go fill the truckbed with ice, an' wine coolers an' beer, an'..."

"Thank ya, now, Miz Quigley," Corny Poe interrupted Ruby as he appeared suddenly from the Family Unity Center. He surreptitiously tugged through his Sunday suit pants at the left leg of his boxers. "But I'm afraid Penni and I are takin' Cornelius Jr., Susie, Patsy and Edgar Allen to a Family Unity Encounter retreat this weekend, and since Daddy's gonna have his hands full runnin' the grocery while we're gone, I just wouldn't feel right takin' Friday night off, too! But we sure do thank ya, ma'am. Come along, Penni!"

As the proud fourth-generation owner-operator of the Poe House Grocery on Main Street, a fourth-generation Elder at the First United Assembly of God's Children, and the father of four young, impressionable children, Corny Poe wanted absolutely no part of any Masked Ball, any drunk weenies or any trucks full of wine coolers and beer. In fact, it was his sincere belief that masked balls, drunk weenies and wine coolers were responsible for all the havoc in today's society, and Corny was hell-bent on protecting his family from the ways of the devil, especially if the devil was gonna be wearing a mask and hanging around with the likes of Ruby and Roy Quigley.

As a church Elder, he was now duty-bound to support and uphold the new Policy on Fast Living, and its *'Free Will, Free Choice'* philosophy, regarding every member's personal decision toward alcohol consumption, dancing and card playing. Corny personally despised alcohol and the accompanying evils it represented, and felt obligated to do everything in his power to offer non-sinful activity options to his community; non-sinful options like his Family Unity Encounter retreats. It was part of his Master Plan. He had to act fast, to convert the straying liberals back to the Mother Church, before they became just like the Methodists, or, God forbid, like the no-good, drunken Catholics and Whiskey-palians!

Penni Poe frowned her cute brow in Corny's direction and patted Ruby Quigley on her blue-plaid polyester shoulder, "Ruby, honey, thank you *so much* for thinkin' of us! But you know, our four little future missionaries need a strong family foundation if they're gonna grow up and do right. Corny organized this special Family Unity Encounter weekend to teach us all about the hidden evils in all them "bite-size" snacks that are so popular now! Did you realize, if ya let your guard down, you can be tempted to eat an entire box of bite-size Curlee-Qs in one sittin'?"

Ruby Quigley's mouth fell open in awe as Penni took her arm.

"I'm *serious*! That's just what those prepared snack cake manufacturers want! 'Specially that company that uses the devil sign on its package! Sure, they put 'fat-free' on the label an' all, but I mean, you gotta be careful! They tell ya, it's ok, just sit down with your coffee and have one li'l ol' bite-size Curlee-Q, but before ya know it, you're thinkin', *'Hey, it's just a bite-size piece! So why not have a few more?'* and POW! Just like that, your whole life becomes one big, bite-size, fat-free Curlee-Q binge! They *control* you! They take over your life, open you to sin!"

Penni Poe paused for a deep breath and patted her perky bosom with a white-gloved hand. Her cheeks were brightly lit with the hellfire and brimstone of the bite-size snack cake world, but she caught Corny frowning at his watch and glancing toward the car…they were gonna be late for dinner at Penni's mother's house.

"Well, my, we'd better go, but listen, Ruby...I've got all those special-order crepe paper streamers and those little paper drink umbrellas you wanted...you just come on over and pick 'em up tomorrow when I'm there...make sure you ask for me, hon, Corny's sister Euladeen's got the week off...you know how every year she goes down to Panama City for the World of Bingo convention...so I'll be Head Checker this week. And thanks again for the party invite!"

Roy Quigley shook his head at Penni and hitched up his robin's egg blue polyester pants. "Too bad ya'll cain't join us, Miss Penni! You're really gonna miss somethin' special! You ain't had a drunk weenie in your mouth 'til you've tasted mine! An' I was hopin' ta teach ya how ta do that dance, what is it, oh yeah, the *Macaroni!* Have ya seen it on tv?"

As Roy demonstrated his prowess on the dance floor, he rared back with a swagger and nearly burst the gold-tone buttons on his blue plaid polyester blazer, which was roughly one and one-half sizes too small for his rotund frame. Ruby's sewing ability was dramatically outweighed by the Bernina 2000's capabilities.

"Yes, ma'am, that there Macaroni dance is a real hoot! An' Ruby's gonna unveil our matchin' costumes for the Ball...lemme tell ya, that Bernina 2000's really been smokin'!"

Ruby blushed to the tips of her dyed-black bouffant, "Oh, shoot, Roy, you are too much! Penni, I'll let ya'll in on a little secret, since ya can't make it to the party! We're gonna dress up like *dollar bills*! Yessir, just like my Roy says, nary a minute goes by in this town without a business transaction involvin' us Quigleys! Between the Quigley Quik-Steak, the Quigley Realty, the Quigley Beauty Box, an' a course Roy's family's original business, the Quigley Funeral Parlor, well, we just count ourselves lucky that we can contribute so much ta the commerce of Chestnut Ridge!" Ruby glanced at a disapproving Corny, "and of course, we do our share fer the church, too!"

Penni nodded and noticed that the drawstring handbag dangling wildly from Ruby's wrist matched exactly the blue plaid of the Quigley's blazers, and that she wore several blue plaid bows down the back of her lacquered coiffure.

"Ruby, when things calm down in a couple weeks, I do want to talk to ya 'bout helpin' out with the costumes for Edgar Allen's school Easter pageant! Ya know, I'm PTA president again this year, and, well, you're the only person I know with a good serger! Those bunny ears can be so touchy! Remember two years ago, those poor little second-graders just looked like albino German shepherds up on that stage!"

"Sure, doll! Just holler at me...just not next Tuesday...that's Miss ShuShu's day ta get groomed, and we try ta keep things real quiet after she comes home."

Corny Poe had heard enough. He stepped over to interrupt the conversation and grabbed his wife by one arm. He steered her toward the car and hollered over his shoulder, "Ruby, Roy, good ta see ya! We got to go! Your mama's waitin' on us, Penni!"

At Penni Poe's departure, Roy Quigley unfastened the straining buttons on his blue plaid blazer and longingly studied Penni's cute pink wool behind while he tried to remember where he'd parked the yellow Quigley Realty Lincoln. When Penni was no longer in sight, Roy turned to Ruby,

"Come on, honeybunny, let's go…we gotta see how that new manager over ta the Quick-Steak's doin' with the Wednesday night rib rush! I tol' him last week that next ta Saturday nights, Wednesday dinner was the real challenge ta the restaurant bizness in this town, an' that if he had any future in fast food, he'd better shore up an' fry quick, 'specially now that the Grits 'N Gravy's gone!"

"Ok, precious." Ruby adjusted a blue plaid bow on her hair tower and walked off toward the parking lot. "Roy, don't you think it's strange how them Poes never go out, 'less it's a church function? I think that Corny Poe just keeps poor little Penni's apron strings too durn tight!"

Ruby walked quickly as she talked, unaware that Roy was about ten paces behind her, searching in vain for the yellow Lincoln. Suddenly Ruby stopped under a pole light and waved her church bulletin in the air.

"Oh, baby, there's the McArdle twins. I need ta ask 'em 'bout extra security fer the funeral parlor during the Masked Ball…remember last year when those kids stole poor dead Mr. Hanes outta the Blissful Rest Room an' propped him up on Amelia Festrunk's porch? Bill! Bull! TWINS! Yoo hoo!!"

As Ruby's plaid posterior waddled off toward the McArdles, Roy leaned against a weathered elm tree in the dark of the church parking lot and muttered under his breath, "Oh, sweet Penni Poe, Penni Poe…yes, Lord, if I had me a good-lookin' hunka red-headed woman like that Penni Poe, I'd keep her apron strings tied ta the bedpost, an' then I'd grease her up real good, and' we'd just do us the Macaroni dance a coupla times, an' then I'd show her *my* drunk weenie, an' poke it right in…"

"EVENIN', ROY!" Fine night, isn't it? You just thinkin' out loud, Roy, 'bout *pokin*?"

Roy turned around hard and hit his head on the lowest branch of the elm tree. He opened his eyes in pain and stared straight into the six-foot figure of Margaret McArdle-Graham, the baby sister of Bill and Bull McArdle. Roy blanched in horror. Margaret served in an official capacity as the dispatcher for Chestnut Ridge's police and fire protection services, of which her brothers were the captains; but she was by far more famous for her services as the town's dreaded resident feminist. A feminist not to be reckoned with, in any form or fashion.

Margaret McArdle-Graham was the steadfast guardian of all town secrets. There was no family feud, no break-in, no dog-on-my-property incident that escaped her ear, but she never breathed a single word of the goings-on to anyone outside the dispatch office. Margaret always minded her own business, much to the chagrin of the town gossips, with one exception. There was one type of criminal activity that could really stir Margaret's blood… abuse against women…and she reacted swiftly against the offenders with ruthless, merciless vengeance. But unlike most women who express empathy for abused wives and children, because they have been victims themselves, Margaret's disgust was not actually based on personal experience. Margaret, reluctantly divorced some twenty-five years previously, had ironically never been physically, or even mentally abused by her husband, but she considered herself a near-victim and figured that only Providence had separated her from the real horror of an actual tragedy.

The fact that her husband left her before she'd even had the *chance* to be abused was a real sore spot in her otherwise comfortable life. Margaret was a wife abuse wannabe, and she longed to join the Sisterhood of the Victims as they paraded in front of Oprah and Sally Jesse, telling their tales with dignity, through all-knowing eyes.

Margaret's ex-husband was Hoot Graham, Will Graham's no-good, fast-talking brother. Despite the fact that Hoot had never laid anything but a loving hand on Margaret, his hasty, sneaking departure from his marriage, and from Chestnut Ridge twenty-five years earlier, had transformed Margaret McArdle-Graham into a full-fledged anti-wife abuse enforcer, whose revenge tactics were well-known, if not publicly admitted or formally prosecutable.

Margaret never intended to become such a legend. She was just a big-boned, plain young woman who'd just started a promising career with the Chestnut Ridge Police Dispatch office. But when a grinning, sandy-haired Hoot Graham returned home to Chestnut Ridge on a hot August day in 1972, after a two-year stint in Vietnam, the first woman he'd seen when he stepped off the Federal Mail train was Margaret McArdle in her six-foot-plus glory. Actually, Hoot ran right into Margaret, as he tried to pick up his regulation Army duffel; but the bag's strap caught a corner of the porter's cargo cart, and in his efforts to free his personal belongings and get on with his life, Hoot Graham accidentally rammed the bag right into Margaret McArdle's big-boned derrier. As she wheeled around in shock and prepared to hurl an unladylike epithet in her assaulter's direction, she unwittingly pressed her ample breasts right into the bandages on Hoot's war-wounded right arm.

As their blushing apologies intermingled in the August morning heat, Margaret and Hoot instantly recognized each other from high school. Margaret immediately felt an overwhelming concern for her old friend Hoot, whose bandaged arm and faraway eyes betrayed the 'aw, shucks' grin he'd managed when he'd said her name in recognition. Whatever unspeakable terrors this boy had suffered in Vietnam, she could erase. It was her duty as a neighbor, as an American and as a single woman...she'd immediately noticed Hoot's left ring finger was naked, and Margaret was fast approaching twenty years of age.

Three minutes after their clumsy, bumbled re-introduction, Margaret McArdle announced that she was gonna buy this soldier some coffee and a cheeseburger, and she'd taken the fifty-pound duffel right out of Hoot's hand and walked along with it like it was a feather pillow. Hoot and Margaret talked and stumbled embarrassingly over each other for five blocks to the Grits 'N Gravy, and there they shared fourteen cups of black coffee, two cheeseburgers no onion and a pack of Camels between them during the hours that followed.

Luckily, it was only nine-thirty in the morning, after the Grits 'N Gravy geezer crowd, and well before the lunch rush gossip mongers. Margaret was pleased to have time alone with her old schoolmate and potential new boyfriend, without the staring eyes of a small town. There was a severe shortage of eligible men in Chestnut Ridge, and if Margaret didn't strike fast, Hoot would be spoken for by the time he walked down Main Street to his father's bank.

Hoot and Margaret were both aimless wanderers at junctions in their lives; right there, in the Grits 'N Gravy, Hoot Graham fell hopelessly in love with Margaret McArdle. Despite appearances, Margaret seemed to be delicate, quiet and needful of a man's attention. Resting on her large frame was a very pretty face, a kind face, a face that smoked Camels and had a steady job with a free apartment. A face that didn't mind if he droned on endlessly about the tragedies of Nam. And right beneath the face were two of the largest breasts Hoot Graham had ever hoped to see, let alone touch with his own bare hands.

In the whirlwind courtship days that followed, Margaret imagined Hoot as her own personal decorated war hero, fresh from the fray, who needed the tender care and attention only she could adequately provide, as she constantly reminded him. Four weeks after the duffel-rump-cheeseburger encounter, Hoot Graham and Margaret McArdle were married at the Wilson County jail by the prison chaplain, with Prisoner Number Three in attendance as a witness. After a two-day honeymoon in Chattanooga (Margaret had always longed to See Rock City), they made their home in

Margaret's sparsely furnished one-bedroom apartment, located above the Chestnut Ridge Police & Fire Protection office. After two weeks of home-cooked food and Margaret's chesty embraces, the very sense of humor that precipitated his boyhood nickname fairly well returned to Hoot Graham.

Six weeks after the honeymoon, however, Hoot Graham's marital bliss crashed to the ground faster than a helicopter in Saigon. Instead of looking through the Chestnut Ridge *Tell-All* Help Wanteds one morning, as Margaret had vocally chided him for the hundredth time to do, he'd read an ad in the *Army-Navy Underground* about a commune in California. A commune for ex-Nam vets only, where a man could go around naked if it pleased him; where he could grow organic vegetables for fast, amazing cash, and where he could learn the intricacies required to become a high-paid time-lapse photographer in his spare time. And all a man had to do was bring his official discharge papers, twenty thousand in cash and a clear conscience. Not bad for a lifetime of free enterprise without Commies, jungles, copters, MREs or wives who expected him to work nine-to-five at a dull job in a dull town.

Six weeks into his marriage, Hoot suddenly realized that he truly loved Margaret…she had given him a gift no other person had been able to bestow upon him...she had given him total confidence in himself, such that for the first time in his life, he realized he was a free adult, able to make a choice and do anything he truly wanted to do. And it was then he realized that he truly didn't want to be married to Margaret any longer than absolutely necessary.

Hoot was never one to take a lead, or even a stand. He'd plodded through school, never failing, but certainly never impressing anyone with his academic abilities; that was his brother Will's job, because the whole town knew that Will would take over the family's bank business. Hoot had been a mediocre football player, a mediocre student, a mediocre son. And then two days after high school graduation, he was drafted; he served as a mediocre soldier and won a mediocre Purple Heart because he'd saved the company's MREs during an attack, thereby preventing the imminent starvation of his comrades.

And now here he was, back in Chestnut Ridge, in what he figured was a mediocre marriage and a mediocre apartment, trying to find a mediocre job. Hoot's dad had offered him any job at the First National Bank, the bank his family had founded and owned for over a hundred years. But deep down, Hoot knew that the serious bank jobs belonged to the college boys, and he had absolutely no intention of ever going to college. And he sure wasn't gonna hang around and be a lowly bank teller, under the direction of the recent college graduate and new bank vice president, Will.

Hoot stared hard at the ad for the commune in California…he reflected on his six weeks with Margaret. His new life wasn't totally bad, with the possible exception of the Tuesday night Tuna Tetrazzini Casserole ritual. At least he did have as much sex as he could ever want, because that Margaret was a real nympho…but this ad…it could be his only chance to start over, clean, take control of his future, and his life!

If he stayed in Chestnut Ridge, he'd just be ol' Hoot Graham, Will's brother, the one who never made good of himself, you know, Margaret's husband. He'd always have to watch his brother's successes, always see the regret and disappointment on his father's face, always have to live in this one-room apartment with Margaret…always have to eat Tuna Tetrazzini Casserole on Tuesday nights…that Commune sounded real good, and he'd always heard that California was full of good-lookin', easy women…But twenty thousand dollars was a lot of money! He only had two measly dollars in his wallet…and Margaret held tight to the checkbook since the day he'd accidentally thrown it in the dumpster! She wouldn't even let him drive the car unless he had a job interview. He couldn't watch football, or boxing, or go down to the Tap Room with his old school buddies…what a great life! Better off in Nam, where a guy could shoot the enemy! Here, the enemy makes a man eat Tuna Tetrazzini Casserole!

The ad for the California commune beckoned to him from its perch on the green naugahyde footstool. Hoot lit another Camel and inhaled deeply. He believed with all his shell-shocked might that this California commune thing could be his one true life's destiny. He could ask his father for the cash, tell him it was a business loan…no, his dad would just put some kind of condition on it, like *'go to college, then we'll see'*…nah, that'd never happen…maybe his mama would give him an advance….no, WAIT!

Hoot ran into the bedroom and rifled through the one dresser drawer Margaret begrudgingly allowed him. He grabbed a silver key ring heavy with at least fifty keys…*there it was*! The key to the family vault down at the bank! Hoot kissed the key ring and leaped onto the bed. Just to spite Margaret, he dropped cigarette ashes onto the awful pink ruffled bedspread and remembered a hazy day some years earlier.

"Son," his father had told him as Hoot prepared to leave for Vietnam, *"I don't ever want you to think that you don't have just as much claim to the family business as your brother. Now I'm right sorry you've gotta go off and fight this war, but it's your duty; you know I fought in W-W-2 myself; and your granddaddy fought in the Great War, and of course, the Major was a decorated hero of the Confederacy…we've got a long tradition of duty, us Grahams. And you remember, Hesperus…"*

Hoot winced at the memory of the given name that he had dodged his entire life.

"You're not just goin' off to fight for yourself, or this family, but you're also fightin' it for your brother Will, since he's in college, and can't go too! Now here, take this key...put it on your key ring...go on, it's the key to the Graham vault down at the bank. Now don't worry, I've got another copy... but you take this key, and when you're out there in those woods, fightin' those no-good Reds, you look 'em right in their slanty eye, boy, and you remember that you got somethin' to come home to! Part of everything in that vault's yours, you know, after you come home safe... and graduate from college, of course!"

Hoot twirled the beautifully ornate old key on his finger in silence as he lay on the lumpy double bed he now shared with Margaret. "I'll never get any of that inheritance," he muttered. "Will's got his hands on it firm, an' I'm always gonna have to bow and scrape, just to get what's rightfully mine. An' I'll be damned if I'm gonna go to college, just to work in a bank! Nope, I want a life of adventure...of risks...ain't nobody gonna tell me what to do, ever again!"

Hoot laughed out loud and stubbed his cigarette into the pink ruffled folds of Margaret's treasured bedspread. As the polyester singed and smoked, Hoot scanned the bedroom closet. He needed a suitcase, but Margaret had destroyed his regulation Army duffel the first week of their marriage because she said it smelled like marijuana, and she, working as the official Police & Fire Dispatcher of Chestnut Ridge, could not have anything in the house that reeked of such a heinous vice.

He looked on the top shelf of the closet and spotted a bright yellow vinyl bag that said "PSYCHO-DELIC" on one side, and decided it would make an excellent substitute. He quickly packed his military uniform, four cartons of Camels and his Alabama football sweatshirt into the bag. Then he searched Margaret's lingerie drawer, where underneath her voluminous white underwear he found the plain white envelope where she stashed the grocery money. He thumbed a couple of fifty dollar bills and stuffed them in his wallet. Then he retrieved a crumpled Quigley Quik-Steak sack from the bedroom trash can, folded it neatly and placed it in his back pocket.

Thus after a full three minutes of laborious packing, on this warm Tuesday in late September, 1972, Hoot Graham was nearly a free man. He tore the commune ad from the *Army-Navy Underground* and put it in his shirt pocket, along with his official discharge papers. He was almost out the front door for good, when he realized that he shouldn't be so ungrateful to his own wife, even if he no longer needed her, or her Tuna Tetrazzini Casserole. Hoot found a blank sheet of paper and leaned over the kitchen table to write his farewell.

"Boobsie," he began, using the pet name Margaret hated with a passion, *"a man's gotta do more than work at a job, live on a budget and eat tuna*

tetra...whatever...every week. Even though you're a pretty good cook, and really great in the sack, I'm just not happy."

Hoot frowned and straightened up. It wasn't easy saying goodbye to your wife after such a meaningful relationship. He pulled out the ad for the commune. How could he impart the ad's excitement into this measly note to Margaret? No time to fret about it; just say it.

"I'm gonna go learn to be a organic farmer and a time-lapse tomato filmmaker, in a sunny, coastal setting, miles from everywhere yet close to the heartbeat of California, and I hope one day we can be reunited after I'm a big success, and then I'll pay you back for all you done for me. Or at least, buy you a beer and a carton of smokes. And pay for a new bedspread, since I burned a hole in the one you already got."

Hoot suddenly felt sharp pangs of guilt stab him in the stomach. *"I know this is a big surprise to ya, Boobsie, but let me tell ya that if I'd stayed just one more day, for one more dose of tuna tetra...whatever...well, then you'd have had me, hook, line and sinker, and I'd never have the courage to, what is it you're always tellin' me...carve that dee-em! Now don't be mad, sugarplum, it's really all your own fault! You had so much faith in me and told me to get out there and live my life, so that's what I'm doing. But if you want a divorce, just get my daddy's lawyer to fix it and send me the papers. I wrote my new address on the back of the bank statement, since you look at it every night, right after you check the grocery money envelope. Thanks for the loan, I'll pay you back. Be safe, love Hoot."*

Hoot folded the note and placed it next to the half-empty pack of Camels he left behind. He glanced at the kitchen clock. It was nearly eleven o'clock; Margaret usually came home for lunch and a smoke break at eleven sharp, but on Tuesdays, she had to wait until twelve-fifteen for her break, because she had to conduct the weekly Chestnut Ridge Police & Fire Protection Emergency Alert Siren Test. Hoot realized with a grin that his sudden choice of escape dates was pure fate, because Margaret would not be able to leave her switchboard until twelve-sixteen, and by then, he'd be on the noon express bus to Nashville!

He also realized, however, that despite her inability to leave the office, she would be able to see him exit the apartment through the clear plate-glass windows downstairs. And she'd know he wasn't exactly dressed for a job interview. He looked out the kitchen window. The fire escape! At the back of the apartment! It was perfect! She'd never see him go.

Hoot shouldered the yellow vinyl PSYCHO-DELIC bag, locked the back door and climbed gingerly down the fire escape ladder to the alley behind the Dispatch office. With a light whistle, he quickly walked the three blocks to the First National Bank of Chestnut Ridge, where his brother Will was learning to be a bank officer, just like three other generations of eldest Graham sons before him. As Hoot entered the busy bank, Will waved at him from behind a teller cage. Hoot waved back and smiled his infamous "aw, shucks" grin. He approached the old walnut desk that belonged to Miss Iva Jean Dupree, the bank secretary.

"Mornin', Miss Iva Jean! Don't *you* look pretty today!" Hoot held up the PSYCHO-DELIC bag for Miss Iva Jean to see. "Why, if I didn't think Margaret would whup me good, I'd just leave this here bag with ya…it goes right with your outfit!"

Miss Iva Jean Dupree was a mass of silvery hair and canary-yellow starched cotton, with huge yellow-ball earrings dangling from her ears and a matching yellow-bead necklace around her thin, prim neck. She had worked at the First National Bank of Chestnut Ridge for more than thirty years, faithfully serving the Grahams and her fellow citizens, and she considered Hoot Graham nearly like a son.

"Oh, Hoot, you are just the *sweetest* thing! But now, you know that yellow is Margaret's favorite color, too, and I'd never be caught dead takin' anything yellow right from under her nose! I heard she took karate lessons! And she's such a *big* girl, too! Now, how can I help you, sug? Need to see your daddy? He's workin' on month-end, but I know he's always got time for you!" As she spoke, the bright yellow-ball earrings slapped Miss Iva Jean on her cheeks and left little red spots from their impact.

She smiled and patted Hoot on the shoulder, "You comin' to work with us here real soon? How's that bum arm doin'? *Painful*, I know, you poor boy!"

Hoot ignored her first question in favor of the second, "Thank you, Miss Iva Jean, why this arm's just about healed…in fact, I'm on my way over to the Vet hospital in Murfreesboro for a checkup! And I'm in kind of a hurry, so don't bother Daddy, but I do have a little favor I wonder if you could do for me…it's sort of for my mama…"

Hoot's puppy-dog plea shot clean through Miss Iva Jean Dupree. "Hoot Graham, I can't even believe you think you have to *ask* me for a favor! And you, wounded in service to this great country. Whatever do you need, sug?"

Hoot took a deep breath, grabbed his arm and feigned wooziness. He sat down in the old wooden chair next to Miss Iva Jean's desk and spoke in a barely audible voice, "Well, Miss Iva Jean, you know, Mama's birthday's comin' up, an' I wanted to get her somethin' real nice, but I'm a little short on *cash*…no, ma'am, thanks, I don't need a loan…but I figgered it'd be real nice to get her favorite pearl pin outta the family vault, an' have it cleaned up real good for her birthday! Ya know, she loves that pin more than anything, next to my Daddy, an' it's in bad need of a good cleanin'! Ya think ya could let me in to the vault without Daddy's signature? I've got my key to our lockbox, but I don't want Daddy to know, 'cause, well, Miss Iva Jean, to tell ya the truth, ya know how cross-ways Daddy is these days, an' I'm afraid he'll slip up an' say somethin' to Mama, an' then my surprise'll be spoilt!"

Miss Iva Jean grabbed a tissue from her desk drawer and daubed at her misting eyes. This was such a nice, thoughtful boy, so well-mannered, so much more personable than his brother Will...fooey to those old state banking laws regarding Opening Procedures for Secured Vaults! She stood up.

"Come on, sug, follow me!" Hoot dutifully and silently followed the yellow vision that was Miss Iva Jean past the teller cages and down a long, dark hall that led to the vaults. Miss Iva Jean saw that there was no one already in the vault room, and she closed and locked the door behind them.

"Now, Hoot, this is our little secret, right? You know, if I'd a had a son...I'm *barren*, you know ...but if the Good Lord had given me a son, I'd have wanted him to be just like you!"

Miss Iva Jean hugged Hoot so tightly that pain shot through his nearly healed arm, but he endured it like a trouper. Miss Iva Jean found her master vault key and unlocked the shiny steel door that gave passage into the huge rooms with their numbered compartments. Hoot procured his antique key, and Miss Iva Jean opened the cage to the Graham private vault.

"Now Hoot, you hurry up, and if you need any help, you just press this red button, *'k?*" I gotta run, sug, gotta go get your daddy his lunch! See ya!"

Miss Iva Jean planted a wet kiss on Hoot's cheek, then left him standing all alone in the middle of the four-foot square Graham treasure trove. Hoot waited for the click-click-click of Miss Iva Jean's yellow pumps to disappear, then he gazed at the endless rows of steel drawers which held the Graham family fortune.

After a few tense moments spent trying to locate the cash drawers, Hoot successfully removed twenty thousand dollars in large bills and dropped the funds into the Quigley Quik-Steak sack. Then he realized that he needed a little pocket money, so he grabbed an extra five thousand, for good measure. He placed the sack inside the PSYCHO-DELIC bag and patted his shirt pocket to make sure his discharge papers were still intact. As Hoot exited the vault, he did a double-take at the sight of his infamous ancestor, Jebediah Horatio Graham, whose portrait hung inside the vault, in testament to the man who made the Graham family a wealthy one indeed.

"Yeah, I bet you'd a done this same thing, Jeb! You fought them varmints, didn't ya? You know how hard it is to come back home an' be bored to tears, don't ya? Well, I'm doin' you *proud*, Jeb...just like you ...I'm gonna start me a clean *slate*! An' some day I'm gonna come back here, all rich an' famous-like, an' this whole town's gonna kiss my Vietcong-killin' ass! An', Jeb, ol' buddy, now don't ya get the idea that I'm *stealin'* this money! Nossiree! Everybody knows us Grahams *never* steal, cheat or lie! I'm just *borrowin'* it for awhile, so I can get respectable, like my big brother an' my daddy never *dreamed*! Won't they sure be surprised, huh, Jeb?"

Hoot gave a little whistle as he closed the door to the vault. He passed Miss Iva Jean's desk and kissed the top of her silver head as she ordered his daddy's lunch from the Grits 'N Gravy. Then he whistled louder and stepped right out the door of the First National Bank of Chestnut Ridge, be-bopped over to the bus station and caught himself the noon express to Nashville. During the brief bus ride, Hoot scanned the commune ad several times. When the bus pulled into Nashville, he looked out the window and smiled at the downtown branch of the Davidson County Bank & Trust. Hoot clapped the bus driver on the back, then took off down the street with a step so light he might have been floating.

He entered the lobby of the bank and scanned it for the greenest employee he could find, among the two rows of "New Accounts" desks in the lobby. After a thorough search, Hoot settled on a thin young man with a new suit, who looked as if he'd just learned to shave that very morning. He sauntered over and plopped the PSYCHO-DELIC bag down in the center of the young man's desk.

"'Scuse me, mister, but I'm a Vietnam vet jus' back from the jungle, killed me a few thousand Commies, ya know, an' I'd like to open up an account at this here bank!"

Hoot grinned widely as the young man's wide eyes took him in. He watched gleefully as the New Accounts officer moved the PSYCHO-DELIC bag to the floor with a disgusted frown and stiffly shuffled the two papers which had been resting on his desk. This young man would do nicely, Hoot mused, because he obviously did not recognize Hoot as the Son of a Prominent Regional Bank Owner.

"Well, I would be happy to help you, sir, but it's twelve-fifty-five, and I am now leaving on my lunch hour; besides, unfortunately we do not process new accounts between twelve and one o'clock! Please come back after one o'clock, and I'll be happy to assist you then! Thank you, and good day!"

The New Accounts officer stood up from his desk and put on his suitcoat. Hoot retrieved the PSYCHO-DELIC bag from the floor and set it once again atop the young man's desk.

" *'Scuse me*, there, Leroy, but I ain't leavin' an' comin' back in...what...five minutes? I gotta catch me a bus back to base in an hour, an' I gotta open this account *now*, if ya don't mind!"

The New Accounts officer exhaled and cocked his head sarcastically. "I'm sorry, sir, but I have already missed my entire lunch hour, and if I do not go and eat my sandwich this instant, I will most likely collapse in a hypoglycemic faint! See that woman over there? She will be happy to help you, at one o'clock! Please take a seat in the lobby, sir."

The New Accounts officer took a step, but Hoot blocked his exit with one leg. Hoot was in no mood for a lowly bank newbie to come between him and his chance to be a wealthy resident of California, far from the clutches of Margaret and her Tuesday Tuna Tetrazzini.

"*Hold it,* Leroy! I reckon ya don't know who you're dealin' with! I'm Hesperus Graham, from Chestnut Ridge, as in, my daddy owns the First National Bank of Chestnut Ridge. Ya see, little man, my daddy plays golf with Mr. Caldwell, as in *Ernest Caldwell IV*, as in, the owner of this bank! Yessir, they play every Wednesday afternoon! An' did I mention that Mr. Caldwell is also my godfather? Did I? An' did I mention that if ya don't get your scrawny little faggot hypo-whatever ass in gear an' lemme deposit my twenty-five thousand right now, I'll eat ya for lunch? I'm a *Ranger*, ya know! Bite the heads off live chickens, hell, their necks are just 'bout the size of yers! Where's a phone, I'll call Uncle Ernie myself an' get your little shit-for-brains ass fired!"

Hoot grabbed the red telephone on the corner of the desk, dialed a couple of numbers and nodded at the New Accounts officer. "Miss Betty Jan Applewood still his pers'nal sec-atary? The Miss Betty Jan Applewood who babysat me since I was four years old? Hello, hello, *hey,* Miss Betty Jan?"

Hoot talked into the phone, which of course, emitted nothing more than a dial tone, craftily muted through the palm of his hand. The New Accounts officer was humiliated but now duly concerned for the well-being of his career, in light of the grave mistake he had just made with Mr. Caldwell IV's godson. He motioned wildly for Hoot to sit down, removed his jacket and pulled some papers out of his desk drawer. Hoot continued his telephone charade.

"Hey, there, Miss Betty Jan, this is Hoot Graham, you remember, from Chestnut Ridge? Yes, ma'am, that's right. Killed me 'bout three hunnerd Commies, yes ma'am. How's Uncle Ernie?"

Hoot glanced at his watch and decided the New Accounts officer was sufficiently impressed, particularly as the young man was pleading with him to hang up the phone and fill out the New Account application he'd laid on the desk. Hoot nodded and said, "Oh, no, Miss Betty Jan, I just wanted to say 'hey' to him, an' good luck playin' golf with Daddy tomorrow, hear? Tell him to take alla Daddy's money! Bye, now!"

"Now, then, Mr. Graham," squeaked the young man, "did I hear you correctly? You wish to make a large deposit? I apologize, sir, my blood sugar's low. I will need some identification, please. "

Hoot stomped his foot for effect. "I got yer identification, Missy! Gimme that phone back! Let's just call Uncle Ernie, ok? I'll give him the run-down on his new bank officer, here, whaddya say?"

Hoot reached once again for the red telephone, but the bank officer grabbed it.

"That won't be necessary, sir. Didn't you say you have a bus to catch? We should make haste! Here, please fill out these papers in triplicate and sign the bottom."

In record time, the New Accounts officer processed Hoot's new account. Then Hoot made arrangements to wire himself the money in care of the California Coastal Bank, Del Mar branch, the official financial institution of the commune, just like it said on the ad. Despite the obvious fury on the young banker's face, he never uttered a word to Hoot during the entire transaction except to wish him a pleasant journey and to have a nice day. His banking successfully completed, Hoot stood up to leave.

"Now, then, Leroy, you tell Uncle Ernie that Hoot says *'hey!'* I'll write him from my base in California! Secret maneuvers, ya know, can't tell a soul what I'll be doin'! Oh, wait a minute!"

Hoot placed one hand on his hip, suddenly impatient. He raised his voice so everyone in the bank lobby could hear, "Ain't ya gonna tell me all about them free promotions ya got for new account holders? Don't I get a toaster or somethin? That's what yer sign out front says! I mean, twenty-five thousand dollars is a lot of money! I should at least get a six-pack or somethin'!"

Consumed with frustration, the New Accounts officer quickly opened a large cabinet next to his desk. "I'm sorry, Mr. Graham, but that promotion has been over for some time, and unfortunately, the sign out front has rusted tight to the stand, and we are in the process of having it sand-blasted so these things don't happen. I cannot offer you a toaster, or a six-pack, but would you please accept one of these canvas tote bags? It's, well, it's not quite as *festive* as the bag you're already carrying, but I'm sure it will come in handy for something."

Hoot grinned widely and accepted the bag, it was perfect for his next step. He stuck his hand out in front of the young man as if to shake on their respective deals, but he immediately doubled over as if in pain. This sure was a lot of fun.

"*Whoa, Nelly*! Hey, Leroy, listen here, I've still got some real bad problems with my innards, ya know, from bein' wounded an' all…listen, I gotta use your facil'ties *right now*…she's liable to blow any second…*ooh…aahhh…ow*!"

The New Accounts officer paled and backed away from Hoot in hopes of avoiding any potentially disgusting personal plumbing accident near his own desk. He motioned to a hallway immediately past the teller cages.

"Help yourself, Mr. Graham, down the hall. And thank you for banking with Davidson County Bank & Trust! I'll be sure and give your best to Uncle...Mr. Caldwell...call me if you need anything else, although, not for an hour, please, because I'm going to go to lunch!"

The young man disappeared in a flurry of carbon paper. Hoot labored off toward the restroom, where, inside a stall, he donned his military uniform. He crammed his civilian clothes into the PSYCHO-DELIC bag. Then he removed all the wastepaper from the restroom trash can, threw the PSYCHO-DELIC bag into the bottom and covered it with the trash. He packed the canvas Davidson County Bank & Trust tote with the cigarettes, his Alabama sweatshirt and his discharge papers, and set off toward the Nashville bus station, but he took a quick detour to drink a cold beer at Tootsie's Orchid Lounge. When he learned from the bus station ticket attendant that a ticket to L.A. cost nearly one hundred dollars, Hoot decided to enact Emergency Tactics.

He found the L.A.-bound bus, then talked his way onto it by telling the old driver that his commanding officer had gone AWOL, left him with no orders and no cash, and that his unit was en route to a top-secret mission. If he didn't get to Fort Ord in Monterey by Friday, well, there was gonna be a real serious threat to national security. As Hoot pressed a twenty into the driver's hand, the man waved him off toward the back of the bus. Hoot settled into a comfortably-tattered seat and promptly fell asleep. Forty-five hours and countless stops later, Hoot Graham kissed the ground in California and placed the call to the commune that would change his life and make him a wealthy time-lapse photographer.

Back home in Chestnut Ridge, Margaret McArdle-Graham received a new Social Security card with her married, hyphenated name (a sinful feminist act in everyone's opinion) and a goodbye note from her husband of six weeks, both on the very same day. Margaret snubbed out her fifth lunchtime cigarette and stared once more at Hoot's ridiculous note.

Well, what's done is done, she thought. *No need to cry. I should have known there were no good, decent men in the world.* She called the bank and the credit card company and notified them of her impending divorce. Then she returned to her desk at the Dispatch office and radioed her brothers with the news.

Bull immediately offered to put out an all-points bulletin and take justice into his own beefy hands, but Margaret convinced him that there was nothing Hoot Graham had that she wanted any longer. That evening, she called Hoot's mother, and informed her that Hoot had left town to live in a commune, and that she'd be filing for divorce very soon. When Margaret couldn't say whether Hoot would be home for Christmas, Mrs. Graham became hysterical, and Mr. Graham had to finish the conversation. Margaret gave him Hoot's forwarding address and asked if he could recommend a good lawyer.

Mr. Graham then offered Margaret some unsolicited advice on the rigors of divorce, explained why it was to her considerable future tax benefit to refuse alimony and informed her that the most prudent course of action to avoid mutual legal fees was for her to willingly decline any claim on the Graham family fortune. Mrs. Graham picked up the other receiver and screamed at Margaret that she had poisoned Hoot with Tuna Tetrazzini Casserole. Margaret hung up on both of them and smoked an entire pack of Camels.

That's right, Margaret mused, *it's Tuesday. There's one thing to be thankful for.* She turned on the oven, put in the Tuna Tetrazzini Casserole, and set the timer. *It's not so bad,* she said out loud. *Don't be a moaner and groaner, like all those women who stand around the baked goods aisle at the Poe House Grocery, complaining about their lives.* She located her adding machine and made a few calculations.

When she'd announced her marriage, the Dispatch office had awarded Margaret a forty dollar a month raise. Without Hoot, her living expenses would be reduced by nearly two hundred a month! Two hundred a month for beer, pizza, magazines and his own Camels! I'll have two hundred and forty a month extra! I can take a *vacation,* she thought! I can buy a sofa bed! I can eat Tuna Tetrazzini every *day* if I want to! Margaret immediately realized there was a bright side to Hoot's departure. She was tired of picking up after him and dodging him in this tiny apartment that had long been her home. She was sick of doing his laundry, and she was sick of being the sole provider for a three-pack-a-day smoker who didn't seem the slightest bit interested in finding a job and contributing at least the cost of the Camels to the marriage! And I won't have to sleep all curled up on the bed! I can stretch out across that mattress like I used to, so my feet won't hang off! My back will stop hurting! The oven timer buzzed. Margaret removed a steaming pan of Tuna Tetrazzini Casserole from the oven and sniffed it with closed eyes. *This is pure Heaven,* she thought. *An entire pan of Tuna Tetrazzini Casserole to myself! Just like when I was a swinging bachelorette!*

As Margaret sat on the couch and forked her way through the Tuna Tetrazzini Casserole, she remembered that during Hoot-days, she would have lost her temper by now. Every Tuesday, Hoot would pick all the peas and carrots out of the Tuna Tetrazzini Casserole and pile them on the table, under his plate. Then he would stir the remainder of the casserole around and around, until finally he would beg off, complaining that his "jungle virus" had kicked in. He would boldly let absolutely perfectly delicious Tuna

Tetrazzini Casserole go to waste on the Sears Everyday. Not one bite would he eat. Leftover Tuna Tetrazzini Casserole was no problem for Margaret, but leftover Tuna Tetrazzini Casserole that someone else had *breathed on* and *played with* and *wasted*, that was a completely different story.

Day by day, Margaret resigned herself to the fact that her marriage had been a mistake and a failure, and that Hoot was gone. She had more money in her checkbook and more Tuna Tetrazzini Casserole in her fridge, but she was alone, desperately alone. Perhaps, like her twin brothers Bill and Bull suggested, she'd been such a good wife to Hoot that he'd felt guilty and unworthy, and he'd had to leave, to find some way to better himself and repay her, just like his note said. After all, a soldier is pretty worthless in peacetime, they reminded her, and it was pretty obvious that Hoot Graham wasn't cut out for factory work.

After the initial brouhaha surrounding Hoot's departure calmed down a bit, once the scandal was mentioned in public every ten days or so, instead of every single day, Margaret McArdle-Graham called Richard Leigh-Lee IV, at the insistence of Hoot's father, to prepare no-fault divorce papers. Margaret knew that Mr. Graham's offer to pay all lawyer fees was his way of getting her to release any claim she might have on the Graham gold. But she no longer cared. She just wanted the whole thing to go away; she wanted to disappear.

During Margaret's initial consultation with Mr. Leigh-Lee, he explained that as a matter of practice, he would not be handling the divorce personally, but that a young clerk in the firm would do the honors. '*Nevertheless,*' he said, *'I am a junior partner of this firm, and I would like to review with you what your divorce demands and expectations are. Have you prepared a list of demands, Mrs. Graham?'*

Margaret informed her attorney that her divorce demands were fairly well nonexistent, much to his chagrin, as his firm's fees were based on the settlement she would receive. The Grahams and Leigh-Lees were co-owners of the bank and of many other businesses in town, and despite the fact that the Graham family had secured the promise of Leigh-Lee & Sons to obtain Margaret's release on any future claim to their wealth, Leigh-Lee & Sons still had to make a profit. It was up to Richard Leigh-Lee IV to see what he could pump from the well, within the respectable bounds of friendship, of course.

"Do you realize, Margaret…may I call you Margaret?" Richard Leigh-Lee IV flashed a wicked, toothy smile, "Do you realize that you are by law fully entitled to one-half of all Hoot Graham's inheritance, an inheritance that will one day approximate nearly twenty million dollars?"

Margaret nodded silently; Mr. Leigh-Lee continued. "Do you realize that this inheritance includes stocks, bonds and owner-interests in several profitable local businesses? These entities could make you a very rich woman, Margaret. Even after court costs and legal fees, and of course, you would most likely only receive a tenth of the full amount, based on court precedent...you're giving away all claim to a good sum of money, miss!" *And giving this firm a disgustingly small reason to take this case*, mused Richard Leigh-Lee IV.

"Isn't there something you want? Some manner in which Mr. Hesperus Graham may provide for you in the future, to make up for this tremendous embarrassment, this horrible injustice, this unspeakable wrong? He left you, my dear, cold! Unprotected!"

As she listened to Mr. Leigh-Lee drone on, Margaret spied a *Vacation Times* magazine on the chair next to her. Mr. Leigh-Lee suddenly apologized and left to take an important call. Margaret perused the magazine and found an appealing, lifestyle-changing ad of her own.

"Breathtaking Casa del Sol Resort, minutes from Gulf Shores, Alabama. Lose your worries...lose your troubles...celebrate yourself! Pre-paid vacations are our specialty! Low rates! No interest! Fifteen beach-side bars with over a hundred frozen drinks from which to choose! Sports for the active set, including badminton, shuffleboard and bridge! Gourmet meals! Singles Mixers! Divorcee Dances! Nightly Entertainment with Las Vegas-style talent! Hurry! Reservations for the 1973 season are filling fast!"

Richard Leigh-Lee IV returned. "Thank you for waiting, Margaret. Now...where were we? Oh, right. You say you don't want to have anything to do with the Grahams or their money. *Fine*, Margaret, fine. And I don't guess you want to prosecute Hoot...*Hesperus*...for undue stress or embarrassment, or to recoup some of the expenses you incurred during your marriage? Well, that's ok, it's perfectly legal, you know, and..."

"I want to go *here*." Margaret stood up and shoved the Casa del Sol Resort ad in Richard Leigh-Lee IV's surprised face.

"I want to go here for two weeks every year on my vacation, and I want *him* to pay for it! I want a double room, so I can take a guest if I want to, and I want everything paid for, the whole nine yards, including a plane ticket! Until the day I die!"

Richard Leigh-Lee smiled. He was getting through to Margaret, even if her demand was a tad unconventional. "I *see*. Well, first of all, Margaret, I don't think there's an airport in Gulf Shores...but we'll check into it. So...you don't want any of the stocks, bonds, properties or investments, but you want two weeks a year, for the rest of your life, at Casa del Sol Resort...*fine, fine*! But Margaret, what happens if Casa del Sol *closes*? What if they go out of *business*? Wouldn't you just rather have the *cash*?"

And keep things simple for my staff, Richard Leigh-Lee IV thought. *Save me the expense of checking all this out and making the annual reservations? Give me an immediate cash windfall, instead of an annual percentage on some ridiculous two-week stipend?*

"No, from the looks of this place, Mr. Leigh-Lee, it's very successful. It won't close. I'm sure of it. No, I want two weeks a year there, with one exception..."

Richard Leigh-Lee brightened; here must be the cash cow. "Yes...what is that exception?"

Margaret leaned over and whispered, "When Hoot Graham drops dead in that California commune, I want an airline ticket to take me to where he is before they bury him!"

Richard Leigh-Lee IV cocked his head, "I see, so you can escort the body back here? You are most thoughtful, Margaret, but I'm sure the family would..."

"No, I didn't say anything 'bout escorting him back here...nope, I just want to be there when he's dead. Because I want to kiss his naked, no-good, leavin' ass, right in front of his commune buddies, an' dump an entire batch of Tuna Tetrazzini Casserole on his head! Oh, and I guess, when he is dead, I'd like an extra week at the Casa del Sol, since I'll be a widow, right? Gotta have time to mourn, isn't that what they say?"

Richard Leigh-Lee IV tried in vain to persuade his firm's newest divorce client that this was a most unusual, and not at all lucrative move on her part, but his client merely waved the Casa del Sol ad and puffed on a cigarette. After four months of legal haranguing with the Grahams, in which Richard Leigh-Lee and his clerks ran up quite a nice tab for researching the ins and outs of the details associated with an annual stay at Casa del Sol, Margaret McArdle-Graham received her divorce and a notarized pledge from the Graham trust administrator that her decrees would be made good. She refused to remove "Graham" from her legal name, however, and after the ensuing ugly battle with the Leigh-Lee & Sons senior partners and the Graham family, Richard Leigh-Lee IV promptly turned to drink.

With her divorce in hand, things finally began to calm down. Margaret McArdle-Graham insisted she was not at all bitter, but she was damned well tired of everybody in town asking her if she was all right, if she needed anything and if Hoot had abused her. All divorcees are abused, people said, in one way or another. Margaret heard so much talk about abuse, she began to wonder what she'd done wrong to escape it. As far as she knew, she wasn't an abuse victim, but what if she'd missed something?

Maybe she had been a victim, after all! She decided she would investigate abuse, to determine exactly what Hoot had done to her, so she could guard against it in the future! A woman alone had to be extremely careful, even a woman alone who was over six feet tall and approaching two hundred pounds. After all, during two weeks a year at Casa del Sol Resort in Gulf Shores, Alabama, anything might happen!

Unfortunately, although there were quite a few divorced women in Chestnut Ridge, no one actually wanted to share their experience or their expertise with Margaret. She agonized in vain with no one to talk to, to share with, to learn from...she was mentor-less and nearly ready to call it quits, until one late night, weepy and unable to sleep, Margaret heard a commercial on the all-night radio station that changed her life.

"Single gal...are you branded with the stamp, 'divorcee'? Are you tired of wearing a 'D' on your chest for all the world to see? He got the trash compactor, and you got the trash? Confused, with no one to talk to? Are you dealing with abuse and denial? Too petrified to ever date again? Subscribe today to 'Today's Divorcee' magazine! Twelve issues for nine-ninety-nine...we know what you're going through...you don't enter the murky world of Divorce alone! Stand up for your rights with Today's Divorcee!"

Margaret immediately called the all-night radio station, but the phone rang endlessly without answer. She threw on her tattered chenille bathrobe, grabbed her car keys and drove out to the station's tower at the edge of the county. "Let me in! It's an emergency!" She shouted as she pounded and pounded on the heavy door of the concrete block building. Finally, a bewildered deejay opened the door and reached for his gun at the sight of Margaret bursting past him.

"How do I get it?" she screamed. "How do I get *Today's Divorcee?* It's an *emergency!* I *need* it!"

The deejay rubbed his eyes and told Margaret to stay put while he changed the record that had ended thirty seconds ago, and that was now rubbing hours of use off of the turnplayer's needle. Then he jotted down the name of the advertising agency that had placed the *Today's Divorcee* ad and gave it to a grateful Margaret, who planted sloppy kisses on his cheeks.

For ten days, Margaret's life was a blur of cold Tuna Tetrazzini Casserole, Camels, Fresca and double shifts at the Dispatch office. She'd sent in her subscription to *Today's Divorcee,* along with ten extra dollars so they could mail her three back issues. Every day at noon, she drilled the Postmaster as to whether he'd received any magazines for her from Yonkers, New York. She told her brothers she was working double time because she was going to go on an unscheduled vacation, in a couple of days, when a friend from school was coming to town. "You know, we're gonna do some girl stuff," Margaret told everyone.

Finally, the first new issue and the three back issues arrived in the noon mail. Margaret immediately told Bull she needed her vacation. Then she went home, unplugged the telephone, dished out some cold Tuna Tetrazzini Casserole and settled in with her newfound, printed friends. There were stories of heartache, of desertion, of financial difficulty too horrible to imagine. There were custody battles, shifty lawyers, tales of unpaid alimony, unfair judges, and pages and pages of abuse. After engulfing every word and every ad in the four issues of *Today's Divorcee*, Margaret had still not fully defined how she had been abused, or whether she had been abused at all, but she now realized that she was not alone in her fight.

If only Today's Divorcee had been available to me months ago, she thought. *I nearly lost my life but for the sake of a magazine ad on all-night radio.* Margaret McArdle-Graham stood in the middle of her tiny apartment and made a solemn vow. She would devote her life, right then and there, to the elimination of wife abuse, to help other victims, as she should have been helped.

In the weeks, months, and years that followed, Margaret subscribed to every magazine that was remotely related to divorce and wife abuse. She became a charter subscriber to *Playgirl*, and she bought every feminist manifesto ever published. She checked out mounds of library books on psychology, on criminal habits of rapists and assaulters, and on personal defense. Margaret became a self-styled expert on women's rights and the hate crimes of men.

When she finally did take her first two-week vacation at beautiful Casa del Sol Resort, Margaret was forced to leave behind one suitcase full of books due to the airline's weight limit. After taking a fifteen-minute walk on the beach and drinking three umbrella drinks in rapid succession, she adjourned to her double room with an ocean view, and remained there for the duration of her stay, ordering room service, so she could read her manuals and learn how to further defend herself against the Evil Ways of Men. She returned home refreshed and renewed, albeit without a tan, and she decided it was time to go public.

She posted bright, bold signs all over town (most of which were promptly removed) which declared, "DIVORCED WIVES OF THE ROUND TABLE, UNITE! FIRST MEETING, 7:30PM, TUESDAY, APARTMENT OVER DISPATCH OFFICE."

Margaret made a double batch of Tuna Tetrazzini Casserole; she had no round table, but the small card table in the middle of her meager living room would do nicely, she decided. The first meeting of the Divorced Wives of the Round Table was a rocky success, at best. Seven recently divorced women attended, but most of them had not experienced abuse, other than an occasional late alimony check or an embarrassing incident at the Poe House Grocery in front of the ex-husband's new girlfriend. Stella Stanley, fresh from her third marriage, announced her hope that the club could hold future meetings at the bar across the county line, so they could meet men.

After Margaret led the discussion on Public Use of Personal Defense Tactics and handed out Anti-Abuse Diaries and Abuse Victim Checklists to everyone present, two of the ladies informed Margaret that the Divorced Wives of the Round Table was not for them. No matter to Margaret; the much-needed support system had begun. She was personally insulted, however, that they declined any Tuna Tetrazzini.

Over the course of the next few months, Margaret and the Divorced Wives of the Round Table became well-versed in abuse terminology. But it was only Margaret who could spot a victim at ten paces, and she could pinpoint the perpetrators every time, most likely from all her years working at the Dispatch office, and the two weeks spent in Gulf Shores memorizing abuse manuals. She was proud of her new skills; she tested herself in public by selecting prime abuse candidates as they shopped at the Poe House, unaware of her or her checklists and diaries. She would stand in the produce section, near the entrance, and when a likely victim, or victim-to-be walked in to do a little innocent shopping, Margaret immediately jotted down critical characteristics of the unwitting study participant (apparent physical marks, jaundiced skin, sunken eyes, plaster casts). She would then stroll casually through the grocery with only a bag of potatoes in her cart, and she always maintained at least a three-cart distance from the said abused, to avoid discovery.

Margaret became quite bold with one poor woman who sported a neck brace and pushed a cart containing three runny-nosed, sticky children. *Definite serious case here,* Margaret noted, but when she handed the woman a piece of paper on Divorced Wives of the Round Table letterhead, which read, *"It's your lucky day! You don't have to live like this!,"* the woman screamed, and raced through the Poe House Grocery yelling, "Oh, my God! We've won the contest! I just knew it!! We've won the cartful of steaks! Mr. Poe! Mr. Poe! We've won!"

It took Corny Poe and Margaret nearly twenty minutes to calm the woman and return the Porterhouse steaks to the meat cooler. As Margaret sheepishly confessed to Corny that she was performing top-secret police research that couldn't be revealed to the general public, the woman fainted in Aisle Three, and after they cleared aside her screaming, tearful children, they brought her around and learned that she was from Ohio, visiting her sick mother in Chestnut Ridge, and that she was down to her last twenty-five dollars for groceries, which is why she was so excited about the possibility of winning Porterhouse steaks. Margaret handed the pale woman a hundred-dollar bill, apologized to her, and to Corny, and subsequently stayed out of the Poe House Grocery for nearly two weeks. But it still didn't stop her from pursuing her prey, or their innocent victims.

Since the Poe House Grocery proved to be a less-than-ideal testing ground, Margaret decided to conduct live, in-the-field Perpetrator Identification Training Classes. She packed the remaining Divorced Wives of the Round Table into a borrowed police van, and they drove to Pop's Top, a rundown bar outside the city limits. After nearly crashing the van into a tree while Stella Stanley tried to honk the horn at a former beau, Margaret successfully parked the vehicle behind some bushes, where they could keep their vengeful eyes posted on the entrance. For about three minutes, the Divorced Wives of the Round Table watched in hushed concentration for a potential perpetrator to exit the bar.

"Does everybody have their Potential Perpetrator Identification List?" Margaret asked in a whisper. "Watch out for braggards, false bravado, alcoholism or weapons," she cautioned, "and especially watch out for any signs of military service. I have firsthand experience with *that* type!"

"I thought you tol' us that wife abusers was sneaky...that they could be plain ol' bizness men an' upstandin' members o' the commun'ty!" one of the Wives asked.

"Just read your lists and watch out the windows!" Margaret snapped. "Abusers come in all sizes and shapes, it takes years of training to recognize every single type!"

After an hour of frustrating inactivity, the only thing slightly resembling a Potential Perpetrator was an underage kid who waited in front of Pop's Top for an old bum to bring him a bottle of beer. The Troops were getting restless. Margaret decided it was time to strike – they were losing valuable time and energy.

"Divorced Wives of the Round Table! There's our man!" Margaret pointed at the boy in front of Pop's.

"Miss Margaret," one of the Wives exclaimed, "that's just Ginny Bevers' boy, and he ain't no wife abuser! He's just tryin' to get a beer, why he cain't be more than fifteen!"

"SHUT UP! I'm an expert at spotting a Potential Perpetrator, and this one's got the LOOK!" Margaret's voice ratcheted up a notch or two in defiance.

"Shit, Margaret! He ain't even got a wife! I bet he ain't even got a girlfriend! Hell, his pecker's prob'ly not even three inches long yet!" Stella Stanley shouted and waved a nail file in Margaret's face. Then she smiled, "'course, 'member what they always say...it ain't the size of the ship, it's the motion of the ocean!"

Stella kneeled on the van's front seat, and gyrated her hips so hard she fell down on the floor board and let out a loud guffaw. The Divorced Wives of the Round Table whooped with laughter, which rocked the police van and shook the bushes outside. Margaret clenched her fists in anger.

"SHUT UP, YOU MORONS! I can see you're all hoodwinked by this man! He could probably black both your eyes with one two-second swipe of his fist! He's probably wanted for abuse in Metro Davidson County! Look at his eyes! Look at the tell-tale way he leans against that wall! He's just oozing with Male Abuse Hormones! Are you with me, or not?"

Margaret reached over to open her door and defend the Divorced Wives of the Round Table from certain abuse at the hands of this Potential Perpetrator, but Stella Stanley laid her elbow into Margaret's gut and slammed one hand on the police van's horn.

"Hold it, Margaret! You're actin' a fool! You leave that boy be!"

The other Divorced Wives of the Round Table yelled at Margaret and tried to separate her from Stella Stanley. The police van rocked and swayed. The boy looked over toward the bushes, and as he noticed the five screaming, stomping women inside, engaged in some kind of catfight, he took off in a cloud of dust, not wanting to be recognized outside of Pop's fine establishment. The Divorced Wives of the Round Table managed to calm Margaret by throwing her out of the van and onto the dirt. As the Rookie Divorced Wives of the Round Table stood over her, Margaret fumed.

"This is how you repay me! Each and every one of you has displayed completely unprofessional, intolerable behavior for the Divorced Wives of the Round Table! That's it! I am disbanding this group on the spot! Right now!"

Margaret stood up and slapped a cloud of dust from her camouflaged pants. "As of this moment, right now, this group is finished! All you people want to do is socialize! But I'm tellin' you, there are Evil Abusers out there, and you could be the next victims! Don't come cryin' to me when it's your turn for tears! You had your chance! I'm goin' back to town…here…here's a quarter…call your ex-husbands to come and get ya! Just see how long it takes 'em! An' what they'll do to ya after they catch ya here!"

Margaret slumped into the police van and sped off with the side doors wide open. Stella Stanley stomped the ground.

"That bitch! I ain't gonna walk back to town, and I ain't gonna call nobody, neither!" She looked at the other ex-Divorced Wives of the Round Table, who were most bewildered at their predicament. Stella picked up Margaret's fallen pack of Camels and offered it around the group.

"Hey, look, we're already out here…why don't we just go inside an' git us all a beer, an' figger out what we're gonna do. I mean, it's Friday night! This here place is safe enough for a group of good-lookers like us! After 'while, I'll call Bull McArdle an' tell him his sister's done gone an' left us out here…he'll come over an' git us, I'm shore…whaddya'll say?"

The ex-Divorced Wives of the Round Table huddled briefly for their last Official Act, and decided Stella Stanley was right. They took turns brushing their hair and applying lipstick using a battered discarded hubcap for a mirror. Then they entered Pop's Top en masse, for an evening of entertainment. Thus, the final meeting of the Divorced Wives of the Round Table was a huge social success, at least for the majority of the participants.

As Margaret silently drove back to town, she realized that Stella Stanley had not only gotten the best of her, but that she'd dropped her Camels in the dirt. She sighed. The life of a wife-abuse fighter was a lonely, solitary life, but her dedication was undiminished. *Here I am,* she thought, *trained with all kinds of knowledge on How to Spot Abuse, How to Defend Myself Against Abuse, and how to Identify Potential Abuse Perpetrators, and not one single person in this town cares to protect themselves.* Then she remembered a passage from her favorite book, "The Abuse Prevention Handbook,"

'Do not despair when poor, innocent victims resist your efforts to assist them. Abuse victims do not fully understand their situation, until someone takes control and shows them the sad state of their lot. Be bold, be brave, and continue on your path...those who mock you today, may need you tomorrow.'

Every damned one of those Divorced Wives of the Round Table is gonna need my help someday, Margaret mused. *I guess it's just up to me to point that out to 'em. They're helpless, they are. Ok, I'll just work by myself. It's better that way anyhow! Easier to stalk the perps, she reminded herself. They'll all come 'round, someday. But I can't stop...I have important work to do.*

Thus, as Hoot Graham settled into his new life in a California commune, as he learned to grow organic okra and corn, and change camera lenses, Margaret discovered her own life's destiny: to assist the Meek, the Needy, the Victims, whether they realized their plight or not. And as a result, thanks to detailed articles in the Chestnut Ridge *Tell-All,* and the toothy exchanges of the coffee-klatch gossips, no self-respecting man in Chestnut Ridge dared to strike his wife or girlfriend, for fear of the infamous and terrible wrath of Margaret McArdle-Graham.

Margaret reviewed every incident that came across the Dispatch desk for Abuse Potential. And what the police weren't allowed to handle legally, Margaret handled privately. Despite her brothers' suspicions, Margaret was careful to leave no trail of evidence that might point to her. *Without clear proof,* Margaret rightly reasoned, *there can be no charges.* And after ten years on the dispatch desk, Margaret knew all the tricks for avoiding clear proof. Soon, her charity and safe-haven offers to women in Chestnut Ridge were legendary, but not nearly as legendary as the black-belt results of her after-dark encounters with the abusers themselves. Margaret's suspected escapades would have made the CIA proud.

The most notorious Margaret incident occurred in February 1993, during the Great Ice Storm. A certain Bubba Briley tied his wife Wilma to a metal trash can in fifteen-degree weather, on the assumption that she was having an affair with the sanitation engineer himself, and on the assumption that the heat of Wilma's passion would protect her from the cold, until said sanitation engineer made his rounds, on the next regularly scheduled trash pickup, in about three days.

The police deposited a thawing, dehydrated-but-alive Wilma at the station, where Wilma refused to press charges, fearing that she might lose Bubba, her trailer, and the convenience of trash pickup on Mondays and Thursdays. Noting Wilma's obvious inability to control her own miserable life, Margaret took an early lunch break and invited a grateful Wilma to join her. Margaret drove straight to the bus station, and put a confused and dripping Wilma on the bus to Memphis, to visit her mother. Margaret gave Wilma the standard Margaret McArdle-Graham Wife Abuse Information Kit, which included nearly one-hundred Xeroxed pages of articles on *How to Spot an Abuser, How to Say No without Bruises,* and Margaret's personal favorite, *How to Cripple a Man in Three Seconds.* From the bus station, Margaret telephoned the Dispatch office, and promptly informed the relief dispatcher that she suddenly needed a few days off, to attend to some urgent family business, out of town.

"Oh, yes," Margaret said sweetly, "I've already told Bull and Bill...I'm just letting you know. See ya soon!"

No one saw Margaret for the next two days, and the relief dispatcher didn't even mention Margaret's absence to Bill and Bull, because she assumed that since they were Margaret's brothers, they were already aware of their own family's emergency. It didn't dawn on her to question why they were still on duty, instead of attending the family in its time of need.

On Thursday of that same week, however, the police responded to an anonymous call, informing them that they might just want to buzz over to the Happy Trailer Estates, where they found a butt-naked Bubba Briley staked to the roof of his mobile home, nearly frozen, with a thin and brittle layer of ice covering his goosebumped skin. A note was around Bubba's privates that read, *'YOU FORGOT TO TRASH THE FROZEN CHICKEN PARTS.'*

When the relief dispatcher asked Chief McArdle how the McArdle family emergency was going, and did he know when Margaret would return, Bull realized that his poor demented sister had struck once again. He quickly informed his officers and the Chestnut Ridge Tell-All that the Bubba Briley incident was a police matter, under secret investigation, and there would be absolutely no discussion of any details to the public, or to the press.

Bull forgot to pre-empt the communications of one Latisha Buckley, however, who resided in the trailer next to the Bubba Briley brood. Mrs. Buckley's husband worked nights for the Chestnut Ridge Utility District during ice storms, which meant that Mrs. Buckley, a jittery woman, did not sleep while her husband was away. Thus, Mrs. Buckley heard a wild commotion in the middle of the night, and therefore personally observed out her bedroom window that a naked-as-a-jaybird Bubba Briley was tied to the roof of his trailer. Early the next morning, once her husband was sound asleep, Mrs. Buckley cranked up the engine in the bucket truck parked in front of their home, raised the bucket to the sky, and using her husband's zoom lens, snapped several photos of Bubba Briley in all his birthday suit glory.

Latisha Buckley made a hundred copies of those photos, and sold each and every one for a dollar to all her friends and neighbors. A sheepish and slightly frostbitten Bubba Briley brought a photo to Bull McArdle and asked if it counted as concrete evidence of the crime committed against his person.

"Naw, Bubba, sorry, son! All we got here is a photo of you and your family jewels 'toppa your roof! Ain't no evidence of nobody doin' nothing to ya! For all we know, you decided ta sleep up there after a good drunk! I mean, Bubba, it ain't like you've never done nothin' stupid before, is it?"

Bubba Briley had to admit that the Chief of Police was right. He quietly went to Memphis and returned home with a bouquet-laden Wilma, and nothing was ever said about the incident again. There was, however, an astounding increase that month in fatherly attendance at Chestnut Ridge church services and PTA meetings.

So when Roy Quigley found himself face to face with Margaret McArdle-Graham on this particularly cold Wednesday evening in February, after uttering smutty thoughts aloud, regarding Penni Poe and what he would like to do with said Penni Poe's apron strings, Roy began to sweat profusely under his blue plaid polyester jacket. Despite the dark, Margaret's eyes were hidden behind official FBI-regulation mirrored sunglasses (obtained through the Shopper section of *No Victim Today* magazine) and Roy began to wish desperately that Ruby would come back and rescue him before it was too late.

"Well, well, Miss Margaret! Hey! Hi! How...how in the world are ya doin'? I was jus' gonna go find Ruby, see, she's over there talkin' ta your brothers, see her? See yer *brothers*, right over there? Yeah, I reckon you done heard me mumblin' ta myself! Well, I just cain't seem ta remember where in the hell...HECK, where in the HECK I parked the Lincoln! An'...well, hey, how you doin'?"

"Quit babblin', Roy Quigley! Where's Ruby? I need to talk to her 'bout some SEWIN' I need done for the Policeman's Auction next month."

Margaret lit a Camel and aimed her mirrorred sunglasses directly at Roy, waiting for his reply.

Roy pulled a blue plaid handkerchief out of his pocket and wiped a cascade of sweat from his brow, despite the cold night air. "Is it just me, Miss Margaret, or is it real warm this evenin'? Ruby? Well, like I just said, she's over there somewhere talkin ta yer brothers…see…that's her, there she is, the sweetie, I can see them cute bows in her beehive hairdo and…can you see outta them sunglasses, Miss Margaret?"

"Like I was sayin, Roy, I need some SEWIN' done. Ruby ever made any APRONS? You know, aprons …" Margaret took a deep draw on the Camel, and blew smoke in Roy's sweat-soaked face. He blanched.

"Aprons? Did you say aprons? Hmm…hmmm now, well let me see…aprons…well, I don't know…" Roy wiped his brow again, this time with his church bulletin. Then he nervously tried to roll the soggy bulletin into a tube. Margaret cocked her head and sighed,

"You know, Roy, aprons….with LONG STRINGS that can be TIED REAL GOOD to stuff…like BEDPOSTS! Like you might see in those sex magazines where they grease people up real good…" Margaret tapped the ashes of her cigarette so they fell just in front of Roy's patent leather slip-ons.

"Aprons, Miss Margaret? With long strings, huh? Listen, uh, I gotta git over ta the Quik-Steak for the rib rush…it's All You Can Eat Ribs night ya know, an' that new manager's gonna run clean outta sauce…but lemme ask Ruby 'bout this for ya, ok? You take care now, see ya, Miss Margaret! Bye!"

Roy Quigley made haste to retreat from Margaret, but as he did, he turned several times to wave his church bulletin tube in her direction and to make sure she wasn't following him. He grabbed Ruby by the arm, but then when he realized Margaret was watching, he gave Ruby a huge hug, and led her by the hand to the car. Margaret drew on her Camel and chuckled lightly to herself. It was good to see the effect she still had on men, but oh, how different their reaction now, versus twenty-five years ago, when they used to laugh at her, and taunt her about her height and her inability to keep her husband at home…yeah, look at that miserable Roy Quigley! Now there was definitely a response! A reaction! She was in full control!

Margaret snubbed out the Camel into the church parking lot. Inner peace was so nearly at hand, after twenty-five years of article reading, twenty-five years of soul-searching, twenty-five years of aiding and avenging innocent victims of abuse. For twenty-five years she had waited for her deliverance, and now, thank you, God, it was here. Oh sweet dreams do come true, Margaret mused. Yesterday, her big brothers had given her the best birthday present she'd ever received. Bill and Bull, the hulking, grey-haired, fifty-two year old twins, slowly and cautiously informed their baby sister that lo, and behold, Hoot Graham was back in town to document on videotape the entire year-long preparations surrounding the 136th Chestnut Ridge celebration.

"Now, we don't wanna upset you or nothin'," Bill started, "but Hoot's been keepin' hisself real hid at his brother's house since Christmas, an' we figured you'd best hear it from us first. I guess we're sort a lucky you ain't already laid eyes on him...but ta tell ya true, Sissy, I b'lieve ol' Hoot's plumb afraid to be seen in public! 'Fraid you'll pounce on him, or worse!"

Margaret instantly dropped to the sofa, in that same one-bedroom apartment she'd shared briefly with Hoot, and cried big alligator tears onto the new Stain-Pruf carpet.

"I'm so happy, boys! So happy! You have no idea how happy this makes me! This is my chance to resolve my inner conflict! To be at peace with the world! Oh, Stella Stanley told me this day would come! All I gotta do now is keep cool, wait for the right time, make my MOVE..." Margaret wiped a hand across her streaming eyes and looked up lovingly at her twin brothers, who were at once most uncomfortable, and most concerned.

"Now, Sissy, WHOA, gal, jus' hold on a minute, here!" Six-foot-seven inch Bull McArdle rared back and pulled his official police-issue Sansabelt slacks over what would have been a seventh-month pregnancy bulge on a woman.

"Now, there's no cause ta git upset or nothin', 'cause Hoot's mindin' his own bizness, he's done moved over ta the Fluffy Pillow Motel on his brother Will's dime, an' well, you jus' need ta calm down! Git a holt of yourself, Sissy! No need ta do nothin' rash! You know, the onliest reason Hoot's in town is 'cause Will's uppity wife Dorothy wants ta record all this here Festival bizness on tape, so's I guess when she's old an' grey, she can watch herself! But now, you don't need ta git all upset, an' go off half-cocked...you an' Hoot's been divorced for 'long time, an' ain't no need for revenge, or nothin!"

"Bubba's right, Sissy!" Bill McArdle adjusted his own Sansabelts. "Hoot'll be gone a'fore we know it, an' me an Bubba'll keep a real close watch on him, you know we will! Now don't you worry 'bout nothin', you jus' leave ol' Hoot 'lone...HEY! I got it! Why'nt you take your vacation early, an' go with Euladean Poe to Panama City for a few days! She's leavin' in the mornin' for that World of Bingo convention!"

Bill propped one Big-and-Tall-Man's leg on Margaret's new oak coffee table, revealing one eight-hundred dollar custom elephant skin boot, size fifteen. Bull helped himself to a Coke from the fridge and opened it with his teeth.

"Now you listen here, Sissy," Bull said between swigs, "Hoot Graham was all shot up when he done came home from 'Nam, an' he jus' wasn't right in the haid. Now Hoot was a good boy…you 'member, we played ball together on the State Championship team…now I know in my heart, he really did love you, Sissy! But he was jus' so lost, an' messed up, an' ya can't blame him for tryin' ta put his life back together agin, can ya? I mean, he's always sent you them yella flowers every year for your birthday, ain't he? And sendin' 'em to ya for Valentime's, even if ya do thow 'em in the trash ever' year…so there's no need ta git hiss-tercal, 'cause we ain't gonna let nothin' happen to you…or to Hoot, right, Bubba?"

The two twins exchanged looks over Margaret, who continued to stream tears of joy all over her new sofa. They weren't at all concerned that anything in the slightest would happen to Margaret by Hoot Graham's hand…their consuming fear was that poor Hoot Graham would suffer unspeakable atrocities at the hands of their baby sister and her midnight antics. As the Police Chief and the Fire Chief of Chestnut Ridge, they were duty-bound to uphold the safety of every citizen and keep Margaret in check. They had their hands full with the Festival preparations, and they didn't need any more "secret investigations" in their files.

"Right, Sissy, you listen to your Bubba," said Bill. "Now you've had you a good life here in this town, ever'body says so, an' how you're the best durned dispatcher…you know you're up fer National Dispatcher of the Decade at the convention, ain't ya? In Tupelo? So don't go and screw up your one chance ta git recognized! You know that Fay Bailey's just dyin' ta take your job if anything was ta happen, ta make you have ta resign, now, darlin!"

"An, Sissy, you know we ain't never mentioned this, an' don't take it wrong, we love you, you know, but me an' Bull had a helluva time fixin' things after the Bubba Briley thing…so just calm down, breathe real deep…"

Margaret McArdle-Graham stared at her brothers in disgust. "Well, good grief, you boys must think I'm some kind of crazed animal or something! I'm not gonna hurt one hair on Hoot Graham's head! All I wanna do is talk to him, pick his brain a little…if he's got one…and see if he's up to a reconciliation, that's all! I mean, he was my husband, you know, and I need a man to take care of me in my old age, don't I? Do you think he'll still find me attractive, Bull? Should I go have Stella put a rinse in my hair? Now, hand me my cordless phone! I've gotta make some calls! I've gotta go shoppin'! I gotta buy me some clean guest towels, and stock up on Camels!"

Bill ran thick fingers through his grey hair as Bull adjusted his Sansabelts and paced back and forth across the tiny living room, swinging the Coke bottle in mid-air. Bull stopped and waved a beefy finger at Margaret, "Sissy, whaddya mean, a reckonsil…a reckonsil…honey, whaddya mean? You wanna git back together with Hoot? Sissy, don't you think a vacation at your place in Guf Shores'd be real nice this time a year? You got all them comp time hours built up, an'..."

"Oh, Bull, hush up! I'm not leavin' town as long as Hoot Graham's here! What I'm tryin' to say is that I've had a change of heart after all these lonely years! I just didn't do right by him the first time, that musta been why he left me! Most folks don't ever get a chance to set the record straight, now, do they? No, and if me and Hoot can start over, now that we're both so mature, and now that he's found himself...well, maybe now we can be happy together!"

Margaret blew her nose loudly. *Yep, we'll be together in a really BINDING way...from which there'd be no escape. Oh, how long a wait for this glorious day...*

Bill and Bull stared at their daydreaming sister and shook their heads. As bachelors, they would never understand their baby sister, or any other woman, for that matter. And they would never have guessed that after twenty-five years of anger since Hoot's departure, Sissy would so eagerly want to take him back into her life, and this tiny apartment. Yep, they had a lot to learn about women...an awful lot.

"Well, then, Sissy, you jus' take it easy, now, an' let us know what's happenin', ok? You hear? Ok, baby, we gotta go back on duty..." Bull kissed the top of Margaret's head.

Bill nodded, "You call me tomorra an' let's go get us some a that new frozen yogurt over to the place where the Grits 'N Gravy used to be, ok?"

He hugged his sister, and then he and Bull walked down the steps to the Chestnut Ridge Police and Fire Protection office. As Margaret watched her brothers leave, a distinct wave of calm covered her like a warm blanket, much like the calm that descended on her now, as she watched Roy Quigley adjust his rearview mirror to see if she was still monitoring him. She waved at Roy as he stuck his head out of the yellow Lincoln to back out of the church parking lot.

"Bye, now, Roy! 'Member about those APRONS!" Margaret called cheerfully. Roy nearly crashed his Lincoln into another car at the sound of Margaret's voice.

Men are such easy marks, Margaret mused. *Hoot-days are back,* she pondered, *but oh my goodness, they were gonna be so very, very different from the last time! So different, and so much more fun!* It was time to get started. Margaret McArdle-Graham inhaled one last puff of her cigarette, dropped the butt onto the church parking lot, and smashed it with the toe of her sensibly-heeled dress pump. As she looked up, she saw Dan Gastineau nearly run smack into Miss Amelia Festrunk with his fancy black BMW. Miss Amelia was crossing the street to get into her dilapidated Pontiac and apparently Gastineau didn't intend to afford Miss Amelia her pedestrian right-of-way.

Gastineau honked, lowered his window, and waved his fist angrily at Miss Amelia, "GET OUTTA THE ROAD YOU STUPID OLD BAG! GO BACK TO YOUR CLINIC AND STAY THERE!" He revved the BMW and sped off into the dark.

Amelia Festrunk, visibly shaken, leaned against the big hood of her old car, gasping for breath. A small crowd quickly gathered around her to offer assistance; someone ran to fetch water, another person waved a cell phone to call Doc Kimball. *What a little shit,* Margaret fumed. *That Dan Gastineau thinks he's God's Gift to Women! He nearly killed one of the most upstanding, good and moral women on the face of this earth, right in front of a church!* Yep, Margaret thought to herself... *Hoot-days are back, but I've had that plan laid out for years... there's no reason I can't pursue two Abusers simultaneously! That damned Dan Gastineau's caused enough trouble for women in this town...* Margaret suddenly realized she had a great deal of work to do, and it was time to get to it.

CHAPTER NINE - BABY LOVE

Last Friday in February 1999; Gastineau & Gastineau, CPAs, Chestnut Ridge

"Now, son, I realize full well you're a grown man, out of graduate school, and that sometimes you have a good head on your shoulders...look, I don't really want to give you a lecture; but *your mother* wanted me to remind you about your behavior last year at the Masked Ball, and call to your attention that not only did your escapades cause *you* a great deal of financial, emotional and personal agony, but that you also dragged the good Gastineau name into the toilet right along with you. Your mother and I have spent the past twelve months breaking our backs going to planning meetings and fundraisers for over fifteen different charities in this town, just to restore some kind of dignity to my great Gastineau name!"

Dan Gastineau, chief executive officer of Gastineau & Gastineau, CPAs, stood behind his desk and glanced sideways into the gilded baroque mirror which hung next to the Vanderbilt University diploma on one wall of his richly furnished, historic-district office in downtown Chestnut Ridge. As he smoothed his salt-and-pepper hair, he silently reminded himself that he was long past overdue for a facial with Stella Stanley at the Quigley Beauty Box…the laugh lines were evident again, and it was time to hit the tanning bed. He straightened the paisley ascot at his neck and looked back at his son.

"Now, look, Roland, I know it's no picnic studying for the CPA exam next week, but you're a Gastineau, and Gastineaus are smart. Of course, I never had to crack a book in school, you know, used to just waltz in there, schmooze those teachers, and, well, they'd give you the benefit of the doubt, if you know what I mean! But lemme tell you, son, even though you have to work a lot harder than I ever did, I'm proud of you! I've waited ever since the day you were born to hang your name in gold letters on the front of the business that my great-great granddaddy founded in this town, in this very building. With you joining this firm, there's no limit to our growth! Couple'a years, you'll be a partner, and if you bring in the kind of money I expect you to, you'll be drivin' your own Beemer in no time! Then I can think about retiring, and you can support me and your mama in our old age, haha!"

Dan Gastineau crossed over to the long corner window. He leaned one arm against the windowpane and sighed deeply. "Yeah, we're gonna make a killing in the tax law business, Rollie! Long as you don't trip up again, right, son?"

His son said nothing, but hung his head and rolled his eyes. Dan Gastineau didn't notice; instead he turned to face Roland, and began to pick at the cuticles of his left hand.

"What a great package we can offer potential new clients, *'I'd like to introduce my son Roland, the tax lawyer...sure he's good, his rate is five hundred an hour.'* I've waited for that all my life, and it's almost here! Which is why I asked you to step in here a minute, son. See... I just want to remind you that we don't want our partnership to get off to a bodacious start with any shenanigans at the Masked Ball tomorrow night, that's all... course, since I've arranged for Danita Kay Leigh-Lee to be your date, she'll keep you honest; you won't have a chance to pull any stunts like you did last year. Man, she's a homely girl...but smart! Very smart! Oh, did I tell you we've got a chance at getting the tax account for Roy Quigley's entire business empire? Your law degree is the key to that one, boy!"

Dan Gastineau chortled and sat down in a leather chair behind the highly polished walnut desk which had been used by generations of Gastineau accountants in this very office. Twenty-six year old Roland Gastineau drummed his slender fingers in rapid succession on the desk's glass top and shook his head.

"Dad, look, I don't need a lecture, ok? I know I was a real pain in the ass last year...but my whole life was in turmoil, and I mean, I really had a lot of stress! After all that stuff with Bonnie Lou... well, I promise I won't embarrass you and Mom at the Masked Ball this year! I know how important our image is in this town, as businessmen, and now that I've joined the firm, well, I intend to uphold my reputation, too, I mean, it's my livelihood, my future, right? But dad, you've got to quit telling people I'm a *tax lawyer*...when you drop out of law school in your final semester, you are not legally a lawyer! And you can't call yourself one! So please just say that I *'specialize'* in tax law, or else we'll get sued, and I'll go to jail!"

Roland looked up at his father and ran slender fingers through the mass of dark black straight hair that framed his handsome face with its bright blue eyes. He took a deep breath...might as well get it off his chest, since Dad brought it up...*again.*

"Look, dad...I am upset about why in the hell I have to take Danita Kay Leigh-Lee to the damned Masked Ball. I mean, I'm all for business alliances and everything, but I think you've gone a little bit off the deep end this time. Danita Kay is a real *dog,* Dad! I could have any...go to the Masked Ball with any eligible woman in Chestnut Ridge, and Danita Kay is definitely *not* my first choice!"

Roland stood up and smoothed his khakis as his father continued to pick at his fingernails. "I mean, I realize we've known the Leigh-Lees for years and all...hey, I'm sure it's hard for Danita Kay to get a date, but it's really not very fair of you to just up and decide my 'civic duty' for me! I mean, what will prospective clients think when they see me with Dogface?"

"ROLAND! That'll be enough of that kind of talk! Danita Kay Leigh-Lee is a very smart, sweet girl, and a very capable lawyer in her own right! Did you realize she graduated second in her class at Harvard? *Graduated* is the operative word there, son. Yeah, and if we want to avoid any kind of concern on the part of the Leigh-Lee & Sons firm regarding our intent to steal away their big-business customers, then we've gotta reinforce the idea that together, our companies can assist each other! We can bring them legal clients, and they can bring us tax accounts! And that way we can avoid an all-out calamity just in case you happen to also provide perhaps the tiniest bit of pseudo-legal tax advice to certain particularly sensitive tax customers, if you're so inclined! Gotta beat 'em to the punch, boy, didn't they teach you that in school? Or were you sick that day, havin' a fit over that big-tittied cheerleader?"

Roland exhaled loudly and sat his long legs into an antique chair, shaking his head. "See, Dad, this is where I have a real problem. I mean, when I left UVA...well...I'm just not real comfortable giving out tax law advice...it could put us in a real bind, and I don't really agree with your idea to build a new business angle around that part of my background...it won't fly. It's not right!"

Dan Gastineau slammed his hand down on an IRS manual atop his desk, then instantly regretted his action, because his large gold pinkie ring jammed into his knuckle and caused him a great deal of pain.

"DAMMIT, ROLAND! I'm tired of having this discussion! You were only *one course shy* of graduation from law school when that bimbette got pregnant and you lost your senses and dropped out! And if you're not careful, you're gonna continue to pay for that error in judgment for the rest of your sorry life! And then to top it all off you had to tell the entire town about the real reason you left UVA! Now grow some balls, son, and get with the program! You're joining this firm, you're gonna pull your own weight, and you're gonna have to fight tooth and nail to get clients in this measly town, so get used to it!"

Dan Gastineau wanted to take another glance at his image in the gilded mirror, but sensed that his son, who in recent weeks seemed to be developing a hot temper, was preparing to stand and leave the room, so he switched gears. He tugged on the waist of his polyester slacks, and put one hand to his temple as if he had a severe headache.

"Look, Rollie, I'm sorry. I'm real worried about you, son. You've got so much pressure next week with the CPA exam, tryin' not to let me down! Hey, I know you're gonna pass it with flying colors on the first try, because you are a Gastineau! So now let's not get all caught up with formalities like *'who didn't actually get which degree after three years of money and work down the drain,'* and let's realize that for all intents and purposes, you've accomplished everything but one final, and very minor, requirement for the purposes of practicing tax law. And I just bet you could take a correspondence course from UVA and finish your degree...did you call them yet? I mean, in essence, son, once you've got CPA status, you might as well practice tax law, with or without a diploma, right? I just know you're gonna ace that test! Aren't you?"

Roland ran his palms across the thighs of his khakis. In twenty-six years, he'd made one mistake, out of a mostly successful life, but it had been a doozy, and he doubted his father would ever let him forget it. Roland Daniel Gastineau, only child, was the epitome of good looks, good grades and good behavior in Chestnut Ridge. Since the age of twelve, his one dream was to become the family's first tax attorney, and take over the family firm. And Roland stuck like glue to his plans, day in, day out, never failing anyone, until last spring. Would Dad ever cut him some slack? Roland had suffered terrible pain on a lot of levels, but his father would never understand, because his father just wasn't cut from the same cloth.

Daniel Gastineau married Roland's mother Isidore the day after they both graduated from high school, which meant that he'd pretty much been able to get laid any time he'd wanted, right through college and graduate school! In those days, it was okay to get married before you graduated, you could even start a family. But Roland had other plans. He was a serious student, and he didn't want any distractions, not sports, not girls, not anything. And this had always been a sticking point with his roving, party-loving father, who never understood Roland's lack of girlfriends or socializing...not that Roland actually lacked for the attention of women… he was one of the most strikingly handsome young men most women ever laid eyes on.

But Roland was so hell-bent on fast becoming a tax lawyer and pleasing his parents, he'd never really had time for women in general. Until Bonnie Lou Morgan. And then when Roland found the right girl, and blew it, well, Dan Gastineau didn't have the tolerance or empathy for that scenario, either.

Roland was never interested in casual relationships, or in easy marks. Which is why Bonnie Lou Morgan was so irresistible to him. Bonnie Lou Morgan, at five-foot-two, one hundred pounds of natural blonde beautiful green-eyed action, was the most perfect woman he'd ever tried to woo and win. Ok, so she was actually the *only* woman he'd ever really even noticed during his intense march toward becoming a tax attorney.

But Bonnie Lou hit Roland like a ton of bricks. She was beautiful, her family was top-notch Virginia society, she was a cheerleader and athletic, she was popular and smart. Well, no, she wasn't really smart, but that was even better, because she left it up to Roland to do all the thinking. In Roland's eyes, Bonnie Lou Morgan was his ideal of a perfect tax lawyer's wife. But Bonnie Lou's one tragic flaw was that she didn't really need Roland. Which is exactly why Roland desperately needed Bonnie Lou Morgan.

Late in the fall of his last year at UVA law school, Roland hotly pursued Bonnie Lou, after their accidental meeting in the undergrad library, where Roland was returning some books for a friend. There, right between the stacks, he'd glimpsed his own Personal Vision of Loveliness, Bonnie Lou Morgan (he didn't actually know her name right away, so at first she was just The One). Roland, usually a model of self-control, stared open-mouthed at Bonnie Lou as she stood near the library entrance. As Bonnie Lou turned to leave, Roland's heart stopped briefly, jarring him back to life. He suddenly called out, "WAIT!" and was reprimanded by the librarian, a tiny waif of a woman with blue hair.

Roland ran after Bonnie Lou Morgan, caught her in the library foyer, and gently touched her UVA-sweatered arm, that perfectly proportioned arm, damn, that powerfully bicep-ed arm! He introduced himself, asked if they'd run into each other in Torts or Professor Hicks' class, or at the Law library, and Bonnie Lou Morgan began to laugh softly and shake her head, "No," to each question Roland could ask.

Finally, tiring of this endless, meaningless interrogation, Bonnie Lou suggested that perhaps Roland had seen her at a football game, where she was on the UVA cheerleading squad, you know, *'Bonnie Lou Morgan, of the UVA cheerleaders?'*

Roland caught his breath. No, third-year law students didn't have much time for football. To which Bonnie Lou angrily replied that it was a tragic shame that the grad students at UVA were so apathetic when it came to what was truly important in school. What if *every* UVA student failed to support the athletic programs? What if no one went to the football games? The cheerleaders just simply couldn't do it all!

Trying desperately to buy some time with this UVA Angel, Roland nodded quickly in empathy, looked sheepish, suggested, maybe you could help me change my ways, we could promote athletics among the grad school population together. But Bonnie Lou just gave another soft laugh, tossed her head, and stomped off, leaving a disheveled and smitten Roland Gastineau in the UVA undergraduate library.

But Roland was no quitter. He had found The One, and he knew it was his destiny. All the years of serious studying and avoidance of distracting temptations had paid off, and it was still early October, so he had plenty of time to entice Bonnie Lou Morgan into matrimony and a blissful life in Chestnut Ridge before graduation next spring. In his first romantic flush, Roland took great risks with his study time in light of his class load, and spent hours trying to locate Bonnie Lou Morgan on campus. He went to every remaining UVA football game, just to see Bonnie Lou cheer in her perky UVA sweaters and culottes and little flounced skirts and sneakers. And was Bonnie Lou in great shape! She could do those all those awesome jumps and flips and leaps, landing perfectly on the shoulders of some lucky undergrad punk with a megaphone. Oh to be those shoulders. To be that megaphone, touching those red sultry lips....

With the help of his lifelong friend Wink Jackson, III, son of the Senator-from-the-Great-State-of-Tennessee Winslow Jackson II, Roland managed to obtain official UVA Athletic Student records and locate Bonnie Lou Morgan's entire life history, as well as her address. They discovered, in fact, that she'd been awarded a full gymnastics scholarship two years earlier.

Wink's daddy even discovered Bonnie Lou's hometown (Roanoke, Virginia), her father's occupation (real estate magnate estimated to be worth six-to-eight million, easy), her car make, model and license (1992 BMW 325i convertible, red, tag "UVA YLR"), and her GPA, a two-point-five in Physical Education training...barely good enough to hang onto her slot on the cheerleading squad.

Thus primed, it was only a matter of time for Roland to make The Big Pitch, and swoop upon Bonnie Lou Morgan in an effort to convince her to spend her remaining days as his wife. Roland was fully aware that he'd probably have to promise to build her a gymnastics studio in Chestnut Ridge where she could teach little Olgas and prepare them for the Olympics, so she wouldn't get bored or fat in the midst of a gymnastics wasteland.

But all of those kinds of details could be easily dispatched. The major difficulty was to get close enough to Bonnie Lou Morgan to *talk* to her, and with his L3 class schedule, Roland had a serious problem on his hands. He'd worked too hard to screw up even the slightest slack in grades. So Roland spent his days in class, his evenings in the law library, and his sleepless nights thinking of Bonnie Lou Morgan and how he'd make her happy for the rest of their lives together.

On December ninth, Roland determined that his most prudent course of action would be to suspend all further Bonnie Lou pursuits until after Christmas break, because his Spring semester in L3 was going to be a relative cakewalk. In keeping with his lifelong goal to graduate with honors, Roland had spent the last three summers holed up in his apartment at UVA, reading the textbooks for each coming year; he was way ahead of the other L3s, and he figured he could afford a little leisure time, no problem. Of course the fact that Bonnie Lou Morgan departed UVA for home after finals on December ninth was also a major contributing factor in Roland's decision to wait until the start of the new year.

Over beers at Adelphi's Pizza, huddled at their usual corner table, Roland and Wink Jackson discussed the 'Pop the Question to Bonnie Lou Plan.' After Roland steered Wink past all his concerns, like, didn't Roland think it would be a good idea to date some *other* women first, for an objective comparison, and wasn't Roland taking things a bit too seriously with someone he'd never really *talked* to, they were able to get down to brass tacks.

Wink had it all figured out...UVA was gonna play in the Peach Bowl, and Bonnie Lou would obviously be preoccupied with Peach Bowl-type activities, which meant she wouldn't be able to fully devote her attention to Roland's serious request regarding matrimony, or at least, *dating*, until her return on January fourth, with the rest of the official UVA Peach Bowl entourage. Then Roland could sweep Bonnie Lou Morgan right off her feet, and he'd be sure to have her undivided attention and make his case. Roland wisely agreed with Wink that his chances with Bonnie Lou would be dramatically improved in January, what with the post Peach Bowl letdown, no football games to cheer (UVA had a separate basketball cheering squad), and no Winter Olympics on television that year. He figured that Bonnie Lou Morgan's attention would be pretty much guaranteed-available for him, sans extraneous sports distractions, just like Wink said. But he knew a good soldier does not go into battle without weapons, or training, no matter what the odds.

So Wink offered very valuable information gleaned from his sister, the flight attendant... just as expected, Bonnie Lou Morgan would return to school that afternoon from the obligatory Peach Bowl commitments on a three o'clock flight. Roland thanked Wink and made tracks to the airport, Gate B-Three.

When Bonnie Lou Morgan stepped off the plane, she was the last of the UVA Cheerleading squad to do so. Her Peach Bowl experience had been terrible: the airline lost her luggage, and, horror of horrors, she'd had to wear a size XXL sweater and a borrowed pair of cheerleading panties to the nationally-televised Peach Bowl. But the panties were the wrong color for the rest of the outfit, they were *navy*, and the skirt was *white*, so Bonnie Lou was deathly afraid that those obnoxious Peach Bowl tv cameramen would focus on her contrasting bottom throughout the entire game! Luckily the tv cameras paid extremely close attention to the players and the actual game, and focused only partially on Bonnie Lou Morgan's breasts, which flopped around like lemons in the gunny sack of a sweater she'd been forced to wear.

Bonnie Lou's exit from the return flight portrayed in one vivid visual image the total misery of her Peach Bowl trauma. After four days, her luggage still could not be found, and as it contained her industrial-strength mascara remover, Bonnie Lou Morgan was now wearing four days' worth of mascara. She looked a bit like a raccoon as she stomped off the plane after having searched every overhead luggage compartment on board (no one bothered to inform Bonnie Lou that the plane in which she'd ridden to the game was an entirely different one from the plane in which she'd returned).

So when Roland Gastineau called out, *"Bonnie Lou!,"* from his perch immediately outside the arrival gate, and when he'd thrust three dozen beautiful red roses and the huge Valentine chocolate box in her face, Bonnie Lou was so overwhelmed by the kindness shown to her by a total stranger, she'd just stopped dead in her little UVA cheerleader Ked-tracks and stared hard at Roland Gastineau in mascara-ridden confusion.

"Do I *know* you? Can I help you? Is it Valentine's already? Oh...it's *YOU!* From the library. Mr. Questions. WHAT'S your name?" Bonnie Lou was visibly exhausted, but her curiosity (and her reluctance to let go of the roses) got the best of her.

"Madam, I, Roland Gastineau, am your humble servant. Your chariot awaits, and I implore you to allow me to escort you to your home, post haste."

Roland copied these words from a book of *Classic Quotes for Lovers,* and committed them to memory two days prior, confident in the knowledge he could memorize romance much more easily than he could depend upon his ability to ad-lib under pressure.

Bonnie Lou Morgan looked around, hoping her fellow cheerleaders wouldn't see this fruitcake...except for maybe Johnny Stearns. She wouldn't mind at all if Johnny Stearns saw these gorgeous red roses and this box of candy. Johnny Stearns, Head Tumbler, had broken up with Bonnie Lou (it was mutual, she'd assured him) just a week before Christmas, probably so he wouldn't have to get her a present. If only Johnny could have seen this guy, with these beautiful roses...well, maybe this guy had *money,* for a change! Bonnie Lou was so tired of paying for all of her dates with that bum, especially after he'd practically moved into her townhouse...and he never put the toilet seat down! And he was such a liar, she saw his hands on Pookie Anderson at practice last week...that was no accident!

Bonnie Lou sized up Roland Gastineau — he was actually very good looking, once you got past the sort of nerdy exterior, but he was obviously nervous. And tall, nice butt...good face, ok hair.... maybe he wasn't so bad, and she'd dreaded the prospect of taking a cab home from the airport. Cab drivers were so low, always saying things like, "*Hey, baby, show me your pom poms!*" She decided she'd take a chance, and at least save the cabfare.

"Sure, ok, you can give me a ride, if we can go straight to my house. I'm really exhausted, and I've had the worst trip...and I have got to take off this makeup! How did you know I'd be on this flight? Mmm…these roses smell so good!"

Roland was so exuberant at Bonnie Lou's acceptance of his offer, he immediately grabbed her hand and began to pull her through the airport at a fast trot, in one big red-rose-and-Valentine-candy-box blur. As they arrived at Roland's car, a 1968 red VW Beetle, Bonnie Lou momentarily had second thoughts, but the car was cute and clean, and after Roland quickly mentioned that his real car was a Mercedes convertible, at home in Chestnut Ridge, for safekeeping, Bonnie Lou immediately warmed up to Roland and his taste in automobiles. It remained an unspoken fact that Roland hadn't actually yet acquired a Mercedes Benz…but it was the very first thing on his post-graduation list to do, after securing Bonnie Lou's hand in marriage!

About halfway home, Bonnie Lou Morgan suddenly realized she was ravenously hungry, and although she ordinarily would never have broken her unwritten rule about eating in public wearing day-old mascara, let alone *four-day-old* mascara, she could no longer ignore the angry violent pangs emitting from her midsection.

"Uh, Roland, is it....uh, *Roland*, do you think we could stop for a pizza, or something, I mean, I can get it to go so you don't have to wait while I eat, but I really need to get some food! All they gave us on the plane was peanuts, and my metabolism just cannot tolerate nuts...they give me....well, I can't eat them!"

Roland clutched the steering wheel of the VW and said a silent prayer of thanks to God. This was working out amazingly well. "Hey, sure, no prob! Ever been to Adelphi's...on the square?"

Bonnie Lou shook her head *no*, and stroked the dark velvet of one of the roses. Adelphi's was probably some goofy grad school hangout where all the waiters had their body parts pierced.

"Well, hey, they have the best pizza in town, and it's always *fast fast fast*! They know me and we'll get great service! We can be there in three minutes!"

Roland sharply turned the Beetle, and began to tap the steering wheel in time to the radio, which was tuned softly to the local Alternative station. Bonnie Lou preferred Top Forty, but she'd recognized a few of the songs during the short ride from the airport. Grad students always listened to the strangest music...what were they trying to prove?

Bonnie Lou Morgan was beginning to be a little bored with her Knight Transport, but she was so hungry she was sort of trapped...at least until she had dinner. In any case, an hour later, in the dark, cozy environment at Adelphi's, among the scant remnants of a sixteen-inch stuffed pizza with extra mushrooms, after two pitchers of beer and some kind of rich Italian bottomless-layer-of-whipped-cream kind of pastry, after many, many friendly nods from the nice waiter, who appeared to know Roland personally, and over something delicious she couldn't pronounce that tasted like coffee, Bonnie Lou Morgan realized she was actually relaxed, enjoying herself, and a little bit horny.

Who needed Johnny Stearns, when there were rich law students? Roland had made it quite plain that he'd be picking up the check, and he'd made it quite plain that his family had money. The hour over a shared pizza gave Bonnie Lou ample opportunity to stare into Roland's eyes, and she confirmed her original suspicion that he was in fact amazingly good-looking. He was very smart too, but sometimes she just laughed at his comments, because she didn't have the foggiest idea what he was talking about. And he sure did talk an awful lot.

He never even gave her the chance to tell him about herself, because he kept on going on and on about some place called Chestnut Ridge in...where was it...*Arkansas*? And how he'd like her to go there, and meet so-and-so....but Roland's mumblings were a blessing to the exhausted Bonnie Lou, because she hadn't really felt like talking much, particularly to someone who was practically a total stranger. Even if he did insist on paying for dinner.

The only potential glitch in the evening was when Roland attempted to discuss the merits of Shakespearean sonnets with his new enamorata, and Bonnie Lou replied, "Oh, yeah, sonics...I think I learned those in grade school. Uh, Roland....Roland Gastineau, that's so formal. Don't you have a nickname?"

"In undergrad my frat name was Gas Station, because no one could ever pronounce my last name. But that's it...except for my friends who still call me Rollie."

"Well, then, *Gas Station*," Bonnie Lou said with a flick of her tongue as she licked her dessert fork clean. "I could get used to having my own personal airport escort...what else do you do? Any experience with domestic services? Hey, Gas Station...you wanna check my oil?"

Roland nearly dropped his cappuccino in response to the little giggle and smile Bonnie Lou now offered. She shifted a bit in her wooden chair, feeling warm and sensual, and wondering if Roland's physical attributes were as gifted as his mental capabilities. She rubbed Roland's leg with her foot, but then realized that she was mistakenly coming on to the table leg. A nervous Roland began to babble.

"Domestic stuff? Well, I can make a great soufflé, with an old family recipe. And I'm great at sleeping! L3's never get enough sleep!"

Roland's innocent comment about sleeping was totally re-interpreted by Bonnie Lou, who had gone without Johnny Stearns' physical attentions for two stressful holiday weeks. She leaned forward and whispered across the table to Roland, "Sleeping is my *second favorite* activity in bed...I'll bet you can't guess what my first favorite is… hey...you're kind of cute. What do you think? Are we ready to leave?"

But Roland didn't budge. Bonnie Lou was amazed that Roland didn't respond to her come-ons! *Maybe he doesn't want to have sex with me…no, that's absolutely impossible!* She leaned forward, closer to Roland, who was finishing his frothy cappuccino. "I'm *sooooo* relaxed! But I could really use a good backrub…you have excellent hands for a grad student! What else you got that's good?"

Bonnie Lou stretched perfect cheerleader arms over her head and rolled her neck seductively from side to side. Roland quickly paid the check and helped her with her coat. Then they whisked out the door and into the ice-cold VW. At Bonnie Lou's doorstep (she lived in a townhouse written off by her father as a business investment...athletic dorms were so *nasty*), Roland originally intended to remain the true Southern Gentleman he was, and he moved to kiss her lightly on the cheek, thanking Bonnie Lou for the enjoyable evening. But Bonnie Lou grabbed Roland's puckered-up-to-kiss face between her red-wool gloved hands, and shoved her cappuccino-tasting tongue right between Roland's lips.

"You have a really cute butt, Roland! You know, if you were so desperate to meet me, why didn't you just give me a call?"

Roland, gasped for breath in amazement at the fact that The One had been so bold! He had not anticipated this question, but like the quick-thinking law student he was, he said, "Well, I just wanted to leave a more indelible impression, I guess."

"In-edible...what do you mean....you want to *eat* me? Mmmm....sounds like *fun!*"

Bonnie Lou ran one gloved finger down to the waist of Roland's khakis, and then up his body to the side of his face as he protested.

"No, *indelible. Permanent.* I wanted you to remember me and our evening together."

Roland was intensely aroused. He deeply inhaled the frigid January air and tried not to think about all the Spring reading he was supposed to do.

"Does the poor law student have to study tonight? Can the poor law student come in and light the little cheerleader's pilot light? It's *very* cold out here!"

Bonnie Lou began to kiss Roland all over his face with cute cheerleader-type kisses. Roland Gastineau made the gentlemanly but incorrect assumption that Bonnie Lou Morgan needed assistance with the heating system in her residence, due to her most recent absence, relative to her requisite Peach Bowl duties. This proved to be a serious misjudgment on Roland's part; however, after three rolls in the hay with Bonnie Lou Morgan's personal heating system, after much up-close-and personal testing of Bonnie Lou's pilot light, Roland had sufficiently redeemed himself to overcome any misgivings in Bonnie Lou's eyes. In fact, Bonnie Lou was most impressed with Roland's stamina, as well as his butt muscles. Forgetting Johnny Stearns was gonna be a picnic, Bonnie Lou Morgan decided.

On that early January evening, Roland's plan worked so much better than anticipated, and not only had Bonnie Lou Morgan dropped her guard, she'd also dropped her panties and her bra, in one fell swoop. For the next three days, Roland Gastineau and Bonnie Lou Morgan knew the meaning of Paradise Found, Heaven on Earth, True Love and Passion. They didn't leave the townhouse, Roland skipped the first three days of Spring semester classes, and Bonnie Lou refused to answer the telephone calls of her fellow cheerleaders, as well as those of Johnny Stearns.

They existed on sex, delivery from Adelphi's, and marshmallows toasted over a firelog in the den. *Wait til my family meets her,* he mused. *I wonder if we'll have blonde children, I wonder if that old warehouse at the edge of Chestnut Ridge is still for sale...it'd make a great tumbling academy...*

For the next four weeks, Bonnie Lou and Roland thrashed about passionately before classes, between classes, and in many cases, during classes they did not attend, ceasing only for quick trips to the convenience store around the block, or if Wink Jackson's secret-code telephone ring came through, warning Roland of impending trouble with an inquiring professor or an overdue assignment. On those days when his L3 responsibilities could no longer be avoided, Roland cranked out his most inspired and efficient work, then returned to the townhouse with more red roses for Bonnie Lou, who was only taking two gymnastics courses to satisfy her parents' and UVA requirements. Since Bonnie Lou and Roland's own private townhouse-oriented gymnastic efforts were in fact quite challenging and strenuous, Bonnie Lou's instructors were suitably pleased with her performance on those rare appearances she made in the gym, so they remained fairly silent and unobtrusive.

Then one day in early February, four weeks after their new life together began, a red States Airlines van pulled up in front of the townhouse, carrying Bonnie Lou's errant suitcase. At this point, Bonnie Lou had totally written off even the slightest possibility of ever actually receiving her suitcase, so at first she was pleasantly surprised. Bonnie Lou thanked the driver of the van, and went upstairs to unpack the suitcase, looking for enough clean underwear to possibly forestall laundry for another day, which in translation meant more time for Bonnie Lou to fondle Roland's cute butt. Roland was in the kitchen, in his UVA LAW boxers, eating a toasted marshmallow and reading a two-day old newspaper. He suddenly heard thunderous noises emitting from the bedroom, presumably from Bonnie Lou.

"OH SHIT. OH MY GOD. SHIT. OH MY GOD. SHIT. *SHIT.*"

Roland bounded up the stairs to Bonnie Lou, whose face was beet red, but who still looked quite sexy despite her bunny slippers and UVA running suit.

"What is it Bonnie Lou? Do you have to use that kind of language? What's wrong?" Roland took another bite from his marshmallow, offering it to Bonnie Lou, who shook her head in an emphatic no gesture.

"MY SUITCASE IS BACK!" Bonnie Lou pointed at the Samsonite, which lay on the bed.

"Yes, hon, I can see that. Great! Anything missing?" Roland took another bite of by-now-cold toasted marshmallow.

"Yeah, something's missing, alright. MY BRAIN! *YOUR* BRAIN!" Bonnie Lou flung herself on top of the bed and began to cry. "MY LIFE AS A CHEERLEADER IS OVER! WHAT THE HELL AM I GONNA DO?"

Giant tears spilled onto the comforter around Bonnie Lou's hidden face. Roland took the last bite of marshmallow and joined Bonnie Lou on the bed.

"Mhoney, mwhat'sm mthe mmatterm? Mwhat ism it?" Roland helped Bonnie Lou sit up cross-legged on the bed and handed her a Kleenex.

"YOU JUST DON'T GET IT, DO YOU, ASSHOLE?"

Roland, wide-eyed, tried to remove the marshmallow from where it was stuck on the roof of his mouth before he was required to say anything else. He shook his head back and forth. He silently wondered what it was that he was supposed to "get."

Bonnie Lou sobbed and screamed, "I AM A COMPLETE IDIOT. WE HAVE BEEN SCREWING LIKE RABBITS FOR FOUR WEEKS, AND I AM A COMPLETE IDIOT. MY BIRTH CONTROL PILLS WERE IN MY SUITCASE, WHICH MEANS THAT FOR FOUR WEEKS, I HAVEN'T TAKEN MY BIRTH CONTROL PILLS, WHICH MEANS THAT I NOW KNOW WHY I'M *LATE*, WHICH MEANS THAT I AM PROBABLY *PREGNANT*, YOU DUMBASS! AND IT'S ALL THE AIRLINES' FAULT! THEY LOST MY BIRTH CONTROL PILLS AND I'M GONNA *SUE* THEM! YOU'RE A LAWYER! *YOU* CAN SUE THEM FOR ME, BECAUSE *YOU'RE* THE ONE WHO DID THIS TO ME!! AND THEN I'M GONNA SUE *YOU!*"

Bonnie Lou threw herself face-down on the bed, and bawled. Roland instantly threw up, leaving a sticky marshmallow coating all over the comforter, and all over one of Bonnie Lou's cute little bunny slippers.

"GROSS! GO IN THE BATHROOM! GROSS! WHY ARE *YOU* THROWING UP, I'M THE ONE WHO'S PREGNANT! YOU *MORON!*"

Bonnie Lou hopped off the bed and threw the soiled bunny slipper after

Roland, who ran into the bathroom and shoved his face under the faucet, gasping for air.

BONNIE LOU PREGNANT!? THE FAULT OF THE AIRLINES?! LAWSUITS?? Roland, being the dedicated law student he was, tried to imagine how in the world he could sue the airlines for negligence for the delayed return of birth control pills, as ice-cold water from the faucet gushed over his forehead and down his face. To his knowledge, there were no legal precedents for something like this, but he did not really want to disclose this information to his client at present. Bonnie Lou stopped sobbing and dried her eyes, and Roland saw her reach for the raincoat that hung on the back of the bedroom door. He grabbed a towel and mopped his frozen face as Bonnie Lou buttoned her raincoat and slipped on running shoes, tears streaming down her face.

"I'm going to the drugstore and get a home pregnancy test, which is what I should have done last week, but I've been so busy buying marshmallows, and going to class, and screwing, that I, oh, shit, just *shut up*!"

Bonnie Lou stormed out of the room and out of the townhouse, leaving a dazed Roland to wipe his face and clean up his mess. He had to call Wink...Wink would know exactly what to do...Roland took a deep breath. It was going to be okay. Bonnie Lou would simply return, take the test, and they'd know "in a matter of minutes without a doubt," just like those ads on tv said. Then he could slap himself back into reality and finish the semester, and they could get married next summer, like he'd intended. It would all be okay very soon.

The evil home pregnancy test, however, immediately transformed the veritable Roland-Bonnie Lou Winter Wonderland into Hell on Earth, in just three easy and accurate minutes. Bonnie Lou was definitely pregnant; Roland had never seen such a staggering shade of blue in his life. The next two days were a complete and total blur to Roland. He couldn't eat, couldn't sleep, and began to speak in fatherly tones to Bonnie Lou, the only natural thing to do in this newfound fatherhood situation, since he assumed it was his responsibility to take care of her. Bonnie Lou, however, did not *need* another father...she did not require his advice, his opinion, or his presence in her bedroom. Bonnie Lou Morgan banished Roland Gastineau to the couch, until such time as she could bring herself to talk about her present status. Bonnie Lou was mortified that something like this could threaten her position as Head UVA Cheerleader next fall, and she slept for two solid days.

So for those two days, Roland made lists. He wrote down all the positives of the situation, as well as all the negatives. When he'd filled an entire UVA SCHOOL OF LAW legal pad with negatives, compared to only one-tenth of one sheet with positives, it became blatantly apparent to Roland Gastineau that he'd somehow lost total control of his life, and that this was the kind of stunt that even Wink Jackson couldn't fix. *WINK*! He'd forgotten to call Wink! Roland grabbed the pink princess phone from the kitchen.

"Hey, Wink! WINK! How's it goin, man? Great! Great! Listen, I've gotta talk to you...no, not about the briefs...I've really gotta talk to ya ASAP - can you meet me at Adelphi's? In thirty minutes? It's life or death…life…just be there!"

Roland and Wink conducted a key strategy meeting at Adelphi's, over a sixteen-inch stuffed with extra cheese, while the waiter provided constant coffee and water refills during the course of two-and-a-half hours. Roland barely touched the pizza; Wink did most of the talking. His eyes rolled around in his head in disbelief at Roland's predicament. He was a short, stocky young man with a tendency to gain weight, and his easygoing manner made him everybody's friend.

"Rollie...man...when you get *in*, you get in *good*, don't ya? No flies on you, boy!"

Roland rested his head against the back of the booth and sighed. "I mean, Wink, it's not like I wasn't planning to marry her anyway, right? So why can't we just take a quick trip to both sets of parents, announce our engagement, plan the wedding for June like I wanted to, and who's gonna be the wiser?"

He added quite possibly the tenth packet of sugar to his cold coffee and continued to stir. Wink Jackson shook his head.

"Naw, man, listen to me, *one more time*. It's February eleventh. So she's a coupl'a weeks along at the most, we think, I mean, like I know any of this stuff, what the hell do I know about these things? Ok, so I figure she's gonna drop somewhere in the October-November area, right? So that means that in June, about the time you're plannin' to walk the Big Tux Road of No Return, she's six months along, which means *whoa, Nelly*, she's definitely gonna be totin' the big watermelon seed into the church. You can marry her, but you can't marry her when it's *obvious*, man! Nope, you got to speed things up a bit, like say, spring break, March wedding, or somethin'!" Wink took another hefty bite from his seventh slice of pizza and wiped his mouth.

Roland absent-mindedly stirred his cold coffee. "But I can't get married in March! How am I gonna fit a wedding in during mid-terms? My mom will kill me if she can't have a garden wedding like she's always talked about! My parents aren't gonna fly two hundred people up here for a quickie wedding! They're gonna want a typical Gastineau party! With historic Gastineau cheese soufflé!"

"Roland, my man, *you are missing the boat, son! The clue bus is leavin' and you are still standin' at the corner, Rufus!"* Wink slammed his fist on the wooden table, scattering empty sugar packets to the floor. "We are talkin' shotgun wedding here and you are worried about your mom's goddamn preference for finger sandwiches over cocktail weenies! You are way beyond details, my man, way beyond!"

Roland and Wink looked around the nearly empty restaurant, thankful that the crowd was thin. Wink took another bite, swallowed it nearly whole, then took a swig of his own cold coffee.

"Now, look, Rollie, I have been your friend for a long time. And I ain't about to let you just totally screw up your life, even though you've pretty well helped yourself along already. The way I see it, you got two options: *Option A*, you take a drive to the mountains and visit a doctor, all very reputable and sanitary, of course, and then you write Bonnie Lou a nice little check for a couple'a thou', and send her on her way, so she can finish out her senior year cheering UVA on to victory! Or *Option B*, you marry this girl A-SAP, set yourself up in her townhouse, finish the semester and graduate, and POOF, your plans aren't ruined, they're just shoved forward a little bit. Now me, I personally wouldn't have that option, because my daddy's insistin' that I interview and try to get a job with a big Washington firm, but you've been plannin' on goin' inta business with your daddy for twenty years…so a little thing like a baby sure isn't gonna stop you, really."

Wink gulped down some ice water.

"Naw...it's just gonna mean that you don't get to hang out for a few months after graduation and drink beer on the beach like you'd planned! Instead, you'll be puttin' cold washcloths on Bonnie Lou's forehead and bringin' her pickles an' bon bons in the middle of the night, but hey, you can handle it, bud! I'm right there with ya, Rufus!"

Roland realized that Wink was right. The baby was just kind of the formal, physical glue to seal his relationship with Bonnie Lou, the relationship he'd intended to be legally binding and lifelong in the first place.

"But what the hell do I do about Bonnie Lou's ridiculous idea to sue the airlines? I mean, Wink, she is really *serious* about this! She thinks we can get at least a million bucks since it was their fault for losing the luggage containing her birth control pills! Do you think we have a case?" Roland took a sip of his cold coffee and nibbled on a previously discarded pizza crust.

"Is this girl into voodoo or somethin'? Has she put a hex on your brain? What kind of everlovin' hold does she have on you, boy? A *lawsuit*? A LAWSUIT? Were those the only birth control pills in the state of Virginia, Rufus? The girl was too dumb to remember that she didn't have her birth control pills, and she just happened to have sex ten thousand times in a four-week period! Ok, everybody has occasional memory lapses now and again. Totally understandable, for some people. But for four weeks? You two screwed like

Bugs Bunny day and night for four weeks and she forgot to take her pills for four weeks, and she's gonna blame it on the airlines who lost her tiny little suitcase over New Year's, before she even knew your *name*? *Four weeks*, we're talkin'!"

Roland closed his eyes in agony as Wink continued through a mouthful of pepperoni.

"And by the way, where in the hell did you deposit your smarts during that time, my man? *Four weeks*, didn't you once happen to think, boy this is really great, nice tits, tight ass, but hey, shouldn't I be concerned about preventin' the little ol' offspring situation? Shouldn't I maybe *ask her* what we're doin' about that little remote possibility, just in case?"

Roland looked sheepishly at Wink, whose chin was smeared with tomato sauce. "You know, Wink, I was havin' so much fun, I didn't even consider it, because I think that deep down, in my heart, I knew Bonnie Lou and I were going to get married and have kids...ok, I haven't even asked her yet, but I planned to! I mean, I snooped around once in the bathroom cabinet, and found an old pack of her pills with all those little foil things popped out...I guess I just assumed she was taking care of everything! She was so confident and so horny all the time! Don't birth control pills make women extra horny?"

Wink opened his wallet and put down a twenty to cover the check. "Roland, for somebody so book smart, sometimes I think you are the stupidest person in the whole wide world. For someone who's had three years of training to be on guard, be on the defensive, argue and fight back, you've been sunk like the *Titanic*! I think it's a real good thing you're gonna go into tax law, Rufus, because you'd be shot down in a courtroom so fast it'd make your head spin! Now you know I'm with ya, man, whatever you decide. I gotta run; you call me later when you know what you're gonna do. And don't forget we gotta test next week!"

As he watched Wink leave Adelphi's, Roland already knew what he had to do. "Thanks Wink, I owe ya."

When Roland arrived back at Bonnie Lou's townhouse four hours later, he discovered she'd emerged from her two-day bedroom siege and had dramatically improved her appearance by showering and changing into a clean UVA running suit. She was seated on the couch, sans bunny slippers, and she'd lit a fire. She saw the roses in Roland's hands, and she smiled.

"Oh, sugums, I'm so glad you're back! I've got this whole mess figured out, and as soon as you take off that old nasty coat, we can talk about everything!" Bonnie Lou patted the empty sofa cushion next to her.

"Bonnie Lou, you just sit right there and listen to what I have to say. I'm only gonna say this once, and I don't want you to interrupt me, no matter how difficult that might be, ok?"

Roland hung his coat in the closet, then approached the sofa, handed Bonnie Lou the dozen red roses, and knelt down in front of her on his left knee.

"Bonnie Lou...I pursued you with a vengeance last fall. From the first moment I laid eyes on you, I knew you were the only girl in the world for me. And our relationship has been such a whirlwind, but I feel so close to you, I know in my heart that we are meant to be together forever. We are destined to be partners."

Roland fished around in the pocket of his khakis and produced a little black velvet box. He covered both of Bonnie Lou's trembling hands with his own, around the velvet box.

"Bonnie Lou...I want to share the rest of my life with you. I want to be the best tax lawyer in the state of Tennessee, maybe even the whole country, and I want you to be my cute little perky gymnastics teacher wife, with your own gymnastics studio. You can even pick out the colors and the location. I don't care what it costs. But Bonnie Lou Morgan..."

Roland opened the black velvet box to expose a one-carat, emerald-cut diamond solitaire ring. "Will you marry me?" He looked pleadingly at Bonnie Lou, whose eyeballs swelled with strain as they tried to get a closer look at the enormous diamond ring.

"Oh, Roland! It's beautiful! What size is it? Is it two carats, or just one? Is it white gold, or platinum? You know I can't wear white gold, don't you? Did you get it at Ayers'?"

Roland shifted his weight to the other knee. "Bonnie Lou. You haven't answered my question. Will you be my wife?"

He squeezed Bonnie Lou's cheerleader hand tightly, expecting just one word to make his life's dreams complete. Bonnie Lou leaned back against the couch and pouted.

"It hurts my feelings that you didn't ask me what kind of ring I really wanted! I mean, shouldn't you have asked me first? What if I wanted a marquise cut?"

Roland released Bonnie Lou's hand and stood up. "Bonnie Lou, are you gonna marry me or not? I'm still waiting for an answer!"

"Well, Roland," Bonnie Lou put the ring on her wedding ring finger, and admired her hand as she spoke. "That depends. Can we exchange this ring for a different style? Emerald cut really isn't my taste, and..."

"DAMMIT, BONNIE LOU! YES! THE RING'S NOT THE MAIN ISSUE HERE! I MEAN, WE'RE TALKING WEDDINGS AND LIVES, AND YOU'RE GOIN' JEWELRY SHOPPING! DO YOU WANT TO SPEND THE REST OF YOUR LIFE WITH ME OR NOT?"

Roland waved his arms as he spoke and nearly knocked over a lamp.

"Well, I guess...I mean, I don't really know you very well..." Bonnie Lou held her ringed hand under the lamp for a closer look at the stone. "And I don't really know if I want to teach gymnastics or not. There's already a huge gymnastics studio in Roanoke, and I don't know if I could compete with them."

ROANOKE? Roland was stunned. He sat down on the stone hearth and ran his fingers through his hair. He took a deep breath and spoke very quietly.

"Bonnie Lou. We won't *be* in Roanoke, honey. I'm gonna join my Daddy's CPA firm in Chestnut Ridge, in Tennessee, *remember?* You'll have plenty of opportunity for students there. And how much better do we need to know each other? I'd say we've pretty much run the gamut! Exhausted the possibilities...cleaned the clock!"

Bonnie Lou stood up,

"Well, I can just tell you right now that there is no way in hell I'm gonna move out of Roanoke, Virginia! And I'm not even sure I want to have this baby, while we're on the subject! As soon as you came home today, I was going to tell you that I'd found a good doctor who can take care of things! And I've made an appointment! All you have to do is pay for it! *Nothing* is going to stop me from being Head Cheerleader next year, especially not a stupid baby!"

Bonnie Lou cried, and rushed up the stairs into the bedroom. Roland was thoroughly confused. His plan was so simple, so easily activated. Why didn't she see how everything fit together, how this baby was just the glue they needed to seal their love? Roland was extremely dazed, and he could no longer think any independent thoughts. After a few useless attempts to roust Bonnie Lou from the bedroom, Roland lay down on the couch and slept like a rock for the next eighteen hours. He was awakened by Wink Jackson pounding on the front door. For the past few weeks, Wink Jackson had operated as the Roland Gastineau stand-in, until he could stand in no more. Wink hollered through the front door and insisted Roland let him in for a talk.

"Rufus, I have done everything I can for you, man, but it's no good. At the rate you're goin', if you don't get your butt outta this townhouse and into class, you're gonna flunk out for good! The dean told me he understands your 'medical predicament,' and he's willing to cut you some slack on account you're his top student and you've obviously been smacked with the love stick! He's makin' an exception, Rufus, you hear me? He never, *ever* makes an exception, but he's offering to give you a little more time, you know, take your exams in private, one-on-one with him, if you'll just start comin' back to class and do your papers. It's a one-shot chance, Roland, and it's the only favor he's ever given anybody, and you gotta get your ass in gear, or you're not gonna graduate! He's about to write you up!"

Roland opened the townhouse door invited Wink into the living room, and told him about the latest state of the union. Then he went to the kitchen to make some coffee, and smiled at his friend, "Look, Wink, I really appreciate everything you've done for me, but I can't leave this townhouse until I convince Bonnie Lou Morgan to marry me and keep the baby!"

Wink swallowed hard and waved his hands, "What do you mean, keep the baby? Is she thinkin' what I think you mean she's thinkin'? Well, then, you already got your answer, Rufus, and you'd best be gettin' back to class! Congratulations, you got your life back, son!"

Roland shook his head, "No, I gotta hold tight a few more hours. She's upstairs, still sleeping I guess. She's not real sure she wants to go to Chestnut Ridge…Maybe you could talk to her? What time is it? I must have really been out!"

Wink clapped his hands together and pointed them at Roland. "Rufus, did she give you an answer yet? A yes, or a no?"

At the lack of a response from Roland, Wink shook his head. "World, meet Rufus dumbass! I can't believe what a total dumbass you are!"

Wink took the coffee mug Roland handed him as the phone rang. "Let the machine get it," Roland muttered. After four rings, the machine kicked in, and both Roland and Wink listened in horror as Bonnie Lou's voice put an end to their entire discussion.

"Roland, this is me...I'm at a clinic, and I've had an abortion. Don't try to find me...I'm leaving school for the semester, I got a medical leave from the Dean. Just please get your things out of the townhouse and lock the door when you leave. I'm real sorry, but no baby is gonna interfere with me being Head Cheerleader next year! I've just worked too hard, and there's no way I'm ever gonna live outside of Roanoke! Your ring's next to the toaster. See ya! Go UVA!" The answering machine clicked and rewound.

Wink closed his eyes and hung his head, "You thought she was upstairs, sleepin', huh?" Then he shook his head silently, stood up, drained his coffee, and clapped Roland on the back. "Come on, Rufus, let's get outta here."

In ten minutes' time, Wink packed Roland's clothes and the engagement ring into a paper grocery sack while an evaporated Roland sat on the couch. Then Wink helped Roland with his coat and led him out the door of the townhouse. He put the grocery sack in Roland's car, which was parked across the street, and they walked in silence to Adelphi's, where Wink ordered them each a shot of whiskey and a beer. It was ten in the morning. Wink looked at his friend, who suffered excruciating pain.

"I know how bad this whole thing has hurt you, Rollie. I can't believe she did that...I don't know what to say, Rufus, but you're better off, because she's gotta be the coldest woman I've ever tangled, and you know I've tangled a few!"

Roland drained his whiskey and waved at the waiter for another. Wink continued, "I know it's hard to swallow your pride, return that diamond...I know all that. It never would have worked, man...she just isn't Chestnut Ridge material! Her priorities weren't in line with yours! You can do so much better! I'm tellin' ya, it's all for the best, Rollie. I've always said that everything happens for a reason."

Roland slapped his hand on the wooden table as giant tears streamed down his face. "You know, Wink, that's just what Bonnie Lou always used to say..."

He drained the second whiskey, and then drank his beer mug dry. Wink threw back his own whiskey, and wiped his hand across his mouth. He handed Roland a clean paper napkin to wipe his face.

"Come on, man, let's go see the Dean. Let's put some closure on this thing! Let's get you back on track with your life! We can just make it to class this afternoon, and then we can catch that hockey game tonight on the tube while I bring you up to speed on your notes."

Wink laid a twenty on the table to cover their drinks and stood up.

"Wink, I don't want to finish law school. Because if I finish law school, then it's like I'm still happy, and doing things according to my plan, and we both know that's not reality any more. I have to face facts...my life will never be the way I imagined. If I quit school now, I can hang out at home until May, get an accelerated MBA this summer, then join my dad's firm next fall. What's one more Gastineau CPA without a law degree? We've always just been four-year business grads, with an occasional MBA thrown in, so it's not like I'm breaking any rules or anything!"

Wink knew that Roland was in no mood for further discussion, and he had to get to class. They shook hands, and Wink sauntered off, leaving Roland alone at Adelphi's, where he proceeded to drink four more rounds of whiskey, until finally, the devoted waiter cut him off. Roland hailed a cab and slept in his own bed for the first time since early January. Roland desperately wanted the next morning to dawn like a clear beginning, but an incredible hangover cloud hit him right between the eyes. He sat on his bed clutching an aspirin bottle and a Coke, and re-traced every Bonnie Lou minute. Then he showered, ate a stale Pop Tart, and sat in his living room in the dark. If everything did in fact happen for a reason, then perhaps Roland Gastineau was not at all destined to become a tax lawyer. Perhaps the last twenty years of his best-laid plans had become an impenetrable shroud that prevented him from seeing his true destiny.

Perhaps he was meant to be an MBA-CPA, not a tax lawyer, and this was the only way the Powers That Be could get through to him. At least now he was looking objectively at the entire situation, and he could say he'd made his own decision, versus taking the easy way out like Bonnie Lou did yesterday, without even asking him.

Roland turned on the television, and tuned in to CNN, but all he saw was an ad for the U.S. Marines. What would the Marines do in this situation, he wondered. Then a commercial appeared for an easy home pregnancy test, and Roland threw the remote control against the wall, an action which caused the ON/OFF switch to activate and turn off the tv. He shuffled over to his desk.

All the years of good grades, indescribably tough law classes and jerk professors down the drain. Roland looked up as his mail was shoved through the slot in the apartment door by an invisible hand. He walked over and sat down on the floor. He flipped through the envelopes...mostly credit card offers, and subscription notices for various law reviews...a notice from the Dean. He opened it slowly, and read its contents.

"Gastineau, Roland. 9 February, 1998

Dear Mr. Gastineau:

You are hereby informed that your lack of classroom attendance and failure to perform the required Law III assignments are grounds for your immediate dismissal from the UVA School of Law. As you have made no response to our previous communications, we therefore assume you are no longer in the pursuit of a law degree, and that you have waived your right to an audience with Dean Wiggins. You are formally assigned an Incomplete on all Spring semester classes, and in order to be considered eligible for Law III completion in the future, should you so desire, you must obtain express, written permission from the Dean's office, after a minimum mandatory one-year probationary period.

Registrar, School of Law, UVA"

Roland noticed a handwritten note at the bottom, from Dean Wiggins. *"Come to my office before February 15, Rollie, and we'll talk. I can help you and am willing to accommodate you as you are such a brilliant student. Please do not allow a single lapse in judgment to ruin your entire career in the practice of law."*

Sorry, Dean...no turning back now, Roland mused. *There's no way I'm gonna stay on this campus...what if I ran into Bonnie Lou? I'd probably break her perfect little cheerleader neck, and then I'd be in jail, besides just being in heartbreak prison.* Roland tore the letter into tiny bits and scattered them into the dirt of the giant cactus plant his mother had sent him last Easter. His mother! Why hadn't he thought of it before? She was so gentle, so delicate, so wise. She always knew exactly what to do in absolutely every situation. And unlike his father, Roland's mother was never angry, or judgmental, or vain. Just dependable, and fun, and steady like a rock. It was then he noticed a letter from his mother in the stack of unopened mail; her beautiful, flowery handwriting on the front of the envelope. Roland tore into it, and snuggled against the warm blanket of his mother's words, which wrapped around him in his bleak apartment.

"Feb. 8. Dear Rollie:

Just wanted to let you know how proud I am of you...it was so good to see you at Christmas, even if only for two days. You are working so hard, I worry about your health. I've been trying to reach you, but I guess you've been spending all your free time in the law library, or chasing wild women, ha ha. Your father is fine...he is training a new assistant comptroller at the firm and is most cranky. I've been anxiously tending my greenhouse with all the orchids I'm growing for the Masked Ball centerpieces again this year. Wish you were here to help me...you're so good with orchids, dear, you have just the right touch. Next year I'm not going to do this...too much work! I say that every year, right? Ha ha. Rollie, I hope you know that you are already an immeasurable success in the eyes of your family. You are a model son, and even if you were to come home this minute, and never finish your law degree, you would have surpassed all our expectations and would have exceeded everything the Gastineau family has ever achieved. Of course, your father would never admit that you had outdone him, but he's so proud of you. I just hope that all the hard work you're doing is really worth it to you, son, because you cannot hide in a law library forever...someday you've got to get out and experience real life. You have a strong constitution and I wish you every happiness, but sometimes you must take a leap and have an adventure. Take a new, uncharted path. My goodness, I'm drifting! I hear my orchids calling. Do please eat right and try to get enough rest, and please give my love to Wink. We hope to hear from you soon, maybe you can come home for spring break, even if only for a day or two.

With much love and confidence, Mom, xxxooo"

As he re-read the letter, tears streamed down Roland Gastineau's face. He held his mother's wisdom to his chest, and sobbed heavily, until he had no more strength. Then he wiped his eyes on the sleeve of his sweatshirt and read the letter once again. Leave it to my mom to know when I need her, Roland thought. She has always been my guardian angel, and here she is one more time.

I can go home, he thought. It's not like I'm a bum...shit, I've got two degrees and three years of grad school behind me, and I could run rings around those MBA students at Vanderbilt! Roland knew what he should do, and he stood up, flicked on his computer, and began a letter of his own to Dean Wiggins:

"February 12, 1998
The Honorable Dean A. Wiggins,
University of Virginia School of Law
Dear Dean Wiggins:

Thank you very much for your kind offer to extend to me official courtesy with respect to the continuation of my studies. While I appreciate your efforts and kindness, permit me to beg your pardon and inform you that I will be leaving the UVA School of Law permanently as of today. I intend to pursue an accelerated MBA at Vanderbilt this summer, as an employee of my family's tax business, and I would be extremely grateful if I could call upon you to write me a letter of recommendation for immediate entry into that MBA program. I trust that despite my performance this semester, I am in overall good standing both as a student and in terms of fees, and ask that all official correspondence be directed to my permanent address in Chestnut Ridge, where I will reside until the Vanderbilt Summer term begins in May. Thank you again for your concern, assistance, and friendship over the past three years.

Sincerely,
Roland D. Gastineau"

Roland signed the letter with a flourish, sealed the letter in an envelope, addressed it, then began to pack.

In roughly two hours' time, Roland Gastineau successfully removed every meager and visible trace of his existence from the small apartment. He phoned his landlady, begged lenience with his lease due to a 'sudden family matter,' and packed the Beetle until it was so loaded the left tire developed a bulge. He taped a note on his neighbor's door, entitling him to any furniture in Roland's apartment he wished to seize, as Roland would not be coming back, or taking the furniture with him. Then he phoned Wink, knowing that Wink would be in class and he'd get the machine.

"Hey, Wink, it's Rollie. I had to face facts, man, so I wrote the dean a letter and I'm outta here. Do me one last favor and take the ring back for me, when you get a chance...I'm gonna drop it off at your place on my way outta town. If you can't return it, pawn it or something! No, I'm not crazy, and I'll fill you in in a few days. Gonna do that MBA-thing at Vandy this summer. Thanks for all your help, Rufus, but I just gotta get outta here for awhile and go see my mom. Call me at home if ya need any help cheating on your exams!"

Then Roland called Bonnie Lou Morgan, knowing he'd get her machine as well, and knowing that she'd definitely check her messages because she was once more available to Johnny Stearns.

"Uh, Bonnie Lou, this is Roland. It's February twelfth. I just wanted you to know that with your careless little toss of the proverbial cookie, so to speak, you've devastated my life, and I'm quitting school. I thought I knew you better, and I

truly did love you and want to marry you. But not now. I'm going home, and I never want to see you again, ever. I'm going to be totally honest with my family about what happened, but I know you won't be able to do the same thing. So I just want to leave you with one thought: every time you see a little kid, just remember, you killed one that could have looked like me, with my cute butt muscles... a little kid that would have loved you like me. Screw you, and screw UVA!"

Roland replaced the receiver and unplugged the phone from the wall. He took one final look around his apartment, then closed the front door and locked it. He was leaving his UVA life forever. He drove aimlessly around campus for about an hour, silently paying homage to the death of his dream, then gunned the Beetle toward Tennessee.

A day later, Roland arrived at his parents' home in Chestnut Ridge, and for another two days after that, there was much yelling and shouting, and many phone calls to Dean Wiggins and Wink Jackson and Winslow Jackson III, but Roland wouldn't budge from his plan to pursue an accelerated MBA in lieu of a law degree.

Roland's mother brought her son hot cider in his favorite mug, patted his head several times a day, and told him in her slow, rhythmic voice that she was proud of him for trying to do what he felt was right, and for sticking with his guns, despite his father's opposition. She'd never intended for her letter to elicit quite this reaction, she told him, but she was pleased that Roland felt good about his new career choice, and that he'd at least tried to do right by the once-pregnant girl.

Privately, although concerned for her son's well-being, Izzy Gastineau was thrilled to be able to spend a few months with Roland. She looked forward to hours in the garden, walks about town on her son's arm, and discussions of her favorite philosophical topics with Roland, who inherited her intelligence as well as her sense of goodness in the world. Her husband Daniel definitely was not at all interested in anything except making money and looking good; he was no partner to her, and so the depth of Izzy Gastineau's good-natured personality was cast about on the innumerable charity groups she served, as she tried to right some of the wrongs imparted by Daniel and his slick business affairs. A few months with Roland would be a welcome change for Izzy Gastineau, and she couldn't deny it, despite her heartache for her only son.

After Roland's first week back home, his father traveled to a CPA conference, and the mood in the Gastineau house was decidedly improved, even jovial. Izzy was caught up in final preparations for the Masked Charity Ball; in her eyes it was merely a contrived social event which meagerly benefited the Senior Center, but one which in any case allowed her an excuse to spend months tending prized orchids which would be given to the elderly after the Ball.

She solicited Roland's help in the greenhouse, as she made final preparations to harvest the orchids for the Masked Ball centerpieces, knowing the mindless activity would draw Roland out. On the afternoon before the Ball, as they misted the last centerpiece prior to delivery, Izzy put down her gloves and stared hard at Roland.

"What is it, Mom? What did I screw up now?" Roland ran his fingers through his hair, leaving a trace of potting soil on his forehead.

"Nothing dear, don't be so negative! But, Rollie, I was just thinking...why don't you go over to Bessie Thibodeaux's dress shop and rent yourself a tux, and come to the Ball with your father and me? You need a party, and I would love to dance with my handsome son! What do you think?"

Roland raised his garden-gloved hands over his head in mock fear. "No way, Mom. It's gonna be hard enough dodging nosy questions for the next few months, I don't need to push the situation! Besides, Dad's already pissed off that I've ruined his family name! I don't want to rub salt in the wound in public!" He sat down on an overturned garden pail and removed his gloves.

"But that's my point, son! Everyone who your father thinks is important in this town attends the Masked Ball! And if you can be there in fine style, and present your case firsthand, regarding...what was it your father wants us to say...your *'troubled decision to leave the law and seek training in a more 'ethical' profession?'* By showing up, then it's certain that your version of the details will be delivered to the masses, instead of retold by gossipmongers who may be tempted to change the plot! You've got a Grade-A chance to take control of the situation, Roland! It would really help your father! Might get him off your back, you know!"

Roland looked lovingly at his mother, whose grey, pinned hair was beginning to unravel, due to the many small floral implements she'd stuck in it temporarily. "Mom, I don't know...Dad will think..."

"He will think it's an *excellent* idea, because it will help him save face, which as we all know is the only real problem he has with your decision anyway! You can redeem yourself and emerge a hero, overnight! I'll spring for the tux, if you'll give me the first dance!"

Roland blinked at his mother. He could use a night out, and Chestnut Ridge society was always good for a laugh, if nothing else. He slapped his hands on his knees and stood up.

"Mom, you're a genius! I'll see you later! Let's go to the club tonight for dinner! I'll be back before five." Roland hopped off the pail and dashed out the door.

"Rollie! Wait! Where are you going?"

"To Bessie's! To rent a tux!"

That Saturday evening, the Gastineau family, decked out, and nearly at peace with one another, given their mission to restore Roland's dignity, departed in high style and their BMW for the Masked Ball. Sometime during cocktails, Daniel Gastineau publicly toasted his son's bravery at having fought a terrible battle with the dreaded legal eagles and his own inner conscience, and who now emerged victorious to earn an MBA at Vanderbilt in unprecedented speed, in preparation to join the family firm in September.

As the orchestra played the pre-dinner waltz, Roland whisked Izzy around the parquet floor to thunderous applause, and he heard snippets of conversation bantering his name about with the likes of Sir Galahad, Atticus Finch and Robert E. Lee. It was almost as if the entire evening was dedicated to the brave, upright young Roland Daniel Gastineau himself, and how he'd left the Terrible, Dreaded Evils of Law School in order to Uphold an Important Principle. It was uncertain exactly what principle he was upholding, of course, but it was after all a party, and principles had no place among ball gowns and cocktails.

Sometime in the middle of dinner, Roland became aware of the fact that nearly every woman in attendance, regardless of age or marital status, was flirting with him. He began to gather quite a collection of business cards with *'my private number'* written on the back. After dessert, Roland and his father toasted their future success with bourbon on the rocks, and it became apparent to Roland why most men prefer the taste of bourbon to wine, because bourbon took the edge off, but allowed you to continue to function fairly normally. So Roland continued to order bourbon on the rocks from the endless stream of white-jacketed waiters bounding around the ballroom.

In the late portion of the evening, Roland's bourbon began to dramatically alter his conscious state, and he stripped himself of his tuxedo jacket, his cuff links and his cummerbund. He then informed his parents that it was perfectly fine for them to go ahead and leave, because he'd just catch a ride after he helped the Committee ladies gather up the floral centerpieces for delivery to the Senior Center the next day. Dan Gastineau was most satisfied that his image had been reclaimed to the good, thus Roland waved his parents out the ballroom door, and waved in a new, wildly erotic era in the Chestnut Ridge social scene.

After his fourth dance with buxom Betty Gooch, Mayor Barney Gooch's wife, to which they bumped and ground to their own personal version of *"Tiny Bubbles,"* Roland completely removed his shirt, leaving only the bow tie around his neck, in a kind of male striptease dancer effect. Betty's orange-sequined evening gown had somehow become strapless, placing it in a now-constant state of motion down her bosom as she moved, and her once-French-braided hair was now quite in fact akin to a spiked combat helmet.

For the most part, the remaining party-goers were content to ignore Roland's antics, forgiving any improprieties due to his recent scholarly stress and strain, which was becoming ever more apparent. Roland's striptease with Betty Gooch, however, was another matter, as she was not only a married woman, but also the Mayor's married woman, and as such, was duty-bound to serve as the model of decorum for Chestnut Ridge females.

When the orchestra, fully enjoying the sudden turn of the evening's otherwise dull events, launched into *"Do Ya Think I'm Sexy,"* Roland grabbed Betty by the bow on the back of her dress, which caused the front of her gown to shift dramatically and reveal part of one nipple, as they raced to the dance floor with shrieks of hysteria. As Roland began to pump his hips directly in the face of a kneeling, screaming Betty Gooch, Mayor Barney Gooch loudly encouraged the orchestra to take an unscheduled break, *immediately*, or he would stop payment on their check.

When the music stopped, Roland began to wail loudly and directly at Betty, "DO YA THINK I'M SEXY?" as he danced around her in a circle. Betty, who could do nothing but giggle loudly and scream "YES, OH GOD, YES" at the top of her lungs, was finally lifted off the floor by her husband and his business partner, leaving Roland to grab another bourbon from the only waiter still serving anybody anything. Then Roland decided it was time for a speech. He wobbled to the center of the parquet dance floor, and adjusted the bow tie, causing it to snap loudly onto his bare chest.

"LADIES AND GENNELMN. PLEASE SHUT UP RIGHT NOW SO I CAN TALK. THANKKKYOO."

Roland took three big gulps from his bourbon, then wiped his mouth with the back of his hand, "YOU'LL PROB'LY HEAR REAL SOON WHY I REALLY LEFT SCHOOL. I DID THE DIRTY DEED. I GOT A GIRL PREG-NANT. P-R-E-G-NANT. BUT SHE HAD AN ABORTION, BECAUSE SHE DIDN'T WANT TO MARRY ME AND MOVE HERE, BECAUSE WE DON'T HAVE ANY GYMNA....GERM....ATHLETES WHO CAN TWIST AND JUMP. SO I QUIT SCHOOL, BUT NOW THAT I'M HOME, I CAN DO ODD JOBS AT REASONABLE RATES UNTIL MAY, WHEN I GO TO A DIFF'RENT SCHOOL TO BE A PCA...CPA. SO CALL ME. I PROMISE I'LL KEEP MY DICK OUT OF YOUR WIVES' PANTS. I'M REAL GOOD WITH ORCHIDS, BY THE WAY! DOES AN'BODY WANNA BUY A REALLY BIG USED DIAMOND RING?"

With this final word, Roland Daniel Gastineau collapsed onto the dance floor, without spilling a drop of his bourbon. Immediately, every woman in the room ran to Roland's prostrate side and began to pat him on his hand, on his face, on his beautiful, rock-hard chest, and scream "HELP! CALL 911!"

Betty Gooch tore away from her husband (and part of her dress) and quickly loosened the bow tie from Roland's neck. "GIVE THIS BOY SOME ROOM SO HE CAN BREATHE, BARNEY! HE'S HAVING A TRAUMA!" Betty caressed and kissed Roland's head, and surreptitiously slipped his bowtie down her orange-sequined cleavage.

During this unexpected medical frenzy, the men in the room seemed content to remain seated and discuss things like the high school basketball stats. But in the end, an ambulance was proffered and whisked a stuperous Roland Gastineau away into the night, and onto the ER table at the Festrunk Clinic. His stomach was pumped to remove the deadly demon alcohol, under the personal supervision of Amelia Festrunk and Doc Kimball, still sporting his Masked Ball tuxedo stained with pink crab dip.

For the next two months, Roland Gastineau sustained the wrath of his father, the silent pity of his mother, and wrote endless apologetic notes to the various and sundry community leaders and their wives who had witnessed his "scene." Roland became a model of dutiful generosity, donating money and time to virtually every charity society, in an effort to overcome his bourbon-infused antics, and once again restore his family's good name.

After much bowing and scraping and gripping and grinning, by late April, just prior to his departure for Vanderbilt and the accelerated MBA program, Roland Gastineau had sufficiently pleased the Chestnut Ridge community movers and shakers that his penance was complete, and they immediately turned their limited sights toward the errant behavior of the next deserving soul.

Izzy forgave Roland immediately, of course, being his mother. Dan forgave him, but could not forget the incident, and seemed particularly bent on making it a permanent reminder of failure for Roland. Even though Roland whizzed through the accelerated MBA program at Vanderbilt that summer and fall, even though he graduated first in his class at the December ceremony, even though Roland spent every waking hour after graduation studying for the CPA exam, Dan Gastineau made weekly and often daily references to his son's error. Not only did he mention the real error itself, but more specifically, and much more damaging, in his eyes, was the grave error committed at the Ball. The Confession. Which was why today, in his father's office, nearly one year to the date since The Confession had occurred, Roland had endured enough. If he listened to one more snide reference about The Confession, he would rip the silk ascot right off his father's tanning-bed-browned neck.

"Yeah, Dad, I'm gonna ace the CPA exam. And I'll be a perfect gentleman at the ball, I won't even take a drink, just to please you and Mom. I'll even be nice to Danita Kay. Why, I'll be so nice to her, she'll probably think I'm going to *propose*! I still have that damned ring, you know! Wouldn't you just love that! How much of a signing bonus will you pay me if I marry Danita Kay, and, what is it you say so often, 'firmly consolidate the two best legal and tax entities in three counties'?"

Roland stood up and breathed heavily in his father's direction. His blue eyes flamed, "Yeah, I'm goin' to that damned dance. But after I do all these things, I'm gonna ask you just one favor. It's nothing very major, just a little thing I need you to do for me."

Dan Gastineau checked his ascot in the gilded mirror. Italian silk was *so* temperamental. Never wanted to stay in place, no matter how he tied it every morning. He had to look extremely good today; AnnElise Leigh-Lee was coming over for what she called a private consultation. Could mean anything, he mused with a grin. He noticed Roland in the mirror, obviously upset about something.

"Sure, son, anything for the new partner, even if we did have to change the nameplate on your office from 'tax attorney' to 'tax specialist'! *That* cost a pretty penny! What is it?"

Roland stood up and uncharacteristically clenched his fists. "I'm gonna ask you to shut the hell up about My Mistake, The Confession, the whole Bonnie Lou thing, OK? After I ace this exam, I never want to hear another word about it, ok? Can you do that for me, dad? Can you drop this damn thing? Because if you can't drop it, dad, I'm gonna go crazy, and I can't be responsible for my actions!!! If you don't stop bringin' it up every damn day, dad, I'm gonna leave this town and you won't have a two-hundred dollar an hour tax specialist to kick around any more, you got me? I'll go work for the Caldwells, in Nashville!"

Roland's face reddened, his fists were white-knuckled, and he was now leaning directly into his father's personal space behind the great walnut desk. Dan Gastineau tugged again at the silk ascot, never taking his eyes off the dashing-and-in-control image in the mirror.

"Hey, sure son, no problem. All you had to do was *ask*! You're far too sensitive, Roland, you need to grow some balls! Maybe they would have taught you that in law school, if you'd stuck around and finished. Now if you'll excuse me, I have an appointment."

Early March 1999; Amelia Festrunk's Office

"Mayor Gooch, what your Lilliputian mind has apparently forgotten is that you gave me your word nearly eleven weeks ago that you would personally appoint Henry Bailey Chairperson of the Festival Parade Vehicles committee. I don't like reading in the *Tell-All* that as of your last Festival board meeting there has in fact been no such appointment made. Would you care to explain?"

Amelia Festrunk arched her back against the worn pillow supporting her spine against a dilapidated office chair. Had Barney Gooch been across Amelia's desk instead of talking to her on the phone, he would have been paralyzed with fear at the rage on her face.

"Mayor, I'm warning you. I don't want you to wait until your next meeting! I want you to call on Mister Bailey *today*, this afternoon, in the next hour and inform him of his appointment. Because if I call Mister Bailey this evening and find out he hasn't been informed of his new position, I will personally phone Will Graham and have my money withdrawn from your Festival account! And then I will set fire to the sign you've so tackily displayed on the grounds of my Clinic! Good. But I'm warning you, Mayor, from now on Leonard will be attending all your meetings in my absence. He speaks for me so don't disappoint him or piss him off, do you understand? Very well, I believe you have a phone call to make! *Good day*!"

Amelia slammed the rotary dial telephone onto its cradle in fury. She leaned back in her chair and removed her glasses, rubbing weary eyes. *There's absolutely no excuse for Gooch's inaction! He's had my money in an interest-bearing Festival account for nearly three months!* She swiveled her chair to the small window behind her and stared out into the courtyard of the Clinic. An orderly assisted a patient in a walker in painstakingly slow progress around the sidewalk. She closed her eyes briefly, but was interrupted by a knock at the door.

"Yes, come in, it's open."

AnnElise Leigh-Lee entered in a flourish of Prada, Ferragamo and enough heavy jewelry to bankroll an emerging nation. She closed the door behind her and gave Amelia Festrunk a formal but polite smile.

"*Bonjour*, Miss Amelia. I hope you're not in the middle of anything important...but by the look of your desk, it does seem you might be *un peu* behind in your reading. I don't imagine you've read the latest report by the Board on our intent to trim excessive staff positions by the beginning of the second quarter..."

Amelia glared at the intruder, who casually flipped through a foot-high stack of reports on the corner of the old nurse's desk.

"...*c'est dommage*...doesn't appear you've been doing much reading at all. Well, no matter...we've tried to discuss this with you rationally but I'm afraid that time is past. I shall be frank...I...*we*...the Clinic Board...have decided that your retirement is at hand. Now despite what you may believe, this is not a pleasant task for me, because I have the utmost respect for your dedication. However as I am the only other voting woman on the Board I assume I was selected to convey this sad news to you out of some kind of chauvinistic compassion, to stir up as little *malaise* as possible. Miss Amelia, you may retain this office for your personal use in your charity work as a courtesy at no cost to you, but you may no longer make use of the Clinic staff to provide your clerical assistance. In fact the Board has decided that MayBelle's office will be renovated for an executive secretary, so perhaps you and Miss MayBelle can share this office and she can assist you."

AnnElise waited for a response from Amelia, but none was offered. She continued. "*Mais oui.* Now, with respect to your living quarters. We are not cruel, nor do we wish to relocate the three remaining members of the Festrunk family offsite. Thus you, MayBelle and Leonard may remain in your apartment. Note, Miss Amelia, I said *apartment.* Leonard must remove himself and his belongings from Patient Room Number One *immédiatement*... that wing will be demolished next month to make way for a new parking garage."

AnnElise reached inside her Gucci bag and retrieved a sheaf of documents. She thrust it in front of Amelia. "Now, this is a letter of resignation which the Board has prepared for you. It simply states that you wish to retire and enjoy your golden years doing volunteer work. It will be published in the *Tell-All* and also in the Nashville papers. This is a copy of a lengthy tribute written about you by several leading citizens; it will also be published. The Board will host a reception honoring you and your family next month. Please sign this official Termination of Employment...your pension and all your stock will of course remain untouched; however, despite your majority stockholder status, you will no longer have a vote on matters concerning the Board."

AnnElise smiled shark-like at the tired old woman in the tattered office chair. Amelia refused the Mont Blanc pen offered to her and instead signed the termination papers with a Bic. She knew she had no legal recourse because she had been warned that this day would come unless she adhered to the actions prescribed by the Board in their stream of puerile reports. As she signed her name a certain wave of relief washed over her. The battle was over. The war, however, had just begun.

"My goodness, AnnElise, I must say I never thought you had the balls to do something like this. I remember when you were a fresh-faced young thing newly married from Charleston, before you were corrupted by Richard's money and lack of social graces. I say *balls* because I know you wear the pants in your family…you have to, don't you, because you spent your inheritance ages ago and if you don't manage a tight ship, watch Richard like a hawk, there'll be no more spa vacations or foreign automobiles or shopping trips to Beverly Hills, will there? That would certainly prevent you and Tiffany from having the cosmetic surgery *du jour*…no doubt you'd both have to do something drastic like get a job! How strange that Danita Kay is so genuine and sweet. Perhaps you had an illicit affair just like all the ones your husband has enjoyed over the years, *n'est ce pas*?"

AnnElise Leigh-Lee stiffened and snatched the papers from the old woman. Her cheeks ruddied and she clenched her jaw taut. Amelia laughed out loud and started throwing Board reports into a metal trash can. AnnElise slammed a hand down on Amelia's desk.

"Listen to me you old *bitch*…every single person on that Board is sick and tired of being forced to worship at the altar of St. Amelia Festrunk! You're as money hungry as the rest of us and don't pretend to be anything else! But you're *right*…I'm the only one with the balls to challenge you! Now go tell your bimbo of a sister and that *imbécile* of a brother the good news. You have five days to clear them out or we'll take legal action and it won't be pretty!"

Amelia grabbed AnnElise by one arm in a surprising show of strength. She jerked the younger woman and grinned wickedly. "Don't *ever* insult my brother or sister like that again, missy or I'll have your tight little designer-clad ass slapped in jail so fast you won't see it coming! I may be old but I still wield a lot of power in this town. I'll play your game…but this is just the first move, trust me! I don't have to be on the Board to influence decisions around here…now get out of my office before I call security!"

AnnElise winced at her release and ran in a flushed dash from the room. Amelia laughed heartily as she threw the remaining Board reports into the trash. Within two minutes MayBelle and Leonard appeared at the door. MayBelle began to cry. "'Melie, is it true? They fired you from the Board? Oh, I can't believe it! I'm so sorry!"

Leonard nodded but said nothing. Amelia put her hands on her hips and smiled. "No tears, MayBelle! Remember what Mama always used to say! Listen up…we knew this day was coming…and if I'm not upset about it why should you be? Leonard, I'm sorry but you'll have to clear out of your room and move into the third bedroom in our apartment."

Leonard nodded and grinned. "Okay, 'Melie. It ain't no big deal. We're a fam'ly, gotta stick tagether.

MayBelle pulled a large pink lace hankie from her bosom and daubed her eyes. "But 'Melie, are you gonna just let those awful people get away with this? Daddy wouldn't have and from what you've told me, Granddaddy *never* would have taken this lying down! He'd have fought tooth and nail, I imagine!"

Amelia sighed pensively. "MayBelle...Granddaddy never would have been on that Board in the first place, because it would have taken too much time away from his 'doctorin.'" If I'd behaved more like Granddaddy and less like a Board member, well, who knows..."

MayBelle shook her head as Leonard wrapped an arm about her shoulders. "No, 'Melie, don't you say that! If not for you...think how many times you fought the Board to do what was right, and how many people's lives you saved because you did what you believed in?"

Amelia lowered her eyes to the floor. She didn't want to rehash history now. Then she smiled. "Cheer up, kids! I've got an entire filing cabinet of Board documents to clean out so MayBelle can move into this office with me! MayBelle...you've always wanted one of those Red Cross uniforms...I say we go sign up first thing in the morning!"

MayBelle smiled and shook her fist in the air. "Right, 'Melie! Leonard, you'll come too?"

Leonard nodded. Amelia waved her bony arms about the office. "Good. No more talk about this then. They're gonna give us some kind of shindig next month, so we'll have to act happy about all this until after that's over and done with. Leonard, don't go dog-cussin' anybody in public, okay? Like Daddy used to say, we've gotta wear our game faces!"

Amelia ushered her siblings from the room and sat down weakly in her chair. *That was a command performance if there ever was! I'm too old for all this carrying on.* Looked at the piles of paperwork on her desk. *None of this matters a hoot now, for certain! Time to get down to serious business...time to step up my plan. Where's that phone directory?* She dug in the bottom of an overflowing desk drawer and removed an indexed spiral book. Flipping to *P*, she ran a finger down the page until she located the name she needed, then dialed the number.

"Hello...Doctor Parker? Doctor Avery Parker, junior? Yes, this is Miss Amelia Festrunk...yes, fine, thank you. I'm calling, doctor, because I understand that as a college professor of Civil War history you might also have some contacts in the field of genealogy? Yes, I want the absolute best expert in the country...I see...can you repeat that again for me please...Doctor E. A. Gray of Richmond, Virginia. Yes...five-one-four-seven...yes, I have it. *Excellent!* Thank you so kindly, Doctor Parker! No, no, that's all for now, I'm sure. *Good day!*"

Amelia hung up the phone and let out a satisfied sigh. She checked her watch. Why wait until tomorrow? College professors kept unusual hours…perhaps Dr. Gray would be in despite the time difference. She dialed the number and was surprised to get an answer on the second ring, and even more surprised to hear a woman's voice.

"Doctor E. A. Gray? Genealogy expert? Hello, my name is Miss Amelia Festrunk. I am calling from Chestnut Ridge, Tennessee, and I…yes, that's what I said…Chestnut Ridge, Tennessee, and…*beg pardon…yes, Doctor Gray…*as far as I know there is only one town in the state with this name. *Pardon*? Would you please repeat that last statement?"

Amelia Festrunk's hand began to shake and her heart raced. She tried to steady the near-rapture in her voice. "*I see.* Yes, that's extremely interesting! In fact, Doctor, I received your name from a professor at MTSU, Doctor Avery Parker, and, well, frankly, I made this call as an extreme longshot. You see, I have information on that *very subject* and…umm…well…let's just say that the timing is finally right for me to share that information with others. Yes…and I'm sure you can understand that as this is a *sensitive* matter, I wanted to first tell my story to a certified professional. Oh, Doctor Gray, I'm so happy to talk to you, that's exactly right! Yes, I'd love to meet you…but I'm afraid I won't be able to travel for a few weeks and…what? You're planning a trip to Chestnut Ridge? Excellent! Here's my number and…oh, of course, your caller I.D. Well, in any case…please give me a call when you confirm your travel plans. I would consider it an honor to serve as your personal Chestnut Ridge tour guide, for you see, I am the last person alive who was with Hardy Bailey on that fateful day. Yes, those newspaper clippings are correct, as are *you*, Doctor Gray. Homer Festrunk was my grandfather, and I was there and watched him die at the hand of that terrible man! I look forward to hearing from you. *Good day*!"

Amelia gingerly replaced the telephone as if the simple action of disconnecting could somehow sever this newfound rescue line. *Oh my God! This woman's research is unbelievable! 'What a coincidence,' she said! 'I'm working to clarify a little-known post-War period in the town of Chestnut Ridge, hoping to uncover a trail of missing money and inheritance rights on behalf of a local Richmond family.'*

*I can't believe this is happening! This woman has a Ph.D. in history! She's an expert! Absolutely credible! I don't have to worry about being believed or laughed out of town…she'll corroborate my story! Damnation, she can tell the story herself while she hands out her certifiable-expert Ph.D. business cards! That's it! I don't have to break my promise! I don't have to tell that old killing bastard's story! This woman can 'do my job' for me… no one will ever know…*Amelia's heart leaped and she picked up the phone once more. This called for a celebration. She dialed Henry Bailey Used Cars.

"Henry! Amelia Festrunk! Fine, thanks and you? Oh, *really*? Well, congratulations, Henry, I can't think of a better man to serve as chairman of that committee than you! Now, Henry…how are we doing with respect to locating my late-model Cadillac? I see. Mmm..no, that won't do. It must be absolutely loaded with extras and in top condition. Henry, what would you charge to act as my agent…find me a *brand new* Cadillac? I'm a very busy woman and I don't have the time nor the patience to search for the right automobile. By the way, I think my sister MayBelle's in the market for a Cadillac as well, although she goes more for the sportier models. And Leonard will be needing a new truck…no, it will be his personal vehicle, we are all retiring from Clinic work. *Excellent!* Henry, give me a call soon! *Good day*!"

Amelia Festrunk put on her heavy white sweater and grabbed her purse. She turned off her office light at four-thirty in the afternoon…something she had not done in over sixty years. She waved at the astonished clerks in the admitting office, then she fairly skipped down the administrative corridor of the Festrunk Respite Home and Birthing Clinic. *Henry has his committee position and with any luck he'll earn a nice commission on a couple of cars for the Festrunk family. A history professor in Richmond, Virginia is coming to town to corroborate my story and spill the beans on the misdeeds done to the Baileys oh so long ago to set the record straight. My battles with the Clinic Board are over and I can do exactly as I please, with absolutely no regard for schedules or patients or critical decisions. There'll be no lost public face thanks to that ridiculous resignation letter and tribute, and it will be hilarious to watch the Board members squirm at my retirement reception. I think I'll insist on champagne and caviar. No doubt about it, Saint Amelia…life is indeed good after all! Oh, God…excuse me…but about my little death wish? Let's just postpone that for awhile, whaddya say?*

CHAPTER ELEVEN - SHOW US THE WAY

Mid-April, 1999; Quigley Funeral Parlor

"I HEREBY CALL THIS HERE QUARTERLY MEETIN' A THE CHESTNUT RIDGE CITY COUNCIL, AD HOC CHESTNUT RIDGE SONS A GLORY FESTIVAL COMMITTEE, TA *ORDER*!"

Mayor Barney Gooch banged an old wooden gavel on an even older wooden podium and looked around the crowded Peaceful Slumber room at the Quigley Funeral Parlor. Barney figured there were at least one hundred of Chestnut Ridge's top movers and shakers present, and most of them were seated in the Funeral Parlor's appropriately respectful yet multi-functional gold vinyl-cushioned chairs.

The Chestnut Ridge city flag hung suspended from faded ceiling tiles by two paper clip chains, fastened in haste by Miss Eustacia Gober, who had been appointed Official Sons of Glory Festival Scribe by the Mayor, in an effort to properly record the goings-on at all Festival meetings. Upon her appointment, Miss Gober immediately seized control of meeting protocol, and determined that the florid mural which adorned the main wall of the Peaceful Slumber room, and which depicted Ruby Quigley as the Angel of the Lord, was in poor taste for a city gathering. As the new arbiter of official Chestnut Ridge political decorum, Miss Gober took it upon herself to hang the city flag directly in front of the main portion of the mural; the portion which was most offensive in Miss Gober's eyes, because Ruby Quigley's Angel of the Lord's cleavage was much too revealingly buxom. As any good Bible Bee knew, angels were far too holy to be concerned with cleavage.

Barney Gooch quickly surveyed the room; he hated these meetings, because they never accomplished anything. Nobody in town shared his vision for Chestnut Ridge; all they cared about was this measly Festival. But Barney knew that the Festival was just one peanut on the sundae, so to speak. Chestnut Ridge had serious business investment and prime development potential, and the Sons of Glory Festival was his chance to bring new money and industry to town, especially if that new money and industry would like to locate itself on the hundred-acre tract of land he owned, conveniently located right behind his office supply business warehouse.

As a business owner, and after an eleven-year tenure as Mayor of Chestnut Ridge, Barney could read people as easily as a first-grade primer. He knew that each and every one of the citizens in this room most likely did not share his desire to expand the town's borders or tax base, but it was high time they got off their country duffs and modernize. But first, they had to get through the Festival, now only eight months away, and it had to be the best durned thing they'd ever done. Thus in the twilight of an early April evening, Barney pounded the gavel once more and spoke loudly in his best official Mayor's voice.

"Now, at our *last* meetin', we got off ta a real bad start, seein' as how we wasted two hours talkin' about how a certain preacher in this commun'ty enjoyed hisself a little too much at the Festival Marketing Mixer, an' how certain folks think that another certain person, who is ta remain *nameless,* mighta put Ex-Lax in them whores doovers we was all eatin' at that Mixer, an' so we didn't get nothin' done! An' so tonight, I'm gonna crack my whip, an' ya'll are gonna pay 'tention!"

Barney Gooch ignored the scowl aimed in his direction by Mrs. Forrestine Culpepper, whose revered husband had indeed imbibed much too much alcohol at his first civic cocktail function. *That was last month,* Forrestine fumed silently, *give me a break!* Mayor Gooch continued with the official agenda,

"Now our *first* order a bizness is 'bout them chaser lights that Miz MayBelle Festrunk has donated, ta go 'round the peri-mter a the Festival billboard over ta the Clinic...kinda like them lights 'Meel-yo Rod-ri-gez put up on his house last Christmas...ya'll 'member... them things is still flashin' pink an' orange ever night...anyhow, ya'll may not realize it, but I been very person'lly involved with this whole billboard thing...Miz MayBelle can attest ta that, cain't ya, Miz MayBelle...there she is... she don't look a day over sixty! Now with them chaser lights, hey, ya'll can see 'em clear from the Highway...there's no way anybody's gonna miss that billboard! We're gonna get Festival traffic in here from I-24, sure's shootin'!"

Barney rared back in anticipation of a thunderous ovation, pleased with his announcement, and pleased that his personal assistance to MayBelle Festrunk had thus far eluded discovery, despite the many compromising positions into which Miz MayBelle had trapped him during their frequent 'sign committee' meetings. *It's all for a good cause,* Barney told himself. *I'm givin' an old lady some attention, and I'm gettin' the best-durned billboard location for this Festival in the whole county.* Barney waited for the good citizens to rightfully acknowledge the donation of Miz MayBelle's chaser lights, but it did not happen.

"Who's gonna pay fer the 'lectricity to *run* them lights, Barney? We ain't gonna stand fer no extry taxation, fer no tacky, kiss-my-ass Las Vegas flashin' lights! Jus' 'cause my baby sister thinks she's a hot-shot with the handouts, don't mean I ain't got no say!"

Leonard Festrunk, newly retired Head of Environmental Services at the Festrunk Clinic, was readily on guard against the burden of unfair taxation, despite the fact that up until last week he had lived in a vacant patient room at the Clinic for over forty years and had never paid one dime in property tax to the good City of Chestnut Ridge. A loud, crackly voice from the center of the room retorted,

"Shut up, Leonard! You ain't paid fer nothin' yer whole miserable life! Maybe you oughta just donate the e-lectric'ty, since you Festrunks own pert near half the town!"

Seventy-five year old Raleigh Poe, father to son Cornelius and daughter Euladean, and co-owner of the Poe House Grocery, hated the Festrunks with every valve of his ailing heart. Raleigh's wife Mary Louise died of inexplicable causes after delivering three cases of overly-ripe bananas to the Festrunk Clinic in July 1977, and Raleigh was convinced that the Festrunks were somehow directly responsible for her mysterious and untimely demise. Yet another voice reared its head from the crowd of concerned Chestnut Ridge citizens,

"*YOU* shut up, Raleigh Poe! Yer a fine one ta talk, livin' in that ramshackle house behin' the grocery! Hell, ya ain't even got 'nuf sense ta patch yer own roof! I seen you last Thursday, durin' that downpour, rainwater fillin' up yer house so fast, 'nuf ta hold a swim meet in yer front room! Miss Mary Louise is prob'ly rollin' over in her grave of embarrassment, way you've let that house fall ta pieces! Yer prob'ly just lettin' it rot so's you ain't gotta pay no *improvement* taxes!" Henry Bailey hollered, his round, red-headed face beetish with anger.

"*Henry Bailey, don't you talk ta me 'bout rot*! Just 'cause you tricked my daughter Euladean inta marryin' you don't give you the right ta talk ta me thataway! At least I don't live in no damned rickety RV parked on some no-good USED CAR LOT! I shoulda been 'pointed Vee-hicle chairman but you prob'ly bribed the Mayor inta 'pointin' you!"

Raleigh Poe's face drew taut as the anxious citizens of Chestnut Ridge settled in for round eighty-seven of the Raleigh Poe-Henry Bailey town meeting fights. Fay Bailey, Henry's ex-wife, seated in the back row of gold-vinyl chairs, let out a loud moan. She specifically chose her seat to ensure that the view down the front of her taut leopard-skin tube top would not be obstructed from the eligible bachelor policemen who always stood against the back wall of the Peaceful Slumber room. Fay, who was filing her four-inch long, scarlet red fingernails, leaned over to Bessie Thibodeaux and muttered, "*Damn!* I knew I shoulda got me some popcorn 'fore I came in here! These two have done got started early, an' now I ain't got nothin' in my gut! Bessie, honey, you got any gum or go-betweens in that big purse you're totin'?"

Bessie shook her head *no* as the loud exchange between Raleigh Poe and his new son-in-law continued. When Euladean Poe did the unthinkable by marrying Henry Bailey, town failure and Catholic to boot, Raleigh said that

Henry had obviously worked some kind of papist black magic on his daughter, since everybody knew that if Euladean had any self-respect at all, she never would have entered into the marriage of her own free will. No matter how much Euladean professed to love her new husband, Raleigh believed he knew better; the fact that Euladean no longer lived in the ramshackle Poe residence, cooking, cleaning and seeing to her father's every need also contributed to his wrath.

Now, seated next to her up-and-coming husband, from her second-row perch in the Peaceful Slumber room, Euladean Poe Bailey put down her knitting (Euladean was not much for City affairs, but since Henry was recently appointed as a committee chairman, she was obligated to stand by her man) and looked at her father, who was still red-faced from shouting at Henry.

"Daddy, please don't insult my husband! We're happy as can be in our home, it's just as good as those durn double-wides, only we don't have ta worry about dyin' from the fumes comin' off all that cardboard furniture! Besides, daddy, Henry's right! You really should see ta gettin' a new roof put on! Mama would be havin' a fit! You're gonna catch the pneumonia! And Henry earned that appointment as chairman, fair and square!"

Barney Gooch realized he'd lost control of the meeting, after only five minutes. He banged the gavel, hooked a thumb in his Confederate-flag motif suspenders, and frowned in an official mayoral capacity at the room full of unruly attendees.

"*ORDER! ORDER!* Now, looky here, Raleigh, Henry, Leonard! Ya'll are doin' the SAME thing ya'll did ta the last meetin', an' I ain't gonna have it, YOU HEAR?! Ain't nobody gonna have ta pay extra fer no 'lectricity fer them blinkin' lights, 'cause Miz MayBelle's already took care of it, ain't ya Miz MayBelle? Right! An' we thank ya!"

Barney banged his official mayoral gavel once more and raised one hand into the air for official mayoral silence. "Now, Miz Elspeth Kimball's gonna bring us up ta date on the Pub-liss-ty efforts for the Festival! Miz Elspeth?"

Cornelius Poe stood to interrupt. "Mayor, I need a word if ya don't mind. I got me two pages a signatures here sayin' Henry Bailey's not qualified to be the Festival Parade Vehicle Committee Chairman! This here petition…"

Corny waved two pieces of paper in the air. "…this here petition says Henry Bailey's got an unfair advantage over the rest of us, seein' as how he's got easy access to all them used cars on his lot. That's unfair advantage, that is…if one of us reg'lar citizens had been appointed, we woulda had to round up cars fair an' square, not just go out to our front yard an' see which ones would start on parade day an' slap a Festival banner on 'em!"

A few people clapped and there were murmurs in the crowd. Henry Bailey sank into his chair as Euladean patted his leg. Barney rolled his eyes, then banged his gavel for order, but Leonard Festrunk rose and waved his lanky arms in the air.

"Hey, order! Ya'll listen up! Corny Poe, you ain't nothin' but green of envy! Why on earth would anybody with haif a lick a sense 'point anybody other'n Henry Bailey ta be the Vee-hicle Chairman is beyond me, an' ya'll been *knowin'* I'm simple-minded!"

A few chuckles bounced around the room as Leonard smiled. "Now, look here. Corny Poe...if you was ta be the Vee-hicle Chairman...you'd have ta high-tail it over ta Murfreesboro an' git a bid on some cars, wouldn't ya? An' they'd jack that bid up so high but you'd got no chaince but ta pay it, am I right? Well, you'd be a robbin' us tax-payin' citizens a our hard-earned money! Don't it make more sense ta have Henry Bailey, what's a local bizness man an' a car dealer ta boot, give us his best deal on the use a his veehicles? Nah, you an' alla yer Poe rel'tives'd rather screw us taxpayers outta our money jus' so's you kin drive the lead car in that ol' parade! Jus' like you screw us on the price a milk an' coffee an' a loaf a bread! Am I right? Huh, ever'body, ain't I right?"

A round of applause grew louder as the sense of Leonard's point hit home. Corny Poe clenched his hands into fists and glared at his fellow taxpaying citizens. He pointed a stubby finger at Leonard.

"Well, that's great! Let's just all resign an' let them Pope-worshipin', Virgin-Mary-idolators take over our Festival, right now! An' while we're at it, let's just buy us a buncha them rotary beads so's we can thow 'em from the cars in the parade! Git everybody ta convert! Would ya'll be happy then? Huh? We're talkin' about *Henry Bailey!* Of the murderin', thievin', drunk, no-good, Pope-worshipin' Catholic Baileys! Has everybody gone stir crazy? An' if ya'll don't like the Poe House prices, then ya'll can just danged sure shop in Murfreesboro an' pay the diff'rence in gas!"

Barney Gooch banged his gavel for order and yelled sternly at Corny. "Corny Poe...what'd I tell you jus' this mornin' 'bout this? It's over an' done with an' there ain't no more discussion. Now, Henry, ever'thing all lined up with them cars?"

Henry Bailey blushed and nodded and waved one hand. He had nothing to say and wanted only to disappear. Barney banged his gavel again.

"Good. You 'member you're person'lly responsible fer the well-bein' an' safety a them beauty pageant gals, so don't be takin' no chainces with bald tires or such, you hear? Okay, Miss Elspeth...your turn!"

Barney sat down at the head of the City Council dais, which was really three card tables placed end to end at the front of the Peaceful Slumber room. All eyes turned toward Elspeth Kimball, who was late-thirty-ish, with mousy brown hair and horn-rimmed glasses. Elspeth, the Chestnut Ridge

Postmaster, did not like public gatherings, as she was painfully shy.

Recently, in a shocking display of public service and human contact, Elspeth Kimball volunteered to chair the Sons of Glory Festival's Publicity committee, in an effort to challenge herself and further overcome her fear of human contact. Now she stood in the midst of a packed Peaceful Slumber room and began to speak in a barely audible voice.

"MIZ ELSPETH! Please speak up! We cain't *hear* ya!" Barney could see that his Doc's efforts to coach Elspeth on the finer points of addressing the community had not yet taken effect.

"Oh...my...I'm sorry, Barney...I mean, *mayor*!" Elspeth blushed to the roots of her mousy brown hair, and continued, eyes facing the floor, "In my official capacity as Postmistress, I tried my best to obtain a postage discount for our Festival efforts, but I am sorry to report that the Federal Postmaster General has denied our request. I briefly considered taking the matter to Washington, to Senator Winslow Jackson III, but I do not want to be accused of fraternization or taking advantage of my civil servant status, so I'm afraid we'll have to go to alter our plans."

"Thank ya for yer efforts, Elspeth. Let's have them altinates." Barney Gooch was concerned that the evening's lengthy agenda would cut into *Andy Griffith* at ten o'clock, and Barney Gooch hated to miss *Andy Griffith*.

Elspeth breathed deeply, wrung her hands and nodded. "Certainly, Mayor. I have decided to use my position as Postmaster to override the Federal Law Number 5,430-B, Section twenty-seven, which states that no item or document shall be placed in a postal box without appropriate postage. I have decided that as we are promoting goodwill and furthering education by celebrating the 136th anniversary of this town, it is therefore appropriate for us to place tastefully-worded fliers in the mailboxes of all Chestnut Ridge citizens. I will *personally* drive around and take care of this on my days off this fall! Thank you for listening to my report."

Elspeth Kimball bowed and immediately took her seat, beaming with the relief that she was now finished with her quarterly Publicity duties. Fay Bailey stood up and waved her nail file in the air at the Mayor in disbelief.

"*That's it?* That's her big idea a pushin' this Festival? Hell, you'd have ta be *dead* if ya live here an' already don't know what's happenin'! No damn piece a paper in our mailboxes is gonna cut it! You got ta git the word out, girl! When I win the Mrs. Chestnut Ridge Pageant, I wanna be seen by people from Nashville! I wanna be on TV! An' I don't give a rat's ass if any local yokels show up...they already know I'm a looker! We got ta git *regional!* We got ta git *national!* Hell, call up that guy…what's his name…Jerry Springer…he'll put us on the map! I gotta get seen, so's I can get me an agent! I ain't gonna let all my sangin' talent go ta waste!"

Fay, a part-time hairdresser at the Quigley Beauty Box, had been married and divorced five times, thus she whole-heartedly believed that the title of Mrs. Chestnut Ridge should easily and rightfully become hers. In addition, she was convinced that with her sweep of the pageant's talent competition, based on her planned performance of a Loretta Lynn medley, she would leave town forever, and embark on a hugely successful career as a country singer.

Fay's reputation as the town sleaze had absolutely no effect on her whatsoever, and the fact that one of her local conquests, Estéfan Rodriguez, had come out of the closet immediately after their tryst ended did little to cause Fay any worry regarding her physical or sexual superiority over other women. Barney Gooch banged his gavel once again.

"Now, Fay, there ain't no need ta be *rude!* Elspeth ain't finished, are ya, Elspeth?" Barney nodded at a stricken Elspeth, waiting for her continuation of Plan B. "Go 'head, honey! What else you got?"

Elspeth cleared her throat and stood again. "*Well*... I think it's important to have small, attainable goals, so we should start with our own Chestnut Ridge neighbors first, and then perhaps it would be okay to expand our territory a bit, but I must inform you, my authority as Postmaster does not extend beyond our city limits! I am not at all comfortable placing fliers without postage in the mailboxes of bordering towns!"

"DON'T YOU PUT ANY FLIES IN *MY* MAILBOX, MISSY! FLIES GIVE ME A YEAST INFECTION, AND THEN I'LL HAVE TO GET A PELVIC EXAM!"

Mother Nell Graham, parked in her wheelchair at the back of the room, dozed on and off during the meeting, and despite the fact that she no longer owned a mailbox, she felt obligated to express her opinion. At Mother Nell's outburst, Elspeth suddenly looked as if she might vomit. Then, to Elspeth's rescue, Avery Parker, Jr., Ph.D., rose to speak. The crowd immediately hushed out of respect for Chestnut Ridge's resident celebrity. Dr. Parker, one of the town's handful of African-American residents, was a noted historian who taught at a nearby college. The revisionist textbooks he authored were dedicated to clarifying the historical accuracy behind notorious American legends, and their publication success resulted in nationally publicized speaking engagements. Chestnut Ridge townspeople were much more interested in receiving proper credit as the noted Dr. Parker's neighbors than they were interested in Dr. Parker's serious scholarship.

Dr. Parker's fellow citizens, after overcoming their initial concern at the installation of Dr. Parker and his family into Chestnut Ridge's most exclusive subdivision, had come to realize that he, his school-teacher wife Diana, and their son Rex were fine people, and that perhaps Dr. Parker's involvement in the Sons of Glory Festival would translate into much-needed national fame and resulting fortune.

"Perhaps we are overlooking our primary Festival goals, ladies and gentlemen."

Dr. Parker was tall, with bifocals and a graying black beard. His strikingly beautiful wife Diana was seated next to him, radiant in an emerald green dress that glowed against her milky brown skin.

"Let us not forget that this Festival is dedicated to preserving the memory of the return of commerce to this town, one hundred and thirty-six years ago. Let us remember that although many of the town fathers were, in fact, Confederate *deserters*, they assisted in the re-birth and restoration of the grist mill; they founded a bank, and they married the single women, providing a stable base for trade and the continuation of life in an almost extinct rural community."

Dr. Parker's booming voice waxed eloquent across the fascinated faces in the Peaceful Slumber Room. He continued, "And let us not fail to remember that our primary goal with this celebration is the remuneration of much-deserved honor to the memory of those men and women, versus any residual tourism, commercial benefit, or beauty pageant prizes we might also reap! Those things are *secondary*, ladies and gentlemen, and I *caution* you to avoid turning this event into a *carnival!*" Satisfied with his scholarly admonition, Dr. Parker sat down next to Diana, who beamed proudly at her husband.

"Thank ya, Doc Parker! Elspeth, we'll talk 'bout *Plan C* at the Special Details meetin', ok? NEXT ON THE AGENDA..." Mayor Gooch was interrupted.

"Barney...*Mister Mayor*, you just hold on one minute!" Corny Poe stood, red-faced, with clenched fists. " 'Scuse me, Doc Parker, I don't mean no *disrespect*, or nothin', but I got me a question to ask. You keep talkin' 'bout these so-called 'deserters'...now, I ain't educated or nothin', like you, I mean, I'm just a good ol' country boy that works in a grocery store, but seems to me that a feller who's *new* in town shouldn't oughta be goin' around sayin' that another feller's ancestors were low-down 'deserters' in the War Between the States! 'Specially if that feller ain't from 'round here, an' none of us knows nothin' 'bout what kinda ancestors he's got, like maybe they was jus' cottonpickers, if ya catch my meanin'!"

The Peaceful Slumber Room had never more fully deserved its moniker. Dr. Parker, caught off guard, cleared his throat and stood once more.

"*Certainly*, Mr. Poe! Of course I mean no disrespect, either, and I'm proud to say that Diana and I appreciate the warm welcome we have received into this town! You see, Mr. Poe...please recall I've got a Ph.D. in Civil War History and Related Issues of American Pre-20th Century Behavioral

Patterns...it is an established fact that the 44th Regiment of the Tennessee Riders, those brave souls who fought for what they erroneously believed to be the winning side in the Civil War, stumbled upon a stolen Union payroll...we will never fully understand the circumstances, but it is believed that the commanding officers orchestrated the entire affair...and in possession of such substantial funds in that day and age, used those funds to start the very instruments of commerce we today treasure, the same businesses many of the people in this room inherited, and now operate!"

The once-frozen crowd in the Peaceful Slumber Room began to stir; rumors of this accusatory tale had popped up here and there over the years, but had always been put down to the wanton ramblings of demented geriatrics. Dr. Parker strode up to a small chalkboard that rested on an easel beside the door, used by Ruby Quigley to record in fourteen-karat gold chalk the names of the deceased as they rested silently in the Peaceful Slumber Room.

Dr. Parker reached for the gold chalk like the professor he was, and wrote the words "HISTORY" and "TRUTH" on the blackboard, much to the consternation of Ruby Quigley...that was fifteen-dollar-a-box gold chalk he was using. Ruby made a mental note to write up a receipt for ain-kind city council tax donation.

"Let us recall from our schooldays, ladies and gentleman, that when you go in search of *History*, you also go in search of *Truth*, and though that Truth may set one *free*, it may often be a tad *unpleasant!* Now, mind you, everyone, I personally believe that it makes no difference whatsoever whether the funds that saved this town were stolen, or stumbled upon accidentally; and it makes no difference whether their distribution into local commercial vehicles was intentionally planned to control the town, or an act of kindness to impart an economic rebirth upon the thirty-odd citizens who originally lived here. The important aspect, let us not forget, is that Chestnut Ridge survived the war much better than its neighboring burgs, which now remain nameless in the annals of history! This town owes a great debt to its founders, certainly, whether they were in fact thieves or benefactors!"

Dr. Avery Parker tapped the end of the chalk against the blackboard in emphasis, and as it broke in two, he smiled and returned to his seat, satisfied that he had adequately explained himself to his accuser. Ruby Quigley, angry at the broken chalk, decided to speak to Barney Gooch about the misappropriation of private property for city business. Corny Poe's face purpled and a great spreading blotch appeared on top of his bald head. He pointed at Barney Gooch. "Are we gonna sit here an' let this *nigger* call our great-great-granddaddies *thieves*?"

Pained gasps escaped the throats of several citizens. Corny Poe had just called Dr. Parker the *n-word!* In *public!* Corny Poe, who supposedly stood for Christian Love, Do Unto Others, and Love Thy Neighbor! Raleigh Poe stood up next to his son and waved his fists into the air, shouting his support. Henry Bailey leaped up to the podium and screamed for Bull McArdle to remove Corny from the meeting. Forrestine Culpepper fanned herself and loudly mumbled the Lord's Prayer. The Peaceful Slumber Room was in total turmoil, despite Mayor Gooch's gavel-banging attempts to maintain control.

"CORNY! EVER'BODY! YA'LL SET DOWN! You're outta ORDER!"

Hizzoner the Mayor suddenly stood on top of one of the dais's card tables and whistled a piercing note through his two front teeth. Ears in the Peaceful Slumber room were quickly covered, seats were taken. Barney wildly pointed his gavel directly at Corny Poe, and nearly fell off the card table in the process.

"Now you owe Doc Parker an 'pology, Corny, or Bull McArdle will haul you off ta jail fer disruptin' the peace!"

Penni Poe hung her head in dire embarrassment. First the Policy on Fast Living...then the Sweet Jesus Sweet Potato…now this. The Poe House Grocery was gonna suffer and she'd never be able to afford to send her four children to the seminary. Penni sharply pinched her husband on his thigh, and he yelped. Corny's entire scalp burned with crimson fire, and he stammered,

"..uh...uh...I'm real sorry, Doc Parker...I didn't mean that...see my blood pressure's been actin' up agin, an' them pills Doc Kimball give me ain't workin' right...an' I'm real sorry! I 'pologize. You an' your fam'ly's real nice folks. But I just don't like to thinka *my* family as a bunch of *crooks!* I mean, ever'body knows the real crooks 'round here are them Baileys! Any stealin's been done here, it's by their doin'!"

Avery and Diana Parker exchanged tight-lipped glances, and Dr. Parker raised his hand. "Apology accepted, Mr. Poe. I should have placed myself in your shoes and thought twice before I opened my mouth. I don't mean to imply that your relatives might have been, uh, anything but the honorable soldiers they *must* have been. As to your accusation of the Bailey family, Mr. Poe, a colleague of mine may have stumbled upon evidence quite to the contrary. We may all shortly learn that the Baileys of Chestnut Ridge have been done many grave injustices and that they may in fact be descended from a revered Virginia family."

For a split-second the Peaceful Slumber Room was again silent, but then howls of laughter rocked the air. People held their sides and doubled over, pointing at Henry Bailey, who ran from the room with Euladean behind him. Sixteen-year-old Peter Paul Culpepper, quiet, bookish son of Reverend Cameron and Forrestine, raised his hand, and the Mayor motioned in his direction, thankful to perhaps change the subject. "Yes, Peter Paul. Stand up, son!"

Peter Paul Culpepper stood, "As the Teen Section Editor of the *Chestnut Ridge Tell-All*, I'd like to spend some time with Dr. Parker and get the real story! The people have a right to *know!* What other lies and falsehoods need to be corrected, Dr. Parker? Was there a conspiracy or official cover-up of this incident? Shall I contact the *National Inquisitor* and set up an appointment? Maybe the local business owners should all redistribute their wealth to everybody in town, you know, sort of like an apology for their wrong doings?"

The room buzzed with alarm. Barney Gooch banged his gavel once more and nervously laughed. "Ha ha ha ha, Peter Paul...let's talk about this some other time, ok, son? You just sit down...now LET'S US GET BACK TA THE AGENDA..."

"Oh, Mayor...Mayor...*yoo hoo*...I *agree* with the good doctor, and where did he get his tie? Everybody in this town knows the real saga...my daddy told me that back in the sixties Mr. Richard Leigh-Lee III tried to set the record straight...course they nearly ran him out of town on a rail...up his butt! OOH! Anyway...Mayor...I request permission to speak!"

Horry Graham, sporting a bright chartreuse silk shirt and yellow-polka-dotted ascot, waved at the Mayor, who reluctantly nodded for Horry to stand.

"As a business owner in this town, as the only local epicurean expert, and as a descendant of my ancestor, town father and, *oooh, scoundrel*, Major Jebediah Horatio Graham, I must also agree with Fay Bailey! I feel it is necessary to broaden our publicity efforts! We simply must inform the masses about our little hootenanny, especially if our own version of *Peyton Place* will be unveiled! Dr. Parker's on to something! Let's bare all our dirty laundry, it'll sell, sell, sell!"

Horry hopped up to the blackboard and waved his hands wildly for everyone to pay attention. "Ya'll hush now! *Listen*...far be it from *me* to carnivalize the Festival celebration, but the Nashville papers are always hungry for a good, juicy scandal! I mean, publicity is not limited to simply stuffing flyers in a mailbox, Elspeth! I think Miss MayBelle's flashing light idea is *SUPERB*! You know, in New York City, they advertise by spelling out things in lights. And Mr. Kevin's salon in Memphis has a flashing pink neon sign that says "CURL UP AND DYE," right off of I-40!"

Horry waited for nods or signs of encouragement, but none were offered. He clapped his hands to his face with disgust at the silence of his fellow citizens. "WELL POP MY PANTIES, DIONNE WARWICK! *Kids...hello... what are we missing here?* WE need a MUSICAL...A PLAY! All the best festivals have one! In San Francisco they do opera... on ICE!"

Horry waved his hands over his head in excitement and giggled, oblivious to the suspicious stares of several citizens regarding his behavior, his suggestions, and his mode of dress. Barney Gooch rubbed a sweaty palm over an even sweatier forehead. He knew he'd never make it home in time for *Andy Griffith*.

"Well, ha ha ha, Horry, those sure are some...*ideas*, I guess, but now, 'member, folks, we just about busted our budget when we decided to stage a re-enactment o' the famous Grist Mill Repair, an' I don't see how we're gonna raise the fifteen-thousand dollars that big insur'nce company's makin' us put up for li'bil'ty at the Festival...a musical's not up our alley, son!"

"Mayor Gooch, may I be 'lowed to say somethin', as an observer?"

Hoot Graham spoke up from the extreme far-right corner of the room. A hush wafted over the audience. This was Hoot's first public appearance since his social faux pas at the Charity Masked Ball in February, where he had covertly videotaped the ball-gowned breasts of every female in attendance under the auspices of giving free screen tests, in hopes of finding a new lead in his next film.

Hoot's camerawork created quite a stir, particularly one month after the Ball, when a young boy innocently inserted what his mother believed to be a *Baby Animals* video from Roy's Tape House into the VCR, and promptly reviewed a sampling of the finest breast close-ups in modern times. When questioned by Bull McArdle, Hoot stated that in California, body cinema was meant to be shared, and that he was not responsible if Roy Quigley recognized true filmmaking genius and distributed it for the public to enjoy. Hoot was nearly booted out of town, except that Dorothy Graham personally promised to keep him under tight rein. Dorothy was determined that Hoot would document her Festival organization efforts on film, in preparation for the tribute which would surely come her way after the Festival. She had her eyes on the National Daughters of Charity Association Presidency, and a documentary detailing her lifelong community service was a requisite for entry.

As Hoot now prepared to speak, all eyes scanned the room for Margaret McArdle-Graham, who had lain suspiciously low during recent months. She stood next to her brother Bull in silence. Hoot, dressed in fatigues, a flak jacket, and a "Roy's Tape House" gimme cap (traded for the breast tape), looked around the room at once-familiar faces, whose names he could no longer remember. He let fly one of his famous aw-shucks grins.

"Now, I know I been gone from here for over twenty-five years, an' I want ya'll ta know that me an' my family's patched things up, ok? An' since I'm a successful film an' video magnet from L.A., my sister-in-law Dorothy asked me to come over an' videotape some a these Festival events. You know, my nephew Horry's got hisself a good idea, even if he ain't no snappy dresser...why don't we jus' plan us a *show*, kinda like that movie a few years back, what was it, *'Hollywood Does The Civil War*? Ya'll 'member, the one where that guy who looks like Peter Pan got all o' his friends to pose in costume, an' then he took black an' white pictures, an' then he got some famous people to read a buncha ol' letters...an' it dragged on for 'bout three weeks...anyway, ya'll can put on a show 'bout this town's history, I can tape the whole thing, an' we can SELL it ta PBS or somethin' and make some REAL MONEY! Uh, for the kids."

The Peacefully Slumbering crowd snapped to attention, it was awfully hard to hold a grudge against Hoot Graham for too long, he had such a nice smile, and he definitely had Hollywood connections, everybody said so. Mayor Gooch, intrigued by the idea of unexpected wealth in the city coffers and attention from big-time Hollywood moguls, motioned for Hoot to continue.

"Now ya'll may not believe this, but during my bigtime career in L.A., I did learn a few things 'bout directin' an' stage lightin' an' stuff, an' I'd be happy to help out...it'd be my way of payin' ya'll back for welcomin' me back home... thank ya, Dorothy, fer puttin' me up, too!"

Hoot nodded at his sister-in-law, Dorothy Graham, Festival Chairwoman, seated on the official dais next to Mayor Gooch. Dorothy was not particularly willing to expand her relationship with Hoot much past what was required to capture her Festival duties and triumphs on videotape, but she was also not one to let a perfectly good chance to accept praise in public pass her by. She nodded hesitantly.

Ruby Quigley jumped up, "Well, I shore can sew the costumes, better'n anything ya'll can git on Music Row in Nashville! My Bernina'll do rhinestones like there's no tomorra!"

Peter Paul Culpepper stood on top of his chair and announced, "Mayor, as everyone knows, my dream is to be a playwright in New York someday. And as part of my Senior English project this fall in Mrs. Diana Parker's Exceptional Students class, I'd be willing to write a play, or a musical, if Mrs. Parker would give me credit for it as my class project!"

All eyes turned to Diana Parker, who slowly stood. "Well, Peter Paul, that's quite an offer! How could I refuse such a gesture? I will grant your request on one condition...that you include in your effort several characters of color, in order to present a racially balanced, *historically accurate* viewpoint."

Most of the Chestnut Ridge citizens present clapped loudly in support of Peter Paul Culpepper's offer and Mrs. Parker's decision. They weren't exactly sure how Peter Paul would respond to Mrs. Parker's demand, however, as according to the historical account of the town founding which was posted in the City Library, there had been only three blacks living on the outskirts of Chestnut Ridge in 1863 when the 44th Regiment of the Tennessee Riders descended upon the skeleton town. But they were confident that if anybody could pull it together, Peter Paul Culpepper could. He had a way with words that could make Jesus himself sit up and pay attention. Peter Paul's self-written Christmas and Easter recitations on faith and charity and the true meaning of love had converted many a "C & E" church attendee into full-fledged, fifty-two-week-a-year members.

"Aw right, then, it's 'greed that Peter Paul Culpepper'll write up somethin' an' we'll organize a Play Committee ta work out the details. I guess we can use the High School Gym-torium for the stage. Let's keep it under thirty minutes, though Peter Paul, ok, son? Them Gym-torium bleacher seats is real uncomfterble. An' now I'm tellin' ya, we ain't got no more funds ta spend on this thing, so ya'll are gonna have ta raise the money yoursevs!"

The Mayor recognized Margaret McArdle-Graham's raised hand.

"Mayor, I'd like to nominate Mr. Hoot Graham as Executive Director of the Play Committee, tonight! He's obviously the man with the most expertise in these things!"

Margaret's eyes, hidden behind the regulation, ever-present FBI sunglasses, were full of joy at this opportunity to set her plan in motion. She had been patiently waiting for four months...well, twenty-five years and four months...for this chance. Nearly every person in the room gasped upon Margaret's suggestion, however, fearing that they were about to personally witness some kind of terrible Margaret Activity, right in here the sanctity of the Peaceful Slumber Room itself. The Mayor shelved any potential Margaret concerns in his haste to get home to *Andy Griffith* and hollered, "GREAT IDEA, Margaret! Hoot, you accept?"

Hoot Graham stood up again and shot out another aw, shucks grin. "Well, how'do, Margaret, darlin'! Good ta see ya! You're lookin' as purty as ever...I'm real honored that you can forgive an' forgit! Yessir, Mayor Gooch, I'll do it! I ACCEPT!"

The room thundered with applause. Show business had come to Chestnut Ridge! Hoot Graham! L.A. connections! Real money! Bessie Thibodeaux raised her hand, and rose to speak.

"T'ink you be needin' some lumber, for da scenery?" Bessie offered. "I gots boards behin' my shop...you haul 'em, you keep 'em, *cher!*"

A pious Corny Poe raised his hand, "On behalf of the Poe House Grocery, me an' my daddy'll donate lemonade for the rehearsals, and my wife Penni'll bake ginger snaps! Much better'n them processed snack cakes!"

Penni Poe, alarmed at Corny's generous offer of *her* baking services, glanced painfully at her husband, then smiled meekly at the crowd. Perhaps Corny could salvage his tarnished reputation with donated food and drink. Estéfan Rodriguez stood up, put one hand on his purple silk-shorted hip and glared at his fellow citizens from behind purple sequined eyeglasses.

"Mayor! *Oh Mayor!* You know I'm a legitimate actor, remember I was in that Nashville Escort Service commercial? Well, let's get *real*, I'm the only person you should consider for the lead in this play, *natch*!"

Estéfan crossed his arms with a nod and dared the citizens to challenge his claim, but an awkward silence floated over the crowd. They didn't really have much experience with escort services, or young Latinos with a penchant for sequined eyeglasses and tap shoes. To the best of their recollection, there weren't any Latinos among the Founding Fathers, either...that could be sticky. Estéfan's father, Emilio, stood sheepishly, and raised a hand toward Mayor Gooch.

"My wife and I weel clean thee heem-toreeum for free after thee practeeces and thee cho!" Emilio waved his hat at his neighbors as his wife smiled proudly. As the first and only Hispanic family in a thirty-mile radius, they were somewhat of a curiosity, particularly after their son Estéfan suddenly came out of the closet last summer. Hardworking, gentle people, they were readily and surprisingly accepted by the folks of Chestnut Ridge when they arrived in 1990, fresh from South Texas, in an effort to start a new life and own a piece of America.

Emilio and Esperanza headed North to Kentucky, to stay with a distant relative whose successful brick-laying business demanded their assistance. But Emilio and Esperanza had bigger, better dreams. They planned to open a Mexican restaurant, based on the market study they performed during their long drive from Nogales, Mexico, in which they observed that there was a severe shortage of authentic Mexican restaurants in Tennessee.

As Emilio and Esperanza drove in and out of various small towns in their search to identify an ideal restaurant site (Estéfan knew they were really lost and just using the restaurant research as an excuse), their dilapidated Chevy truck broke down just outside of Chestnut Ridge, and coincidentally their market study efforts terminated.

As parts for the truck were on backorder for two weeks, and as Miz Ethel, the proprietor of the Fluffy Pillow Motel offered them not only a room at reasonable rates but also the opportunity to join the motel's janitorial staff, Emilio and Esperanza shoved the Mexican restaurant idea aside for a few years. Soon the Rodriguez family owned their own cleaning business and a neat three-bedroom home in one of Chestnut Ridge's older neighborhoods. Business was going so well, in fact, that they were not at all concerned that their client list was increasing faster than the local labor supply; there were plenty more Rodriguez family members in South Texas, and some of them were already en route.

And aside from the nasty incident when Esperanza's accidental use of a caustic fluid ruined a section of vinyl flooring at the Poe House Grocery, causing an incensed Corny Poe to paint over the *Rodgriguez Cleaning Service* sign with the words "SPIC 'N SPANS GO HOME," the Rodriguez family for the most part enjoyed a happy, suburban lifestyle.

Emilio's attempts to indoctrinate Estéfan into the janitorial business were met with total rejection and utter distaste, however, which then resulted in Estéfan's diverse career experience as an actor, a bank teller, a housepainter, and now, the maitre d' at Chéz Horatio. Last summer, Estéfan suddenly announced that he was gay *and* that he intended to pursue a career in ice-carving. Fortunately this declaration, although it shocked his family and the town, did not result in the loss of much business for either the janitorial business or the restaurant, and Estéfan had yet to actually depart for the ice-carving circuit. Barney Gooch was now truly impressed at the feverish pitch of volunteerism within the walls of the Peaceful Slumber room.

"Well, great, 'Meelyo, 'Speranza! I'll be durn! Hear that, ya'll, ain't nobody gonna have ta clean up the Gym-torium, thanks ta 'Meelyo an' 'Speranza!"

"I'll make every Thursday *'Festival Play Day'* at the bakery, and donate sixty-percent of every pound cake I sell to the cause!" Juliette Kimball's proclamation caused muffled groans from the citizens.

Juliette, petite, green-eyed wife of Doc Kimball, ran the Sweet Things Bakery, much to the chagrin of the good doctor. She was quite scatter-brained, and with the exception of her chocolate eclairs, her other baked goods frequently suffered from total omission of key ingredients such as flour or sugar. Doc's attempts to persuade Juliette to close her business endeavor were to no avail and finally, after Dan Gastineau advised Doc to let Juliette be, since the Sweet Thing's average annual loss equaled twenty thousand dollars, a much-needed tax break for Doc, Doc decided to keep his mouth shut and let Juliette bake to her heart's content.

Juliette's pound cake was well known in Chestnut Ridge, because every Thursday, she sent three of the rock-hard delicacies to the Chestnut Ridge post office with Elspeth, who offered free samples to all postal customers. And every Thursday *night*, Horace Whitsett threw the pound cake samples in the dumpster, after he used them as doorstops while he unloaded the unsorted mailbags. Some of Elspeth's regular postal customers occasionally amused themselves by taking bets on which ingredient would be missing from this week's pound cake, but it was difficult to secure the regular services of a taster to make an official determination.

Even the Festrunk Clinic, which usually sought handouts from patrons willing to aid the sick and needy, dreaded the appearance of Juliette Kimball's bright red-paneled truck. Amelia Festrunk made it a habit to personally take possession of Juliette's baked donations, so she could then promptly send them to the medical waste incinerator, because on one occasion in April 1985, Juliette's delivery of some innocent-looking doughnuts resulted in esophageal lacerations on four patients. The resulting lawsuits would have caused the total collapse of the Festrunk facility, had it not been for the swift intervention of Richard Leigh-Lee IV and his legal experts who determined that as said dessert was not printed on the hospital menu, it was therefore not an officially sanctioned patient selection, and all resulting claims were thus null and void.

Barney Gooch banged his Mayor's gavel in an effort to stifle some of the rising excitement exhibited by the citizens at their decision to stage a theatrical extravaganza. He glanced at the Agenda, took a deep breath, and said in his most sincere voice,

"Why, thank you, Miz Juliette! Ain't that great, folks? I'm sure we'll all do our part an' go get those pound cakes, now won't we? An' I'm sure Doc Kimball supports Miz Juliette's offer, and that he'll lend his services as well, if ya'll catch my meanin'! "

Mayor Gooch's head throbbed; he was really concerned that this meeting would never end. "Aw right, what's next on the 'genda, Miz Dorothy?"

Dorothy Graham smoothed her helmet of platinum hair, adjusted bifocals and read aloud, "Police and Fire Protection Services Discussion." As she looked around the room for the Chiefs McArdle, Dorothy grabbed the Mayor's gavel and banged it on the card table in front of her. Barney Gooch leaned over and whispered politely in Dorothy's direction.

"Uh...Miz Dorothy, that's the 'ficial Mayor Gavel, an' you really shouldn't use it, ma'am. Only the Mayor can bang that gavel, *ok*? BULL, BILL MCARDLE...WHERE ARE YA'LL? TIME'S A-WASTIN'!"

"*YO, MAYOR*! Bill's over ta the station, workin' a five-oh-three, but I represent botha us." Bull raised his solid frame from its perch against the back wall of the Peaceful Slumber Room. He had selected this location as it conveniently offered an optimum view of Fay Bailey and her leopard-skin tube top. Dorothy Graham peered over her bifocals at Bull and spoke in a perturbed voice,

"Chief McArdle, can you elaborate for us please, your plans to protect the safety of our citizens and our property during the week-long festival activities? And I do hope they are significantly more detailed than the so-called security plans you provided for the Masked Ball...trained monkeys could have performed better, and last year...well, don't get me started!"

Dorothy Graham squarely eyed Ruby and Roy Quigley, remembering the stolen body of Mr. Hanes, and then briefly focused her gaze on Roland Gastineau, seated in the fifth row. Izzy Gastineau patted her son's leg and smiled solidly at Madame Chairwoman.

"Well, Miz Graham, Mayor, we ain't really got no 'ficial Plan or nothin', but ya'll have my word that we done hired some extra boys from Murfreesboro for the Festival. Now, they're gonna cost ya, 'bout eighteen dollars an hour, I figure, an' that'll be, let's see, ten boys for eight hours on Saturday, an' then twenty boys for sixteen hours times eighteen an hour times four days...well, Miz Graham, that'll be a *bunch*! Heh, heh, ya'll best bring yer checkbooks!"

Dorothy Graham crossed her arms and frowned, "Mayor, the Safety Committee specifically requested a written evacuation plan for these events, to prevent any accidents or injuries! Mayor, I am sorely disappointed in the casual attitude our Chief of Police is taking, as usual, and I expect you to address this at once!"

Mayor Gooch was a tad fed-up with Dorothy Graham's attempts to constantly take control of his Festival, chairperson or no chairperson. "Well, now, Miz Dorothy, I'm sure these boys got somethin' figured out, they come from a long line of pro-fessional law en-forcers, an' I reckon it'll all be ok, won't it Bull!"

"Mayor, I *insist* there be a formal, written plan of action, including emergency evacuation, and that it be submitted in triplicate to the Festival Committee chairperson by next Tuesday!"

"Uh... Miz Graham, ain't *you* the Festival chairperson, ma'am?"

Dorothy Graham removed her bifocals and stared at Bull McArdle with a squint. "Yes, Chief McArdle, you know that I am. *Why*?"

"Well, 'cause I jus' think that since we're sittin' here, an' all, well, ma'am, that we can jus' discuss this rashnul-like, an' I can draw somethin' on that chalkboard over there, if ya want. Now, it won't be in triplicate or nothin', 'less ya'll can find me two more chalkboards!"

Howls of laughter rocked the room as the crowd watched Dorothy Graham for a terse retort. Bull McArdle hitched up his official issue Sansabelt police slacks and hulked over to the chalkboard. He wiped the words "HISTORY" and "TRUTH" away with one palm, which he then promptly wiped on one leg of his Sansabelts. He picked up one of the broken pieces of gold chalk, but then substituted it for an unbroken piece out of the box, as Ruby Quigley silently fumed. Bull drew a circle and some arrows on the chalkboard with a flourish.

"See, here, Miz Graham, it really ain't too complicated, follow 'long now...this whole Festival's gonna take place over t' the High Schoo', in the ball fiel', an' there's lotsa ample parking all *'round* the ball fiel', so's we figure anybody needs ta *'vacuate*, all they gotta do is get in their *car*... start the *engine*...an' *LEAVE!*"

Another loud round of laughter circled the room as Dorothy Graham grabbed the gavel from Mayor Gooch's fat, sweaty palm and banged it wildly on the table once again.

"CHIEF MCARDLE, I WARN YOU THAT AS FESTIVAL CHAIRPERSON, I WILL NOT BE RESPONSIBLE IF THERE IS A DIRE EMERGENCY, AND IF SOMEONE IS KILLED IN THEIR EFFORTS TO EVACUATE! WHAT ON EARTH DO WE PAY YOU FOR IF YOU CAN'T EVEN DEVISE A SIMPLE LITTLE PLAN TO PROTECT OUR LIVES? WHAT IF A TERRORIST PLANTS A BOMB? WHAT IF THE PAGEANT CONTESTANTS ARE KIDNAPPED?"

Tiffany Noel Leigh-Lee, seated next to Forrestine Culpepper, gasped at the prospect of being kidnapped from the Sons of Glory Festival Queen Pageant, but Forrestine patted her leg in silence. Horry Graham stood up, pointed at his mother, cupped a hand to the side of his mouth, and shouted to the crowd, "Chief McArdle, ignore that girl! She's been having a terrible time with the change lately, and her hormones are totally out of control!"

Bull McArdle turned beet red at the mention of female hormones, and as the meeting attendees continued to laugh, Mayor Gooch seized the gavel from a horrified Dorothy and attempted to take over once again.

"ORDER! ORDER! YA'LL SHUT UP RIGHT NOW!!!"

"IT'S HORMONES, ALL RIGHT, SPELLED W-H-O-R-E M-O-A-N, THE GRUMPY BITCH! SHE'S TRYING TO POISON ME, TOO!"

Mother Nell Graham waved a wobbly arm at Dorothy from her tethered wheelchair.

"*Mr. Mayor*, should I strike those last comments from the official Ad Hoc committee meeting minutes? This is most certainly *not* a biology class and I do not believe that bodily hormones are on the agenda!"

Miss Eustacia Gober, legal secretary by day and Festival Scribe by night, waited for a response from the Mayor. She was positive that comments regarding hormones were totally unnecessary and inappropriate.

"Yes, Miz Gober...strike away, please! Miz Dorothy, thank you fer yer respectful 'pinion, we'll see what we can do 'bout a 'vacuation plan, right, Chief? Miz Dorothy an' me'll get with ya tomorra, Bull. An' Horry, that's no way ta talk 'bout yore momma, son! Now, what's next...yes, Miz Forrestine?"

Forrestine Culpepper patted her towering beehive hairdo, stood, smiled and waved at the audience, as she instructed all her Culpepper Beauty students to do, prior to addressing any group, no matter how large or small.

"Mr. Mayor, *thank you!* I would just like to say that with all this talk of billboards and police protection and plays and donated baked goods, we have neglected what is of course the most important aspect of the Festival week! The Chestnut Ridge Sons of Glory Festival Queen Pageant! And, most importantly, the Miss American Beauty Pageant's broadcast at the close of the Festival. May we *please* concentrate on this for a few moments, your honor, as it represents so much to so many young impressionable women, future voting citizens of this town?"

Mayor Gooch, momentarily sidetracked by a glimpse of Fay Bailey adjusting her leopard-skin tube top, shook his head. "Now Miz Forrestine, you know we gotta stick ta the 'genda, and next on the 'genda is the 'ficial readin' o' the Festival Schedule. We'll come back ta you in a minute...maybe...Miz Izzy Gastineau, please read off yore list, ma'am!"

Izzy approached the podium, carrying what appeared to be an entire ream of paper, far too many pages for the comfort of the fidgeting audience.

"Mayor, Madame Chairperson, respected citizens of Chestnut Ridge. I hold in my hands the final, approved Schedule of Events for Sons of Glory Festival Week, and have made sufficient Xerox copies, at no charge, I might add, thanks to the donation of Gastineau & Gastineau, CPAs. If my son Roland will please distribute the copies, we can all follow along."

The crowd reluctantly took copies of Izzy's Schedule of Events and settled in for the reading. Izzy forgot that her bifocals hung from a chain around her neck, thus she was forced to hold the Schedule of Events at arm's length in order to read it. She cleared her throat and spoke in an official voice,

"DAY ONE, Friday, December 29, Grand Opening Parade down Main Street, ten o'clock *sharp*, followed by Keynote Address, Dr. Avery Parker Junior. Grist Mill Repair Re-enactment, eleven o'clock, *sharp*! Lunch on the Festival Grounds and associated post-Christmas Crafts Fair will begin at noon and continue throughout the Festival! In case of inclement weather, and I do not mean *cold* weather, but rain or snow *only*, all outdoor activities *except* the Grist Mill Repair Re-enactment will move into the high school gym-torium! Chestnut Ridge Elementary School Historical Fathers Spaghetti Supper, six o'clock *sharp!* Festival Queen Debutante Presentation and Dinner/Dance, catered by Chéz Horatio, by reservation only, black tie, admission fifty dollars per couple, eight o'clock *sharp*!"

Izzy paused to look around the room, satisfied that there were no questions or concerns, and that everyone was following her meticulously prepared schedule of events. As she droned on with her reading, Billy Gooch, the Mayor's twelve-year old son, sleepily fell over in his chair. Billy wore an orange hunter's cap with the flaps stuck out perpendicular to his head, in direct defiance of his mother, who had previously instructed him to remove his cap when inside the Quigley Funeral Parlor. Billy was seated next to his best friend, Rex Parker, the son of the eloquent and scholarly Dr. Avery Parker, Jr. Suddenly Billy woke up and loudly whispered in Rex's face and slapped his leg.

"Whuh? Hey, *homey*, I done fell asleep!"

Rex, an excellent student, was very well-mannered, but since the beginning of summer break, he had lapsed into very low-rung behavior after spending all his free time with Billy, a grave concern to Rex's parents.

"Yeah, you weenie! Hey, *Honky!* What'd you do with my marbles?" Rex's loud whispers caught the attention of his mother, Diana, who frowned in reproach.

"DURN! I forgot! I'll bring 'em to ya tomorrow, an' we can git us some worms and go fishin'!" Billy scratched his ear and then waved his waxy finger in Rex's face. Rex grimaced and hit Billy's knee.

"I can't, I told ya! I'm three chapters behind in my Swahili Home Schooling course, an' if I don't catch up, I'll have to spend all summer in Chicago with my stupid ol' aunt and go to some stupid African-American summer school! Now go on and go fishing by yourself — quit waiting on me! Maybe next week I can go!"

"Ah, shoot, Rex, it ain't no fun fishin' by myself! Whaddya learnin' Sweeli for anyhow...ya'll goin' on a trip to Sweeli-land or somethin'? Cain't you listen to a Sweeli tape in the car or somethin', 'steada havin' ta do all this book-learnin' every day? Man, we sit our butts in school all day, and then ya gotta come home an' learn some more! It's summer, homey! Can't you jus' go fishin' for a half hour?"

Billy tugged on the zipper of his camouflaged, down-filled hunter's vest, which he wore despite the fact that it was not hunting season, and that it was approximately eighty degrees inside the Peaceful Slumber Room. Billy Gooch's bulky frame was a carbon copy of his father Barney's, except that he had a great deal more hair.

"Homey, you're missin' out! I stole my daddy's new jigs outta his tackle box, and I was hopin' you'd help me break 'em in! I mean, it's not every day you get to try the latest Am-Bass-Adore jigs! Come on, *boy*, where's your guts?"

Rex frowned at Billy. "What'd I tell you 'bout callin' me that? My dad says that's disrespectful, to call blacks *'boy'*, and I don't like it! Maybe I *will* jus' stay home an' study all summer!"

Izzy Gastineau dutifully continued from the front of the room as the crowd restlessly followed their handouts. Billy punched Rex on the arm. "Hey, homey, I tole you 'bout 'boy'! My daddy says that the only time ya'll should take offense ta that is when somebody's givin' ya'll an order or somethin', like *'Hey, boy, fetch me some more tea!'* It don't mean nothin', man! Oh, I done forgot...can you lend me five bucks? I gotta get me some gum, and I done spent all my 'llowance when we went to the movies yesterday!"

Rex fished around in the pocket of his neatly creased khakis. "Here...I got a dollar-seventy-five...nope, that's all I got to spare!"

Rex quickly handed Billy the money before his mother caught sight of the loan. "You'd better pay me back by next week, you hear? You *promise*, Billy? You *swear*? Swear on Mary Alice Peterson's titties?"

Billy made a cross over his heart. "I swear all right, but I ain't gonna swear on no stupid girl's titties! Mary Alice Peterson ain't even got no titties, Rex! Why you always got to bring her up? You oughta jus' forgit her...You know's well as I do no black man can truck with no white woman!"

Suddenly, Rex felt his father's strong fingers around his upper arm, and he saw his father's angry face immediately in front of his own. "*Son, if you and Billy don't hush, you will be severely punished when we return home! Now lower your voices! We are gonna have a talk, young man...I don't like the things I hear coming out of your mouth! I think a few weeks in Chicago will take care of that, plain and simple!*"

Rex nodded at his father's stern words and motioned for Billy to keep quiet. His goose was cooked. Chicago was a done deal. No more fishing with Billy...no more *Playboy* magazines down by the woods...no more cigarettes behind Billy's dad's workshop. He was never gonna fit in around here if his father kept treating him like the nerd most people besides Billy said he was! Billy, bored with Rex's mandated silence, thumped Rex on the knee and quickly dashed out of the room. Rex didn't care if his parents said Billy was a no-good redneck...he and Billy were best friends for life, and no summer in Chicago could ever change that.

Izzy Gastineau completed her official duties and breathlessly folded the Schedule of Events and prepared to leave the podium, when Forrestine Culpepper interrupted her.

"*Excuse me*, Isidore...again, let's not forget that at that point, the festivities are by no means *over*! The Miss American Beauty Pageant will take place in our town, will be nationally televised, and will be most likely won by one of our fair beautiful Chestnut Ridge maidens! And many of our young, impressionable schoolchildren, who are coincidentally students of the Forrestine Culpepper School of Beauty & Pageant Instruction, will participate in a musical number dedicated to our glorious town. Trust me, this is *not* something to miss!"

Izzy nodded and made a note on her copy of the Schedule of Events. "Correct, Forrestine, I shall add that immediately! Will attendance be open to everyone, and is there an admission charge?"

Forrestine, dutifully pleased at this fortunate turn of the topic in her favor, displayed a large white leather portfolio emblazoned with a bright red rose and the words "MISS AMERICAN BEAUTY PAGEANT."

"*Naturally*, as I have been instrumental in bringing this event to our town, I have been appointed as the official ticket sales representative for the state of Tennessee. This is, of course, one of the most popular televised events of the year, and as it will be the first beauty pageant event of the new millennium, let me strongly suggest that if any of you wish to participate in this historic occasion, you see me immediately after this meeting. Tickets are seventy-five dollars each, cash only."

Mayor Gooch nodded. "Miz Izzy, I reckon you'll have to revise that fine schedule anyhow, seein' as how we're gonna insert a musical extravaganza inta the week, somewheres! Any suggestions?"

Horry Graham waved his arm in the air. "Let's just *bag* the Community Millennium Party on Sunday and have the play then. I mean, parties for the masses just don't work! They are a catering disaster!"

Fay Bailey stood up one hand on her hip, and pointed her emery board at Forrestine Culpepper in emphasis. "Hey, shut up, you green-shirted doughboy! I wanna have me a kick-ass millennium party in this town like ever'-body else is havin' in this whole danged country! Hell, that's the only reason we're havin' this Festival over New Year's, 'steada in the middle a January when this danged town was really started up!"

Fay, pleased with herself for having drawn attention to what she considered a major issue, tugged at her tube top and waved her arms. "Naw, I say let's jus' cancel the whole damned Festival Queen pageant anyhow, ya'll know Chastity Weatherford's gonna win it lock, stock and barrel...ain't nobody give a care 'bout all them debataunts...let's just have us that Mrs. Chestnut Ridge pageant and be done with it! Ya'll ain't gonna b'lieve my talent act, nossir!"

In her chair next to Forrestine Culpepper, Tiffany Noel Leigh-Lee gasped for air and gripped Miss Forrestine's arm like a vise. "*Miss Forrestine!*" she whispered harshly, "You said Chastity Weatherford wasn't going to *enter* the Festival Queen pageant! You said she already had enough regional titles to enter Miss American Beauty *without* this one! I can't believe Chastity Weatherford's going to try and steal my crown!" Tiffany Noel's eyes brimmed with tears.

"Now, now, Tiffany Noel! Please do not cry in public, you'll cause a scene, and run your mascara! I had absolutely no idea Chastity Weatherford intended to participate in this pageant, and I will most certainly get to the bottom of this after the meeting! Dry your eyes, child, people are staring!" Forrestine Culpepper silently asked God to quickly reveal the Hidden Purpose of this most recent Challenge, but received no immediate reply.

"Miz Bailey, please sit down, an' stop wavin' that nail file at me! We ain't gonna cancel no beauty pageants, I ain't gonna break no little girls' hearts, heh-heh, I done enough a that when I was in high schoo'! I think Horry's idea is a right good one, so's let's us take a vote! All-in-favor a cancelin' the town Millennium Party say-aye!"

"AYE!" The bulk of the crowd responded, primarily out of staunch opposition to Fay Bailey, and because they had no other ideas and were ready to leave. Fay stomped her feet and pointed a red-nailed finger at Forrestine Culpepper.

"Miz Izzy, please amend yore 'genda to 'flect the addition of the play an' the cancellin' a the party. An' if Miz Fay Bailey cain't keep her comments ta herself, Chief McArdle can escort Miz Bailey outta the meetin'!"

This was glorious news to Chief McArdle, who had been admiring Fay Bailey's shapely behind, packed into black spandex pants, for over an hour. Regretfully, Fay Bailey had no more to say, and thus no further reason to stand, or be removed by Chief McArdle.

"Now, any final bizness we need ta 'tend to?" Mayor Gooch had missed *Andy Griffith*, but if he hurried, he could just catch *Mayberry RFD*.

"Barney Gooch! Don't fergit 'bout that proposition I suggested last meetin'!" Ruby Quigley waved both arms frantically over her head at the Mayor, who tiredly nodded,

"Oh. Aw right... Ruby...go 'head!"

"Well, I think it's real important that we reca-nize the bizness people in this town, an' their efferts ta help with the Festival! I still think it'd be a good idea ta do like what they do with th' Olympics, you know, have "O-FFICIAL" stickers made fer the bizness windas, so's people knows they're tradin' at places that support the Festival. Ya know, like, 'Quigley Realty, O-FICIAL FESTIVAL REALTOR', an' 'Quigley Quick-Steak, O-FFICIAL FESTIVAL FAST FOOD,' an' 'Quigley Funeral Parlor, O-FFICIAL FESTIVAL MORTICIANS' an' all!"

"Ruby...if *you* wanna be in charge of somethin' like that, go right ahead! But I'll remind ya ta be fair about decidin' who gets ta be *Official*, and who gets to be *Ordinary!* I better not see all them 'ficial Bizness stickers on every Quigley-owned door in Chestnut Ridge! All in favor of Ruby Quigley headin' up the Official Festival Bizness Sticker Committee, with Bessie Thibodeaux as co-chairman, to keep it honest, say 'AYE'!"

"AYE!" the attendees responded, even if they did think that it was courting tragedy to designate an Official Festival Mortician. Bessie Thibodeaux, surprised at the Mayor's assignment of her person to a committee without her permission, said nothing, but smiled at Ruby Quigley. Roland Gastineau stretched his long legs and sighed, as his mother patted his knee absent-mindedly.

"Mom...how much longer is this ridiculous excuse for a meeting gonna continue? I'm really beat, and I've got a six a.m. breakfast meeting with a new client tomorrow!"

Izzy Gastineau leaned over to whisper in Roland's ear, "OH! There are my glasses! Well, anyway, Roland, just a few more minutes, dear, and then we'll be home. This means so much to your father!"

"But Mom, it's nearly ten o'clock and I haven't said anything yet! Maybe we should raise our hands and just go to it..."

"LAST ON THE 'GENDA IS MR. ROLAND D. GASTINEAU, NEW PARDNER, GASTINEAU & GASTINEAU, CPAs. MR. GASTINEAU, PLEASE."

Barney pursed his lips. He knew that Roland Gastineau was an innocent young man, and that it had been the whiskey working Roland's legs as he cavorted with Betty at last year's Masked Ball. But it was a blow to a man's ego when his own wife slept with another man's bow tie under her pillow.

"MR. GASTINEAU....Oh! There ya are! Yer up, son! Let's go! Hit's gittin' late!"

Roland ran fingers through his thick hair, smoothed his suitcoat, and stood. "Thank you, Mayor Gooch!"

He walked over to the gilt-laden blackboard, but much to Ruby Quigley's relief, did not reach for any chalk. He cleared his throat, a handsome, strong young throat, observed Fay Bailey. From her chair in the last row, Danita Kay Leigh-Lee also took note of Roland. Their one and only date at the Masked Ball in February caused Danita Kay to spend every night since thinking of Roland and his charms. He'd been the perfect gentleman...so suave, so funny, so strong...and he smelled so good. They'd enjoyed only two glorious dances, but that was fine with her. She would have sat down in the dirt at his feet, just to be with Roland, and just to gaze at his amazing face.

But there was no way she could ever let anyone know her true feelings...she was an attorney, she would inherit her father's firm, she was expected to remain steadfast, be the smart one. And she knew she was no beauty like her sister Tiffany, so it was pretty easy to pretend that she didn't really ever care to fall in love or get married. But as Roland spoke, Danita Kay melted in silence.

"Ladies and gentleman, I would like to present an offer from the firm of Gastineau and Gastineau, CPAs, toward the financial liquidity of this festival. Now, as many of you already know, I joined my father's company last spring, as a full partner, and now I am a fully licensed certified public accountant."

Roland glanced at Izzy, who beamed with pride. "Well, I'm a firm believer that a man should contribute something back to the town that gave him a good foundation, helped raise him. And to that end, I would like to offer my services to the Sons of Glory Festival...I will be happy to donate my time to keep the books and record the proceeds of this great event, and then file appropriate tax reports with the IRS. My rough estimates, which the Mayor and Mrs. Graham have, in *triplicate,* I might add, show that I'm offering to give the equivalent of ten-thousand dollars' worth of my time, free of charge."

Loud "oh my's" and "how nices" danced around the room and finally someone broke into applause. Roland blushed and lowered his eyes, but then smiled and waved for the clapping to stop.

"Please, ladies and gentleman, this is a small token of what I can do to help this community! I will set up a special Festival Accounting office in a location of the committee's choosing, and I'd like a few volunteers to help me with some of the initial tasks...anyone who is interested please let Mrs. Graham know as soon as possible. Thanks."

Roland walked back to his chair during more thunderous applause. Maybe now his father would be satisfied that Roland's post-Confession, post-Mistake debts were paid in full. In any case, Roland liked to please his mother, and the present glow on her face was worth a few boring weeks working with the Festival morons. As he took his seat, Roland noticed the sea of waving female hands that immediately raised at his request for volunteers.

"MAYOR! SIR! I'LL VOLUNTEER! I'LL HELP ROLAND! PLEASE SIGN ME UP, MRS. GRAHAM!"

A bevy of loud, female voices crushed the air of the Peaceful Slumber room, and Mayor Gooch banged his gavel repeatedly for order. Roland's shoulders slacked as he realized he was the subject of the commotion, and he turned to stare at his mother,

"*Great!* Did you see that? Fay Bailey raised her hand, Mom! Wow, I really get the pick of the litter in this town! First I had to take the Frump Queen to the Masked Ball, where she spilled champagne all over my jacket because she's blind as a bat, then she called me every day asking to borrow my CPA books! And now I've got Mrs. Five Time Alimony in Spandex on my committee! Mom, *help me!*"

Izzy Gastineau patted her son lovingly on his broad shoulder. "Fay Bailey is harmless, she'll lose interest right away, and Roland, I do wish you wouldn't speak of Danita Kay like that. She is such a *nice* girl… and blonde...you said yourself you have a thing for blondes! Maybe you should look beyond Danita Kay's appearance, and into her soul!"

Roland slapped his knee and said in a low voice. "Mom, it's pretty damned hard to get past those big Coke bottles starin' me in the face, let alone try and find her *soul!*"

He crossed his arms and pouted like a child, silently fuming. Izzy perused her copy of the Meeting Agenda.

"Barney...Barney...BARNEY!"

Betty Gooch shouted from the back of the room where she had been arguing with her son Billy over the forbidden hunting cap. Her husband pretended to ignore her, but finally caved in,

"Ma'am, if you wish to speak, then please 'dress me with my 'fficial title!"

Barney Gooch banged the gavel and waited for an angry Betty to stand. Eustacia Gober stopped her note-taking to determine whether Betty's protocol error would be corrected, or whether she would have to intervene in the interest of proper parliamentary procedure.

"Well, excuse me, *Mister High and Mighty Mayor, sir,* but I been wavin' my hand back here for ten minutes and you been ignorin' me just like you do at home! What I'm tryin' to say is that I wanna sit on Roland's Tax Committee! I'm good with manipulations, you know!"

The Peaceful Slumber room exploded with loud guffaws. A red-faced Barney Gooch cocked his head angrily in Betty's direction and leaned on the wooden podium, which wobbled precariously.

"Yes, ma'am, I do believe ever'body in this here room's done already seen how you're good with manipulations! I think the best place fer you ta sit is at *home,* with yer husband! Now, next on the 'Genda…"

Betty rolled her eyes and ignored Barney. "Excuse me, Mayor...but I am not speaking to *you*...Miz Graham, please sign me up for Roland's Tax Committee...is that a *problem?*"

Dorothy Graham looked over her bifocals at Betty and then looked at Barney, who was angrily drumming his fingers on the podium. She turned toward the other members of the Sons of Glory Festival seated at the dais. Betty Gooch's unmitigated, lusty display with Roland Gastineau at last year's Masked Ball remained the top incident in the town's annals of inappropriate behavior, but it was not her place to tell Betty to back down.

"Why, *thank* you, Betty, you can go down on the Tax Committee...I mean...I'm sure Roland would *love* to have you...uh, Betty...please see Roland after this meeting to feel him out on, uh, *just see Roland after this meeting!*"

Barney Gooch slammed the gavel down on the podium with such force that the handle broke off, the hammer flew across the room, and landed in Forrestine Culpepper's beehive hairdo.

She screamed, "WELL! I HAVE NEVER IN MY LIFE BEEN TREATED SO RUDELY! FIRST INSULTED, THEN IGNORED, AND NOW *ASSAULTED!* AS FAR AS I'M CONCERNED THIS MEETING IS OVER!"

Forrestine grabbed her black patent leather purse and her "MISS AMERICAN BEAUTY PAGEANT" portfolio, and prissed away in a flash, with the majority of the gavel still stuck in her hair. All eyes watched her go, and then they turned to look at Tiffany Noel Leigh-Lee, who was most perplexed. There was no chapter in the Forrestine Culpepper Beauty & Pageant Instruction Curriculum on What to Do When Your Mentor Storms Out of An Important Public Gathering With A Gavel Stuck In Her Hair.

"THAT'S IT! MEETING ADJOURNED!" Barney Gooch pounded what was left of the gavel on the wooden podium with a barely audible thud. "BETTY! YOU COME UP HERE RIGHT NOW! LEAVE, EVER'BODY! ADJOURNED! GO HOME! BETTY! *BETTY!*"

Betty did most certainly not go up front toward her husband. She sent Billy outside into the warm spring night with the car keys, and then she marched right over to a sheepish Roland Gastineau, who remained seated in his gold-vinyl chair next to his mother, in an effort to avoid just such a confrontation. Barney tried to catch Betty, but he was overwhelmed by a mob of ladies from the Chestnut Ridge Morality Foundation who wished to express their distaste at the lack of dress code restrictions during city meetings. Izzy Gastineau stood up to talk with Juliette Kimball, and Betty held her hand out to Roland and whispered,

"*Roland!* You're so sweet to donate your time like this! Now anything you need, you just holler, ok? Let's get together tomorrow night, just us, at the Quik-Steak. I can meet you at seven, we got a lot to catch up on, don't we? I'm sorry I didn't get to see you at this year's Masked Ball…I got a hold of some bad cheese dip, and I had to spend the whole night in the bathroom pukin'! Did you know that I still sleep with your bow tie under my pillow! And I bought a copy of that record, *Do Ya Think I'm Sexy!* Do you still dance?"

"*Oh, Roland,*" Fay Bailey waved and sauntered over, and nudged Betty Gooch out of the way, vying for Roland's attention. "Whaddya say we have us the first committee meetin' at my place? On Tuesday…oh, I'm so sorry, Betty…I forgot that's yer bowlin' night…guess you'll have ta miss!"

"Excuse me, Mrs. Gooch, Ms. Bailey."

Danita Kay Leigh-Lee sat down next to Roland and shoved massively thick eyeglasses far up on her nose as she perused her computerized personal organizer, unaware of Roland's previous propositions.

"Roland, I'd like to volunteer to be on your committee, so I may monitor the accounting process, if you don't mind. I'm studying for my CPA, you know, and I'd like to observe the intricacies of charity work. I'd like to suggest a lunch meeting, at Leigh-Lee & Sons, we'll foot the bill, of course, say tomorrow at noon?"

Roland quickly clapped Danita Kay on the back, a most unexpected heroine rescuing him from the clutches of Betty and Fay. "Hey, great, Danita Kay, *great!* The more, the merrier! Betty, Fay, just meet us there at noon, and look, if there's anybody else you wanna add to this committee, just tell me, I've got plenty of room on my dance card!"

Roland laughed skittishly and then said, "I mean, there's a great deal of *work* to be done to properly record Festival finances!"

He ran his fingers through his shiny black hair as Danita Kay closed her personal organizer and stood to leave. Betty Gooch, obviously disappointed, frowned, "Hmmm...well, I guess lunch'll be all right, but I'm more of a night person, as Roland knows. Danita Kay, I imagine you busy lawyers work most nights, don't you?"

Danita Kay removed her Coke-bottle glasses and rubbed her eyes as she shook her head,

"No, Mrs. Gooch, right now, I'm still studying for the CPA exam since Daddy's decided I should become a tax attorney, but personally, I suggest we meet during the day, it's much more professional, don't you agree, Roland?"

Roland didn't hear a single word Danita Kay said, because he was too busy staring at Danita Kay's eyeglass-less face, which to his amazement was very soft and beautiful, despite the red rings the heavy lenses made on the tops of her cheeks. *I don't remember seeing her like that before! I guess she never took off her glasses when we went to the Masked Ball...but those are the prettiest eyes I've ever seen! And what a cute little nose! With freckles!*

"*Huh?* Oh, sure, Danita Kay, whatever you think! Gotta run, see you ladies tomorrow!"

Roland dashed over to help his mother retrieve scattered Official Sons of Glory Festival Schedules from the floor. Fay Bailey sauntered off after Bull McArdle, and Betty Gooch shouldered her purse and turned to Danita Kay, who was cleaning her eyeglasses with one corner of her tailored, sensible business suit.

"Danita Kay, I know just what you're tryin' to do! I know you're tryin' to get your hooks in that boy! You know, one trip to the Masked Ball doesn't mean *a thing*. I heard Roland's daddy arranged that date anyhow, an' I sure as hell didn't see ya'll cuttin' a figure on the dance floor that night. 'Course, you *know* Roland and I go waaaay back..."

Danita Kay placed her eyeglasses back on her head and smiled a polite, professional smile. She had a speech all prepared for just such a run-in with Betty Gooch. Danita had to be very careful; no one could ever guess how much she truly desired Roland Gastineau. She couldn't bear it if people knew she wanted something they thought she could never attain.

"Mrs. Gooch, don't worry. The whole town is familiar with your interest in Roland, it is quite legendary. And yes, we did attend the Masked Ball together, because our families are old friends, but I'll let you in on a little secret. You see, I do have an interest in Roland, because he's the only person in town with enough credentials to steal my clients, and I'm not going to let that happen. I have a firm to run, and one must know one's competition, Mrs. Gooch! Good evening!"

Danita Kay click-click-clicked out of the Peaceful Slumber Room into the night. Betty Gooch breathed a sigh of relief relative to the ensured safety of her designated Young Stud. As she stepped outside, Barney's hand grabbed her shoulder,

"Hon, now look, don't go gittin' all mad at me back there...if ya wanna be on that committee, then that's jus' fine, but I 'member what happened last year, with that boy, an' how long it took ya ta get back some esteem in yer sef...now I know you was jus' *playin'* that night...it was all them beers talkin', an' I know you ain't got no feelins for that boy, right? *Right, Hon?*"

Betty Gooch crossed her fingers behind her back and looked at Barney, "Oh, Barney, really! I'm just tryin' to help a good cause, that's all. Now let's go home, Billy's waitin' in the car." Betty walked hand in hand with her husband toward the parking lot and silently mused, *and if my sexual satisfaction ain't a good cause, then I'll be damned if I know what is...*

CHAPTER TWELVE – WHEELS IN MOTION

Late May, 1999; Amelia Festrunk's Apartment

"No, Doctor Gray, I'm not angry…just disappointed. For two months I've looked forward to meeting with you…of course now that I'm retired it's certainly no skin off my nose that you have twice cancelled your trip here. A startling discovery? Well, yes, Doctor Parker did mention something about that at a civic meeting last month…no, I wasn't present but I did read his account in our pitiful little excuse for a newspaper. Really? My, yes, that is *quite* an impactful ruling. A federal judge? Goodness, they are serious aren't they? This family must be paying you well…no, I don't mean to imply…certainly I realize your career is also on the line. Yes, of course that's good news! I expect it will take something like that to prove the circumstances and the story. This kind of revelation won't be taken lightly here, believe me. Have I spoken of this to anyone? Doctor Gray, you may be assured I am the personification of secrecy. Yes, I realize this is your life's work…do you not also see that this announcement will most likely affect my life and many others? And now with a federal judge's intervention…gracious me, this is far more than I ever imagined…any other witnesses? No, there weren't…but I do have a friend… a friend since childhood. She was privy to all my secrets and I to hers. However she is quite demented, I'm afraid and…yes, she's the one I mentioned. Yes, I'll keep trying. My schedule for the fall? I have no plans for travel, if that's what you mean. Yes, I think that would be a fine time for you to make a trip here…I shall write it in *pencil,* Doctor, in case it changes. Yes, to you as well, Doctor, *good day.*"

A shaken Amelia Festrunk hung up the phone in her tiny apartment kitchen. MayBelle and Leonard were out test-driving cars with Henry Bailey and she'd taken the opportunity to check in with the genealogy professor in Virginia, much to her dismay.

Not coming until fall because she needs more time to verify new facts! Amazing facts! And she's sworn me to secrecy until she arrives because there's a federal judge involved! Granddaddy…this has your handprint all over it…how on earth can I sit still while everybody's getting ready to put on costumes and playact in what they believe to be the true story of the founding of this town! Well, I have no choice. A few more months won't matter a hill of beans, unless I drop dead or get hit by a bus, but I bet you've got that all taken care of, don't you? Oh, Granddaddy…I'm scared. This is really getting serious. I don't want people to hate me like they hate Henry. I've got to talk to Nell…I've got to find a way to tell her everything. She'll back me up. I wonder if she's at home? Today's the first play rehearsal…maybe Dorothy's at play rehearsal and I can talk to Nell…

Amelia walked to her bedroom and stared at an old photograph of herself with her best friend. Their hair was in braids and they both wore navy sailor dresses with huge collars. They held hands and stared sassily at the camera, daring the photographer to capture their vivacity on film forever. Amelia caressed the photo with a brush of one hand and sighed.

Oh, Nell...I had the perfect opportunity to talk to you in private at that ridiculous reception last month...you were actually lucid and there we were sitting together at the head table while everybody was in the buffet line piling food on their plates. But then they started the speech-making and toasting and photographing and by the time it was over, you were fast asleep in your wheelchair and Will rolled you out to take you home. Every time I drop by to see you that bitch Dorothy practically slams the door in my face. Something's not right with you...I think she's doping you up to keep you out of her hair. Oh, Nell, I need to talk to you...I need you. And Leonard needs you, too. He's driving me crazy cooped up in this little apartment with nothing to do except go to the Red Cross three times a week. He's miserable...he needs something to take care of...someone to look after...he needs his son, Nell...maybe since I'm telling my big secret I should persuade you to tell yours, too...before it's too late.

Amelia went into the kitchen and poured herself a glass of iced tea, then sat on the front porch swing to wait for MayBelle and Leonard. The heat steamed off the Clinic courtyard, much too stifling for May. *'Gonna be a hot one, 'Melie'.*..Granddaddy said that every morning of the summer, rain or shine. As if somehow stating the obvious would make it more tolerable.

She glanced up as she heard a car door slam; Leonard's unmistakable shuffle and the heavy thud of MayBelle's pink pumps grew louder as they came up the courtyard sidewalk to the front porch. MayBelle's face was bright with excitement, like a child on Christmas morning.

"Oh, 'Melie! We did it! We found the perfect car for me, and the perfect truck for Leonard! That Henry Bailey is the nicest man! I think we must have looked at every car in the county, but Henry, he didn't complain once. Come see, 'Melie...I'm so excited! A brand new Cadillac Coupe! Well, it's not *exactly* brand new...it's two years old, but Leonard says it's "cherry," whatever that means. And guess what? It's *pink*! What are the chances? Henry told me you wanted me to have a brand new car, but I told him I'd rather take pink and used than new and blue! Come on, 'Melie, let's go have a look-see and you come with me to the Poe House...but first I'm gonna pull right into that uppity AnnElise's circle driveway and honk my new horn about three hundred times, just because I can! Come on!"

Leonard winked at Amelia and nodded. "Yep, 'Melie, it's a doozy! MayBelle's gonna have ever' bach'ler in fifty miles a here comin' 'round ta go fer a spin! Got big whitewalls, too! 'At Henry, he's a good egg, I reckon. An' he done waived the sales tax…he knows how I ain't payin' no taxes ta no fed'ral gov'ment!"

Amelia smiled at her beaming, elderly siblings, wondering when they had all grown so old. "Leonard…did you get a truck?"

Leonard shrugged his shoulders. "It's nothin' but a Ford, jus' like always…I tole Henry I ain't havin' none a them foreign cars…yep, a Ford's good 'nuff fer me, I reckon. She's a beaut…gotta big engine an' the radio works real good…but I ain't havin' none a them 'lectric windas or doodads…I tole Henry I ain't a fancy man like him. Yep, she's only got twelve thousand miles on 'er…Henry got 'er offa some lady in Antioch done dropped daid of a heart 'tack, it's near as new an' no new-car taxes ta boot! Come on, 'Melie, let's us go see."

Amelia scooted off the front porch swing and followed Leonard and MayBelle to the Clinic's staff parking lot. MayBelle's pink Cadillac and Leonard's shiny red truck were parked side by side in the spaces marked "FESTRUNK FAMILY VEHICLES ONLY." The ancient green Pontiac rested next to the new cars in the third space. MayBelle reached with pride into her bosom and retrieved a remote keyless entry device.

"Watch this, 'Melie…" With a loud pop the Cadillac's trunk opened and the security lights blinked and flashed and the horn honked. Leonard shook his head and laughed.

"MayBelle…I tole ya not to push that red button! It's the blue button ya want, hon!"

MayBelle giggled and gingerly closed the trunk. "Oops! I forgot. There! Look inside, 'Melie! That's real leather! How do they get that leather pink, you think?"

Amelia sat down in MayBelle's new pink palace and admired all the gadgets as Leonard looked under the hood. MayBelle clapped and giggled uncontrollably. Then they followed suit in Leonard's new red truck, although there were not nearly as many appointments to be noted. MayBelle again pulled her keychain remote from the bosom of her dress.

"Well, who's riding with me to the Poe House? Anybody need anything from Gooch Office Supply? Oh, my…it doesn't seem right, all of us getting new cars, does it? We are being much too selfish…let's take them back and donate the money to the Clinic…"

Amelia smiled and waved a finger. "MayBelle, hush! We've spent every waking moment of our lives donating time and money to that Clinic and look where it got us! It's about time we have something new to be proud of and besides, we've got more money in the bank than we can ever spend even if we donate most of it to the Clinic anyway. So let's all enjoy this! Granddaddy would have, you know? No, dear, you go on by yourself, I'm a little tired. Please be careful…you're not used to driving that car yet!"

Leonard nodded. "Yep, you take it easy like I tole ya, baby sister. Later on I'll show ya how to put the gas in…'Melie, MayBelle tole me she wants ta learn herself ta put gas in it…says I been gassin' up the cars 'roun' here fer too long an' it's time she learnt it herself!"

Amelia and Leonard waved at MayBelle, who roared out of the parking lot in her new car. Amelia patted Leonard on the back. "You pay cash to Henry, Leonard? Was he excited?"

Leonard nodded and pulled a wad of bills out of his overalls. "Yep, 'Melie, I did an' he shore was. Here's what's left…he tole me ta tell ya he's still lookin' fer yer car…you shore are picky, 'Melie…fer somebody what's drivin' a train wreck. 'At Henry Bailey…he done made us a good deal. 'Melie…he's a good man…why's people laughin' at him all the time? I 'member his mama…she was a real sweet lady…ever since that day I foun' her sittin' an' cryin' back behin' the ol' incin'rator I was a friend to her an' Henry, too. They ain't never had a break their whole lives…an' that ol' dump 'partment they done lived in…I musta fixed that furnace fer her a thousan' times…Henry tole me today if it warn't fer me lookin' in on them they'd a been real bad off. Made me feel real good ta hear that, ya know, like I done somethin' important in my life, sorta like Granddaddy an' Daddy too."

Amelia swallowed hard and clenched her jaw. *Tears are not the solution, Amelia.*

"Leonard Festrunk, you are every bit the good man they were and more. I had no idea you'd been helping the Baileys all these years, but I'm really proud of you. You know Granddaddy helped them too, in his own way. I wish I'd taken more time in my life to notice people outside the Clinic who needed our assistance. I wish I'd been more like Granddaddy, and you. You two are my heroes, you know that?"

Leonard blushed and rubbed his jaw. "Aw, 'Melie, hush, it warn't nothin'. But I reckon I ain't never wanted ya ta know 'cause I's afraid you'd jus' tell me ta stop, like alla them other folks what tole me them Baileys was trash. Well, they ain't trash, 'Melie. They's good, decent people, an' I'd rather be friends with 'em than with mosta the folks in this town. Reckon ol' Henry nor his mama never made fun a me fer bein' simple-minded…they always acted like I was somebody special. It makes me sick ta see how them city fellers is treatin' Henry on that p'rade committee…they got him playin' step 'n fetchit an' goin' ever' which way an' he don't even care, he wants it so bad. It ain't right, an' that ol' Corny Poe an' Barney Gooch is what's behin' it, fer sure. All their Christian char'ty my ass…they's best be lookin' in their own backyard, huh?"

Amelia smiled and nodded at her brother. The intricate pattern of lines on his face had deepened in the weeks since he'd moved into their apartment and been relieved of his duties at the Clinic. "You know, Leonard, it's true, they have no right to judge anybody. And the older I get, the more outspoken I am, if that's possible, because I know I've always said my mind. Leonard…we need a project, and I can't think of a better one than to help Henry Bailey reclaim his dignity in this town. If Granddaddy was alive, he'd expect us to do no less. What do you think?"

Leonard lit a cigarette and took a deep drag. "'Melie, I think that's a fine idea. Course ya know I ain't the idee man in this fam'ly…you jus' tell me what ta do an' I'm in. Uh, you *got* any idees?"

Amelia Festrunk cocked her head and looked at her brother over her trifocals. "Leonard, I think I just might…I think I just might."

Early August, 1999; Fluffy Pillow Motel, Chestnut Ridge

"*INCOMING! INCOMING!*" Vietcong Choppers whirred overhead, slicing the thick jungle air like a warm, homemade yeast roll. Corporal Hoot Graham reached for his can of warm, stale Budweiser, took a mighty swig, and then removed all his clothes, except for his boots.

"*CORPORAL!* WHAT IN THE *HELL* ARE YOU *DOIN*, MISTER? PUT YOUR CLOTHES BACK ON! YOU'RE OUT OF UNIFORM, SOLDIER! NOW HAND ME A BEER!"

The barking officer's invisible face disappeared as the choppers buzzed right over camp. Bullets hammered the muddy ground and splayed dirt clods all over Hoot's naked body. He looked up at the sky and squinted.

"*Aw, shucks*, git on outta here! You think I'm 'fraid of a little *mud*? Naw...not me...but I gotta keep them clothes clean, I gotta big 'pointment in L.A., with the Main Man of Time-Lapse Tomatoes!"

Hoot sat down naked on a tree stump and drank his Budweiser as he watched the choppers crash into the steep green hillside across from the Grits 'N Gravy.

"Bet them boys wish they'd a got themselves a big ol' fluffy biscuit a'fore they exploded," he observed, as horrible black flames shot up into the sky and engulfed chopper fuselage in a giant burning cloud. The ground rumbled and the air crackled.

Out of nowhere came the tramp-tramp-tramp of non-regulation bamboo sandals. Hoot craned his head back to drain the Budweiser, but upon raising his head, he noticed the barrel of a pistol pointed at his brain. At the end of the pistol, a Charlie smirked, and cocked the trigger. A group of motionless Charlies in coolie hats stood behind the pistol-packing Charlie.

"Hey, man, what's goin' on? Ya'll want some beer? I think yer choppers over there are pretty done in for...hope ya'lls legs ain't tired, 'cause yer gonna be walkin' back to yer rice paddies, you buncha no-good Kung Fus!"

Hoot reached for an unopened beer can and tossed it at the Charlie holding the pistol to his head. The Charlie dropped his gun in order to catch the beer, then he opened the can and slurped greedily. One of the other Charlies gingerly reached for the first Charlie's pistol, but Hoot slammed his official Ranger boot down on it, winked, and said,

"*Now, boys*, let's us all jus' have another round an' *chat* awhile, ok? Yeah, I been staked out here fer some time, Charlie...'scuse me, *Charlies*. Ya'll sure do get a lotta rain in this here country, man! My toes are 'bout to rot off...but I gotta guard them rations, I got me a medal, you know, and I got me some time-lapse photography to do on them yella squash plants over there! Say, you boys got any weed or hash or anythin'?"

Suddenly, and for no apparent reason, Charlie, and all the assistant Charlies, dropped to their knees and began to whimper. Hoot tossed the beer can into the jungle, then stood.

"Now ya'll don't need ta be *whinin'*, there's plenny a beer here fer all a ya'll. Hey, it's been nice talkin' ta you boys, but I gotta go get me a shower an' lose all this mud! Don't want my pecker to dry up and fall off! Got me a *date* later with Fay Bailey....whooo, *doggies*!"

"HOLD IT, HOOT GRAHAM!" A woman's deep voice bellowed from the jungle. That voice...it was sort of familiar...somebody he knew...

"*Mama?* Is that *you?* Mama, what'd I tell you 'bout comin' out to visit me like this! I got *work* to do! Now you jus' turn 'round an' go home...wait...lemme get ya a beer fer the road. Here's one fer Daddy, an' his Elks, too! Mama, I sure hope you rubbed yerself with six-twelve, 'cause them skeeters'll suck ya dry!"

"HOOT GRAHAM! HIT THE GROUND!"

Hoot jumped with a start and turned to face a very tall, solidly built woman in a United States Marines uniform decorated with hundreds of medals...there were so many medals they were pinned to the woman's back, and they ran down the sides of her trousers. She wore mirrored sunglasses, and she held a bullwhip.

"HIT THE GROUND, I SAID...*NOW!*"

The medaled Marine cracked her bullwhip onto the jungle floor as the Charlies whimpered. Hoot swallowed hard. *Margaret!* What was Margaret doing in the jungle? Her dispatch unit jurisdiction stopped at Murfreesboro, thousands of miles from Vietnam! He reached over to offer a can of Budweiser to Margaret as a peace offering, but she stood motionless, waiting for him to follow her orders.

"*Aw, shucks*, Margaret, honey, what are *you* doin' here? You know I tole you never to visit me at the office! I been lookin' fer a job real hard, now, *hon*, but I gotta little sidetracked, what with them Charlie Choppers explodin' over there, and then I had ta finish this six-pack before breakfast. Here...don't you wanna beer?"

Margaret McArdle-Graham cracked the bullwhip into the steamy green and it snapped like a thousand firecrackers at New Year's. "You're gonna be *punished*, boy! You left me without saying goodbye, you burned a *hole* in my pink, ruffly bedspread, and on toppa that, you didn't even eat your Tuna Tetrazzini Casserole! Brother Culpepper says it's a *mortal sin* to waste food. Now, get over there next to that big tree...WONG LI...*HONG KONG SAIGON TAI PEI KUNG PAO*!"

When did Margaret learn Vietnamese, Hoot wondered...*musta been night classes over to the commun'ty college...she's pretty good, though, man, looka them Charlies scatter!* Two of the Charlies grabbed Hoot by the arms, and put some kind of jacket harness contraption over his torso.

"Hey, *hon,* can I at least put on my pants? I reckon these Charlies have seen enough a my privates! I mean, I gotta save them fer you, darlin'!"

"SHUT UP, CORPORAL! NAKED WE FOUND YOU, AND NAKED YOU WILL STAY! *MAI TAI, TSING DAO TAI WU...CHOP SUEY!*"

Two of the Charlies scurried off, and then Hoot heard the sound of an engine revving. From out of the jungle a large crane rolled over the underbrush, driven by yet another Charlie. The first two Charlies motioned for the crane to pull closer to where Hoot stood, and then a long cable was lowered from the top of the crane. One of the Charlies attached a giant meat hook from the cable to a smaller hook on the front of Hoot's harness. Gears cranked and clanged. Hoot looked a little nervous.

"Hey, *babe,* I really wish I could stay here and play this little *game* with ya, you're lookin' real pretty today with alla them doodads hangin' all over your clothes, but I gotta protect them MREs! I got me a *medal,* you know, and...WHOAAAA!"

Hoot was jerked into the air by the crane. The cable jerked to a stop, swinging a naked Hoot Graham wildly back and forth over Margaret's head.

"HOOT GRAHAM, I BEEN WAITIN' TWENTY-FIVE YEARS TO SEE THIS DAY, AND I BEEN SAVIN' TUNA TETRAZZINI CASSEROLE EVERY TUESDAY SINCE YOU LEFT ME! *NOW* LET'S SEE HOW HUNGRY YOU ARE! *WANG CHUNG! KAMIKAZE! TAI CHI!*" Margaret cracked her whip and it snapped against Hoot's naked legs.

"*OUCH,* hon, now there's no need ta get violent! *WHOA*! What are you guys gonna do...oh, good, you're lowerin' me down now...good, 'cause I gotta go finish that six-pack an' this harness ain't too comf'terble...what in the *hell* is that?"

Harnessed Hoot was swung around to a clearing and then lowered just above ground level over a large tarp with some kind of soft-looking, foam-rubbery stuff on it. As he swayed back and forth, Hoot tried to get a good look at the foam-rubbery stuff below him...but instead he caught a good whiff.

"*MARGARET!* DON'T YOU *DARE!* I TOLE YOU TWENTY-FIVE YEARS AGO I AIN'T GONNA EAT NO DAMNED TUNA TETRAZZINI CASSEROLE, AND I STILL AIN'T GONNA EAT IT *NOW!* PUT ME DOWN, MARGARET! DAMMIT, PUT ME DOWN! I AIN'T GONNA EAT IT, I TELL YAMMMPH...."

Hoot was lowered face-down onto the Tuna Tetrazzini Casserole tarp for a few seconds, until he got good and covered as he wiggled for air, then he was jerked back up by the operator at Margaret's command. Noodles, soggy potato chips, and mashed green peas stuck to the front of Hoot's entire body. He gasped for air.

"MARGARETMPH! PHPUT ME DOWNMPH!" Hoot was lowered and raised several times, until Margaret felt she'd sufficiently made the point that Tuna Tetrazzini Casserole was not to be wasted, and she was not to be reckoned with.

"*RIK-SHA! OBI WAN! KABUKI-WA!*" The cable-Hoot contraption swung around again and flopped Hoot over onto his back, and there he dangled over base camp.

"NOW FOR THE BIG FINISH, BOY!" Margaret motioned at the crane driver, who deposited a Tuna Tetrazzini-laden Hoot onto the ground face up. The Charlie crane-driver killed the motor, and four more Charlies tied Hoot's hands and feet to wooden stakes driven into the damp ground.

"Hey, now, darlin', this is gittin' a little ridicaluss, ain't it? Come on, Boobsie, honey, lemme up outta here, an' let's us go git us a cheeseburger over ta the Grits 'N Gravy, my treat! Margaret....*Margaret*!"

"*GEISHA! CHOW MEIN*!"

Immediately all the Charlies disappeared into the thick, steaming jungle. Hoot raised his head, and saw Margaret remove her shirt, then her trousers. She was wearing a neon yellow bra and panties, although any potential sexual excitement for Hoot was somewhat dimmed by the fact that Margaret was also wearing muddy, regulation boots, and the fact that he was covered in slimy Tuna Tetrazzini.

"Margaret, *hon,* whatcha doin'?" Hoot asked skittishly as a big wet noodle slid down his nose. "Come on, now, *sweetie*, lemme up so's I can gitchoo that check I owe ya for the grocery money I stole....I been keepin' tracka the int'rest after all this time, so's you're gonna be one rich little gal...*honey*...*sweetie*...LEMME UP!"

Margaret stood over Hoot and cracked her bullwhip into the air. She shook her hair wildly into the wind and laughed. "MMM...can't you just *smell* that *delicious* Tuna Tetrazzini Casserole! Doesn't it just make you HUNGRY! I tell you what else would go *real good* with that casserole, too, Hoot...wanna guess?"

Hoot smiled weakly and shook his head. Margaret knelt down in her lemon yellow lingerie-clad fury and slowly caressed Hoot's Turkey-Tetrazzini Casserole-smothered person. Despite the fact that he was tethered and somewhat concerned for his own safety, Hoot couldn't help but become aroused; he was just a lonely soldier out in the field, after all. Margaret stared happily at Hoot's groin.

"THERE we go, THAT'S what I been waitin' for, like a *good boy!*" Margaret kissed Hoot's belly, and then she pulled a very long knife out of her bra. "I think there's *nothin'* like a good ol' HOT DOG to go with Tuna Tetrazzini Casserole, Hoot...whaddya YOU THINK...I like my hot dogs BIG and JUICY, just like THIS!!!"

She raised the knife over her head and prepared to strike.

"AAAGGH! MARGARET!!! *NOOOOO!* MARGARET!! DON'T DO ITTT!!!!"

Hoot bolted upright in his room at the Fluffy Pillow Motel. He was drenched with sweat, and his breaths came shallow and fast. He swallowed hard, got his bearings, and stood up next to the window. He looked through one of the plentiful moth holes in the bright orange polyester curtains, but nobody was outside...the parking lot was empty. Another bad Margaret dream...third time this week, ever since Margaret snuck up behind him at the bank last Tuesday... '*I'm jus' waitin' for Will ta take me over ta the laundrymat*,' he'd said nervously... '*I know*,' Margaret had replied, '*every Tuesday since you came to town...see, I know, 'cause Tuesday's Tuna Tetrazzini day....*'

Hoot sat on the edge of the sagging mattress and looked around the dingy motel room he'd called home for the past eight months. It was good of his brother Will to put him up here, pay the bill and all, but he sure wished they could have moved him into the old homeplace...at least he'd have been safe from Margaret there. But Will's wife Dorothy had gone and remodeled everything inch of that house, and now it was way too high-falutin' for the likes of Hoot Graham. Will's own kids had been kicked out, and Mama just rolled around in her wheelchair all day long yelling at everybody about nutmeg and the Elks club.

Hoot glanced at his watch...ten-fifteen...what day was it...*Saturday?* He had to be at the Gym-torium at one o'clock for play rehearsal. Hoot lit a Camel, sat back down on the bed and leaned against the headboard. He noticed something red and unfamiliar on the floor. He walked over and reached down beside the orange vinyl chair next to the window. *Hmmm...unless my memory fails me, I don't recall havin' any red garter belts in my wardrobe,* Hoot thought...*I pretty much got rid of all that stuff years ago*...then he smiled and took a big puff on his Camel. *Oh yeah*...he remembered...*Fay Bailey is inta wearin' these babies! OH YEAH,* he grinned...*me and Fay had us a TIME last night! That Fay Bailey is one wild woman...*

Hoot chuckled and turned on the ancient television, but a Woody Woodpecker cartoon was the only program of interest. *Yep, ol' Woody got him some action last night, all right! That line 'bout makin' demo tapes fer my next L.A. picture is workin' like a charm,* Hoot mused. Fay Bailey loved his script ideas, and she was particularly interested in his tripod, proving again Hoot's theory that women will do *anything* to get a taste of Hollywood.

Yeah, ol' Fay Bailey was probably good for a couple more romps in the hay, and then he'd have to send out for reinforcements, which in this town was gonna be a stretch. It'd been three weeks since he'd enrolled Fay in Hoot Graham's Finer Points of Cinematic Technique School, but Fay was no dummy. Pretty soon she'd figure out that there was no new L.A. picture, no parts for an aging 44D sexpot, and no legitimate need for a part-time hair-dresser's assistant on some non-existent Hollywood backlot.

Wonder if ol' Betty Gooch is still interested... but she's got such a bad case of the Hormone Hots for that skinny Gastineau boy it'd be a miracle to even get her behind the bleachers like in high school...what'd we call her...oh yeah, Ready Betty...she's still a looker, but now she's goin' after fresh meat.

Hoot decided to take a shower. *I gotta get ta work*, he mused as hot water ran over his skin. *Two months a rehearsals and I ain't even read that play yet, and that damned Peter Paul Pussy Playwright's gonna get me kicked outta town if I don't do some directin'. Like I care 'bout that durned play! But it's workin' out perfect... Will's payin' my tab, everybody's treatin' me with respect...all I gotta do is lay low til December...til ever'body's at that stupid Festival Parade, then get myself over to the bank, and make another withdrawal from that family vault...a man's gotta keep up his reputation!*

He turned up the hot water and let it run down his back. *Yeah, since Will decided ta let me off the hook about the twenty-five thousand I stole...I got me a clean slate! And Mister College Boy...what a dumbass...I still got me that vault key! After Daddy died nobody was 'round to remember I still got it! I can just about take whatever I please this go 'round, and just get myself on a plane to Mexico, and whaddya know, Joe, I'll be Makin' Margaritas with Maria at Sunset!*

Hoot whistled happily as he dried himself and flexed his flabby muscles in the bathroom mirror. *"Oh, sugar, no, I don't think you need ta dye that hair a yours,"* Fay Bailey said last night. *"Now, 'course, I can do some mean things with a good color rinse, but ya got 'distinguished' writ all over that face...must be all that clean air out there in L.A....and that grey fits ya, bein' a big director, an' all...people sit up and take notice of ya, sugar, you got...what is it they say...you gotta good aurora!"*

He dressed in his official L.A. Director's outfit: worn-out commune fatigues, a khaki shirt, an ascot, which was really only a red bandanna, and an old flak vest. Hoot lacked the Official Director's Stuff directors actually carry in the pockets on their flak vests, so he simply packed the pockets full of wadded-up toilet tissue. *It's in the details*, Hoot told everybody, *that's what the Big Secret to Directing is, it's in the details.*

Now if only he had a hot car to ride around in, he'd be set. Hoot couldn't think of many Big-Time Hollywood Directors who were forced to walk everywhere or depend on their brothers for transportation, except maybe for that skinny twerp with the big glasses from New York who filmed everything in black and white, the one who used the same actresses in every movie. *He probably walks everywhere, but I gotta get me some wheels,* Hoot realized... *'specially if Margaret's after me.*

He lit another Camel and sat back on the lumpy mattress. That Margaret had just plumb turned strange...he'd heard a few stories about how she'd turned into a real man-hater, all on account of him leaving her! *You just can't ever tell with women,* Hoot thought. *I did her a favor by goin' to that commune...cut her livin' expenses in half, sent her flowers on her birthday each and every year...an' them Gulf Shores vacations she's been takin' for the last twenty-five years... she can't be too mad at me...nah, I gave her the best six weeks of her life! But she must be ticked at somethin'...seems like ever' time I look around, there's Margaret in them damned mirrored sunglasses...well, she ain't gonna tie me to no tree an' hang dead chickens on my privates, by God!*

Hoot tugged at his bandanna-ascot and exhaled smoke rings. *She's followin' me all right...figured it was Will makin' sure I was stayin' outta trouble...but it's her...*Hoot heard a car turn into the parking lot. He waited a few minutes, then carefully peeked out the largest hole in the orange polyester curtains. A Chestnut Ridge Police Dispatch van slowly circled the empty parking lot, driven by a *woman with mirrored sunglasses*!

Hoot stepped away from the window with a start and leaped into the bathroom. It was legit...Margaret was watching his every move. What did she *want?* He didn't have a dime...she was real well off...almost time for her to retire with a big, fat pension...*maybe she's jus' tryin' ta spook me,* Hoot thought. *Maybe she's curious ta see what kinda wild, Hollywood life I been livin'...she's jealous...ain't that jus' like a woman...she's prob'ly goin' through The Change an' needs some hot Hollywood lovin'...* Hoot heard the crunch of gravel outside his door and his heart pounded...every inch of his body stiffened...finally the van drove off and squealed onto Main Street. Hoot let out a long sigh.

I gotta get me a bodyguard, he decided. *A sidekick, ta 'lert me 'bout Margaret...an' I gotta get me a car...wonder if Will'd spring a loan for a used car? Nope, prob'ly not...but who's gonna know it if I's ta say I was in the market for a car? An' if I'm gonna be in the process of lookin' for a used car, I oughta call up that fool Henry Bailey to pop over here an' take me for a few test-drives now! Henry'd be doin' his job, helpin' me find a good deal on somethin' sweet...a good salesman jus' keepin' his eye out...HENRY! He's been watchin' his backside his whole life! He's used ta lookin' out fer stuff! He'd be a fine watchdog...think I was his new asshole buddy! His only asshole buddy!*

Hoot whistled at this latest flash of Big-Time Hollywood Brilliance. He picked up the phone and dialed the motel operator, Miz Ethel, who was also the motel housekeeper, the motel night clerk, and the motel owner. Miz Ethel was quite determined to sell her motel just as soon as the Sons of Glory Festival was over, a decision most assuredly affirmed after eight months of putting up with Hoot Graham. "Yeah, Hoot, whaddya want *today?*"

Hoot cleared his throat and stepped into his best Big-Time Hollywood Director voice, "Uh, hello, madam, this is Mr. H. Graham, in suite eight..."

"Oh, yeah? *Let's see...Mr. H. Graham*...oh, *yeah,* you're the only customer we got right now...and since you been here since *January,* uh...*H.,* I'd say we're pretty much on *speakin'* terms! You set fire to that lampshade again?"

"Uh, no, ma'am, thank you...would you be so kind as ta please locate fer me the car dealers in town who do business in the previously owned automobile market...I need me a nice '68 Cadillac convertible, cherry, with whitewalls. Could you do that fer me, darlin'? It's *urgent,* I have ta take a *meetin'.*"

Miz Ethel squawked into the phone, "Sure, '*H'!* Why don't I jus' walk my fingers through the whole yella pages, since we AIN'T GOT BUT ONE CAR DEALER *IN* THE WHOLE DANGED TOWN...hold the line...*by the way, H*...you and Miss Love Potion was gettin' a little outta hand last night...I better not find no pieces a plaster all over the floor like last time! I reckon your brother Will ain't plannin' on payin' to remodel this whole motel in your honor!"

Hoot slammed the receiver down onto the cradle, but the phone immediately rang back and he picked it up to hear Henry Bailey's voice, a voice which sounded as if it had recently rolled out of a deep sleep.

"Mr. Bailey, this is H. Graham, the Executive Director of the Festival Theater Group...yes, how'do. I'm in the market fer a previously owned vehicle...I want me a nice, sensible car, *no frills*...just leather, whitewalls, kick-ass stereo, convertible top, a course...what can we do 'bout this, Mr. Bailey? Any suggestions? *Cash,* of course, Mr. Bailey, an' I'm in a bit of a hurry! Mr. Bailey...sir, are you there? I ain't got all *day,* ya know!"

Henry Bailey swallowed hard in a sleep-dazed stupor. The only person who ever called him this early was Amelia Festrunk. Who was H. Graham? He didn't have *anything* on the lot that even came *close* to H. Graham's needs...H. Graham...H. Graham...H...*HOOT!* Hoot wanted a used car! Of course! Every Big-Time Hollywood Director needs a car! And Hoot was in the thick of play rehearsals! He was a busy man!

"Uh, Mr. H. Graham, Director, sir...was you plannin' on comin' over ta the lot *today?*"

Henry Bailey had not entertained a customer on the Henry Bailey Used

Car Lot in over three weeks, and Euladean, bless her heart, was working double shifts at the Poe House to make the RV payments. *Just because you made you a good bit a money on that Festrunk fleet deal don't mean we're on easy street, Henry! I'm takin' all that money an' puttin' it in our PCB fund so's we don't haveta eat cat food when we're old!* Henry blinked back to the caller who was talking far too rapidly for such an early hour of the morning.

"My good man, it is customary in L.A. fer pur-veyors of fine automobiles to person'lly select the i-deal vehicle fer that potential *buyer*, an' then *pick up* the buyer at his place of residence, fer a simple test drive."

Henry cleared his throat, "Ya mean ya want me ta drive over in one a my cars an' git ya at the Fluffy Pillow Motel?"

"Yes, Mr. Bailey, that is *exactly* what I mean! I will expect you at my suite in, shall we say, ten minutes? If you're not too busy fer a cash customer, of course!"

Henry Bailey looked at his watch, cleared his throat again, and lapsed automatically into his official Henry Bailey Used Car Lot Sales Manager Voice, the voice reserved especially for cash customers. "*Well*...course I cain't be gone offa the lot fer *too* long...an' I'll have ta inspect my *inventory*, ta see what a 'scriminatin' buyer like yersef needs...that'll take a while...I mean, we got acres an' acres a clean, dependable, low-mileage used cars, ya know...better give me fifteen, ok? 'Less a course we git swamped with customers, an' all...I'm a might short-handed today...I...uh...I had ta send my sales staff over ta the Best Buy Auto Auction...we're workin' a major fleet deal with an important bizness-man, much like yersef, ya know...but I'll be there directly, you jus' sit tight!"

Henry didn't wait for Hoot's reply. He was so excited he slammed down the phone, got out of bed, danced a little jig and said to himself, *"Killer, you are so good! My sales staff's workin' a major deal! HA! Gotta check my acres an' acres a inventory! HA HA!"*

Henry pulled on pants and shirt for their third straight day of strenuous automobile sales negotiations, grabbed his 1967 red Camaro necktie, threw it around his neck and snatched the magnetic AUTO DEALER license tag from the sales desk, which doubled as the RV's kitchen table. Then he went out into the August morning heat to personally inspect the inventory on behalf of his discriminating buyer, H. Graham.

There were exactly seven cars on the Henry Bailey Used Car Lot, and three of them featured the very latest in state-of-the-art blown engines. Of the four remaining vehicles, one was a thirty-year old postal service jeep with the seats ripped out, which Henry momentarily considered, as it would be ideal for carrying heavy L.A. filmmaker equipment, although it was not as well-appointed as H. Graham requested. There was also a tasteful, brown 1982

K-Car, which exactly met H. Graham's whitewall criteria, but the fact that its entire floorboard was rusted out made for somewhat of a rather noisy ride. Henry immediately ruled out the 1979 four-door Fiat, because it was presently without tires, and he wasn't about to risk good money on retreads until he learned H. Graham's mindset regarding fine Italian engines...they required such fastidious maintenance and loving care.

Henry spotted the 1977 El Camino...*a real pretty shade of yellow,* he noticed. *Not much rust...eight-track player works if ya hold yer mouth just right...not a convertible by definition, but with that truck bed, you could set a whole mess a lawn chairs back there and go to town! A Babe-Mobile for an L.A. Director if there ever was one! Yep, H. Graham, you'd look tray chick in this vee-hicle,* he decided. He did another little jig and walked back to the RV to get the El Camino keys.

He stood in his Sales Office/Bedroom and splashed on a little after-shave to prevent discovery of the fact that he had not yet showered. Then he decided to call Euladean over at the Poe House Grocery. *Gotta keep the wife happy,* Henry remembered, *like that planet-watchin' feller's book said. Gotta communicate.*

"'lo, Miz Penni, how're you doin' today? Can I speak ta Euladean, please...thank ya...'lo, hon, it's me...guess what? Hoot Graham's gonna buy hisself a used car, from guess who? That's RIGHT! ME! I'm gettin' ready ta go inta my *sales meetin',* so I gotta run, but I'll call ya later...the El Camino...a right good car, sorta the Cadillac a the small trucks, I always said! Gotta go, hon, talk at ya later! *Love ya!* Bye!"

Satisfied that he had legitimized his diligent sales efforts to Euladean, Henry took a big swig from the milk carton in the tiny RV fridge and combed his stringy hair. He looked at his beaten face in the bathroom mirror and pointed at his image,

"Now, Henry, H. Graham has deep L.A. pockets, an' yer gonna play hardball on this here price...yer gonna say, '*well, Hoot, I cain't let her go fer anythin' under three...yeah, thousand...three thousand...'less a course you got some 'portant role in that play yer directin', then I might be persuaded to drop another five hunnerd or so...ya know my tenth-grade teacher Miz Novella Brainerd always said I had theatercal talent...*' Now let's go sell us a car, Killer!"

Henry sauntered out to the 1977 El Camino and placed the magnetic Auto Dealer License plate on the back. He gave the vehicle a quick once-over, mentally noting its few minor defects, such as the gaping rust spots on the wheel wells, the barely noticeable, ripped yellow vinyl seatcovers which spat pieces of foam upon the passengers, and the arm rests which were bound to the doors with silver duct tape. Yep, a Big-Time Director's car if there ever was!

He cranked the ignition, and after three attempts, the El Camino's engine shook off its cobwebs and sputtered into drive. Henry drove the car slowly around the block just to make sure there were no last-minute maintenance items that needed disguising, and then he pulled onto Main Street, heading for the Fluffy Pillow Motel and his waiting cash customer.

Yep, gonna get me in real good with Hoot Graham. An' when he gits back to Hollywood, he'll remember jus' who it was gave him the best deal...he'll be so happy he'll prob'ly want me to move to L.A. and manage his whole director-car fleet! Yep, swimmin' pools.....movie stars....

Hoot Graham held court from a tattered lawn chair in the barren parking lot of the Fluffy Pillow Motel. He took a drag on a Camel and blew smoke rings into the late August sky. He decided that the first stop on this critical test drive would be the Quigley Quik-Steak, where he would make an invaluable impression on Henry Bailey by treating them both to brunch, as it was nearly eleven-thirty. Hoot would sign the tab with a flourish, and Henry would never know they were dining on Will's dime. Then, with the convertible top down, they would motor over to The Beauty Box, to personally enjoin Fay Bailey's red garter belt with its rightful owner.

After a brief interlude at the Poe House Grocery, to stock up on Camels and beer, it should be nearly twelve-forty-five; Main Street would be packed with its usual Saturday traffic, and Hoot would instruct Henry to drive along slowly, to afford the good people of Chestnut Ridge ample time to gawk at the Famous Big-Time Hollywood Personality in their midst. Image was everything, and it required lots of hard work.

Upon sufficiently pleasing his public, Hoot would then be deposited in front of the Gym-torium, where he would inform Henry that the convertible would do nicely, he'd have the cash by Monday, and since the deal was done, would it be too much trouble for Henry to return at five and deposit Hoot back at his executive residence, after a brief stop by the Quigley Quik-Steak for a light supper? It would be during this light supper that Hoot would explain to Henry how he had been personally hand-picked to serve as H. Graham's Bodyguard...Hoot had all afternoon to concoct the details. It was gonna be a cakewalk...

As he stubbed the Camel into the cracked pavement in front of his executive suite, Hoot heard a godawful rumbling, coughing engine noise. He looked up to see a faded yellow El Camino pull into the parking lot and jerk to a stop with a loud grind. Henry Bailey, wearing a rumpled short-sleeved polyester shirt, ancient work pants and a red tie, exited the El Camino with a huge smile and stuck out his hand in Hoot's direction.

"*Mornin',* Mr. H. Graham, sir! Ain't it a fine day ta be in the market fer a clean, dependable, low-mileage used car?"

Henry's right hand remained outstretched in Hoot's direction, despite the fact that Hoot made no effort to leave his lawn chair, let alone shake Henry's hand. Hoot frowned and sighed deeply.

"Good mornin', Mr. Bailey. Cain't nobody in this town folla *instructions*...I specifically require a *convertible*...preferably late model...perhaps ya mean to take me to your lot, ta person'lly select the car a my choice?"

Henry Bailey walked over to Hoot's lawn chair, again trying to shake hands with the Big-Time Hollywood Director, to no avail. He clapped his hands together and then pointed them in the direction of the El Camino.

"Well, now, Mr. H. Graham, sir, ya see, we was *fresh outta* late model convertibles...yep, I done sold the *last one* jus' yesterday...if I'd only *knew* you was interested, I mighta coulda held it fer ya...them's the breaks I guess, but see here, this El Camino's a looker, ain't she?" Henry opened the passenger door to the El Camino and strategically stood in front of a large rust spot.

"Looka them whitewalls! Got an *eight-track* player...ya don't see *them* babies ever' day, now, do ya? *Classic!* Yep, she's air conditioned, an' I figure a busy Hollywood director like yersef, he needs more than jus' some ol' *convertible*...why, the bed a that Camino can hold all yer filmmakin' 'quipment, or ya can fill it with lawn chairs an' gitchersef an Igloo fulla them fancy wine coolers, an', well, H., you gotta reg'lar *Babe Magnet!*"

Henry drew a deep, anxious breath as he waited for H. Graham's response. Hoot threw his head back in mock disgust and rolled his eyes. He loosened the bandanna-ascot on his neck, and stared at his chewed fingernails.

"Mr. Bailey...may I call you Henry? I'm sure this is a fine automobile but my heart's set on a convertible...I gotta protect my image, and I can't drink Thunderbird when my tongue's set on *champagne!*" Hoot feigned a prima dona Director's pout, and shook his head. "I'll have ta look over in Murfreesboro...I know a coupl'a boys over there...maybe I can rent somethin' fer a time..."

Hoot slapped his knees to stand. Henry Bailey wiped sweating palms on the seat of his work pants. "Looka here, Hoot...I mean, H. Graham...you know what this car is? Why, it's the *mother* of them SUV's ya see ever'where! Them four-wheel drive vee-hicles, why they was *born* on the success of this here El Camino...the first double-duty automobile! With this here fine car, ya know what ya got? Ya got yersef *flex-a-bil'ty!*"

Henry waited for Hoot to move out of the lawn chair, but when no sign of motion was apparent, he opened the El Camino's tailgate, then its hood, waved at Hoot, and continued.

"Hoot...*H*...I can make ya a *real sweet deal* on this here El Camino...you know what I can do? I'm gonna pull out *all* the stops fer *you*, ol' buddy...you got needs, I unnerstand, H.... *but you don't wanna be goin' over ta*

Murfreesboro fer no car...that's clear 'cross the county line, an' a savvy bizness man like yersef, you gotta consider the *tax* sitiation! Why don't we jus' come to a 'greement an' you can lease this here vehicle! Jus' like ya'll do in Hollywood!" Henry slapped the engine block as Hoot watched with a bored stare.

"I'll let ya have it fer a hunnerd dollars a week, up til ya gotta go back ta L.A.! Unlim'ted miles, a course, an' I tell you what...we'll even waive that there secur'ty deposit, if you'll give me a part in that fancy play yer directin'! How 'bout that, H.? Whaddya say? That's a Henry Bailey Deal a the Century! Lordy, I oughta *fire* mysef fer givin' such a great deal! But what are friends for, H.?"

Henry crossed his arms over his chest and rared back, satisfied with his crack negotiations. Hoot hoisted himself out of the lawn chair, and meandered over to the El Camino. He waved a hand lightly over its faded yellow hood and rested one foot on its rickety front bumper.

"Well, if I was *interested* in an El Camino, I'd be a *fool* ta pass it up! But I *ain't* interested in no El Camino, so I reckon I'll jus' have ta talk ta somebody else!"

Henry Bailey eyed the empty parking lot of the Fluffy Pillow Motel. Everybody in town had seen Hoot thumbing rides for months, when he wasn't riding shotgun in his brother Will's Lincoln Town Car. He shook his head at Hoot in true Used Car Sales Manager empathy. Henry let out a deep sigh as he stared at Main Street.

"Guess it gits old fer you Hollywood types, takin' them cabs ever'-where...'course, now, we ain't got no cabs 'roun' here since Newt's bizness closed...must be hard thumbin' fer rides an' callin' yer brother all the time ta take you places..."

Hoot scowled and removed his foot from the bumper of the El Camino. He readjusted his bandanna-ascot and lit a Camel. Henry looked at his watch, and took aim for the kill.

"Well, then, Hoot, I best me on my way...gotta meet a reg'lar customer back at the lot...I'm workin' another fleet deal! Good huntin' in Murfreesboro...they don't make house calls like *I* do, though..."

Henry twirled the El Camino keys in Hoot's direction, then climbed inside the car and cranked the engine, which thankfully started on the first try. Hoot tugged at his bandanna-ascot as Fay's snide remark of the previous evening roared through his head... *'sure is strange a Big-Time Hollywood director don't have no car, with all them 'portant meetin's ya got ta go to'*... He had to play this part to its fullest...his adoring fans were at stake, and ultimately, his chance to sneak into that family vault one more time...

"HENRY! Wait a minute! Ya know, yer a smart man! Yer right, a convertible's a high-risk vehicle, fer theft an' all...maybe I oughta jus' take your advice an' lease this little beauty...'course, I can't pay more than fifty dollars a week, I'm onna expense account...but fer fifty dollars a week, this jus' might do!"

Henry curled his lip and cocked his head as if calculating some intricate formula. Hoot reached his right hand into the driver's window and clapped Henry on the shoulder. Henry shifted the El Camino into reverse. "Ah, Hoot...naw, I just cain't part with her fer less than seventy-five, 'course now if ya wanna give me a part in that *play*, like I was sayin', well, *maybe* I could go down ta *sixty-five...*"

"SOLD, my good man! I'll take it! 'Course I'm *plumb outta cash* right now...I been entertainin' folks all week with this Festival, ya know...my accountant's s'posed ta wire me some more money... them damn accountants...never wanna work on the weekends! An' hey, buddy, I got a part in that play with yer name on it! Now let's go git us some brunch, my treat! Oh, but you gotta *meetin'* ta git to..."

Henry bit his lip as if deep in thought. "Well, now, Hoot...can I call ya Hoot? Hoot, you're my payin' customer, an' it's my duty ta take you wherever you need ta go! When we git ta the Quik-Steak, I'll jus' call my 'sistant manager an' have him take over...no problem! That's the name a the car bidness, Hoot... *flex-a-bil'ty an' customer service*!"

Hoot climbed into the passenger's seat of the El Camino, and his attention was immediately drawn to the fine glimmer of silver duct tape on the armrest, because the tape pulled the hairs on his forearm. But he was too elated with new-car joy to care...Will would surely spring sixty-five dollars a week just to be relieved from daily chauffeur duty! He might even spring for *eighty-five*, and then Hoot'd have some pocket cash! Gotta figure out how to work that through Henry, he mused, make it official. Phase I of the Automobile/Bodyguard Plan was in motion. Hoot readjusted his bandanna-ascot in the El Camino's rearview mirror as Henry drove toward the Quik-Steak.

"Henry, can ya clean her up real good fer me? Git her washed an' waxed? An' do ya mind takin' me 'round fer a coupla days, 'til we git the papers all signed next week, after my accountant gets back in? I lef' my driver's license's back in L.A....s'posed ta come in the mail next week. I tell you what...jus' fer bein' so accommodatin', I'll get my accountant ta pay ya three weeks in *advance*, ok? Hey, Henry...pull inta the Beauty Box fer a minute...I gotta schedule a session with my stylist."

Henry reluctantly pulled into the parking lot of The Beauty Box, but quickly noticed that his ex-wife's car wasn't perched in her usual spot under a large maple tree. Henry didn't want to enter into a shouting match with Fay right in front of H. Graham, Hollywood Director and Henry Bailey

Used Car Customer. Hoot checked his look in the rearview mirror one more time, and got out of the El Camino.

"Henry, I'll be right back. How 'bout crankin' that eight-track up a bit! Let's us listen ta some music, son!"

Hoot slammed the car door and swaggered up the concrete steps of The Beauty Box. Henry saw Stella Stanley look out the window in front of her hydraulic chair. *She's prob'ly gonna tell Fay I was here. Oh well, I gotta right ta be on public property! I gotta right ta do my bizness, an' if that means takin' a good customer 'round town, then it ain't none a her bizness ta say nothin'!* Henry found an old eight-track tape in the glove box and shoved it into the tape player on the El Camino's dashboard console. He pressed several buttons, and finally the tape clicked and played.

Henry didn't recognize the melody, so he turned down the volume; he wanted to be able to hear himself think in case Stella Stanley came out of The Beauty Box and screamed at him to get off her property. He could see Hoot inside, talking with his stylist. *Must be a new girl,* Henry thought. *Reckon no ordinary beautician could handle Hoot's Hollywood Do.* Then Henry saw Hoot dangle some kind of red elastic thing in front of the stylist...*must be one a them newfangled hair devices*...Funny...Hoot didn't *look* like he wore a hairpiece, but then, he probably had the best fake hair money could buy. Henry leaned his head against the yellow vinyl interior of the El Camino and closed his eyes.

Inside The Beauty Box, Fay Bailey was prickling with the anticipation of an unannounced gentleman caller. Hoot swooped over to Fay's hydraulic chair, spun her customer around, and pulled Fay off to one private corner. He planted a big, wet kiss on her lips and ran one meaty finger down her breastbone. Fay giggled between chomps on her chewing gum.

"Hey, sweet thing," Hoot whispered into Fay's ear, or at least, he tried to get close enough to whisper, but Fay's gigantic silver earrings got in the way. "Looky here what *I* got! How're you holdin' up them *panties,* hon? I'd hate fer 'em ta fall down 'round your ankles in the middle a the street...never know when some poor fella might just *poke* ya right there in *public!*" Hoot waved the red garter in Fay's face as she giggled.

"Hoot Graham, you gimme back my garter! It don't hold up no panties, you *fool!* Besides, I ain't even *wearin'* panties!" Fay smacked her gum and waited for Hoot's reaction. Hoot took a deep breath and let out a whistle.

"Well, sug, that's just *fine* with *me!* Listen here, you git yourself dressed up tonight...we're goin' over ta the Elks Lodge Moonbeam Dance! An' no need fer you ta pick me up, darlin...which is a right good thing, since yer car ain't outside...in the shop again? Yeah, well, I got me a *chauffeured limousine,* an' I'll be by at seven-thirty! Now you be ready, hear?"

Hoot swatted Fay's behind and chuckled at the astonished look on her face. Her Big-Time Hollywood Director had come through, after all. Fay nodded silently as Hoot stepped outside. She'd have to cancel all her afternoon appointments and go home early with a sick headache...what should one wear to ride in a limousine, with a *chauffeur*?

"STELLA! COME HERE THIS MINUTE! YOU AIN'T GONNA BELIEVE THIS! STELLA! STOP COMBIN' OUT MIZ MAYBELLE AN' GIT OVER HERE!"

Hoot opened the door of the El Camino and slid into the front seat. Henry Bailey's head was propped up against the cracked vinyl headrest, and he snored loudly. Hoot turned the ignition switch half a turn so he could play with the eight-track. The tape player clicked a few times, then Hoot recognized his favorite song. It was fate.

"Hey, Henry, *wake up*! I ain't got all day, I gotta be at play rehearsal! An' I gotta *eat!* Let's go! If you're gonna hang with a L.A. personal'ty, son, you best be gittin' with the program!"

Henry opened his eyes and rolled his head in Hoot's direction, checking the parking lot to make sure Fay wasn't hiding anywhere, waiting to sabotage him. "Sure, Hoot! Quik-Steak, here we come!" Henry fumbled with the ignition and started the car. Hoot turned up the eight-track volume. "WHOA, this here's my favo-rite song in the whole worl'! Listen up, Henry..."

What should have been a raspy, male baritone voice sounded more like a group of tortured cats as the ancient eight-track tape curled around the playback head. Hoot slapped his knees and sang at the top of his lungs,

"YOU KNOW I AIN'T HIS DADDY 'CAUSE HE AIN'T GOT MY GOOD LOOKS! SO GIT UP OFF YER HIGH HORSE AN' JUS' LEMME OFF THE HOOK!"

The distance to the Quigley Quik-Steak was a mere three blocks, and Henry parked the car in the last vacant parking spot. "I ain't never heard that song before, Hoot. You gotta real nice sangin' voice, though." Henry turned off the engine and got out of the car.

"Why, thank ya, Henry! Yeah, that's sorta my theme song...you know, alla them L.A. women wanna jus' *throw* themselves at ya when you're famous...then they 'xpect ya ta pay 'em child support! Say, listen, I gotta little proposition fer ya...let's go inside and talk, biznessman ta biznessman."

The two businessmen stepped into the Quik-Steak and Hoot waved at the lone waitress, "How do, yes, ma'am, two fer *brunch*, please!"

Brunch was not a regular feature of the Quigley Quik-Steak, nor was it a regular feature of any restaurant in town save Chéz Horatio, so Hoot and Henry had to settle for "Ruby's Rump Roast Special." They both wolfed down their meal, then ordered coffee and chess pie. Hoot pushed his plate aside, lit a Camel, and offered one to Henry, who declined.

Hoot decided now was the time to discuss with Henry the bright prospect of Henry's new career in the Personal Bodyguard industry, particularly as Hoot had scrapped plans for a light supper with Henry, in favor of a social engagement at the Elks Moonbeam Dance with Fay, and particularly as he needed Henry to serve as chauffeur and drive them to said social engagement. Hoot shot Henry an "aw shucks" grin as Henry slurped coffee from a chipped mug.

"Henry...I seen what a *savvy* operator you are...yer pretty much a *legend* in this town...now I know you had some hard times, but you're livin' proof that a man can rise above his troubles! You been ta the school a hard knocks, an' ya gradgiated! You know what it's like ta be hated, an' scorned, an' chased after...but ya showed 'em all by risin' up outta the trash heap! So Henry, that's why I need your help!" Hoot winked at Henry and twirled a spoon in his coffee.

Henry sat back in wide-eyed wonderment as the waitress delivered his second piece of pie. H. Graham, Hollywood Film Director, was asking *him* for assistance...maybe he needed an entire fleet of clean, dependable, low-mileage used cars...maybe he wanted Henry to star in his next movie...a movie about hard knocks biznessmen. "Sure, Hoot, anythin' ya need!"

Hoot smiled and exhaled. "I knew I could count on ya, Henry, no matter what them other folks say. See, us Hollywood types...we got all kindsa pressure on us, day an' night. We got people callin' on our public lines, on our private lines, on our cell phones, faxin' us stuff, it never stops! I got deals workin' all over the country...*hell*, all over the *world!* Sorta like them deals you're workin' all the time, ya follow?" Hoot took another draw on his Camel.

Henry nodded his head...he didn't know about private lines or cell phones, or faxin'. He'd never seen Hoot actually *use* a cell phone...*but that don't mean he ain't got one...probably leaves it in his execative suite at the Fluffy Pillow Motel, too overwhelmed by pressure, a man needs his privacy.* Hoot blew smoke rings across the aisle of the Quigley Quik-Steak.

"Henry, what I'm 'bout ta propose is sorta, well, sorta *unconventional*...see, lotsa people in this town are a might *jealous* a what I've accomplished...lotsa people in this town are right stirred up 'bout my success...Henry...lemme jus' lay it out on the table...I'm bein' *follad!* Near's I can count, there's 'bout three or four differ'nt inda-vidgyals chasin' my tail...this mornin', right before you came over ta my suite, somebody was scopin' me out... I'm a right lucky man ta be sittin' here even *talkin'* to ya!"

Hoot swallowed a big gulp of coffee and looked around the Quigley Quik-Steak as if in fear. He saw Henry's reaction out of the corner of his eye.

Henry slowly chewed a huge bite of pie as he looked around the room for a suspicious character. Hoot continued.

"So what I'm thinkin', as we're drivin' over here, you know, my mind's workin' all the time, Henry...I could really use me a Best Boy...ya know, ta take my calls, keep me straight, make sure I get ta my appointments on time...and a course, perform some *special* duties."

Henry immediately stopped chewing...everybody'd *heard* stories about Hoot's bread not being buttered on the same side as most folks...strange L.A. sexual behavior might be accepted in Hoot's business, but Henry Bailey was a resolved woman-lover, and nothing on earth could change that. Henry was intrigued, however, to discover exactly what a Best Boy was...maybe it was some fancy word for an important Hollywood fleet manager...He took another bite of pie and smiled at the waitress as she poured more coffee into his cup. Hoot eyed the waitress's shapely behind as she trotted off to the next table.

"Now, in *Hollywood*, there's *Boys*, and there's *Best Boys*. An' ever'body wants ta be the *Best Boy*, but only a chosen few ever make it...do ya understand what I'm tellin' ya, Henry? You got all the makin's of a Best Boy!"

Hoot took a swig from his coffee mug. Henry put down his fork and swallowed, frowning.

"Hoot, that's real *nice* of ya, ta think of me as a Best Boy, but I gotta go on record, *right now*, I am a *one-sexual* man...none a this *bi-sexual* or *tri-sexual* stuff! Now I ain't never been outta Chestnut Ridge, but I don't think we get too many Best Boys 'roun' here, 'ceptin' that Estéfan Rodriguez...he done come outta the cupboard, like they say...maybe ya oughta go talk to *him!*"

Hoot chuckled in a deliberately condescending fashion. "*Aw, you ign'rnt hayseed!* Henry, listen here! A Best Boy ain't got nothin' ta do with *sex*...well, ok, he does scope out Hollywood Babes for the boss...but the Best Boy's the Hollywood Director's Main Man! He's the one who really runs the show...tells the stars what ta do, advises 'em on their next project, an' he even *drives 'em ever'where* so he knows *'xactly* their whereabouts! A good Best Boy keeps the Star and the Director happy...but the real deal, Henry, is that ya'd be doin' *double-incognito-duty*...you'd also be watchin' my back fer me, keepin' me *safe!* Do ya realize, Henry, the chance I'm offerin' ya? You'd be like...like, well, the most important person *next* ta H. Graham!"

Henry took a gigantic bite of pie and chewed it with a great deal of difficulty. After a few silent seconds, he worked the pie over to one side of his mouth, and said, "Hoot, I'd be real honored to work with ya as the Best Boy, if yer *sure* there's no hanky-panky involved, an' if you'll show me the ropes! An' if it won't interfere with my car lot too much...I gotta wife ta support, ya know!"

Hoot slapped his palm on the formica table and whistled. "Well, doggies,

I just knew I could count on ya! It's all settled, Henry Bailey is now the 'ficial Best Boy fer H. Graham! Now, the first thing you gotta do is get that El Camino stocked fer the swar-ee tonight, and then ya gotta pick me up at six-forty-five..."

Henry grinned with pride. "I cain't wait ta tell Euladean! She's been after me to git a part-time job! How much do Best Boys make, Hoot? What's the goin' rate? You mean we're goin' to a Hollywood-type party tonight?"

Hoot's face suddenly turned sour, and he lowered his head.

"Henry. I thought better of ya. Why does ever'body think that if they work with a Hollywood celebr'ty they're gonna make a lotta money? Do I look like I got money ta *spare?* I mean, do I got dollar bills fallin' outta my pants legs? All my cash is tied up in foreign investments! I gotta buy scripts, hell, my accountant won't even let me have a *checkbook!* Henry, a good Best Boy works fer the *fun* of it, fer the chance ta be *next* ta the celebr'ty, ta pick up actin' and directin' tips, ta meet movers an' shakers! Fer the *honor* a watchin' after the boss! An' before long, the Best Boy has his *own* network a movers an' shakers, an' he becomes a celebr'ty too, an' then the money jus' starts rollin' in! It's sorta like the Mafia, Henry, 'cept you don't carry a gun, an' you can quit anytime ya like!"

Henry frowned. Being a Best Boy sounded like a once-in-a-lifetime opportunity, but Euladean wouldn't approve if there was no monetary compensation involved.

"How much time do I gotta spend practicin' at bein' a Best Boy, before I can git me this here network a Hollywood movers an' shakers, Hoot?"

"Well, if ya work *real hard*, I mean, night an' day fer a few months, an' if ya watch my back real good, then we'll Make the Introductions. That's where I write letters tellin' ever'body how good a Best Boy you are, an' how you should be hired as a *Producer* on my next picture...an' lemme tell ya, Producers? They make as much as a hunnerd-thousand dollars a film!"

A hundred thousand dollars! For a few months' time, learning at the feet of the great H. Graham! Henry was skeptical, but he might never again have such a chance to be so close to greatness. "I dunno, Hoot, I gotta tell ya, Euladean ain't gonna be too happy 'bout me bein' gone much from the car lot...can ya talk to her for me?"

Hoot choked on his coffee, cleared his throat and wiped his mouth on a napkin. "Naw, Henry, that wouldn't be right...I don't wanna excerpt no undue influence on her or nothin'...but I tell ya what...you go over ta Roy's Tape House later on this afternoon, an' rent you a couple a big-budget movies, *'Attack of the Five-Headed Possum'* or *'Death At the Dollar Cinema.'* You sit Miss Euladean down in front of the TV, an' fast-forward them babies ta the end credits...you'll see the name, 'Eddie Harley' listed as Best Boy.

Now Eddie was one a the best Best Boys in the bizness, an' you wanna guess what he's doin' now? Well I'll tell ya...he's workin' for *Stallone*...yep...as in *Sly...the Rock-Man*...makin' a bundle! It's up ta you, Henry...GEEZ LOUISE look at the time!"

Hoot drained his coffee cup, pleased with this latest con. His commune buddy Eddie Harley had indeed served as a Best Boy, which was nothing more than a gofer, on those very shoestring-budget flicks, right before Eddie'd lost his mind and been admitted to the L.A. County Sanitarium. The fact that Eddie was not presently working with Stallone, or with anyone at all, was a minor detail, an *undiscoverable* minor detail.

"What's it gonna be, Henry? I gotta get me a Best Boy! I been too long without one! My life's at stake!" Hoot drummed his fingers on the formica tabletop and looked around the room as if he was bored.

Henry pursed his lips and glanced out the window of the Quigley Quik-Steak. This was his big chance to impress Euladean, and the entire town, the town whose citizens had laughed at him his whole life, and at his ancestors before that. He looked at Hoot.

"Hoot, why don'tcha jus' tell Bull McArdle 'bout them people followin' ya! He'll take care of 'em...he's yer ex-brother-in-law, ya know!"

Hoot sadly shook his head. "Henry...it's always been my philos'phy ta never take them police away from their sworn duty...they got enough ta do without watchin' my butt ever day!"

Hoot was probably right, Henry mused. Just last week some vandals broke all the windows at the deserted Grits 'N Gravy. Crime was quickly creeping into Chestnut Ridge, he'd told Euladean. *I gotta keep this armed pistol by the bed at night...we got too many valuable, low-mileage used cars on the lot people'd wanna steal.* And Henry could handle himself...all those years of harassment in school, in the Army, his whole life...Henry made up his mind. He'd show them...he'd be the best Best Boy Hoot Graham had ever seen...better than this Eddie Harley...and then he'd become famous in his *own* right...he could see it now... *'HENRY BAILEY'S USED CARS & BEST BOY SERVICE'* emblazoned on a beautiful red sign suspended from the top of the RV.

"Ok, Hoot, you got yersef a Best Boy! What's my first assignment, Boss?" Henry stood up and jangled the El Camino keys. Hoot smiled and slapped his thigh.

"Well, we gotta make a supply run...gotta get me some smokes ta help me deal with all the stress at them play rehearsals. An' then there's makin' sure that I got my privacy...keep that Peter Paul Pussy...Peter Paul *Culpepper* away from me when I'm directin', an' make sure them props is ready, an' bring me refreshments an' such. But we'll go inta all that later. The most important thing you gotta do, Henry, is watch my back, warn me if

Marg...I mean if somebody's sneakin' 'round or watchin me!

"Now, 'bout tonight. After play rehearsal, you're gonna go fill up the limo with an ice chest fulla wine coolers, great idea you got, by the way...an' then you're gonna pick me up at six-forty-five, an' we'll go pick up my date...which I personally hand-picked as a potential actress fer my nex' picture. Then we're gonna get ourselves over to the Elks Moonbeam Dance...now, course, if you wanna bring Euladean 'long, that's ok, but you gotta remember, you're gonna have ta keep your *mind* on your *bizness*, ok?"

"Ok, Hoot. Was you gonna pay fer lunch?" Henry nodded at the unpaid check laying on the table.

"Oh, right! Here, you go on out ta the limo and git her warmed up. I'll be right there, soon as I sign my tab."

Hoot grabbed the check and swaggered over to the cash register. Henry went outside and started the El Camino. *A Best Boy!* What a strange thing Fate was! If only Miz Novella Brainerd could see him now! Not only did he have promising acting talent, he was a Best Boy! For a Hollywood Director! And in just a few minutes, Hoot could help him explain it to Euladean, while they bought smokes at the Poe House! Henry remembered he was supposed to be watching Hoot's back, so he looked through the car windshield into the Quigley Quik-Steak. Hoot stood at the cash register and Henry saw that Mr. Director was involved in an altercation with the waitress.

"Now look here, *missy*, I'm H. Graham, Executive Director of the Sons of Glory Festival Play, an' I got me a *tab* at this fine dinin' establishment! Where's Ruby? Where's Roy? You jus' go ask 'em an' they'll tell ya!"

The waitress popped her bubble gum loudly in Hoot's face, pointed at the cash register, and said sarcastically, "Well, *sir*, this here note says 'DON'T 'LOW HOOT GRAHAM TO CHARGE NO MORE FOOD PER HIS BROTHER WILL OVER TO THE BANK.' So I guess your credit's done been called *in*, Mr. Executive Play Director!"

Hoot gasped in mock despair and stepped away from the register in order to give the Quik-Steak patrons a good earful of what he was about to say. "I AM SHOCKED! I EXPECT THIS IN L.A., BUT NOT IN MY OWN HOMETOWN! DO YOU REALIZE WHO YOU'RE DEALING WITH? MY BROTHER OWNS THE BANK! SOMEBODY FORGED THAT NOTE! HAS MARGARET MCARDLE-GRAHAM BEEN HERE?"

"Hoot...uh, what's the problem?" Hoot turned around to see his brother Will.

"Will! Good grief! Some damned fool's sayin' my credit's no good! *Can you believe it?* You jus' tell 'em what the deal is, Will...that we got ever'thing taken care of, ok? I gotta get over ta practice...say, Dorothy's doin' a great job, you oughta be mighty proud..."

"Hoot, let's step outside." Will dropped a twenty next to the cash register and motioned to the waitress to cover Hoot's check, then he pulled Hoot out the front door. Henry was about to leave the El Camino and pounce on the person standing next to his Boss, but he decided that Hoot's own brother was no serious menace. Will stammered and sighed.

"Hoot...I don't know how to say this...I know you're down on your luck right now, and I realize Dorothy's the one who asked you to come here and film the Festival, but I've spent about a thousand dollars a month on your hotel bills, your restaurant tabs and your groceries at the Poe House since *January*...and in this town, that's a lot of money! Now you're my brother, and I'd give you my last nickel, you know that, but Dorothy's been on my case, saying that we should have kept receipts of everything so we could claim you as a dependent...Hoot?" Will smiled and put a hand on his brother's shoulder, which sagged toward the floor.

"I get it, big brother. I'm good enough ta docament yer wife's every move at this here festival...I'm good enough ta direct this here play an' make ever'-body rich an' famous...but I ain't good enough ta live in yer house, or stay in a motel or eat three squares on yer dime...I'm jus' surprised it took so long fer this ta happen...guess I'll jus' pack up an' head home...get me a big project shootin' time-lapse fer some old client..." Hoot moved toward the car, but Will stopped him.

"Hoot...just hold on a minute. Nobody's saying you're not welcome. But you've got to tone it *down* a bit...I know you gotta eat, but when I get the bill from the Poe House and Corny tells me you bought everybody in the place a five-pack of T-bones, you can see how I might be a little *concerned!* I may own the bank, but I can't print more money! Now what I *told* Ruby and Roy was that I'd pick up your *lunch* tab every day. You can come over to the house for dinner, and you can eat breakfast at the Poe House bakery, ok?"

Hoot's face turned bright red with anger. "If it don't beat all, bein' put on an expense account by my own family... I got me an image ta protect! Jus' 'cause I'm a might shorta cash don't mean I ain't made somethin' of myself! If ya'll had ever come out ta L.A. ta see me, but I guess you was too durn busy ta check on your own flesh an' blood!"

"Now, calm down, let's shake hands and start over, ok? I promise you won't be embarrassed again, I'll see to it personally. What time should I pick you up for dinner tonight?"

Will raised his eyebrows in anticipation of Hoot's response. Hoot drew a deep breath, glanced at Henry who was revving the El Camino's engine and twirling a toothpick in his mouth, and looked at his big brother.

"Will...it's plumb embarrasin' fer a grown man, fer a successful director, ta depend on his fam'ly ta cart him around ever'where! Now I got this opportun'ty...jus' hear me out...see Henry Bailey out there, in that yella El Camino? Well, he's wantin' ta get inta actin' an' the movie bizness, see, an' so's I tole him that if he'll drive me 'round town fer awhile, I'll give him some pointers an' all, an' he said he'd help me carry my equipment while I'm filmin'...you know my war wound's been actin' up again. So you don't have ta worry *no more* 'bout takin' me all over town. It'd be only *fair* ta give Henry some gas money, don't ya think?"

Will looked Hoot up and down and quietly asked, "And how much gas money do you think Henry will *need?*"

Hoot closed his eyes tight and wiggled his fingers as if to calculate an intensely complex gas mileage reimbursement formula. "Oh, I figure 'bout eighty-five dollars a week'll do...that El Camino's a real gas guzzler, ya know! Gotta make it worth the man's while!"

"EIGHTY-FIVE DOLLARS A WEEK!" Now Will's face turned red, his blood pressure rising. Then he remembered his manners, and his poor brother's plight. He hated conflict. "Sorry...ok, *look*, Hoot...if you *promise* to stick to this agreement, watch your spending, tone it down, then I'll pay for Henry's gas...but only if he'll send me the bill *directly*...that way I'll have a receipt!"

Will smiled weakly as Hoot shook his hand. "Thanks, Will, you're the best brother a man ever had! Look, I gotta run...need me ta take care a that bill back there?"

Will shook his head with a faint smile. "No, Hoot, it's paid. Just go on to play practice and do a good job...everybody's counting on your expertise, you know. And don't take this out on Dorothy, she's under a lot of strain right now!"

Hoot clapped his brother on the back and waved, then got into the waiting El Camino where his theme song blared into the greasy air wafting over the Quigley Quik-Steak.

"*PHEW!* What a melluvahess *that* was! Ol' Will was a might shorta change, an' I had ta bail him out! But he's gonna straighten out my accountant fer me! Here's the deal on that car lease...ever' week, I'll drop by your lot, an' you'll give *me* twenty dollars...then you'll write outta invoice fer *eighty-five dollars,* be sure ta write it up as 'gasoline' fer tax purposes...we'll go over all that as parta your Best Boy trainin'...and send the bill ta *Will* over at the bank. Ain't it great how things work out? See, you're gettin' paid fer bein' a Best Boy after all! You've already made money! You're gonna make eighty-five dollars a week, so there ain't nothin' Euladean can say, now is there?"

Henry nearly swallowed his toothpick as he whistled in amazement. Hoot had serious connections. Best Boy was definitely an opportunity of a lifetime, pay or no pay. "Shore thing, Hoot. You want us ta go ta the Poe House now?"

"Drive on, my man, drive on! Now, like I was sayin' bout tonight..."

Henry drove the chugging El Camino to the Poe House Grocery and parked it in a handicapped spot near the door, because Hoot told him that Best Boys are expected to break the rules, and when they do, they're cut some slack, because they're Best Boys with a Best Boy attitude.

"Now, Henry, you jus' keep an eye out an' if anybody suspicious comes 'round, you holler, ok?"

Hoot went inside the Poe House while Henry posted surveillance from the El Camino limousine. He broke out in a sweat fearing Euladean would come out and ask him why he was still with Hoot Graham, and why he was driving the car that Hoot Graham was supposed to have bought several hours ago. And then there was this whole Best Boy situation...Henry's sweat glands began to work overtime. He turned around and looked out the back windshield of the El Camino, when he heard Euladean's voice.

"HENRY! What are you *doin*?"

Henry jumped so high he hit his head on the dome light of the El Camino. It was Euladean, fresh from her break, returning to the Poe House. She leaned into the car and gave her husband a peck on his head.

"Sug, why're you sittin' out here in this heat 'bout to die? How'd it go? You sell Hoot this car? What'd ya get?"

"Hon, I did right better'n that! I *leased* it to him, fer eight...fer sixty-five dollars a week, right up thew nex' Janyary! So we make a little *now*, an' we make a little *later*, 'cause we'll still own this car to sell to *another* 'scriminatin' consumer! An' guess what?"

Euladean frowned at hearing the word, 'lease,' but sixty-five dollars a week was better than nothing."What, sug, hurry up, I gotta get back inside!"

"Darlin', yer lookin' at the new Best Boy to H. Graham, Executive Director! Yep, it's me! I'm gonna hang with Hoot fer a few weeks, learnin' the ropes, an' then he's gonna interduce me ta alla his Hollywood connections! An' I'm gonna produce his nex' movie! Ain't that great? *Sug*? Did ya hear what I said? Producers make a hunnerd thousand dollars a movie, an' Hoot says I got the makin's!"

Euladean Poe Bailey frowned sternly at her husband. "Just exactly what does it mean, ta be Best Boy? There better not be no Best *GIRL!* Where's Hoot? He's nothin' but trouble, an' I didn't get you all straightened out just ta see you waste your talents on ol' Hoot good-fer-nothin' Graham!"

Euladean looked in the Poe House windows to spot Hoot in line. Henry got out of the car and rubbed his wife's shoulders.

"Naw, sugar, it ain't like that! I gotta organize all kindsa important details fer the play, an' fer the Festival! I gotta supervise stuff fer Hoot, so's he can do his *job*, that's all! Now, course, I tole him I cain't be gone offa the car lot durin' the day, so's I'm gonna do all this stuff at night, see? An' yer workin' so many four-ta-twelves lately, ya won't even miss me, right sug?

Henry decided he should come clean. "An' besides, sug...Hoot's payin' me ta do all this! Uh, *ten* dollars a week, on toppa the car lease!"

No need to give Euladean exact figures, Henry mused. Man's got to have some private pocket change. He nuzzled his scruffy chin under Euladean's neck and she giggled.

"Well, I guess it's better than nothin', Henry. I 'member back in school, Miz Brainerd always said you had talent...but you know how Hoot's been hangin' all over your ex, an' I better not catch you doin' the same...that Fay's a snake-charmer, an' she'll charm your snake right offa you if you're not careful! Sug, I gotta run...Corny's out doin' a charity carwash this mornin', so we're short-handed. See ya later, lover, bye!"

Euladean blew a kiss at Henry, and he got back in the car with a sigh of relief. Hoot exited the Poe House with three bag boys each carrying a full sack of groceries.

"Easy, there, son! Put 'em in the back *HEY*, watch out! Them bottles 'll break! That beer's imported from St. Louis!"

The bag boys loaded the car, then stood around waiting for Hoot to give them a tip. He fished around in his pockets and gave them each a dime.

"Here you are, my men! Thank ya kindly!" The bag boys scowled at Hoot, then one of them flipped him a bird, but Hoot was too busy thinking about his new bodyguard and his hot date with Fay to notice.

"Drive on, Best Boy, drive on!"

Hoot removed his bandanna-ascot and used it to wipe the sweat off his forehead. Henry turned down the eight-track and looked at his new employer.

"What all d'ya buy, H.?" Henry was anxious to learn about the critical grocery requirements of Hollywood Celebrities.

"Well, fer starters, got us some Camels...an' an ice chest, an' some wine coolers an' ice an' Dixie Chips fer tonight! An' a few other sundries...stuff us Hollywood Directors need."

"Oh...we gonna tote all that stuff inta play rehearsal?"

Henry was getting sleepy...usually at this time of day, he organized a sales meeting for three minutes, and a post-sales meeting nap for twenty.

"Henry, drive down main street, yeah, don't *never* take side streets when you're drivin' a Hollywood Director 'round, ok? First rule of a good Best Boy is stick ta the main roads, gotta please our fans! Good...ok, now, you're gonna take all this stuff ta my executive suite an' get ever'thing good an' chilled, then run back over ta play practice an' I'll start teachin' ya the ropes. That'll give me a chance ta alert ever'body to the fact that you're my Best Boy, an' let 'em know that things is gonna be *different!* Henry...quick, honk the horn!"

Hoot casually waved a hand at a passerby, a passerby he mistakenly believed was Betty Gooch.

"Henry...your first job as Best Boy's gonna be ta get this vehicle cleaned up, an' get us a sign...we gotta let the public know jus' who's ridin' around town! You can add that ta your list this afternoon!"

Henry shifted in the driver's seat. He was in dire need of a nap, but apparently Best Boys did not indulge in the luxury of nap-taking. "Hoot, don't take this wrong, or nothin', but do Best Boys get a break anytime?"

Hoot nodded as he scanned Main Street for his adoring public. "Of course, Henry! Whenever I'm asleep, or in a big meetin', or with a cute little...when I'm in a *script* conference, you can take a break! I ain't gonna treat you no worse than I expect you ta treat me! Here, pull up in front a the Gym-torium, an' jus' let me off...drive real slow...ok, now get out, open my door fer me, an' then salute me."

"Sure, Hoot...but ain't that gonna look kinda silly?"

Henry was beginning to wonder if there was an official Best Boy manual so he could get a better handle on what was actually required of him.

"Naw, Henry! Trust me! You got natural talent fer this, son!"

Henry parked the El Camino in front of the entrance to the Gym-torium, where fifty people waited impatiently in the August heat for Emilio Rodriguez to open the door and let them in. They stared at the dingy, rusted car in suspicion when they saw Henry Bailey get out, walk over to the passenger door and open it. But at the sight of their Executive Director, someone in the crowd began to clap, and others followed suit. Henry's salute was lost in the shuffle as Hoot greeted his enthralled fans...fans who were desperately counting on Hoot's expertise to lead them all to Big Hollywood Careers and Big Hollywood Paychecks.

"Thank you, thank you ladies and gentleman...please make way, we gotta strennyous rehearsal today...*that will be all, Henry.* Please prepare the bar fer tonight's swar-ee."

Hoot strode dramatically up to the door of the Gym-torium as Henry returned to the driver's seat of the El Camino. "Uh, Mr. Graham, sir, the door's locked," someone called as Hoot tried to open the door with a flourish.

Henry hollered out the passenger window, "Mr. H. Graham, is a Best Boy s'posed to pick locks?"

Hoot rolled his eyes in disgust at his Best Boy's faux pas. "That will be *all*, Henry, run 'long an' see ta your duties!" Hoot shook his head in mock frustration and muttered, "Good help is *so* hard ta find!"

Suddenly the door to the Gym-torium opened from inside, and all the adoring fans followed their great director into the building. Henry sped off in a cloud of black smoke. *Let's see,* Henry thought. *Gotta get the limo cleaned, gotta ice down the coolers, gotta find some lawn chairs an' make us a sign...maybe I can work in a catnap*...Henry pulled into the Fluffy Pillow Motel parking lot just as the motel owner/housekeeper was leaving Hoot's room.

"Hey, there, Miz Ethel! How you doin? Listen, I gotta deliver some stuff here fer H. Graham, can you let me in? I'm his Best Boy, but he done fergot ta give me a key!"

"You're his *what?* His *Best Boy?* Now you look here, I told Hoot I don't 'low no *funny stuff* at this motel! Henry Bailey, I'm surprised at you! Does Euladean know about this? You'll break her heart!"

Henry shook his head and waved his arms, "*No,* Miz Ethel, it ain't what ya *think!* I'm as one-sexual as the day is long! Ya see I'm workin' with Hoot...*H*...as his Best Boy...out there in Hollywood that's what they call a *Producer*...I think...anyhow, Miz Ethel, we gotta big meetin' tonight an' I gotta get ever'thing ready while H. is over ta play practice!"

Miz Ethel didn't like the sound of this Best Boy business, but she was one of the few people in Chestnut Ridge who was kind to Henry Bailey. "All right, Henry, I'll open the door...are you tellin' me you're gonna need an extra key? Ya'll better not be doin' nothin' *strange* at my motel! Hoot's already done some plaster damage, and he's wearin' me out callin' me ever' five minutes! But I know you're a good man...maybe some a that'll rub off on Hoot! Here ya go..." Miz Ethel opened the door to Hoot's Executive Suite. "Bye now Henry, you stay outta trouble!"

Henry carried all the groceries inside, and noted that Hoot's executive suite seemed like any ordinary motel room, except that it had an extra lamp. He iced down the wine coolers, put the Dixie Chips in a separate bag to prevent crushing, and then made a sign out of a paper grocery sack and a tube of shoe polish he found in the bathroom. Henry was no artist but was pleased with his handiwork, which read, "LIMO OF H. GRAHAM & BEST BOY." Now he needed some tape, so he inspected Hoot's grocery purchases. First he encountered two twelve-packs of honeybuns, ten boxes of assorted fancy cookies and four six-packs of Budweiser. *Guess Hollywood Directors need reinforcements for those late-night sessions,* Henry noted.

The rest of the grocery sacks contained cartons of Camels, a few Hollywood gossip magazines (*gotta keep up with the competition,* Henry surmised), a bottle of chocolate sauce and a box of Pre-Lubricated, Extra-Pleasurably Ribbed condoms in Wild and Exciting Neon colors. Henry quickly put the condoms back in the grocery sack...he was still not convinced that a Best Boy's job was entirely on the up-and-up.

Henry looked at his watch...one-thirty...he had plenty of time to take a short nap before completing the rest of his Best Boy tasks. He realized he was hungry, so he opened the honeybuns and ate two. Then he stretched out on the bed, careful to avoid placing his shoes on the clean spread. After roughly thirty seconds, Henry was fast asleep, and he would have stayed that way all afternoon if the phone had not rung. Henry pulled the receiver onto his head as he lay coma-like. He could hear Miz Ethel's loud voice.

"Henry...you okay? What're you doin'? This ain't no *flophouse*...get outta there, 'fore I have ta charge Hoot extra fer overnight guests!"

A groggy Henry replaced the receiver, then looked at his watch. Three-thirty! There was Best Boy business at hand! He used the executive suite washroom, guzzled down a wine cooler and grabbed the El Camino keys. He stashed the "LIMO OF H. GRAHAM & BEST BOY" sign in the glove box and started the engine.

Henry sped off down Main Street with music blaring from the eight-track. *I could get used ta this,* Henry realized. *This beats the hell outta sittin' at that Used Car Lot all day long...*"YOU KNOW I AIN'T HIS DADDY 'CAUSE HE AIN'T GOT MY GOOD LOOKS! SO GIT UP OFF YER HIGH HORSE AN' JUS' LEMME OFF THE HOOK!"

The car lot! Henry turned the El Camino around and pulled into the lot. He opened the RV, found a scrap of paper and a pen, and wrote "BACK IN AN HOUR...MAJOR DEAL." Then he found some tape, stuck the sign to the door of the RV, and threw the tape into the El Camino's glove box. He sped back up Main Street into the hot August sunshine.

Henry stopped at the red light on the corner of Main and Pecan, and noticed a crowd of squealing teenagers in front of the First United Assembly of God's Children. A large white banner was suspended over the church parking lot, proclaiming in garish red block letters, "RIVER JORDAN DRIVE-THRU CAR WASH & BAPTISM, FIVE DOLLARS."

Henry Bailey was a charitable soul, and he was also in need of a car wash, in compliance with his new role of Best Boy. When the traffic light changed, he veered into the church parking lot and pulled up behind a white van that was in line for a wash. In front of the white van, a pickup truck was sudsed and soaked by three wet, slippery boys in shorts.

Just as Henry decided the wait might be too long, his brother-in-law Corny Poe stuck his face into the El Camino's open window. Corny's bald head was as red as a vine-ripe tomato from the heat. His t-shirt was thoroughly soaked, and it stuck to his pudgy chest, making Corny look as if he was a contestant in some kind of bizarre wet t-shirt contest.

"Well, if it isn't my Pope-worshipin' brother-in-law! How're ya doin'? Boy, I haven't seen *this* car in a month of Sundays! I 'member when my cousin wrecked it...never thought *anybody* could drive it after that! Welcome to the

River Jordan Drive-Thru Car Wash & Baptism! You heard about that hy-eenous play they're doin' for the Festival? Well, *some* of us don't agree with the way it's portrayin' our ancestors...so a group of us concerned citizens is raisin' money to stage a little play of our *own!* A play based on God's *truth* about this town, with family values, 'steada teachin' our children that our forefathers was nothin' but a buncha *thieves!*"

Corny wiped a soapy palm on his shorts. Henry nodded in silent agreement, believing it prudent not to mention that he'd just been appointed Best Boy to the hy-eenous play's director. He decided to skip the small talk and cut to the chase.

"That's real swell, Corny! You sure do a heap a good work! Yeah, I need me a good car wash on this fine automobile...reckon ya'll can help me out? I'm in a bit of a hurry..."

"No problem, there, Henry, no problem at all! You're *fam'ly,* unfortunately!"

Corny motioned to several idle teenagers who were flirting beside the water spigot. At his signal, they ran over to the El Camino with soap buckets and sponges, and began to scrub the sin from Henry's car. Corny knelt down beside the El Camino and stared hard at Henry with a tremendous look of piety and calm on his scarlet face.

"Henry, guess you noticed our sign. Henry, do you believe in the power of the Holy Spirit? You may have thought you needed a quick car wash today, but your poor soul was crying out fer *salvation!* The power of the Holy Spirit took over, an' drove you right here, to this spot! How's your soul, Henry? Henry, you been saved? I don't mean saved like you white trash Catholics do it...no, I mean have you really been *saved,* Henry? Have you ever looked the Devil in the eye and told him that Jesus is your personal savior?"

Henry was suddenly very uncomfortable with the current direction of this conversation with Corny. He shifted in the driver's seat and noticed that one of the teenagers had spewed soap foam onto Corny's head. Corny, however, was deep into his ministerial Christian duty, and continued.

"Now I *know* you been through some *powerful* torments in your life...married to that devil temptress...livin' with the shame of the demon alcohol in your fam'ly tree...goin' to that idolator's church! Have you given yourself to *Jesus,* Henry? Have you taken up the cross? Do you feel a sense of overwhelming joy when you wake up each day, Henry? If you just repent, *right now,* Jesus Himself will meet you at the gates of the River Jordan Drive-Thru Car Wash and Baptism! *Jesus Himself* will bless you with a simple spray of the hose! And then, Henry, you'll be with me, and Penni, and Daddy, and your sweet wife Euladean in Heaven...because if ya *don't* accept Jesus today, Henry, you're gonna be on the wrong side of the fence at that big Car Wash in the Sky, sittin' there with all the resta them heathens, wishin' you'd been sprayed here today, like Jesus commands!"

Corny Poe stood up stiffly; saving souls for Jesus was very hard on one's knees, but then he remembered his Sweet Jesus Sweet Potato, a bit shriveled, but still carrying the face of the Savior, and nevertheless a reminder of his calling. He leaned over to Henry through the window and said in a low voice, "Henry...do it fer Euladean...she loves you so. Henry...Jesus loves you, too! Search your heart...shall I spray you, Henry? Will today be the day you have a clean car *and* a clean soul?"

Henry glanced at his watch and realized that he was very late for play rehearsal on his first day as Best Boy, and that if he entertained a discussion with Corny on the merits of soul-saving, he'd be even later. He looked up at Corny and nodded, "Ok, I guess, Corny, sure, count me in! Will it take long?" Corny ignored Henry's question, raised his arms and shouted, "PRAISE GOD! Another soul saved fer Jesus!" A host of car-washing-soul-savers circled around the suds-laden El Camino, linking arms and singing a hymn. Corny motioned for the hose.

I sure hope he's gonna let me close my windows first, Henry wondered. *It won't do fer a Big-Time Hollywood Star to ride around in a wet El Camino...that'd put an end to my days as Best Boy before they even start.*

"Uh, Corny, wait a sec...lemme put up this here winda an'...*AWWW! CORNY!!!!"*

Corny Poe aimed the Holy Hose smack at Henry Bailey's face and proceeded to spray a heavy stream right into the open window, splashing water all over the El Camino's dash, its yellow vinyl seats, and its floorboard.

"PRAISE GOD, HENRY BAILEY! YOU ARE *SAVED!* YOU WILL JOIN YOUR BROTHERS AND SISTERS AT THAT GREAT CAR WASH IN THE SKY! PRAISE GOD! *That will be five dollars, please! Jesus loves you!"*

Corny held out his hand as a dripping Henry angrily thrust a soggy five-dollar bill toward it. Miraculously, the engine re-started, and Henry pulled out of the First United Assembly of God's Children parking lot as Corny exclaimed,

"Another soul cleansed here today, brothers and sisters, at the River of Jordan Drive-Thru Car Wash & Baptism! Praise God! Now let's all hope he comes to church tomorrow so it'll take!"

Henry drove back to the Used Car Lot, opened the RV, and found a few old undershirts in the rag bag. He wiped down the interior of the El Camino, swearing under his breath all the while at Corny's zealous, watery attempt to save his soul. After examining his handiwork, he decided that the impromptu baptism was actually beneficial, because the seats, dash, and floorboard of the El Camino were now much cleaner than before. At least it might appear to Hoot that his Best Boy was also an accomplished car detailer.

Henry threw the rags in the dirty clothes hamper, then took a shower...there was no telling when a Best Boy might have another chance to get cleaned up. He left a note for Euladean that he'd be working late with Hoot, but that he'd call as soon as he could. *Love ya, sug, your Hollywood Best Boy,* he signed it. Then he removed the "BACK IN ONE HOUR...MAJOR DEAL" sign on the RV's picture window, in favor of the sign that read, "CLOSED."

As the interior of the newly-baptized El Camino dried in the hot August sun, Henry grabbed the roll of tape from the glove box and fastened the "LIMO OF H. GRAHAM & BEST BOY" sign to the passenger door. He checked his watch...Hoot was gonna fire him on his very first day if he didn't burn some serious rubber. He sped over to the Gym-torium and parked illegally in front of the entrance, ever-ready for Hoot's return.

This is it, Henry Bailey...don't screw up! Let's go, Killer! Gotta make Miz Novella Brainerd proud of ya, even if she has been stone dead these twenty years...she was prob'ly one a them sightseers, could tell the future, an' all...knew I'd be famous some day!

Henry took a deep breath and walked inside the Chestnut Ridge Senior High School Gym-torium, ready to give H. Graham his Best Boy best. Who'd a thunk he'd ever be a Best Boy...and soon, real soon, a rich man?

CHAPTER FOURTEEN – THEATER OF THE ABSURD

Mid-August 1999; Chesnut Ridge High School Gym-torium

"All right, everyone, let's have some quiet for our Director...QUIET! QUIET, PLEASE!"

Peter Paul Culpepper loudly clapped his hands in frustration at the fifty-odd actors assembled in front of the Gym-torium's makeshift stage. It had been a tedious, hot Saturday, and to say that the Festival play rehearsal was not going smoothly was a vast understatement of the truth. Peter Paul Culpepper was exhausted, and fed-up.

"Now, since we're behind schedule...I think we should omit scene four today and concentrate on the most critical part of this entire play...*scene five*, where the thieving Town Fathers are discovered after stealing the Union Payroll from the innocent Federal soldiers they have just mercilessly murdered. Mr. Director, don't you agree? *Mr. Director*?"

Mr. Director Hoot Graham, at the back of the Gym-torium, was otherwise engaged in a state of mesmerization with an unidentified, chesty, giggling redhead; thus, he was ill-prepared to discuss the rehearsal of scene five, or any other scene, at this exact moment in time. Peter Paul Culpepper frowned and examined his clipboard with an exasperated sigh.

Six days, almost to the minute, it had taken Peter Paul Culpepper to write this great epic of Chestnut Ridge, *"The Golden Secret."* Yet after almost ten weeks of rehearsal, not one single actor fully knew his lines; not one prop, costume or backdrop was ready and not one person involved paid him the slightest attention. The fact that he was the playwright made absolutely no difference to anyone; the fact that he was the Assistant Director made even less of an impression.

The sole source of motivation to this little troupe remained Hollywood Hoot Graham and his plan to film the play and sell it to a major network, or at least to PBS; despite his dubious and supposed L.A. connections, in the opinion of Peter Paul Culpepper, high school senior and aspiring playwright, Mr. Graham was simply not doing his job. Pointing an ancient, cracked light meter toward the stage every so often, to "take readings," was not, in his estimation, a director's only task. Peter Paul looked at his clipboard and yelled, "All right, people, let's get crackin'! *Where* are my *dead soldiers*? *Where* is the besmirched Negress?"

Reluctantly, the three dead teenage soldiers climbed the rickety stairs to the stage and milled around, mumbling about how they would much prefer to be playing football. The besmirched Negress, alias Betty Gooch, head wrapped in a red kerchief and boot-black smeared on her cheeks, stubbed out a cigarette and slouched to stage right. With a final glance at Mr. Director, who remained enthralled at the back of the Gym-torium by his enchanting guest, Peter Paul Culpepper yelled for *Action*, as he had done at every rehearsal to date. *Somebody has to get this hulking theatrical monster off the ground,* he thought to himself, because he would be the one to suffer if it didn't, at the hands of his Senior English teacher, Diana Avery.

"People! *Let's go*!"

The besmirched Negress exhaled a white cloud of smoke, snubbed out her cigarette, then wrung her hands and moaned loudly, in an untrained, overly dramatic and noticeably non-Negress voice,

"Oh, me, oh, mah, wha's l'il ol' me ta do? I done been besmirched by dem Johnny Rebs, an' now dey done gone an' headed fo' de Massa's house…I shore hope dey'uns don't fin' dem Boys in Blue, Lawd, no, seein' as how dey carryin' dat payroll, fo' dem hon'rable Fed'rals, who done been fightin' to set us free!"

The besmirched Negress staggered awkwardly toward the dead soldiers, who were tangled in a furiously giggling heap, stage left. She knelt down over the dead bodies, raised her hands to the sky, and then toppled over onto the pile in an act of sheer grief.

"Oh, Lawd, hab mercy! Dem Johnny Rebs done killt dese poor souls! I best see if dey done took de gold! *Oh, Lawd, Lawd, it's gone*! Da gold is gone, gone! An' dese boys is dead, dead, on de cold, cold groun'! Dese poor, poor boys who…*HEY! YOU BETTER STOP GROPIN' MY TITTIES, YOUNG MAN, OR I'LL WHIP YOUR SORRY LITTLE ASS!*"

The besmirched Negress jerked one of the dead soldiers to his feet, and shook him hard, stage left.

"You're s'posed to be *dead*, and that mean's *no touching*! Do you get it? *DEAD*! I'm tryin' ta do some bodacious actin' an' this kid's playin' touchy-feely with my bosoms!"

Betty Gooch tore the kerchief from her head to reveal roots in dire need of a dye job and stormed off the stage. Her fellow actors, including the three dead soldiers, laughed hysterically. Peter Paul Culpepper threw his clipboard onto the floor and screamed,

"THAT'S IT! YOU ARE SO IMMATURE, JASON! THIS IS A SERIOUS PLAY WE'RE DOING HERE, AND IF YOU CAN'T ACT YOUR AGE, THEN JUST LEAVE!"

These were musical words to Jason's ears; he quickly unbuttoned his dead soldier's jacket and threw it onto the stage floor.

"Hey, I didn't touch that old *bag*! But she's floppin' her titties on me somethin' fierce! Just like she did at that dance with Roland Gastineau! I don't wanna be in your old damned play, anyhow, you wimp! Go find somebody else ta be dead! Come on, ya'll, let's go!"

Jason departed in a huff, with the other two dead soldiers following dutifully behind. They were stopped at the door, however, by Mr. Director himself, whose red-headed distraction had mysteriously vanished. A disgusted Peter Paul Culpepper watched in anguish as Mr. Director intervened in the dead soldiers' exit.

"Hey, now, *men*! What's shakin'? Come on, ya'll can't let a little thing like this put a halt to your actin' careers, now can ya? I mean, if ya'll wanna leave, ok, git on outta here! But... *an' I'm real serious now*...ya'll are prob'ly missin' out on the opportun'ty of a lifetime! I'm tellin' ya, this play may be may not 'xactly be Big Time, but once I get this stuff on film, it's gonna hit the airwaves, boys! It's gonna put this town on the map! Trust me on this! But I reckon, if ya'll don't wanna be part of it, if ya'll aren't inter'sted in havin' pretty women chase ya all over town, like that fella, what's his name, Leonard D. Capacheeno? Well, then we'll jus' see ya'll later!"

The three ex-dead soldiers grunted and looked at each other. Jason grumbled, "Sorry, Mr. Director. But she's just *askin'* for it, ya know? I mean, we're up there, bein' dead, an' she just plops down and wiggles her titties right on my *head!* What am I s'posed to *do?*"

Mr. Director grinned, "Take it like a man, son, jus' take it like a man!"

The three dead soldiers wisely pondered the sage advice given to them by Mr. Director, and suddenly saw their terrible predicament in a new light. They decided to postpone their walk-out and followed Mr. Director as he sauntered toward the stage. Hoot adjusted his bandanna-ascot with a perturbed look and threw his arms to the sky. Then he exhaled deeply and hopped up on the platform. He kicked a couple of props, threw a script into the air and turned toward his audience in a blaze of fury.

"Ya'll are nothin' but a bunch a rounders! I ain't never seen a lazier group a people in all my life! Ten weeks, I been *sweatin'*, an' *toilin'*, an' whatta we got? ZERO! We ain't got diddly-squat to get on film! Now I'm tellin' ya...I'm tired a wastin' my precious time! I got contracts back in Hollywood fer sixteen movies! Spielberg's left me so many voice mails it done broke the machine! I ain't jus' hangin' out here fer my *health*! An' how d'ya'll think poor Peter Paul Puss...poor Peter Paul feels, huh? He's done busted his balls ta write this here play, an' ya'll are jus' steppin' all over it! Like it was *trash*! That's it! I'm outta here! *HEY! BEST BOY!* Let's go! I'm goin' back ta L.A., *tonight*! No...right *now*, dammit! We're goin' back ta L.A., an' ya'll can jus' do this by *yerseves*!"

Mr. Director quickly surveyed the shocked crowd of thespians as his tantrum took effect; everyone stood completely still and silent, and the eyes of some of the women brimmed with tears. The Best Boy appeared from behind the stage, still wearing his costume; the costume of a Civil War-era widow woman. A part, Mr. Director had assured him, that was vital to the success of the plot.

Mr. Director scooped up his Roy's Tape House gimme cap, his bottled water and his ancient light meter, and thundered off across the Gym-torium. The Best Boy, who at this exact moment resembled more of a Worst Woman, hustled to keep up as he unbuttoned his dress and fumbled with his wig. The other actors slowly removed their meager costumes and dispersed; their days of fame and glory had come to a screeching Hollywood halt. Peter Paul Culpepper sulked around the Gym-torium, retrieving copies of his precious script. *Someday,* he muttered to himself, *someday I'll be a famous playwright in New York City and all these goobers will be so sorry they didn't pay attention to me now! Just wait! Goobers! Hicks! Every one!*

Backstage, in the Ladies' Dressing Room, constructed from flattened refrigerator cartons placed end to end, Stella Stanley, Official Play Makeup Artist, scoffed.

"That Betty Gooch'll flag 'em down at any age, the ol' hussy! An' did ya git a load a them *roots*? She's cancelled ever' 'pointment she was s'posed ta have with me fer the last three weeks! The only reason she's in this here play is she thinks that poor Gastineau boy'll fall in love with her if she's a big-time actress! But I reckon if I's married ta Barney, I'd most likely do the same! Man can't even *see* his pecker over that tub a lard he's carryin' around!"

Stella snubbed out a cigarette as Ruby Quigley plopped down in the Official Ladies' Makeup Chair so Stella could remove her Federal Spy makeup. Ruby fumed.

"All I gotta say is it's *oblivious* who the important folks are in this town! Look who's got the best parts! I mean, come on, MayBelle Festrunk playin' a twenty-year old? While the rest of us is gotta be dolled up like slaves, or old widdas, or *Yankees*! My daddy's prob'ly rollin' over in his grave, seein' me all got up like a Yankee spy! Roy won't even talk ta me when I git home from practice! But Miz MayBelle's sure got lotsa 'tention!"

"I heard that, Ruby Quigley! I can't help it if you're just jealous that you've had to work for a living! Pardon me, I'm sure you do quite well for yourself, in a blue collar fashion, but really, now, that's just not the same as owning half the town and living in leisure off the interest, is it? Isn't that what you always say about me and my family? I heard what you said about us driving around in our new cars, too, acting like we're something special!"

MayBelle Festrunk unbuttoned her costume and pointed a pudgy pink finger at Ruby Quigley. "Well, let me tell you one thing! For sixty-five years, my sister and I have lived our lives at the hospital aiding our fellow citizens. We drove old cars and wore old uniforms so we could put every single extra nickel back into that Clinic, because it was our duty, and we were proud to do it! Now my brother and sister and I put up half the money for this play and all I wanted was a little bitsy bitty part; I can't help it if Barney Gooch recognized my talent and insisted I get a starring role! But it's about time this town recognized what the Festrunks have done!"

MayBelle Festrunk stuck her tongue out at Ruby Quigley, and sat down on a milk crate to wait her turn at makeup removal. MayBelle had been surprisingly selected to portray the Young, Upstanding, Righteous Female Citizen in Peter Paul's play. Her character's role was pivotal; it was the Young, Upstanding, Righteous Female Citizen who would catch the Scoundrel Johnny Reb Thieves in the Act, and after a long battle with her conscience, instead of turning them in, forced them to revitalize the town by using the stolen gold to repair its broken grist mill and feed its hungry masses. The fact that this plotline was far from the historic truth was not an issue to the playwright or his technical advisors, nor was it an issue that a late sixtyish woman with blue hair was playing the role of a twentyish fair maid. MayBelle was awarded this prime role shortly after she donated no less than five thousand dollars to the production company's coffers, at the personal request of the Mayor.

"Ladies, ladies," Stella said through a mouthful of bobby pins, "let's us not have another go 'round on this, ok? Ruby, there's parts enough fer ever'body, hell, there's still parts Hoot ain't got filled yet! Besides, ya look real good in that Fed'ral Spy jacket! It's real slimmin'!"

"Oh, Stella, yer just sayin' that 'cause I'm yer boss! I'm sorry Miz MayBelle, this menopause stuff is givin' me the hormone fits, I know ya'll have always been nothin' but help to ever'body here. Hey, Esperanza! Come on in here, honey! How in the world yer gonna get all that boot-black offa yer face…yer gonna git a rash! Stella, better order some more a that extra-strength cleansin' crème. I guess Betty Gooch just got in her van an' drove home with alla that stuff still on her cheeks! Lordy be, I hope she don't run into Roland at a traffic light!"

The actresses in the Ladies' Dressing Room hooted with laughter at the thought of Betty Gooch with her bad roots and boot-blacked face, sitting at a stoplight opposite Roland Gastineau. Esperanza removed her Slave Number Two costume, careful to avoid smearing any boot-black on it, as she pulled it over her head.

"Thees ees *stupido*! I khave no need of thees stuff! My skeen ees already dark eenoff! An' I tell choo won t'ing! Meesis Lacy, thee library, shee say, *'Esperanza, only tree slaves een dees town back 'den, an' all mens!'* Dees ees *stupido*! *Loco!*"

Bessie Thibodeaux entered the Dressing Room. She wore tattered cotton rags and a necklace made out of large blue feathers. Woven into Bessie's thickly plaited hair were several African Tribal artifacts, as interpreted by Stella Stanley, who cleaned out her kitchen cabinets and volunteered a pair of red enameled chopsticks, an old Troll doll with green hair, and a string of Mardi Gras beads. Bessie's costume, Dr. Avery Parker insisted, should ultimately represent the authentic clothing that an African slave woman would have worn in protest of her situation, to remind her fellow slaves of their individualism; Stella Stanley, however, quickly tired of the individual effort required to dress the actress for the part, and so everyone overlooked the fact that chopsticks and Troll dolls were not inherent to the slave era. Bessie gingerly removed the African Tribal artifacts from her hair and sat down.

"Why we wearin' dis silly stuff, anyhows? I look like t'at crazy woman outside town, used ta put t'at ol' chicken on a leash an' walk him up Main Street! It ain't right, I gonna tell you!"

Ruby Quigley wiped her face with a wet washcloth and stepped out of Stella's chair so Miz MayBelle could take her turn. "Ya got that right, honey! I done talked ta Carol Lacy myself, an' she fired up that there micro-fishin' machine an' showed me an art'cle in the Nashville paper, from eighteen an'eighty, that says the very same thing! They was countin' farms, or somethin', back then, an' this reporter got all side-tracked an' started talkin' 'bout how Chestnut Ridge made such a mirac'lous recovery after the War Between the States; an' how parta the reason was 'cause they didn't have ta give no land ta no slaves, 'cause they was only three slaves here, an' they'd already done moved on when the Yankees found out 'bout this ol' town in the first place! Chestnut Ridge wasn't nothin' but a handful of dirt farmers on the brinka starvation! We ain't never owned no slaves, or treated nobody bad, 'ceptin' maybe them Baileys. And Lordy be, they deserved it! Oh, sorry Euladean."

Euladean Bailey, official Costume Mistress of *"The Golden Secret,"* stepped into the Dressing Room, oblivious to Ruby's comment. She carried an armload of costumes that had been hurriedly discarded in the middle of the Gym-torium floor by the men. She dropped the pile on the floor in disgust and began to sort through it and hang up the clothes.

"I swear, don't ya'll get tired of pickin' up after these men every day! I mean, do ya think their mommas just didn't ever teach 'em how to do *nothin*? Ya know, Ruby, I talked with Miz Lacy too, an' it got me ta thinkin'... I dug up in my daddy's attic last week when he was over in Chattanooga for that Meat Purveyor's potluck. An' I found my Granddaddy Poe's journal...he wanted ta be a writer, ya know, an', anyhow, one day he'd got *his* daddy, Mr. Prospero Poe, ta talkin'...back in nineteen-ten...old Prospero was 'bout seventy years old, you know he was one a the foundin' citizens a this town, an' ya'll ain't gonna b'lieve what *he* said..."

All eyes were steadfastly glued to Euladean Bailey in anticipation of some earth-shattering confirmation of the truth to the town's past. Euladean suddenly broke into one of her famous sneezing fits, which happened only when she became excited. After counting about two dozen sneezes, Euladean's audience nearly lost interest, but then as quickly as the sneezes had begun, they simply stopped and Euladean continued without missing a beat.

"...an' *he* said, that all them soldiers in the 44th Regiment a the Tennessee Riders was followin' orders from their officers, you know, the Major an' the Captain an' the Lieutenant, an' so they broke camp behind the grist mill, because it was so cold an' windy that night. He said they were goin' 'bout their bizness regular-like, doin' Army stuff, an' that suddenly, outta nowhere, came these young gals carryin' steamin' pies an' hot coffee! 'Course wouldn't ya know one a them was my great-great grandmomma, later on after she married ol' Prospero...anyhow, they told those men ta strike their tents an' they done took 'em to the cave over yonder, ta hide from the Yankees. An' then, when they found out the War was 'bout over, an' they decided ta stay right here, 'cause there was lots a widdas with farms, an' lots a stuff broken, like the grist mill. An' a course they opened that quarry."

There was an awkward silence in the Ladies Dressing Room; Euladean Poe Bailey was a God-fearing woman and a friend to many, and although her friends had come to terms with her marriage to Henry, they couldn't deny the misdeeds of his forebears and the tales of murder and scandal surrounding the quarry's demise. Undaunted, Euladean continued. "Weren't no talk 'bout slaves, or gold, or thievin'!"

"Was there a besmirched Negress?" MayBelle asked. She was quite concerned that the play's content might be too lascivious for children.

"No, it didn't say nothin' 'bout no Negresses, besmirched or reg'lar...Prospero said that them three slaves b'longed to a rich widda woman but they done run off when they caught sight of the Major an' his men. Then one came back 'cause he was starvin', an' the widda woman sent him off agin ta get parts for the mill, an' that time he never came back."

Stella Stanley slopped a thick layer of cold crème on MayBelle Festrunk's face. "Now looky, Euladean, ya know I've dated me an Army man er two in my time...they cain't just stick aroun' somewheres just 'cause the *pie's* good an' there's broke stuff ta be *fixed*! I mean, they gotta folla orders from headquarters an' stuff!"

Euladean nodded her head. "I know, but accordin' ta ol' Prospero, in this journal, them officers had a meetin' once they was in that cave, an' after a coupla days, the Major told ever'body the Yankees would be comin' soon an' they was all free to go home, or free ta stay put, an' most a the men stayed put, livin' in that cave fer 'while I guess, an' married the widda women, an' the young gals, an', well, here we all are! An' far as ol' Prospero's journal says, no Yankees ever did come here, 'cept ta buy limestone from the quarry, said they came to that quarry every week with ten horse carts an' left with them carts fulla limestone. Nothin' 'bout thievin', or carryin' on with slaves or Negresses, an' well, 'scuse me, Miz MayBelle, but there warn't nothin' 'bout no Young Upstanding Righteous Female Citizen, neither."

Bessie Thibodeaux slammed her broad hand down on a copy of the script. "Here is what I t'ink! I am American! No slave, no African Princess! And I ain't gonna dress up in no more costume like t'at crazy Chicken Woman, t'at Doc Avery an' his missus, they be rewritin' da hist'ry an' tryin' to make us look like fools so's he can give him a big speech! Ain't nobody in dis place treated me bad! T'is play is not right! I'm have a talk wit' Mr. Will, *cher*!"

Diana Parker abruptly entered the Ladies' Dressing Area. She was obviously furious, and her eyes shot hot rockets toward Bessie Thibodeaux. "Mrs. Thibodeaux, I'm sorry you feel put out about interpreting your ancestral mode of dress. But it was heavily researched by my husband! Would you prefer that we just simply *ignore* the inclusion of any persons of color in this theatrical representation? Would you prefer to just omit your entire *race* and pretend like everyone else around here that we never *existed*? Perhaps if you ladies looked around you, you might realize that this play is about symbols...that it is a chance to right some of the injustices and wrongs committed against women, against persons of color, and if you are not willing to participate in a portrayal of Truth, and make a statement for your sex, for your race, then..."

"Hey, now Miz Parker! Don't get all riled up!" Stella Stanley wiped Miz MayBelle clean and motioned for her next victim. "But, listen up, some a this stuff in that play ain't even happened here! I mean, we been tol' there weren't but three slaves in the whole county! An' everyone of 'em was men, not a black woman in the bunch! An' I ain't *never* seen no slave women all dolled up like some Voodoo Witch in any ol' war photos, neither! Least, that ain't how they do it on TV! An' if that money *was* stole from the Yankees, then how come ain't nobody was arrested, an' how come ain't none of us ever heard tell 'bout it, an' it ain't in them old newspapers, or over t' the town records, or nothin'? An' if it's true them Yankees was comin' here ever' week ta buy limestone outta that quarry, how come they never got all riled up an' tried ta git their stolen gold back?"

Diana Parker pursed her lip. "I had greater hopes for all of you. I expected that you would all willingly participate in this town's effort to right a great injustice! I had dreams that the "have nots" could somehow humble the "haves" into doing what is right! Force them to acknowledge their mistakes, right their wrongs...make amends for the past...my husband swears that this town was founded on stolen money, whether you ladies care to acknowledge it or not. And the fact remains, the people of this town have certainly not practiced inclusivity!"

Ruby Quigley adjusted a bright red bow in her black bouffant. "Miz Parker, everybody knows you an' your husband are smart…ya'll are just about the smartest durned folks we've ever had in this town, 'cept for Doc Kimball. An' ya'll know we love ya like fam'ly. But I swear, this whole play thing's gone too far! I mean, I know how much it means to ya'll's people to get some kinda apology for slavery, for discrim'nation, an' all that…but Miz Parker, we ain't had much a that in Chestnut Ridge! We're jus' plain ol' poor folks! Course, we only had them three slave men, if ya b'lieve Miz Lacy's newspapers, an' Bessie an' her sister, an' then ya'll moved here…an' Bessie, well, she ain't been complainin', she's always been treated like one a us an' now she got her own shop! An' 'Melia an' Esp'ranza...lookit how successful they been here, there ain't been no discrim'natin' goin' on! An' ya'll done moved inta one of the nicest neighborhoods in town an' ain't nobody said nothin', 'cept they didn't know why ya'll would wanna live here when there ain't but a handful a ya'lls people in town an' ya'll might stick out like sore thumbs, but it don't matter none to us! But I don't see how we can put on this play an' not tell the truth! An' alla this stuff in this here play just ain't the truth, lease not 'cordin' ta what we've heard from our own momma and grandmomma's lips! An' what's in them newspapers in the library, an' now what we done found out's in ol' man Poe's journal!"

The other women in the Ladies' Dressing Room mumbled softly in agreement with a surprisingly eloquent Ruby Quigley. She continued."I mean, we all 'preciate what Peter Paul has wrote…don't get us wrong…I cain't barely write out my grocery list, let alone somethin' like this…but that boy told me hisself it ain't the same play he wrote after your husband got through with it. All we know is we live in a sweet little town, outside a Nashville…an' we done heard legends all our lives 'bout how our fam'ly had somebody that fought in that War Between th' States…an' how they helped this town survive when all that was 'round was a buncha no-good Yankees wantin' ta starve us outta our homes! I signed up ta help with this play 'cause I thought it'd be a way to pay back their mem'ry, not stir up a buncha mess an' embarrass me an my ancestors!"

Stella Stanley took a long drag from a cigarette and nodded. "Miz Parker, maybe yer husband's right…maybe alla the people in this town just mighta come down from a buncha thieves…but ta us…we been knowin' 'em all our lives as heroes…an' fer some a us, that's all we got. Ya'll callin' our folks thieves an' liars ain't much differ'nt than us makin' fun a you if yer great-granny was a slave, er me sayin' Esperanza's mama's a tortilla-eatin' wetback, which she ain't...I reckon it's painful whichever side ya take, ain't it?"

Diana Parker nodded her head in the silence of a woman who is suddenly ashamed of herself. She drew a deep breath and sighed. "Well, I must say I am continually amazed at the depth of feeling the townspeople of this community have for their past, heroic, or not. My husband and I do not mean to diminish any heroism, or bravery, that might have been experienced here all those years ago. But we do feel, based on evidence, and historic research, that along with that heroism and bravery, the true facts of the situation should surface. Unfortunately, I suppose, those facts may never be discovered…and I guess our trying to assign the truth it is as unforgivable as ignoring it. But my husband is very dedicated to his Revisionism…"

An elderly woman's voice pierced the confines of the Ladies Dressing Room. "Have we ever considered the fact that those who recorded the history of our town were perhaps the first Revisionists? That they recorded the version they wanted to be told, whether it's true or not?"

All eyes in the Ladies Dressing Room turned to see Amelia Festrunk standing next to a refrigerator box. Diana Parker nodded her head. "Indeed, Miss Festrunk, that's precisely what my husband and I are trying to communicate, and..."

"Did we ever stop to think that perhaps the way they achieved their success and good fortunes was by manipulating the lives of others and preventing the shocking circumstances about the founding of this town from *ever* being told?"

Diana Parker held her head triumphantly and inhaled, but Amelia Festrunk pointed a bony finger in her direction.

"Mrs. Parker, don't be so quick to hitch your team to my wagon. I'm afraid we are not of the same mind. I agree with these women...it is all good and proper to wish to see wrongs be righted, but to exaggerate the facts is to do no more than perpetuate the wrong in the first place. We have a long, unfortunate history of mistreatment in our fair city, right under our noses. The real story in this town is not comprised of white versus black...it's not about stolen money, either. It's about a few men with skeletons in their closets who resented the surprisingly esteemed Virginia bloodlines of another man they considered to be the scum of the earth, and how they schemed for sixty years to keep that man down for their own benefit. That's the real story here, and it's not being told! But it will! You watch, it will be!"

Amelia Festrunk stormed off with the unmistakable thud of her orthopedic pumps. Stella Stanley puffed a smoke ring into the air and sighed. MayBelle Festrunk wrung her hands and said in a low voice, "Something's not right with 'Melie...I'm worried about her. Ever since the Board...ever since she resigned, she has been acting strange."

Euladean Bailey hung the last pair of Confederate trousers on a rod in one of the refrigerator cartons. "Well, it all don't matter now, since Hoot Graham's done gone back to Hollywood! My poor Henry…he was so excited ta have a part in this play, even if he was dressed up like a widda woman."

In the sweltering parking lot of the Gym-torium, the Best Boy was hurriedly trying to locate his car keys, amidst the endless folds of a calico widow woman's costume. Hoot stood impatiently beside the passenger door to the El Camino, waiting for the Best Boy to start the car, turn on the air conditioning and cool the vehicle to his liking. In a fury, Henry Bailey jammed the ignition key into the switch, cranked the engine, put the air conditioner on full blast, and sat back in disgust, realizing he was still wearing the dress that was now unbuttoned to reveal his hairy chest. Hoot, in no mood to wait around while the Best Boy changed clothes, reached a hand inside the car, and, satisfied he would not burn his tender Hollywood director skin on the vinyl interior, sat down with a thud and a scowl.

"Well, whaddya gotta say fer yerself? Huh? Ya'll just ain't serious 'bout this play! Ya'll ain't serious 'bout nothin', 'cept makin' money! Nobody wants ta work 'round here! *Jus' gimme the cash! Fork it on over!* Makes me sick, I tell ya, *sick*! None a ya'll know the meanin' of a hard day's work!"

Henry hung his head and sighed. "You wanna stop off at the Fluffy Pillow before we hit the road, H.? I'll help ya pack yer bags."

Hoot frowned at Henry. "What are you talkin' 'bout, Henry? I ain't goin' nowhere! Are ya so ign'rant ya don't realize what jus' happened in there? That was fer *effect*, son! That was a fine example a Mo-ti-va-tion, Hollywood-style! Ya gotta make 'em sweat, make 'em feel real low…then after 'while, ya build 'em back up again, an' nine times outta ten they give it their best shot! Man, don't ya'll ever read the *papers*, Henry? Don't ya'll know nothin' 'bout *nothin'*?"

Hoot rested his head against the seat and closed his eyes in disgust. Henry clicked his tongue and sighed. He knew the Used Car Business and that was it. This Best Boy stuff was the hardest job Henry'd ever had to learn; it was even worse than working on the assembly line at the suitcase plant in Murfreesboro. Henry drove the El Camino to the exit of the Gym-torium parking lot, but stomped his foot on the brake, nearly sending Hoot through the windshield.

"What the hell…Henry! What're you doin?"

"Look, Hoot! What's that? What're *they* doin'?"

H. Graham and his Best Boy stared ahead at the sidewalk outside the Chestnut Ridge Senior High Gym-torium. Approximately twenty people carrying large picket signs paced back and forth, blocking the El Camino's exit. Henry recognized his brother-in-law Corny and put the car in park, but left the engine running for H. Graham's ultimate comfort, as only a Best Boy should.

"Just a sec, H., lemme go see what's happenin,'" Henry hitched up his calico dress, and walked over to Corny, who had stopped pacing in order to straighten his picket sign and tug on his creeping boxer shorts.

"Hey, Corny, hey ya'll…Corny…what's goin' on? What're ya'll *doin*? Awful hot ta be out here, don'tcha think? 'Bout near a hunnerd degrees, I'd say!"

Corny Poe scowled and held his picket sign in front of Henry's face. Written in bold, red letters on neon-yellow poster board were the words, *'HOLLYWOOD LIES! WE ARE NOT THIEVES! BOYCOTT THESE LIARS!'*

"Whaddya think 'bout *that*, Henry Bailey! Mr. *'Best Boy*! Ya'll through playactin' for today? Ya'll through lyin' 'bout our ancestors, tired of puttin' all them falsehoods on stage? Feelin' a little guilty, Henry, 'fraid you're gonna *BURN IN HELL*? I see you're wearin' women's clothin', too! So now you're one a them across-dressers? *SODOM AND GOMORRAH*!"

Henry wiped his sweaty forehead with one sleeve of his calico dress and shook his head, "Corny, what is you talkin' 'bout? I think ya been standin' in the meat locker too long, yer brain's done froze up!"

"*Stand aside, Devil*! That play you're doin', it's nothin' but a buncha lyin' bout this town's forefathers! They didn't steal no gold! And they sure didn't assault no nigra women...no self-respectin' white man'd ever do that! Afercan Voodoo an' such! It's the work a the Devil, I say! Ya'll let that kiss-my-ass-Doctor-Avery-Parker-Junior dictate ever' word a that play, an' it's all LIES! An' I ain't gonna stand up here, an' let ya'll put LIES 'bout my *family*, an' my *town*, on stage!"

"But Corny…that's just plumb ridic'lous! Doc Parker's a famous scholarly! He's done researched the whole thing! An' he helped Peter Paul write ever' word of it! Hell, Peter Paul Culpepper's yer own preacher Culpepper's *son*! Ya think he's gonna put somethin' out ta the public that ain't *true*?"

"*HUSH, SATAN*! Brother Culpepper' ain't what he seems, neither! He's the *real* devil behind all this! But how would you know? All dolled up like a *woman*! Yep, playactin' an' tellin' lies, right here at the Gym-torium! An' you, Henry Bailey, married to my sister! You oughta be ashamed a yourself! *BE GONE, LUCIFER!* Your velvet tongue ain't gonna sway me, no sir! Now get outta my way! We got the work a the Lord ta do here!"

Henry Bailey absent-mindedly swished his calico skirt in an effort to get some cool air to his legs. He eyeballed the picketers, who were now frowning in Corny's direction at the length of his break from the picket process in the late summer swelter. H. Graham revved the engine of the El Camino as a secret code that he was ready to depart for his next meeting. Henry took a step toward his brother-in-law, hands on his hips.

"Corny Poe, you git outta *my* way! I gotta git the Director ta Hollywood, he's gotta important conf'ernce, so's you just back off, an' let us pass! I don't know what yer so worried 'bout, anyhow! The way I see it, the only three fam'lies who done got any *real* money in this town is the ones who oughta be worryin' 'bout lies! The Grahams, the Leigh-Lees, and them Festrunks, maybe we oughta ask 'em jus' how *they* done got all their money… They're prob'ly the ones who did the stealin', if there was any stealin' ta do!"

Corny raised one eyebrow; he'd always resented the social position and success of the three most wealthy and influential families in Chestnut Ridge. Henry waved his arms in the thick humidity.

"Hell, Corny, if yer mad, then git mad at how come the Poes an' the Baileys ain't even mentioned in this daggum play! What's the big deal, anyhow? All we're tryin' ta do is raise some money fer this town, so's we can all a us benefit! Hell, yer a biznessman, jus' like me! Or maybe ya got 'nuff sales over ta the Poe House, ya don't *need* no more? Huh? Tell me what the deal is, Corny! *TELL ME*!"

Corny Poe clenched his teeth, put down his picket sign and reached for a crumpled brown paper bag. He shoved the open sack at Henry, who frowned and looked inside. A moldy, withered brown mass lay on the bottom, emitting a very foul odor. Corny shook the sack in Henry's face and Henry grimaced and covered his nose and mouth.

"*This*! This is the big deal! This is the Sweet Jesus Sweet Potato, an' I'm the one chose by God ta give it to! I been carryin' this Sweet Jesus Sweet Potato 'round since winter, when the Good Lord revealed it to me! Here, look on it, Satan! Look at the power a the Lord!"

Corny again thrust the sack into Henry's face. Henry rared back and glared at Corny,

"What in *tarnation*! Corny, what in the *hell* is a Sweet Jesus Sweet Potato? Looky here, ya set down in my car over here, an' I'm gonna go call Doc Kimball, ya got heat frustration or sompin'…here, gimme that thing…"

"*REPENT, DEVIL*! Don't you *touch* this with your heathen fingers! This here's the Instrument a God! Can't you see *the very face of Jesus* on this veg-'table? Can't you see it's a *sign*, a sign that I'm the only one in this miserable town holdin' the Keys ta Heaven? You oughtta get down on your knees *right now*, an' thank me for revealin' it to ya! I'm talkin' 'bout dancin'! Drinkin'! Carryin' on! Lyin'! Across-dressin'! An' playactin'!"

Corny Poe put his picket sign down on the ground and waved his arms wildly. "Henry Bailey, someday you're gonna be dead, an' you're gonna be sittin' with alla them other Pope-worshipin' Catholics, an' them

Whiskeypalians, jus' starin' at the sweet face a my baby sister Euladean, across the Fence. An' you know why? 'Cause my sweet baby sister an' me'll be in Heaven sittin' at the Right Hand a God, an' you an' alla these playactors is gonna be sittin' on the Big Stage a Hell! You, an' Doctor Avery Parker Junior, an' Brother Culpepper, an' them Quigleys, an' them Leigh-Lees, an' Festrunks, an' Grahams, an' everybody else in this town who don't take up the Sweet Jesus Sweet Potato, an' follow *me*!"

Henry Bailey looked to his left and to his right, to see who might be listening, as his brother-in-law suffered this tragic meltdown. Of course, the fact that he himself was standing on Main Street wearing a bright yellow calico dress never crossed his mind. It was obvious that Corny could not be appeased; with his best Best Boy brainpower, Henry devised a Plan. He had to get Hoot to the Fluffy Pillow Motel before real hell broke loose. And he had to appeal to his self-righteous brother-in-law in the only language he could fully understand.

"Corny, look, I warn't gonna say nothin', but, well, listen here..." Henry leaned up to whisper in Corny's bright red ear, "Ya 'member that day ya baptized me in the El Camino? At the River Jordan Car Wash & Baptism?"

Corny nodded his head skeptically.

"Well, see, look, this is awful hard fer me ta *say*...look at me, I done got the shakes! See hear, this Angel 'peared in the bathroom mirror a my RV...in the middle a the night...right over the sink! I ain't even tol' Euladean! An' this Angel, it tol' me that you was gonna baptize me that day, in the El Camino, an' it tol' me that there's gonna be a holy veg'table laid down in this town from up yonder! Yeah, it tol' me how Brother Culpepper's doin' wrong, an' leadin' his flock ta ruination, an' it tol' me somethin' else..."

Corny Poe held tighter to the Sweet Jesus Sweet Potato paper sack. "*What*! What did it say? You better not be messin' with me, Henry! I'll smite ya! I'll smite ya *hard*!"

"That there Angel tol' me ta follow that vege'table...said it'd be reveal-ed unto-eth me...It tol' me that ta git Brother Culpepper, I had ta show him up in public! That Angel tol' me that Peter Paul Puss...Culpepper...would write this here play, an' that it'd be fulla lies, an' then Brother Culpepper'd swell up with pride at his son, an' insist on bein' the Narrator, an' then the Angel's gonna come down and...what'd you say, smite 'em, *hard,* in the middle a the third act!"

Corny Poe pursed his lips. "You're mockin' me, Henry Bailey! I don't believe one word you're sayin! You're mockin' me..."

Henry rolled his eyes with his best Used Car Sales Manager nonchalance."Well, now, ya believe what ya like, Corny Poe, but I'm tellin' ya ever'thing that Angel's said's done come true! I don' got baptized by you at the River Jordan Car Wash…an' ya jus' showed me that there Sweet Jesus veg'table, didn't ya? An' guess what? We're tryin' ta git outta this here driveway, so's we can git over ta Brother Culpepper's office…*why, you say*? 'Cause he done called Mr. Director H. Graham, an' asked him could he be the *Narrator*! So's we gotta git over there fer a readin! 'Course, I already know it's a done deal, since my bathroom Angel told me 'bout it. So Corny, yer messin' with the Lord yer own se'f! Now ya'd best git outta the way, so's that bathroom Angel don't come down here an' smite *you* hard right here on this picket line!"

Corny rubbed his furrowed brow, and lovingly set the Sweet Jesus Sweet Potato brown paper carrying case on the ground by his feet. For months he'd prayed to God to deliver to him the means to rid Chestnut Ridge of Brother Cameron Culpepper; it might be at hand.

"All right, Henry. Even if you are an idolatrin' Cath'lic…I can tell you gotta different look about ya since you was saved over t' the car wash…I'll let ya'll pass, but if this is all a big joke, I'm tellin' ya, me an' the Sweet Jesus Sweet Potato squad are gonna come an' find you! Hey…Henry…please don't say nothin' to Euladean 'bout this, ok? Let's keep this Angel stuff just between us, right?"

Henry saluted Corny, and leaned down and awkwardly made the sign of the cross over the Sweet Jesus Sweet Potato sack. "Ya got it, my man! I'll let ya know what happens, ok?"

Corny directed the Sweet Jesus Sweet Potato Squad to stand aside as Henry pulled the El Camino out of the Gym-torium parking lot, with an angry H. Graham in tow. When they were safely on Main Street, Hoot asked, "What in hell was that all about? I ain't accustomed ta long delays, ya know!"

Henry winked, and looked in the rearview mirror. "Oh, nothin', just my brother-in-law. He's all pissed off 'cause he don't got no part in the play. Say, H., I know ya been lookin' real hard fer a good Narrator fer this show…ya know, it's not *my* place ta suggest somebody, but ya might wanna consider Brother Culpepper…he's a real fine speaker, an' he can pack in an audience! I mean, since his son's the playwriter, an' all. 'Course now, the Brother, he stutters a bit, but it ain't real noticeable, once he gits ta goin'!"

Henry chuckled and imagined what Brother Culpepper would say if he knew Corny Poe was worshiping a moldy sweet potato. *Sackerlidge, I bet…*"Say, Hoot…ain't you used ta be some kinda veg'table phatogerpher? Ain't that how you got yer big start out there in L.A.?"

Hoot examined his fingernails and said nonchalantly, "Yeah, sure! One of the best! Why?"

Henry cocked his head, "Well, see here…there's this…uh, reckon I might just have a little job fer ya, if yer interested in makin' some cash on the side...ya still got yer equipment?"

Hoot Graham winked and grinned, "I sure do, Henry, an' the ladies are still linin' up ta see it! Oh, you mean my *equipment!* Heh, heh I got so much stuff, lenses, an' film, an' all kindsa photo *ap-parati*...that's an industry term...worth a lotta money, Henry, gotta keep it in a vault in L.A. But my ever'day camera's over at Will's house, under lock an' key! I'm a little rusty, you know, with alla them movies I been makin', but I can still shoot with the best of 'em! What kinda job you got?"

Henry's brain whirred. He had to work it all out just right. No sense telling Hoot everything yet. "Oh, well, one a my customers has this vegetable he's been growin' all summer, thinks it'll win big at the County Fair; he might need a photo or two..."

"Well, that's right up my alley! Bring 'em on! We oughta do it here real soon, while I'm takin' my leave a absence, makin' ever'body think I'm back in L.A. 'til they get desp'rate for me ta come back an' save their asses. We'll have ta do it real secret, though...I'm gonna have ta lay low for 'while...I's thinkin', maybe I oughta check outta the execative suite, an' rest a spell over ta Fay's...she needs me ta check out her plumbin'! Heh, heh, yeah, I'll get that camera, an' we can shoot yer buddy's veg'table, no sweat."

Henry wondered how much time he had to work out his incriminating sweet potato photo scheme. "When was you figgerin' ta practice again? What if they replace ya, Hoot? Ain't ya worried 'bout keepin' yer Director slot?"

"Element'ry, my dear Best Boy, element'ry! The Town Meetin's in a coupla weeks...we'll just let 'em stew, then I'll breeze in, an' act like I've taken pity on 'em, an' bail 'em out. Have 'em eatin' right outta my hand! Whaddya think?"

Henry grinned. This Best Boy stuff was finally beginning to click. "I think that's a great idea! An' in the mean time, ya can sharpen yer phatogerpher skills, an' git us some publiss'ty! Ya need a Best Boy fer that, H.?"

"Henry, in the first place, my skills don't need no sharpenin'! An' in the second, I *always* need a Best Boy! That reminds me...my Best Girl's gonna be wonderin' where I am..."

The creaking El Camino pulled into the parking lot of the Fluffy Pillow Motel, where a furious Fay Bailey was seated on the ground, in front of Executive Suite Number Eight. Henry stiffened and began to sweat. The sight of his ex-wife always gave him stomach cramps.

"*Uh oh,*" Hoot said, "looks like my Best Girl's a might teed off! Henry, my man, whyn't ya go get us some a them wine coolers an' Dixie Chips, an' then come back in a few...I'll pack my gear, an' then ya can d'liver me ta my new execative residence! An' on the way, we'll swing by Will's an' get my camera…where's this veg'table of yours at?"

Henry gripped the steering wheel as Fay approached the El Camino. "Uh, Hoot, I ain't sure… I'll be back. Look, I gotta go! See ya!"

Hoot barely stepped clear of the El Camino as Henry jammed the accelerator to the floor and sped off in a cloud of gravel. Hoot grinned at Fay,

"Hey, sugarplum! How's my Sex Kitten? *Meow*!"

"Don't you Sex Kitten me, you *jerk*! I been waitin' here fer thirty minutes! I had ta walk all the way from the Beauty Box, 'cause my car's done blown a gasket! An' now my mascara's runnin', so yer gonna have ta gimme five minutes so I can redo it afore my video session!"

Hoot's heart stopped… he'd forgotten about his promise to Fay that today he'd videotape her singing her pageant talent competition medley, so she could send it to The Nashville Network, at the request of her new agent. *If she's pissed 'bout that, how's she gonna take it when I tell her I'm movin' in for awhile, ta lay low?*

"Honeybunch…there's a change in plans…now, Fay, baby, don't look at me in that tone a voice! See, last night, I was puttin' in a test roll, an' the danged camera froze up! So Henry took it over ta be fixed this mornin', but it ain't gonna be ready fer three weeks! Can ya b'lieve that? An' on toppa that, Miz Ethel's plannin' ta fumigate this entire hotel, an' it must be somethin' powerful, 'cause I gotta find a place ta stay fer a while…I can't go ta Will's, I ain't sure *what* I'm gonna do…I guess I could live in the back a the El Camino, sleep out here in th' open…but the problem is…that El Camino ain't got no phone, an' I'm waitin' fer Merle Haggard ta call me 'bout that document'ry he's wantin'…"

Fay lit up like a Coleman lantern. "*Merle Haggard*? *The* Merle Haggard? Only my fav'rite singer! Only one a my insp'rations! Yer tellin' me, yer gonna be workin' with Merle Haggard? *HOOT!* Ya think he'd listen ta my Loretta Lynn medley? Would that be askin' too much…ya can talk to him from *my* place…I reckon ya can *stay* there, too…for 'while..."

At the sight of Hoot's self-satisfied grin, sparks flew from Fay's eyes. "*Hoot Graham*! You'd better not be lyin' to me! I gotta lot at stake, here! It's my dream, it ain't jus' some hobby!"

Hoot grinned. "Honeybunch…have I *ever* lied to you?"

CHAPTER FIFTEEN– A PEARL OF GREAT PRICE

August 18, 1999; Chestnut Ridge High School Gym-torium

Billy Gooch looked sheepishly around the corner of the Gym-torium's red brick exterior. Exactly one hour after the close of the first day of school on a warm Thursday afternoon, he was on a mission. He'd heard a rumor that one of *"The Golden Secret"* widow women had mistakenly worn her corset home, and that her size 44DD brassiere had been left behind in the Ladies' Dressing Room, locked tight in the Gym-torium. At least, that's what Gus Tatum had told him this morning in homeroom, when he'd dared Billy to break into the Gym-torium and snatch it.

Billy was determined to get that bra; with a size 44DD brassiere in his possession, he would not only be the most respected boy at Chestnut Ridge Middle School, he could also make a small fortune from his buddies, who were completely mystified by the world of women's undergarments. And best of all, Gus Tatum, his arch-enemy, would be silenced forever and humiliated in public when Billy pulled that 44DD bra right out of his jeans pocket.

Nobody out front of the school, Billy observed. *It ain't even locked...door's wide open...Mr. Rodriguez must be cleanin'.* Billy dashed beneath one of the Gym-torium windows and peeked in. From his secret habit of eavesdropping on his father's phone conversations, Billy knew the play's props and dressing rooms were still intact; nobody wanted to dismantle anything until after the town meeting, so a vote could be taken on whether to replace Hoot Graham with another director and go on with the show.

Billy looked left then right, and seeing no one, darted inside the Gym-torium and hid behind a section of bleachers. He listened for signs of movement but heard only the pounding of his young heart inside his chest. He snuck behind the refrigerator cartons that made up the Ladies' Dressing Room and climbed under a pile of old sheets, commandeered from various Chestnut Ridge households to serve as Federal tents in Act Two. Billy stayed put for a full ten minutes, listening and waiting to make sure he was alone; then he stood up and surveyed the Dressing Room for clues to the treasured and elusive 44DD bra.

He noticed two makeup tables made from plywood sheets laid on top of concrete blocks. White Christmas tree lights were strung around a shard of broken mirror propped up on top of one of the plywood sheets, like those fancy Hollywood makeup mirrors you see in the movies. Billy, with all the wonderment of a twelve-year old boy, stepped closer to the plywood vanities and looked at the vast array of makeup bottles, cold crème jars, cans of hair spray and bobby pins resting peacefully, waiting for the next rehearsal.

He opened a large metal tin of boot-black, stuck in a finger, but disgustedly smeared the goo on his blue jeans. *Ain't no bra here over here*, he murmured. Then he caught a glimpse of an old closet rod, wedged into one of the refrigerator cartons, upon which hung several women's costumes. *Bingo*! Gotta be over there someplace! Billy greedily rifled through the costumes; a couple of frilly women's blouses, a few skirts, a hat or two...but dang, no bra.

He scanned the Ladies' Dressing Room for more potential bra hiding places. Just a few piles of shoes, a couple of scripts, some empty soda cans. He got down on the floor under the plywood vanities for another look, but there was no sign of the 44DD. As he was about to give up in frustration, Billy noticed a strange heap of something soft and brown on the floor near the tent sheets. He crept over and gingerly touched the topmost article...*pantyhose*! A pile of women's pantyhose right here on the floor! Or at least, that's what he *thought* it was...he'd often seen his mother standing over the ironing board, wearing nothing but her pantyhose and bra, as she hurriedly ironed something to wear to work at his dad's office supply store. He carefully pulled up pair after pair of silky pantyhose in pubescent wonderment and held them aloft, as if they were fragile. They smelled faintly of women's perfume and shoe leather. And they were so *small*! How did women get into these things? What was the point, anyway? Why not just wear socks?

Well, *goldurnit*, Billy slapped his knee with a silent chuckle, at least pantyhose was something! Not as good as a 44DD brassiere, but better than nothing at all! He wadded a couple of pairs into the pockets of his blue jeans, then realized that the hunger pangs in his stomach were in need of an answer. He stood up and looked around the corner of the Ladies' Dressing Room and started to walk out onto the Gym-torium floor.

Suddenly, a dark shadow passed by the door to the hall. Billy drew back and breathed heavily. He slowly poked one eye around the corner of a refrigerator carton. Probably just Mr. Rodriguez, mopping the hall floor. He waited a minute, heard nothing, then raised his foot to take a step.

"Hey, now, whadda we got here? You doin' a little *snoopin'*, boy?"

Billy Gooch froze in terror. He turned around to face the haggard grin of six-foot-six Leonard Festrunk who stood behind one of the refrigerator cartons, watching Billy's every move.

"Uh, Mister Leonard...*hey*! Uh, well, see, my Mama done left her good shoes in here, see, an' I was jus' gittin' 'em for her, that's all! HEY! You been watchin' me the whole time, or what? Spyin's against the law!"

Leonard Festrunk twirled a wooden toothpick in his mouth. "It is, is it? Yep. I been here the whole time, watchin' ever' second! I seen what ya been doin'! Goin' thew them women's clothes like shoppin' at the salvage store! Ya find yer Mama's...whaddya say, *shoes*? 'Zat what ya got in them pockets?"

Billy covered his blue jeans pockets nonchalantly with both hands. "What I got in my pockets, it ain't none a yer beeswax, Mister Leonard! Now I gotta git, my Mama's waitin' on me at home an' I gotta do my chores's afternoon...so's if you'll 'scuze me, I'd best be..."

"This what ya been lookin' for, boy? It's a whopper, I'll say!"

From one bony hand, Leonard Festrunk dangled an enormous white brassiere into the air. Billy's eyes widened in disbelief, and he gulped for air. Leonard smiled and shook the bra in Billy's direction.

"Come over here, boy, let's take a good gander at this, jus' me an' you!"

Billy stared suspiciously at Leonard, but after Leonard winked and smiled at him, Billy figured it was ok. He exited the Ladies' Dressing Room and sat down next to Leonard on the bleachers. Leonard stretched the giant bra out between his widespread arms while Billy gawked in astonished silence. It was the most amazing thing he'd ever seen, with the exception of a centerfold photo Gus Tatum had showed everybody earlier that summer.

"Where'd ya *git* that?" Billy asked. Leonard chuckled and admired the bra as he spoke.

"Well, I been doin' a little work fer this play, too, ya know! Them sets over there, I built 'em! Them plywood makeup tables, I fixed 'em! You know I ain't never had no schoolin' like my sisters, but I'm good with my tools an' all, an' I sure ain't got much else ta do since the Clinic done let me go an hired that fancy new maintenance engineer! So I decided I best be givin' this here play some help, seein' as how my baby sister MayBelle's in it, an' seein' how my ancestors is who done started this danged town in the first place!"

Leonard Festrunk admired the bra's huge cups as he spoke. "An' I come up here today ta figger out how ta make a cannon, fer when they hang the deserters in the last act...there's s'posed ta be a cannon goes off...I dunno...this whole thing's a buncha hogwash, there warn't no hangin's or cannons in this town, but anyhow, I reckon I gotta help out somehow. An' when I got here, I had ta go let my water out, you know, an' I jus' dashed inta that women's restroom over yonder, figured nobody's around, an', Lord, have mercy, this bra-zeer was swingin' from the hook on the backa the door! It's a mighty fine specimen! Sure would like to see the gal that it b'longs to! Them's some pretty fine titties, I'd wager!"

Billy Gooch gaped at Leonard Festrunk and blushed. No grownup had ever talked to him about stuff like this before! But then, Billy remembered, everybody said Mister Leonard was "special." That's what they said when they really meant that a person was slow...what did his daddy say...*Leonard wasn't the sharpest knife in the drawer.*

"You mean, titties can really git that *big*?" Billy looked up in earnest at the old man, who slapped his thigh and laughed.

"Shore as shootin', young man! I 'member one time, back in the war, this ol' friend a mine come home an him an' these peckerwood officers took us ta one a them striptease joints over ta Nashville…they had alla these fancy dancin' gals, well…I'm guessin' they had titties big as watermelons…now this *here* bra-zeer…" Leonard waved the bra through the air in front of Billy.

"…this *here* model ain't *nothin'* compared to the ones them fancy dancin' gals had…this one gal, why, her titties was so big, they had ta use duck tape and wood screws ta keep her bra-zeer on! Them things coulda *killed* ya if they was ta flop 'round! Whadda way ta go, though, whadda way ta go!"

Leonard dropped the bra and convulsed in waves of laughter on the bleacher seat next to Billy. Billy snatched the bra from the floor, and blissfully ran a hand over one of the stiff cups. Leonard took a tattered handkerchief out of his back pocket, and blew his nose, right in Billy's ear, but Billy was so mesmerized by the bra he didn't even notice.

"You think whoever owns this bra's gonna come lookin' for it?" Billy asked.

Leonard pursed his lip in deep thought. "Well sir, I'd say that a gal that's got titties this big, she'd best be havin' a spare 'round the house…'cause if somebody this stacked's wavin' 'round loose on Main Street, whosever gits in her way's gonna git hurt bad from the backlash, an' it'll be on the front page of the paper, boy!"

Leonard shook with laughter as Billy considered Leonard's logic.

"So, you reckon if I took this bra with me fer a while, it wouldn't do no harm, then? I mean, if I was ta *borrow* it, jus' fer a coupl'a days… I'll bring it back, I swear…"

Leonard's face hardened, then he pursed his lips and sighed. "*First*, boy, it ain't yers ta *borry*! I'm the one done found it, so's it's *mine*. Second, what's a boy like you need with a bra-zeer, anyhow? You one a them faggot-y fellers? You figurin' on wearin' it 'round the house?"

Billy grimaced and stuck out his tongue. "*No way, José!* I ain't gonna wear no girl's bra! And I ain't no faggot, neither, I'm jus' as tough as anybody! I jus' wanna take this thing ta school an' make ol' Gus Tatum green when he sees what I got! I could make me some *serious money* showin' it off ta the fellas! HEY! Whaddya need it fer, *yerself*? You got some girl ta give it to, or what? You got you a wife?"

Leonard's eyes darkened, and he lowered his head. The lines on his face deepened, and Billy noticed Leonard's hair was completely white and his hands knobby. "No, I ain't got me no girl, not no more. Once't upon a time, back durin' W-W-Two, I's just a young thing…but I had me the sweetest li'l gal ya ever did see …she'd come an' tap on my window of a night, an' slip in between the sheets with me…then she'd high-tail it outta there, long b'fore mornin', an' git on home…but then the war ended, an', well... that's been over fifty years ago, boy, but I can still see her face lit up like a firecracker in the moonlight…shinin' in that hospital room…oh, Lordy, she was a looker! Warn't much in the titty department, though."

Billy wondered how old Leonard Festrunk was. For years, he'd seen Leonard trudge into his dad's office supply store, every Monday afternoon, coming to pick up items for the Clinic. They rarely spoke, but Leonard always winked at Billy and waved, and Billy always waved back. Leonard never paid for anything; he never carried any money, and he couldn't sign his name, so Barney Gooch always drew an "X" on the receipt, and Leonard would trace it with one bony hand.

And every Monday, time and again, Leonard would look Barney Gooch in the eye, and say, "Remember, now, Mayor, we don't pay no taxes on this here stuff…ya got it figgered right? I ain't payin' no taxes ta no sonsabitch pol'ticians!" And every Monday, Barney Gooch would sigh, and say, "Yep, Leonard, it's right as rain!"

Billy shifted on the bleacher, "Hey, Mister Leonard, how come you live in that ol' hospital anyhow? Don't you ever git tired a livin' in jus' one room, no yard ta play in, or nothin'? Alla them sick people right there with ya?"

Leonard smiled and plopped a plug of chewing tobacco in his mouth. He worked the tobacco around to his left cheek, then pulled a small brass cup out of his shirt pocket. He spat in the brass cup and blinked.

"Son, I ain't livin' there no more, the Board done seen ta that. But looky here, the Leonard Festrunk School of philos'phy is open fer bizness. Here's the deal... a man, if he's d'rectly inclined, he gits himself some schoolin'. He spends ever' danged day cooped up in a room with some ol' ugly hag, an' a buncha goofy kids, an' a whole messa rules an' reggalations. Ain't time for no in-dee-pendent thoughts in that there school, gotta stick ta the program. An' then he gits outta school, an' he gits him a job…an' he gotta stick ta the program there, too. Can't think fer his own self, gotta do what the boss man says. An' he makes him some good money, but he gotta give mos' of it ta the damned fed'ral gov'ment, so's they can piss it away, an' then he's gotta give the rest ta the little woman, an' feed the young-uns, so's he never gits nothin' fer hisself. An' he spends his whole danged life *workin'* an' *workin'*, ta git him some free time, an' finally, when he's purt' near seventy, an' he's 'bout caught up, an' he don't owe nobody no more money, he retires ta do him some thinkin', or fishin', or whatever he pleases. But then, 'bout a week later, he gits the cancer, or a weak heart, an' where does he end up? In the *hospital!* An' he has ta sell ever' thing he owns jus' ta pay the bills! An' then, them doctors an' nurses jus' take over! They start tellin' him what ta do! An' then, the damned fed'ral gov'ment'll only give him 'bout a tenth a what he done put in, so's his money runs out, an' he dies, plumb broke, miserable-like."

Billy Gooch frowned at Leonard Festrunk, impatient for the point to the story. Leonard spat into his brass cup.

"Son, *I* decided I was gonna live my life *differ'nt!* I ain't gonna sit in no classroom, or work fer no boss man, an' spend all my life payin' bills an' workin' hard jus' to end up in the hospital, on the damned fed'ral gov'ment's charity! I figure, if I jus' go 'head an' live in the hospital *now*, well, I'm beatin' the system! An' it worked fer more'n sixty years! I ain't been sick a day in my life...'cept sick of them Clinic board members tellin' me what ta do, but I got used ta that a long time ago. I don't owe nobody no money, I ain't got no wife tellin' me what ta do ever' minute of ever'day, an' I ain't gotta pay no taxes ta no cheatin' sonsabitch pol'ticians!"

Billy nodded at Leonard. He really had some strange ideas, but they made sense, in a way. Why should a man work all his life when he could just lay out and do his own thing?

"Mister Leonard, I don't care what they say about ya. I think yer a pretty smart guy. Maybe that's what I'll do, too... I'll make me a cabin out in the woods, an' hunt an' fish an' live off the land. I can take care of myself, ya know! Whadda I need with alla that ol' book learnin', anyhow? An' I don't need no mom or dad always tellin' me what ta do! Night an' day, day an' night! Make yer bed! Clean up yer room! Help me out at the store on Saturday! It wears me *out*!"

Leonard realized he'd made an impression on the boy, and he thought better of it. "Well, now, Billy, listen up. I's a grown up man before I made my decision, ya know I musta been 'bout fourteen, an' anyhow I'd already done been kicked outta ever' school in the county 'cause I never did learn my letters on accounta I's simple-minded. Then my folks was dead, I didn't have nobody ta raise me 'cept my sister, an' she was always busy runnin' the Clinic. I reckon I ain't never had me no op'tun'ty ta do nothin' else. But now you listen here, Billy... I'll tell ya true...ya got good parents, an' I've seen ya 'round town... ya got lots a friends, don'tcha?"

Billy nodded. Leonard nodded back. "Yeah, well I never had me no friends, well, 'cept that ol' gal done snuck inta my room, she was a special friend. Nossir, I ain't had no friends, 'cept you! You knowed how I always wave at ya when I come ta yer daddy's store ever' Monday? An' ever since ya was knee-high to a grasshopper, I seen ya wave back! An' it sure made me feel good, somebody was ta notice me! An' now ya an' me had this here talk today, jus' like pals!"

Leonard picked up the bra from Billy's lap and folded it neatly. He spat into the brass cup, and clapped Billy on the back. "But now ya wanna rush off an' show that bra-zeer 'round ta yer friends at the schoolyard. I never had nobody ta show nothin' off to when I was in school! Ever'one was always leavin' me by my lonesome, they all said I was dumber than a doornail. If I'da had some friends, maybe I'da stayed put, an' gradgiated, maybe my life woulda been happier…not so lonesome-like…ya never know…"

Billy shifted again on the hard bleacher seat. He wasn't sure where Leonard was headed with this story, but he really didn't feel like being lectured by the town idiot.

"What I'm tryin' ta say, Billy, is ya oughtn't ta be chargin' yer *friends*, son, if they's yer friends. It ain't right ta make money offa people what trust ya. Naw, you take that bra-zeer, an' you show it 'round fer *free*, then ya bring it on back ta me. I'd like ta keep it, as a soovy-neer, but you can borry it anytime. An' look Billy… yer smart, I figger…ya stay in school, an' learn all ya can learn, an' be successful like yer daddy. He's a respected man, yer daddy. Got him a good bizness, he's a good mayor ta this here town, he's got him a pretty wife, got you fer a son, an' a big ol' house on a hill. Yep, I don't reckon a man could be more happy than that…djew?"

Billy looked at Leonard and thought he saw a tiny tear in the man's right eye. He was embarrassed, and didn't know what to say. He stared at the huge bra in Leonard's large hands, anxious to change the subject.

"Ok, Mister Leonard, thanks fer lettin' me borry it. I don't wanna rip off my friends, I jus' wanna see ol' Gus Tatum's face when I waltz up an' wave it at him! He's always hittin' on me, givin' me a hard time! Just once, I wanna fix him good!"

Leonard tousled Billy's hair absent-mindedly. He looked Billy straight in the eye. "Well, now, I'm doin' you a favor…so's you gotta do me one back, that's the deal. If'n you'll be my friend, an' help me with som'pin', I guess I can let loose a that bra-zeer fer a coupl'a days. Now look here…I gotta figger out how ta make a cannon fer this here play, an' I could sure use some help from a friend. Ya think ya could help me work on it? I ain't too good at figurin' out stuff, but if somebody could git me started, I'm good as gold. Reckon you could do that?"

Billy nodded and grinned. If he couldn't make money off the bra, he still had the hidden pantyhose…that could earn him a little extra cash, and he could still keep his bargain with Leonard.

"Yes, sir, Mister Leonard! Sure! Oh, boy, thanks! Whatcha got ta work with fer that cannon? Hey…wait a minute…why're you worryin' 'bout it? Mr. Hoot's done left town fer Hollywood, an my daddy says the play's prob'ly gonna get canned, anyhow!"

Leonard stood up and stretched his lanky arms. "Aww, that's a buncha hoodoo! Hoot ain't lef' town…he's shackin' up over ta Fay Bailey's, watchin' them soap oprys! He's got Fay cookin' him his meals, an' doin' his laundry, an' no tellin' what else! Hoot Graham ain't nothin' but a big liar, he ain't no

Hollywood di-rector! You jus' wait…he's jus' hopin' ta git ever'body riled up an' make 'em think they cain't live without him, an' then he's gonna show hisself at the town meetin' an' wait for ever'body to beg him ta come back! An' come back he will, 'cause he ain't got nothin' better ta do! Heh heh, folks say I's simple-minded, but reckon I know what's what!"

Billy curled his lip; Hoot Graham holed up at Fay Bailey's house? He decided he'd better tell his father about that…he didn't think Mister Leonard would lie about something as important as the play. Leonard spat into his brass cup.

"Now I got me an assignment, ta git them cannons built, an' I ain't gonna waste no more time waitin' on no Hoot Graham ta git it done, neither!"

He pointed at a pile of flattened grocery cartons. "Them boxes is all I got, an' some boot black. But I ain't no good at renderin' stuff…an' this here cannon, it's s'posed ta fire at the end a the play. Ain't got no idea how that's gonna happen, no sir!"

Billy Gooch stuffed the bra down his shirt and clapped Leonard Festrunk on the back. "Well, Mister Leonard, ya leave that ta me! I won first prize in the sixth-grade science project 'cause I done blew up my volcano the best in the class! We'll figure out somethin', I promise! Ya know what we need? We need my buddy Rex…he's a black man, but he's a lot smarter than anybody in the whole school, an' if anybody can figure out how ta make a real live cannon, he can! But now, I gotta git home or my mama'll whup me."

Leonard nodded his head with a big grin. "Well, sure as shootin'! Tell ya what…I'll meetcha here tomorra…'bout noon, an'…"

Billy shook his head in protest. "I cain't, Mister Leonard! I got school tomorrow, dadgummit!"

Leonard pursed his lips. "Ok, how's 'bout after school? Say 'long 'bout four o'clock? Tell you what… I'll spring fer the cookies…git some from the Clinic, an' we'll have us a cookie or two, an' we'll start workin'! Now, ya best git 'long home!"

Billy nodded and extended his right hand toward Leonard, who spat into the brass cup. Leonard wiped his palm on the seat of his workpants, then shook Billy's hand hard, and smiled. Billy ran off and called, "See ya, Mister Leonard! And *thanks*!"

The next day was the most glorious day of Billy Gooch's seventh grade experience; it included the premier of the 44DD bra on the school playground and the sale of thirty-second glances at women's pantyhose to the tune of over twenty dollars. After school, Billy Gooch and Rex Parker trotted happily toward the Gym-torium. Leonard Festrunk was waiting anxiously with a bag of chocolate chip cookies. Billy stopped suddenly on the street and looked at Rex with a serious face.

"Now, 'member, homey, what I tol' ya. Ol' Leonard, he's a might slow, but he's a right nice man. He lent me that bra, on the condition I didn't charge nobody ta see it…but he don't know 'bout them pantyhose, so you keep yer big trap shut, you hear?"

Rex nodded. "I told you I won't say anything, honky! How much money did you make, anyhow?"

Billy smiled widely and held out ten fingers. He flashed them twice. "Twenty bucks, my man, twenty bucks! 'Nuf ta git that new fishin' rod outta layaway at the sportin' goods store! Can ya go fishin' tomorrow, or you gotta study again, like you did all summer in Chicago? Homey, ya sure missed a heck of a good bit a fishin'!"

Rex frowned behind his eyeglasses, "Don't remind me, honky! I hated every minute of it! My Aunt Pearl is one crazy old woman, and I don't ever want to see her again! She made me take a nap every day, she wouldn't let me go outside, and I had to listen to Swahili tapes, French tapes, and do math problems six hours a day! Talk about *torture*! I did get to go to a Cubs game a coupl'a times with my cousin, though, that was pretty fun. And I saw Michael Jordan on the subway, once."

"Aw, yer crazy, homey! Michael Jordan don't ride no subway! He's got him a big-ass limo, I seen it on TV!"

"Hey, you weren't even there! How'd you know? I'm tellin' you, I saw Michael Jordan on the subway, and that's that! You just shut up and believe me, or I'll tell Leonard you charged everybody in school to see those pantyhose!"

Billy bit his lip and frowned. "You do an' you'll answer ta me, son! Now if you wanna go fishin' with me an' use my new rod, you jus' hush up, hear?"

Rex laughed and skipped down the street. "Make me, honky, make me!"

Billy ran after his friend and as they careened into the brick entrance of the Gym-torium, Leonard Festrunk appeared and waved.

"Howdo, Billy! This yer smart friend?"

Billy nodded and said, "Yep, Mister Leonard, I'd like ya ta meet Rex Parker, my best friend. He's real smart, ya know, his daddy's Doc Parker over to the univers'ty, an' I tol' him 'bout yer cannon, an' he's already got an idea how we can do it! He's gonna blow us ta kingdom come! Rex, this here's Mister Leonard Festrunk."

Rex Parker adjusted his glasses and shook Leonard's huge hand. "I'm real pleased to meet you, sir. It sure was nice of you to lend Billy that bra! You shoulda seen the look on Gus Tatum's face! It was great!"

Leonard smiled. "Well, good, good! Come on, ya'll wanna cookie? Miz Davenport's specialty, choc'late chip…here, let's us set down a minute an' visit. I got us a Co-cola, too."

The three new acquaintances entered the Gym-torium and sat down on the bleachers. They each took swigs from a huge plastic soft drink bottle Leonard offered, and munched cookies. Billy and Rex talked with their mouths full and told Leonard about the popularity of the infamous bra and the impressions they'd made on all their friends. When they were finished eating, Leonard wiped his palms on his workpants and led the boys to the back of the Gym-torium.

"This here's the 'ficial prop room. I gotta build me a cannon fer the last part a the play, fer when they hang the d'serters. Rex, I knowed yer daddy help write this here play, but I gotta tell ya, son, it ain't all of it true...reckon you've heard that already, though."

Rex nodded. "Yessir, but it's ok. I'm stayin' out of it. But I told Billy I'd help you do this, because it sounds like a lot of fun, I like to blow up stuff, and, well, because of that bra and all. My dad's real smart, too smart, I think. He wants me to study all the time, like he does, and I'd just as soon go fishin' with Billy. We're gonna live in the woods one day, you know."

Leonard grinned. "I like fishin' too, Rex! I tell ya what...when we git this here cannon built an' workin', let's us all go fishin'...I'll drive us over ta the lake one Sat'dy, an' we can have us a time! Ya'll like ta do that?"

Billy and Rex shouted and jumped up and down. "Yessir! That'd be great!"

Leonard motioned for the boys to be still. "Ok, now looky here. Afore we git started, I got ya'll a li'l present...it ain't much, but I wanted ya'll ta know how much I 'preciate yer help. Here, open it."

Leonard proffered a brown paper sack, which was clumsily fastened with silver duct tape. "Go on, open it up!"

Billy and Rex rolled their eyes, and Billy tore into the package. He pulled out two bright white t-shirts and gave one to Rex. Printed on the front of each shirt was a large red and blue Confederate battle flag, known as the "Stars and Bars." Under the flag, in blue letters, were the words, *"True Freedom = States Rights. Screw the Federal Government."*

Billy and Rex simultaneously pulled their new t-shirts over their school clothes. "Man! This is *great*, Mister Leonard! Where'd ya git these cool shirts?"

Leonard beamed as the boys admired their gifts. "Well, sir, I ain't one ta shop in no mall or nothin', so's I git lotsa them cat'logs, an' I was thumbin' thew one the other day, an' I seen this here Confed'rate flag...my sister MayBelle, she read it ta me, an' I figgered we might jus' need 'em fer the Festival...I done ordered two hunnerd of 'em...figgered they'll go like hot cakes!"

Rex admired his t-shirt and nodded hard. He'd always admired the Stars and Bars and had recently wondered why, if his father was such a noted Civil

War scholar, they had no fine examples of this flag in their own home. Wouldn't his father be proud to see this!

"Yessir, they sure will! These are so cool! You gonna sell 'em? I'll help!"

Leonard shook his head. "Thanks, but I ain't gonna sell 'em... I'm gonna *give* 'em away ta anybody wants 'em! An' seein' as how ya'll are helpin' me with this cannon, I wanted ya'll ta have 'em first! Good! Now, let's git us ta makin' a right-proper cannon!"

Rex pulled a crumpled sheet of paper out of his pocket, and reviewed his cannon design with Leonard and Billy. They spent the next hour modifying Rex's design and carefully drawing its components on the sides of several flattened cardboard boxes. As they were about to use Leonard's official Swiss Army knife to cut out the first section, the beeper on Rex's watch sounded.

"Dang! I hate that thing! Mister Leonard, that's Rex's official 'git'-cher-ass-on-home' watch…ever' time it beeps, he takes off runnin' fer home, else he'll git in trouble, won't ya, homey?"

Rex nodded with a sigh. "Yeah, honky, and I don't feel like takin' any heat my first week back from Aunt Pearl's…I sure as shootin' don't wanna get sent back there again! Mister Leonard, sorry I gotta go…but I could come back tomorrow…it's Saturday, and my music lessons don't start for another week. Would that be ok?"

Leonard smiled and shook Rex's hand. "Son, I reckon that'll be jus' great! You shore are a smart boy, jus' like Billy said! Now you best git 'long home… I'll be here tomorra when ya'll come back…ain't got nothin' else ta do."

Rex gathered up his books and ran out of the Gym-torium calling, "Bye, Billy! Bye, Mister Leonard! Thanks for the cookies! And the t-shirt!"

Leonard eyed Billy. "That shore is one nice young man you got fer a friend, there, Billy. He talks good, he's smart, an' he's a happy little fella, ain't he? Yep, you're right lucky, I'd say. I'm glad I met up with 'im, an' I shore am glad I thought ta bring them shirts over here today…djew see 'is face light up? Well, here let's us cut out these drawin's."

Rex Parker walked in the front door to his family's comfortable, sprawling house and headed for the kitchen. He saw a note from his mother, saying that she would be home by six, that he shouldn't snack too heavily before dinner, and that he should study his African Culture textbook until then.

Rex drank a big swig of milk straight out of the carton, as he'd seen Billy do, wiped his mouth with the back of his hand, grabbed a piece of fruit from a basket on the countertop, and went into the den. He sat down on the sofa, kicked off his shoes, scattered his schoolbooks on the coffee table, and leaned back against the sofa cushions. In three minutes' time, Rex Parker was fast asleep, after nary a bit of African Culture studying, and still dressed in his new Confederate battle flag t-shirt.

At exactly six o' clock, Dr. Avery Parker and his wife Diana arrived home. They found their son sleeping peacefully in the den. Diana Parker stood behind the sofa and gazed admiringly at her only child,

"Look, Avery. He must have been studying, just like we asked him to...and look! He was going to eat an apple, instead of eating chips straight out of the bag like that Billy Gooch does...I think your Aunt Pearl worked another miracle, dear, just like we hoped! Now if he'll just make some friends tomorrow at the African Heritage Youth Center in Nashville...maybe then he'll forget all about this bad crowd. Did you tell him about tomorrow yet, Avery?"

Dr. Parker put one arm around his wife's shoulders. "Mmm, not yet... I'm glad Aunt Pearl was able to do some good with him. Rex was succumbing to extremely bad influences around here. I hope we've done the right thing, keeping him out of private school for one more year...you know I really want him to get the best education, but it's going to be so hard to see him leave and live three hundred miles away at such a young age. Let's hope we can enjoy this last year together, as a family. He'll be in college, soon, you know, Diana."

Rex stirred on the sofa and rolled over, rubbing his eyes. He looked up at his adoring parents, and smiled.

"Hi, Mom, hi, Pop! What's for dinner?"

Diana and Avery Parker froze simultaneously as they gazed in horror at the Confederate Stars and Bars that glared back at them. They exchanged silent glances and Dr. Parker removed his arm from Diana's shoulders. In a taut voice, he said,

"*Son...what is that you're wearing, and what on earth possessed you to bring it into this house?*"

Rex's smile faded; he was still half-asleep. "Huh?" He looked down and remembered the gift from Mister Leonard.

"Oh, yeah, Pop, isn't this neat? Me and honky...*Billy* both got one, for helping Mister Leonard build a cannon for the town play. Mister Leonard ordered a bunch of these shirts, and he's gonna give them out at the Festival. But he gave us the first ones, isn't that cool, because we're helping him over at the Gym-torium tomorrow, I figured it'd be okay, since it's Saturday."

Dr. Parker slammed his hand down on the kitchen countertop behind him. "NO, Rex, it's NOT okay! You will be otherwise *engaged* tomorrow, at a rally in Nashville, at the African Heritage Youth Center. So you can just forget about any more work with Mister Leonard...is that Leonard *Festrunk*? The old man who can't even read and write? You've been spending your study time with Billy Gooch and a man who can't even *read and write*, a man who isn't allowed to carry any money because he can't even think straight?

Did you learn *anything* in Chicago with your Aunt Pearl? And I suppose you walked home wearing that disgraceful shirt...insulting your entire race! Have you just gone completely *insane* and decided to throw your whole *life* away? *Rex*? Diana...I can't deal with this right now...*look* at that *shirt*! I cannot believe this is happening..."

Dr. Parker quivered in anger and stormed into his office, slamming the door behind him. Rex looked innocently at his mother, who sat down beside him on the sofa.

"What, Mom? What did I do now? He gave me the shirt fair and square, for helping him, I promise!"

Diana smoothed her hair and cleared her throat. She spoke with great control, "Rex, do you know anything about the symbol on that shirt you're wearing? Do you realize what it means?"

Rex shook his head, and stared down at the Stars and Bars. "It's some neat Civil War design...sort of like the American flag, only the stars and stripes are a little bit different...I'm not really sure what *'True Freedom = States Rights. Screw the Federal Government'* is all about, but I guess it's some sort of joke or something."

Diana frowned and grabbed Rex by the hand. She squeezed it tight, and said quietly,

"*Rex*. Our ancestors were brought over to this country as slaves...*SLAVES*! In *chains*! Naked as the day they were born! In foul, stinking ships, lashed to one another! They had no *food*, they had no *water*, they weren't allowed to go to the *bathroom*, they were separated from their families, and sold into *slavery*, Rex! They were owned by white people and forced to pick cotton, and do hard labor, and they lived in *unimaginable squalor*, for over two hundred *years*!"

"I know, Mom! But what's all that got to do with this *shirt*? We're not slaves anymore! What's the big deal?"

Diana nearly jerked her son by the ears, she was so incensed. "*REX*! The South supported slavery, and this was the flag used by the South during the Civil War! This was the flag they raised, the flag that said, *'All men are not created equal'* so they could keep us *down*! We were slaves! They made money off our sweat, and misery, and inhuman condition! This is the flag that stood for *slavery*, Rex! And you have brought it into this *house*, and you are wearing it in *public*, and your father and I are *horrified*, and we are *heartbroken*, because we have spent our every waking minute of our entire lives fighting for the rights of our people! And now, to have our own son wear this, this symbol of HATE! I just can't even believe you would *do* this to us!"

Diana Parker began to sob and held her face in her hands. Rex was sick to his stomach. A giant tear rolled down his cheek.

"But Mom, I didn't know that's what it meant! These flags are all over the place down here! I just thought it was some kind of Southern way to show American pride! Billy's got it on a cap, and I've seen it on license plates, and it's on fireworks stands at the Fourth of July picnic! Slavery's been over for a hundred years, it's not like we're still fighting a war, or anything, Mom! Nobody ever told me about this flag…how was I supposed to know?"

Diana looked up through her tears. "Son, your father is one of the world's most renowned experts on African Heritage and the Civil War. Don't you realize, *you* of all people should have known not to display this? Not to wear it, or bring it into our home, or be *associated* with anyone who approves of it? Can you understand that, Rex?"

Rex nodded and began to cry. "Mom, I *swear* I didn't know! Nobody's ever *told* me! Just because Pop knows all that history stuff, it doesn't mean that *I* do! *I'm* not a professor! I'm just a *kid*! I mean, we learned about the Civil War in school, but they sure didn't say anything about all this! How would I know, Mom? Besides, you and Pop are so busy going to lectures, and rallies, and meetings, and leaving me at home…you expect me to know everything that you do, but you never take the time to tell me, so how would I, Mom? *How would I*?"

Avery Parker came into the den and placed a gentle hand on his sobbing son's shoulder. "Rex, it's ok, son. Diana, he's absolutely right. He's only a child, and we've expected him to behave as an adult…as both of us with our Ph.D's behave…I'm sorry, Rex."

Rex wiped his eyes and nodded.

"It's ok, Pop…I'm sorry I wore this shirt, but I promise I didn't know anything about all that stuff…I'd never do anything to hurt you and Mom, I swear! But I'm not sure what I'm supposed to know anymore! Why do I have to study Swahili? Nobody else does! And why do I have to go to some stupid rally tomorrow? I want to be here, with my friends! It's hard being the smartest kid in school, ya know, and being black too! I'm just trying to fit in! Maybe my friends are all white, but I like 'em! Why can't you?"

Avery and Diana Parker exchanged looks. Dr. Parker sat down on the fireplace hearth across from Rex, and folded his hands. He took a deep breath, bit his lip, and sighed.

"Son, there are some very nice people in this town. And there are also some very ignorant, very backward people in this town, just like in any town. And although living here is ideal for my work at the university, it's not the best place to raise our son, because unfortunately you are exposed to a very limited line of thinking. But you have the brains, the common sense, the potential, that very few children ever have, and we want you to make the most of those gifts, and grow to be a fine, independent man, to make your own judgments, to pave your own way."

Rex wiped his eyes. His mother patted him on the shoulder."Rex, honey, there is nothing wrong with your school, or your friends, for the most part. But there is so much more in the world for you to learn. And that is why...that is why..."

Avery spoke up. "That is why you will be going away to school next year, to a school in Atlanta where different viewpoints are examined, and studied, and where the African-American heritage is valued as a contribution, not a quota."

Rex's heart stopped. Going away to school? *In Atlanta*? He couldn't breathe. He couldn't speak. He couldn't imagine...

"...and until that time," Dr. Parker continued, "until you are able to go away to school in Atlanta next year, I've just spoken to your Aunt Pearl. She has agreed to make the ultimate sacrifice for you. You know how she loves you, Rex. And she has offered to come here and live with us this year, to help prepare you for your Atlanta departure. You must focus, Rex, you must make a concentrated effort on your studies, and it is obvious that after only a few days at home, you cannot be trusted to work on your own. And your mother and I can't exactly quit *our* jobs. Diana, Aunt Pearl will arrive tomorrow evening. You'll need to get a hold of a good contractor to finish the room over the garage for her. That way, Rex, when you come home from school, there will be someone here to look after you, to guide your studies, to reinforce the kind of behavior that we expect in this family."

Rex felt as if he'd been struck by a car. He couldn't look at his parents. He just stared blankly at the floor. Diana shifted stiffly on the sofa.

"Avery, we did not discuss this as an option. Now I know your Aunt Pearl has Rex's best interests at heart, but I'm not sure that living with us under the same *roof* is the best plan; you just said that with Rex in Atlanta next year, this will be our last year together, and you know, your Aunt Pearl is so hyper-critical of everything I do that..."

Avery Parker rose from the hearth and raised his hands in protest."Diana! I've made up my mind! We have to act swiftly, and we have to act now! Rex's education is our topmost priority, and there will be no further discussion! I know how you feel about my Aunt Pearl...she can be a little difficult, I realize. But it's done. Now, dinner? I know, Rex, let's order a pizza, after all, it is Friday night, and then we can look at that rally brochure together. Some of the finest people in the Civil Rights movement will be there tomorrow, it will be thrilling!"

Rex Parker didn't smile again for days. When he didn't show up at the Gym-torium on Saturday, Billy called the Parker house and was informed by an icy Dr. Parker that Rex was no longer able to participate in the cannon project, that he would be otherwise engaged, and that he would no longer be allowed to associate with Billy after school, as he would be preparing for his entrance examinations into a prep school in Atlanta. Billy shrugged, and he and Leonard Festrunk set to work on the cannon, using Rex's design. After a miserable day at the African Culture rally in Nashville, Rex went sullenly to his room, to await the dreaded arrival of Aunt Pearl. He could hear his mother slamming doors and banging pots, in protest of her husband's decision to send out for unwanted family reinforcements. Rex was distraught, and he buried his head in his pillow and sobbed until he fell asleep.

He slept so soundly that he never heard his Aunt Pearl arrive, he never heard her loud argument with the taxi driver over the fare, and he never heard his mother come into his room and cover him with a blanket. He slept right through supper, and didn't wake until he heard an annoying gurgling sound coming from the guest bathroom.

Rex sat upright in bed...he realized he was still in his clothes and that it was Sunday morning. Then he realized that the annoying gurgling sound in the guest bathroom was emitted by Aunt Pearl, as she followed her strict morning gargling regimen. His summer of Aunt Pearl horror had now become his year of Aunt Pearl terror, and life, as he knew it, was over.

Rex plopped back on his pillow. *I could just slip out the window,* he thought. *Just climb down that tree and run as fast as I can over to Billy's....no...to Mister Leonard's! He'd help me! Maybe he'd hide me someplace! Just until we could get some food, and sneak into the woods, and build our cabin! No Aunt Pearl, no Swahili tapes, no...*

"Rex, dear, time for breakfast! You must be famished! Please wash and come to the table!"

He was doomed. He'd waited too long. *Should have made my escape last night,* he realized. *Could still go, right now...but that bacon smells great...are those biscuits, too? Maybe I'd better eat...then I can think straight.* He changed clothes, washed his face, and lazily tromped downstairs. His Aunt Pearl sat on one full end of the den sofa. Her ample frame was draped in an ensemble including a turquoise silk caftan, a matching turquoise turban with jewels on the front, and turquoise bedroom slippers trimmed in white fur. She raised her flabby arms with a great grin and motioned for Rex to come near.

"My lands, look at this child! Avery Rex Parker III, I do believe you've grown six inches since I saw you last! Diana, whatever do you feed this boy? Rex, honey, you feel cold! Diana, I told you it's much too cold in here! This child is *frozen*! Come here, honey, and let me see your tongue...do you have a virus? Diana, where is your hot water bottle?"

Rex reluctantly hugged his Aunt Pearl. From the kitchen, amidst lots of banging and clanging, Diana Parker yelled, "Aunt Pearl, you just saw Rex last week! I doubt if he's grown that much in seven days! And in *this* house, we keep the thermostat set at 74...he's just fine, aren't you, Rex?"

Rex nodded and sat down next to Aunt Pearl. "Yes, ma'am. I'm just fine, thank you. How was your trip, Aunt Pearl?"

Aunt Pearl opened her mouth to speak, but Diana called that breakfast was ready, so Rex and Aunt Pearl padded into the kitchen. Avery Parker sat at the breakfast table, deep into the Sunday paper. Rex volunteered to say the blessing, because he knew from past experience that if Aunt Pearl took a turn, breakfast would be cold, and his mother would be even angrier. After giving thanks, Rex complimented his mother on the food, then pre-empted Aunt Pearl from supplementing his abbreviated prayer by once again asking her about the trip to Chestnut Ridge.

"Well, it was absolutely the most *terrible* trip I've ever taken, that's how it was. Oh...these are *canned* biscuits? I don't know that I've ever eaten *canned* biscuits before...don't worry, Avery, tomorrow I'll bake you some of my nice, fresh, *scratch* biscuits for breakfast!"

Aunt Pearl spread the equivalent of a third of a jar of marmalade on a biscuit as Diana stared in silent disapproval.

"What do you mean, Aunt Pearl? Was the flight okay?"

Rex smiled at his mother. Pleasing Aunt Pearl would not be nearly so difficult as keeping the peace in this house now that two battling women shared it, he realized.

"My lands, child, is any flight ever okay? Lord have mercy, those pilots, they're not but about twelve years old, I think! And taking off in a *thunderstorm*! Like they had permission from God Almighty! And O'Hare Airport, you know it's just about the nastiest place on earth...all those foreigners... they don't wash properly! And I forgot to bring my toilet seat covers, so I was about to pop by the time I got here! Well, you know I just dropped everything, I mean *everything*, to come here for you and your father, Rex, on the spur of the moment, so I didn't even have time to eat lunch yesterday, and I refuse, I mean, *refuse* to eat that airport food...ten dollars for a tuna sandwich, uh-uh, I'm not paying *that*!"

Aunt Pearl plopped half of a marmalade-laden biscuit into her mouth in one bite and reached for the plate of bacon. She removed five pieces of bacon from the plate in succession, then grabbed another biscuit.

"*No eggs*, Diana? I always make eggs with my bacon and biscuits, don't I Avery? Soft-scrambled, just the way Avery likes them. But then, I never served canned biscuits, either."

Diana gripped her coffee mug tightly. "Avery and I must watch our cholesterol, Aunt Pearl. We don't usually eat eggs, out of concern for our health."

Aunt Pearl grimaced over her bifocals at Diana, then glanced at Avery.

"Well, child, maybe the genes on *your* side are weak, but our family's been eatin' eggs for two hundred years, and none of *us* have ever suffered, have they Avery? But our genes are better than most, I suppose. All this talk about watching cholesterol and counting calories...well, that's fine for *you* Diana, but this child here is *growing*, and he needs some *eggs*! Rex, honey, tomorrow your Aunt Pearl will make you some eggs, just like I made for you at my house, ok?"

Rex nodded, then smiled sheepishly at his mother, who rose quickly from the breakfast table to pour herself another cup of coffee. Aunt Pearl buttered her fourth biscuit. Avery hid behind his newspaper.

"You know, speaking of tuna sandwiches, Avery, Rex, you know my neighbor, Mrs. Bartow, she got a tuna sandwich at the O'Hare Airport one time, and it had a *rat's tail* in it! I know, because I went with her on the train back to the airport, and we had that little tail in a plastic bag, and we marched right up to the desk of that airlines, and we shoved that plastic bag in that little girl's face, and told her we wanted to speak to the manager! You'd a thought they would have given us proper compensation, at least paid our subway fare, and they should have given Mrs. Bartow a free ticket, she wanted to visit her sister in Hawaii, of course...not that we didn't try, I'm telling you, we were there, talking to that uppity white man for *three hours*, but they said that rat's tail was a *bean sprout*! Now I'm asking you, who ever heard of putting *bean sprouts* on a tuna fish sandwich? Lord knows, that was a *rat's tail*, and those people will get what's coming to them one day!"

Aunt Pearl jammed a biscuit into her mouth and reached for another slice of bacon. Diana returned to the table, pursed her lips and grabbed her own untouched plate of food in disgust at Aunt Pearl's recital. Dr. Parker re-folded his newspaper and smiled at Aunt Pearl as he took a sip of coffee.

"Aunt Pearl, thank you so much for coming here on such short notice! Rex and Diana and I are very pleased to have you here. I've already hired a contractor to start work on your room, and it should be done by the end of the month. Until then, I do hope you'll be comfortable in the guestroom. Did you sleep well, Aunt Pearl?"

Aunt Pearl wiped her mouth daintily with a napkin, took a sip of coffee, smoothed her turban, and sighed."Well, *no*, Avery, thank you for asking, I didn't sleep well *at all*."

Dr. Parker frowned, and tilted his head to one side. "Was your bed too soft Aunt Pearl? We can get a new mattress, or..."

"No, dear, it's not the mattress."

"Maybe it was a little too cold in your room? Diana prefers it to be a little cool in the house, but we can set it up a bit tonight if that would help."

Diana scowled at her ingratiatingly kind husband. Aunt Pearl idly stirred her coffee and shook her head.

"No, dear sweet boy, I don't mind sleeping with four blankets...I'm sure I'll get used to it...well, I shouldn't say *sleep*...I didn't sleep at all."

"Aunt Pearl, are you feeling all right? Maybe you were overtired from your trip."

"Well, Avery, to tell you the truth...I had a *heart attack* last night. But I'm much better this morning. Although I am surprised that no one could hear me *suffering*...this hotel you're living in must have three-foot thick walls, I suppose...I might have been dead before anyone came to my aid...I'm lucky it was just a small heart attack. I don't think I'll have any permanent damage...I've had them before, you know. But I'm feeling right as rain, now, dear, thank you for asking, such a sweet boy!"

Avery and Diana exchanged looks, and Diana had to bite her tongue to keep from laughing out loud. She stood up from the breakfast table. "Excuse me, I think something's still in the fridge...I mean, the oven."

Rex stared in amazement at his great Aunt Pearl, a medical miracle, who buttered a fifth biscuit. Dr. Parker set his newspaper aside.

"Aunt Pearl, I didn't realize that people who have heart attacks could just go back to *sleep* and then come down for breakfast the next morning, without any symptoms, or pain, whatsoever. Are you positive you just had a heart attack? Should we go to the hospital?"

Aunt Pearl stopped buttering her biscuit and waved her knife at Avery. "I *know* what I had, young man, and it was not *just* a heart attack....it was a *series* of heart attacks...and thank the good Lord it's just not my time to go yet. God needs me to work with your son, here, since your own wife can't stay home and take care of her own child. Now like I said, Avery, I've been havin' heart attacks for the last twenty years... I have at least one or two a week, you know. But I don't go to hospitals, no, sir, I just trust in the Lord. Now, pass me that bacon platter."

Rex handed the bacon to Aunt Pearl, who took three more pieces. Dr. Parker winked at Rex, and picked up his newspaper.

"Well, Aunt Pearl, I'm certainly glad to hear you're feeling better this morning. Now you know, any time you need assistance, even in the middle of the night, you just need to call out, and we'll come help you immediately. I'm sorry we didn't hear you in your agony."

"Oh, Avery, bless you, child, but you know that when a person has a heart attack, he can't talk or move! I just had to lay there and suffer in silence...but I did have to go to the toilet about seven times, and I just assumed that with all that flushing, you might have checked on me, to make sure I wasn't dehydrated... but I suppose Diana didn't want to wake you, I know how soundly men sleep."

Diana looked up from the kitchen sink where she was forcefully scrubbing an already-spotless frying pan, and said sarcastically, "Aunt Pearl, I most certainly did *not* hear the toilet flush last night…I, too, am a sound sleeper. Perhaps we should get you a bell to ring…in case you need us? Or perhaps I should just set my alarm to ring every hour and come check on you *personally*?"

Aunt Pearl waved her biscuit in the air, causing marmalade to drip off one side. "Child, goodness no, if you were to set an alarm, it would wake Avery! It's just a little old heart attack, that's all! Now, if it was my gall bladder, well, that's another story…but as long as I stick to my diet, my gall bladder shouldn't be a problem."

Diana pondered the volume of Aunt Pearl's breakfast. "And exactly what type of diet would you be on, Aunt Pearl?"

"Well, it's not so much a *diet* as it is a *lifestyle*, you know. Everything in moderation…eat only when I'm hungry, no desserts…it's all in combinations, too."

"Combinations, Aunt Pearl?"

"Well, of course, Diana, didn't they teach you anything about nutrition at that fancy girl's college you went to? Combinations are what clear the blood of impurities. Look here, child, see this biscuit? Covered in butter? But it's not going to clog my arteries, because I've blocked that devil butter with orange marmalade! The natural cholesterol fighters in the oranges just chop up that butter so it can pass right through me, and most likely, it'll pass here in just a few minutes! Combinations are the key to healthy eating, Diana, *everybody* knows that."

Just then Aunt Pearl's face took on a strained appearance, and she set her biscuit aside, and wiped her mouth quickly. "Excuse me, dears, but just like I said, train's passing on through!"

Aunt Pearl dashed from the table and into the half bathroom. Diana cleared the remaining dishes from the table in disgust.

"Avery Parker, we have to talk! This is not going to work, and you've got to make a decision… your son gets an education, or you get to keep your wife!"

Dr. Parker spoke from behind his newspaper. "Diana, it's just for a few months! And in a couple of weeks, she'll be in her own room over the garage, with her own kitchen, and we'll never even know she's here. Besides, we're not doing this for ourselves, dear, we're doing it for Rex. It's the least we can do for his future!"

Rex realized that his mother's pained face was the key to his liberation from Aunt Pearl.

"You know, Dad," Rex said matter-of-factly, "aren't you worried that Aunt

Pearl will fall down the stairs or something? I mean, she's pretty old, and out of shape, and, well, you know what she does every night..."

Avery Parker set down the paper and frowned at Rex to keep quiet. Diana stopped scrubbing the frying pan."What? What does she do every evening, Avery? What are you talking about, Rex?"

Avery inhaled sharply through his nose and glared at Rex, who innocently ignored his father.

"Well, mom, I don't really think I should say...but when you spend two and a half months with someone, in their house, you know stuff...I mean, it's probably ok and everything, but, well..."

"Spit it out, Rex!" Diana dried her hands anxiously on a paper towel.

"Well, every night, after she thought I was in bed, I'd hear all this clanging around, so I'd stand at the top of the stairs, out of sight. Aunt Pearl got this big brown bottle out of her locked china cabinet and drank the whole thing in two gulps. Then she'd go in the kitchen, dig around in the pantry, and come back and put the bottle in the china cabinet. Pretty soon, she'd start singing, and sometimes she'd dance, but most of the time, she'd just giggle and have trouble walking up the stairs. One night, she fell down and started laughing real loud, though, and I had to help her to her room!"

Avery frowned at Rex. "Young man, that will be enough! I know what you're up to, and it won't work. Diana, this is utterly ridiculous!" He looked at his watch.

"Great, I'm late for my golf game! We'll discuss this later. Diana, did you pack my cooler yet? With bottled water? I'll be back around three. Goodbye."

Diana handed her husband his cooler. Avery kissed her quickly on the forehead, clapped Rex on the back, and anxiously rushed from the kitchen. Diana stared intently at her son.

"Rex, are you telling the truth? Does Aunt Pearl really drink something from a bottle every night?"

Rex nodded in earnest. "Yes, mom, I *swear*! I asked her about it, and she got real angry with me, and said it was her cough medicine that she needed it for her lungs, because it's so cold in Chicago. I promise! Hey, if you don't believe me, look in her suitcase! I bet she brought it with her!"

Diana was secretly horrified. If what Rex said was true, Aunt Pearl might very well be an alcoholic, and Rex, her precious, only child had lived an entire summer on peril's doorstep. Diana Parker was not about to entrust her son with that same alcoholic in her own home, no matter what Avery had to say about it. Rex put his juice glass in the dishwasher.

"Mom, is it ok if I go upstairs and start on my homework? I've got a lot of reading to do, and since I was at that rally all day yesterday, well, I don't see how I'm going to be able to get it all done if I don't start right now!"

Rex crossed his fingers behind his back at the lie but there was no way he was going to spend the day with Aunt Pearl. Diana cleared the dishes from the table and quickly put away the leftovers.

"Yes, Rex, you get started on your homework. I'm going to finish the dishes, then I've got some work of my own to do today. I'm not sure what we'll do with your Aunt Pearl…oh, Aunt Pearl. Are you all right?"

Aunt Pearl's turban shifted slightly on her head as she stormed back into the kitchen and stared at the empty breakfast table."Well, I guess you decided that breakfast is over? My goodness, I'm glad I ate a small bite before I had to excuse myself, or I'd never have gotten anything at all!"

Diana rolled her eyes. "Aunt Pearl, I'm sorry, I thought you were finished. The bacon and biscuits are in the fridge, you're welcome to help yourself. But Rex and I both have a lot of work to do today. I'm afraid you'll be on your own until Avery returns from his golf game later."

Aunt Pearl opened the refrigerator and shuffled through its contents, looking for the bacon and biscuits. "Now don't you worry about me, Diana, I'm going to make myself a grocery list; when Avery comes back, he can take me to the store, if you don't mind. No, you and Rex just go about your business, ok? But I would like to finish my breakfast…what did you have planned for lunch?"

Diana's mouth fell open, then she snapped it shut. "Well, Aunt Pearl, it's already eleven, and we just finished a rather large breakfast, for our standards, anyway, so I really didn't plan on cooking anything until tonight…"

Aunt Pearl dropped the butter in shock. "What? No lunch plans? *My Lord*, things are different now! I never would have *dreamed* of not having a good, hot Sunday meal ready for my family! What about Rex? He's a growing boy, he needs to be fed and watered, Diana! And I don't mean hamburgers, or pizza, either!"

Rex tried to rescue his mother. "It's ok, Aunt Pearl, I always make myself a peanut butter and mustard sandwich on Sundays, while Dad's at the golf course, because on Sunday nights, we go out for piz…"

Diana clapped her son loudly on the back and interrupted. "We always have a nice, home-cooked dinner on Sunday nights, like a roast, or a turkey, or something, don't we, Rex? And since your Aunt Pearl is our guest, why don't we let her decide what she would like me to prepare! Aunt Pearl, what is your pleasure?"

Rex's eyes opened wide at his mother's blatant lie, but he didn't say anything. Aunt Pearl studied the meager contents of the refrigerator.

"Hmmmm…you know, I've been thinking about pork chops ever since I got on that airplane. Wouldn't a good mess of pork chops just hit the spot?"

Diana smiled weakly. "Well, Aunt Pearl, that sounds wonderful. But I'm afraid I don't really cook much pork…it's so *fatty*…what about…"

"Oh, gracious, child, I didn't mean *you'd* cook them, Lord, you with all your low-cholesterol fol-de-rol, why, who'd want to eat an ol' dried-up low-fat pork chop? Not me, and certainly not Avery and that precious boy! No, I'm talking *fried* pork chops, with pan gravy...Diana, you've never tasted a good pork chop until you've tasted Aunt Pearl's pork chops, right Rex? And I'm sure Avery would be *grateful* to get a good, hot meal for once!"

Rex nodded enthusiastically. He loved his Aunt Pearl's cooking. Suddenly he realized he faced a terrible dilemma. If he worked this just right, he could probably make his mom so upset she'd send Aunt Pearl back to Chicago, one way or another, and he'd regain at least some of his freedom. But if Aunt Pearl stayed, she'd cook for them every day, and wouldn't that be a welcome change from the frozen food and meager meals his mother scraped together after her long work days.

"Yes, ma'am! I *love* your pork chops, Aunt Pearl! Mom, they're so good! Ooh, the *gravy*! And will you make your special mashed potatoes, Aunt Pearl? The ones with the little onions in them?" Rex's mouth watered at the thought of pork chops and mashed potatoes.

Diana crossed her arms over her chest. "Well, thank you, Aunt Pearl, that would be lovely! Let me show you where the…"

Aunt Pearl raised her fleshy arms in protest. "No, no, Diana, you go do your 'important' work, I know how you career girls are! I'll just make myself at home in this kitchen, and if I don't find what I need, which I'd guess is just about most *everything*, I'll write it down, and Avery will take me to the grocery this afternoon! Now go on, you two, this is my kitchen now! You just leave the cooking to Aunt Pearl!"

A beaming Rex and a wistful Diana left Aunt Pearl in the kitchen, and made their way to their respective rooms. Rex promptly locked his door and fell asleep after reading two pages of African culture. When Avery returned after his golf game, he was greeted at the door by Aunt Pearl, dressed in a brightly colored African print dress, matching turban and sandals.

"I'm ready to go to the grocery now Avery, so please don't be long showering. We are having pork chops this evening, and you how involved that is. I've already rearranged this entire kitchen, it was an absolute *mess*!"

Avery, in anticipation of his Aunt Pearl's pork chops, hurriedly showered, greeted Diana, who was deep into her lesson plans, and escorted Aunt Pearl to the Poe House Grocery, where Aunt Pearl spent a Parker family record of four hundred dollars on groceries. Avery carried all the groceries into the kitchen, as Aunt Pearl put them away. After unloading the grocery sacks, Avery opened a bottle of water, and watched Aunt Pearl tie on her favorite cooking apron, the one with the Swiss milk cow on it, the selfsame apron she wore when he was a boy.

"Aunt Pearl, you know I can't ever thank you enough for coming here. I was in a real quandary, Rex lapsed right back into his old habits. Now I want you to feel like this is your home, too, Aunt Pearl, and if you notice anything about Rex, or this household that I need to correct, or be aware of, then you just tell me, ok?"

Aunt Pearl washed her beefy hands in the kitchen sink. "Avery, honey, I love that child like he was my own, and that's the *only* reason I'm here! It just *galls* me to see how your wife ignores that boy in favor of her career. She doesn't *cook*, and this house, well, it's a *train wreck*, I can't soft-pedal it, Avery. And you know I don't *ordinarily* speak my mind, but Lordy-be, you are too soft on her! Have you seen the amount of dust under that sofa? A woman's place is in the home, not out gallivantin' around in the business world. Now it's none of my affair, I know, but why can't Diana just come on home after school's out at three and look after Rex? Where on earth does she go, answer me that? She messin' around on you, son?"

Avery swigged some water from the bottle. "Aunt Pearl, Diana is quite an authority on African American literature, her work is as important to her as mine is to me. She has an office at the university library, and every day she goes there after school and works on the textbook she's writing. We both get home by six-thirty or seven, at the latest, but I can't ask her to cook and clean after we've both had such a long day, now can I?"

Aunt Pearl guffawed. "Textbook writin'! She should leave that to the men, and stick to child-raisin'! If she had, you wouldn't be in this mess, and I'd be back in my own house in Chicago, tending my roses, instead of having to walk on tippy-toes in the house of my own flesh and blood!"

Avery waved one finger slightly at his aunt. "Now Aunt Pearl, I respect your opinion, and I agree with you, if Diana was around more, Rex wouldn't be in this situation, but I'm going to have to ask you to keep it our little secret, ok? Diana is not at all happy that you're here, I'll be perfectly honest with you. She's going along to please me, and because she knows it will be best for Rex. So you two are going to have to get along for the next nine months, I don't want any arguing, or accusing, or tattling, ok? Will you promise me that?"

Diana Parker stood in the upstairs hallway and fumed. How *dare* this old woman come into her home and accuse her of not doing her job! How *dare* she say that a woman had no right to a meaningful career, or that her house was a train wreck! *A train wreck*! And how *dare* her own husband talk about her behind her *back*! Diana clenched her fists in a fury, then took a deep breath. She could hear Rex snore from behind his locked bedroom door.

This is ridiculous! I have lost control of my own home! And this old witch thinks she can...thinks she can...

Diana remembered her morning conversation with Rex. She eased back quietly toward the guest room, careful to avoid the floorboards that might creak and tattle. She peered into Aunt Pearl's room. The bed was made with nary a wrinkle; Aunt Pearl's belongings were completely put away. Diana crept into the room, eyes scanning it for potential brown-bottle hiding places. She'd show that fat old bag, and her chauvinist pig husband, too! No damned alcoholic was going to accuse *her*, in her own *house*! Diana gingerly opened the guest room bureau; Aunt Pearl's giant white panties filled the entire top drawer. Disgusted, she searched the other three bureau drawers to no avail. Then she carefully opened the closet door to a shocking array of loudly-colored caftans and house slippers. On the floor in a corner of the closet was Aunt Pearl's suitcase. Diana tiptoed over and quietly pressed open the locks, but the suitcase was empty.

Satisfied there was nothing in the closet, under the guest bed, or between the mattresses, Diana stepped into the guest bathroom. She ran smack dab into the clothes hamper and froze with one leg in the air, crane-like, but after a few silent seconds, she padded to the medicine cabinet, where no fewer than thirty bottles of Aunt Pearl's various and sundry medications, for her mysterious medical ailments, were neatly arranged in alphabetical order. Diana opened the linen closet door, and ran one hand behind and between all the guest towels and linens, finding nothing. Even the pocket of Aunt Pearl's gaudy red bathrobe was bare.

As she was about to end her search for the elusive brown bottle, Diana noticed that the top to the toilet tank was turned backwards. She mindlessly picked it up, in order to replace it correctly, and noticed a dark brown, corked bottle inside the tank, nestled comfortably next to the flush valve. Diana's eyes flew open wide, and she snatched the bottle from its cove. She pulled out the cork and sniffed....*RUM! Rex was right! Aunt Pearl is an alcoholic! Wait until Avery hears this!*

Diana corked the bottle tightly, then raced down the hallway to Rex's room. She tapped on the door, and a sleepy-eyed Rex opened it. "Whuh...hi, Mom, is it time for pork chops?"

Diana's eyes blazed. "It most certainly is *not*! Look what I found in your Aunt Pearl's bathroom! Hidden in the *toilet tank*! Is this the brown bottle you told me about? *Rex*?"

Rex rubbed his eyes and stared at the bottle his mother shoved in his face. "Yes, ma'am, that looks like the bottle Aunt Pearl keeps in her locked china cabinet. It's her cough medicine."

Diana snorted and shook her head in triumph. "It most certainly is *not* any damned *cough medicine*! It is *RUM*! *Alcohol*! Your Aunt Pearl is a *drunk*! Come with me right now!"

Diana Parker grasped Rex painfully around his arm and jerked him to the stairs. "Watched my only child all *summer*, drinking and doing no telling *WHAT* in that house, and comes in here and criticizes *me* and my *housekeeping* and my *career* and my ability to raise my *child*, and my own husband *agrees* with her, and *OVER MY DEAD BODY*!"

As she shouted this last statement at no one in particular, Diana, pulling Rex, reached the top of the stairs that led into the kitchen where Aunt Pearl was chopping onions for her special mashed potatoes, and where Avery Parker, Junior was happily sampling quarters from a deep red tomato that his Aunt Pearl had lovingly sliced for him. Diana's loud voice startled Aunt Pearl, who only seconds before complained to Avery that the poor excuse for kitchen knives she'd found in this house were dreadfully dull and needed sharpening in the worst way.

"*OUCH! MY LORD GOD IN HEAVEN I HAVE SLICED OFF MY THUMB!*"

Aunt Pearl raised a hand to the sky as blood oozed steadily from a deep cut. She swallowed hard, staring at the thumb which remained solidly attached to her hand, and which was in absolutely no danger of falling off, then she promptly fell to the floor in a large heap. The kitchen knife flew up into the air and landed with its blade stuck in the vinyl floor.

"OH MY GOD, AUNT PEARL!" Avery jumped off his barstool with a tomato quarter in each hand, but finding himself unable to grab Aunt Pearl, shoved the tomatoes in his mouth.

"MHEMPH MEMPH! MDIANMMA! MHEMPH!"

Rex raced down the stairs and helped his father gently lift Aunt Pearl's head. "It's ok, Dad, her thumb's still attached, see?"

Avery nodded furiously and tried to chew the tomatoes in his mouth. "MPHESS, MPHI MPSEEMPH. MDIANMA!"

Diana Parker stood her ground at the top of the stairs, and held out a dark brown bottle in Avery's direction. "DO YOU SEE THIS? YOUR PRECIOUS AUNT PEARL WAS HIDING THIS BOTTLE OF RUM IN THE *TOILET*! AVERY! DO YOU HEAR ME? SHE IS A *DRUNK*!"

Avery Parker ignored his wife and began to tap Aunt Pearl on her cheeks. Rex placed a cold dishrag on Aunt Pearl's forehead and silently wondered if this meant there would be no pork chops for dinner. Aunt Pearl opened her eyes and said woozily,

"Lord, Avery, did you save my thumb? I think I heard it fall into the garbage disposal, Lord have mercy, don't turn on that garbage disposal! Rex, honey, you'll have to fish around in there and find it and put it on ice, child, so they can sew it back on! No organ donor's thumbs for me, no sir, I'm not gonna meet St. Peter at the Pearly Gates wearin' somebody else's digit!"

"Calm down, Aunt Pearl, you didn't cut off your thumb, but it's a pretty bad gash. Do you think you can sit up for a minute? Rex, go see if we have any gauze in the medicine cabinet! Diana! Get Aunt Pearl a drink of water, and..."

Aunt Pearl opened her eyes wide, stared at the ceiling, and gasped.

"Lord, Avery, stop lyin' to me, I *know* I cut it off because I'm already havin' those ghost pains where it used to be! Oh Jesus God, it's St. Peter himself, coming to get me...*what a beautiful white chariot,* I wish you all could see it! *Lord have mercy,* there's Lawrence, riding shotgun... *Lawrence...*you should be ashamed of yourself, dyin' and leaving me all alone with that big mortgage, now hold those horses so St. Peter can come and get me...Lawrence...this is Rex, your grand-nephew! St. Peter, I'm sorry about my thumb, but my nephew's *wicked, lazy wife* scared the breath right out of me, and...*LAWRENCE*! Move out of St. Peter's way, so he can find my thumb..."

"AUNT PEARL! You stop that this instant! You are not dying, and you did not cut off your thumb! Now sit up here and have a drink of water... *DIANA*! I *asked* you to get Aunt Pearl a glass of water, now hurry up!"

Diana Parker stomped over to where her husband and son were trying to raise Aunt Pearl from her romp with the dead. She angrily waved the brown bottle in Avery's face. "*First of all,* Doctor Avery Parker Junior, if *you* want your Aunt Pearl to have a glass of water so badly, then why don't you get up off your sorry ass and get it *yourself*! And *second of all,* if Aunt Pearl's so thirsty, why don't we just give her a big gulp out of this *bottle* I found inside the *COMMODE*! It's full of *RUM*!"

Aunt Pearl bolted upright and reached for the brown bottle as her bleeding thumb sprayed Avery's tan slacks.

"*You give me that*! I might have known your wife would snoop around in my bathroom, Avery! And I'll have you know, *missy,* that's my special cough medicine, that Doctor Jackson Jefferson prescribed for me, to clear my lungs, because I have the *tuberculosis*! Never mind that I cough so hard at night, my lungs come clean out of my mouth and I have to stuff them back in, but *no,* Aunt Pearl, you're not allowed to have any cough medicine in *this* house! Oh, Lord, Avery, do I have to bleed to death before I get any medical attention? There's nearly five pints of blood on this floor, oh my sweet Jesus!"

Aunt Pearl lay back on the floor, moaning, but tightly grasped her bottle with her non-injured hand. Avery scowled at his wife.

"I can't believe this, Diana! Look what you've done to Aunt Pearl! She dropped everything to come here and help us, and not only have you caused her to injure herself, you've become a common *snoop*! I want an explanation!"

Diana shook her fist at Avery. "Don't you yell at *me*, Avery Parker! This is not my fault! I heard every word you and your precious Aunt Pearl were saying about me! That woman is a drunk, and she's not staying another night in this house!"

Rex gingerly wrapped gauze around his Aunt Pearl's thumb, but he soon realized it was having no effect whatsoever, so he calmly walked to the telephone and dialed 911.

"Yes, ma'am, I need an ambulance…my aunt has a severe injury…917 Mountain Shadow Road…no, ma'am, that's just my parents fighting in the background…yes ma'am, I'm ok, we're all just worried about my aunt. Please hurry!"

Rex patted his Aunt Pearl on her turbaned head as his parents screamed at each other. "Don't worry, Aunt Pearl, the ambulance is on its way. You'll be ok, I promise."

Aunt Pearl smiled weakly at her nephew and said in a low voice, "Rex honey, listen up, here, take your Aunt Pearl's cough medicine, and pour me a little into that water glass right quick, ok? Oh, God, the pain of losing a limb...it's just so horrible...go on, now, Rex, hurry up and get your Aunt Pearl that cough medicine..."

Aunt Pearl winked at Rex, but Rex wasn't in the mood to risk his mother's wrath, even though his parents had just stormed out of the kitchen.

"No, ma'am, I can't do that. You need to go to the hospital and get that thumb stitched, and I don't think you should be drinking anything but water right now, Aunt Pearl. Here, take a sip…"

"*LISTEN HERE, YOUNG MAN, don't you sass me*! You uncork that stopper and pour some cough medicine into that glass *right now*! If I have to spend three weeks in the hospital while they re-attach my thumb, I need to take some extra cough medicine to tide me over!"

"Aunt Pearl, you won't even have to spend one night in the hospital! Look, here's the ambulance now! Stay right here, and I'll go open the front door."

Rex realized his parents were oblivious to the arrival of the ambulance, primarily as they now stood on the back porch shouting simultaneously at one another and waving their arms. He ran to the front door and opened it for the paramedics, who flew by as he shouted, "KITCHEN! TO THE LEFT!"

In his haste to greet the paramedics, however, Rex left the brown bottle in Aunt Pearl's possession, and she'd managed to sit up long enough to pry it open with the kitchen knife that was stuck in the vinyl floor next to her landing site.

"There she is…Aunt Pearl, these men are going to fix your thumb, and…AUNT PEARL! Did you drink out of that bottle?"

Rex lifted the brown bottle from his aunt's hand, and realized half the contents had disappeared down Aunt Pearl's throat. He looked at one of the paramedics, who began to inspect the wound in question. Aunt Pearl moaned loudly and lay back on the floor. She closed her eyes. Rex handed the bottle of rum to one of the paramedics.

"Hey, mister, sir, you better take this bottle to the hospital, too."

"Why's that, son?"

"Because I think it's full of rum, at least, that's what my mom says, and I think my aunt here just drank about half of it when I ran out to let you guys in."

The paramedics eyed one another and grinned. "Well, yep, guess we'd better take it with us, then, for testing! Ok, ma'am, we're all ready to go...do you think you can walk to the ambulance? Ma'am...can you hear me? Ma'am, can you tell me your name? Can you open your eyes?"

The paramedics waited anxiously for Aunt Pearl to respond...she was a very large woman, and they did not relish the idea of lifting her onto a stretcher or carrying her to the ambulance.

"Son, what's your name...Rex...ok, Rex, did your aunt hit her head on anything?"

"No, sir, she cut her thumb with a vegetable knife, and then she fell down on the floor, but she didn't hit anything on the way down, if that's what you mean. And she's been sitting up a couple of times and she's talked to us, so I don't think she has a concussion or anything."

"Well, thanks, Rex! You're a smart guy! She's gonna be just fine, I'd say!"

"Thanks, I'm a Boy Scout, and I've had basic first aid training. Ummm, my parents are outside...having a discussion...should I go get them?"

Aunt Pearl opened her eyes in dismay as the conversation drifted away from her injuries and her dire state of medical emergency. "Whuh...where am I? Who am I? Lawrence, don't you leave me! St. Peter, come back here this instant! Did you save my thumb, young man? Did they tell you I'm already having ghost pains? Rex, honey, get these men some ice so they can save my thumb! Do you have any Demerol in that bag of yours? I need some Demerol right now!"

The paramedics rared back as they caught a whiff of Aunt Pearl's cough-medicined breath. "Ma'am, you've just got a bad gash on your thumb and a few stitches will take care of it. There's really no need for you to ride in the ambulance. We'll wrap this good and tight, and your family can take you to the ER."

Avery and Diana entered the kitchen and stared curiously at the paramedics who were talking to Aunt Pearl. Rex smiled sheepishly and said, "I called for help."

Aunt Pearl suddenly closed her eyes and made no response to the paramedic's comments or questions. He stroked her cheek and patted her hand, then nodded at Avery.

"It's just a deep flesh wound, sir, and I really don't think you'll want to spend three hundred dollars for a ten-minute ambulance ride when I can wrap this for you and you can take her to the Clinic, but it's up to you. Ma'am...*ma'am,* I'm a paramedic. Can you hear me? You're going to be just fine...you've got a bad cut to your thumb and your family is going to take you to get it stitched. Do you think you can walk to the car if I assist you?"

Aunt Pearl blinked, frowned, and looked the paramedic straight in the eye. "Young man, I am sixty-nine years old, I have survived over a thousand heart attacks, I have tuberculosis, my gall bladder is ten times its normal size, my thumb has been severed and I have just lost seven pints of blood. *I will thank you to pick me up, put me on that stretcher and carry me to that ambulance right now, the way God and Medicare intended!"*

August 19, 1999; The Leigh-Lee Mansion

AnnElise Leigh-Lee pursed her lips in anger and plopped a stack of papers in her lap in a huff. She glanced around the room at the thirty women gathered in her parlor…thirty of Chestnut Ridge's most elite socialites, thirty women who should have been peacefully selecting menu items for the Sons of Glory Festival's Cotillion Ball, but who were now engaged in no-holds-barred warfare about whether or not to serve Stuffed Crab Balls or Sassy Shrimp Roll-Ups.

"Well, I never! And I thought you were my friend! Dorothy Graham, you know we always serve stuffed crab balls at this event! That recipe has been in my family since the late 1600s, it is a Charleston society *staple,* and it is much more elegant to eat something with one's fork than it is to shove a common seafood eggroll into one's mouth with one's *fingers*! But I should have expected nothing less from the woman who approved our Festival Vehicles committee to be chaired by the white-trash likes of Henry Bailey!"

All eyes turned to Dorothy Graham, whose pink linen suit perfectly matched her pink-lipsticked mouth. She casually adjusted her helmet of platinum hair with one hand, then smiled gracefully.

"My, my, AnnElise, that temper is *so* unbecoming! And Sassy Shrimp Roll-Ups are not *'common seafood eggrolls'* dear…they are a respectable hors d'oeuvre, designed by my son Horry for Chéz Horatio; and may I remind you that they are by far the most popular appetizer in town, according to the guests at Horry's restaurant...guests who are the upper crust of society and who will be in attendance at this event in the first place!"

"You know, Dorothy…we are all so sick and tired of hearing about Horry and Chéz Horatio…that silly little restaurant survives in this town because it's the only place to eat anything that's not batter-coated, short of driving to Nashville! And *you…*you wouldn't have anything to do with it, until you realized you could get your picture in the paper every time Horry hosts an Elks banquet! *Mon dieu,* Dorothy, you are so transparent!"

Dorothy's surgically enhanced cheekbones flushed the same tone of pink as her suit. "And you're *not,* Miss *Let's Speak French to Make Ourselves Look Important*? Let me tell you and everyone in this room…I hate to disappoint you, but this is not Charleston! This is Chestnut Ridge! And it's about time we serve something that was created by a native Chestnut Ridger, not some three-hundred year old, moldy Charlestoner! Now my husband's great-great grandfather founded this town and I'm proud that my son operates one of the top businesses here, as did his ancestors before him. I say we need to honor our *own* for a change, and serve fare that respects our roots!"

"Oh, Dorothy, let's not even discuss roots, shall we? If you put any more bleach on that hair of yours, it's going to fall out right into your lap! And dear, we don't say 'Charlestoner', we say *Charlestonian*...but you can't possibly be expected to behave with proper social decorum, so I suppose we'll just have to ignore your little *faux pas, n'est ce pas*? Now, then, I say we take a vote....all in favor of serving Stuffed Crab Balls, the same tried-and-true Stuffed Crab Balls we have always served at this *soirée*, say, *'aye.'*"

Silence hung heavy in the room as AnnElise waited for the sound of her comrades' allegiance to Stuffed Crab Balls. After a few lengthy and uncomfortable seconds, AnnElise spoke again.

"Well? What are we waiting for, *mes amis*? Surely you don't want to see your daughters forced to eat with their hands at the Cotillion ball! Remember, they will be wearing white gloves, and...yes, Isidore?"

Izzy Gastineau stood up from her chair and smiled sweetly. She sported a pair of reading glasses atop her head and another pair around her neck.

"Oh, AnnElise, you know, dear, I tend to agree with Dorothy. I mean, we have been serving virtually the same menu for years...I think it would be fun to try something new, and Dorothy's right, Horry is a home-town boy, and those Sassy Shrimp Roll-Ups are delicious! We can always revert back to the Stuffed Crab Balls next year! What do you say, girls, aren't we all up for something new? And by the way, Dorothy...and I'll say this for the record... I think Henry Bailey is doing a wonderful job as Vehicles chairman! Now, who's for Sassy Shrimp Roll-Ups?"

The girls clapped in enthusiastic agreement, primarily as it was nearing noon, they were ready for lunch, and the smell of Delilah's delicious chicken casserole tickled their carefully powdered noses. Dorothy Graham clicked her tongue in approval, then sarcastically said,

"Wonderful...and all those in favor of *Stuffed Crab Balls*?"

Again, an uncomfortable silence hovered over the ladies, until Dorothy banged her Festival Chairwoman gavel on the coffee table, much to the chagrin of AnnElise.

"*Done*! Now, ladies, I believe it's time for lunch...yes, Isidore?"

Izzy Gastineau reluctantly waved a hand. "Madame Chairwoman...aren't you forgetting something?"

Dorothy exhaled. Upon her arrival, Izzy Gastineau whispered to Dorothy that Roland had discovered something amiss with the Festival financials. It was time to swim the backstroke.

"Oh, yes, ladies, there is one other matter we must attend to. You all know that Roland Gastineau has been working many, many selfless hours on the Festival books, and let me just say, Izzy, that boy is a *wonder*! I had no idea he wanted to audit those books so quickly, that was quite a surprise, and he finished in record time, I must say!"

A round of applause filled the parlor, and Izzy blushed and nodded. AnnElise raised her hand.

"Excuse me, *Madame Chairwoman*, but you always seem to forget that my daughter Danita Kay is also working closely with Roland and has donated a great deal of her time as well!"

The ladies erupted in another round of applause, but Madame Chairwoman promptly cut it off with a loud bang of her gavel.

"Ladies, thank you, we must press on. So, I'm thinking, we should create some kind of plaque, or trophy, in recognition of the efforts of these two fine young people. Anyone have a problem with that? No, I didn't think so. Very well, then I suggest we adjourn, and..."

Izzy stood up meekly and wrung her hands. "Dorothy, I'm sure Roland and Danita Kay will deeply appreciate our recognition of their hard work, but isn't there something *else* you need to tell us... that little *discrepancy* Roland detected in the Festival account...shouldn't we talk about it, because we have to purchase that insurance bond by next Friday, if I'm not mistaken?"

Dorothy's face flushed in horror; a little discrepancy she could handle, but she'd completely forgotten about the purchase of the bond. This would not be pretty, and obviously Roland had discussed the results of his unscheduled audit with his mother. Dorothy was trapped.

"Oh, yes, thanks, Isidore, I nearly *forgot!* Now, as Izzy was saying, Roland discovered a minor, uh, inconsistency in the bank account, and..."

AnnElise tossed her head. "Inconsistency? What kind of inconsistency? What do you mean, Dorothy? Izzy do you know about this?"

Izzy nodded and spilled her terrible secret. "Roland says that the account is fifteen thousand dollars short for some reason...we only have two thousand toward the purchase of the Festival insurance bond. And it's due by next Friday!"

Stunned gasps filled the room as hands rose to surgically augmented bosoms in disbelief; Dorothy pretended to ignore the beads of perspiration that appeared on her coiffed scalp.

"Ladies, ladies, it's no big deal! Basically, girls, we have done an excellent job managing our funds, but let's face it, things just don't cost what they used to, and to be truthful, the Budget Committee completely underestimated our total expenses..."

AnnElise, chairwoman of the Festival Budget Committee, stood up in and stomped her feet.

"*No we didn't, Dorothy Graham*! You've obviously overspent, and I'd like to know where the shortage is! Fifteen thousand is no small sum! And since you're the only one with access to the bank account, I suggest you tell us *immédiatement*!"

Dorothy glanced sideways at AnnElise and frowned. These were not waters she wished to tread at this particular moment. She looked at her watch.

"Ladies...it is eleven-fifty-five, and I know most of us are due at the Children's Library Board meeting this afternoon. I suggest we adjourn for today and review this item next time."

AnnElise waved her arm dramatically into the air. "*C'est tout! Finit*! That's so typical, Dorothy! No, I say we stay here and discuss this over lunch! Fifteen thousand dollars is a no inconsistency, in my opinion, it's robbery and I'd like to know how we intend to correct it! Ladies, the deadline for purchasing that insurance bond is next week and I believe it is urgent we address this situation now, *n'est ce pas*?"

The ladies nodded and murmured in agreement. AnnElise rang for Delilah, who instantly appeared wearing a light blue maid's uniform and cap.

"Delilah, there has been a change of plans. We will be having *déjeuner* here in the parlor, so would you please prepare the buffet cart and trays? *Merci*."

Delilah disappeared and Dorothy Graham pursed her lips. "Well, I was under the impression that as the Chairwoman of this Festival, I had the right to call for a vote, but I see that once again my good friend AnnElise has taken over. Very well, after lunch, we'll review the..."

AnnElise smiled and flashed perfect teeth. "There's no need to wait, Dorothy, dear. Please continue. Delilah will bring our lunch momentarily, so please, do inform us about this terrible shortage of funds. I'd specifically like to know where the shortage is...do you have an itemized list of expenditures?"

Dorothy's cheeks turned pink once again. "I do, in fact, but..."

"Then I suggest we all take a look at it. Shall we pass it around as we break for *un petit toilette*?"

The ladies nodded and scattered for a bathroom break. AnnElise snatched Roland's itemized Festival Accounting Report from Dorothy's hand and scanned it in haste.

"Ball decorations...three hundred, Xerox copies...two-fifty, printing... twenty-five hundred, police protection...eight hundred...postage, fifty-seven...these expenses seem in order...wait a minute. Miscellaneous...*fifteen thousand dollars*! *Mon dieu*, Dorothy, what on earth! How in the world do you spend fifteen thousand dollars on miscellaneous?"

Several ladies gathered around AnnElise and looked over her shoulder at the Festival Accounting Report. Izzy Gastineau bit her lip; Juliette Kimball turned to Dorothy and asked in a meek voice, "Dorothy, dear, surely we have receipts and details of these miscellaneous charges, don't we?"

Dorothy blanched. She'd thought it a foolproof scheme; a few months prior, after brown-nosing the current National Daughters of Charity Association president, and after learning that the NDCA needed a fifteen thousand dollar grant to purchase a computer system for the new West Palm Beach headquarters, Dorothy decided that as an NDCA presidential candidate, a fifteen thousand dollar donation would serve her in good stead toward an election victory. After all, she reminded herself, it's not really an election…it's a *contest.* The NDCA presidency was just the first step; after a year she'd be well-ensconced in West Palm society and would no doubt have charmed all of the eligible and more importantly, wealthy elderly men in the area. Filing for a divorce fromWill would be Phase Two in her lifelong plan for a luxurious future...she could smell that salt air and feel the perpetual tan on her skin now.

But Will refused to give her the money because he didn't want his wife living in West Palm Beach for a year, and she knew he didn't like all her NDCA friends. *Social climbers, that's what they are! Why do you need to hob-nob with all those people from West Palm and New York, honey? You're just sweet little Dottie Chatwick from Chestnut Ridge! You've raised two of the finest children on the face of God's earth! You've got respect, all the money you can spend, you shop in Nashville and Atlanta on practically an unlimited budget, you redecorate this big old house every six months to suit you...why do you need those people...social climbers!*

But Dorothy ignored Will's protests. *What Will Graham doesn't know about yachts, expensive champagne, chateaus on the French Riviera and estate jewelry would fill volumes,* she lamented in silence. *If I don't get out of this morbid little town I'll go crazy,* she told herself. *The NDCA presidency is my only ticket.*

Dorothy was desperate for the fifteen thousand dollars. She'd already promised the NDCA that the check was in the mail. She couldn't retract her donation, or risk tarnishing her reputation, after she'd come so far. She needed a plan. And as luck would have it, Will left town to attend a conference on the very same day he'd refused her the NDCA donation. With the divine hand of Providence, Will gave Dorothy the checkbook to Hoot's expense account and asked her to pay Hoot's bills during the week he was gone.

In the secrecy of her bedroom after Will's departure, Dorothy examined the checkbook register. To her utter delight, only one simple entry of thirty thousand dollars, written in Will's hand, stared back at her from the register's top line. There were no other entries...no recording of checks written, no deposits to be added, no withdrawals to be balanced. Will Graham was simply a terrible bookkeeper and apparently had no idea what the balance in his own bank account was. And why should he? *The Grahams don't pay over-*

draft fees or service charges, honey! Just transfer more money! We don't worry about a few nickels here and there! She placed a simple phone call to the automated bank information line and learned that there was just a little over fifteen thousand dollars in the account. Lady Luck smiled down on Dorothy that day, indeed.

It could not have been any easier, writing a fifteen thousand dollar check for cash at the bank in Smyrna and getting a money order made out to the National Daughters of Charity Association. Will would never even notice, based on the lack of accounting displayed in the check register. But after two days, Dorothy was suddenly swamped with bills from the Fluffy Pillow Motel, the Poe House Grocery and the Quigley Quik-Steak. *Shit! He'll get angrier if I don't pay those bills than he will at the fact the money's not in the account! How in hell can I get my hands on the money to pay Hoot's expenses*...then Dorothy smiled a huge smile. *It's perfect! I'll just call the bank and have them transfer more money into Hoot's account!*

She didn't factor in the refusal of the bank to transfer one red cent into Hoot's expense account, however. *Damn! Only Will can approve transfers! Ridiculous! Married to the bank owner and not a nickel to my name!*

During her regular tryst with Dan Gastineau at the Peacock Inn the following day, Dorothy discussed with him her bill-juggling headache. Dan informed her that due to an error on Will's personal income tax, he would shortly receive, via wire transfer, a neat fifteen thousand, two hundred dollar refund of which he was as yet unaware. An ecstatic, if not naked Dorothy, leapt from the bed, tore through her purse, handed a deposit slip to Dan and demanded that he instruct the IRS to wire the refund into Hoot's expense account. He protested severely, but Dorothy skillfully found his Achilles' heel, and soon, Dan moaned with the pleasure of total compliance. After he stopped moaning he couldn't promise, however, when that IRS refund would materialize; it was the fifth of the month...the bills were past due and Will's return imminent...*why don't you just borrow the money from the Festival account to pay those bills, Dorothy? You're the Festival Chairwoman, don't you control the checkbook? But don't you write any checks, honey...never leave a paper trail! Just go to the bank and have them transfer the funds into Hoot's account. Then you write those checks and pay Hoot's bills like you're supposed to. You can tell Will you need extra clothes money to cover all those ball gowns you bought in New York! He'll never know the difference and you can pay the Festival Account back over time! Nobody will be the wiser!*

That was it! She could kick herself for not thinking of this sooner! She had an *out*! To the best of her recollection, all the Festival expenses had been paid; its current seventeen thousand dollar balance was merely a buffer, just sitting there doing nobody any good. She'd withdraw fifteen thousand, deposit it in

Hoot's account, then pay it back as soon as she could convince Will to increase her clothing allowance for a few months. *I might not even have to pay it back*, she mused, *because in a few weeks, the Festival's advertising revenue will roll in, and then the advance Festival ticket order money will follow and with all those silly transactions to be recorded, nobody will pay the slightest attention to a momentary few-thousand dollar blip in the account.* Dorothy was so happy, she let Dan wear her bra the way he'd always wanted.

But the next day, as Dorothy returned home from personally paying the last of Hoot's bills with borrowed money from the Festival account, she was greeted in the driveway by Will's protegé, Harper Collingwood III.

"Mmm, mmm, *hello baby*! Dorothy, you look beautiful in that shade of blue! Why don't you invite me inside…you're looking about a quart low, I'd better check your oil…"

Dorothy sneered at the nattily dressed young man who in her opinion was nothing short of an up-and-coming twit, sent to Chestnut Ridge by his wealthy family in Nashville to learn the banking business at the hands of Will Graham. She was sick to death of his leering glances and rude suggestions. He was a skinny kid with no sense whatsoever and the only reason she tolerated him was that his old-money family often invited the Grahams to Nashville's to-die-for social events.

"Harper, you know full well that Will's coming home this afternoon so just shut up! What are you, *twelve*? You haven't even learned to shave yet! Besides, my Swan Ball invitation just arrived this morning, so I don't need any more social favors from you! Now, I'm not going to bed with you and that's final! Get out of here, I have important work to do!"

Harper laughed and leaned against his BMW. Dorothy tossed her head and stomped past him in the driveway, heading to her front steps. He caught her arm with a twist and let out an evil laugh. "Oh, I'm sure you do have important work to do, Dottie baby! Gotta go cover up that fifteen-thou you 'borrowed' from Hoot's expense account, don't ya? Gotta fix everything nice and neat before Big Daddy gets home!"

Dorothy froze in terror; she searched for Harper's eyes behind his mirrored sunglasses. "Ouch, you're hurting me, Harper! What do you think you're talking about? Do you want me to call the police right now? I've asked you to leave!"

Harper loosened his tie and grinned. "You know, I thought something was up when Will called me in a huff last week and asked me to keep an eye on things…he said, let's see, something about fifteen thousand dollars you wanted for a charity gig…something about, what was it, oh, yeah, he wouldn't let you have it but he figured you'd just take it out of Hoot's account while he was gone. Now, see, Dorothy, if I was just some stupid kid like you think I am, I would have just sat my ass down in Will's chair all week and played computer games. But I do have half a brain, and I've been watching that account very closely. And today, by golly, what a *coincidence*! A check came in made to "Cash" for...let me see...oh, yeah, fifteen thou! How 'bout that? With *your signature*! Dorothy, you'll have to drive a little farther than Smyrna next time. But what I don't understand is how you transferred fifteen thousand back into that same account. Guess you had to pay all of Hoot's bills before Will gets home ...where'd you get all that money, Dorothy? I know Uncle Will keeps you on a tight leash! Oh, my, I wonder what we're going to do about this? Let's see...it's a little past eleven...Will's due back around two?"

Dorothy's jaw clamped tight. She stormed over to the great granite front porch steps, knowing Harper would follow. She pressed internal buttons to activate her personal fountain display as tears streamed down her face. She collapsed in a helpless heap on the steps and sobbed. A confused Harper Collingwood III sat down next to her, waving the flailing hands of a young man confronted with a crying woman.

"Hey, Dorothy, it's ok...I'm sorry...I won't say anything about this, I won't, but you can see how it looks..."

"Oh, Harper, I can't believe you think I'd do something as low as steal from my own husband! The man I've loved for thirty years! The man I've slaved for and cooked for and cleaned up after!"

Dorothy sobbed heavily into a pink tissue while her mental cogs whirred into motion. Harper rubbed a hand across his forehead in frustration.

"Well, Dorothy, you can see why I might think that! I mean, come on, there it was in black and white on the computer screen! Shit, Dorothy, your signature was on the check! I mean, ok, so I didn't go to Harvard, but I'm no dummy!"

Dorothy daubed one eye and blinked through tears at Harper with a pretty pout. "Harper...you've got to believe me...I can't...oh, this is so embarrassing! Look, you swear you won't tell anyone about this? Ok...see, my mother died of Alzheimer's...and...and...it's getting me, too, Harper. I'm forgetting things. Lots of things, every day. I know I should go to the doctor but I can't stand the idea of all those needles, all those hospitals...leaving my babies and my man all alone...see...I had some Festival business to take care of...you know, of course, that I'm the Festival Chairwoman."

Harper nodded. Dorothy continued.

"Well, we have to rent ten *extremely* large tents for the Festival in case of bad weather and the only vendor in the area is in Smyrna. I had to go and meet with him last week and write him a deposit for fifteen thousand to hold those tents, or he threatened to let those dreadful stock car people have them the same week we need them! Can you *imagine*?"

Harper shook his head, trying to comprehend the difficulties faced by the Festival Chairwoman with respect to tent procurement.

"So anyhow, this horrible man…oh, you've no idea how insulting he was! I was so flustered! And he simply would not take a check. I had to go to the bank in Smyrna and present him with cash! And of course, that's against all Festival policies! But I was desperate for those tents, Harper, I had to do it! Well, you see what's happened, don't you? I wrote the check out of the wrong checkbook! But I paid it back, that's the deposit you noticed. It's the Alzheimer's! Oh my God, how can I tell Will? How can I tell him I'm dying, Harper? How can I? It will kill him!"

Dorothy sobbed and rocked her shoulders in agony as Harper Collingwood III exhaled and felt sick to his stomach. Accusing one's mentor's ill wife would not go unnoticed, he felt certain. Maybe as her disease progressed she'd forget about it…

A shamed Dorothy bit one finger and sobbed. Harper gulped back a wave of nausea. "Dorothy…it's ok, I promise! I'm so sorry I accused you. I…well…you know, I'm just trying to do a good job here, so Uncle Will and my dad will be proud of me. I guess I took it too far. But Dorothy…Will's eventually gonna see those financial records. You're going to have to tell him about your Alzheimer's sooner or later."

Dorothy's fountain mysteriously ran dry and her tone turned sour. "What do you *mean*, when Will sees the financial records? Harper, do you realize that man hasn't made a single entry in the check register of Hoot's account in six months?"

Harper's eyes widened. "Well, yeah, Dorothy, he doesn't need to! Bankers don't do check registers any more! Everything's on computer now! First thing Will does every morning is call up all his accounts and check the balances…then he does it again at noon and right before he leaves. That man knows where every nickel he owns is every minute of every day, I've never seen anything like it!"

Dorothy's stomach knotted; she was sunk. "Harper, look…I don't have the courage to tell Will about my condition yet! Besides…there's this new Alzheimer's treatment…in *Memphis*…at *St. Jude's*…I'm going to go there and be treated and it's my hope…*my prayer*…that I'll be cured before I have to tell Will anything but good news! Please, please help me. You've got to help me cover this up and keep it from Will. Please, Harper!"

Harper rolled up his trouser leg and scratched his very muscular calf absent-mindedly. Dorothy stared at Harper's leg in surprise. *He's no skinny kid after all…he's rather built! Didn't somebody tell me he's a soccer player?* Harper stood up and adjusted his tie.

"Ok, sure. I'll figure out how to change the records in the computer somehow. All Will usually looks at is the balance, not the activity reports, so if the money's there, he won't think twice. I'd better go."

Dorothy swallowed and smiled admiringly at Harper's stunningly taut behind. "Well, Harper, you silly boy! Going so soon? Can't I thank you properly for your trouble? *Come with*?"

Harper froze. He didn't care for the way Dorothy Graham was looking at him. Ten minutes ago she was a hot-blooded, attractive older woman that he would have eagerly engaged in a round of horizontal recreation. Now she was Alzheimer's-damaged goods and he didn't want any part of that at all.

"Uh, no, thanks, that's ok."

Dorothy licked her lips seductively and caressed Harper's left ear with a manicured fingernail. Harper took a step back. "Uh, no…uh…look, I've got to go…gotta take care of this before Uncle Will gets back…I tell you what…how 'bout a raincheck? I'll call you next week, ok?"

Harper dashed to his BMW and roared out of the driveway, leaving a disappointed Dorothy to ponder her latest work of fiction. *That little geek better not say one word about this to Will! Oh, well, if he does…I'll just tell Will that he tried to rape me, right behind the bougainvillea! I'll tell him Harper forced me to steal that money or he'd rape me! Will knows how much I've complained about that twit's staring at me…he'll surely believe his own wife over a silly bank teller!*

It took several martinis and a long hot bubble bath to calm Dorothy's nerves after her close call; as she dressed to greet Will, Harper called with the news that her transactions were well hidden, and in the nick of time, as Will stopped by the bank on his way home from the conference. *Everything's fine, he didn't notice at all,* Harper'd said. Dorothy wrung a soapy sponge onto the smooth skin of a belly that was too-taut for a middle-aged woman. *Perfectly orchestrated, Dottie! If Will gets curious he can see that I paid Hoot's bills…the account balance is all in order and there's no real proof that I took anything from the Festival account…besides, I'm the one who has the Festival checkbook! I'm the only one who writes the checks!*

But Dorothy's memory, with or without Alzheimer's, was not as finely tuned as her plot; she had forgotten all about the ghastly Festival insurance bond and Roland Gastineau's audit. And now while the Committee ladies enjoyed Delilah's cooking, although somewhat fretfully, Dorothy's mind raced for a solution. Dan told her just this morning that Will's tax refund remained outstanding, there was some kind of delay and it might not materialize for months. Roland's audit of the Festival account and his amazingly swift report of the financial error to the Committee could ruin her. *Why can't that damned Roland be more like his father? What a goody-two-shoes!* It appeared she was sunk. She had to think fast.

"So, Dorothy, dear, where were we?" AnnElise sipped daintily from an iced tea glass. "Oh, yes, you were going to tell us about those fifteen thousand dollar 'miscellaneous' expenses!"

Dorothy's face clouded and she felt sick. She raised one hand to her head, and sighed. "You all will have to excuse me, I'm afraid...I am not feeling well today, my doctor has me on a new kind of thyroid medication, and it's wreaking *havoc* with my system...I think I need to go home and lie down."

AnnElise shot a sarcastic look around the room and smirked. "*Mais non, cheri*! If you are feeling ill, you shouldn't drive! Here, dear, here's a pillow...put your feet up on this *chaise!*"

She gestured to a gold-brocade sofa and waited for Dorothy to protest. Dorothy stood gallantly, knowing she'd been trumped, and moved to the sofa. She sat down and slowly removed her pink pumps, then reclined on the sofa and closed her eyes with a faint moan.

"Yes, thank you, that's much better. All of a sudden, I feel as if I might faint, and I seem to have a horrible sick headache; oh dear, the room is swimming!"

Juliette Kimball patted Dorothy's shoulder and dipped one end of a linen napkin in a pitcher of ice water. "Here, Dorothy, darling, just pat this on your temples and you'll be all right. Would you like me to call Doc?"

Dorothy nodded *no*, and continued to moan softly. AnnElise wasted no time. She crossed the room to the chair where Dorothy's briefcase full of festival papers rested on the floor.

"Well, ladies, as the Vice President of the Festival Committee, I'll take over for Madame Chairwoman, if there is no objection."

There was of course no objection, because everyone was now extremely curious about the fifteen thousand dollar shortage, and wanted to know just how their hard-earned charity funds had been squandered. Dorothy raised her head and said weakly,

"AnnElise, go right ahead, search my papers if you must! But you'll find that everything is in order, we have just overspent a little here and there, and it all adds up, you know, over time!"

As Dorothy lay on the sofa, and as the ladies waited in anguish, AnnElise rifled through the manila folders to no avail. Everything truly did appear to be in order, as Dorothy said. After fifteen minutes of vain searching, AnnElise straightened the folders and stuffed them back into Dorothy's briefcase, and Dorothy, who had watched AnnElise from the corner of her eye, smiled a tiny smile and instantly regained her composure. She sat up slowly and put on her shoes.

"Well, I suppose you are satisfied now, AnnElise? After you have insulted me, and embarrassed me completely, in front of all our friends? I told you, there is nothing, absolutely nothing out of line with respect to this Festival! And I fully resent…uh, AnnElise…*AnnElise*…there's nothing in there… that's my private folder…those are my personal papers…*please do not open*… ANNELISE!!"

As she replaced Dorothy's Festival papers, AnnElise discovered a hidden pocket in the briefcase. A hidden pocket that contained a single cream-colored envelope. AnnElise held the envelope aloft for all the ladies to see, then she sat down next to the coffee table and opened it. A single bank electronic transfer order in the amount of fifteen thousand dollars fell out. Dorothy's signature was on the bottom line of the form. AnnElise shook the envelope and a second slip of paper fell into her hand. AnnElise stared at the order, then gasped dramatically, her hands to her face.

"*Ça alors! Sacré bleu*! I don't believe it! Ladies, look at this! Dorothy, how could you?" The slip of paper contained, in Dorothy's handwriting, the words, "IOU $15K."

Dorothy sank back on the sofa and didn't care that the heels of her pink pumps snagged the gold brocade fabric. She was doomed. Her head pounded. Juliette Kimball dabbed a linen napkin at her teary eyes. AnnElise waved the withdrawal slip in disgust.

"I don't need to see anymore. It's obvious we've been robbed by our own Chairwoman! This is so *scandaleux*, I just can't believe it, right under our noses!"

The Festival Committee Ladies looked at each other in confusion. Dorothy Graham, pillar of the community, bank president's wife, was misappropriating Festival funds! They gasped and swooned. Their hard-earned money, money they had raised, and cajoled and begged for; money they had sold baked goods for, and served punch for, held countless benefits for and had plans for, all that money had vanished into the hands of Madame Chairwoman, leaving them and their Festival high and dry. AnnElise Leigh-Lee stepped over to the sofa where Dorothy reclined with one arm across her eyes. She pointed in anger at Madame Chairwoman.

"Perhaps we should hear from the thief herself; perhaps she should inform us, in her own words, as to the whereabouts of that money…I'm sure you have an excellent reason for its withdrawal, Dorothy, and I'm sure we'd all love to hear it, *maintenant!*"

Dorothy's head ached; it was all Hoot's fault! All she'd done was ask him to find her a reliable videographer, to document her do-good deeds during the Festival year. She couldn't even be considered for the National Daughters of Charity Association presidency without that tape. But Hoot insisted on moving back to town, to personally record her merits, and then he'd hit them up for financial support! None of this would have happened if all those stupid bills of his hadn't come pouring in…

"Dorothy…we are *waiting…*"

Dorothy raised her head and surveyed the angry eyes of her Festival comrades. She would not disclose anything…a year in a West Palm Beach high-rise was at stake. *Damn that Hoot, anyway, and….Hoot! That's it! Hoot's skipped town! He's already in hot water!* Dorothy's mind hummed….if somehow, they would take pity on her, she could remain in control of the Festival. She needed tears, *lots* of tears. The fountains were summoned.

"Oh, dear…" Dorothy sharply pressed her manicured nails into the palm of her unseen hand until giant, salty drops welled up in her eyes and spilled down her cheeks. From there it wasn't a stretch at all. She hung her head.

"All my life, I have wanted to be somebody. You don't know what it's like to be the youngest of five beautiful sisters! In high school, I was too short to be a cheerleader. And even when I finally won Homecoming Queen, don't you remember, the newspaper printed my sister Lucy's name on the photograph! And in college, my mother was a Delta legacy, so I had to pledge Delta, but back then, the most popular girls were all Kappas!"

AnnElise sighed and crossed her arms impatiently. This was the umpteenth performance of Dorothy Drama Live & In Person, however, the rest of the audience was captivated.

"…and then, *by the grace of God*, Will Graham married me, and I finally felt like I had done something right with my life. The Graham family! Town founders! Owners of the bank! And they wanted me! But it was a curse, because I was expected to act like a Graham…to give freely of my time, to be generous…to do good. And so I did, but nobody ever saw me…don't you understand? I was, and always will be, *Will's wife*! *Mrs. Graham*! The Grahams always get the accolades! I can never contribute anything of my own, because Will never allowed me to work, I had to stay home and raise my precious twins…"

AnnElise coughed at Dorothy's remarks, but Dorothy continued, undaunted. "And the only reason I wanted to be Festival Chairwoman, was so I could meet the National Daughters of Charity Association presidential requirements and work like hell to win the election, to prove to everyone that I, *little Dottie Chatwick*, could do something of worth! That I, *little Dottie Chatwick*, could win the NDCA presidency all by myself, without the Grahams or their money, and then maybe everyone in town would really be proud of me, and then I could give something back to Chestnut Ridge!"

The Festival Ladies each silently observed the fact that the sweat from their own brows and the work of their own hands had also contributed to the Festival, and thus to Dorothy's bid for the NDCA presidency, but they said nothing; one of their own was obviously distraught.

"And so that gives you an excuse to steal from your own sisters, your fellow charity workers, whom you have known for thirty years?" AnnElise was bored with Dorothy's pity party. Dorothy wiped a hand across her brow.

"I didn't steal anything....I might as well tell you...oh, this is so embarrassing...*I am being blackmailed*!"

Juliette Kimball blew her nose loudly into one of AnnElise's best linen napkins as Izzy Gastineau patted her on the back. Loud "oh mys" and "my goodnesses" pierced the parlor. Several ladies took their seats in a swoon; this was entirely too much excitement for a typical socialite luncheon in Chestnut Ridge.

"That's right, I'm being blackmailed, and our Festival organization is being held *hostage*!"

AnnElise shook her head in disbelief. "What are you saying, Dorothy? Really, this is getting ridiculous! We have proof right here that you've stolen the money! Why can't you just confess and then maybe we'll opt not to press charges!"

Juliette Kimball stomped her foot. "AnnElise, that's enough! Let Dorothy finish! Dorothy, dear, do you need a hankie?" Juliette handed a pale green lace handkerchief to a grateful Dorothy.

"Thank you, Juliette. I'm sorry you can't find it in your heart to believe me, AnnElise, but what I am about to tell you is true. And it's all Hoot Graham's fault! You all know that Hoot came here to spend this year with us, to film the Festival activities for me, so I could submit my tape to the NDCA and get elected president. And when I win, *as you have all probably forgotten*, this town will receive a twenty-thousand dollar stipend, to compensate for a year of my time, since I won't be here to organize fund-raisers and supervise charity events!"

AnnElise clicked her tongue in disapproval, but Dorothy ignored her. "Do go on, *cheri*, this is *trés* fascinating."

"Well, *most of you don't know this...* when Hoot arrived, Will and I vacated our master suite, and offered it to Hoot. But he refused to set one foot in the same house as Mother Nell...his own mother! Let me tell you, that man has absolutely no compassion for the ill...he won't even eat a meal with us! Well, all his cash is apparently tied up in film projects, so he couldn't afford to stay in a hotel long-term, and he threatened to go back to L.A. As you can imagine, I was at my wit's end...but Will knows how much our town needs me to win that NDCA presidency, and how the entire Sons of Glory Festival depends on us! So out of the goodness of his heart, he offered to pay all of Hoot's expenses out of his own pocket! For an entire year!"

Dorothy waited for the Festival Ladies to gush forth empathy, but it didn't happen. She sipped from a glass of iced tea and continued.

"Remember when Hoot showed up at the Masked Ball and videotaped everyone's cleavage? Well, that's when it started. And I have to go on record right now...what I am about to tell you is *classified information*...and if you don't believe me, you can ask Richard, AnnElise, because he's the one who is handling this case, unbeknownst to all of you! Let me tell you, the FBI is involved because it's a blackmail operation and if you gossip about this, or if Hoot finds out we're on to him, you'll all have to answer to the *Feds*! And while you're standing there accusing me, I've been putting my very life and the lives of my children, on the line every day!"

Dorothy covered her eyes for effect and managed to squeeze out a few more effective tears. AnnElise's eyebrows arched at the mention of her husband handling a legal case involving the Feds; some of the Festival Ladies covered their mouths with their hands. After a few more sobs, Dorothy strategically wiped mascara from underneath her eyes and took a deep breath.

"Where was I? Oh, yes. You all remember the tape that was found at Roy's Tape House, the one with our cleavage on it? That is only the tip of the iceberg. Apparently Hoot installed secret cameras in the men's bathroom at the country club that night, and in addition to our cleavage, he has, on tape, a record of some of our most prominent citizens engaging in, shall we say, improper acts in the bathroom!"

Two of the Festival Ladies screamed, then instantly blushed, hoping that no one actually suspected them of participation in the improper bathroom behavior. AnnElise waved a hand at Dorothy in dismissal.

"This is absurd! It's probably just Betty Gooch doing what she always does at the festival...oh, excuse me, Isidore, but you know what I mean!"

Dorothy frowned and shook her head. "No, AnnElise, it wasn't, and I strongly suggest you keep your comments to yourself...as I said...these were prominent citizens, very close to many of you..."

Madame Chairwoman glared at AnnElise as she said these words, and never batted an eye. The room was still and silent. AnnElise blanched in horror...*she'd put a stop to Richard's roving...Miss Gober watched him like a hawk...but he certainly was in the bathroom for a long time that night, she remembered...oh my God...Hoot has Richard on tape! The Feds caught him and they're forcing him to prosecute Hoot!*

Dorothy continued. "The day after the Masked Ball, Hoot paid me a visit. He showed me the tape, and let me tell you, I was just sick to my stomach! I had to take a tranquilizer and go to bed with a headache! But the worst..."

All ears strained to hear Dorothy. Delilah rolled a beverage cart into the room, but was promptly dismissed by AnnElise in a huff. "...the absolute worst thing is that Hoot dubbed his voice over the tape, you know, he's a very accomplished director...and, well, basically what he did was create a

Sons of Glory Festival commercial…I mean, on screen are these people doing what God intended for people to do to procreate the species, but you hear Hoot Graham's voice saying, *'Don't miss the Chestnut Ridge Sons of Glory Festival, folks! December 29-January 1, Chestnut Ridge Tennessee. Tickets available at all area businesses, including…'* and then there's a long list of businesses, most of which are owned by the very people sitting in this room! Can you imagine if anyone saw that on television? We would all be ruined!"

Izzy Gastineau grabbed at one of her multiple pairs of glasses and looked through the bottom lenses at Dorothy. "But Dorothy, dear, nothing like that would ever get on television, surely!"

Dorothy shook her head in protest. "Isidore, you are so wrong! We are all so isolated in this town! After Hoot showed me that tape…he forced me to watch it *twice*, by the way…he handed me an 'invoice' for fifteen thousand dollars. And then he told me that if I didn't give him the money, he was going to mail a copy of that tape to a buddy of his in L.A., a buddy who owns a porno tv network. And he told me that this buddy would broadcast that tape on international cable television, and that he'd also put the tape on the Internet, so people could see it night and day, even if they didn't have cable! Can you imagine how I felt? I would have agreed to anything, to keep our good names good and our Festival intact!"

Dorothy once again sobbed and pressed a tissue to her eyes. Juliette Kimball and Izzy Gastineau rushed over and hugged her. The Festival Ladies murmured in shock; they had accused Dorothy Graham of stealing when in fact, she had covered for all of them, as best she could.

AnnElise was still not convinced. "So what you're telling us, *mon ami,* is that you gave in to Hoot's demand, and you paid him the fifteen thousand? Why does Hoot Graham need fifteen thousand dollars? That's not much money to a man who'll inherit the bank one day!"

Dorothy gulped iced tea and daubed at one eye. Her mind whirred into overdrive. This was beginning to get very complicated, and she hoped she could remember everything later.

"All he would tell me was that it was for some kind of gambling debt. At first, I refused…where would I get that kind of money? Will keeps me on a very strict household budget, and I couldn't very well tell him about his own brother blackmailing us all, could I? Besides, Hoot said if I told anyone, all he had to do was visit the post office, and drop that tape in the mail! I couldn't bear to see my friends shamed! I tried to stall him. I pawned my grandmother's diamond brooch, but it only brought two thousand! I gave that to him first, to buy more time. Oh, Grammy, please forgive me!"

Dorothy sobbed uncontrollably until she was satisfied that everyone felt her pain. She looked up through tear-stained eyes at the Festival Ladies, all of whom gazed at her in sisterly concern. She daubed at her eyelids, then sighed.

"I made Hoot promise to give me a few more days to get the money, and by some miracle, he agreed. But he reneged on his word. One day he'd been drinking and he came to the house and held me at *gunpoint*! I had nowhere else to turn! I knew the Festival account was available, so we drove to the bank and I got the rest of the money and gave it to him. Then... *I can barely speak about it*...he tried to *seduce* me, right in my own Mercedes, but I kicked him in the groin and shoved him out of the car!"

The Festival Ladies gasped at the terror Dorothy had endured on their behalf. This was much too much to ask of a Madame Chairwoman, they were certain. Dorothy prepared for the big finish.

"I didn't know what to do...I knew we had to get that money back, to pay the insurance bond! And I am a terrible person, because I've been praying each and every night that God would come and take Mother Nell home to Glory, because I know how much she's suffering, and because I know that in her will, she's left me her entire estate and all her jewelry. I have prayed to God Almighty every night to end poor Mother Nell's misery, to grant her wish, just so I can repay the Festival account and get that insurance bond! Oh, girls, can you ever forgive me?"

Thirty pairs of arms reached out in love to Dorothy Graham, Madame Chairwoman. Countless tissues and sips of iced tea were volunteered, and in general everyone was in a daze. Everyone except AnnElise, who stood deep in thought next to a window of the parlor.

"Dorothy, *ma cher*...if Hoot told you not to tell anyone, then how are my husband and the FBI involved, *hmmm*? Doesn't that contradict your little *story*?"

Some of the Festival Ladies scowled at AnnElise; she could be so cold. But Dorothy refused to disembark from the S.S. Fabrication.

"AnnElise, it's very simple. The Feds have been watching Hoot for quite a while, apparently, and I've had to give several legal depositions...Richard has been there each time. I presumed he was acting on Hoot's behalf, but he certainly does jump when the Feds bark their orders!"

AnnElise waved her arm impatiently. "So why don't they just slap Hoot in jail and get the money back, and then we can all get on with the Festival! I don't understand all the secrecy, really, Dorothy."

"First of all, AnnElise, no one knows where Hoot is! After he stormed out of play practice, he vanished into thin air. And second, Hoot told me that there is more than one copy of the tape, and that if I so much as threaten him, he can have it broadcast internationally within twenty-four hours. So we are all at the mercy of Hoot Graham, I'm afraid. At least, that's what the FBI told me. We can't make a move until Hoot does."

Juliette Kimball wadded a tissue and sighed. "Without the money, we can't buy the insurance bond, so I guess there won't be a Festival...everyone will be so disappointed."

Dorothy blanched. The S. S. Fabrication struck an unforeseen iceberg; the Festival couldn't just *stop*...she would be blamed, the truth would come out, and she'd never get elected NDCA president. It was time to take back control. She stood up.

"Well, if we hadn't gotten sidetracked today, thanks to my good friend AnnElise, I was about to make an announcement that should please all of you! There is a light at the end of this dismal tunnel!"

Everyone looked at Dorothy in anticipation of some glimmer of hope for the Festival, amidst this terrible turmoil and sordid story. Although the financial resources of every woman in the room could have easily been tapped to purchase the insurance bond many times over, that would involve telling husbands, and as Dorothy promised strict confidence to the FBI, they couldn't break that vow. Dorothy smoothed her pink suit and ran a hand under her platinum bob.

"As God is my witness, there is no way this Festival will be canceled! I have spoken to my children... of course, they know nothing about all the terror I have endured at the hands of their uncle, and I certainly can't tell them. I simply said that our coffers are somewhat low, and that if they would refund the twenty thousand dollar deposit we paid them toward Festival catering, we could use it to buy the insurance bond. Then after the Festival, I said, we will be *flush* with cash, we'll pay them back, with interest, of course. And because they love their mother so much, they agreed, on the condition that none of us mention another word about it!"

The Festival Ladies clapped loudly as Dorothy beamed like a Cheshire cat at the success of her latest plot twist.

"So, ladies! There is absolutely nothing to worry about, except our respective committee duties! I'll have the money for the insurance bond in plenty of time. Now, please, everyone, remember that our good names and future successes depend on total secrecy in this matter! Please don't even tell your husbands, or Roland, Izzy...about this...the Feds were adamant! On that note, shall we adjourn?"

The Sons of Glory Festival Committee became a bevy of hugs and relieved sighs. Dorothy beamed at her triumphant escape; *Mama always said I was quick on my feet,* she remembered. *I've got to go talk to Richard this minute,* she realized, *AnnElise will start picking him apart the minute he gets home tonight.*

As the ladies of the Festival Committee filed out of the room, Dorothy Graham snatched up the electronic transfer slip and the IOU, stuffed them into the envelope and reached for her briefcase. AnnElise bid goodbye to her last guest, then stood, arms crossed skeptically, at the door to the parlor.

"Well, Dorothy," she said with a sneer, "you certainly recovered nicely from that little brush with danger, didn't you *ma petite*? Have you given yourself enough time to replace that fifteen thousand before next Friday? You may have fooled those other biddies, but I know you're up to something sneaky, and I'm going to laugh myself silly when it brings you down."

Dorothy snapped her leather briefcase shut and smiled at AnnElise. "Dear heart, I'm sorry you weren't elected to be the Festival Chairwoman...but please stop taking it out on me. You are only making yourself look bad in front of our friends, and all this scheming to get me fired is really adding lines to your face. And I mean what I say, AnnElise...don't you dare mention this to anyone...if we are discovered, the Festival will come to a screeching halt, which means your precious Tiffany Noel will be ineligible for the Miss American Beauty pageant. And you will be forced to use over-the-counter cosmetics like a white-trash housewife, after your husband's law firm is disgraced on international television. Thank you so much for lunch."

Dorothy Graham sauntered victoriously out the front door, got into her red Mercedes coupe, and drove away. AnnElise stomped her feet on the parlor floor and shouted, "*DELILAH*! Where is my portable phone! I've got to call Miss Gober right now!"

There were fortunately no immediate public repercussions from Dorothy's fiction workshop. The next day she took to her bed with a sick headache; at least, that's what she told Will and the maid. Little Dottie Chatwick had hit rock bottom, and she was in the worst predicament of her life.

I've got to get a grip on things, she thought. *There must be a way out of this mess, without compromising my Festival authority, without letting anyone know the truth. All I need is fifteen thousand dollars to pay back the fund and buy that bond before next Friday and then I can just tell everyone that the matter has been taken over by the Feds, and that even I don't know what's going on. Once that money's back in the account, then surely they will all just forget about it and leave me alone!*

Dorothy propped herself up on one elbow to think. *But how to get my hands on fifteen thousand... I've exhausted all my contacts*, she muttered aloud to no one in particular. *Oh, dammit, why did I ever think that Richard would help me...I can't believe I was so foolish...* But foolish she had been. After the Festival Committee meeting, Dorothy went straight home, washed her face, freshened her makeup and donned a red, lowcut sundress with matching sandals. She'd immediately stormed right over to Richard Leigh-Lee IV's office, where Richard himself quickly changed his shirt and tie and splashed on cologne while Dorothy waited impatiently in the executive reception room. Richard's eye had been favorably glancing at Dorothy Graham for ten years and he was not one to miss an opportunity.

I'm here in strictest confidence, she'd said. *No one, not even Will, must know that we have spoken, it's a matter of utmost confidentiality.* And in his best confidential lawyer manner, Richard Leigh-Lee IV had assured her that the words spoken within would remain there forever. *What's on your mind, Dorothy?*

*I have some 'information' you might wish to discover, Richard. It is very embarrassing and very unpleasant, but you are my friend and I think you should know. It concerns your wife...*Richard's ears pricked up at the sound of what might be any morsel of dirt that he could use against AnnElise and regain control of his liquor procurement and his dignity...*Yes, Dorothy, please go on...*

Before I tell you anything, you must promise that you will do me a favor. I need fifteen thousand dollars from my trust fund, the one Will's daddy set up for me when I first married Will...I need it in cash and I need it before next Friday and I don't want any questions, you'll just have to trust me, Richard. Do you promise? Can you do this for me?

There was a sense of gutter-girl urgency and danger to Dorothy's voice that Richard had never imagined could flow from such a pampered, spoiled socialite. It excited him and he was intrigued, but it would be virtually impossible to secure any of the trust fund's assets without Mother Nell's written permission; however, since he realized Dorothy was not privy to that minor detail and because he so desperately needed revenge on his own wife, he nodded slightly, as if in compliance. Dorothy was such an easy mark...on seeing her glowing smile when she believed he would help her, he realized he could probably make a secret request of his own.

Dorothy, you know these last few months have been terrible for me...AnnElise has gone off the deep end...I have seriously contemplated ending my own life...I can see you are terrified of something...I promise not to ask questions...but are you in physical danger?

Dorothy breathed deep, and spoke in a near-whisper. *Richard...I will cut to the chase...your wife has been caught in a compromising situation, and apparently, it's not the first time, except that in this case, it's on tape and if we're all not very careful, that tape will get into the wrong hands, and you'll find yourself out of business, and disgraced.*

Richard put on his best panic-stricken face; he raised a hand to his temple, then drained his glass dry and refilled it once more. *AnnElise... AnnElise...what a beauty...I knew I never deserved her love...I just can't give her what she needs...oh, God, this hurts, Dorothy! This hurts so much!* He crossed the room and sat down on the leather sofa next to the bearer of his bad news. Dorothy hugged him tightly and as she did, he managed to get an eyeful of the freckled cleavage her red sun dress innocently displayed. He looked up at her with soulful, lost eyes.

But Dorothy...I don't understand...how did you get involved in all of this? How did you find out about my wife...oh, God, you're not a couple of lesbos, are you?

Dorothy swallowed hard and shook her head emphatically. She hadn't counted on Richard asking any questions about how she'd discovered AnnElise's infidelity. Her web was getting more tangled with every minute; she decided she'd better spill some dirt on herself, to cover her tracks.

Richard...I am so ashamed...but I must tell you the truth...I have been having a secret affair with Dan... Will's never home and he just doesn't love me anymore...so last week, Dan wanted us to get, well, you know, kinky. So he put in a tape, but it was the wrong one...and there on the screen was AnnElise...with Dan...doing the nasty. And then he showed me a tape of one of our little meetings...I was so ashamed! Of course, after that, well, I've broken it off. But I had to tell you, Richard, I just had to. But now Dan's threatened to sell us all down the river if I talk, and if I don't give him fifteen thousand to cover his...his gambling debts. He says he'll put the tape on the public access channel...he wants to steal all your tax accounts, you know...Dan wants fifteen-thousand dollars before Monday...I'm so distraught, I called the FBI, in fact, they may call you, Richard. Oh, this is so terrible!

As she sobbed, head in her hands, Richard smiled a faint smile and thought to himself, *this is certainly old news. AnnElise has boinked virtually every man in town, unbeknownst to Dorothy and I'm not surprised Dan Gastineau's on the list. But what a tasty tidbit of info...Dorothy also doing the dirty deed with Dan Gastineau, the very man who is scheming to steal all my clients away from me with his own son. But something's not quite right...this business with the FBI...that doesn't make any sense...*Richard put his beefy arms around Dorothy and held her as she cried.

Dorothy, sweet Dorothy! Please don't cry, there, there, dear. It's all right, I will be ok and so shall you. I have suspected this for a long time...and I thank you for being a true friend. What shall we do? What did the FBI suggest? To whom did you speak?

Dorothy wiped her eyes in silence for a full minute; again, Richard had asked a question she'd never thought to anticipate. *He didn't give me his name...just his badge number. And I lost the piece of paper...but you'll know if he calls you. Really, this is silly, but he said that we should just ignore the whole thing...but I had to tell you Richard...I had to let you know that your wife is not what she seems. You be careful, Richard...be on guard for any strange behavior at home...if she says anything about a tape, or the FBI, you just smile and keep your mouth shut...and of course, you know I won't say a word to Will or to anyone. Now when should I come over to get that fifteen thousand?*

As he inwardly laughed at what a terrible liar Dorothy was, Richard noticed that she had much too quickly regained full composure. *Badge numbers! Gambling debts! Just ignore it!* Good God, the local FBI agents were *crying* to get their hands on stinking Dan Gastineau and his borderline illegalities! No, there was likely no videotape; Dorothy was up to something, but it was best to just play along, work it to his full advantage, *right now.* He might never get another chance. He took Dorothy's delicate hands in his own and pressed them softly. He smiled and leaned his head closer so he could whisper in her beautiful pink ear.

Dorothy, honey, now you listen to me. I never said I could get you that money! You breeze in here, all hot and bothered and you didn't let me finish! Now I don't know what's going on, Miss Dottie Chatwick, but there is no way I can get you any of that trust fund until Mother Nell kicks...unless she gives me a written codicil or a verbal order! Would you like me to talk to her for you? Look...I know Dan, and he's no blackmailer. Tell me the truth, Dottie...what's the money really for, hmm? Will won't spring for that Paris designer Cotillon gown? One of your girlfriends wants to open a little business? Dorothy, honey, if you need money so urgently, why don't you just go ask Will...I mean, he owns the bank!

How in the hell does he know Dan's not blackmailing me? Dorothy reached out and slapped Richard Napoleon Leigh-Lee IV hard across the face. Her eyes blazed and her cheeks clouded. She stood up and pointed. *Damn you, Richard! You said you'd get that money for me! I need that money and I need it now! And it's none of anybody's business why I need it, I just need it! But I can't go to Will, or Mother Nell, or any of the rest of the stupid Grahams, oh, dammit, I'm so sick of asking for money!*

Dorothy sat down and sobbed into the leather sofa cushion as Richard rubbed his cheek and reached for his whiskey. He had Dorothy over a barrel...a steamy, hot, sex-filled barrel. He stood up, walked over to his desk and sat down in his leather executive chair.

You know, Dorothy...I can see you're in a real bind, and we've been friends for thirty years. Here's the best deal I can offer...you may not know this, but Mother Nell called me last week from the hospital and told me she wants to amend her Last Will & Testament. I've already made the revisions, all I need is her signature. I realize this might be painful for you, honey, but, well, is she near death, Dottie?

Dorothy raised her head and shouted, *Hell, no, she's just having her feet scraped!*

Richard smiled and continued. *Well, ok, anyway she called me. And you know how she loves Danita Kay, so I promised her I'd send Danita Kay over there to get her signature. Now, what Mother Nell doesn't know is that Danita Kay's been really busy with a huge land deal...hell, she won't even have time to look at the paperwork, she's just be-bopping over there on her lunch hour to get Mother Nell's signature. Now...Dottie...I'm willing to meet you halfway on this, if you're willing to do your part...*

Dorothy brightened and wiped her eyes. She could guess by the look on his face what he was thinking. *Richard, I've got to have that money! Yes! I'll do anything! Anything you say!*

Richard sighed and his heart pounded wildly inside his chest. *Fine, Dottie, Fine. I'll just insert a tiny phrase into that Last Will & Testament that says you can have up to fifteeen thousand dollars without express permission from Mother Nell, before her death. I'll stick it in there where no one, even Danita Kay, will look for it and as soon as we get that signature, you'll have your money. But Dorothy, it's Friday afternoon...even I can't make your Monday deadline, honey...look, after we get a signature, you'll have to take a notarized copy to the courthouse and then one to the bank and then Will's got to sign all the paperwork to get you the money...no, that won't do, will it?*

Dorothy was losing patience. *Richard! Stop playing with me! You've got to figure it out! I've got to have that money! You're a lawyer...fix it!*

Richard Napoleon Leigh-Lee IV crossed the room and stood in front of Dorothy, admiring her beautiful face, despite its mascara streaks and disheveled bangs. He bit his lip. *Dottie, honey, there is only one solution. I will personally give you a bridge loan...you'll have your check, it will be our little secret and when Mother Nell goes to that big nut factory in the sky, whenever that might be, you can pay me back. I'll even waive the interest! But you've got to do your part, Dottie...*

Richard stroked Dorothy's smooth, surgically enhanced cheekbone. He gazed into her blue eyes and licked his lips. *You've got to do for me what you did for Dan Gastineau...you've got to make me feel like a real man again, Dottie...you've got to meet me at the Peacock Inn on Monday afternoon at two with your prettiest negligée and your highest heels...I'll bring the champagne, the roses and the money. But like I said, if I do my part, then you've got to do yours!*

Dorothy Graham was sick to her stomach. She smelled Richard's whiskey breath on her neck and she saw his eyes look her up and down. She knew she had no choice if she wanted to buy that Festival insurance bond and save her NDCA presidency bid, but she did have a smidgen of negotiating power left.

All right, Richard, you win. But if I have to do this, then you have to loan me twenty-five thousand dollars, or it's no deal.

Richard smiled at the ease of his success. He kissed Dorothy's hand graciously and bowed. *Twenty-five thousand it is, sugar plum, but for that kind of money, we'll have to do it at least twice and there will most definitely be several positions involved, to cover the deal from every angle, so to speak!*

Dorothy grabbed her shopping bag and her purse and let out a disgusted cough. As she opened the door to Richard's office, he called out sweetly, *Monday, two o'clock, Dorothy. Don't be late!*

She'd taken to her bed with a sick headache, and now on Saturday morning, Dorothy's head pounded as she remembered that terrible hour spent in Richard's office. She rolled off her elbow and leaned back against her satin bed pillows. She couldn't believe she agreed to prostitute herself for twenty-five thousand dollars when she was worth at least fifty. But then she remembered, she'd done it with Dan Gastineau for the past eight months for free. At least this way, she'd have something to show for her trouble. After she repaid the Festival account, she could go shopping to her heart's content. She reached for a piece of dry toast and took a bite. As she chewed, she stared at a picture of the twins on her vanity.

I still haven't talked to Hester and Horry, she thought. Her lie about Chéz Horatio loaning them back the catering deposit back could still work...but Horry would pitch a sissy fit and tell Will and then she'd be completely sunk. But maybe it was worth a try...maybe she could just talk to Hester, alone. *That's it! I'll take Hester to Elizabeth Arden for the day! We'll get rubbed, and oiled and pampered and Hester will feel so good, she'll do anything for her sweet mama!*

Dorothy sat up and punched buttons on her portable phone; she booked two all-day sessions at Elizabeth Arden, then dialed Chéz Horatio. It was only nine o'clock on this Saturday morning, but she knew Hester was probably already at the restaurant.

"Hello, Hester? This is your mother. How *are* you, dear? You know, it's been so long since we've had any time together...I was wondering, could I come over there in a few minutes, and let's have a talk, just us girls? There's something I need to discuss with you...good, I'll see you soon!"

Dorothy rang for the maid, said that her headache was gone and that she'd be leaving to spend the day at the spa in Nashville. She dressed and put on minimal makeup, then dashed over to Chéz Horatio in her red Mercedes. Hester unlocked the restaurant door and smiling, gave her mother a big hug. Dorothy reciprocated with a light peck on each of Hester's cheeks.

"Good morning, dear, how *are* you? Where's your brother?"

"He's in the back, taking kitchen inventory so he can send Estéfan to the produce market later. We've got a big group coming in tonight and they've requested an all-vegetable meal."

Dorothy frowned, then she touched Hester lightly on the arm. "Hessie, dear, I have a surprise for you! You and I are going to Nashville, to Elizabeth Arden for an entire day of pampering! I know how hard you've been working and I never get to talk to you anymore, so…finish what you're doing, get your purse, and let's go, ok?"

Hester pushed a strand of hair behind one ear and stared blankly at her mother. Dorothy tried to ignore Hester's mismatched skirt and top, her lack of makeup and her poor choice of earrings.

"Mom…you mean *today*? That sounds great, but today is Saturday…our busiest day of the week! I can't leave the restaurant today…Horry would kill me! Every table's booked for tonight and people have already started to call for reservations this morning and well, I just can't, Mom! What about one day next week?"

Dorothy inhaled deeply and pursed her lips. "I *see*. You are too busy to spend a few hours with your own mother, the one who labored *over thirty-six hours* to bring you into this world. Well, I understand. My needs come second, they always have. No, that's fine, you just go about your business, take your little phone calls, roll up your little napkins. My issues can just wait…"

Dorothy was about to stomp off in a huff, knowing full well Hester would follow, when she noticed Estéfan Rodriguez approach the door. He wore a t-shirt that said "PURPLE PRIDE," a pair of extremely short denim cut-offs, and what appeared to be patent leather tap shoes with purple socks. His black hair was cropped close to his head, except for one long strand on the right side of his face that was dyed purple. He sported a thin gold ring in his right ear.

"Hey, toots, what's shakin'? Morning, Mrs. Graham! Girl, that color is so you! To die for! Hessie, baby, could you get me a double 'cino pronto, *por favór*! *This* Cinderella stayed out way too long past midnight and my pumpkin is in pain!"

Dorothy grimaced in total disgust at Estéfan's display. She turned to say something to Hester and noticed that Hester absolutely beamed. Her cheeks were flushed, she gazed at Estéfan dreamily and as he walked past her toward the kitchen, he swatted Hester on the bottom and she giggled.

"Hester! What is the matter with you? Hester…look at me! *Please* don't tell me you have a *crush* on that boy?"

Hester looked up from the cappuccino machine with a start and cocked her mouth in denial. "Mom…I mean…*Mom*…what do you *mean*? *Him? Estéfan? Me*, a crush on *Estéfan*? No way, Mom, no way! Don't be silly! Now, what were we talking about? Oh, yeah…hang on a minute, Mom, let me just take this to Estéfan and I'll be right back."

Hester didn't wait to find out whether her mother was interested in waiting, but instead raced to the kitchen with Estéfan's cappuccino. Horry was making notes on a legal pad and Estéfan was standing very close behind him, looking over his shoulder.

"Here, Estéfan, here's your double 'cino, I put cinnamon on top, just like you like it!"

Hester grinned and waited for Estéfan to notice the special touch she'd added to his drink, but he was deep in some kind of urgent vegetable discussion with Horry. *He's so handsome,* Hester thought. *Look at those arm muscles! Look at that tight butt! He could have been a male model. Maybe I should send his picture to Vogue...*

"HESTER! I cannot wait here all day, you know!"

"Oh...yeah, coming Mom!" Hester wiped her hands on her apron, but Horry grabbed her by the shoulder.

"*Hessie*...is that the Dragon Lady I hear out there? Please, Hessie, I can't be distracted today! This vichyssoise recipe is very demanding!"

Hester nodded and glanced at Estéfan, who leaned his head on Horry's shoulder in an effort to better see the legal pad. "It's ok, Horry. She's leaving right now. Estéfan...when you have time, will you show me again how to fold the napkins into tulips? I just can't get the hang of it."

Estéfan murmured a yes but never took his eyes off Horry and his legal pad. Hester dashed out to where her mother waited impatiently in the restaurant foyer.

"Sorry, Mom. Ok. Look, I can't go to the spa with you, but why can't we just sit over here at this table, have a cappuccino and some biscotti, we have those ones you like from Italy, and we can talk now? I'll just turn on the answering machine so we won't be bothered."

Dorothy scowled, and was about to protest, when the image of a naked Richard Leigh-Lee flashed through her mind. "Certainly, dear, that's an excellent idea. I'm sorry, I forget just how busy you twins are with this restaurant. You know, your father and I are so proud of you!"

For forty-five minutes, Dorothy Graham donned the mantle of a Caring Individual and poured her heart out to Hester, claiming that there was an unexpected family emergency involving a cousin in Canada whom Hester had never met. Dorothy desperately wanted to help this young woman, Cynthia was her name, because she had been impregnated by some roving sailor, then abandoned without a penny. She needed fifteen thousand dollars to cover the baby's delivery expenses and had called Dorothy in the middle of the night. She'd thought about it, but there was no way she could go to Will...he just wouldn't understand, because he'd never liked her side of the family. *You are my last hope, Hester ...I have no money of my own...you know your father keeps me on a tight leash...but we owe this girl our Christian charity...she is my family! All the way over here, I kept thinking...what if this happened to my Hessie...and what if the only person she could turn was two thousand miles away? Hester, you must give me the money, today! Cynthia is counting on us...*

Hester blinked large tears from her eyes. "But *Mom*! I can't just write you a check for fifteen thousand dollars! What will Horry say? We are doing well, but we go through a lot of cash in a week, to buy produce and meat, and pay our staff and expenses, and then there's our mortgage!"

Dorothy nodded in understanding. "Yes, I'm sure dear. But I have an idea. Remember the twenty thousand dollar check the Festival Committee gave you as a retainer for the catering? Didn't you tell me that money is in a special account? Why not just lend me *that* money? The Festival is months away, and since you're not using it for anything, it's just sitting there, isn't it? Well, this girl's child is much more important than the Festival, sweetheart! I have to send her that money by the end of the week, or she'll be kicked out of the unwed mothers' home, you know, in Canada they have socialized medicine and everything is done by cash up front. I can't send her out into the street to have her baby!"

Hester took a bite from a biscotti, which was soggy with Cousin Cynthia-inspired tears. "Mom! If I lend you that retainer money, what am I supposed to do in October, when I have to start ordering Festival supplies and pay for them in advance?"

Dorothy smiled and patted Hester's hand. "Simple, dear! October is months away! You and I will just go to your father together and tell him what we've done. You know he'll give *you* the money, because you know how he loves this restaurant and how much he's looking forward to the Festival! He'll bail us out, I just know it! We just need more time to convince him, trust me!"

Hester twirled a spoon in her cappuccino mug. She and Horry had no secrets, she couldn't imagine going behind his back, no matter what the cause. And all those professional businesswoman lectures she'd attended with Juliette Kimball had taught her to follow her first instincts when it came to money; her first instinct now was to hang on to that deposit, and send her mother packing.

"I'm sorry, Mom, I just can't do it. I'd really like to help, and I admire what you're trying to do...but I just can't. If Horry knew, he'd blow a gasket and then Daddy would find out anyhow. It's just not how we operate, it's not good business. Couldn't we talk to Daddy together? Can't you just get a loan or something?"

Dorothy slammed a fist on the table and splashed cappuccino all over her blouse. "*NO,* I can't get a loan or something! I've tried every option! Do you know how miserable it makes me feel, to have to beg my own family for money? You are just like your father and all the other Grahams…selfish! *Selfish, selfish, selfish*! Fine, Hester! If you won't help me, I'll find someone who will!"

Dorothy snatched her purse from the table and stood up angrily. Hester blinked back tears. "Mom, I'm really sorry! But you're asking me to compromise my business and lie to Horry and to Daddy and I just can't do it! I really think if you'd just talk to Daddy, he'd come around! He's always so good-hearted…just like Estéfan…"

Dorothy's eyes flamed. "Let me tell you something, *missy*! That boy you're so fond of…he's not *right*! What kind of man goes around wearing tap shoes and purple socks? And those shorts are so tight his family jewels are dragging the ground! You listen to me, Hester Graham…you need to get over him, because that boy is a *QUEER!* Do you even know what that *means*? He likes *boys,* honey! He will never love you, even if you spend *three* days at Elizabeth Arden! When are you going to get your head out of your ass and slap on some makeup and decent clothes and realize that unless you pay attention to yourself, you will *never* have a husband?"

Hester's bottom lip quivered as she watched her mother storm out of the restaurant and get into her car. She picked up a cappucino cup in silence, feeling guilty that she hadn't been able to offer her mother the money she needed for their cousin Cynthia. Maybe she could get Cynthia's address and send her a card and diaper coupons. Hester placed the cappuccino cups and biscotti plates in the bar sink. She looked through the round kitchen door window, but Estéfan and Horry were nowhere in sight. She made her way through the kitchen, back toward the cooler, where she heard muffled sounds.

Mom's so wrong, she thought. Estéfan is all man…he's a Latino, that's why he's different than most of the guys around here. All Latinos dress flamboyantly…a lot of them wear earrings…but he's definitely not queer…he pats me on the butt, he's even kissed me a couple of times on the cheek…no, my Castilian Prince will notice me one day…he's just so into his work…he's a true professional…he's kissing my brother in the cooler.

Hester screamed and slammed the cooler door closed. As she'd rounded the corner, following the muffled sounds in an attempt to locate Horry and Estéfan, she noticed the cooler door wide open. As she peered inside, she saw Horry and her Castilian Prince, lip-locked in what was most definitely not a kiss shared by men friends!

She slumped to the floor and sobbed. *How could I be so stupid? I don't know what's worse, the fact that Estéfan's gay, or the fact that my mom was right! I can't believe this! My own brother, stealing my boyfriend right out from under me! How blind can I be?*

She heard fists pounding inside the cooler.

"*Hessie! Hessie,* open the door! It's not what you *think*! Estéfan was just showing me how it feels to get your lip pierced!"

Hester sat on the floor, unmoving, and unmotivated to open the door. The pounding continued, and she recognized Estéfan's voice.

"Hessie, *bebé, cara mia,* please open the door! *Mi corazón,* Hessie, it's a little too *frio* in here, please, let us out!"

Hester edged closer to the door's seal and shouted, "Hey, no shit, it's cold in there! It's a *cooler*! But I'm sure you two can figure out a way to keep warm! Lip piercing, my ass! I can't *believe* it, Horry! I trusted you my whole life and you have kept this from me...and you, you sorry little fop...you smiled at me and patted me on the butt and kissed me! You're nothing but a whore in tap shoes!"

Hester kicked the cooler door and sobbed. She'd hurt her own mother because she'd wanted to avoid going behind Horry's back. All her dreams about Estéfan, her Castilian prince...it was all shit. Her mother was right, she'd never find a husband. Nobody deserved such a stupid, stupid girl...

"HESSIE! YOU OPEN THAT DOOR THIS MINUTE! I AM GETTING FROSTBITE!"

"Oh, I'm sure you can figure out a way to keep yourselves nice and toasty for a few minutes, Horry! *HORRY*! Agh, even your name says it all! How could I be so blind? So stupid? I just thought you were odd, you were an artist! Give me a *break*!"

Hester stood up and walked out of the restaurant kitchen. She grabbed a pen and wrote out a sign that said "CLOSED DUE TO FAMILY EMERGENCY." She posted the sign on the front door, then reached for the phone on the reservations stand. "Hello, Juliette? Hey, this is Hessie. Listen, we've got a bit of a problem...we've got to close the restaurant for a few days...the health inspector's on our back and we don't want to take any chances...Horry is...Horry is out of town and I've got to handle this by myself, so I'm just gonna close for awhile, I wanted to let you know, nothing's seriously wrong, ok? If anybody asks, would you please just say we took a few days off? Thanks...sure, I'll let you know...take care, *bye.*"

Hester hung up the phone, then immediately picked it up again. She dialed information. "Chestnut Ridge...yes, I'd like the number for Ms. Margaret McArdle-Graham, please...oh, it's unlisted? Well, what about the number for the ...let me see if I've got the name right...the Abuse Victims Support Group? You do? Great...thanks!"

She scratched the support group's number, which was really Margaret's home number as well, onto a scrap of chartreuse paper. She folded it and placed it in her wallet for safekeeping. Horry and Estéfan pounded and kicked the inside of the produce cooler door in a rage. She took another sheet of chartreuse paper and grabbed a large felt-tipped pen. She wrote "GO TO HELL" and placed a small piece of masking tape on the paper.

Hester walked quietly over to the door and taped her sign to it. She looked carefully at the steel latch; it had never worked properly and Hester knew that if Horry gave it a really good, swift kick, it would probably fly open without a problem. But she didn't want to be found guilty of murdering her twin brother and his Latino sexual plaything, no matter how angry she was at their behavior. She ran a finger over the latch and lifted it ever so slightly. *One good kick and they can be out of there*, she decided.

With her conscience eased, Hester shouldered her purse and strolled out the door of Chéz Horatio. She walked the fifty-odd steps to her cottage, opened the door, bolted it behind her, and threw her purse on the sofa. She reached for the phone; it was time to call in a professional, so she dialed the number of the Abuse Victims Support Group and burst into tears.

CHAPTER SEVENTEEN – PASSED HISTORY

August 20, 1999; Festrunk Clinic

She arrived at the Festrunk Clinic to have her eighty-three-year-old feet scraped of three-inch thick calluses. But the pain in her feet was mild compared to the pain Mother Nell endured at the hands of her hospital roommate, Aunt Pearl Parker.

Aunt Pearl was admitted to the Clinic through the ER after her near thumb-severing kitchen knife incident. Upon further examination, it was discovered that Aunt Pearl's blood pressure, her serum cholesterol and her blood sugar were all severely out of whack; apparently her "combination dieting" had fallen short and Pearl Parker was moments away from total heart failure. The serious nature of her illness, however, did not stem the unceasing flow of conversation from her perfectly healthy jaws, much to the consternation of Nell Graham.

Because of the severe Chestnut Ridge summer heat and the resultant effects on the elderly town citizens, the Festrunk Clinic was filled to capacity and the administrator had no choice but to bunk Aunt Pearl in the huge suite typically reserved for wealthy patients, the one used frequently by Mother Nell. After her foot-scraping, Mother Nell was heavily sedated for two days, thus oblivious to Aunt Pearl's existence and the fact that Aunt Pearl could and did maintain happy banter with the wall. On day three, however, Mother Nell was taken out of sedation and the good times rolled. She successfully lobbed her bedpan, a box of tissues, a plastic water jug and an IV cart at her chatty roommate; Mother Nell was much stronger than she looked. After the orderlies restrained her, Mother Nell continued to shout obscenities at Aunt Pearl for nearly two hours until the Clinic Administrator tracked down Amelia Festrunk, the only person in town who could get through to Nell Graham.

Amelia, in her Red Cross volunteer uniform, ordered everyone to leave the room, including Aunt Pearl, who was wheeled out for an extra session of exercise. Amelia then engaged in a stern, private talk with the *grande dame* patient.

"Nell, what's all this commotion about? Can't you just sit here like a lady and behave yourself for once?"

Nell Graham scowled at her old friend. "Bullshit! I'm no lady! You have to be *treated* like a lady to *be* a lady, and look at me! All strapped in like a mare in a stud barn! They're poisoning me, 'Melie! I've been calling and calling for you but you never come! I saw those orderlies put nutmeg in my food and I'm telling you, they're poisoning me! And now they've put some old nigger woman in my private suite, and all she does is lay there and jack her jaws! I mean, what good's an old nigger woman if she won't even clean the bathroom?"

Amelia pursed her lips and crossed her arms. "Nell Graham, you know how that kind of talk upsets me! If you can't be civil, I'll just leave."

Nell sighed and plopped back against her pillows like a child. "Ok, how 'bout this…there's some old *colored bag* in my room and I want her *OUT*! But why should you care, you haven't been to see me at all! I bet the only reason you're here right now is because you and all your liberal bones beat a path down here to make sure that old…*colored* gets better food than me so she won't file some damned lawsuit against your precious Clinic! You always did put the Clinic first, don't know why I'd expect it to be different now!"

Amelia sat down on the edge of Nell's hospital bed and untied the patient restraints. Nell rubbed her wrists. Amelia looked deep into her friend's eyes and realized that she was completely lucid, for the first time in months. "Nell Graham, you listen to me. I don't work here any more! Do you remember seeing me at the party a few months ago, the party where we ate pink cake and sat together just like old times?"

Nell smiled and nodded. "Of course I remember! Don't talk to me like I'm a stupid half-wit! Why does everybody treat me like I'm a lunatic?"

Amelia ignored her and continued. "Well, don't you remember, that party was to celebrate my retirement and MayBelle's and Leonard's, too. We're not part of the Clinic any more, Nell. We're all working over at the Red Cross a few days a week. So I can't just waltz in to see you anytime like I used to and besides, they've had you so sedated that when I did visit, you probably didn't even know I was here, did you?"

Nell's eyes filled with tears and she shook her head. "I'm sorry…I'm not myself these days. But what do you mean, you're not with the Clinic? What a bunch of horseshit that is, now you stop…*oh, 'Melie, what's happened*? You swore the only way you'd leave this Clinic would be on your deathbed! You said you'd never quit because you owed it to your granddaddy to help people! 'Melie, you're not a quitter… this Clinic…it's your life! It's your pride and joy! *OHHH!* They *forced* you out, didn't they? That bitch AnnElise and those other socialites on the Board…they made you quit and you didn't stand up to them, did you, you pussy? Oh, 'Melie, how *could* you? How could you do that to MayBelle? And *Leonard*? Oh, my Leonard…"

Amelia Festrunk swallowed hard and stared at the tiled floor. She felt a cool hand on her face and turned to see Nell smiling at her, just like when they were young girls. "Amelia Festrunk, you listen to me! Nobody worked harder in this town to do right than you! And don't you let the jealousy of a few uppity men and women drag you down, either! Don't let them win,

'Melie! Don't give in and feel sorry for yourself or think that you didn't finish your work! You may not run things here anymore, but if I know you, you're still beating yourself up trying to help folks in this town, aren't ya? You're up to something, I just know it…spill it, 'Melie…what's goin' on?"

Amelia saw Nell wink and she laughed. "Nell, you know me better than I know myself. How I've missed you. I have so much to tell you…are you tired, or do you think we could have a little chat?"

Nell looked around the room and waved her arms in exasperation. "Well, shit, how in the hell do you expect me to have a little chat when there aren't any cigarettes in here? And you know I can't have a decent, proper conversation without a spot of bourbon, now don't you? What does a gal have to do around here to get taken care of? And have you taken a gander at those orderlies? They are the most godforsaken ugly bumpkins I've ever seen in my life…not one good butt muscle in the bunch, and half of 'em probably like boys anyhow, just like that queer grandson of mine!"

The two old friends laughed out loud until tears spilled down their cheeks. Amelia squeezed Nell's shoulders and fluffed up the pillows behind her head. Nell sipped some water from the plastic cup Amelia offered her and cocked a finger in the air.

"Look here…I've missed you too. And you know the reason I've been off my rocker for so long? Well, I'm telling you, I'm being overmedicated! That bitch Dorothy screws around with my prescriptions…she slips pills into my food when she thinks I'm not looking! And my mind's shot to hell because of the drugs, so I forget where she's put the pills and end up eating them anyway… I stay in a foggy haze most of the time! But I still hear what everybody says about me…all this horseshit about 'dementia'…but I'm telling you it's not dementia, it's *Dorothy.* She wants me to die so bad she can't stand it and she's helping me along! You've got to stop her, 'Melie! I know Doc Kimball knows something's goin' on but he's afraid to do anything because he thinks Will'll call his loan. Listen…a few nights ago when the bitch was out of town and that old bag they call a nurse was asleep, I called Richard and told him I want to revise my will. I'm cutting the bitch completely out…I'm leaving everything to Leonard. Richard's bringing the papers here on Tuesday, I think. But even he doesn't believe me…he thinks I'm crazy as a loon and he's just happy to put in some billable time. Look, I need you to read those revisions…make sure he's changed what I want changed. You've gotta help me, 'Melie! Oh, Lord, how can I ask you again? I always depend on you so, don't I? And you've never called on me for anything. I owe you so much!"

Amelia set her jaw and reached for one of Nell's bony hands. She gripped it tight and said in a low voice. "Nell… you don't owe me a thing! We are best friends and that's that! But I've got a big mess of my own, Nell...I've got a big mess to fix and I don't know what to do. And when you hear what I have to say you're gonna think I'm the biggest coward and fake that ever lived. My whole life's been a lie and I didn't even realize it. Are you sure you're up to this?"

Nell grinned. "Shit, Amelia! Don't get me all cock-teased and then decide to keep the goods to yourself! Spill it, girl! Spill it!"

Amelia Festrunk's heart spilled out to Nell Graham like water rushing out of a downspout after a flash flood. She told her every word of what happened that cold December day at the quarry so many years before; the pain of watching Granddaddy die at the hands of an old drunk, the promise she'd made to Granddaddy and purposefully ignored out of spite for his murder. Then she told Nell every detail of the dream she'd had in December, on the very anniversary of Granddaddy's murder, and how it finally dawned on her that after years of hatred and blame and working to preserve Granddaddy's memory, she'd ignored the one final request Granddaddy'd made and expected of her. She hadn't done the one thing he'd asked and people had suffered because of her stubborn hatred. And now she was such a coward, she was depending upon a complete stranger from Virginia to come and bail her out so she wouldn't have to stand alone when the wrongs were righted. Nell stared at her friend and soaked up every word; when Amelia was finished, Nell leaned back gently on her pillows and exhaled.

"Amelia...I used to think you didn't ever get any titties because you just didn't want to be bothered with them! But now I know why...it's because you've been carrying this horrible load on your chest for seventy-seven years and those poor babes couldn't grow up over it!"

Amelia chuckled. "Nell, look who's talking about flat-chested! Nell...what am I gonna do? I'm such a big huge coward! I had that dream eight months ago and yet all I've done is give Henry Bailey a few car sales...I'm scared to death to say anything without that professor here to verify my story, and Lord only knows when she's gonna get serious and show up! The Board went after me and won, Nell, they threw me out and nobody said boo! And if I try to set things straight without somebody to back me up, I'll be sittin' in a room with you and we'll *both* be overmedicated!"

Nell bit her lip and reached for a cigarette, a cigarette she'd not smoked in over ten years but reached for anyway out of force of habit. She patted the bed and the pillows in vain.

"Well, 'Melie, at least we'd be roommates again and maybe between us we'd hook a piece of young ass...look here, you can't fool me...you never were any good at playing dumb and scared! You're only the bravest, toughest broad in the whole county...don't sit there and tell me you're a coward.

It's just that you're so smart you know what's what. You already know the answer, don't ya? First of all, and this is very hard for me to say but I'm gonna say it anyway…first of all…you've gotta tear down that marble pedestal you've had your granddaddy on for the last seventy-seven years. 'Melie…he may have helped folks, but he was nothin' but a man, plain as day and some folks said he was no Boy Scout back before the War. Gal, you've lived your life as a tribute to somebody that may not have deserved it any more than the fella that shoved him over that quarry pit. I know that's hard to hear, 'Melie, but it's true. I should have told you this years ago before it was too late…you should have married and had babies…but you were so dead-set on dedicating yourself to this Clinic on account of your granddaddy you wouldn't have listened to me anyhow. Don't you know everybody in town's called you Saint Amelia since we were about twenty years old?"

Amelia nodded and shrugged her shoulders. "Yeah, I know. I was just trying to do the right thing. If you'd been there that day, Nell, watched him fall over…I'll never forget it, ever."

"You old bag of bones, you *did* the right thing! You did it four thousand times over! But get on with it, gal! It's old news! Did you ever stop to think, *'who's gonna keep me company when I'm old?'* This Clinic can't, for sure! I may not have lived my life with the man I loved, but at least we had a child together and at least we had our love and our memories. Maybe this is your granddaddy's way of telling you to leave the hatred behind and get on with your life…course he sure as hell took his *time* tellin' ya, didn't he? Now me, I can still get it on with the best of 'em if they can get past all my wrinkles! But I can't see you havin' a fling, Amelia…you sure should, honey, you sure should! I can't quite see you cuttin' loose now, though…"

Amelia smiled and nodded. "Hey, I bought MayBelle a Cadillac and I got Leonard a new truck! And Henry's trying to find me a new car too, but he says I'm too picky."

Nell rolled her eyes. "Picky ain't the word for it! Even if you are trying to do right by poor Henry I bet he's wishin' you never set one foot on his car lot! But it's not enough, 'Melie. You're right, you've gotta come clean with the story, but hell, you've waited this long, a few more weeks isn't gonna set the world on fire. You need that gal from Virginia to stand up there with you…look, we both know that once a gal gets wrinkles on top of wrinkles, nobody gives you the time of day but they're poppin' a pill down your throat or askin' you if you want another blanket! You need that professor to back you up, or everybody'll just think you've finally lost your marbles and they'll forget all about your decades of hard work. They'll remember you as "that old crazy Festrunk woman" and you'll go up in flames every time you hear it. And that brings me to something else, 'Melie, along the same lines…"

Amelia raised her eyebrows. "What is it?"

Nell took a deep breath. "You know how much I love your brother. You wanna talk about cowards... I was such a big one I could never tell anybody that I loved him. He's the best man in the world to me and it hurts me so much the way people treat him, just because he can't read or write. I always felt that if I could pipe up and tell folks how much I loved him, it would prove that he was a real man and not just a simpleton. If folks knew that Hoot was Leonard's son, maybe they'd look at Leonard in a different light. Now, don't get me wrong...I know Hoot's no model citizen...he's all full of bull and piss and vinegar, just like Leonard. But Hoot should know who his real daddy is. And Leonard should be able to be proud of his son in public. Don't you think? I've wanted to come clean on this to everybody for so long, but I was nothin' short of chicken shit. Don't talk to me about cowards, 'Melie. You're looking at the Queen, right here."

Tears spilled from Amelia's eyes. "Nell, it's not too late...for either one of us. Leonard's so miserable...they made him move out of his room at the Clinic and he's in the apartment with me and MayBelle. He's so lonesome, Nell. He needs something to give him a purpose again... I think it's a great idea...what should we do?"

"Well, hell if I know. When's your professor woman getting here?"

Amelia frowned. "She's supposed to call me on Monday to confirm but the last time we spoke she'd planned to come here next week. Why?"

Nell bit her lip. "We can't spring all these surprises at *once*, 'Melie, or we'll drop dead before we can enjoy 'em! Like I said, I think Richard's comin' over on Tuesday with my revised will...if your professor comes next week, we only have a few days to figure out how I'm gonna come clean about Hoot and Leonard. But dammit, you gotta stop me from takin' any more of those godawful pills so I can keep my wits about me! I want to be there when you tell your story and I want to see the look on everybody's face when I tell them I love Leonard Festrunk and that Hoot is his son! And I wanna watch the bitch Dorothy keel over dead when I tell her she's not gonna inherit my money after all these years, despite what my danged fool husband promised her! Hell, this is more fun than when we snuck off to New York after graduation! You sure you're in?"

Nell raised a crooked pinky in Amelia's direction. Amelia raised her own pinky and they hooked fingers together, shaking them in the air as they had done when they were schoolgirls.

"I'm in, Nell. What should we do first?"

Nell bit her lip. "I know you don't work here any more, but you'd best become a fixture in this room. Dorothy calls every day and hounds the doctors to keep me medicated I'm surprised I'm not already in a casket six feet under! Now, what are you gonna do about movin' that old darky out?"

"NELL! You stop it or you can just forget about getting any help from me, you hear? That's Pearl Parker, she's Doctor Avery Parker's aunt from Chicago and she has every right to be here. The Clinic's full because of the heat so you'll just have to grin and bear it. She's on a low-fat diet and exercise regimen for three weeks and then they're gonna do a heart bypass on her. You should be out of here in a few days."

Nell frowned and gripped Amelia's arm. "*Hell, no*! If I go back home I'll be dead in a matter of days! You've gotta figure out how I can stay here for a while! You're a nurse, make something up! Hell's bells! *That's it!* Why can't I hire you as my private nurse? Then you'd have every reason to be in this room anytime you want! You can keep the bitch out and take a look at my will and throw all those fool pills in the trash. And as soon as we have that taken care of, we'll slap everybody on the back with the news about Leonard and Hoot!"

Amelia blinked and swallowed. "*Oh*...that is a good idea. There's nothing anybody could do about it, either, because I'm still certified and now I certainly have the time on my hands! You're sharp as a tack, Nell. You know what? I've got private nurse contracts in my filing cabinet from when I used to hire myself out years ago...or they *were* in my filing cabinet, now they're at home in a box. Let me run and go get one right now...once we've put it on paper, nobody can argue with it. We'll need a witness, though..."

At that precise moment, a sour-faced orderly wheeled an unhappy Pearl Parker back into the room. Aunt Pearl daubed at her glossy forehead with a bright pink handkerchief and sighed.

"Lord have mercy, I think this young man bought his driver's license at the K-Mart! He rammed me into the wall so hard my pelvis is fractured! Just look at the bones pokin' out of my privates! Hurry up! I bet I've lost four pints of blood just comin' down the hall! Get me a nurse! I need a doctor! I have a broken pelvis and I'm gonna sue this place for every penny it's got! Oh, Lordy be, the pain! Get me a Demerol I.V. right now, young man, or I'll have your uppity white ass on a platter!"

Amelia motioned for the orderly to stop and winked at Nell. He released Aunt Pearl's wheelchair and rolled his eyes. Amelia waved him from the room and spoke in a low voice.

"Mrs. Parker...I'm Amelia Festrunk, former CEO of this Clinic. Although I recently retired, I do apologize for the terrible way in which you've been treated. Uh, Mrs. Parker...I am a nurse and I would be happy to examine you for injuries. *In fact*, Mrs. Parker...I may have information on your case that you might be keenly interested in receiving...that's why I'm here. You see, I've just informed Mrs. Graham here about a critical oversight in her medical care and she intends to file a very large lawsuit against the Clinic. We're talking *millions*, Mrs. Parker, *millions*. But I don't imagine you wish to be bothered with such trivial matters right now, in light of your impending heart surgery."

Pearl Parker's mouth gaped so wide she could have swallowed a grapefruit whole. "GOOD GOD ALMIGHTY I *TOLD* AVERY…oh, 'scuse me. Yes, ma'am, I would indeed be very interested to hear what you have to say! And I can tell you one thing, right now…no smart-alec whitey doctor's gonna cut on me, no sir! There's nothing wrong with my heart that a little nip of brandy won't take care of…it's all a big Medicare scam, that's what it is! You betcha I'll be bothered, Miss Festrunk! Don't you worry about my heart…I've been having heart attacks every day for nigh on thirty years but believe me, my golden chariot's not ready! Ever since my nephew's wife tried to murder me with the kitchen knife…you know she severed my thumb in three places…ever since then, I see heavenly visions. The Lord warns me about folks, tells me what to do. Shouldn't you examine my pelvis now?"

Amelia shook her head. "No, uh, I can assess from here the fact that your pelvis is probably not broken…however I'm sure that doesn't make it hurt any less. Mrs. Parker, before we talk I must go and get the proper paperwork. It will only take a few minutes and I'll be right back. Can you sit here quietly in your wheelchair and say nothing of this to anybody until I return, in about five minutes? Will you be able to sign the papers, Mrs. Parker? It could be worth *millions* to your future."

Pearl Parker winced dramatically and waved a hand in the air. "Oh, Jesus, be my strength! Yes, Lord, I hear you! Yes, Lord, she may be wrinkled as a prune but I do believe her, Lord, Lord…oh my…oh my…*OHHHH!* Ok, Miss Festrunk…the Lord's performed another miracle on me…He's taken my pain away so I can sign those papers…but He's only givin' me fifteen minutes, so you'd better get the lead out. Oh, and Miss Festrunk? The Lord sure would appreciate it if you'd bring me back a big jelly doughnut…He's not at all happy about the quality of this hospital food. And while you're at it, honey, bring one for Nell, too, ok? She's about the skinniest whitey I've ever seen!"

CHAPTER EIGHTEEN – OUT OF THE BAG

Monday, August 23, 1999; Henry Bailey Used Car Lot

Henry Bailey ran an ice cube around his sweaty neck and looked out his Sales Office window, the one that doubled as the window over the kitchen table of the RV he shared with Euladean. He'd just endured a particularly exasperating telephone conversation with Amelia Festrunk, who was for some unknown reason in an extremely surly mood. All he'd wanted to do was ask her if she'd consider a Cadillac he'd located at the auto auction, but instead he'd been forced to listen to a lecture on how young people these days had no respect of the elderly and how they thought nothing of canceling plans at the last minute. Something to do with some gal from Virginia coming to visit her, as far as Henry could tell from Miss Amelia's angered screeches.

Henry sighed with the dread of a man who would in a matter of minutes be forced to enter the sweltering late August heat and open his car lot for business. Then he brightened as he remembered there was yet another critical phone call to make, thus one more reason to stay inside the air-conditioned RV. He'd been so busy in the last ten days playing step-and-fetch-it for holed-up Hoot Graham there'd been no time for his own agenda. He dialed happily and bounced his head in time to some silent rhythm.

"355-6729...Yes ma'am, may I speak ta Penni Poe, please? Thank ya...Bum-dee-dum-dum-dee-ba-ba-doo...*hey, Penni*! It's Henry Bailey, how're ya doin' today? Yes ma'am, ya got *that* right, it's hot as blazes out there...look, Penni...ya gotta minute? There's sompin' I need ta ask ya...look here, this ain't none a my bizness...but ya know how much I love that gal Euladean, an', well, ya'll are *fam'ly*, so here goes. I been noticin' Corny's actin' a might *strange* lately...*ya know what I'm talkin' 'bout*? I mean, he's been totin' 'round that brown paper sack a his sompin' fierce...what's *in* that sack, Penni? I see...ya cain't tell me...well, lemme tell *you*, hon, whatever's in there, I reckon it's 'bout ready ta meet its Maker, 'cause it stinks ta high heaven! I mean, t'other day, Corny sailed past me over ta the courthouse, *I was workin' a big fleet deal with the city ya know*...anyhow, we gotta whiffa that brown paper sack, an' I'm tellin' ya, they just 'bout had to inspecticide that whole buildin'! Look...the reason I'm callin'...*are you ok, Penni*? Do ya need ta talk ta somebody, 'cause me an' Euladean's always 'vailable for ya, ya know that, don't ya? Uh huh....I see...ya want me ta try an' talk ta Corny fer ya? Look here...I got me an idea...why don't I jus' *steal* that paper sack, an' then it won't give ya no more trouble! Don't ya think that's a good idea? So whyn't ya jus' tell me where Corny keeps that durn thing, an' I'll snatch it when he ain't lookin'...ya know, I done my time in the Army, an' I had *me* somma that *reconcile trainin'*, ya know...I'd be in an' outta there so fast, Corny'd never suspect nothin'....oh...well, ok, Penni, I guess ya know best...no, no, I promise. Yep, I swear, I swear I won't say nothin' 'bout this ta nobody...it's our fam'ly secret. Ok, hon, you take care, now, *bye*."

Henry Bailey slammed the receiver down on the phone. *I gotta git my hands on that durn Sweet Jesus Sweet Potata. I gotta git it so Hoot can take a pitcher of it...I mean, if this ain't the finest oppatun'ty ta git Corny Poe, I reckon I don't know what is...alla them years he's done laughed at me an' poked fun at me an' alla us Baileys...tellin' me I ain't goin' ta Heaven, 'cause I'm a Pope-lovin' Cath'lic...sayin' he'll be laughin' at me from the other side a the fence! I'll show you, Corny Poe...I got the VM and the JC on my side, ol' buddy...*Henry looked at the clock. It was ten forty-five and the Henry Bailey Used Car Lot was scheduled to open for business at eleven, but he was still wearing his tattered green bathrobe and boxer shorts. He opened the fridge, took a swig from a carton of orange juice, then sauntered into the RV's tiny bathroom.

He shed his clothes, turned on the shower and stared at himself in the mirror while he waited for the water to warm. As he showered Henry performed his usual Las Vegas act, which consisted of two Elvis tunes and the crowd-pleasing big finish wherein he dried himself and snapped wet towels in the air to "*God Bless America*." He wiped condensation from the mirror, then combed the meager strands of red hair that clung desperately to his scalp. He made two fists and shadow-boxed his reflection.

"*Hey, Killer*! You are one happenin' guy, Mister Best Boy! Mister Used Car Salesman a the Month! Mister Chairman a the Parade Vee-hicles committee! Yeah, I gotta figger outta way ta git my hands on that sweet potata...I had me a prime oppertun'ty that day I was tellin' Corny 'bout my Bathroom Angel but I screwed up...an'...*HEY! KILLER! BATHROOM ANGEL! THAT'S IT!*"

Henry danced a little jig and waved his comb in the air. "Oh, Bathroom Angel...Bathroom Angel, where are you *at*?"

Henry looked around the bathroom in anticipation of a Heavenly Sign. Then he grabbed a damp bath towel, draped it over his shoulders regally and said to the mirror in a high-pitched falsetto voice, *"Why, here I am, Henry Bailey, an' don't ya cut a fine figger of a man! If I wasn't an angel I reckon I'd git me some a that! What can I do fer ya today?"*

Henry cleared his throat and spoke in his non-nonsense Used Car Sales Manager voice, "Well, *hi, there,* Miss Bathroom Angel! Where ya been keepin' yersef? We been clean outta sightin's 'round here lately an' I got some 'portant bizness ta take care of! I gotta git my hands on that Sweet Jesus Sweet Potata! Ya got any ideas?"

Henry placed an angelic hand to his face and looked soulfully to the heavens. Then he adjusted his bath towel angel wings and said, *"A course I got me some ideas, they're payin' me ta be the Bathroom Angel, ain't they? You think bein' the Bathroom Angel's a buncha jus' sittin' 'round, playin' cards an' eatin' chips? Hell, no! I gotta work ta keep this here towel an' these here wings!"*

Henry bowed his head and pouted into the mirror. "Look here, I'm real sorry, Bathroom Angel. Please don't smite me er nothin'. But how'm I gonna git that potata? I need yer help!"

The Bathroom Angel spread its damp wings and flew around the toilet, then slipped on a wet spot but amazingly regained control of its flight pattern without serious injury. It returned to the mirror and made a pronouncement.

"Henry Bailey, you listen up real good, 'cause I'm only gonna say this once't. Hey...you payin' 'tention ta me? I'm fixin' ta make me a decaration...ok, here goes...this here's the words a the Main Man."

The Bathroom Angel pointed sheepishly up to the sky and continued, but in a deeper voice that clearly resembled Henry Bailey's Deal of the Century tone. "THIS HERE'S HENRY BAILEY, WITH HIM I'M PRETTY DURN PLEASED. HE GOT HISSELF A NICE HOME, BIZNESS IS PICKIN' UP AN' HE TREATS HIS WIFE REAL SPECIAL-LIKE. *HENRY BAILEY.* YOU TELL THAT HOLY ROLLER GOOFBALL CORNY POE THAT I GOT ME A SPECIAL PLAN FER THAT SWEET POTATA. TELL HIM IT'S DONE ROTTED CLEAN THEW AN' IT'S TIME FER STEP TWO. *HENRY BAILEY.* YOU TELL THAT CORNY POE THAT I SAID TA GIVE YA THAT SWEET POTATA RIGHT NOW AN' I'LL SEND HIM A SIGN NEXT WEEK, 'LONG 'BOUT FOUR P.M. IN THE AFTERNOON."

Henry Bailey dropped to his knees in solemn reverence, but as he did he hit his head on the bathroom sink. He rubbed his temple and prayed, "Oh, Lord an' Bathroom Angel we thank ya fer this here insp'ration an' we thank ya fer this day an' we'd be right thankful even more if ya was ta send us a coupl'a suckers...*customers*...lookin' fer a good, clean, depend'ble used car. AMEN!"

Henry stood up, crossed himself, and admired his physique in the mirror as he removed his soggy wings and giggled with glee. "Killer, yer as sharp as the keys on yer Memaw's pianna! How can Corny argue with the Bathroom Angel? That's just it! He *cain't*! Hee hee...."

Henry dressed, hung the OPEN sign on the front door of the RV and sat down in his Sales Office with the latest issue of *Hot Car* magazine to wait for the coup'la customers he felt sure the Lord would send his way. It was just too hot to sit in his usual Sales Manager perch on the RV's redwood deck. His phone rang twice, but one call was a wrong number and the other was Hoot, still staked out at Fay Bailey's, laying low and waiting for the right time to make his reappearance and rescue the Festival play. Henry looked outside his Sales Office window; Main Street was dead. The sweltering August heat wreaked havoc with the used car business and the business of Chestnut Ridge in general.

At eleven thirty Henry realized it was time for lunch. He turned the OPEN sign over to read CLOSED, then he dialed the Poe House Grocery and asked for Corny. He told Corny in a trembling whisper that he'd had another visit from *You Know Who* and that he had a special, personal message to deliver. They agreed to meet at eleven forty-five at the receiving dock of the Poe House. Henry hung up the phone, stripped off his Camaro tie and whistled as he locked the RV. After walking the first block in the hundred-degree heat, Henry wished he'd driven the Mustang, but he continued on with four blocks to go and mopped sweat with an old red rag as it dripped from his saturated brow. His white short-sleeved shirt stuck to his back and arms, so he unbuttoned it down to his navel to catch what little breeze there was. His pace picked up as he rounded the last corner and entered the Poe House and after waving hello to everyone, he walked directly over to the Frozen Food section, opened a cooler door and stepped closer to the cold air as it stung his skin. He was getting nice and cool when Euladean swooped up behind him and swatted him on the behind.

"HENRY! What'd I tell you 'bout stickin' your head in them coolers! It's bad for business! And just look at you! You look like common white trash...button that shirt! Wipe off your face! Pull up your pants! You're gonna embarrass me half to death!"

Henry did as he was told and smiled at his wife, then gave her a peck on the cheek. "Hey, sugar plum! It's hot as Hades outside, an' I'm watchin' our budget, ya know, like ya done tol' me, so I hoofed it over here ta save gas...ain't ya proud a me?"

Euladean patted Henry's shoulder and nodded. "Yes, Henry, I am. Corny says you all gotta meetin'...what's that meetin' *about*, Henry? You gonna wise up an' take that Produce Manager's job? Corny's in the back, by the dock."

Henry gave his wife a stern look. "Well, now, I reckon that's between me an' Corny, don't you? I better git back there, don't wanna keep the man waitin' too long. See ya, hon."

Euladean lovingly tweaked her husband's bright red ear as he strode off to meet with her brother. *Somethin's not right...Corny hates Henry's guts...he's only offerin' that job to Henry on my account...and Henry'll never take it. What on God's green earth are they up to?* She wanted to sneak back to the receiving area and eavesdrop, but the canned music that played over the loudspeaker suddenly stopped and her father's voice shouted,

"CLEAN UP ON AISLE SEVEN...EULADEAN...QUIT YAMMERIN' AN' GIT OVER THERE! AND GIT YOU A MOP!"

Henry found Corny in the receiving office at the back of the store; the tiny room smelled of ripe fruit and was crammed full of broken chairs stacked with papers, boxes, plastic milk crates, old ledgers and approximately thirty jumbo packages of toilet paper. Henry raised a hand in greeting as he watched Corny tape a note to one of the toilet paper packages. He saw the Sweet Jesus Sweet Potato sack tucked into the pocket of Corny's grocer's apron; the odor emanating from Corny was terrible, and it was all Henry could do to keep from gagging.

"Hey, Corny! What's with alla them toilet paper rolls? Ya plannin' ta wrap Brother Culpepper's house this weekend, heh heh?"

Corny raised his head and looked at his brother-in-law, and that brother-in-law took a step back and steadied himself on the doorframe. Henry could not believe what he saw. Corny Poe sported huge blackish-purple circles under each eye. His face was hollow and jaundiced and what little hair remained on his head stood straight up in the air. His shirt and produce apron looked as though they hadn't been washed in weeks and something resembling crankcase grease was caked under each of his fingernails. It was obvious to Henry, despite his complete lack of medical training, that this was a man on the verge of insanity. Corny stared at Henry for a second, then slowly stepped over some boxes and put a hand on the toilet paper packages. He said in a low, serious voice,

"No, I ain't gonna wrap no houses, Henry. This toilet paper's *sacred*...it was on special the day I found the Sweet Jesus Sweet Potato and these here packages were all stacked up in the produce section, you know, merchandising. 'Course, I moved 'em right away, after gettin' the Sign...I figured the Lord might need a roll or two, if he feels like sendin' me another message. But Penni keeps puttin' 'em out on the shelf, so I had to round 'em all up again this mornin' and now I'm puttin' a note on here tellin' everybody to keep their unclean hands offa the Lord's holy *scrolls*!"

Henry Bailey smiled faintly at Corny. He rubbed his chin and nodded. "Well, that sure is a good idea, I reckon...never know when the Lord might need him some *tee pee*...look here, we need ta talk, Corny, an' I ain't got all day, ya know, I'm workin' me another big fleet deal, so we'd best git to it...hey, uh, Corny...ya know, I's in such a hurry ta git over here an' d'liver yer message from the Bathroom Angel, I plumb forgot my lunch an' my wallet. Ya reckon you could jus' grab us one a them pizzas from the deli? What I got ta tell ya, you ain't gonna wanna hear onna empty stomach!"

Corny looked aimlessly around the receiving office and muttered, "Sure…sure…I'll be right back. Go get yourself a cold drink from the cooler, make yourself at home."

Corny patted his pocket, which caused a cloud of Sweet Jesus Sweet Potato stench to waft about the room, then he left the office in a daze. Henry grabbed a soda from the cooler in the warehouse marked "EMPLOYEES ONLY." He gulped it down in three swigs, then threw away the can and helped himself to another, and he grabbed one for Corny.

Corny returned with a large veggie pizza, hot from the Poe House Grocery Deli, some paper plates, and a fistful of paper napkins. He led Henry to the edge of the receiving dock, much to Henry's chagrin, because despite the shade, the heat simmered all around them. Corny sat down on the edge of the dock and hung his legs over the side. Henry did the same.

As Corny said a rather lengthy blessing, Henry helped himself to three large wedges of veggie pizza, before Corny could put his filthy hands on it. They ate in silence and Henry noticed that his brother-in-law didn't seem to be too interested in his lunch; he just stared ahead into the parking lot. When he did move, it was in slow motion. As Henry reached for a fourth slice of pizza, Corny set down his plate.

"Well, Henry. You said you had somethin' to tell me…well, out with it."

Henry swallowed a huge bite of pizza and wiped his mouth with the back of one hand. He swigged from his soda can. Corny grimaced in disgust.

"You know, gluttony is a *sin.* What is it, Henry? It's about that no-good sumbitch Culpepper bein' the Narrator, ain't it? Are you playin' with me, Henry? Come on, spit it out!"

Henry looked around to make sure they were alone and he said in a somber, low tone, "Corny, this mornin' I was mindin' my own bizness, gittin' ready ta open the Lot an' who do I hear messin' around in the powder room but the Bathroom Angel hersef! 'Course I done fell right ta my knees…them angels 'spect ya ta prostate yersef, ya know. Anyways, that bathroom done filled up with light an' the Bathroom Angel started flappin' her wings real hard, she pert near knocked that new towel rack offa the wall, an' then I done heard this loud voice, louder than the track at the Dixie Five Hunnerd! *'Henry Bailey,'* it said, *'you take this here message ta Cornelius Poe, or I'll smite ya with my own two hundred trillion hands!'* An' then it gave me the message an' then alla the faucets turned on by themselves an' the commode started flushin' over an' over an' over an' the mirror fogged up. An' when I stood up an' wiped off the mirror, the Bathroom Angel's starin' back at me, smilin' an' she tells me not ta screw up, 'cause she says you an' me's the denigrated drivers a this here Lord's Plan!"

Corny swallowed hard and wiped his brow, leaving a pizza sauce trail on his forehead. He desperately wanted to hear his special message from God, but he had a hard time dealing with the fact that the Lord had chosen Henry Bailey, a no-good, white-trash, Pope-lovin' loser, when he, Cornelius Poe, was the very picture of an upstanding and righteous man and almost a Senior Elder at the First United Assembly of God's Children.

Corny motioned for Henry to hurry up. "So what is it, Henry? What's the message? Does God want me to unveil the Sweet Jesus Sweet Potato and take over the pulpit this Sunday, get rid of that scheming, no-good liberal Brother Culpepper? Is that why He gave me the Sweet Jesus Sweet Potato, is it the very Instrument of the Lord?"

Henry shook his head and folded his hands. He pressed his two pointer fingers together and aimed them at Corny's chest. "*Nope*! You ready? I'm gonna give you this here message fer-baitin'...so don't stop me mid-stream...ok, here goes..."

Henry raised his hands in the air and shook them a few times for effect. Then he closed his eyes, leaned his head back and delivered the Bathroom Angel's message in a monotone voice, nearly word for word. When he was finished, he blinked his eyes open and rubbed his temples as if delivering the message had physically drained him. He reached for his soda can and winked at Corny, whose mouth hung wide.

"Henry! *I don't believe it! That can't be right*! The Lord *gave* me the Sweet Jesus Sweet Potato! Why would he want to *take* it from me? Now, in the hour of my need?"

Henry shook his head. "'Member what the Good Book says... *'I done brought ya inta this world, an' I can take ya right out, too,'* or maybe that was that Bill Crosby fella...anyways, look, Corny, I don't write this stuff, I'm jus' the deliv'ry man. Now...you'd best be handin' over that Sweet Jesus Sweet Potata...like I said, I got me that big fleet deal workin' this afternoon an' I don't feel like gittin' smited by the Lord in fronta alla my customers!"

Corny looked as if he would cry; he was the very picture of bewilderment. He could not believe God wanted him to relinquish his precious Sweet Jesus Sweet Potato to a heathen idolator like Henry Bailey. He stared at his feet as they hung over the edge of the dock.

But who am I to question God's plan, he wondered. *Look at what Noah had to do...it took him thirty years to build the Ark...and Moses, he didn't wanna go find the Holy Land, he liked Egypt just fine...and he told the Lord He was crazy and the Lord nearly burnt him to a crisp...and Abraham...at least God's not makin' me take my kids off some place...Penni'd have a fit.*

Corny realized he had no choice if he wanted to remain on God's good side; he reached down into his grocer's apron and gingerly removed the stained brown paper sack that contained the Sweet Jesus Sweet Potato. He carefully unrolled the folded bag and stuck his face down into the top for a goodbye gaze. An overwhelmingly rotten odor wafted out of the bag and over Henry and he nearly gagged.

"*Hey, Corny*! Close that thing up, will ya? My nose ain't used ta alla them holy 'romas like yers is…yer gonna make me puke up alla that pizza! C'mon, hurry up, now…I gotta git!"

Corny folded the bag closed, caressed it with a loving hand and reluctantly handed it to Henry, who took it in his arms like a baby and bowed his head.

"Oh Lord an' Bathroom Angel…we thank ya fer this here message ya done sent us…an' Lord, please bless my brother Corny…help him ta know in his heart that he done right…an' please, Lord, help him ta git hissef cleaned up real good…since he ain't the custodial a this potata no more, it's ok fer him ta shower off real good, *with soap*, an' scrub them fingernails an' such. We're waitin' fer yer next move, Sir, *oh,* an' if ya need any scroll-writin' paper, jus' look in Corny's office. AMEN."

Henry carefully stood up with the paper sack and saluted Corny. "Well…that's that, I reckon. Don't you worry, I'll take good care of 'er, an' soon's the Main Man tells me the next step, I'll holler at ya."

Corny nodded as giant tears rolled down his face. Henry turned to leave, then he remembered something. "Uh, Corny…you know, I ain't said nothin' 'bout this ta nobody…an' I guess you won't neither? Like, if you was ta tell Penni er yer daddy, er Euladean…we might both be smited inta statues right where we's standin.' Ok, pard? Is that a big ten-four?"

Corny nodded again. "Don't worry, Henry. Penni's barely speaking to me these days; she's making me sleep out in the shed. Daddy and Euladean have been too busy runnin' the store to notice, so there's nothin' for you to worry about. You know, Henry…I feel pretty good right now…I mean, it's kinda nice not havin' to worry about the Sweet Jesus Sweet Potato for awhile...maybe I can get some sleep… eat a good meal…can I come visit it, Henry?"

"Well…the Lord didn't say nothin' 'bout visualization…let's us jus' wait fer the next move, ok? Yeah, you go git some sleep…and take you a *shower or two*, pard! Yep! Don't that Lord jus' beat all! See ya later, Corny!"

Henry walked down the steps of the receiving dock and out into the blazing afternoon. *I need ta git me a good gander at this veg'table, ta see if there's anythin' left ta photagraph,* he thought to himself, *but if I open that bag, I'm gonna git swarmed with flies, an' I'll prob'ly git arrested fer carryin' a health hazardous in public!* He glanced across Main Street and noticed that the Jebediah Horatio Graham Memorial Park was deserted. Henry crossed against traffic, then found a patch of shade at a picnic table under one of the park's large oak trees. He inhaled deeply and held his breath so as not to offend his nose with the odor of the sweet potato. He opened the bag and dumped the potato out onto the picnic table, where it lazily rolled to a moldy stop.

"Whew, doggies! Woodja look at that!"

The Sweet Jesus Sweet Potato was definitely past its prime as a religious relic; it had shrunk considerably and was now only about five inches long. On one end, a bulging, furry, black mold patch sprouted spores; there were at least a dozen yellow, craggly eyes growing out from all sides and smack dab in the middle, where previously Corny had claimed to see the face of Jesus, there now rested a puddle of green, oozing goo. Henry backed away from the picnic table for some fresh air and whistled through his teeth.

"Man, oh man...this is gonna make one helluva photo shoot...I can see it now...Hoot an' his Best Boy'll git us a close-up a this here nasty thang...prob'ly haveta use some kinda boom lens, I reckon...an' then, we'll blow that sucker up ta 'bout twenty feet high, an' plaster it in the parkin' lotta the Poe House Grocery! An' then I'll git me a banner, it'll say, 'ON SALE TODAY...FRESH FROM HEAVEN...SWEET JESUS SWEET POTATAS...HURRY WHILE THEY LAST! SEE CORNY FER DETAILS'"

Henry clapped his hands with glee. "Oh, man, oh man, I cain't wait ta see Corny Poe's face, an' the face a his damned daddy! I jus' hope Euladean don't take it too person'l...seein' as how we's still newlyweds."

Henry looked at his watch. He was supposed to meet Hoot at Fay's house in twenty minutes so they could determine a clandestine location for the sweet potato photo shoot, and they had to be careful. When Hoot stormed out of play practice and fictitiously returned to L.A., Festival play preparations came to a screeching halt; disappointed actors who spied Hoot running the streets of Chestnut Ridge just might do something drastic, Hoot'd told Henry. *Gotta lay low, make 'em miserable, make 'em die to get Mister Director back in action, save the day...*

Henry was itching to get back to Best Boy training; he'd just gotten his feet wet and *wham,* Hoot goes into hiding and sends everything into a tailspin. And in Henry's opinion, Hoot was way too comfortable over at Fay's. She cooked for him, did his laundry, and no doubt gave out free samples of her womanly charms. Hoot'd never focus on the play, and there would go Henry's chances at becoming the best durned Best Boy ever.

Henry rubbed his sweaty neck and realized he had to get the Sweet Jesus Sweet Potato back into its carrying case. The challenge, he noticed, was how to put it back in the bag without exactly touching it...*I ain't touchin' that nasty thang...I ain't gonna me no get busonic plague, er no elephantitis C...*He noticed a large stick on the ground beside the picnic table. He spoke out loud, *"Killer...you are one smart son-of-a-gun! I'll jus' push that potata with a stick, right offa the enda the table an' plop it back in that sack!"*

And that is precisely what Henry tried to do; the sacred religious relic, however, possessed a mind of its own. Henry gave it a light push with one end of the stick and it rolled a half-turn in the direction of the sack. After about ten more pushes, Henry succeeded in moving the potato approximately three inches from the edge of the table. *One more good shove is all she needs,* he muttered to himself. *Yep, here goes...here goes...sweet potata...come to papa...come to papa...OH SHIT!*

Henry eyed the ground in sorrow. The Sweet Jesus Sweet Potato, in all its apostolic glory and free will, changed directions and landed in the dirt with a stinking plop. It then bounced onto Henry's work shoes, where it deposited its final remains in a small explosion. Gooey, black gunk clung to Henry's shoes. The air stank like sulfur and dead animals and Henry gagged and coughed. He faced a heavenly dilemma. There was no way he wanted to touch the putrid refuse, but he had to wash himself of the stench immediately.

"*DAMMIT*! There goes my pract'cal joke! I shoulda never opened that durned bag! Killer, you have done screwed up agin! *Man,* that stuff stinks ta high heaven!"

Henry scanned the park...there were no water fountains. Then he noticed the new Quigley EZ-Care Car Wash across the street. He reached into his pants pocket; four quarters and a nickel...surely he could get a couple of good pulls on the hose with that. Henry stepped stickily across traffic and slipped into one of the corrugated metal bays at the EZ-Care Car Wash. He inserted two quarters into the slot, pressed a button and aimed the spray gun at his feet.

"*YEEOWW!*" The water gushed out with intense force and stung Henry's skin. He took turns washing first the left foot and leg, then the right, holding it there as long as he could stand it. After about five minutes, the stream of water dripped to a trickle; Henry's time was up. He looked down at his shoes. The black goo stuck fast where it had landed, but at least now it smelled more like Super Raspberry Foam and less like sulfur.

Henry decided to return home and change; there was nothing he hated more than taking two showers in one day and his shoes were completely ruined. He hung the hose into its holder, but turned as he heard a woman call his name.

"*HENRY! YOO HOO! HENRY BAILEY!*"

It was Ruby Quigley and her dog, Miss Shu-Shu. Ruby wore a lime green pantsuit with what appeared to be shards of broken glass glued all over the front. Her matching lime green shoes sparkled as she walked and Henry noticed Miss Shu-Shu's collar matched Ruby's shoes exactly. He didn't know what to do; he waved and smiled sheepishly.

"Hey, Miss Ruby! How're you doin' today?"

"Well, I'm just fine, Henry, I'm just fine, an'…HENRY! Where's yer *car*? Why are ya standin' in the middle a the Quigley EZ-Care Car Wash without a *car*? An' you're all *wet*! Oh, honey, did Euladean drive off an' leave ya here? Did ya'll have a newlywed's spat or somethin'? OH MY GOD…Henry…what on earth is all over yer feet? An' what is that *bodacious smell*?"

Henry laughed skittishly. "No, Miss Ruby, me an' the missus is doin' jus' fine. See here, uh…well, I was jus' walkin' 'long Main Street, mindin' my own bizness, ya know, on my way to a sales meetin'…*I'm closin' another one a my big fleet deals, ya know*…anyways, these here fellas in a ol' beat-up tank done tossed sompin' at me an' took off laughin'! An' whatever it was, it don' hit me an' 'sploded sompin fierce! An' it stinks ta high heaven…'course, I reckon ya already know that…an' I cain't git this stuff offa my self!"

Ruby Quigley picked up Miss Shu-Shu and absent-mindedly stroked the dog's face. "Lordy-be, ain't nobody *safe* any more? Henry, ya come on with me, over ta the Quik-Steak. We got some grease remover over there that'll work wonders…listen up, though…I'm drivin' the truck today…whyn't ya ride in the *back*…Miss Shu-Shu ain't feelin' too good these days…I don't want her ta get sick from them fumes comin' off yer shoes!"

Henry climbed into the back of the pickup; the ride gave him a chance to devise his alternate plan for Corny's humiliation. Ruby pulled up to the service entrance of the Quigley Quik-Steak and made Henry wait outside with the dog while she went in to locate the grease remover. Surprisingly, only half of the bottle was needed to remove the last traces of the Sweet Jesus Sweet Potato from its final resting place on Henry's shoes. Henry offered to pay Ruby for her trouble, but she wouldn't hear of it. She had other plans.

"Lordy-be, Henry, if I cain't help a fella citizen in distress! But listen up…ya know I'm in charge a sellin' these Official Festival Business Sponsorship Signs, right? Well, I gotta tell ya…they ain't movin' as fast as I'd like. Now, me an' Roy, we got 'em in every winda of our shops…there's four at the Quigley Realty office, six right here at the Quik-Steak, we even have some at the Funeral Parlor…an' lucky for you I was fixin' ta put some over at the car wash…"

Henry laughed. *"Heh…heh…lucky fer me!"*

"So, Henry. Lemme show ya these here signs…see, yers could say, *'Official Used Car Lot of the Sons of Glory Festival'* What do ya think about that? Ain't that a pretty shade a red? An' fer the low, low price a six hunnerd dollars, you can lock in that Used Car Lot slot…ya know, we're only sellin' one sign per business category!"

Henry choked and coughed. "*Six hunnerd dollars*? Ruby…that's more than I make in a *month*! I cain't afford no six hunnerd dollars fer no sign…an' hey…I oughta git me a discount…I already got the only Used Car Lot in town, so don't that make me o-fishul without buyin' one a them signs?"

Ruby pursed her lips and frowned. This was precisely the argument she had faced all over town, from every business owner. "Henry, everybody local knows that! But alla them tourists that's gonna come into town don't know it! You gotta *advertise*…you gotta impress 'em! I tell you what…I'll come offa that price…how 'bout three hunnerd?"

Henry shook his head. "Look here, Ruby…I think it's great, what yer tryin' ta do…but ain't no tourist gonna be in the market fer no used car when he's here fer the Festival! He's gonna be winin' an' dinin' an' carryin' on! That'd be a waste a my good, hard-earned money! Besides, Euladean'll skin me 'live if I spend another nickel this month."

Ruby raised an eyebrow. "Henry Bailey…this Festival's gonna 'tract national 'tention. There's gonna be folks here from ever'where. The odds are in yer favor…somebody's car's gonna crap out an' Lord knows we ain't got a decent mechanic in this town. This may be the golden opportunity a yer car-sellin' life! How 'bout two hunnerd an' ya can pay me *next* month?"

Henry took a deep breath and stared off into space. Horse-trading was his chosen occupation; there was no one better at it than he. "One hunnerd, an' I'll do ya some cross-marketin'…I'll tell ever' one a my customers from now 'til the Festival that the best durned food in town is over ta the Quik-Steak…an' like ya said, I don't have ta pay 'til next month…deal?"

Ruby extended her hand. She knew cross-marketing was very trendy, and very lucrative. "*Deal*! Now, you need me ta take ya someplace, Henry? I gotta git over ta Gooch Office Supply an' see if I can unload a sign over there. I tell you what, I been tryin' ta git that Betty Gooch on the telephone every day for three weeks! That line a hers is always busy! An' then I gotta take Miss Shu-Shu to the vet…we got us a brand-new glass dinin' room table, an' honey, yesterday, Roy set down Miss Shu-Shu's doggie biscuit on toppa that glass, 'cause the phone rang. Lordy-be, Miss Shu-Shu got under there an' jumped up ta get that biscuit an' gave herself a *concussion* when she hit that the underside a that glass tabletop!"

Henry gave Miss Shu-Shu his best Used Car Sales Manager look of extreme empathy; *what a stupid dog*, he thought. "Hey, no thanks, Ruby, I'm gonna re-group here an' go see Euladean at the groc'ry. Thank ya agin, I'll be waitin' fer ya ta bring me that sign! Hey, Ruby…could I use yer phone?"

Ruby directed Henry to the small manager's office at the back of the Quigley Quik-Steak. Henry thanked her again and as she darted out to scream at the cook, Henry dialed Fay's house, let it ring three times, then hung up and dialed again. It was his secret code for Hoot.

"*H.!* It's me, Best Boy! Listen, I'm workin' me a fleet deal from a remote location...yeah...so I ain't sure when I can make it over there...I'll holler at ya later, gotta go, *bye.*"

Henry flipped through the phone book on the Quik-Steak manager's desk and then dialed the number for the Sweet Things Bakery. "*Hey, there,* Miss Juliette! This here's Henry Bailey...yes, ma'am, we's both doin' fine! Uh, I got me a special request...can you bake me a sweet potata pie? *Yer kiddin'*...they's on *special*? Well, I'll be durn! Put me down fer one...I'll be there ta pick it up, say, in 'bout an hour...but listen...can you take a piece a paper, an' put my name on it an' stick it on toppa that pie an' put it in yer front winda? An' hey, Miss Juliette, it's real important you don't say nothin' 'bout me askin' ya ta put my name on that pie ta nobody, ok? I'll explain later...ok, great. See ya, *bye*!"

Once again, Henry found himself walking in the torrid heat toward the Poe House. He whistled at his good fortune...what were the odds that sweet potato pies would be the featured Pie of the Week at the bakery? He had to find Corny and deliver God's latest message before he requested visitation with the now-vaporized Sweet Jesus Sweet Potato. He slipped behind the Poe House and dashed into the receiving office where Corny sat on a box, his head in his hands.

"Corny! Am I glad ta see ya! I done had me 'nother hit from the Bathroom Angel, soon's I left here!"

Corny's eyes opened wide and searched Henry's person for the brown paper sack. "Where's the SJSP? How come you're all wet? Ugh...what's that smell? *Henry, where's the SJSP*?"

"The whu...*oh*...here, Corny, sit down...you ain't gonna b'lieve this..."

In a breathless voice, Henry told Corny how the Bathroom Angel had descended upon him in broad daylight, right in the middle of the Jebediah Horatio Graham Memorial Park, while he rested peacefully in the shade and prayed for guidance with his big fleet deal. *She just hung over the picnic table, suspected in mid-air, Corny...an' she snatched up that brown paper sack right outta my hand! 'Course, I prostated myself agin, but she tol' me ta git offa the ground an' git mysef over ta the Bak'ry, that there was gonna be a sweet potata pie with my name on it in the winda an' that you an' me was ta git over there at two o'clock an' git it. Then she done tol' me that we's ta take that there pie an' don't wrap it up or nothin', but stick it in yer Frozen Foods cooler at the Poe House, with a sign on it sayin' 'SWEET JESUS SWEET POTATA PIE...PROSTATE YERSEF AN' PRAY, 'CAUSE THE END IS A COMIN.' An', oh, yeah, she said we'd still be gittin' a message from the Head Dude in a coup'la days...*

Corny's eyes filled with tears. Henry's Bathroom Angel stole his Sweet Jesus Sweet Potato, as if a stupid pie could take its place. "Aww, Henry, this just sounds like a bunch a bull! How come I ain't seen no Bathroom Angel? I go to church two times a week and I'm fixin' to be a Senior Elder! It ain't fair, I tell ya, it ain't fair! I can't put no unwrapped pie in my cooler! The Health Inspector'll close me down! It'll drive away all my customers! An' how come you're all wet?"

Henry put his hands on his hips. "Ok, hey, fine, Mister Non-B'liever! I'm all wet 'cause that Bathroom Angel tol' me I stunk sompin' terr'ble from carryin' that potata 'roun' all afternoon! An' she done called up the Holy Hosepipe an' sprayed me off good! But hey, Corny, if you ain't gonna b'lieve me...I ain't yer judge an' fury!"

He looked at his watch; it was one-forty five. "Well, I'm headin' over ta the bak'ry! Ya comin' er not? I reckon it's been nice knowin' ya...hope it don't hurt too bad ta git smited!"

Corny wrung his hands. He had to go to the Sweet Things Bakery or he'd never know if Henry's Bathroom Angel was legit. And if it *was* legit and he didn't go, then God probably *would* smite him for his sinful disbelief and he'd never get his name on a Senior Elder plaque. The Lord certainly didn't make it easy on a man.

"Awright, Henry, I'll go. Lemme tell Penni I'm leavin' for a while. You wait here, I'll be right back."

Henry grinned and whistled a tune. As he and Corny walked to the Sweet Things Bakery, Henry relayed to his brother-in-law the finer points of big-volume used car selling he'd read about in the latest issue of *Used Car News.* As they approached the bakery, Henry took a deep breath and crossed his fingers. Juliette Kimball was very absent-minded and he just hoped to goodness she'd put his name on that pie and put the pie in the window. He strained his eyes...there it was, plain as day! Henry smiled and grabbed Corny on one arm.

"LOOK! THERE IT IS!"

Corny Poe's mouth gaped wide. Several people standing in front of the shop next door stopped their conversation and stared at the wet man and his filthy friend pointing at a pie in the bakery window. Corny edged closer to the Sweet Things Bakery window and gently pressed his fingertips to the glass. It was *real!* Henry Bailey was telling the *truth!* He turned around to face Henry, and tears of joy rolled down his ruddy cheeks.

"Oh, Henry! I'm so sorry I doubted you! Oh, Lord, please forgive me! Henry, I've gotta pray right now for mercy..."

Corny dropped to his knees, but Henry grabbed him by the arm. He didn't need any Main Street incidents to interfere with his new plan. He whispered, *"Hey, Corny! We got all day an' night fer prayin'! But we gotta git in there an' git that pie an' put it in yer cooler, like the Bathroom Angel said! C'mon, pull yersef tagether!"*

Corny stood up and wiped his eyes. He followed Henry into the bakery, but immediately they began to cough and choke; the Sweet Things Bakery was filled with grey smoke and smelled of fire. Henry grabbed the soggy handkerchief from his back pocket and put it over his nose and mouth.

"MIZ JULIETTE! IS YOU IN THERE? YA GOTTA FIRE, MISS JULIETTE, AN'..."

Juliette Kimball appeared from the kitchen carrying a small battery-powered hand-held fan. Her curly brown hair was full of flour and her cheeks were black with soot. She aimed the fan at her two customers to clear the air.

"Hey Henry! Hey Corny! Don't worry! It was just a little grease fire...more smoke than flames and it's out now. Gracious, Corny, will you please open the door to get some air in here? What is that godawful odor?"

Henry wasn't sure if Miss Juliette's comment referred to Corny's lack of personal hygiene, or his own SJSP-covered shoes, but he said nothing. "Miz Juliette, ya sure yer ok?"

She laughed and wiped her face with a towel, smearing the black soot on one cheek. "Oh, my, yes, thank you, Henry! I was trying a new recipe for a Millennium Cake...it's *very* involved, you know, and it said to *'thoroughly grease the bottom of the pan.'* Well, I guess I wasn't myself this morning, too much on my mind I suppose and I just slathered shortening all over the bottom of the *outside* of that cake pan! So when I stuck it in the oven at four hundred degrees, well, you can just imagine the *flames*!"

Henry chuckled. He noticed more big tears streaming out of Corny's eyes, but he figured it best not to call it to Miss Juliette's attention, hoping Miss Juliette would put it down to the smoke-filled bakery instead of a recent religious experience. He reached for his wallet.

"Miz J., , I b'lieve you gotta pie in that winda with my name on it! How much I owe ya?"

Juliette looked in the direction of Henry's pie. She raised her hands and shook her head. "Not a thing, Henry Bailey, not a thing. That pie's already been paid for...the most angelic-looking woman I've ever seen came into the bakery bright and early today...she's not from around here... at least, I didn't recognize her...anyway, she bought a doughnut and then she did the strangest thing...she paid me for that pie and told me to give it to a deserving person...she said I'd know him when he called. Isn't that *odd*?"

Henry nearly swallowed his tongue. The hairs on the back of his neck stood to attention. This was not part of his secret agreement with Miz Juliette, but you never could tell, maybe she was just playing around; maybe she thought she'd lend an extra element to Henry's surprise. He returned his wallet to his back pocket and looked at his sweet potato comrade, who was now crying uncontrollably. Henry scratched his ear; whoever paid for his pie, it sure had convinced Corny. He shook his head and accepted the boxed pie Miss Juliette offered to him.

"Well, Miss J., I sure do thank ya! That sure is a strange story ya done tol.' Ya say ya ain't never seen this gal afore?"

"Whuh..whuh...what did she look like?" Corny mumbled through his sobs.

"*Henry, is he ok?*" Miss Juliette stared at the bawling Corny in confusion. Henry sidled up to the counter, closer to Juliette.

"Yep, he's ok, he just gotta big whiffa that smoke in his lungs an' he's 'lergic, ya know. He'll be awright in a minute, I reckon. So, Miss J., what *did* that gal look like, anyhow?"

Miss Juliette's eyes widened, and she ran a flour-dusted hand through her hair. She pointed at Henry. "Say, Henry, before I forget, since you're the chairman for the Festival Vehicle committee, well, Doc's trying to do right by local merchants, and he's looking for a weekend car, you know, maybe a nice convertible with leather seats. But he wants top grain leather...do you have anything on your lot that might be top grain?"

Henry put a thumb in the waistband of his pants, and rared back in Used Car Sales Manager concentration. "Hmmm...well now, prob'ly what I got ain't *the* top, but I got plenny a stuff *near* the top...uh, Miss J., you was 'bout ta tell me 'bout that gal that done paid fer this here pie..."

"Oh, she was very, very tall, with broad shoulders, and she had the most beautiful skin I've ever seen...long blonde hair and deep blue eyes...and she had on a white gauzy dress, it came down clear to her ankles, almost and sandals. I didn't see her get in or out of a car, I guess she just walked over...must have been at the courthouse on jury duty, or something. Well, boys, I've got to get back to my baking! You enjoy that pie now, you hear? *Those are farm-fresh sweet potatoes!*"

Henry's stomach flip-flopped as Juliette left the front of the bakery. The Mysterious Pie-Paying Angel was too close to Henry's tall tales for comfort. He needed some fresh air.

"C'mon Corny, let's *go*!"

They walked quickly back to the Poe House, oblivious to the heat. Corny chanted prayers under his breath. Henry silently wondered whether it was really a good idea to play a joke on Corny after all; he wasn't much on religion, but he did believe in God. Was the Head Dude trying to give him a warning? Nah...probably not. Like Juliette said, it was probably just a girl from out in the county come to town for a traffic ticket or a tax stamp or something. He couldn't stop now; he might never get another chance to put one over on the Poes. They walked to the back of the grocery, into the receiving office and Henry set the pie on the desk. He looked at Corny, who no longer cried or chanted.

"Ok, my man…let's us git sompin' we can make us a sign with!" Corny nodded and left the office. He returned in a few minutes carrying a large piece of neon-yellow poster board and a red magic marker.

"I thought red'd be a good color, seein' as how it's the Lord's words, an' seein' as how red's the color of blood, which will come at the end a the world."

Corny was really starting to get into this, Henry realized. He nodded. "Right as rain ya are, Corny! Now then…what was it that Angel tol' me…"

"'*SWEET JESUS SWEET POTATO PIE…PROSTATE YOURSELF AND PRAY, BECAUSE THE END IS AT HAND.*' That right, Henry? Wasn't that what you said she said?"

Henry blinked. "Yeah, *goldurnit*, word for word! Man, Corny, you got one a them photogenius mem'ries or sompin'? Ok, here, I ain't much fer sign-makin' so you put yer hand to it, ok?"

Corny was more than ok; he was positively astonished that Henry would appoint him Holy Sign Maker. Maybe he'd misjudged Henry Bailey all along. In his best block letters, Corny wrote out the Bathroom Angel's message. He had to turn the poster board over, however, and start again on the backside, because he'd miscalculated how much space the exact wording would require and he ran out of room for the word 'HAND'. Corny propped the completed sign against a box and he and Henry admired it. Corny searched a desk drawer for a roll of masking tape and proceeded to tear off tape strips. Then he carefully plucked the sign from the desk and carried it toward the door, when Henry stopped him.

"Hold it, there, pard! What're ya doin'?"

"I'm gonna go put this sign up on the cooler door, out in the grocery an' put the pie in the cooler, just like the Bathroom Angel said!"

Henry rubbed his chin. "Ya *know*, Corny…with alla my experience at interpolatin' the Lord's words here lately…here's what I think…it's the middle a the *afternoon*…if you was ta go out there *now* an' hang that sign in fronta alla yer customers…well, ain't nobody gonna respect it proper an' the mirac'lous pow'r a this pie's gonna be wasted afore it has a chance ta do some good…nah, listen up, I think I knowed what the Lord wants us ta do…"

Henry relayed his plan. He was very tired; it was past his afternoon nap and devising so many schemes and alternate schemes in one day sorely taxed a working man.

"So, Corny. Ya jus' do like I say, come in here tonight after closin' an' set it all up. Then in the mornin', ya jus' go 'bout yer bizness, like nothin's changed. That Bathroom Angel tol' me we ain't s'posed ta say nothin' ta nobody 'bout this, else we'll git smited. Them angels sure got smitin' on the *brain*...anyhow, don't ya tell yer daddy er Penni, not *nobody* 'bout our messages! 'Member, we're s'posed ta git another message real soon."

Corny frowned. "But what am I supposed to do in the mornin' when alla my customers start laughin' an' carryin' on an' Daddy, an' Penni, an' Euladean start askin' me all kindsa questions? Hey, Henry...you think I oughta play my *Streets of Gold* gospel tape over the loudspeaker, ya know, for effect?"

Henry grinned. "Corny, that's a *great* idea! Put 'em in the mood, I always say...now quit worryin' 'bout what's gonna happen...ya gotta *b'lieve*, son! Ya gotta have *faith*! That Bathroom Angel ain't let us down yet, nossiree...if anybody asks ya any questions, you jus' look 'em in the eye an' say, *'IT WILL ALL BE REVEAL-ED UNTO YOU.'*"

Corny's face knotted with worry. "You really believe that, Henry? You *do*, don't ya! Henry Bailey, an' you a Pope-lovin' idolatrous Catholic! I had you figured all wrong an' I'm right sorry! *'IT WILL ALL BE REVEAL-ED UNTO YOU.' 'IT WILL ALL BE REVEAL-ED UNTO YOU.'* Henry...you really think it will all be reveal-ed unto us?"

Henry slapped Corny on the back and grinned. This was going to turn the entire town inside out; he couldn't wait to tell Hoot. "*Yes, Corny, you betcha I do! I sure as shootin' do!*"

CHAPTER NINETEEN – SAVING FACE

Tuesday morning, August 24, 1999; Gastineau & Gastineau, CPAs

Roland Gastineau stared out the window of his newly-appointed corner office at Gastineau & Son, CPAs. He silently prayed that the slow, steady rain would put an end to the incessant swelter of the past two months. It was a long time since he'd spent a summer at home and Roland had forgotten how the humidity could hang around you like a heavy curtain, crushing your brain and obliterating all but the coldest of images: frosty lime margaritas, snow skiing, a certain UVA cheerleader loved and lost. He checked his watch; it was ten o'clock and his father had harshly told him to be at the hospital no later than eleven to pay a visit to Mother Nell Graham. Mother Nell was supposedly revising her will today, although how Dan Gastineau knew about it completely baffled Roland. Dan told Roland to pay the old bag a visit, to see if she might wish to place her expectedly brief financial future in the hands of a certified tax attorney such as Roland.

Roland sighed, slumped in his chair and drummed his fingers in time with the raindrops. He hated working for his father; his lifelong dreams of a future in the family tax business had been dashed after he'd witnessed his father's motives and tactics firsthand. *He's lucky he doesn't get his certification revoked. Hell, he's lucky he doesn't get put in jail! I hate all this pressure he's putting on me, the underhanded way he wants me to get new clients, and sneak around at community functions for gossip about who I can lure away from other firms. It's not ethical.*

Roland picked up the phone to check his voice-mail; he punched in the code. There were twenty-seven messages! Twenty-seven! *I've only got two clients,* he thought. *I hope there's not an emergency...Dad will really have a fit if he thinks I ignored somebody...*He punched in another code, grabbed a pen and listened to the first message.

"*Hi, sug!* It's me, *Betty-boo*! Listen, Rollsy, why don't I just come over there to your office this afternoon, and let's go get a cool one at the Whippersnapper in Smyrna, whaddya say? I've been tryin' to get to you for *three weeks*! I dang near had to bribe your secretary to get your direct number! Anyway, you can reach me on my portable...973-2284...call me! *Kisses*!"

Roland grunted in disgust, and played the next message.

"Hey, sug! It's me again, your Betty..."

Roland erased that message, too, and fast-forwarded.

"*Roland Gastineau, if I didn't know better, I'd think you were trying to avoid me!* Now, look, I'll be at your office around three...I won't take no for an answer, sug, and..."

Roland erased the third message and twenty-four others, all from Betty Gooch. This was *ridiculous*! He had done everything short of embarrassing the woman in public in an effort to rid himself of the Betty Menace. Last week, she followed him to the Quik-Steak where he'd reluctantly agreed to meet Roy Quigley to talk business over a greasy lunch. The minute Roy stepped away to take a phone call, Betty plopped down in Roland's lap in front of God and all the Chestnut Ridge busy bodies.

He'd shoved her aside as politely as possible and told her point blank that he had a girlfriend. Of course, he *didn't*, but what did it matter; Betty was either too dumb to take the hint, or too much of a sex-starved female to care. The only reason he'd been able to ditch her that day was because when Roy saw Betty as she ran her fingers seductively up Roland's leg, he hollered out to the entire lunch crowd that, he'd forgotten to put Betty Gooch on the dessert menu and did anybody want a piece? Betty steamed off in a huff.

Roland stared out at the rain. It was obvious he'd have to vacate his office before Betty showed up at three; he could tell his dad he was out prospecting, but then he'd have to prepare a written report on the results. He pounded his desk. *I have no life! I have to write reports for my father about every move I make! And now I'm not safe on the streets, thanks to this oversexed middle-aged bimbo! What have I done? Why did I quit law school? Why did I come back here? What was I thinking? Where's Wink when I need him? What would he do?*

Dan Gastineau burst into Roland's office without so much as a knock or hello. "Son, I hope you haven't forgotten to go see Nell Graham this morning...it's nearly ten-thirty. Here's a list of potential clients I've pulled for you. I'd like you to set up at least three appointments per day, until you get enough accounts of your own to justify that big salary I'm paying you! Now, this one here... rumor has it they *really* need a tax attorney and..."

Roland stood up and pounded his new desk. "DAD! Stop it! I'm *not* a tax attorney! You're gonna get us all put in jail!"

Dan Gastineau adjusted the silk ascot at his neck and toyed with the large gold pinky ring he wore on his left hand. The same pinky ring given to him by his late father; the pinky ring that he told his wife Isidore was so heavy he couldn't also be expected to wear a wedding band.

"Roland, this is getting really tiresome. If you don't want to work here, fine, just say so."

"Ok, Dad, *I don't want to work here*! If you're gonna make me tell lies and pretend to have qualifications I don't have, then I don't want to be associated with this firm, ok? I've already screwed up law school...I can't afford to screw up my CPA license, too. Is that *clear* enough for you, Dad?"

Dan Gastineau stared out one of the spacious windows in his son's office.

Kids today have absolutely no respect for their parents...I slaved for years to put this boy through expensive schools, and then he blows it. I spend ten thousand dollars to renovate this corner office for him and now he's too lazy to work in it. He has no clue how the real business world operates...in my day, we had respect for our parents' sacrifices, we had motivation, it was called poverty... yeah, motivation...take every penny in town away from the Leighs and the Grahams and the Festrunks...my family helped found this town, but did we ever get any breaks from anybody? Did we ever get invited to all those high-class snooty balls?

"Dad...did you *hear* me? I *quit*! Just tell me how much I owe you, for college and for grad school...but remember, I worked the whole time and had scholarships, so I probably don't owe you more than about fifty thousand, but I'm sure you've kept the meter running and you probably know exactly how much you shelled out to raise me when I was a little kid..."

Dan Gastineau slammed a beefy hand on Roland's desk in anger. "ROLAND! Shut up! You are losing it, boy! I knew that fancy-ass school would make you think you were too good to work with your old man. Did I go to a high-brow college? Did I have time for a fraternity or law school? Hell, no, I was a husband and a daddy and a student...I had a family to support...you are nothing but a spoiled little *twerp*! All right son...I'll make you a deal because I'm sick and tired of arguing with you and I'm sick and tired of your bad attitude. *You want out?* Ok, when you bring me enough new clients whose combined annual billings exceed a hundred thousand dollars, then you can have out, lock, stock and barrel! And we'll call it even, zero balance, paid in full. *Satisfied?*"

Roland ran his bony fingers through his thick black hair. He couldn't believe his ears...his dad was actually going to let him go! He stuck out his hand. "*Shake*...ok, Dad, it's a deal. New clients, combined annual billings a hundred thousand...you *promise*?"

Dan Gastineau smiled wickedly through his anger. *That's one way to get his sorry ass moving,* he decided. "Son, of course I promise. Everybody but you knows I'm a man of my word, you ungrateful little shit! Happy hunting!"

Dan exited the office in a huff and Roland plopped down in his chair. Find new clients...a hundred-k in billings...it would take a few months, but now at least he was motivated, now at least he had a *goal!* And then he could leave this miserably hot scrap-heap town, move someplace...someplace *cool*...Seattle, maybe. He looked at his watch...gotta get to that hospital! He grabbed his sport coat, straightened his tie and smoothed his hair.

If I could get Mother Nell's estate business, that would be a great start! She's always liked me, she's always been kind to me, I'll remind her how I used to send her homemade birthday cards, even when I was in undergrad! And I always used to bring her flowers from my mom's greenhouse...and that time I fixed her bro-

ken doorbell. I just hope she's in a good mood today...it all depends on whether she's taken her medication and whether she's in a good mood...

Unfortunately for Roland Gastineau, Mother Nell was *not* in a good mood. At the hands of her new private nurse, Amelia Festrunk, Mother Nell was secretly being weaned from all the unnecessary drugs that were warping her mind. And although Nell considered this a vital part of her recovery, the side effects of this new therapy included a state of full cognizance and alertness, which meant that Nell was forced to listen to Aunt Pearl Parker drone on and on with Amelia about the fictitious medical malpractice suits and her near-broken pelvis. For the first three days, Nell adjusted to her new state of awareness by taking lots of naps; by today, day four, Nell was fully caught up on sleep, and napping was no longer an option, although she pretended to nap to avoid Pearl's attempts at conversation. Amelia had been forced to return home early that morning to search for her trifocals so she could review Nell's revised will when it was delivered by Richard Leigh-Lee IV. While Amelia tore her home apart in an effort to locate her glasses, Nell and Pearl Parker engaged in all-out combat.

Aunt Pearl was furious at the meager, low-fat diet dictated to her by the physician. While Nell's breakfast consisted of scrambled eggs, two slices of whole-wheat toast with butter and jelly, grits, two slices each of sausage and bacon, and a cup of coffee with heavy cream, Aunt Pearl received merely a slice of melon and a glass of juice. Of course, Aunt Pearl ignored the fact that Nell Graham weighed only about a hundred pounds dripping wet, while she was nearly a hundred pounds too "ripe" as she described it.

After wolfing down her melon and draining her juice, Aunt Pearl noticed that Nell had not even touched her food; she assumed that since Nell was deep into a mid-morning nap, she would probably not wish to eat a cold breakfast, thus the food was up for grabs, for someone who was in dire need of sustenance and sausage.

Aunt Pearl tip-toed, as much as it is possible for an obese elderly woman to tip-toe, over to Nell's breakfast tray and swapped it for her own. She greedily gobbled down eggs, bacon, sausage, toast and grits; then she drained the coffee in one gulp. She wiped her mouth daintily with a Festrunk Clinic paper napkin and re-swapped the breakfast trays, before tucking herself neatly back into bed. Nell watched Pearl perform this little maneuver from beneath nearly-closed eyelids as she pretended to nap. *I'll fix that sneaky bitch...next she's probably gonna steal my purse!*

A half-hour later, Amelia had not yet returned and Nell was 'awakened' by the nurse so she could take her medication. *I've got to create a diversion! I can't take those pills now, I've come so far! Where in the hell's Amelia?*

When the nurse congratulated Mother Nell on the excellent volume of breakfast she'd managed to eat, Nell screamed bloody murder and threw the empty coffee cup at Aunt Pearl. There ensued a raging verbal battle between Mother Nell, Aunt Pearl, two orderlies and the nurse regarding whether or not Mother Nell had indeed eaten her own breakfast and whether or not Aunt Pearl, whose stomach rumbled loudly from ingesting so much fat after days of low-cal fare, was telling the truth. While the nurse and the orderlies argued with Aunt Pearl, Nell quietly slipped her medications under the pillow, mission accomplished. *Oh, where in the hell's Amelia?*

It was now ten o'clock and the Breakfast Commandos declared somewhat of a cease-fire. They opted instead to try and out-do each other in the Competitive Illness Olympics. Aunt Pearl was first out of the gate.

"*Lord have mercy*, Nell, you think *you've* got it bad, you think *your* feet hurt, well, let me tell you about the forty-seven corns I had cut out of my feet last year! I'm surprised I can still walk after all that digging! I'm allergic to anesthesia, you know, so they had to cut out all of those corns while I was still awake! I bit clean through a steel pipe and then every one of my teeth fell out, *right there on the operating room floor*! I lost about a hundred pounds after that, because they put me on a liquid diet!"

Nell was not impressed; she tossed her blue-grey curls and hollered, "Horseshit! You *wish* you had it so bad as me! Two years ago my damned daughter-in-law put an earwig under my pillow and that earwig crawled right inside my head and I could feel it in there chewing on my *brain*! But I fixed it, yessir! I put a piece of gum on my hearing aid and stuck it in my left ear. That earwig climbed right inside that hearing aid to get at that gum and then I flushed the whole thing down the commode! My brain cells grew back and the doctor told me I was a medical miracle!"

Aunt Pearl was rested and ready for the Second Heat. She crossed her arms and snorted. "Hmmph, I *doubt* it! I'm the *real* medical miracle around here! I've had over three hundred heart attacks and last week, when I came in here I'd lost *seven* pints of blood! I looked like *whitey*, I'd lost so much blood! But that's nothing...yesterday, while you were sleeping...that big, old ugly orderly came in here and he *molested* me! He stuck his hand up my gown and tried to *feel me up*! And then he grabbed a hold of my *bosoms* and shook 'em all around, but I *bit* him! I bit him so hard, he screamed and there was blood all over the floor and I nearly passed out cold, I was so upset! You slept through the whole thing!"

Aunt Pearl, satisfied she had topped Mother Nell, settled back against her pillow and arranged her bedcovers. Nell sat up and pointed a shaky finger at her roommate. No one was gonna get the best of her.

"Pearl Parker, if you got felt up yesterday, the earth would have stopped turnin' in its tracks! No man in his right mind would touch you, you heifer!

Now in my day, I had to beat 'em off with a stick! I probably had a hundred and fifty men before I got married, but lordy-be, did I have me a time, they were beggin' in the streets for me! Hey! *Sexpot!* Next time that orderly comes at you, you tell him to wake *me* up! I need a good pelvic exam! I'll show him what it's like to bed a *real* woman!"

Nell turned away from Aunt Pearl to see Miss Danita Kay Leigh-Lee standing quietly next to her bed. Danita Kay was obviously unaware that she possessed coveted ringside tickets to the Competitive Illness Olympics. She was smartly attired in a navy blue pinstripe suit and matching pumps and Mother Nell noticed she'd cut her once-frumpy hair into a very stylish do. Danita Kay's Coke-bottle-thick glasses were gone.

Nell panicked momentarily; Amelia had cautioned her that she must continue to act demented, lest anybody suspect their shenanigans. She laughed loudly and wildly swatted the air in front of Danita Kay; Danita Kay accepted the gesture as par for the course for poor old Mother Nell Graham. Nell continued to swat the air for a few seconds, then turned her head back toward Danita Kay and hollered.

"HEY, GAL! Come over here and give your Aunt Nell a big kiss! You're awfully dolled up… is that war paint on your face? You got the hots for some doctor? You are one cute button…but you better watch out for your maidenhead, gal, the orderlies around here'll snatch it right out! Hey, where are your glasses? Don't bump into my bed…you know you're blind as a bat!"

Danita Kay blushed, smiled and gave her Aunt Nell a kiss; Nell Graham was of course not her real aunt, but the Leigh-Lees and the Grahams had been commercially and socially entwined for so long it was inconsequential.

"Hi, there, Aunt Nell. Yes, ma'am, mom took me to her hairdresser and then to the spa; I had a full makeover. I got contacts, too. I decided it was time for me to pay more attention to my appearance, now that I'm a professional. But I tried not to go overboard… I mean, it's good to make a positive impression on the jury but I don't want to be consumed with vanity like Tiffany. I want my clients and the judges to take me seriously."

Danita Kay smiled softly; she wanted Roland Gastineau to take her seriously, too and hoped he would be smitten with the results of her new visage, so recently instilled at the hands of her mother's expensive professionals. Two weeks ago, at a Festival Accounting meeting, she'd stepped into the bathroom and overheard Betty Gooch tell Fay Bailey that Danita Kay was by far the homeliest girl in town and that she posed absolutely no threat in the great battle for Roland's attentions. That was a battle cry, as far as Danita Kay was concerned and she had rallied with every beauty resource that money could buy. Danita Kay Leigh-Lee had been successfully transformed into an attractive, stylish young woman, and she was out to wage war for Roland Gastineau.

Aunt Pearl threw her hands into the air and guffawed. "It's a sin, I tell you, it's a sin what you young people spend to impress each other! My nephew's wife, the one that tried to murder me and severed my thumb in three places...she spent four thousand dollars to buy her some mammaries! *Heh!* She should have bought her some *sense*, might as well have just torn up that money and thrown it on the ground!"

Danita Kay walked toward the hefty black woman in the bed next to her Aunt Nell and stuck out her right hand. "I don't believe I've had the pleasure...I'm Danita Kay Leigh-Lee, attorney at law. *And you are?*"

"I'm Pearl Parker ...Doctor Avery Rex Parker junior is my nephew...I came here last week to try and put my grand-nephew Rex on the straight and righteous path, since his own mother neglects and abuses him, and she's so ungrateful she tried to murder me. She severed my thumb in three places and I lost *seven pints of blood.* And then an orderly slammed me into a wall and broke my pelvis...did you say you're an attorney, young lady? I'd shake your hand, but my ghost pains are kicking in and I'm sufferin' terrible!"

Danita Kay smiled politely and walked over to pat Aunt Nell's hand. "*Likewise*, I'm sure. You are just the picture of health, Aunt Nell. I hear you'll be going home soon, if you behave yourself! Here are the papers Daddy prepared for you at your request...it's all very routine, everything is in order, so if you will sign on page three and then again on pages five, seven and twelve. Can I get you anything, Aunt Nell?"

Nell looked quizzically at Danita Kay as if the young woman was from another planet. She blinked several times in rapid succession. *Amelia Festrunk you'd better get your skinny schemin' ass over here right now or I'm screwed!*

"Danita Kay, isn't that *sweet*, you pretending to be a lawyer, just like your daddy! Hell, what are you, in seventh grade by now? Where in God's name is your father with those papers? How dare he waste my time sending you over here! I don't have time to play games! I've got a Ladies meeting this afternoon and Will's quarterbacking the big game tonight! *HEY!* You wanna buy a raffle ticket for the high school, honey?"

Danita Kay cleared her throat. "Aunt Nell...I *am* a lawyer...remember, I graduated from Harvard last year? I joined Daddy's practice...he sent me over here because I'm fully capable of assisting you with these revisions. Look, here's your will, you just need to sign a few places."

Mother Nell's wrinkled fingers searched the top of her blue-grey head for her glasses in vain, until Danita Kay pointed out that she was already wearing them. Nell peered sheepishly at the Revised Last Will & Testament and glanced at the wall clock. She feared something bad had happened to Amelia. She waved the will in the air and pointed a finger at Danita Kay.

"I want to read every page, gal. I don't want to be buried in that damned city cemetery next to any Elks members! It was Elks that killed my husband and they're trying to poison me, too! Where's my purse? Get yourself a dollar and go get some candy while I read this."

Danita Kay smiled. "Aunt Nell, you take your time. Your purse isn't here...you're in the hospital, remember? I'll just wait over there in that chair."

"WHO STOLE MY PURSE? PEARL ALREADY STOLE MY BREAKFAST! DID SHE STEAL MY PURSE, TOO? YOU PLANNIN' TO RUN OFF WITH THAT ORDERLY, PEARL, SINCE YOU FINALLY GOT YOURSELF A MAN?"

Danita Kay patted Aunt Nell's arm and shook her head. "Aunt Nell, calm down, your purse is at home, safe and sound. Now you just relax and look over those revisions!"

Nell pretended to scan the pages with a shaky, shriveled finger. Danita Kay sat down in an ancient Festrunk Clinic wooden chair to wait. Aunt Pearl, exhausted from her turn at Olympic competition, snored loudly. Suddenly there was a light tap on the door and Dorothy Graham breezed in.

*"Hello, Mother Nell...*my *God,* is that *you,* Danita Kay? I heard you'd been to the day spa but I never *dreamed* they could really do anything for you! That hair is *stunning*! So much better than that stringy nonsense you were so fond of! And *makeup*! I've never seen you wear makeup! That shade of lipstick is so *charming*! And *oh,* RK or contacts? I hear you're doing very well for yourself, dear, your mother is extremely jealous, you know, since she never finished college! Don't let me disturb you, Danita, I'm just here to visit with...*oh!* Mother Nell! What are you *reading*?"

Nell shoved the revised will under her bed covers as Dorothy reached for it; Dorothy Graham would soon find out about the change in Nell's posthumous plans, but it wouldn't be today, in a hospital room...finally she'd cut that tramp completely out any inheritance, and everyone in town would laugh and laugh and point their fingers.

"DOTTIE CHATWICK...GET OUT OF HERE! I'VE BEEN IN THIS HOSPITAL TEN TIMES IN THE PAST YEAR AND YOU'VE NEVER VISITED ME ONCE! WHAT ARE YOU AFTER, GAL? YOU THINKING I'M ALMOST DEAD, SO YOU'LL GET YOUR MONEY?"

Dorothy Graham laughed skittishly, "*Now, Mother Nell!* That's no way to talk! I was in the neighborhood and I thought I'd stop by!"

Dorothy patted Mother Nell's pillow and lifted the bedcovers, trying to get a glimpse of the papers Mother Nell shoved out of sight, but Nell slammed a hand down on the blanket. Dorothy rolled her eyes and turned to Danita Kay. She knew exactly why Danita Kay was there and exactly what Mother Nell was supposed to sign...and she had paid dearly for the two sentences that Richard had supposedly inserted into the will's text. She intended to sit in that room and witness Mother Nell's signature; it was her right, after her unspeakable humiliation yesterday at the Peacock Inn with Richard. What she did not know, however, was that the revisions Nell Graham would sign into fruition actually included the complete transfer of Dorothy's inheritance to an unwitting third party.

On Saturday, upon Hester's refusal to loan her any money, Dorothy locked herself in her room to mentally steel herself in preparation for the dreaded tryst with Richard Leigh-Lee IV. Her one stroke of luck was that Will was out of town at yet another banker's golf tournament until Tuesday. *At least I don't have to face him*, she mused. Dorothy refused her maid's offers of food or her phone messages, claiming she had a sick headache and that on doctor's orders she was to stay in bed.

On Monday at noon, as she had devised no alternative plan, Dorothy knew it was time to face the music and Richard. She rifled through her expansive closet and located a red, lacy negligée given to her by Dan Gastineau. Then she found a pair of spiked red satin heels and put both items in a small duffel bag. She went into the bathroom, shaved her legs and took a shower, then grabbed a bottle of extra-strength hand-sanitizer from the cabinet and threw that in the bag. She might have to get *close* to Richard Leigh-Lee IV, but she would not wear his nasty germs around all day.

It was an easy forty-five minute drive to the edge of town and the thick copse of trees that hid the entrance of the Peacock Inn and Dorothy arrived precisely on time. She checked in to her standard suite. The staff was very discreet; it was the only elegant hotel in the county and the majority of the illicit affairs conducted by the rich and famous locals took place within its exquisitely furnished rooms. Will knew nothing about Dorothy's love nest, because she paid the bills out of her grocery account; Dorothy didn't eat much and Will ate most of his meals at Chéz Horatio. Richard arrived a few minutes late, bearing two dozen red roses, a bottle of chilled champagne and a small suitcase. Dorothy met him at the door in the red negligée and heels. He tried to kiss her with his mouth open but she turned her head, so he licked her cheek. She groaned in disgust.

"Richard, I *never* do open mouths! Are you planning to stay for a *week*, or is that thing full of all the medical paraphernalia you need to sustain a hard-on?" Dorothy asked, as she nodded at the suitcase.

"Ah, Dottie-doll, ever the charmer! And such a toilet mouth, despite all the money Will spends to keep you in high-maintenance style! No, I'm not staying a week… but I do plan to savor this memory for the rest of my natural-born life, unless of course, you come to your senses and realize that I'm the man you need to fulfill your womanly potential!"

Dorothy clucked her tongue in sarcasm as Richard loosened his tie and opened the suitcase. Dorothy gasped. Inside were a video camera, a tripod and a very long extension cord.

"*What in the hell do you plan to do?* Don't you think for one minute I'll let you *tape* this sordid little episode! I only let Dan Gastineau do that once, because I actually *enjoyed* screwing him, but look where that got me!"

Richard giggled and waved a signed check in Dorothy's direction. "Babycakes, you don't have much of a choice, now do you? I've got your money, your twenty-five thousand, Dottie Chatwick, Whore-of-Plenty! But if you don't do exactly as Big Dick says, you won't get a penny! I didn't fall off the turnip truck yesterday, Dottie. I know you and your wily ways and I'm not sure I believe a word you told me last week...that was quite a little story... all that talk about illicit videotapes gave me an idea...so I decided to take out an insurance policy of my own."

Richard set up the tripod and took the camera out of the suitcase. He gave Dorothy a good, long, lascivious gaze. "I'll give you your money, after you give up the goods, so to speak; but I know how the world turns. Years from now, somehow this will all get out in the open and if you decide to flap your mouth and accuse me of anything, I'll have all the evidence I need to keep myself out of jail. And while I'm waiting for the shoe to drop, I sure can have a good time watching our little adventure in my bedroom every night; it's been lonely since AnnElise moved me out five years ago...*hey, Dottie*...just think of this little meeting today as some of your precious charity work...I need a woman in the *worst way*!"

Dorothy marched in a huff toward the champagne bucket and popped the bottle's cork. She took a giant swig, then another and glared at Richard. "Well, hurry up and get ready. I've got a hair and nail appointment at four-thirty and I refuse to be late!"

There was no hair and nail appointment; but the banks all closed at five and Dorothy had to make that deposit *today*. Richard stripped to his boxers, then told Dorothy to lie on the bed, so he could determine the best camera angle. When he stopped fiddling with the camera, Dorothy retrieved the champagne bottle and drained it dry. It went straight to her head, which was exactly her intention. There was no way she could do this sober. She dimmed the lights in the bedroom, but Richard protested that it would interfere with the videotape. He noticed the empty champagne bottle on the floor and grinned.

"Good job, Hottie-Dottie...nobody knows better than me that too much booze makes a woman ready and a man soft! Now, let's see...oh, yes, *first*, just look into that camera, please and repeat after me: *'I, Dottie Chatwick Graham, am here of my own free will in exchange for a loan by Richard*

Napoleon Leigh-Lee IV in the amount of twenty-five thousand dollars and I am performing all acts you are about to see without duress, on this day, et cetera, et cetera.' Go ahead, Dottie, smile that pretty socialite, capped-tooth smile of yours and focus on the blinking red light..."

Two hours, one long hot bath and a full bottle of extra-strength hand sanitizer later, Dottie Chatwick had her twenty-five thousand dollar loan, if not her self-respect. She'd driven to Smyrna, cashed the check at the giant bank conglomerate so dreaded by her husband and headed straight home, where she'd made out a fifteen thousand dollar deposit slip to the Festival account and written the check to pay for the Festival insurance bond. She changed her clothes, drove to the bank, conducted her banking transactions and promptly called AnnElise Leigh-Lee from the parking lot.

"Hello, AnnElise? It's Dorothy, I'm on my mobile. You'll be pleased to know that I have just deposited fifteen thousand dollars of my *own money* into the Festival account and have personally sent the check to the insurance company for the bond. So you can stop your little accusations of impropriety. I am presently on my way to a meeting with the FBI agent in charge of my case...there apparently has been some kind of new *development*...anyway, I know you'll want to pass this good news on to the committee. And do give *Richard* my regards."

Dorothy didn't give AnnElise a chance to mutter a single word; she turned off the cell phone and rifled through the glove compartment for the pack of Lady Ultra-Lites she kept for emergencies. She plucked a cigarette from the nearly empty pack, lit it and inhaled deeply. *That ought to shut her up,* she fumed. *She probably told everyone in town I stole money from the Festival...well, at least my facelift's not sliding down my neck! And my husband doesn't sleep around, either!* She smoked the cigarette down to the nub and lit another.

That was just about the most disgusting thing I've ever had to do in my whole entire life, she mused. *Well, maybe not as disgusting as screwing Will's father in the back of his Chevy so he'd make me Nell's beneficiary. But that was different. My entire future as a socially prominent citizen was at stake. Hmmm...I guess it's the same thing now, isn't it? No matter what Richard said...I'm no prostitute...I'm just taking control of my life...investing in my retirement! Ugh, that hairy back of his...but my goodness he is well-endowed. AnnElise was a complete fool to move him out...I haven't had a good one like that in a very long time...Big Dick's no joke, is it? Too bad I don't need any more favors from him...a girl could get used to that high once a week or so...*

She pulled down the Mercedes' lighted makeup mirror, checked her teeth and smiled widely. *The bond's been paid, and I have ten thousand dollars in my very own secret bank account! Mad money! It's not much, but it's a start! I'm going to need lots of extra pocket change when I'm living in West Palm...maybe I can add a few grocery money deposits here and there* ...Dorothy grabbed her cell phone, took another deep drag on the cigarette and dialed the Peacock Inn. It was time to cut costs and after her financial transaction with Richard, no matter how degrading, Dan Gastineau could no longer measure up.

"Hello, Morris? It's *Mrs. Jane Smith*...yes, thank you, the room was fine, although I must say the bathtub was gritty, very uncomfortable. Listen, Morris...I'm going to be living out of state for a few months... I really don't *need* that suite again until I return...yes, thank you, please keep me on the mailing list...one never knows when one might need to pop in!"

Dorothy finished the cigarette and flicked it out the car window. *That's a few thousand more I can save for my West Palm account,* she grinned. *Won't Dan Gastineau be heartbroken when he shows up next week for his usual romp in the hay...well, Danny-boy, there are no more free lunches...if you want me, you'll have to pay to play. I've got a West Palm wardrobe to buy, half-caf lattes to save for...and new friends to impress.*

Dorothy opened her mouth to receive the benefits of breath spray. She smacked her lips and said aloud, *"Dottie Chatwick, you are one smart cookie. I think I'll just take you to dinner tonight to celebrate."* She pressed the number of her favorite restaurant into the cell phone keypad and turned the Mercedes into traffic. Dorothy sighed and remembered what her daddy used to say... *ain't it great when a plan all comes together.* She had her money and Richard would never disclose their little secret.

Yes, Dottie Chatwick, you lead a charmed life. And when that old shrew signs her revised will...you'll be in business...then you can repay Big Dick and make another tidy deposit into that West Palm account...I'll never come back to this hick town...

Flush with cash, Dorothy Graham arrived at Mother Nell's bedside Tuesday morning. Richard promised to send his daughter with the papers before eleven and so he had. Dorothy wanted to make sure Richard lived up to his part of the deal. But apparently, Danita Kay had encouraged Mother Nell to review the revisions in detail; this was not part of the plan.

Danita Kay Leigh-Lee stood up from the chair in Mother Nell's room and walked over to the old woman's bedside. It was obvious Dorothy Graham's presence irritated Nell and Danita was due in court in half an hour. She could count on one hand number of times she had witnessed civility between Dorothy and Nell Graham. Danita Kay didn't know what was in that revised will; she only knew her father had burst into her office this morning in a panic and asked her to do him this small favor before her court appearance. *Maybe I should take a look at those papers,* she decided. *I'm a professional and I can't take any chances on behalf of my client...Daddy's been so busy lately…I should really see what the gist of this is so I can advise Nell if there's a problem…*

"Aunt Nell, excuse me…Miss Dorothy, I'm not here on a social call…this is a private legal matter, would you care to step out in the hall, please, while we conduct business?"

The look of concern for Mother Nell's health was instantly wiped from Dorothy Graham's face; no young lion fresh out of law school and the day spa was going to get in her way.

"Danita…*dear*…I'm waiting on the doctor, to discuss Mother Nell's delicate situation in full. Just pretend I'm not here. Perhaps I might be of assistance…Mother Nell, shall I read those papers to you? You know your eyes haven't been up to snuff lately. My goodness, you seem unusually alert…have we taken all our medication today?"

Dorothy slipped a hand under the sheet and tried to snatch the revised will from Mother Nell's grip. Danita Kay slammed a fist down on top of Dorothy's hand, and said in a steady voice, "Mrs. Graham, as Nell Graham's legal representative, I must ask you to leave this room immediately. This is not your affair and you have been politely asked to go. If you don't, I'll call security and have you removed. Aunt Nell, the documents, please?"

Mother Nell smiled sarcastically at Dorothy, who backed away in red-faced anger. The old woman handed the revised will to Danita Kay with a wide grin. She pointed a finger at her daughter-in-law.

"HEY! PUT THAT BITCH IN JAIL WHERE SHE BELONGS! SHE'S BEEN TRYING TO KILL ME SINCE 1971! That'd fix you, Dottie Chatwick! That'd fix you for stealing my son and spending all his money! I know you screwed my husband in the backseat of his Chevy so he'd make you the beneficiary of the Graham fortune! *And guess how I found out?* Will played detective! He was cleaning out some old papers in the family vault last month and guess what he found? *A letter*! A letter from his daddy, my dead good-for-nothing husband! Confessing how you tricked him into it! You curious about these papers? You should be! I'm doing something I should have done twenty-five years ago, when you handed over your babies to be raised by a total stranger so you could play bridge! *That's right!* I'm cutting you out, you white-trash hussy! You may have put one over on Will's daddy, but you don't fool me and I'm taking your little trust fund and throwing it out the window! How do you like that, Dottie Chatwick? Danita, let's put this bitch in jail, right now! Don't worry, Dottie, your pearls will look great with those prison uniforms!"

Aunt Pearl Parker awoke at the sound of Mother Nell's outburst. She rubbed her eyes and shook her head. "*Lord have mercy, I* spent *months* in jail, with Martin Luther King, years ago. They put us all in one big cell, at Cook

County, with only one little coffee can to pee in! And all they fed us were hot dogs and warm milk! You ever eat hot dogs and warm milk? You swell up like a hot-air balloon …I was constipated for a *whole year!* My kidneys exploded and I had to have a *transplant*, and…"

"Excuse me, Mrs. Parker, but do you mind if I close this curtain? I'm trying to conduct client business." Danita Kay abruptly drew the curtain around Aunt Pearl's bed. Aunt Pearl was suitably insulted and in response, turned on *The Price is Right* at full blast. Danita Kay's head pounded; she had to get control of the situation so she could get to court.

"Aunt Nell, as the attorney acting in my father's stead, I recommend that I take these papers and study them in greater detail. There may be some criminal investigation involved here…blackmail, prostitution…I think I'd better have a word with Daddy and with Mister Will. We can discuss this later, in private. Now, you just take it easy and get some rest."

Dorothy watched in horror as Danita Kay snatched up the ticket to *her* West Palm financial future. *Cut me out? No trust fund whatsoever? Richard's clause will never hold up in court if Nell Graham cuts me out completely!* Dorothy's stomach knotted and churned. *This is not happening…Richard played me like a fool… I'm doomed…I owe him money…he has me on tape…Will knows about the afternoon with his father oh-so-many years ago…West Palm is slipping through my fingers…this can't be happening.*

Danita Kay kissed Aunt Nell and motioned a panic-stricken Dorothy Graham to step outside. She spoke in a low but stern voice. "Miss Dorothy, I'll be brief. I don't know what's going on, but I'll find out. And in the meantime, I expect you to behave yourself and show civility to Nell!"

Dorothy fumed, pursed her lips and waved a finger at Danita Kay. "How *dare* you sass me, just because you have a law degree and a new haircut! Now you listen to me, young lady…that old witch is *crazy*! You have no idea what it's like to live in the same house with her, I've put up with it for ten long years! Will's daddy loved me like a daughter and that old woman is lying! That money is *mine*! I've earned it, fair and square, taking care of her all these years! I *have plans* for that money! She *can't* just cut me out! She can't do it! I'll speak to Will about it…*he* won't let her change one word!"

"It seems that Will is the very person who recommended his mother make these changes, according to Mother Nell. Nell Graham can revise her will any way she pleases and no one can stop her. But don't take my word for it…why don't you just give my father a call…he's *your* attorney as well, isn't he? I'm sure he'd be happy to advise you on this matter…now, good day!"

Dorothy stomped her designer-clad feet on the Clinic's tiled corridor floor as Danita clicked away in stylish navy pumps. *Oh, don't worry…he's already advised me on this matter, missy…and I was stupid enough to believe him!* Tears welled in her eyes and spilled down her cheeks. A life of community stature and her well-laid plans had suddenly been sucked down the bottomless pit of deprivation. She reached for her cell phone with a trembling hand.

Danita Kay stepped out of the main Festrunk Clinic elevator toward the hospital entrance and ran smack dab into Roland Gastineau as he darted in out of the rain. Roland glimpsed just enough of Danita Kay's blonde hair to assume he'd once again encountered Betty Gooch; he grabbed his stalker firmly at arm's length and let out a loud grunt of disgust.

"*I can't believe it!* Are you following me all over *town*? What'd you do, implant a secret transmitter in my shoe or something....*oh...oh...I'm sorry, miss...wait...I... is that you, Danita Kay? For real? Uh...hey, I'm sorry...I...*"

Chills raced up and down Danita Kay's entire body; Roland Gastineau grabbed her tightly with those beautiful, strong hands and now looked into her very soul with his electric blue eyes. Beads of rainwater danced on the shoulders of Roland's navy sport coat and crowned his black hair; tiny droplets of water danced across his dark eyelashes. Roland was dumbstruck. Danita Kay Leigh-Lee looked like a completely different person. *Cute, bouncy hair, professional hair,* Roland noticed. *And what gorgeous eyes!* He couldn't stop staring into those eyes, those eyes without Coke-bottle glasses!

Danita Kay cleared her throat and nodded slightly in the direction of Roland's vise-gripped right hand. He blushed.

"Oh, I'm sorry!" Roland loosened his hold, but he didn't let go, Danita Kay noticed. She turned up a corner of her mouth with a tiny smile. Roland took a deep breath. *Man, she's got a really good body under that suit...has she been working out?*

"Look, Danita Kay...I'm having a bad day...I thought you were somebody else...I hope I didn't hurt you...are you ok? I'm running late for an appointment with Nell Graham, and I..."

"What a coincidence...I've just come from a meeting with Aunt Nell; she's resting now. I didn't *realize* she had retained you...or was this strictly a social call?"

Danita Kay waited, smirking, for Roland's reply. He let her go and ran bony fingers through his hair, raining water droplets around his shoes.

"Uh...yeah, uh, it is...it's a social call. Just wanted to see how she's doing...you know, I always used to make her cards and stuff...we've always been buds...so...she's *resting*?"

Roland didn't know what to do with his hands; he wished they were still holding Danita Kay, but that was no longer an option as Danita Kay's little smile quickly turned serious. He thrust his hands into his sport coat pockets and waited for Danita Kay to say something. She turned a very cute nose into the air and tossed her head.

"I know *exactly* why you're here, Roland Gastineau. Well, let me tell you right now, Nell Graham is *definitely* not on her deathbed. Far from it! And she's in complete control of her mental faculties. So, *errand boy*, you can just go back and inform your father that his prospects for putting his filthy hands on Nell Graham's business are *zero*. Do you understand? And next time, watch where you're going. What's the matter, Betty Gooch chasing you all over town?"

Roland's heart pounded and he felt sick. In less than thirty seconds, Danita Kay had hit the proverbial nail on the head regarding his visit to Mother Nell, his status within his father's firm and the fact that he was being stalked by the Betty Menace. It was time to save face.

"Look, Danita Kay...I *swear* I'm just here to visit Mother Nell. My dad may think he can connive his way into the pockets of everybody in town, but *I* don't do business that way. In fact, I'll be leaving his firm pretty soon! I'm just working there for a while to get my feet on the ground, you know, pay him back for all he's done for me. Then I'll be hanging out my own shingle, as they say!"

Roland grinned, despite the fact that he had inadvertently supplied his most ardent competitor with a piece of information that could cause the complete and total ruination of Gastineau & Gastineau, CPAs. Danita Kay overlooked the critical G-2, however and nearly melted on the inside. *You are so good-looking! I want to plop you down right here and kiss those hard cheeks and run my hands through that black hair!* But old habits die hard, and years of shielding herself behind an all-business force field were hard to crack. Danita Kay blinked her eyes and again tossed her head, like she'd seen her sister do so many times.

"Roland, you must be *crazy* to try and compete with your father here!"

Roland's eyes widened and he shook his head. "Oh, I won't be sticking around. As soon as I can, I'm gonna move out West...to Seattle. I'm ready for a major change, you know, nice climate, more progressive environment, good coffee bars...yep, just a few more months in this old burg and I'll be moving on, probably right after the Festival."

Danita Kay's heart sank to her ankles. *Roland leaving?* It was not within the realm of possibilities, it was not what she had planned, it was incomprehensible! The all-business force field popped and crackled, weakened by Roland's blow. She had to act fast, remain cool. With every ounce of effort she could summon, she rolled her eyes indifferently.

"Well, if that's what you *want*, then, hey, go for it! I'm sure you'll do quite well...oh, that reminds me. I need to review the Festival accounting records with you, before the next town meeting. But I'm so booked right now, in fact, I'm due in court in ten minutes..."

Danita Kay casually flipped through her datebook. "I hate to ask this, I don't want to be accused of any professional impropriety, you know I've insisted this committee meet during the day, much to Betty Gooch's regret, but would it be possible for us to meet one evening? For dinner…to *work*, of course…a quiet place, so we could concentrate?"

Roland warmed to the tips of his toes. A quiet dinner with this woman would be absolutely perfect, business or no business. In fact, it was what he had momentarily decided to organize. *Caution*, he remembered. *Take it slow. Don't go overboard like last time. 'Rufus, don't be so pushy!'* Wink said after the Bonnie Lou fiasco. *'Just be loose…let 'em think you're just hangin' out, ya know, casual!'*

"Sure, hey, it's just a *business* dinner! We'll probably turn some heads, though, since we're competitors…congratulations on your CPA, by the way! Dad's worried sick! I mean, it's not like we're *interested* in each other, or anything, right? Hey, *that* would be a kick! Give me a *break*!"

Danita Kay steeled back tears; her instant regret patched the crack in the all-business force field. *Why did he have to say that? He's probably got a girlfriend …probably in Seattle, the bitch…all this makeover crap for nothing… no point getting my hopes up, spending an hour getting dressed just to have my heart broken in public…better to meet at my office, look at those records and then he can go call Miss Seattle…how can I stay here if Roland leaves? My life is over…get a grip, Danita Kay…*

"How about tomorrow…look, let's just keep it simple. Come to my office, I'll send out for sandwiches. It'll be easier than hauling around all those files…say about six-thirty?"

Roland frowned and ran his fingers through his hair. *She sure is quirky; first she says a nice dinner, now we're gonna have sandwiches at her office…maybe we could catch some music after we finish work, or take a walk and talk…I wonder if she likes ice cream…or roses…*

He nodded and waved one hand in the air. "Well, ok…if that's what you want. Can I bring anything? Want me to stop and get a pizza? Or we could work first and then go grab a bite after…"

Danita Kay briskly closed her datebook and shook her head. The force field was again fully operational. She glanced at her watch. "No, thanks, I'll take care of it. I've got to run… at least the rain's stopped. Good day!"

Roland turned and watched Danita Kay walk briskly out the door of the Festrunk Clinic and speed up the block toward the courthouse. He let out a confused sigh. *It's probably nothing…she's just in a hurry to get to court…but she did seem a little testy there at the end…oh, well, no point going to see Nell Graham now, he thought. Don't want to hurt my chances with Danita Kay…guess I could go and say hello, though. Especially since I told Danita I was here on a social call.*

He stepped into the Clinic Gift Shoppe and bought a Get Well card and a small vase of peach-colored roses from an ancient candy striper whose hair matched her pink uniform. He took the elevator to the third floor, to Mother Nell's usual suite. As he rounded the corner, Roland noticed Dorothy Graham leaning against the wall outside Mother Nell's room, cell phone in hand. Her foot was loudly, impatiently tapping the tiled floor. Roland applied his brakes. *Oh, man, I don't wanna get in the middle of some family feud and I definitely don't wanna talk to her about that fifteen thousand dollar discrepancy in the Festival books. I'll just duck in the visitor's lounge until she leaves.* He dipped inside the waiting area, sat down in a chair next to the door and held a magazine close to his face, while an oblivious Dorothy Graham waited furiously for Richard Leigh-Lee IV to answer her call. Roland strained to catch the conversation.

"*No*, I don't *wish* to call back later! Did you tell him that this is *Dorothy Graham*...no, I *won't* hold, it's *urgent....RICHARD! You dirty rotten bastard!* I'm at the hospital, to witness what I *thought* would be my new lease on life and *guess what?* Your precious daughter Danita Kay just waltzed off with Mother Nell's will...*sans signature!* Oh, but wait, there's *more*! Let me ask you, *Big Dick*...did you even *read* those revisions? Do you have a clue why she was even revising the damned will in the *first* place? *Ummm*...you *assumed* they were *routine* in nature? Well, then, *routinely speaking*, as my attorney, can you tell me how you plan to *contest* them, so I can get my damned money after I've been completely *cut out* of the will? *No shit, it's a surprise*! NO I WILL NOT MEET YOU AT THE PEACOCK INN TO DISCUSS IT! *Listen to me*...you'd better *fix* this and I mean fix it in my *favor*, or I'm going to pay AnnElise a little visit, tape or no tape! I have nothing more to lose...my money, my position with the Festival, my reputation, my NDCA presidency, that condo in West Palm Beach...it's all hanging by a damned thread and let me tell you, if *I* hit bottom, *you* hit bottom. *Do you hear*? You have two hours to figure this out and call me back, or I'll drop by your house and you'll be kicked out and disgraced before *cocktails*!"

Dorothy smacked the cell phone against the wall in anger and flung it into her purse. She had to collect her thoughts and figure out what to do; as she exhaled a deep, angry breath, she saw Ruby Quigley racing down the corridor, accompanied by a bevy of nurses and candy stripers. Ruby, decked out in a neon orange pantsuit, with matching shoes and hair bows, waved her arms and nodded furiously as she walked and talked; the nurses and candy stripers raised their hands to their faces and gripped one another in some kind of disbelief. *Oh, God, what has that white-trash realtor stirred up now*, Dorothy wondered. *I've got to get out of here...where's the fire exit...*

"DOROTHY! MADAME CHAIRWOMAN! *YOO-HOO! DOROTHY!*"

Ruby Quigley and her candy-striped entourage came to a screeching halt in front of Dorothy Graham. Ruby's face was extremely flushed; wisps of damp black-lacquered hair hung on top of her makeup-laden cheeks and she gasped for breath. Dorothy tried to step away, but she was cornered, there was no escape.

"Ruby...ladies...what is going on? I thought this was a *hospital*...really, Mother Nell is *trying* to get some rest and I don't think..."

"DOROTHY! YOU AIN'T GONNA BELIEVE IT! YOU JUST AINT GONNA BELIEVE IT! She won't will she? *Nope!* This thing's gonna turn the Festival on its ears!"

Dorothy's wounded countenance drooped in despair; she could not face another problem with the Festival right now. She gripped her designer bag firmly and braced herself for Ruby's news. Amelia Festrunk appeared, flushed and out of breath, her misplaced trifocals swinging from a chain around her neck. She crossed her arms and rebuked Dorothy.

"Good grief, ladies! This is a hospital and Nell Graham needs her rest! Do you think you can keep it down or do I have to send for security?"

Dorothy clucked her tongue and tossed her head. "Shut up, you old bag! You don't run things around here anymore. What are you doing here, anyway? I gave strict orders to the nurse not to let you in to see Nell...you *agitate* her."

Amelia grinned like a Cheshire cat. "I hate to disappoint you, Dorothy, but Nell hired me to be her private nurse. I have a signed contract. One of my responsibilities is to keep you away from her, at her request."

Dorothy fumed in embarrassment. "What a load of crap! You're so old you can't take care of yourself, let alone anybody else! And that woman is demented! Her signature's no good! So you can just tear up your stupid contract and stuff it up your ass! Besides, it seems you're not doing your job, missy! I just came from Nell's room...where were *you*? Obviously not doing the job she *hired* you for!"

Amelia waved a legal document in front of Dorothy's face. "Oh, just on my way back from seeing my attorney and getting this contract filed as evidence. It is legit, you see...under my supervision, Nell's been taken off all those unnecessary tranquilizers. Oh, and did I mention that Nell, on my advice, has filed charges against you for personal injury and mistreatment? We're on to you, Dorothy...multiple prescriptions all over town? Overmedicating a poor old woman just to keep her out of your way and hasten her death? But don't let me dwell on this...it will all be in the subpoena."

Ruby Quigley exploded. "Would you two shut up an' listen ta me? We got us a major incident goin' on an' ya'll gotta hear this right now!"

Dorothy was grateful to change the subject. "What are you talking about, Ruby? My God, you *must* be upset, your hair bows are popping off!"

The candy stripers and nurses nodded in agreement; they'd never seen Ruby so scattered. Ruby patted one orange neon hair bow absent-mindedly. A nurse lightly touched Amelia's arm, as if to shield her against what she was about to discover.

"Well, *first off,* Esperanza's in the ER, passed out cold! Fainted dead away, right there in the Poe House frozen foods! Ya know how Esperanza's got all them warts on her fingers, *both hands,* such a shame, 'course my mama always said warts was from drinkin' too much coffee; anyhow, Esperanza, she pressed them hands up there on that cooler door and when she took 'em off, *praise God,* them warts was vanished! *Gone!* An' Esperanza just plumb passed out, right there by the ice cream!"

Dorothy and Amelia stared in confused silence, waiting for Ruby to continue, which she did.

"An' I heard Juliette Kimball givin' her statement ta Bull McArdle...or was it Bill? One a them McArdles was there, I cain't remember which...an' she said an *Angel of the Lord* came inta her shop and bought that pie...paid *cash* for it...an' it told Juliette she'd know who ta give it to...an' she give it ta Henry Bailey, who give it to Corny Poe, an' somehow, in the middle a the night, that pie moved itself to the frozen foods and, well, *there it is.*"

Dorothy Graham touched her left temple and rolled her eyes. Ruby Quigley's reputation for hysterics preceded her and this was probably another one of her publicity stunts to get attention for the Quik-Steak.

"Ruby...*I'm sorry*...I've had an extremely taxing morning...what *exactly* are you trying to say?"

Ruby scowled at Dorothy as if she'd just dropped in off the moon. "Didn't you just *hear* me? Esperanza's out like a light! The *whole town's* up in arms...I mean, all I did was stop at the Poe House to get Miss Shu-Shu some Perky Poochies...*she ain't been herself since that concussion*...anyhow, here I am, mindin' my own bizness in the pet food aisle an' I hear this awful racket in the frozen foods; so bein' the concerned citizen an' quick-thinkin' execative that I am, I raced over there totin' Miss Shu-Shu an' lemme tell ya, that dog was quakin, I tell ya, *quakin' all over*...an' there it was..."

Several candy stripers shook their heads slowly as if in shock; a nurse clasped her hands as if in prayer. Dorothy tired of Ruby's antics.

"Ruby...I don't have all day...spit it out...*what's going on*?"

Ruby swallowed and leaned closer to Dorothy and Amelia. One of the candy stripers began to weep. Ruby grasped Dorothy's arm and glanced up and down the corridor. She spoke in a loud whisper, "*It's the very face of Jesus*...it's done appeared in the condensation on the door to the frozen veg-

'tables at the Poe House. *It's plain as day,* I seen it with my own eyes. Right under this big sign sayin' *'SWEET JESUS SWEET POTATO PIE…PROSTATE YOURSELF AND PRAY, BECAUSE THE END IS AT HAND.'* There it is, *the face of our Savior,* hoverin' over this special sweet potata pie that some angel bought offa Juliette Kimball. Brother Culpepper's on his way over there right now, an' Barney Gooch's tryin' ta find Hoot Graham, ta take a pitcher before they have ta re-stock the cooler this afternoon, in case it drips off. Barney wants ta put it on a Festival billboard, do some *marketin'.* That's why I high-tailed it over here…I seen your car in the parkin' lot. We gotta find Hoot! You got his L.A. number? What about Will? Can he reach Hoot? We gotta find him!"

Dorothy Graham rolled her eyes and let out a huge sigh of disgust. "Get out of my way, Ruby Quigley! That is the most ridiculous thing I've ever heard. You people need to get a life. I'm late for an appointment!"

Dorothy angrily brushed past the candy stripers, nurses, Amelia and Ruby. She had more important fish to fry and she refused to give this huckster one more second of her valuable time. The candy stripers and nurses stared at Dorothy in horror, appalled that she could be so cold and unconcerned. Amelia turned on her heel and disappeared into Nell's room. Ruby patted a weeping candy-striper on the back and watched Dorothy Graham stomp down the corridor. She called out after Madame Chairwoman,

"Yer a fool, missin' out on a prime Festival marketin' opp'tunity! These here mir'cles ain't happ'nin' ever' day! An' yer gonna be sorry, Dorothy, come Judgment Day! Them designer shoes won't save ya from eternal hellfire, ya know! The Lord don't truck with no naysayers!"

CHAPTER TWENTY – WHERE THERE'S A WILL, THERE'S A WAY

Tuesday late-morning, August 24, 1999; Leigh-Lee & Sons, Attorneys

Richard Leigh-Lee IV hung up the phone and leaned back in his leather office chair. *Two hours?* Only two hours to come up with a suitable explanation as to why Nell Graham was carving Dorothy out of her trust fund and why he had lapsed in performance for his first and second most important legal clients. Only one hundred and twenty minutes to devise a feasible alibi, an alibi that Dottie would believe, without spilling the beans regarding his absolute ignorance of the nature of Nell Graham's proposed revisions. Seventy-two hundred seconds to find a way to reassure Dottie he was indeed her hero, her legal knight in shining armor. How could one man overcome so many legal, professional and personal hurdles in only two hours? He realized his starched white collar was soaked through; it was time for some liquid brain food. Richard opened the door to his executive suite and smiled at Miss Gober, who sported the ever-present grey sweater set, in defiance of the late summer heat.

"Miss Gober…I'll be reviewing some critical documents for the next few minutes. No disruptions, please."

Miss Gober gazed over her bifocals at her boss, the man who had afforded her the chance to see the Holy Land with the Bible Bees, the opportunity of a lifetime that was now only eight months away. Richard Napoleon Leigh-Lee IV was a living, if alcoholic, saint in Eustacia Gober's eyes. She had the passport, the trip tickets and the new Buick LeSabre to prove it.

"Certainly, sir. Let me know if you need anything."

Richard closed his office door and stepped over to his bookcase. He reached behind Dante's *Inferno* and grasped his fingers around a slender bottle. He cracked the seal and downed a third of the contents in one swallow; whiskey warmth enveloped him, soothed his aching head, softened the afternoon's hard edges. After another long pull, he replaced the bottle and returned to his desk. He opened a cabinet door on the bookcase and pressed several buttons on the combination television/VCR, then sat closely to the monitor screen, hands on his knees, and whispered, *"Oh, Dottie Chatwick, you are one hell-cat of a woman, you know that? You gave me the best afternoon of my long and miserable life and all I had to do was slip you a few thousand measly dollars…I don't care if you ever pay me back!"*

Richard stared at the videotape he'd made of yesterday's tryst with Dorothy. He was smitten, he hated to admit. Dottie proved to be worth every penny of his investment, and he would gladly have paid double or even triple for the opportunity. He grinned at the sight of Dorothy Graham, top-rung socialite, in red satin spiked heels, riding him like a bucking bronco and enjoying it, to boot. Yeah, underneath that platinum, high-maintenance exterior was a hot-blooded cracker who needed a good time as much, if not more, than anybody, and she'd obviously been pleased to discover his equipment was fully functional as well as above-average.

But now she had him temporarily over a barrel; Dottie was irate, he knew she wasn't fooling around. Her fury obliterated her ability to think twice about her reputation, her future, or the repercussions of her actions; she wanted that money from Nell and if he didn't get it for her, they'd both be run out of town on a rail. *Maybe that wouldn't be so bad,* Richard mused, *to live on the lam with Hottie Dottie...of course, we'd be penniless, a drunk without a paycheck and a debutante without designer clothes and manicures. It would never work.*

The legal oversight was completely his fault. Nell Graham had revised her will a hundred times in thirty years, but it was all just trivial stuff, why should this time be any different? The old bag couldn't even remember her own name, yet now suddenly she'd decided to cut Dorothy off without a cent, and he hadn't even bothered to take a look at the revisions. Yeah, he'd screwed up big time. And Dottie's clause was such a clever piece of work, too, hidden smack in the middle of the second page. Miss Gober didn't even flinch when he insisted she insert it...but Miss Gober would walk on water for him if she had to, now that she'd shot so rapidly up the pay scale.

But the fact that Nell's revisions completely obliterated Dorothy's right to the money in the first place, well, *that* was a pretty major error and clause or no clause, the inheritance would vaporize upon Nell's signature, and with it his chance to play Dottie's hero. Not to mention he'd look like the biggest fool of an attorney in the western world.

Richard sighed as the videotape darkened; he pushed the REWIND button; the cassette whirred. In twenty-four hours he'd watched the tape as many times. He had to have Dottie again...he craved her touch more than he craved his liquor and that made his hands quiver and his bones cold. *Oh, Dottie...freckled, smooth, sweet Dottie... I can fix this...Nell hasn't signed those papers, Danita Kay's in court...nothing's gonna happen today...I've fixed worse...but I gotta have more time...I'll tell DK that Nell called me from the hospital...she wants to make another revision, get my hands on the original copy...then I'll just disappear for awhile, take all the files...hell, next week, the old crank won't even remember what she wanted to change in the first place...and everything will be fine...*

A series of sharp knocks at his office door made him jump; he quickly closed the VCR cabinet and popped a breath mint into his mouth. Irritated at the interruption, he unlocked the door to find his wife and youngest daughter in the executive reception area, chatting up Miss Gober in the faux-speak they used when addressing a social rung bottom-feeder. He sighed and motioned for AnnElise and Tiffany Noel to step into his office. *This is too close for comfort ...what if Dottie gets a wild hair and storms over here, sees AnnElise...she could erupt like Mount St. Helens...gotta get AnnElise out of here... send her to a spa for a week...buy myself some thinking time.*

"Fine, fine...what a surprise," Richard said flatly, "I've had a terrible day and now my lovely wife is here to make it better. Miss Gober, any calls?"

Miss Gober handed him a sheaf of messages that he quickly scanned; none was from Dorothy, thank God. "Hold my calls again, please, Miss Gober, for a few more minutes."

Richard returned to his desk. AnnElise scanned the bookcases, looking for liquor bottles. He pretended not to notice and silently prayed she'd missed the shelf where Dante's greatest work was hidden.

"So, let's see... how will you both occupy yourselves today...Shopping? Bridge? Lunch at the club? How can I be of service...checkbook run dry? Need a new car to match your outfits?"

AnnElise ignored the sarcastic edge in Richard's voice. Several months ago, she'd put him in his place; she now controlled his every move, as well as the majority of his bank accounts. "Don't be ridiculous, Richard. We are here on a very important matter and I want you to listen fully to what I have to say, before you interject any rude comments. Do I have your word?"

Richard waved his hands innocently at his chest and nodded. He glanced at his watch; in a little over ninety minutes, Dorothy might make good on her threat and he had yet to devise a plan. He'd better listen to AnnElise and listen fast. She sat in a leather armchair next to Tiffany and stroked her daughter's shiny black hair.

"Richard, you know how hard our Tiffany Noel has worked these past eight months, dieting, exercising, clearing her complexion...she is down to her fighting weight and I see no reason why she won't walk away with the Festival pageant crown *and* the Miss American Beauty prize as well. We are so proud of you, *ma petite cherie*!"

Richard cleared his throat; this was old news. He hated the way AnnElise dramatized every conversation as if it was the opening to a Grisham novel. But he dared not interrupt, or he would be there for hours and Dorothy would waltz in and that would be it, his goose would be drawn, quartered and cooked. He nodded and smiled. AnnElise continued.

"*Ah, bien.* There is a situation, however, that we cannot overcome. According to Forrestine Culpepper, who as you know, is a veritable skin *expert*, Tiffany's ability to sustain her tan is impaired. All these months of tanning sessions, under artificial lights, have compromised her pigment production and she has begun to splotch. We visited a dermatologist, but he was a complete *imbécile* who advised us to stop tanning altogether and as we all know, palefaces do not win beauty pageants! Forrestine however, consulted with several national specialists and we now have a *plan*."

Tiffany nodded and smiled excitedly. She winked at her father; he melted into his chair. He wondered silently how much this plan would cost him and whether he would be expected to participate in any manner other than financial.

"*Fine*, fine, I see...you have a plan...an expensive one, no doubt...and *that plan would be...*"

"That plan would be that Tiffany, Forrestine and I are leaving in an hour to catch a flight to Atlanta, where we will then proceed to Athens. We will be spending a month in the Greek Isles, to take in the sun and sea air and where Tiffany Noel will undergo daily sea sponge massages with a professional pigment therapist. I have *personally* spoken to Ari by phone, and he guarantees me that he can manipulate Tiffany's pigment production back into full swing, so she can lose these horrid splotches and regain her tan for the pageants. But it will take at least three, perhaps four weeks, to achieve the final results."

Richard Napoleon Leigh-Lee IV stared at his wife and drummed his fingers on his desk. A month in Greece for most people would cost approximately ten grand; for what AnnElise, Tiffany and Forrestine Culpepper could drop in that time, he could purchase a top-of-the-line Beamer.

"*I see*. Well, it sounds as if you've got the whole situation covered, as usual, my dear. *Ari*, is it? As in, *Aristotle*? Ah, yes, and does this Ari perform his services by the hour, in the comforts of one's hotel room, or does he actually have a legitimate business location, where one might also be persuaded to purchase authentic antique vials of ancient Greek seaweed and hideously expensive ancient Greek bath salts, crushed by the hand of Athena herself, or perhaps obtain services of a more personal nature, offered by *certified vestal virgins*? This is ridiculous, AnnElise! A month in Greece, for a suntan at the hands of some rip-off Greek god? Tiffany, you know I am very proud of you and I have never denied you anything when it comes to your pursuit of pageant honors; but answer me this, AnnElise...if Tiffany is the one with the suntan deficiency, then why must you and Forrestine Culpepper accompany her? On my nickel?"

AnnElise tilted her head to one side and smiled at Tiffany, as if the answer was obvious to everyone. "Richard, Ari is a fully licensed therapist, he operates a certified European spa! He does *not* work in hotel rooms... *I know what you are suggesting...* I have seen his brochure! *Ça alors*, you would send our precious *jeune fille* to Greece for a month with no chaperone? Should she just traipse over there by herself, to be preyed upon by every hot-blooded Grecian who comes along? *Mais non*, I will not stand it! I am her mother and I care about her future! This is Tiffany's one chance to set her life back on track and prove that she has overcome last year's *faux pas*!"

Richard grinned wickedly, "It's not '*Grecian*,' dear, as in the hair dye...I believe we say *'Greek.' Fine,* I don't mean to undermine Tiffany's chances in any way. I would simply like to understand why Forrestine Culpepper must tag along on this bronzing boondoggle...do you realize what a month in the Greek Isles, for three women, at a place run by some huckster named *'Ari'* will cost?"

AnnElise stood up slowly and smoothed her lemon yellow linen pantsuit. She adjusted a diamond earring, then looked Richard dead in the eye. "Well, I can imagine it will cost roughly the equivalent of what you lost when that bimbo legal secretary of yours ran off in your brand new Cadillac, and your gold card, on a Las Vegas shopping spree...would that be about right, Richard? Now, we are leaving in an hour and we shall return in four weeks... and I..."

The door to Richard's office opened slowly and Danita Kay peered inside. Richard's heart pounded; he didn't have the capacity to simultaneously wrangle AnnElise about money and Danita Kay about his misgivings as an attorney. He jumped up from his desk.

"DK! Back from a hard day in court! How'd it go, sweetie?" He kissed his daughter on the cheek. She blushed and nodded.

"It was fine, Daddy, just a routine re-zoning issue. Mom, hey Tiffany... what's going on? Is everything ok?"

Richard watched intently as Danita Kay kissed her mother and greeted her sister. If he could slip out that door...escape from them all...hide from Dottie, until he could figure things out... *THAT'S IT! RUN AWAY! We'll all go to Greece for a month! Give me some time to think, how to handle Dottie, send her a fax or something, send it when DK's off looking at ruins...no, DK won't go...she's in too deep, trying to impress everyone, trying to make partner... WAIT! I'll just take that will and those files on a little Greek tour of their own! Put DK in charge! She'll be beside herself! Oh, Big Dick, you are one brilliant legal eagle! You are...*

"Oh, Daddy, before I forget, about those papers for Nell Graham's signature...it's an awful mess..."

"DK, we don't have time to discuss that right now. We're all going on a *vacation*! That's right! You know, AnnElise, I've been thinking...it's been too long since we took a trip together as a *family*. DK, your mother and sister are heading for Greece this afternoon for a month, so Tiffany can consult with some godawful tan specialist...anyway, you go tell Miss Gober to get our passports out of the vault...we're *all* going to Greece! In an hour!"

Danita Kay, AnnElise, and Tiffany Noel Leigh-Lee stared at Richard as if he was speaking in tongues. He choked back bile; *a month in Greece with my wife, my spoiled daughter and Forrestine Culpepper? I'd rather poke hot needles into my eyes...*

"Richard, five minutes ago you were complaining about the cost to send *three* of us to Greece, now you're suggesting we *all* go? *On a family vacation?* That's a laugh...we haven't done *that* since...since..."

"Since longer than I can remember! That's the problem with this family, we don't see enough of each other! Look, Tiffany's back in shape, DK's a successful lawyer and CPA, you've been preoccupied with the Festival and my nerves are shot...can't we all just take a break? Now, DK, hurry up, collect all the files you need, get that laptop you're so fond of...we can work from Greece just as well as we can from here! *Miss Gober! Call Charlie and get him up here*...you'll need to tell Charlie about the cases you're working, so he can get file the delay motions, and..."

Danita Kay held out a stop-sign hand at her father. "Daddy, I can't just pick up and go to Greece for a month! I've got cases stacked up from here to the ceiling! I've got court dates for two consecutive weeks! And billing is due tomorrow, and then I have to..."

Richard shook his head. "You're right, you and I won't go for a month... we'll go for a *week* and leave your mother and sister in *'Ari's'* hands, no pun intended. Now, I don't want to hear another word..."

AnnElise collected her designer bag and motioned for Tiffany to follow. Tiffany tried to kiss her father on his cheek, but her mother intervened.

"Ah, *ma cher*, remember, you are not to move your facial muscles for another hour, to get the full benefits of the cellophane wrap! Richard, I would say your *petite* mental lapse is the result of undue work stress, but I know that's not the case. You cannot possibly join us. Ari has reserved his last available suite for me and we've already imposed on his good graces by requesting a cot in Tiffany's room for Forrestine. Danita darling, of course you are welcome to come along, if you can get away, we could probably find you a nice hotel close to the spa, but it appears you have a great deal of work to do. Now, then, Richard...Delilah has the number where we can be reached. If you really want to take a vacation, versus simply ruining ours, why don't you go down to Hilton Head and play some golf? Or go to Las Vegas, maybe you'd hit the jackpot, find your Cadillac on some deserted highway, with the bones of your ex-girlfriend inside!"

Richard slammed his office door shut and leaned against it. "AnnElise, if I want to go to frigging Greece with you, you can't stop me! Don't forget who *earns* all the money around here, I'm the one who funds these wild adventures of yours!"

AnnElise's black eyes flashed. "*That* is a bald-faced lie! My family inheritance pays for..."

"Pays for *nothing*! You exhausted that measly, moldy inheritance years ago! Me and my hard work and the hard work of all the Leigh-Lees before me, we're the ones who foot the bill for all your perks, *Madame*...and I am sick and tired of you treating me like a pariah...you're not fooling anyone, you know. The only reason you made such a fuss about Miss Whitaker and my drinking, is to save your own face-lifted face, so you can continue to dangle your Charleston society airs over the whole town! But if you hadn't locked me out of your life five years ago, I might have behaved differently! You want to spend a month in Greece, fine! *Fine!* I'll gladly pay for it, to get you out of my hair! But don't tell me where I can and can't go, *ever again*! *Do you understand, or shall I say it in French?*"

AnnElise could not look her husband in the eye. Where was this sudden boldness coming from? He really was angry...maybe Dorothy was telling the truth...maybe he was about to burst under pressure...was he indeed part of that horrid Masked Ball videotape blackmail investigation? She'd heard that the FBI's tactics could be terribly draining. She crossed to the door and Richard moved away, furiously speechless. Angry or not, in her eyes, he remained a weak, brittle shell of a man.

"Richard. I'll thank you not to discuss *notre affaires privé* in front of the girls. Now, if you'll excuse us, we have a plane to catch. We will call when we arrive in Athens. Danita, dear, I'll bring you a nice present from Greece...Richard, you didn't even notice Danita's new haircut and makeup...take care, *ciao*!"

AnnElise and Tiffany Noel exited Richard's office with a flourish and nearly trampled an eavesdropping Miss Gober. Danita Kay bit her lip and sighed. She patted her father on the back.

"Don't worry, Daddy. If Mom's French blood isn't worked up at least once a day, she's not happy. You know we all love you very much!" Danita Kay smiled at her father and kissed him on the cheek. He plopped down in his leather chair.

"Oh, DK! I do love you. You are my brightest and my best, you work so hard! So diligent, and you never give up on your old Dad. I'm not easy to live with, I know. I only want to be respected in my own home. Is that too much to ask? By the way, hon, you really do look great! Every hot-shot young buck in the district's gonna be coming to the house to court you, you know! Your sister may be the acknowledged pageant queen, but you're the true beauty of the family...I want you to know that, DK."

A small tear welled up in Danita Kay's eye. She placed a sheaf of papers on her father's desk. Richard read the words "LAST WILL & TESTAMENT OF INELLE DUBOIS GRAHAM" and his gut knotted.

"Daddy, thanks...listen, I think you *do* need a vacation...there's something I want to talk to you about...Nell Graham's will...I glanced at it during a court recess. Daddy, maybe Miss Gober's getting sloppy...or maybe it was a clerk in Edits...and I know you're overworked...but there was a clause in the will giving Dorothy Graham immediate access to her inheritance from Aunt Nell. I think Miss Gober got confused... Aunt Nell's cutting Miss Dorothy out altogether. Apparently Mister Will found some letter in the bank vault from his late father, confessing an affair with Miss Dorothy wherein she tricked him into making her Nell's beneficiary over his own sons. Nobody knew anything about it. According to Aunt Nell, Mister Will was so upset about his own wife cheating on him with his father, he advised her to cut Dorothy out...or at least make some kind of revision. And I've heard a few rumors around town that Will's hired a private detective to do some checking up on Dorothy...he suspects something else fishy, I guess. But in any case, that clause...what if Aunt Nell'd signed the will, Daddy? That's a pretty hefty mistake and I don't think..."

Richard Napoleon Leigh-Lee IV beamed at his eldest girl. He took her firmly by the hand. This was working out beautifully. Dottie Chatwick was in a hot soup kettle indeed; she'd no doubt require his help and he'd be only too happy to barter his services for hers. And Danita Kay didn't suspect him at all...she was giving him an out, pure and simple. He could not have asked for a more generous gift.

"I don't think that this firm can stand to be without Danita Kay Leigh-Lee as a *full-fledged partner* for one more minute! Brilliant, my girl! *Fine work*! I knew you had an eagle eye and you've just saved this firm hundreds of thousands of dollars in lawsuits and legal headaches! *Damn*! Let me see that will....MISS GOBER! GET IN HERE! MISS GOBER! HUSTLE! *MOVE*!"

Miss Gober dashed into her boss's office and nervously placed bifocals on her face. She feared the worst. There was a no-refund policy for the Bible Bees Holy Land Pilgrimage. "Yes, sir, what is it? What's wrong?"

Richard smiled at his bone-thin legal secretary. "Miss Gober, I would like to introduce you to this firm's newest partner and I do mean, *full partner*...Danita Kay! With one glance at a seemingly innocent stream of words, Danita Kay has prevented the certain downfall of Leigh-Lee & Sons, Attorneys at Law. She not only rescued us all, she has also preserved the legal reputation of four generations of Leigh-Lees and prevented our most important client from making a tragic financial mistake! Miss Gober, take a memo! Inform the other partners, hell, inform *everybody*, put it in the *Tell-All*, the next issue's tomorrow...*go call them right now*...Danita Kay Leigh-Lee has been promoted to full partner with Leigh-Lee & Sons. And if anyone revs up the nepotism engine, you simply point out to them that Danita Kay's hawk eyes detected a million-dollar mistake that our supposed crack legal staff let *slide*!"

Danita Kay blushed to the roots of her new haircut. "Daddy! *Are you serious*? I've only worked here for a few months! I mean, it was really nothing, I…"

"DK, how do you think the partner game is played? Do you think it's a series of endless hours, winning your share of routine zoning victories, courting the board members at firm functions? *Hell, no!* It all comes down to saving the firm's ass, DK and whoever does it, that's who makes partner! *Guaranteed*! Miss Gober, call a special board meeting! No, wait…I don't need a special board meeting! I'm the Chairman! BAM! You're partner!"

Danita Kay giggled; not only was tomorrow Wednesday, the day her partner announcement would no doubt be featured prominently in the *Tell-All*, more importantly, it was the day of her working dinner with Roland. *Oh, that? Yes, I suppose it was in the newspaper…well, yes, I'm a Full Partner…it was nothing…a million-dollar rescue, fairly routine…but thank you for asking…go tell that to your damned Seattle hussy girlfriend, the one that probably earns minimum wage in a coffee bar and doesn't shave under her arms!!*

"Thanks, Daddy! I don't know what to say! Miss Gober, we'll need to revise this will once more, and I want to launch a full criminal investigation…"

Richard grabbed the papers from his desk before Danita could retrieve them and looked at his watch. AnnElise was safely en route to Athens, out of Dorothy's reach, for the time being. He cleared his throat and put one hand to his temple with a frown.

"DK, as CEO of this firm, I must *personally* review these documents, to determine who made this error; I'll coordinate with Miss Gober for the corrections, I know you've got a helluva caseload…*my God*, if I hadn't asked you to do this for me, to stop by Nell's hospital room and get that signature…I can't *imagine* the repercussions! Don't even want to *think* about them! And I agree…we should get in touch with the authorities about this."

Richard rubbed his forehead as if he was only seconds away from total ruination; in reality, he had closer to an hour. Even with AnnElise unapproachable, there was no telling what Dorothy might do.

"But you know, DK, this is a very delicate matter involving two of Chestnut Ridge's most prominent, respected families. We've got to be very careful…take it slow…find out all the facts. This will take time, DK. And I'm so tired…you're right. I really *could* use a vacation. Miss Gober…hold up a minute on that board meeting announcement…DK…would you mind holding down the fort for me, for a few days? I think I'd like to take off…do some serious reflection on this case… how we can preserve the sanctity of our client relationships and yet see justice done on their behalf…Miss Gober can fill you in on my schedule for the rest of the week."

He paused, and bit his lip. "Look, you two, can you do me a favor? I'd really like to keep my whereabouts a secret…every time I go off to relax, I'm inundated with faxes and phone calls…I'll let you know when I get to my destination."

Danita Kay hugged her father. "Sure thing, Dad! You go relax and focus! This is a pretty big deal for the firm…take your time. Oh, I've gotta run…client meeting. *Bye*!"

Richard Leigh-Lee IV watched his full partner daughter click away in sheer happiness. He folded the revised will and placed it in his coat pocket. Miss Gober cleared her throat, crossed her arms and pointed a finger at her boss.

"Another near-tragedy averted, I presume, sir? Maybe next time, you'll actually get the gist of it before you ask me to add a sentence here and there…"

"*Miss Gober*. Once again, may I take this opportunity to thank you for your excellent, loyal service and the clamped jaw you so steadfastly maintain. But may I also remind you that your recent pay raise *does not*, I repeat, *does not* give you the right to advise me on how to conduct my business affairs! Indeed, Miss Gober, this one was a *tad* too close to the vest…now, if you'll excuse me, I shall depart for my solitude."

"Sir, is there a particular lodge I should call to make your reservations?"

Richard Napoleon Leigh-Lee IV popped a tape out of the VCR behind his desk, dropped it into his briefcase and snorted. "My dear Miss Gober…thank you, but I have absolutely no intention of traveling more than about thirty-five miles from here. Take messages, please, Miss Gober…I'll call you tomorrow."

Miss Gober pursed her lips. "Another one of our little secrets?"

"Yes, indeed. Oh, and if Dorothy Graham should call…please forward that to my mobile. Very volcanic situation Mrs. Graham's in, very volcanic!"

Forward to his mobile she did. Richard was driving happily down the interstate in his black BMW, nearly to his destination, when the cell phone jingled. He pushed a button to activate the hands-free speaker.

"Hello, Dottie! *Right on time*! Must be in your little red coupe…I hear that bad cylinder clicking…you know, sweetie, if you were *my* woman, I'd *never* allow you to drive a single mile in a car that needed maintenance so badly! So, babe, how was *your* afternoon? You know, I've gotta tell you, what is it they say about video cameras adding ten pounds? It just isn't true, doll! You look fantastic on that tape!"

"Richard, *ugh*! This is no game! What's going on? I'm in my driveway and I can be at your house in four minutes, facing AnnElise in five. The shit's hit the fan, Richard. Not only is Nell cutting me out, but it seems Will's after me too. You can't believe what I just found out…I'm being trailed by a private investigator! You'd better have some info and a plan. Well…*I'm waiting…*"

Richard chuckled and waved at the car that passed him on the left, out of sheer joy. "Oh, now Dottie…I don't want you to be embarrassed, but it seems you've blown this entire thing totally out of proportion! First, *heh heh, you'll get a kick out of this…*apparently there was some kind of problem with the clerk staff…some bozo in Edits pulled an old copy of Nell's will…you know, that woman calls me at least three times a week to request some kind of ridiculous alteration. In fact, *this is really funny*, Nell Graham has been threatening to cut you out of your inheritance for the last twenty years! And one time, we actually had to put it in writing and that's the version this shit-for-brains clerk pulled up. Of course, I've *always* been able to talk Nell out of it…*she trusts me*, you know, *like a son*."

"Go on…I'm listening…you've got three minutes left."

Richard swerved to avoid a dead possum. "Yeah, so *basically*, Dottie…the will is in my possession, Nell never signed it and I'll be handling it *personally* from here. Let's give Nell a few days to recuperate in peace, shall we? But as your attorney, Dottie, I'd advise you to give her a cooling off period, before you stop by and pay her any more visits. Now, as for Will…what on earth could he *possibly* be angry with you at, Dottie? Did we overspend our clothing allowance at that trunk show last month?"

"Listen up, asswipe. Did you *hear* what I said? Will's been having me *followed…hello*! Remember yesterday, we screwed like hot monkeys at the Peacock? Your butt's on the line, too, mister big-shot attorney! And now I don't get my inheritance at all! I need that money to pay you back and I need to get to West Palm Beach before Will does anything drastic! I should have known you'd wimp out…you don't have a plan, do you? That's it, I'm pulling out of the drive. You'll be sleeping in the dumpster tonight! Who's to say I wasn't *coerced* yesterday? Who's to say you didn't *rape* me? I know AnnElise is home, because she's always home on Tuesdays, and…"

"Uh uh uh…Dottie, girl! I do wish you'd be a little more discreet on these cell phone airwaves, doll! Not so fast! You didn't let me finish, now did you? Complex legal affairs require a great deal of patience, sugarplum! You'll get your clause, signed with Nell's own hand…I promise! But it may take me a few weeks…or longer…and we'd better consult about this investigator thing."

"Forget it, dickless! I'm turning the corner onto your street. I don't have the privilege of waiting for you to get your ass in gear and do your job! We had a deal and I kept my part of the bargain…now you fix it or I'll fix *you*, do you hear me? Hear that? That's me, pulling into your airstrip of a driveway, right now, as we speak…I'm getting out of the car…I'm walking up to the front door…"

Richard heard Dorothy's expensively heeled feet stomp up the steps. He laughed into the hands-free speaker. "Dottie, honey, take it easy! You can't shop for clothes if you're laid up in bed with a foot cast! Oh, by the way…"

Richard heard Dorothy stop in her tracks.

"*Dottie*…I think you'd better listen to me, honey. *Dottie*…AnnElise isn't home…in fact, she's taking a *bon voyage*, as she would say…let's see…what time is it? Yep, they've just hit the friendly skies for Europe. What did she tell me? *A month or more?* I think that's right. They'll be gone at least a month. You know, if I was you, I'd be very pleased to think that my mortal social enemy was out of town for awhile. You can regain control of that prissy group of women you two count as friends, mix it up real well for yourself."

"*What did you say?* What do you mean, she's out of town for a month? Is this another one of your schemes, Richard? She can't leave town…we've got to vote on the Cotillion menu and organize the floral theme and we have a national press conference in two weeks…"

Dorothy Graham lifted her Oleg Cassini sunglasses and peeked through the massive beveled glass front door to the Leigh-Lee residence. The weight of Richard's words struck home; her mind reeled. *He's right! With AnnElise out of town for a month, I can take total control of the Festival! She won't be there for the press conference! I'll be the only speaker on national television! I'll be fully in charge! And I can sway the ladies on every decision, plan this entire event the way I want it! My vision! My dream! My name on the television screen. Oh, that NDCA presidency is in the bag, Dottie! In the bag!*

Dorothy turned and gingerly backed down the steps. She glanced around to make sure no one had seen her, then whispered harshly into the cell phone. "Richard…you swear this is true? Why the sudden rush to Europe? What could have been such an emergency…"

Richard pulled onto a secluded, weaving, darting country lane. "Oh, Dottie, it's just terrible, *terrible!* Tiffany's skin developed some kind of awful splotch-thing, they went to consult with specialists, to make sure she's cured before the pageant season. So…what do you have to say for yourself now, Dottie Chatwick? *Miss me?*"

Dorothy grunted into the phone and got into her car. "Give me a break. This all better be true, Richard, or I swear, I'll bring you down! You know, as I recall from Hoot's interlude with the police in February, simply *possess-*

ing a videotape of the '*full act*' is a violation of state law! I could turn you in so fast...but I still want that money!"

Richard spied a new liquor store on the left, only three miles from where he'd be spending the rest of his week. He asked innocently, "But Dottie...*why* would you want to show yourself for the money-hungry, twenty-five thousand dollar a day hooker that you *are*? That'd just be the icing on Will's private investigator cake?"

Dorothy clicked her teeth; he wasn't an attorney for nothing. "Oh, shit, all right. Forget it. You just figure out a way to get Nell Graham's signature on some kind of legally binding piece of paper that says I can have my money...and *soon*! Once Will gets back from his stupid golf tournament it's going to hit the fan!"

Richard dove in for the kill. "Dottie...*I need you...I miss you*...I want to see you again...don't you think I have your best interests at heart? Besides...I've come up with a plan for you to get your anxious little hands on the full value of your inheritance, *now*, while Nell's alive, without anyone being the wiser and I know how you can shake that P.I. and strike a compromise with Will...you'll have to tell me what it is you've done to piss him off, though, but there's always a solution, Dottie...remember, I'm your *attorney*...I'm acting on your behalf."

Dorothy swallowed. "What do you mean? What kind of plan? Where are you?"

"I'm at the Peacock Inn, *naturally*! I'm here for the rest of the week and quite possibly the weekend. Now, Dottie...I want you to go home and pack a bag full of lingerie and high heels and leave Will a note that you went to visit a sick cousin, or some such nonsense. When you get here, we'll talk. For awhile. Then we'll work it out, *one way or another*, to the tune of several hundred thousand dollars. Drive carefully, my love!"

Richard turned off his cell phone and belly laughed. Today he had witnessed not one, but *three* certified, verifiable miracles. His wife up and volunteered to leave the country for a month, only minutes away from learning about his act of kindness to Dorothy...his own daughter bailed him out of a legal jam and the potential ruination of his lucrative law firm...and now Dorothy Graham would be coming to him for the second time in two days. *What an easy read! A sick cousin! Oh, Hottie Dottie...give it to me, please!*

Dawn, Wednesday, August 25, 1999; Chéz Horatio Restaurant

Hester Graham unlocked the entrance to Chéz Horatio and ran a hand over the "CLOSED DUE TO FAMILY EMERGENCY" sign she'd posted on Saturday. Then she re-locked the door behind her, turned on the lights and flicked on the cappuccino maker, momentarily forgetting the fact that with Estéfan gone there was no need for cappuccino. It was a little after dawn on Wednesday morning, and her life was in shambles. The events of Saturday weighed heavy on Hester's mind; the discovery that her unrequited Castilian prince was in fact a homosexual was a slap in the face, but she knew she'd survive. However the argument with her mother and refusal to loan her fifteen thousand dollars pounded her conscience. Hester was overwrought with guilt. *I turned down my own mom,* she reminded herself. *How could I? I've got to make it right...but now she's gone off to Canada to help cousin Cynthia all by herself.* Hester fished around in her skirt pocket and retrieved a crumpled piece of ivory stationery imprinted with *'From the desk of Dorothy Graham'.*

'Will, I'm headed for Canada to visit an ill cousin. It's a serious emergency and I can't be bothered with explanations right now. Please make sure my grocery money is deposited ASAP. I'll call. Dorothy."

Hester tenderly folded the note and the scent of her mother's perfume kissed her nostrils. *Oh, Mom, you shouldn't have done this alone...Daddy's really upset; you didn't tell him where you were going, didn't leave a number, he's never heard of any cousins in Canada...he said he would have helped you, but you never even discussed it with him...*

Hester recalled her father's face; she'd stopped by the house late yesterday afternoon to make amends with her mother, but instead found Will sitting on the steps of Graham mansion's wide veranda, next to his suitcase and golf bag. *This note was taped to the front door,* he'd said. *She's never done anything like this...it's not like your mother to dash off and help people...she's been acting very strange lately...and then I found out...*

Hester waited patiently for her father to continue but he didn't; he sighed and ran a hand through his hair. She couldn't decide if he was angry or concerned or just plain tired of her mother's antics, but it seemed to her that this time her father wouldn't just sit idly by. After a brief brace of hesitation, Hester told her father about the argument with her mom. She left out the part about Horry and Estéfan, however; *that would kill him,* she decided. *Better wait for another time...*

They sat together on the veranda for an hour sipping iced tea. *Don't worry,*

Daddy, she'd said, *Mom's very tough, she knows what she's doing. I feel terrible... it's partly my fault... when Mom tried to ask me for help on Saturday, I was pretty selfish; I wouldn't lend her the money she needed to pay cousin Cynthia's medical bills... apparently they're gonna kick her out of the unwed mothers' home if she can't pay for the baby's delivery... I'll make some calls, try to find her... there can't be too many unwed mothers' homes in Canada...*

Hester noticed more than bewilderment about her father; something simmered inside him, just below the surface. Will Graham, normally a very calm man, was uneasy. Hester wrung her hands in silence. *Is there a missing piece to this puzzle? What did he say... wonder what he found out? Are Mom and Daddy having trouble? Oh, please no... I can't take any more...*

She'd kissed her father on his graying head and returned home. After a sleepless night, Hester rose early and now found herself at the desk in her tiny office. She groaned at the paperwork heap that screamed for her attention. Not only did she have to deal with the mysterious disappearance of her mother, but just being at the restaurant reminded her about the secret life of her secret love, Estéfan Rodriguez, the practicing homosexual who was apparently enamored of her twin brother Horry. Talk about a cold, hard slap in the face! On Saturday, after she caught them practicing at homosexuality in the produce cooler, neither Horry nor his paramour had called and no one in town had seen them since. Hester had spent the last three days at home, reading gothic romance novels and fretting, wishing her troubles would simply go away.

Now on this Wednesday morning, Hester looked at her desk, facing a stack of unpaid bills, a reservations book completely filled for the month and the knowledge that her life would never be the same. She pressed buttons on the restaurant answering machine and listened to the messages. Most were from furious patrons, one was from Horry. Hester listened to it three times.

"Hessie, it's me. Look, I'm really sorry about what you saw... we never meant to hide anything from you or hurt you. Listen, Hess... I can't help the way I am! But I have a right to a happy life just like everybody else, and in that stupid town you know I could never be myself! I love you, sis, and I'm sorry this happened the way it did, but maybe it's for the best. Estéfan's helping me find out who I am, Hessie, and we both realized that the farther away from Chestnut Ridge we go, the better our life together will be! So... I'm calling you from Florida... we're on our way to Key West... Estéfan knows some nice gay couples there who'll put us up for awhile until we get on our feet. I'll call Dad in a couple days and let him know what's going on, and he can tell Madam Chairwoman all about it, I just can't face her yet. But Hessie, I do love you. You have my blessing to close up shop and sell the restaurant... we both know I'm not cut out for the business world, it's for the best, don't you think? Kisses!"

So, once more Horry'd left her to take charge, make some decisions and get a grip. She played the next message, from none other than Margaret McArdle-Graham, whom she'd called immediately after realizing she'd been an innocent victim at the hands of her brother and his Latin lover. *I really don't want revenge…I just need to talk to somebody who understands what I've been through…*

Margaret's deep, sultry voice filled Hester's office. *"Hello, Hester, this is Margaret. I'm sorry I missed your call…I worked a double shift on Saturday. I will be happy to meet with you at your convenience; this is nothing to take lightly. You've obviously been burned, and I'm here to help. There are actions to be taken, and if you don't take them, you'll just allow these two to continue their free-for-all hurt spree on God knows how many more innocent victims. I have Wednesday off this week…why don't we get together for dinner…come by the Dispatch Office at six. And remember…you have the Power!"*

Hester stretched her arms, took a deep breath of resolve, then quickly set about paying the bills and clearing her desk. After an hour, she managed to put some semblance of order back into force. She then made a succession of calls to cancel the produce, butcher and dairy deliveries until further notice, with the simple claim that she and her brother were taking a much-needed vacation for a few weeks. *No, business is great, and we'll be back before you know it. But we're both so burned out…we really need some time away.*

She went into the kitchen and unplugged all the appliances. Then she rifled through the diary cooler and checked expiration dates on tubs of sour cream and yogurt and five gallons of milk; there was nothing that was immediately a hazard. She checked the freezer to make sure the various cuts of meat were well wrapped, then snapped a padlock on the door. Next she straightened the dry-goods shelves, making notes on a legal pad to remind herself what to order for re-opening, if that day ever dawned. She scoured the sinks, mopped the floors and cleaned the grease traps. After two and a half hours, Hester Graham was physically spent, but her mind raced. She crouched against a wall and stared at the produce cooler door, the scene of the crime, the place of discovery, the ruination of her world.

I can't believe my own brother! How can one twin be gay and one twin normal? I should have known… Estéfan always stood a little too close to Horry…they were always giggling…and touching each other's clothes and patting each other. Estéfan never looked at me when we talked…I thought he was just shy! And now of course I have to do all the work, close up the restaurant, fix everything! Good ol' Hester will do it! Horry may never show his face around here again…he and Estéfan, his precious Mexican piñata, may never come back…how am I gonna explain this to Daddy? Damn you, Horatio Graham! Damn you Estéfan Rodriguez! You can both just go straight to hell!

The sharp ring of the kitchen telephone knocked Hester off balance and she slid to the floor, then ran to catch the phone. "*Chéz Horatio, Hester speaking*...oh, hello, Margaret, yes I got your message, thanks. Yes, I plan to be there. Oh, that's ok, I know how it is when an employee doesn't show up...I'm sorry you have to work on your day off...ok, I'll see you at six. Thanks!"

As Hester replaced the receiver, the phone rang again. "*Chéz*... oh, *hey*, Daddy. I've been cleaning...*Horry*? Well, no, Horry's not here...uh, he...uh...he's out of town, didn't I tell you? *Oh*, well, yeah, I guess I forgot to tell you *that*, too...yeah, closed since Saturday. Look...Dad, I don't want this to get out, but we...uh...*we failed our health inspection*... it's no big deal, a few minor violations, nothing major. But we can't take any chances with salmonella, you know...so we closed for a few days to scrub the place down with Clorox. Of course there's no family emergency... I *know* that's what the sign says, but I can't exactly say, 'CLOSED BY HEALTH DEPARTMENT' now can I? Please keep it quiet, ok? No, we should be open by the middle of next week...yes, it *will* take that long to get it all done...*no*, Daddy, *please* don't call your friend at the Health Department... I'm *begging* you...remember our rule? This is *our* business. It's nice having a little break, Dad...I...we're both a little worn out. Ok, Daddy, thanks and I'll call you later. Have you heard from Mom? Oh...ok, well, don't worry. Love you too."

Hester hung up the phone, leaned her face against the cold steel of the produce cooler door and bawled. Giant tears streamed down her face. *I can't believe I just lied to my own father...the man who raised me and who loves me and who footed the bill for my future...I pray he doesn't call the Health Department...I've gotta get out of here...gotta talk to Juliette...gotta clean out that damned cooler...damn you, Horry! Damn you!*

Hester wiped her tears with a corner of her apron and entered the produce cooler. She propped the door open with a box of wilted brown lettuce. She dragged box after box of vegetables into the kitchen, then shoved them out the back door and hauled them to the dumpster. *I should donate this stuff to the Clinic...but thanks to my brother and his sloppy sexual practices, I'd be in direct violation of the health code!*

Hester dragged hundreds of dollars' worth of carrots, tomatoes, onions, potatoes, zucchini, five kinds of lettuce, raspberries, strawberries, oranges, plums and kiwis out into the back parking lot. *I never liked kiwis,* Hester muttered, *and I hate the color chartreuse*! She grabbed a kiwi out of the carton and hurled it against the dumpster wall. She laughed wildly as it smashed into a green, mushy, seedy, chartreuse mess that slid slowly down the side of the dumpster. She pitched another and another, until every single kiwi in the box was reduced to sticky, oozy goo.

Exhausted, she sat down on the back step and spied a half-empty pack of Kools and a book of matches on the ground, tucked under a large rock. *Estéfan's cancer sticks,* she mused. *I wonder what it tastes like to smoke?* Hester pulled a cigarette out of the pack, lit a match and held it to the end of the cigarette. She forgot she was supposed to put the other end of the cigarette in her mouth, to draw the flame up into the tobacco and so the cigarette flashed and caught fire, burning her fingers. She stomped it out and lit another, this time correctly, or as correctly as a virgin smoker could. She took a big puff, then swallowed the smoke. It felt wild, reckless, exciting as the smoke tickled her nose, but then it burned her lungs. She coughed for ten minutes. *That's disgusting! Everything about Estéfan is disgusting!*

Hester returned to the kitchen, noticed the black tracks she'd made on the floor by dragging the produce boxes outside and mopped the floor again. She scrubbed her hands with anti-bacterial soap and turned off the kitchen lights. *Juliette should be finished baking by now, it's nearly ten o'clock.* She gathered her papers, the ledger and the reservation book and started toward the door, but stopped and stared at the telephone.

What was it Margaret said? I have the Power? I wonder what that means? I don't feel very powerful at all right now. But I did stick to my guns with Mom, didn't I…that's a first I guess. And I it sure did feel great to lock Horry and his girlfriend in the cooler! Maybe I have more power than I think…Dad's always told me I should stand up for myself more. How dare Mom just run out on Dad…how dare she come to me for money behind Dad's back! She knew I'd give in, that's why! Wimpy Hester will do it, go ask her! Don't even ask her, just tell her, she's such a wuss she won't even flinch! I worked myself into a frenzy all weekend about this but I was right all along! I'm a business owner! I can't be expected to compromise my values just so you could fly off to Canada! You don't care anything about me or Dad do you? Always criticizing me…belittling me because I wasn't a beauty queen…making fun of me for being in love with a fag…but did you ever take five minutes to show me how to look beautiful? Did you ever even spend five minutes talking to me about boys, or love or what I want in my future? All you've done is look out for yourself! That's it, I'll show you!

Despite her despair, Hester felt a new courage surge through her veins; she was on her own now, she would never trust another soul to run her business or her life and she instantly knew that she could do anything she set her mind to. No more meek Hessie, ever again. She was so incensed about her mother's behavior she felt compelled to take immediate action. She put down her books and papers and picked up the receiver.

"Hello, operator? Information for Canada, please…yes, hello, I hope you can help me. I'm trying to find the number of either a…well, I guess her name would be Cynthia *Chatwick*, or the numbers of all of the homes for unwed mothers in Canada. *No, this is not a joke*! Look, I'm calling from Tennessee…my mother is somewhere in Canada trying to help a pregnant, unwed cousin named Cynthia Chatwick…and I've got to find her! There's a family emergency! No, she didn't *leave* a number, that's why I'm calling *you*! Ok, I'll hold…"

Hester breathed deeply; the Canadian telephone system played disco music for her listening enjoyment. *Estéfan loved disco…yeah, well, disco sucks and it's no wonder!* The music stopped and the operator returned.

"*Well*, how many homes for unwed mothers in Canada can there *be*? *Of course I know Canada's a big place*! But isn't this *Information*? Aren't you supposed to be *helpful*? What, did I interrupt your *coffee break*? *Let me speak to your supervisor*…all right, that will be fine. You can leave the numbers on my answering machine. You can reach me at 6..1..5..7..9..3..4..3..9..9..yes, thank you very much!"

I sounded just like my mother, Hester realized. *I'm just as powerful as Mom! That tone of voice really works! That operator wasn't going to help me at all until I threatened her*! Hester giggled gleefully and checked the clock; she had to see Juliette before Juliette went home for her morning nap. She gathered her belongings and checked that the security system was turned on, then she locked the front door. The Sweet Things Bakery was located next to Chéz Horatio. *I think I'll have a chocolate donut today*, Hester decided, *instead of an éclair…it's time to make some drastic changes in my life.* She absent-mindedly turned the handle on the bakery door like she'd done a thousand times before, but to her great surprise it was locked. She looked up and noticed that the counter area was dark; the baked good cases were empty and the CLOSED sign hung in the window, but it wasn't even noon. Then she heard the sound of a shoe slipping on gravel. She gingerly stepped over to the narrow alley that separated the Sweet Things from Chéz Horatio and there she saw a scruffy-looking man wedged in behind two trash cans. Hester squinted and edged closer.

"Mr. Bailey…*Henry*, is that *you*?" Hester stepped over to the trash cans in the alley and Henry slowly looked up. His face was unshaven and it appeared that he'd slept in his clothes. There were dark rings under his eyes and his shoes, which were covered with water stains and untied. He managed a weak smile.

"Hey, Miz Hester, how in the world are ya?"

Hester cleared her throat and knelt down next to Henry. Surprisingly, he didn't smell too bad despite the already-searing heat. "Well, I'm *fine*, Henry, but are *you* ok? You look…well, you look terrible…do you need a doctor? What are you doing in the alley? Are you *sick*? Should I call Euladean?"

Henry nodded his head and rubbed his eyes. "No thank ya, Miz Hester, I 'preciate it, but I'm all right. I've done been thew the ringer an' back, though, I tell ya! Alla them goin's on over t' the Poe House...yest'd'y...I ain't never seen nothin' like it...people over there's makin' spectaculars a themsefs...Miz Esperanza's in a comatose over t' the Clinic an' Miz Juliette's bein' held by the po-lice, an' then alla them Nashville mediator-types come in here, cameras poppin' ever'where an' flashin' them big lights in my face an' stickin' them big megaphones in fronta me, tryin' ta git me ta say sompin'...I cain't take it...I ain't built fer no spotlight...a man's gotta have peace an' quiet, ya know?"

Hester nodded in agreement, although she didn't have the foggiest idea what Henry Bailey was talking about. She didn't know Henry very well, but all her life she'd heard stories about him and his family and how they'd ruined everything they touched. She reached into her purse, pulled out an unopened bottle of water and offered it to him. He drank it half down. Hester smiled and pushed her glasses up on her face. Her stomach rumbled; she really wanted that donut. *Juliette held by the police! Esperanza in a coma! Had she learned the awful truth about her gay son's affair with Horry? Did the whole town know the gist of her family emergency?*

"Henry...what exactly happened at the Poe House? Did you say Juliette's with the police? Was Esperanza in an accident?"

Henry drained the water bottle and recapped it. He rubbed the back of one hand across his mouth and leaned against the brick bakery building. He stretched out to tie his shoes. "Ya mean you ain't heard nothin' 'bout what's happened? Yer 'bout the onliest one in town, then...ever'body else's been down there since yest'd'y mornin'...givin' interviews...watchin' that cooler door...prayin'...moanin' an' carryin' on...it's nothin' but a big Grocery Store Revival, I tell ya! I sure hope yer stocked fer awhile, Miz Hester, 'cause you ain't gonna be buyin' nothin' at the Poe House...cain't git in past alla them mediator-types and photographers. Raleigh's turnin' away alla the deliv'ry trucks...cain't even git 'em in the parkin' lot."

Hester was about to pop; what was going on? "Henry, I've been out of pocket for the past couple of days...do you mind telling me what's up?"

Henry winced and grabbed his stomach. "Nah, I don't mind a t'all, Miz Hester, but ya got anything ta eat in that there bag of yers? I'm 'bout half-starved, an' one a them mediator boys done snatched my wallet right outta my pants...I ain't got no cash, I ain't eat nothin' since yestiddy mornin'."

Hester scrounged through her purse and found a pack of breath mints. She tore open the wrapper and offered them to Henry. "Here, it's all I've got, but you're welcome to it. Now tell me!"

Henry popped three breath mints into his mouth and worked them around in his jaw so he could talk. "Well, Miz Hester...*it's like this...*"

Henry recounted the strange tale of the Sweet Jesus Sweet Potato Pie and how it came into his possession after being purchased at the bakery on Monday by an anonymous blonde, angelic-looking woman. He carefully omitted the history of the Sweet Jesus Sweet Potato, its explosion in the park and the visits by his Bathroom Angel, as well as the fact that he was only trying to play a simple prank on Corny Poe. Yesterday afternoon, when all the pushy reporters began to follow them unmercilessly, Henry and Corny made a pact to discuss in public only that they'd purchased the pie from Juliette Kimball and placed it in the cooler for safekeeping; that was all they would admit. So he filled Hester in on the most current details with the same version he'd given to police chief Bull McArdle and everyone else, including the pushy reporters.

"I reckon it was late Monday afternoon when we done got that pie from Miz Juliette...but I had me one a them big fleet deals a workin'...so Corny tole me, *'hey, Henry, whyn't ya jus' stick that there Sweet Potata Pie in the cooler over here...I'll put a SOLD sign on it, an' Euladean can bring it home after her 4-12 shift'.* But see, Euladean forgot ta bring that pie home. *It ain't no big deal, I tole her, we'll jus' have us Sweet Potata Pie fer breakfast*! But 'bout six ayem yesterday, Corny calls me in a fit. *Git over here, now*, he says, so me an' the missus, we head over t'the Poe House, ta git our pie, but somethin' ain't right. We go ta the cooler, an' there's Corny an' Raleigh...starin' at the cooler door like it was on fire or sompin'. An' I says, *hey, Corny, what you so worked up 'bout, ya done eat my pie*? But don't nobody laugh."

Henry coughed and rubbed his eyes. Hester scanned the alley and waited patiently for him to continue.

"So, I looked over at that cooler door, an', Lordy be, there's my pie but the SOLD sign ain't on it ...no, sir, there's a big, hand-writ sign taped ta the door a the cooler, an' it says, in big red letters, *'SWEET JESUS SWEET POTATO PIE...PROSTATE YERSEF AN' PRAY, 'CAUSE THE END IS AT HAND.'*"

Henry popped three more breath mints into his mouth; Hester frowned. She still didn't understand what all the fuss was about. Henry rubbed his temples and sighed.

"Corny, he still don't say nothin', an' I'm thinkin', *hey, what kinda joke you playin' on me,* 'cept I notice his hands was really a shakin'. Well, me an' Euladean step over closer ta that cooler door... It's fulla consolidation, ya know how in the summer time, you git alla that water build-up on that glass...anyways, right there in the middle a that consolidation...I seen it. The face of Jesus starin' back at me, lookin' all peaceful-like. An' I tell ya, Miz Hester, I tried, but I cain't take my eyes offa it! I was plumb froze up, right there in the Poe House! An' the funny thing was, I didn't care 'bout nothin' else...I had me this good feelin', like ever'thing was gonna be ok...like my whole life was gonna be differ'nt. I felt warm all over, like I was somebody *special*...it's like Jesus was tellin' me without sayin' a word that I's a good man, an' that I oughta be happy, an' take care a ever'body, an' spread alla this love I was feelin' around a bit. An' Miz Hester...I ain't *never* felt that away before...nobody *ever* tole me I was *special*!"

Chills raced up Hester's spine and her arms broke out in goosebumps, in partial relief that her own discovery of Horry and Estéfan might not be the source of all the commotion. "What happened next, Henry? Is the face still there?"

Henry nodded and ate the last four breath mints. He was visibly shaken. "Yes, ma'am, it's still there. Ya know how consolidation us'lly runs down glass, breaks up? Well, this *here* consolidation, it ain't movin', it ain't runnin', or breakin' up, no, sir...it's stayin' put, with the face a Jesus *impact*, it ain't changed a bit since yesterday. Not even when that orn'ry Stella Stanley come up ta see fer hersef...she comes in early ta git cigarettes an' a co-cola afore she goes ta work...well, she seen us all standin' there starin' at that cooler door an' none a us would give her the time a day, but she wanted ta pay fer her stuff an' git. So she huffs over where we're all a standin' an' smacks Corny upside the head an' says, *I'm tryin' ta pay fer my damned groceries Poe*, but Raleigh Poe says, '*Don't you be blasphemin' in fronta the face a Jesus right here on that cooler door!*'"

Henry paused for breath; he was visibly exhausted. He searched his pocket for a handkerchief and wiped his face. He continued.

"Well, Stella smacks Corny on the head agin, ta git him outta the way an' she says, '*Lemme see...what are ya'll talkin' bout, ya'll are a buncha goofy Jesus freaks*,' an' Corny tries ta point it out...but Stella, she's pissed off an' she pops open that cooler door an' wipes her hand all over Jesus' face! Well, we was all screamin' an' carryin' on...she done wrecked our mir'cle but fer real, she ain't done *nothin.*' Her hand warn't even *wet*! There set Jesus, still lookin' all peaceful-like, still settin' up there on that cooler door in the middle a that consolidation! Stella was so broke up she hollers, '*Oh my God, I see it,*' an' she gits down on her knees an' starts prayin'! I seen her with my own eyes! Now she's over there, totin' a big cross back an' forth in fronta the store an' Corny Poe done baptized her right there in Aisle Five at the Poe House!"

"But what happened to Juliette? And what about Esperanza? You said she's in a coma."

"Yes, ma'am, she is. Bout eight a clock, people start comin' inta the Poe House ta do their shoppin' an' word starts gittin' out. Me an Corny an' Raleigh, we tried ta close the store but whores a people kept comin' in them 'lectric doors. I tried ta block off Aisle Five but it warn't no good, them people kept pushin' an' shovin' over ta the cooler. Euladean, she don't like crowds fer nothin', she ain't one ta put up with no nonsense, so she takes off her Timex an' she makes ever'body line up real orderly-like. *'Ya'll can each git one minute ta look at this here door, not a second more...we gotta store ta run, keep them lines straight!'* she says. Well so, Miz Esperanza, she was first in that line, fiddlin' with them ropery beads she totes 'roun' all the time. An' she says somethin' in Mex'can I reckon, an' soon it's her time ta see the Cooler Jesus. She starts yammerin' away in Mex'can agin an' puts her hands flat on the fronta that cooler door. An' then her face gits all glow-y like an' she looks at her hands an' she starts wailin' an' says '*Meeverrugees*', that's Mex'can fer warts, I done foun' out later...an' then she faints deader than a doornail right there at the fronta the line."

Hester shook her head. "I don't get it, Henry. What was wrong with her hands?"

Henry wiped his brow again; Hester noticed the handkerchief was filthy and full of grease. She handed Henry a small pack of tissues from her purse and he rubbed his eyes.

"There warn't *nothin'* wrong with her hands, Miz Hester. Fact is, alla them bizillion warts she done *had* on her hands alla these years, they was each an' ever' one of 'em *gone.* Me, an' Euladean an Stella Stanley, we tried ta git Miz Esperanza ta come to an' while we was workin' on her, Stella says, '*hey, she ain't got no more warts on her hands!'* An then Stella says, '*Them warts was there five minutes ago, 'cause I was watchin' her fiddle with them ropery beads an' they was right there all over!'* Well, we prospected ever' one a her fingers an' them warts was disappeared with nary a trace. It was a certified, wart-removal mir'cle."

Hester breathed a sigh of relief; perhaps Esperanza would yet pull through. *Just wait until she finds out about her son is shacking up with my brother in Key West...she'll pass clean out again...*Henry ran a hand through the strings of his filthy, damp hair.

"Well, after that, half the people in line took off runnin' ta fetch their sick younguns an' their sick mommas an such; an' the other half musta called ever' newspaper in the whole danged state 'cause 'bout an hour later here come alla these cam'ra crews an' mediator-types, stompin' all over each other tryin' ta git inside ta see that Cooler Jesus. But Bull McArdle warn't lettin' 'em in, he got his big shotgun. He told alla them mediator-types they gotta wait fer the Mayor ta git there...then they hauled Miz Esperanza off inna amb'lance, I heard they done sent fer her daughter over ta Nashville. Ain't nobody knows where that goofy boy a hers is at...'Melio's beside hissef. An' then, here comes the Mayor totin' Hoot Graham 'long, ta sup'vise them cam'ra crews."

Hester helped Henry stand. He was shaky and pale; he nodded and swayed. Hester steadied him with a firm grasp and wondered how they'd located her wayward Uncle Hoot, who had supposedly returned to L.A. for a huge film deal.

"Henry, what did you say about Juliette…she's being held by the police?"

"Yes, ma'am, one a them mediator-types heard her tellin' Ruby Quigley 'bout that pie-Angel an' he jammed a megaphone in her face an' started twistin' her words 'round, made like Juliette planted that sweet potata pie in the cooler like a joke! Raleigh Poe, ya know he's such a danged fool an' so hard a hearin', he b'lieved ever' word that reporter was a sayin' an' he pressed charges an' Bull done hauled Miz Juliette off fer questionin'. She's in the pokey like a common crim'nal!"

Henry burst into tears. He held his head and sobbed, right there on Elm Street in the arms of Hester Graham. She patted his back and let him have a good cry.

"There, there, Henry…it's ok. Maybe this will all just die down by this afternoon…I'm gonna get you home, then I'll go over and see if I can't get Juliette out of jail. Does Doc know what's happened?"

"No, Miz Hester, Doc's at a med'cal convention in Tunica an' ya know what that means…he's done turn off his phone an' he's parked his hiney by one a them quarter slots. But when Miss Elspeth heard all the ruckus an' heard her momma's in the pen, she done locked hersef in the post office, cain't nobody get ta their mail. I'm real worried, Miz Hester…there's more a them mediators comin' ta town…I seen 'em on the main road…Barney Gooch run me outta there late last night, said I had no bizness gittin' in the middle a all this even though it was my sweet potata pie in the first place…an' I decided I had ta git me some quite an' I been walkin' 'round town ever since jus' tryin' ta think. I figgered this here alley'd be a good place ta git me some rest…my dogs was barkin', Mis Hester. I hope it's ok, I didn't mean no harm. Them reporters is camped out ever'wheres…waitin' fer sompin' ta happen…there's even one guy from Oster-alia, I think. An' people are comin' in carloads…sittin' in lawn chairs at the Poe House parkin' lot. They been lightin' candles an' singin' songss an' prayin' nonstop. An' then I heard Barney Gooch tellin' Hoot he wants a pitcher a that Cooler Jesus so's he can slap it onna billboard, fer Festival publiss'ty. That pie was mine, fair an' square, Miz Hester. All my life they done shut me out. It ain't never gonna end, Miz Hester…it ain't never gonna end!"

Henry sobbed uncontrollably and buckled over in grief. Hester didn't know what to do, but she remembered she now had the Power to do something. She lifted Henry's face and dried his eyes with a crumpled tissue.

"Henry, come on. Let's get my car and I'll take you home. You need to rest and I've got to get Juliette out of jail. Now can you walk to my car, right over there? Good, let's go."

Hester led Henry to her cottage behind the restaurant and deposited the wilted man into her Chevy Cavalier. Then she took off for the Henry Bailey Used Car Lot. As they approached the corner, they discovered a swarm of camera crews, satellite television vans and reporters carrying huge microphones, all waiting anxiously in front of Henry's RV.

"Henry! *Look*! Why are they doing that? What do they want? You can't even get to your front door!"

"Well, Miz Hester...they done found out that I's the one that got that sweet potata pie from the Pie-Angel. Hoot tole them reporter fellers I was nothin' but a two-bit white trash loser an' ancestral of a murd'rer afore I got that pie an' now I reckon they wanna piece a me."

Hester stopped the car. "Get down, Henry, before they see you!"

Henry scrunched down in the seat. "What am I s'posed ta do, Miz Hester? I ain't been home since yesterday mornin'...I'm so tired my eyeballs is achin'! I don't know where my wife is...I'm 'bout ta starve haif ta death...What am I s'posed ta do?"

Henry sobbed in anguish. Hester bit her lip. "Henry, we're going back to my house. Nobody will think to look for you there."

She turned the car around, headed home and pulled into her tiny garage. When they were safely inside Hester's cottage, she pulled down the shades on all the windows. She disappeared for a moment, then returned with a fluffy chenille bathrobe and waved toward the bathroom.

"Henry, why don't you take a nice hot shower? There's a pack of razors in the linen closet. You can put this robe on...it's an extra one I've never even worn, too heavy for me. You can run your clothes through the washer if you want, it's out in the garage, nobody can see you. Then you get some rest...you can stay out here on the sofa, or lie down on my bed. You'll find some Cokes and some food in the fridge...I'll be back as soon as I can figure out what's gotten into everybody and get Juliette out of trouble. Now, Henry..."

Henry Bailey looked at Hester with the wide eyes of an innocent child. She pointed a finger at his face, and eyeballed him sternly. "Henry...don't you set one foot outside this house, do you *hear*? Don't use the phone or open the door or anything...just get cleaned up, eat a bite and rest. I don't care who comes to the door, or if the phone rings off the hook. I'll be back soon. Got it?"

Henry smiled wanly but shook his head. "Uh, Miz Hester, I cain't stay here. If yer mama finds out I been stayin' at yer house, you been helpin' me, you might as well close up shop right now. Yer mama hates my guts an' I know she'll make ya mis'erble 'bout this, she'll tell all her high-falutin' friends an' ya know what'll happen. Yer right nice an' all, but I cain't let ya put yersef in jepady. Yer a real sweet gal an' ya got yer whole life ahead a ya."

Hester shouldered her bag and headed toward the door. "Henry Bailey, don't be ridiculous! Now go take a shower and get some rest, ok? You worry too much about gossip...besides, my daddy's always said you're one of the finest men in the county but you couldn't get a fair shake. And what my daddy says goes for me, and don't you worry about my mom! It will be all right. Just don't go outside!"

Hester roared out of her garage and pulled onto the street. Henry cried again and walked into the bathroom. He turned on the water, stripped off his filthy clothes and showered. He sobbed loudly under the pelting hot water until he was all cried out. He dried off, wrapped the towel around his waist and stared at himself in the mirror. *I look terr'ble...jus' how Corny looked when alla this here Sweet Jesus Sweet Potata stuff started...an' it's all my fault! I didn't mean nothin', jus' a little goofin' off!*

Henry filled the sink with water, found a new plastic razor and slathered his face with soap. He retraced yesterday's events as he shaved. *God's payin' me back...I jus' don't get it...Corny tole me he put that pie in the cooler an' hung up that sign after midnight, jus' like we said. An' he locked the door, went home, his daddy was sound asleep an' don't nobody else got a key to that place! So he an' his daddy git there at five o'clock in the ayem an' he sees that sign still a hangin'...but he notices there's sompin' on that cooler door...he don't believe it! He gits his daddy offa the loadin' dock...then he calls me an' I high-tail it over there with Euladean...it was s'posed ta be a joke...but now it ain't funny. I ain't never been so scared in alla my life! An' now Corny thinks I gotta d'rect line ta God...ever'thing you said's come true, he's tellin' me...shit, I'm scared ta death! But that face...it's so peaceful-like...it's so powerful! I feel so good when I look at it...I swear I can hear it sayin', 'you are special, Henry Bailey!'*

Henry shaved the left side of his face and stared at his reflection. It dawned on him that perhaps opposing forces were at work, Good versus Evil. Maybe he was being tested, maybe the whole town was being tested by God. The Millennium was at hand. Maybe they were all a part of a big Devil-God contest; maybe Corny, with all his self-righteous preaching, was right: they were all going to hell in a hand-basket. Maybe Corny Poe was the Messenger of God. Nothing made sense. He shaved his upper lip, then the right half of his face with long, slow strokes.

What I don't git is that Pie-Angel...Lordy, Mama tole me not ta talk inta mirrors...said it was the work a the devil...wonder if I done called me up a devil by talkin' ta my mirror, pretendin' ta have me a Bathroom Angel an' instead, this here Pie-Angel's come down ta smite me! What if this big Devil-God contest is all my doin'? Oh, Pie-Angel, I ain't done nothin' I'm proud of! Please, don't come down here an' smite me whilst I'm shavin'! Please fergive me...I'm beggin' ya. I ain't never gonna play no joke on nobody agin as long as I live, I swear! An' if yer the devil then you jus' git on back ta where you came from...this here's a good town, even if ever'body does laugh at me an' my family an' even if they've been a-laughin' all our lives. I cain't hep it if ol' Hardy Bailey was a drunk an' robbed alla them Grahams an' Festrunks an' then kilt hissef afore he done paid 'em back! I've always been nice ta people...I make 'em fair deals on depend'ble, clean used cars...I take back the lemons if I have to...I been doin' good as Hoot's Best Boy an' the Fest'val people an' I'm right friendly...I cain't help it if I've had a forty-year streak a bad luck! I cain't help it if my ex-wife stole me blind an' lied about it! I cain't help it if my forefathers was all thieves! But I ain't no thief, I jus' ain't never had no chance! I been good ta Euladean, I run me an honest bizness...I don't wanna end up 'cross the wrong fence, like Corny says.

Henry wiped the traces of shaving cream from his face with a towel. He got down on one knee, on Hester's plush bathroom rug, and wept.

"Oh, Pie-Angel or Bathroom Angel...or Devil...or God...or whatever you are...I don't wanna be all alone! I don't wanna be watchin' my sweet wife Euladean 'cross no hell-fire fence! I don't wanna be standin' there eyeballin' her an' Corny an' them others, all havin' a good time while I'm hoppin' round on burnin' feet! I ain't no good man, I knowed it, but I do love my sweet baby Euladean an' I cain't stand ta be without her! She's the only one in this whole danged world ever give me the time a day an' cared 'bout me. I been on the straight an' narra here lately, it warn't my fault I's born a Bailey... Please, help me, Jesus, an' Mary an' Joseph an' alla you Pie-an'-Bathroom Angels! Please don't smite me down!"

"*Henry. Henry. Are you all right?*"

Henry jumped. He dared not look up; either the Pie-Angel or the Bathroom Angel was playing a trick on him, throwing its voice from the mirror. He swallowed and said nothing. *Please jus' go 'way an' leave me alone. I'll quit talkin' ta ya, I swear!*

"Henry Bailey, get up offa that floor and come give your wife a kiss, or I'll smite ya myself!"

Henry felt Euladean's strong arms around him; he stood up, and they hugged each other tightly. Euladean began to cry, which reduced Henry to tears once more.

"Honeybunch, how'd ya git in here? How'd ya know where I was? Look at ya, yer as worn out as me! I'm so glad ta see ya! I thought you'd run off an' lef' me!"

Euladean smiled through her veil of tears. "Don't be silly, Henry Bailey!

Hester saw me walkin' home from the store and gave me a lift. She told me not to go home, says there's reporters everywhere. She dropped me off, she's on her way to pick up Juliette Kimball. *Henry...I heard what you said.* Now you listen to me...*you are a good man*! You can't go around believin' everything people say! It's wrong the way people treat you and it's not your fault your family was a buncha lyin' thieves an' suicidals an' alcoholics an' rednecks! But you're not like that, Henry...that's why I married you! And I ain't gonna ever leave, Henry! When are you gonna believe that? *Huh*?"

Henry wiped his eyes with his towel, forgetting his nakedness. "Ah, darlin', it ain't somethin' a man can jus' put outta his mind overnight! All my life people in this town been laughin' at me an' tauntin' me an' tellin' me I was a loser. Hell, even one a them mediator-types is even sayin' it an' he ain't been here but a single day! Oh, babycakes, all I want is ta make us a good livin' an' make you happy, an' be the kinda man you can be proud of. I figgered since we got married, since I been doin' so good at bein' a Best Boy, that people'd start thinkin' I was worth sompin.' But I ain't doin' nothin' but draggin' you down an' I ain't never gonna have no respect no matter what I do. Looky here, Jesus Christ hissef's done 'peared on the cooler door with *my sweet potata pie* an' *still* it ain't made no differ'nce!"

Euladean grasped her husband by the shoulders. "Henry, *stop it*! I don't wanna hear any more of that talk! You are a good man, but you gotta stop listenin' to what folks say! It's just a bunch a gossip! Now, *I* love you and that's enough!"

Henry stroked Euladean's cheeks. "I love you too, Euladean. You reckon I'm a good man? *Am I*? I jus' wanna be a part of sompin'. I jus' wanna be loved, be respected...like Barney Gooch. Is that too much ta ask?"

Euladean flashed her eyes at his. "Henry Bailey, the day you start actin' like Barney Gooch, is the day I whup your ass! Now, hand me a clean towel so I can take a shower!"

Unbeknownst to Euladean and Henry, Hizzoner the Mayor Barney Gooch was right then and there walking up Elm Street, past Hester Graham's house, enjoying the early afternoon sunshine and whistling loudly as he made his way back toward Gooch Office Supply. The rabid events of the last twenty-four hours replayed in his mind.

By mid-morning on Tuesday, the phone at Gooch Office Supply was ringing off the hook. The demand for his inspection of the supposed miracle at the Poe House Grocery grew like a fury. But by far the most important phone call was from none other than Hoot Graham, famous L.A. filmmaker, miraculously back from the coast and eager to regroup and redirect the efforts of the Sons of Glory Festival's Two-Act Play. Hoot informed the Mayor that he felt real bad about leaving the town in the lurch several weeks prior and that play rehearsals would go on as planned, as long as everyone would take their parts seriously and focus, focus, focus. In reality, Hoot was lured out of his lair by Fay Bailey's exciting tales of the appearance of the Cooler Jesus. Stella Stanley called Fay with the news of her morning religious conversion and asked if Fay would accompany her to church. Fay dashed to the Poe House in a fever to personally witness Stella's transformation for herself, then reported the finer points to Hoot. Hoot had grown weary of life at Fay's and this was exactly the kind of incident he needed to coax himself out of hiding. He knew what was coming; international press, countless camera crews, large royalty checks and he intended to get a piece of it. He immediately called the Mayor, they'd discussed things rationally including Hoot's request that Betty Gooch be reprimanded by her husband for disturbing the last play practice, and they'd agreed that there were no hard feelings.

Then, Hoot pointed out to Mayor Gooch that it would be a sad waste of taxpayer trust, should he allow every two-bit journalist with a camera inside the Poe House to photograph *their town's* cooler, make money off *their town's* miracle. Wouldn't it be *preferable*, Hoot asked, to appoint an Official Cooler Jesus Filmmaker, supervised by an Official Cooler Jesus Event Manager? It would cut down on the traffic inside the Poe House, they could control the images that were released, you know, make sure they were appropriate and tasteful; and in turn, offer the good people of Chestnut Ridge additional municipal funds with which to build that new park for the little children. *Remember, Barney*, Hoot warned, *it's all about the children and next year is an election year*!

The discussion ended with the Mayor awarding the city's Official Cooler Jesus Event Management contract, with its Official Cooler Jesus Film Rights clause, to Hoot and his camera crew; the fact that Hoot had no camera or crew was of no consequence. *Hoot, you promise to always film me on my left side? And you promise that the money you make offa this stuff, we'll split fifty-fifty, after puttin' some in fer the city? I'm seein' billboards...I'm seein' CNN...I'm seein' piles a gold coins in the town coffers...or at least, in our personal coffers, right, Hoot? To hell with the Festival...this thing here's got real stayin' power...*

After promising Hoot to meet at the Poe House, Barney told Betty to close the shop early and wait at home by the telephone. It was then that Barney Gooch proved himself to be the efficient civil servant that he was; he took total control of the explosive situation at the town grocery.

First, in the crush of the parking lot crowd, Mayor Gooch pulled a rabbit out of his hat, for all the town to see; he produced Hoot Graham, noted Hollywood producer, noted handler of Big Events, home from L.A. to personally supervise this miracle and its associated film rights for the full benefit of the community. Then, he'd shoved his way through the mass of reporters and television cameras fighting for a way inside and with assistance from Bull McArdle, they'd locked the doors, preventing the media from entering the grocery and stealing their photo ops right out from under them. It was time to personally address the chaos inside, over the loudspeaker of the Poe House grocery.

Ladies and gentlemen, this here's your Mayor, please be calm. There ain't no reason fer pandemonium. Everything is under control. Please git in a solid line down the center aisle, no shovin', no cuttin', ya'll. I have been advised that the approximate waiting time fer the Personal Cooler Jesus Tour is now up to an hour. Everything is under control. I'll be givin' a press conference here shortly and if we're lucky, it'll be broadcast in Nashville and prob'ly picked up by all them other network 'filly-ates. What? Oh, yeah, Raleigh Poe wants me to remind ya'll...while you're waitin' in line, why not take advantage of some a the big specials at the Poe House this week...Hump Roast...oh, sorry, Rump Roast, fifty cent a pound; Eggplant, thirty cent a pound...Frozen Pizzas, two fer five dollar...hey, Raleigh...they can't git them pizzas if the cooler section's closed...hey, ya'll...scratch that deal on the Frozen Pizzas...but we got lots and lots a special items, folks! And don't ferget ta stop by Gooch Office Supply, 419 Elm Street, in beautiful downtown Chestnut Ridge!

With the Mayor's stunning loudspeaker performance, the Barney Gooch-Hoot Graham Cooler Jesus Extravaganza got off to an impressive start. Barney instructed Bull McArdle to seize the Poe House as temporary city property and place it under martial law, by Article 317 of the municipal code. According to the Mayor's liberal interpretation of Article 317, the massive crowds created a health hazard to the town's good citizens and they needed to be controlled.

Next, the Mayor took time from his busy show schedule to personally review the options facing the Poes, who were at this point enraged at the Mayor's decision to take over their store. Option *A*, Barney pointed out, was an all-expenses-paid trip to the city jail if they continued to protest his mandate; or, Option *B*, they could cooperate fully, remain quietly in the second floor office which looked directly over the checkout area and keep a tally of the visitors who would now be taking their Personal Cooler Jesus Tours, as directed by Hoot Graham, Event Manager. Hizzoner promised the Poes fifty cents for every tour-taker, to be paid from the sure-thing international television and newspaper royalties that Hoot Graham was so skillfully negotiating that very moment in the parking lot. The Poes were no fools; certified, broadcastable miracles did not come along every day. They happily selected Option B and divided their ranks into two-hour shifts to record the devoted flock with a series of hash marks made on the back of old cash register tapes.

Hoot Graham proved his mettle and his marketing genius; he borrowed a microphone from a sound technician whom he'd convinced had fought beside him in Nam. He called all the press together in the late morning sun of the Poe House parking lot and relayed the good news that he was in fact their photo broker, as appointed by the Poes and the City of Chestnut Ridge. Over the groans and loud protests of the reporters, Hoot reminded them that if they would all cooperate, they could each achieve their respective goals...photographs, high ratings, increased circulation and a few coins to build a park for poor, underprivileged Chestnut Ridge children. Each crew was assigned a number and informed that photos and film footage of the actual Cooler Jesus Miracle would soon be available for purchase, to the highest bidders.

Hoot's next move was nothing short of L.A. filmmaker brilliant, Barney recalled, as he walked along toward his office supply store. In an effort to procure a camera and a crew, Hoot conducted a raffle. The winner would receive First Right of Refusal on all Official Cooler Jesus images; the pick of the image litter, so to speak, the chance to bring home the bacon and drop it in the laps of the viewers. There were no raffle tickets, per se; each interested party signed a piece of paper pledging to lend his or her camera equipment, sound technicians and personnel to the City of Chestnut Ridge effort, under the direction of Hoot Graham, who retained all future rights. When several members of the press corps protested loudly to Hoot's outrageous plan, he stood on a crate of bananas in the back of Corny Poe's Dodge truck and turned on the charm.

Lemme tell ya'll a story...there was this poor, dusty town without no professional broadcast equipment. We ain't got the money to pay for things like cameras an' microphones an' lights or fancy satellite trucks! We ain't even got a radio station, our little children don't got no decent playground! Half the people in this town can't afford to buy a newspaper, let alone no tv! We're just simple people in a simple town...an' quite simply, if ya'll wanna share in our miracle, ya'll can show us your gratitude when we pass the plate!

The raffle was a success; an Atlanta cable network crew won the exclusive honor of working with Hoot Graham and as he whisked them inside the Poe House, to film the first live shots of the Cooler Jesus Miracle, he realized that with all the other camera crews and their vehicles crowding the parking lot, there was no room for spectators. And spectators were the key to Miraculous Religious Experience success. His mind whirred once more. He quickly returned to his banana crate podium.

Members of the press...ya'll may be interested to note that we got us a family of life-long criminals in our fair town. Three blocks up the road, on Main, is one Henry Bailey Used Car Lot. Now, the Baileys are Chestnut Ridge legends. They been murderin' an' stealin' an' lyin' an' cheatin' fer 'bout a hunnerd years. Henry Bailey himself has lived the life of a loser for forty years. Hell, them Baileys purt near wrecked this whole danged town way back at the turn a the century. Now some folks is sayin' Henry Bailey was hand-picked by God 'cause he got that pie. But some of us better fam'lies 'round town knows that Henry Bailey done stole that pie from the person God intended it for. Now, ain't nobody seen hide ner hair a Henry since yesterday... now if ya'll wanna big story, go find him! Talk about a life a crime! Talk about a fam'ly tree that rotted clean through! Henry's prob'ly givin' interviews at his car lot...ya'll can't miss it, there's a big silver RV parked on the lot. Just go on, knock on the door...and...

Reporters immediately fled in droves toward the Henry Bailey Used Car sidebar. With the parking lot cleared of media vehicles, scores of religious pilgrims pulled in to pay their respects and see the Cooler Jesus Miracle for themselves, upon payment of a modest five-dollar Miracle Parking Fee. While the Official Camera Crew set up its gear inside the Poe House, Hoot instructed Euladean and Penni Poe to draw large signs that read, "PERSONAL COOLER JESUS TOURS...NO CHARGE" and "CITY CHILDREN'S PLAYGROUND FUND...DONATE AND HELP A DESERVING CHILD."

Hoot displayed the signs at the entrance and exit doors to the Poe House, respectively. He gave Raleigh Poe strict orders to keep the line of onlookers, which now spilled out the front door and curved around to the back of the parking lot, in tow. *Raleigh, just keep windin' 'em around the lot, like them rides at Opryland...you see anybody cuttin', just holler.*

Not one to miss a financial opportunity, Hoot asked Penni if her children could help him with a small task. Glad to be rid of their whining, she agreed and Hoot took Cornelius Jr., Susie, and Edgar Alan Poe to the loading dock, where he instructed them to roll around in the dirt. When they were dutifully smeared with dust, Hoot tousled their hair and gave them each a raspberry popsicle. He then deposited three sticky, dusty, raspberry-coated children directly under the sign by the Poe House exit, the one requesting playground donations. He gave little Susie an industrial-sized plastic pickle bucket.

You kids sit right here under this sign until I come back for ya, ok? Anybody gotta potty? Good, now ya'll just sit here and look real sad. Think about the saddest thing that ever happened to ya...but in between feelin' sad, I want ya'll ta smile at each and every one of these people as they come around lookin' at that cooler, ok? Now Susie, you hold up this here bucket until they drop in some money, ok? And if they put in a five, or a ten, ya'll thank 'em real nice. Ya'll are good kids. No, Edgar Alan, you just sit right there...Cornelius, you're in charge, you keep your brother here, ok? Ok, now give me a big smile...that's it!

Barney chuckled at the vision of the Poe children masquerading as filthy street urchins; they'd filled the pickle bucket three times over since eleven and they'd sent Euladean off to take a shower and get more coin wrappers. But by far the high point of the day was when Hoot auctioned off the first photo rights for a hundred thousand dollars; nobody wanted to pay more until the Cooler Jesus Miracle could be authenticated, until they'd proven to their bosses that this one was Legit; but once it hit the air, Hoot promised, the price would skyrocket.

And skyrocket it did; once the first photos were broadcast over the national wires, the offers rolled in. The bidding continued late into the night; hundreds and thousands of religious fanatics poured into town; the Fluffy Pillow Motel was crammed full and the Quik-Steak ran out of everything but grilled cheese sandwiches. Business was booming. The shelves of the Poe House were laid bare as the devoted flock decided that maybe the Miracle Pie's aura might have rubbed off on a loaf of white bread, a twelve-pack of beer or a can of cat food. Ruby Quigley drove to Smyrna, bought every lawn chair she could find and sold them from the back of Roy's pickup for twenty dollars apiece. Everything was rosy; at least, until Henry Bailey approached the Mayor before dawn this morning with a concerned look on his face.

It ain't right ta make money offa alla these here people, it ain't right. An' I'm the one done got that pie, fair an' square, I'm the one God, or that Pie-Angel done give it to...God don't charge no tolls, ask fer donations under false defenses! I want that pie back, so ya'll'll quit robbin' these poor folks! This town don't need no playground, Barney, yer jus' takin' their cash an' stickin' it in yer bank account!

Barney, Hoot and Raleigh Poe quickly huddled at the back of the Poe House. Henry Bailey could shut down their gold mine and that was not an option they intended to exercise. It had taken the reluctant threats of Bull McArdle, at the Mayor's insistence, to force Henry off the grocery property, with the warning that if he opened his mouth to anyone regarding his concerns he would be arrested and taken to the county jail.

The stream of faithful pilgrims swelled throughout Wednesday morning and the photos rolled across the wires. There were no additional wart-removal miracles, however, much to the chagrin of Barney Gooch. By one p.m. on Wednesday, the Poe House Cooler Jesus Miracle was fully under control, it rocked with the circadian rhythm of a full-fledged carnival and Barney decided he could leave for a few hours. He headed over to the office supply store; Wednesday was payroll day, Miracle or no Miracle.

Barney muttered softly under his breath. *And to think, all this happened because a no-good bum like Henry Bailey had him a hankerin' fer Sweet Potata*

Pie. Why in the world would God an' Jesus pick Henry Bailey to be their d'livery boy... 'course, it wasn't really up to Henry... that Pie-Angel jus' said, 'give it to a deserving person' an' he says he happened to be the next feller that gone in there... it shoulda been me... I go ta church ever' Sunday! I know Henry Bailey stole that pie. Jesus, you done lost your everlovin' mind... why'd ya give that pie to a goofball screw-up like Henry Bailey, anyhow? I reckon it don't matter, now, anyway... we've done taken control of the sitiation, an' Henry won't git his hands on nothing' else. Can ya imagine if that reporter'd been able ta interview him, standin' there in fronta the Poe House with his shirt-tail hangin' out? Woulda ruint our image... woulda kilt our Festival publiss'ty!

Barney turned the corner and stepped into the Gooch Office Supply parking lot. It was nearly two o'clock; he'd been up for two days straight. He stopped whistling long enough to fish in his pants pocket for his keys; *good thing we closed up, ain't nobody buyin' no office supplies this week.* Barney grabbed the door to insert his key, but it moved ajar as his hand touched it. He rared back with a start, then slowly pushed the door fully open. The lights were on, but the CLOSED sign hung in the window. *Dang you, Betty! How many times do I gotta tell ya ta TURN OFF THE LIGHTS AND LOCK THE DURN DOOR! We got thousands of people packin' inta town, roamin' all over an' you leave the door wide open fer a day an' a half!*

Barney angrily scanned the store; nothing seemed out of place. *Hell, it's lucky Henry Bailey don't come by here on his way home... he'd a stolen half my stock right out from under me, jus' because I chewed him out in fronta that reporter!* Barney guffawed. *'Course, he woulda had ta make about fifty-seven trips on foot, seein' as how he ain't got one able-bodied car on that mis'rable lot! 'Mister Mayor, sir, I'd like ta offer the use a my vehicles fer the Festival parade.' Gimme a break! The day I 'low the likes of Henry Bailey to associate hissef with that Festival, or anything else in this town will be the day I die!*

Barney headed toward his office, but paused as he heard a loud thud from the far end of the paper goods aisle. The scent of a tantalizing perfume wafted over him; he heard a slight rustle, like the sound a woman's satin ball gown makes when she stands up to dance. The hairs on the back of his neck stood up; he waited, but there were no more sounds, and no more scents.

"Who's there? *Hey*... I got my shotgun in my hands, so don't be thinkin' you can git outta this without a fight, you hear?"

Silence filled the office supply store. Barney gulped in air and swallowed hard. Another soft sound tickled his left ear.

"Billy... Betty... is that ya'll? Ok, now, this ain't funny... the last time ya'll snuck up on me, I had them heart palpiations fer a week an' ta top it off, ya'll run off an' left the store wide open, an'... WHO ARE YOU? PUT YORE HANDS UP!"

Barney Gooch uttered the words despite the fact that his shotgun was locked in the office; a tall, blonde woman dressed in a white gauzy dress and sandals smiled at him from the center of the vast selection of Sticky Notes. He blushed and let out a huge sigh.

"*Ma'am, you done scared me half ta death*! I'm sorry, but we're closed! I ain't sure how you got in here, but…"

"Oh, sorry, the door was unlocked. What a wide variety of interesting things you sell. Businesses in town must rely on you a great deal."

Barney nodded, "Yes, ma'am, Gooch Office S'ply only serves the best folks in town. All my customers is top-notch an' fer the most part they're computerized, up to speed…they buy the latest modren gadgets 'n stuff. Yeah, I only deal with the best biznesses in town an…"

"Why in the world do you think people use these?"

Barney blinked his eyes in surprise. Everybody knew about Sticky Notes, didn't they? You'd have to be from some foreign underprivileged country not to know about Sticky Notes. Not wanting to offend a potential customer, he smiled and nodded.

"Well, ma'am, ya write a little note on 'em, see, an' then ya stick it where somebody'll find it! Pretty clever, huh…ya know, the invention a them things was an accident, I been to their fact'ry, took the official tour an' met the guy hisself, ya know an'…"

"Why not just speak face to face with the person, take time to look into his eyes instead of leaving him a note? Wouldn't that be more polite? Somewhat more thoughtful?"

Barney grew irritated; he was a busy man with a payroll to cipher. He didn't have time to stand here and debate the merits of Sticky Notes with this female intruder, who obviously could not grasp the sensitivities of the modern business arena.

"Uh, miss, can I hep you? You ain't from around here, are ya, don't reckon we been intraduced. Ya must not got no office supply store where yer from, huh? Where *are* ya from, 'xactly? I ain't never seen ya 'round these parts…an' I'm the Mayor!"

The blonde woman smiled and replaced the package of Sticky Notes on the shelf. "Yes, I know you're the Mayor; I was told I might find you here. This seems like a nice town. Have you seen Henry Bailey? Is he one of your best customers, you know, up to speed?"

Barney started to answer her question with a question of his own, like *why are you in my store and what in the hell do you want*, but stopped. *Such a beautiful face…kinda glows-like…there's that smell again…*he shook his head and snapped back to his senses.

"Whaddya mean, is Henry Bailey a good customer? Henry Bailey ain't nothin' but a two-bit thief an' used car salesman an' a bad one at that! Offerin' his *'whole fleet a vehicles fer the Festival parade*! Gimme a break! There ain't a car on the lot that can make it up the block! How do ya know Henry Bailey? Oh, wait a sec...you one a his no-good relations come ta live here in that danged RV? Look here, we got enough people who're unemployed in this town an' we got us enough Baileys ta last a lifetime, ever' one a them is a liar an' a shyster an'..."

Barney's mouth snapped shut; the blonde woman had somehow moved to stand right next to him, but he hadn't seen her take a single step. Her eyes were like endless aquamarines and her hair and eyelashes glinted like corn silk. That delicious scent caressed his nostrils; it was like every good thing his mama had ever baked and lavender soap, all mixed together. The blonde vision pointed a finger at Barney and frowned.

"How do you *know*? How do you *know* he's a thief and a shyster? Did he steal something from you? Did he shyster you?"

Barney frowned. This gal sure talked strange. "Look, I don't hafta explain myself ta you, miss! But ain't no Bailey could ever be trusted, an' Henry's a Bailey, that's all. Now I'm gonna hafta call the cops if you don't git outta here an'..."

The woman closed her eyes as if deep in thought. Barney stared, mesmerized at the sight of her translucent skin. She was a good head taller than he, but it was as if he could see right into her eyes, right through her eyelids. She opened those eyelids and raised a silken eyebrow.

"Barney Gooch...I'm sorry I startled you. I'm sorry I asked you about the Sticky Notes and I'm sorry to have kept you from your payroll. I'm just looking for Henry Bailey. But I would like to ask you a question. Do you know the true meaning of *'Love Thy Neighbor?'*"

Barney broke into a cold sweat; how'd she know his name? How'd she know he had payroll to do? *Oh my God it's the Pie Angel, right here in my store.*

"Ma'am, excuse me...but yer the one that done bought that sweet potata pie ain't ya? Yer an angel ain't ya? Why'd ya buy that pie, angel?"

A tiny smile flicked across the woman's face; she blinked. "Do *you* think I'm an angel? I like to do nice things for nice people, don't you?"

Barney guffawed and slapped his thigh. "Well, sure I do, sure I do! But the joke's on you, pardon me, ma'am, Miz Pie Angel! 'Tweren't none other than Henry Bailey got that pie, Henry Bailey, the town fool! Ya meant that pie fer *me*, didn't ya, ya done screwed up an' now yer back-trackin' so's you can fix it right? The Boss Man's gonna be pissed ain't he? Ya done give that pie ta the wrong feller! I knew that Henry Bailey messed things up agin!"

The woman closed her eyes once more, but this time opened them in a stern grimace. Barney stepped back. She tilted her head down to meet his and spoke in a low, ghostly tone directly into his face.

"Barney Gooch, maybe Henry Bailey's not what you think. Whatever you say he is, don't forget that he is also one of God's children and he is as important and as loved as you."

Barney rolled his eyes. No real Pie-Angel would ever take up for the likes of Henry Bailey. If this *was* the Pie-Angel, she'd soon be demoted for being so stupid. Maybe she was new to her job, like the guy in that movie with Jimmy Stewart. *Her wings musta not be got yet...*

"He's the *runt* of God's children, that's fer sure! An' the gelding, to boot! He ain't got no balls! He ain't never made *nothin'* of himself! Not like me, mind ya, I got my own bizness, I been the Mayor for years an' years...my fam'ly's one a the town founders...I got me a sweet wife an' son...an' I ain't afraid a speakin' my mind, neither!"

The blonde woman straightened. She placed a firm hand on Barney's shoulder. " *'And I say to you, the meek shall inherit the earth. Surely as ye have done it to the least of my brethren, ye have done it to me.'* "

Barney nodded nervously. His shoulder burned where she touched him and yet he felt no pain. If this *was* the Pie-Angel, he didn't want to make her mad.

"Hey, what are you, one a them religious fantastics? Prob'ly come down here ta see our miracle? Yeah, I remember that stuff from Sunday School...so if I be *readin'* you right, yer sayin' that if I do somethin' nice fer Henry, it's like doin' somethin' nice fer the Lord?"

The woman smiled. "*Exactly.* But, lest you forget, it works both ways. If you have done an injustice to someone, or caused another person pain, then you have inflicted that same pain on the Lord as well, haven't you, Barney? I know all about the suffering of Henry and his family. I saw how you treated him this morning. And I'm no fanatic...I'm just a caring person who tries to be kind to my fellow man."

Barney inhaled deeply. Interpreting the Pie-Angel's words was not his bag. He didn't like the sound of what appeared to be an accusation. He was a church-goer and the Mayor and he was not accustomed to being inquisitioned. And how in the hell did the Pie-Angel know about what happened today at the grocery? Something fishy was going on...

"So what am I s'posed ta do? If I go 'round, treatin' Henry Bailey like a *friend*...what's ever'body gonna think? I'm the Mayor a this town...I gotta reputation ta uphold..."

The woman pressed her lips in thought. "Yes, Barney, you do. And so do we all, a reputation of love and trust and kindness. I suggest you let your conscience be your guide. This town has a history of terrible misdeeds against the Baileys and it's never too late to make amends. "

Barney looked down at his feet; *this Pie-Angel sure packs a mean punch,* he thought. *Ain't nobody outside a my mama can make me feel this guilty*...He looked up, but the woman was gone.

"*Hey! Pie-Angel! Come back*! I'll make ya a good deal on a case a them Sticky Notes!"

He walked over to the door and stepped outside. The woman had vanished, no car was in the parking lot. A shiver ran down his spine. *Wait 'til I tell Betty! Just wait 'til I tell Betty!* He fumbled with the telephone and dialed his home number; then he remembered it was Wednesday afternoon...Betty was probably at her regular hair appointment. *Man, she's gonna come unglued when she finds out ol' Stella Stanley's done give up the hair bizness...an' don't Stella sure look right stupid carryin' that cross around all day! Wait'll Betty hears this...be kind ta Henry Bailey...love thy neighbor...gimme a break!*

Early Afternoon, Wednesday, August 25, 1999; The Quigley Beauty Box

Betty Gooch reached for her can of diet soda. She tried to drain the last drops, but her hair rollers created an unforeseen obstacle, preventing her from tilting back far enough to wedge the soda can under the hair dryer's plastic dome and still meet her lips. The Quigley Beauty Box was packed to the gills with angry women in dire need of hair repair; angry women with standing Wednesday appointments who did not like to be kept waiting. Stella Stanley's sudden resignation to convert new souls in front of the Cooler Jesus did not set well with Chestnut Ridge's bouffanted matrons, and Fay Bailey was handling six customers simultaneously. Betty grumbled to herself; she needed a straw but that need was quite low on the totem pole within the frenzy of the Beauty Box, relatively speaking.

She gave up on the soda and checked the time; two-thirty…she'd been there for an hour and a half. But it was preferable to sitting at home waiting for Barney to call her from the Poe House to report some ridiculous new development in the bidding war for Cooler Jesus photos. Betty grinned to herself; Stella Stanley's absence was the key to her newfound hairstyle freedom.

For years, Betty and Stella clashed in a beauty salon battle; Betty dreamed of a short cut and a tight perm to put some much-needed body into her fine, limp hair. Stella refused to perform the operation, claiming that Betty's hair was too fragile and that she would not be responsible for causing one of her most dependable customers to experience baldness at such an early age.

But today was different; Stella was gone and Fay was far too busy juggling customers, telephones and appointment books to care about Betty's tender scalp. *I should have done this years ago,* Betty realized as she'd watched Fay snip her hair to a five-inch length, *but Stella would have whupped my ass if I'd switched to Fay, right under her nose.* Ten more minutes under the dryer, then the long-desired effect would be achieved. Betty reached out to the small table next to her hair dryer chair for today's issue of the *Chestnut Ridge Tell-All.* There on the front page and on the following seven pages were photos and dramatic headlines that recited the fascinating story of the Poe House Cooler Jesus Miracle. *What a bunch of crap,* Betty observed. *What a bunch of dumb-asses, fighting to get their picture taken, saying they believe in the healing power of the Cooler Jesus, everybody wants to be famous.*

She glanced at a photo of her husband Barney who sported a top hat emblazoned with "MAYOR" across the band. He smiled widely, his arm around one of the Official Cooler Jesus Camera Crew members. In a second photo, Barney held his head with one hand and comforted Stella Stanley with another as Stella took time out from her cross-carrying to smoke a cigarette on the front stoop of the Poe House Grocery. *Look at that damned old fool,* she thought. *I'm the one married to him...I cook his food and wash his dirty shorts, hell, I'm the one that glued that sign on his stupid hat and not one damned mention of me anywhere!*

As Betty disgustedly folded the paper, she noticed that the non-Miracle-related news events were crammed together on the back page. Her eyes scanned top to bottom, looking for the business incorporations section; Gooch Office Supply's best sales leads resulted from Betty's efforts to meet and greet the newcomers to the world of Chestnut Ridge entrepreneurism. She let out a groan as she glanced at small headline, *"DUE TO SPECIAL MIRACLE COVERAGE, BIRTH, DEATH AND BUSINESS ANNOUNCEMENTS WILL BE ABBREVIATED."*

Then, unexpectedly, she caught a particular photo out of the corner of her eye. She stared at it; she didn't recognize the woman, but there was something vaguely familiar about that face...she read the headline and then the article, in disbelief. To her shock, Betty Gooch realized that the woman in the photo was none other than Danita Kay Leigh-Lee, who not only had been promoted to full partner, the first full *female* partner, by the way, at Leigh-Lee & Sons, but she had also apparently undergone some kind of major facial transformation. Betty stared at Danita 's photograph.

Must be nice to have a rich daddy to pay for cosmetic surgery and expensive haircuts and a new wardrobe, she fumed. *Must have cost that rich daddy a fortune to change that sow's ear into a silk purse...must be nice to have a rich daddy to give you a good job, a big fancy office and put your name in the paper.*

Betty flung the newspaper across the row of hair dryer chairs at the Quigley Beauty Box. She reached for her soda can, prepared to lob it as well, but Fay Bailey grabbed it, snapped off Betty's dryer and lifted the plastic dome. Fay smacked her gum loudly, then rolled it to one side of her ruby red-lined mouth.

"What's yer problem, miss priss? You only been sittin' here an extry minute er two...cain't you see I got my hands full? Now git over there in that chair an' rinch off yer hair, git that perm'nent solution out, rinch it good an' I'll be there'n a sec. Betty...*BETTY*!"

Betty bent down, picked up the newspaper, flipped it over and thrust it into Fay's bewildered face. "*Look*! Look at that! *You know who that is*? That's *Dogface*... Danita Kay Leigh-Lee, new partner at her daddy's law firm! *Look at that*...how in the world do you explain it, huh? She went from ugly to passable in one week...she didn't look like that at our meetin' last Tuesday! You tell me how that's done, Fay, you tell me!"

Fay popped her gum, studied the photo and placed her hands on her hips. "Body wave, I reckon...see that curl? Yep, it's a body wave, or I ain't..."

"You can't change a *dogface* like Danita Kay into somethin' like that with just a *body wave*, you idiot! We're talkin' major surgery...we're talkin' big bucks! I'd give my left titty to look like that and WHAM, her daddy just goes out and buys it for her!"

Fay sniffed and sighed, "Well, yer the one done said she was the homeliest girl in town, Betty! Hey, maybe she done heard what ya said in that powder room...maybe she done put her daddy's *money* where *yer mouth* is!"

Fay whooped with laughter at her joke, then ran across the room; the smell of burned hair permeated the Quigley Beauty Box. Betty followed behind, incensed.

"She didn't hear me, nobody was in that bathroom but us! She's just like all those other uppity social snits in this town...she likes to flaunt all her daddy's money in my face!"

Fay removed a hot roller from a customer's singed head and fanned the air with a wet towel. "*Don't worry, sweetie, it'll cool off in a sec...yeah, I can fix that*...listen to me, Betty Gooch...you gotta quit takin' it personal ever' time one a them Leigh-Lees er Grahams er Festrunks drops a dollar! When're you gonna start workin' on improvin' yer own social stratus insteada jus' sittin' around here bitchin' about what ever'body else is got? Look a me...I took matters inta my own hands...the day I dropped Henry Bailey, I shot up that social ladder so fast I had men fallin' inta my lap! I ain't never looked back, neither! An now with Stella gone, I'm gonna be RICH! I tell ya, there's big money in hair, Betty, good money! Now, look, Betty...yer on the right track...gittin' this new do, an' I'm proud ta say it's prob'ly gonna be some a my best work...ya jus' gotta take it all the way, that's all I'm sayin'. But if ya don't hurry up and rinch off that perm solution yer gonna be *takin'* it all the way to the *wig shop*, if ya know what I mean."

Betty quickly unrolled her hair and rinsed it in a large rust-stained porcelain sink as she listened to Fay's advice on improving one's social position. Fay lit a cigarette and prepared to tease Mrs. Euling's flaming red locks.

"It's like this, *hon*...I ain't one ta bring up the past, but you screwed up big-time when you married Barney...that man jus' likes ta hear hisself talk! Now, in my book, ya missed the Big Cruise on the Love Boat after that Masked Ball...ya coulda jus' took up with Roland Gastineau right then an' there...ever'body in town expected ya to, so why ya didn't, I cain't say. Ever since, you been chasin' him an' chasin' him with me as yer onliest competition, but I seen how heartsick you been, so I done backed off him. But now, you got a problem. You got dogfaces turned inta beauty queens, hell, you ain't stood a chance...looka how her momma's dolled up all the time an' that sister a hers...Tiff'ny. You know what them two spends on face waxin' a year? Nope, you ain't stood a chance, now..."

Betty wrung the water out of her short locks; she reached for a towel. "So what am I supposed to do? I can't just leave my husband and my son, hell, I own half that business, you know...and Barney'd never give it to me if I got a divorce!"

Faye waved the teasing comb at Betty and flicked cigarette ashes onto the floor. "Honey, ain't nobody said nothin' 'bout *divorce*! Now, me, I ain't had no choice but ta divorce Henry...he was takin' alla my money an' cheatin' on me an' lyin' about it...but you, you ain't in that position! But ya gotta fight fer what's yers! Way I see it, you was first in the Roland Gastineau chow line an' now that line's gittin' longer...you'd best be liftin' yer bowl to the soup pot, if ya catch my drift!"

Betty plopped into a faded pink salon chair and stared at herself in the mirror; damp corkscrew curls framed her face. *It's not exactly like that picture I showed Fay*, she observed. *But she's still gotta comb it out and fix it yet. I think it makes me look younger...I wonder if Roland will notice...I've gotta get to him before he sees Dogface...*

"Fay, get over here and work your magic! I'm gonna do what you said...I'm gonna put on my best dress and all my makeup and some of that Lewd Lady perfume Barney got me for Christmas last year and I'm gonna go see Roland Gastineau...show him the new me! I gotta do something before Dogface does...I gotta make him notice me, make him remember how special we are together! But what'm I gonna tell Barney?"

Fay held the cigarette and popped her gum. "Betty, yer brain cells musta all been in that hair I jus' cut off...look at alla them pitchers in the paper...what time'd Barney git home last night?"

Betty curled a lip. "About twelve...twelve-thirty."

"Well, is them camera fellas gone? *Hell, no*! You think Barney's gonna spend time at home with you insteada gittin' his pitcher took, girlfriend?"

Betty smiled slyly. She'd take Billy to her sister's house, have the evening free. "Fay, you mind if I use the phone?"

Betty dialed her sister and made the necessary arrangements for Billy to spend the night. Then she dialed Roland's secretary. It was time to stop moping and get serious.

"Yes, hello, this is Mrs. Betty Gooch...from the Festival accountin' committee... I'd like to speak to Roland, to give him my report...uh, huh...I see...uh huh...*do what? Shit*...I mean, *you don't say*...well, oh, I remember *now*... silly me! Well, thanks, sure, I'll just fax it over there! Thanks!"

Betty slammed the hot pink telephone onto the receiver. Fay ignored her and teased Mrs. Euling's red hair into a vertical mass similar to the thatch on a troll doll. Betty fumed.

"Mister Gastineau's not in; he's got client meetings all day. But guess where Mister Gastineau's goin' *tonight*? He's goin' to Dogface's office, for a meeting! *A Festival meeting!* And guess who's not *invited!* You, me, we're half the committee and we're not even invited! '*Why not fax your report to Miss Leigh-Lee's office*,' she says! That's it! I'm too late! My life's over!"

Fay stopped teasing and stared at Betty. *Them curls ain't her cup a tea*, she realized, *I done made her inta Orphan Annie, lookit alla that frizz.* Ashes from Fay's cigarette fell into Mrs. Euling's troll hair; luckily, Mrs. Euling was sound asleep and didn't notice.

"Hey, *whiney-baby*! I been *lotsa* places I ain't been asked! What's a matter, yer car don't know the way ta Dogface's office? You been struck lame, cain't ya walk up them big steps ta that front door? You gonna jus' give up, let Miss Makeover steal yer man?"

Betty gritted her teeth. Fay was right; she would show them both, Dogface and Roland. It might take a couple whiskey shots to give her the courage, but she could handle it, no doubt. Anybody who could spend fifteen years married to Barney Gooch, run Gooch Office Supply and keep a wild twelve-year-old in line could easily prove to her secret love that they were meant to be together. No doubt about it.

"Well, then, *dammit*, Fay, hurry up! Miz Euling's out like a light, get over here and work on me so I can get home and get ready! I got one shot at the love of my life and I don't aim to sit here and waste it at the Quigley Beauty Box! You think Roland'll like these curls?"

Just outside Chestnut Ridge, Roland Gastineau shifted in the hard chair in the office of Doctor Avery Parker, Jr. He tried to think of a way to casually sneak a peak at his wristwatch; it seemed Dr. Parker had been lecturing him for hours on the finer points of American Civil War history and he still had several stops to make on this round of cold calls. Dr. Parker stood up from his desk and crossed over to the chalkboard. It was plainly apparent to Roland that Dr. Parker had no intention of hiring Gastineau & Gastineau, CPAs, but that he was desperate for an audience in the lull between summer school and the fall semester.

"Dr. Parker...if I may interrupt...*this is truly fascinating*, but I promised my mother I'd drive her to the airport this afternoon...a distant cousin is arriving from Georgia...I'm sorry to cut this short, but my mom really hates to drive on the interstate!"

Dr. Parker raised his eyebrows, then smiled weakly; the best part of his lecture was at hand. "No matter, Roland, we can resume at this point next time. I can tell you are a serious scholar of history; I suggest you might want to audit my *"Myth vs. Truth: The American Slave's Role in Union Preservation"* class this fall. I'm sure it will fill quickly; shall I put you down?"

Roland stood and coughed; he hoped his mother hadn't planned to be outside working in her rose garden this afternoon for all to see, as there was no scheduled trip to the airport to collect a visiting cousin.

"Uh, well, I don't know, Dr. Parker…it sounds *great*, but you know I'm the Festival Auditor and that's taking *way* too much of my time right now. Maybe next spring…"

Dr. Parker nodded. He tapped the chalkboard and rubbed his hands together. "I see. You know, Roland, it is my opinion that this entire Festival is a dramatic waste of time, energy and resources. We would be better served as a community to erect a monument of some sort on the town square, one that informed the public of the *true* story regarding the founding of this city. The falsehoods which prevail in Chestnut Ridge are anathema, don't you agree?"

Roland knit his brows and nodded slowly; he didn't want to encourage Dr. Parker to open another discussion on this new topic. He was rescued, however, by Dr. Parker's son, Rex, who peered in from the hallway.

"Son, come in, what is it? Roland, you know Rex, my son. Rex, this is Mr. Gastineau. Rex is attending a seminar here on campus for African-American students who wish to pursue the study of civil rights issues. His mother and I have high hopes for this young man!"

Rex extended his thirteen-year-old hand and shook Roland's vigorously. "Hi, Mr. Gastineau, I'm very pleased to meet you. Dad, is it ok if I go to the Student Center with some of the other kids from the seminar? They're showing two Malcolm X documentaries back-to-back and Mom said you could stay here and work until it's over."

Rex watched his father anxiously for a reply; it was given with pride, just as Rex expected. Unbeknownst to Dr. Parker, however, Rex had no intention of seeing any Malcolm X documentaries; Leonard Festrunk and Billy Gooch were picking him up behind the football stadium to study firsthand the finer attributes of the crappie that lived in Stones River. Dr. Parker beamed.

"Certainly, son, here's a twenty…you'd better eat something at the movies, because we're going by the hospital to visit your Aunt Pearl this evening on the way home. But no junk, now! Have fun and pay special attention to the *issues*, Rex, *not* the actors!"

Rex thanked his father, said goodbye to Roland and whisked out the door. Roland shook Dr. Parker's hand. "You must be very proud of your son, Dr. Parker. He's a fine boy!"

Dr. Parker grinned. "Yes, thank you, I am proud of him. It's extremely difficult to properly raise a young child in a place where no credit whatsoever is given to the contributions of his race. We've had a rough go…he was spending far too much time carousing with rednecks and people from the wrong social class…but the matter is well in hand now, thank God!"

Roland grinned and stepped into the hall. "Thanks, Dr. Parker, for your time. I can see why you're so popular with the students! Take care! I'll be in touch!"

Roland stretched his long legs into a near-gallop. *Yeah, I'll be in touch all right, when hell freezes over and pigs fly! What an overstuffed, boring history geek!* On the way to his car, he performed some mental calculations; after the thirty-minute drive back to town and adding the stops for wine, dessert, roses and a shower prior to his meeting with Danita Kay, he would have exactly twenty minutes in which to cram three cold calls.

Bag it, he decided. Danita Kay was far more important. *It's not really a date,* he rationalized, *it's just a meeting…but I've gotta make the right impression.* He started his car, pulled into traffic and dialed the firm's secretary on the cell phone.

"Hey, Marie…look, I'm running late, Dr. Parker asked a lot of questions… but there's a huge traffic jam on I-24…I should have taken the back road, but it's too late now…can you call my last three appointments and reschedule? Thanks. Any messages? Great. I'll talk to you…oh…ok, put him on…"

Roland banged the steering wheel with the heels of his hands; his father demanded an audience. The cash flow gods must be appeased.

"Son…how's it going? Got those ten new clients yet? What's the deal with Parker?"

Roland cringed and rolled his eyes. "Not yet, Dad, but I'm working on it! Dr. Parker wants a second meeting…"

"Well, since you don't have any clients to occupy you, you can come to the Rotary meeting with me tonight…it's been a few weeks since you've made an appearance. Gotta work that crowd hard, Roland, if you intend to pick up some business…"

"Dad, I can't tonight. I've got a Festival accounting meeting…we're reviewing the books, some pretty critical issues." Roland realized his father would consider the Festival meeting a serious waste of billable time. "I'd be glad to cancel, but the meeting's at Leigh-Lee & Sons and you never know who I might see…or spy on…"

Dan Gastineau chuckled into the phone. "Now that's what I like to hear! Maybe your old man's business acumen is finally rubbing off on you, eh? It's about time you figure out how the world works…your competition's already showing you up!"

Roland frowned and slowed the car; a state trooper passed him in pursuit of a speeder. "Whaddya mean, Dad?"

"Well, if you'd get up a half-hour earlier and read the paper instead of lounging around, you'd know that Danita Kay Leigh-Lee was promoted to full partner! She's making her mark, son…she sure knows how to get the ink, that girl! One well-timed article on the back page of the newspaper today…what a coup, that issue sold out because of all that Cooler business at the grocery…talk about free advertising…*only every household in the county saw that announcement*! Maybe I should have hired *her* to work for me, instead of you!"

Roland made a face and mocked his father. "Yeah, Dad, maybe so. Uh, Dad…Dad…you're breaking up…Dad…"

Roland pushed the cell phone's OFF button. *Too bad, daddio but I don't need any of your sarcastic bullshit today, thanks. Danita Kay a full partner? She just graduated! Talk about your blatant nepotism…great…there goes my good impression…hi, Danita Kay, I'd like to ask you to consider dating me, but now that you're a full partner in your family's law firm, I guess it'd be beneath you…sure, I'm on the fast track, too…the fast track to federal prison…*

At six-twenty-five, Roland Gastineau, smelling of soap and dressed in fresh khakis, entered the mahogany-appointed reception area of Leigh-Lee & Sons, Attorneys at Law. In his right hand he carried a dozen pale yellow roses; in his left, a paper shopping bag filled with a bottle of Chateau Margeaux, a tin of English toffee and a copy of his favorite poetry collection by e.e. cummings. The book was a gift to commemorate Danita Kay's promotion; Roland decided e.e. cummings was a safe bet, as his own attempts at poetry had been for naught, lo those many months before.

Miss Gober, aggravated at having been asked to work late in order to properly receive him, curtly informed him that Miss Leigh-Lee would be with him momentarily. Roland sank down into a leather armchair to wait. His stomach knotted and his palms were wet. He noticed that Miss Gober's purse, lunch kit and a paperback were neatly stacked on top of her desk; she held her car keys in her hand, ready to pounce the moment she was released by her employer.

"You may go in, now, sir, through those double doors and the first door on your left."

Roland smiled as he heard Miss Gober's grumbling behind him. He walked down the hall and tapped on what he supposed was Danita Kay's office door.

"Mmm..come in…"

Roland took a deep breath and entered the office. His eyes glazed over; if this was a full partner's domain, one could only imagine what a senior partner's office would look like…*probably paved with gold*, he decided. He took note of the dozen-odd congratulatory floral arrangements scattered around the huge room, crowding the gleaming mahogany furniture. He smiled at Danita Kay, who did not look up from her desk.

"Hey, Danita Kay! If you're busy, I can sit over here, and wait…I'm in no rush…"

Danita Kay studied a sheaf of papers and chewed on a pen. She said nothing. A drop of perspiration tickled Roland's neck. It would be difficult to gauge his chances with said prospective romantic partner if the said prospective romantic partner totally refrained from speaking.

"Uh…congratulations on the full partner thing! Here, I brought you some flowers…'course, I see you've got a few of those already, heh heh, …well, I also brought you a book…uh…uh…that's really great, full partner! I guess your dad…"

"My dad had absolutely nothing to do with it; I *earned* that promotion, fair and square."

Roland gulped; thirty seconds and it wasn't going well. Danita Kay's tone suggested she was angry at something.

"I mean, I guess he's proud of you, that's all. Where would you like these roses?"

Danita Kay let out a sigh and looked up from her paperwork. Roland's heart stopped beating; she was stunning. Her pale blond hair was accentuated by the fire engine red of her business suit; her eyes blazed in the early evening light that spilled into the office from the floor-to-ceiling windows behind her. She waved a weary hand.

"Just put them anywhere…I don't care. Now, here are the Festival records and…"

Roland laid the roses on the sofa table, parked the shopping bag in a tapestry-upholstered wing chair and crossed to Danita Kay. He sat on the edge of her desk, to her surprise. She pursed her lips and frowned.

"Uh, *do you mind*? You'll be much more comfortable in that chair."

Roland shrugged his shoulders and sat in a cushy chair at the corner of Danita Kay's credenza. He slapped his knees.

"Should we eat something first and talk business later? I brought some wine and this great toffee for dessert. I don't know about you, but I'm starved! Hey, how 'bout all that business at the Poe House, huh? I've had three calls from my old frat buddies…one was in Paris, I guess it made the international wire. Talk about embarrassing, huh? Makes me wish I was already in Seattle! "

Danita Kay brushed a strand of loose hair away from her face; *she's a goddess,* Roland mused, *an absolute goddess…how did I miss her, right under my nose? I must be blind…she sure didn't look like this at the Masked Ball…must be the new clothes…*

Danita tapped her pen on the desk impatiently. This was her turf and she would call the shots. Roland's mention of Seattle reinforced her intentions to stick to business. *I've got to put him out of my mind...he'll be leaving soon...and I'll be running the firm in a few months, at the rate I'm going...my work will be enough...look at that hair...those hands...those eyes...*

"I wouldn't know, I haven't had much time to read for pleasure lately. If you don't mind, I would prefer to review these records *first* and then eat if we have time. Now, if you'll note *here*, the problem as I see it goes back to February when..."

For the next hour, Roland endured the merciless drudgery of the Festival accounting records at the hand of Danita Kay. She was thorough, she was efficient and she'd made financial sense out of the shoeboxes filled with illegible, hand-written receipts and notes provided by Dorothy Graham and the Festival Committee. There was simply nothing Roland could add to the program; he was CPA window-dressing. He ran a hand through his jet-black hair and leaned back, blinking in awe.

"Man, Danita Kay! You're *good*! You've single-handedly straightened out eight months' worth of mess! Everything looks perfect, so I guess the audit's complete until after the Festival. Would you like me to take it from here? I probably have more time, now that you're a full partner and..."

"That won't be necessary. Besides, I don't want your Festival obligations to stand in the way of your move to Seattle. When is it, exactly, that you plan to leave? I'd like to know, so I can put together a list of suitable replacements for the Committee."

Roland stared at Danita Kay, who glared back. She was known for her formality with regard to business, but the tone in her voice wasn't right; it was as if she was about to burst a vein in some kind of enraged fit.

Maybe she's angry about the time she's spent on these records, he wondered. *But I never told her to do it by herself, all she had to do was ask for my help. That's it! She's pissed! She thinks I'm ditching my job on this Festival thing and she's pissed off!*

"Well, for *starters*, it doesn't look like you *need* to appoint my replacement, because you're some kind of accounting marvel! As for Seattle, I don't know, off hand. I mean, I'd *like* to move to Seattle some day, but I haven't exactly thought about when I would *go*...there's a lot at stake, I mean, it's not just up to *me*."

Danita Kay's foot tapped nervously under her desk; *Great, so he does have a girlfriend! He's waiting for her to graduate from college, or find a job out there, then he'll join her, the bitch!* She slammed the ledger closed and tossed her head, fighting back tears.

"It must be nice to go through life with no regard for your responsibilities.

Your friend in Seattle must be *very* flexible, *very* laid-back, to sit around and wait for you to decide when you might drop in. But I don't do business that way, Roland. I like things well-defined and organized. The Festival may not mean much to *you*, but this is my home and I will be here after it's over. So, I'll ask you again...what is your time frame, your exit strategy?"

Danita Kay turned her head and looked out the window; she couldn't bear to watch him as he relayed his departure date. Roland gripped the arms of the chair; *is she nuts? What's she talking about? What friend in Seattle...she's shootin' firecrackers at me outta those eyeballs, she's so pissed off!* Then, he remembered the words of his friend Wink Jackson, *'never let a woman, even a friend, think she's got competition, Rufus, she'll tear your heart out and eat it for breakfast!'*

A realization slapped him in the face...*she thinks I have a girlfriend in Seattle! She thinks I'm moving to Seattle for a girl! And she's jealous! Oh, man, Wink, I'm in like Flint...she's jealous, which means she's interested! There's a chance, Rufus! There's a chance. Kid-glove time, my man...gotta give her an out, don't make her look stupid...*

Roland sat on the edge of the chair, in silence, until Danita Kay turned and looked him in the eye. He smiled and leaned close with a tilt of his head. He spoke in a low voice, almost a whisper. "Danita Kay...did somebody tell you I was moving to Seattle for a specific reason?"

Danita Kay's lungs seized; she blinked, blushed and swallowed. "I...I think I heard, yes, I believe someone, it must have been at a meeting someplace...I heard somebody say you were moving to Seattle to join your girlfriend...or was it your fiancée?" *Might as well get to the truth of it right now,* she determined, *no use prolonging the agony.* She braced herself for the worst.

"Danita ...there's no girl in Seattle; there's no fiancée in Seattle...the only reason I want to move to Seattle is because I hate this town, I hate the heat, I hate working for my father and I hate the fact that a guy can't get a good latté around here without driving to Nashville! I'd *love* to move to Seattle, someday. But right now I'm not going anywhere because I've got a really good reason to stay here!"

Danita Kay nearly screamed in shock; *he's not leaving, oh, God, thank you, he's not leaving...*she gritted her teeth in an effort to prevent her excitement and relief from showing. A tough exterior was critical in these situations, they'd always told her in law school.

*But what does he mean, he's got a good reason to stay here...oh, no, there's a girl in town...OH MY GOD, I'll have to see them, every day, holding hands on the street, kissing in public...showing up at social functions together...I can't take it...I will just die...*Danita Kay needed to know the object of Roland's affections; she had to name her pain. She forced herself to speak in a measured tone.

"*Really*, how *nice* for you. And what's her *name*?"

Danita Kay's eyes flashed, ready to mortally wound Roland the second he uttered the name of the woman who had robbed her of the only man she'd ever allowed herself to fall for...

"Her name is Danita Kay... but I've got a nickname picked out for her...what do you think of 'Pooky'?"

Before she could fully comprehend the meaning of his words, Danita Kay felt the strong arms of Roland Gastineau lift her from her leather desk chair. Roland kissed her full on the mouth; a long, deep, soulful kiss that sent shivers to her toes and electricity to the roots of her new hairdo. As they parted, her jaw fell open and she shook her head; words refused to form on the lips that still tingled with his taste. He grinned and gripped her tightly just below the shoulders.

"Danita Kay, I've been a real jerk; I was so caught up in my own problems, I was so pissed off about not finishing law school, so mad at the world, I didn't even *notice* you, what a good, smart, beautiful woman you are! I mean, *damn*, you were my date to the Masked Ball and I didn't give you the time of day! But these last few months, working with you, getting to know you, it's been a real eye-opener. Can you ever forgive me? Could you ever love a loser like me? I don't want to go to Seattle if you're not there. Hey, *I know*...I'll quit my dad's firm and *you* can hire me! I'll be your office boy! I'm great at making copies and I can almost answer the telephone without cutting off the clients! And I'm sure as hell a lot better looking than Miss Gober! You could chase me around your desk any time you wanted!"

A wave of relieved laughter rolled up from Danita Kay's belly; she laughed until tears spilled down her silken cheeks and until Roland held her tightly and kissed her, over and over. *He wants me! He likes me! He thinks about me! It's a miracle and I don't even have a cooler door!* She wiped her eyes and glimpsed the pale yellow roses on the table by the sofa. She crossed the room and sniffed their heavy, fragrant petals. She pulled out a single rose and caressed her cheek silently.

"These are the most beautiful roses I've ever seen...I can't believe you...I'm in shock! Do you know how much I wanted to hear you say this? Are you sure it's not a joke? My sister Tiffany didn't put you up to this, did she? I was so *mad* at you...I thought I'd never see you again, I only wanted the chance to make you notice me, make you like me...you are so funny and charming and smart. I've loved you since the Masked Ball, did you know that? When did *you* know?"

Roland swallowed hard; he knew from Wink's numerous war stories that these were dangerous waters to tread. "Oh, I guess, probably not long after that..." *Once you took those Coke bottles off your face, so I could get a good look at you, once you brought your hair into the twentieth century and put on some lipstick, that was the real clincher,* he wanted to say, but he refrained, like the gentleman he was. He took her in his arms. "So, what do you think, Pooky…me, you, a glass of wine, to celebrate?"

The wine was of excellent vintage; however, it was never uncorked. Roland and Danita Kay opted instead to advance through various stages of undress in their respective pursuits to fully get to know one another. Shortly after they dispensed with most of their street clothes, Betty Gooch tottered into the unlocked lobby of Leigh-Lee & Sons and proceeded to snoop her way toward the muffled giggles she could hear if she really strained hard. She'd downed four shots of Jack Daniel's and her courage was at an all-time high.

The giggles became louder and to Betty's chagrin, they did not exactly have the ring of a Festival accounting meeting about them. As she drew closer, down the long corridor of offices, she heard what she believed to be a man's voice gasp, *'oh, you don't know how long I've wanted to kiss you like this,'* and the fury of a woman scorned was set ablaze.

Betty turned the corner and noticed that a very large mahogany door was ajar; as she tip-toed to the door, the muffled giggles grew louder, accompanied by the unmistakable sounds of heavy breathing. She placed her face so that it barely grazed the open door and peered inside with one eye. She drew quickly back in horror and rage; there, on what she correctly assumed was a very expensive hand-knotted Oriental rug, Roland Gastineau and Danita Kay Leigh-Lee were enjoying what Betty's high school gym teacher would have described as "heavy petting." Roland straddled Danita Kay; they were both clad in their underwear and they were completely oblivious to the fact that they were being watched.

Betty stepped back into the hall and tears cascaded down her make-up layered cheeks. She caught her reflection in a gigantic gilt-framed mirror. Her perm had not lived up to expectations and as Fay suspected, she did resemble Orphan Annie, with the exception that Orphan Annie did not wear smeared, deep purple eye makeup.

It took me two hours to look my best, she lamented, *but it was two hours two late. Dogface stole Roland, right out from under me. Great! And now she's right under him! He never returned my calls, the bastard! He never gave me a chance! I hate him! I hate 'em both, with their daddy's money, their fast cars, their big offices, their cosmetic surgery…*

She reached into her purple vinyl bag, the one that matched her purple vinyl shoes and her purple polka-dotted dress, and found a tissue. She daubed her eyes and noticed that the purple mascara she'd so tenderly applied had crusted into a clingy mass on her eyelashes, blurring her vision. She edged back toward the open office door and tried to get a second look at love lost, which was difficult due to her current mascara peril. Even through the purple blur, there was no doubt about it...Roland and Danita Kay were definitely an item; he would never willingly fit into her plans for a secret romantic interlude, let alone a long-lasting affair that could easily span decades. Betty shuddered as she tearfully watched Roland slip Danita Kay's bra strap down and plant his lips on Danita Kay's chest. She noticed a fire alarm out of the corner of her blurry eyes.

Maybe I should call 9-1-1 to cool them down...wonder if Margaret is working tonight...MARGARET! She'd know what to do...what was it I heard her tell that group of women at the Poe House, all those years ago? 'Never take matters into your own hands until you've developed a thorough game plan. Errors can be costly and embarrassing. Remember the three S's of Abuse Action...Stop, Sit, and Smoke. Work it out in your mind, over and over until you're absolutely sure...'

Betty realized that although she would most certainly enjoy surprising Roland and Danita Kay in the midst of their hands-on accounting session, if she were to strike now, it would be over and then it would be merely her word against theirs. *'Remember the three S's...the three S's...'* She stole a long, final glance at Roland's beautiful purple-tinted back, blinked back more purple tears and ran out of Leigh-Lee & Sons. She hurried to her car, slammed the door and locked it and bawled into the steering wheel. After twenty minutes, she removed the rest of the purple mascara crust with a Quik-Steak napkin, then proceeded to drive home. As she waited at a traffic light, she spotted Margaret McArdle-Graham's van parked in front of the Police Dispatch Office. She ran the light, then pulled up behind it.

She'll probably think I'm nuts, Betty decided. *We're not friends, just a few hellos around town...*she searched the floorboard for the hidden bottle of Jack Daniel's and poured another shot of liquid courage down her throat. *Ah, what the hell...nothing left to lose...Billy's at Mabel's...it's still early! My man's done me wrong, it's my aim to get even! If anybody knows anything about that, it's Margaret! Besides, with all this Cooler Jesus bullshit, nothing else's happenin' around here...Margaret's probably just sittin' around the Dispatch Office, readin' a magazine, bored to tears...*

Wednesday Evening, August 25, 1999; Chestnut Ridge Dispatch Office

Margaret McArdle-Graham sat in front of her computer terminal at the Chestnut Ridge Police & Fire Dispatch Office. In addition to the wireless telephone earpiece and microphone that Margaret wore, she cradled a black telephone receiver between her left ear and neck. In her right hand she held a small cellular phone. Between tokes on a smoldering cigarette, Margaret juggled Dispatch calls with her personal conversations on the black phone and the cell phone with the efficiency of a seasoned veteran.

In a worn plastic chair at one end of the Dispatch Office's tiny Call Center, Hester Graham sat timidly, amazed at the buzz of activity successfully engineered by Margaret. It was a little after eight in the evening; Margaret and Hester had planned a six o'clock Abuse Victim Strategy Session to review Margaret's ideas for Hester's revenge on Horry and Estéfan. But Margaret's replacement called in sick and she was forced to pull another double shift. *If that damned Barney Gooch would approve the budget and hire another dispatcher, this wouldn't happen! He's never liked me, thinks it's funny to see me work my ass off!*

"Don't worry, Hester," Margaret said, "usually after nine or so, things get pretty dead around town and we can talk then."

Hester was disappointed about the delay. She was exhausted; earlier, after checking on Euladean and Henry Bailey, who slept soundly on her bed safely hidden from the Cooler Jesus reporters, she'd sprung a bleary-eyed Juliette Kimball from jail. It took several shouting matches with a harried police sergeant and an appearance from her father to secure Juliette's release, but at last Juliette was free to go, after Will Graham convinced Raleigh Poe to drop the trumped-up charges, or he would call in Raleigh's home improvement loan.

Upon arriving at the Dispatch Office and learning of Margaret's extra tour of duty, Hester tried to beg off and reschedule. But Margaret refused.

"You've got to strike while the iron's hot," she advised, "everything's fresh in your mind, we can't put it off any longer. I bet you could use a good meal…I know just the thing."

Margaret gave Hester the keys to her apartment and Hester returned with a baking dish containing Margaret's notorious Tuna Tetrazzini casserole. Hester warmed the Tuna Tetrazzini in the Dispatch Office microwave, placed a bowl-ful in front of Margaret and sat in the corner chair to enjoy Margaret's home cooking.

Hester ate roughly three bites and then excused herself when she could see that Margaret was in the middle of handling a particularly intense call. She flushed the Tuna Tetrazzini down the commode, bought a package of go-betweens from the snack machine and sat in the bathroom, cramming the crackers in her mouth two at a time. *No sense working Margaret's dander up before our first session,* she figured. *I really need her help. I just hope she doesn't ask me to eat any more of that awful Tuna Tetrazzini...*

Margaret flipped the wireless microphone to the side of her face and spoke into the black telephone receiver. Hester flipped through a dog-eared back issue of *No Victim Today* and silently observed her new mentor in action.

"Yes, *ten-four.* I'm with the Chestnut Ridge Police & Fire Dispatch Office...I'm the Senior Dispatcher...*roger.* Now, as I said, we're conducting an important fire protection publicity campaign and we wish to post several billboards. We'd like to rent the billboard locations I faxed you yesterday...that's a *ten-four. Negative,* we only require these locations for a month's time...what do you mean, you can't let them go for such a short contract? Sir, you are keeping thousands of innocent little children from their right to learn about fire...is that something you can live with? Then may I remind you that this is official City business...I'd *hate* to see those billboards condemned by our Fire Inspector and torn down. Sir, I note that you owe our city approximately ten-thousand dollars in right-of-way taxes... oh, *this is worse than I realized...*just a moment, while I alert Chief McArdle so he can read you your rights... *Ten-four,* I'll hold while you check that *sudden availability...*excellent, the children of Chestnut Ridge thank you. Now, let's discuss the posting schedule...this is a surprise gift for our city, so the posting crews must work between midnight and five ayem...*roger...*of course we'll pay triple wages...*ten-four...*I'll drop by and sign the contract personally. *Over and out.*"

Margaret replaced the black receiver on its base and winked at Hester. Then she paused to take a bite of cold Tuna Tetrazzini and answered a call on the cell phone from her brother Bill, who was busy monitoring the Cooler Jesus situation at the Poe House. She wolfed down the rest of the Tuna Tetrazzini and swung her chair around to face Hester.

"That takes care of the first detail in our little plan; I'll fill you in, then we can divide up the duty roster and make the arrangements. How you holdin' up? Doin' ok? Look, Hester, I've got to make a few calls on another project I'm workin', you're beat, I can tell. Why don't you go lie down on the cot in the break room? There's nobody here but us, it's nice and quiet in there. I'll make my calls and then we can get to work, ok?"

Margaret was close to trapping Dan Gastineau in return for his near hit-and-run involving Amelia Festrunk several months earlier. She also wanted to verify that Hoot had truly departed the abode of Fay Bailey; her revenge on Hoot, although foremost in her mind for twenty-five years, had taken a backseat to the pressing needs of the Abuse Victims at hand.

Hester nodded gratefully at Margaret's proposal, she could barely keep her eyes open. She wandered down the short hall to the break room and stretched flat on the immaculate military-style cot. Shortly after her head hit the pillow, however, she heard a knock at the Dispatch Office door. She also heard Margaret's angry shouts at a 9-1-1 caller who was apparently intoxicated and who seemed to have difficulty providing Margaret with his correct home address. Hester took it upon herself to open the Dispatch Office door and peered out at the makeup-streaked countenance of a woman with a mass of tight, frizzy curls. It took Hester a few seconds to realize that the woman was Betty Gooch, sporting a new hairstyle and smeared purple eye makeup. Betty sobbed and hugged Hester; Hester didn't know Betty all that well, but she tried to comfort her just the same and invited her inside the Dispatch Office.

Margaret continued to shout at her 9-1-1 caller, so Hester led Betty to the break room and sat beside her on the cot. Betty sobbed for five minutes and as she had no tissues, Hester offered her a rough paper towel from the dispenser located next to the break room sink. Betty wiped her eyes and as her tears subsided, she managed a weak smile.

"Thanks, Hester. I didn't mean to go all slobbery on you...I've had a really bad day. Is Margaret here?"

Hester nodded. "She's working a rough call. Are you ok?"

Betty nodded and screwed up her face as if she might cry again, but this time she controlled herself. "Yeah, I'm ok. But I really need somebody to talk to. Somebody who understands the way I feel, somebody who can tell me what to do about it, you know? UGH! *Men*!"

Hester did know, although she didn't have a clue as to the exact circumstances of Betty's need. "I'll go get Margaret. Can I get you a Coke?"

Betty smiled and shook her head and Hester returned to Margaret's cubbyhole. Margaret held a cigarette to her mouth and inhaled sharply.

"Hey, babe, sorry about the noise. Man, that was a loser if I ever heard one...guy ran over his wife's dog with his pickup truck, but he was so drunk he couldn't remember the name of his own street! There's no shortage of idiots in this town, I tell ya! Hester...what's the matter?"

Hester relayed the sudden appearance of Betty Gooch and Margaret snubbed out her cigarette. She removed her wireless telephone headset and placed it on Hester, whose eyes widened in protest, but Margaret patted her reassuringly on the back.

"Hey, it's no big deal...you just watch this red button...when it flashes, you punch this green button and talk into the mike. Get the caller's name, address and phone number and type them into the computer...the computer automatically alerts the officers on duty. I'll be right back. If it's life or death, holler at me…I wanna check on Betty…*it's ok, Hester, you can do it*!"

Margaret dashed out of the call station and Hester faced the computer screen. She muttered a prayer under her breath that the red button wouldn't flash and thankfully, it didn't. After about ten minutes, Margaret returned, leading Betty Gooch whose red, swollen eyes further complimented her Orphan Annie curls.

"Now, isn't this *cozy*? Betty, you sit in that chair. Hester, you park on that milk crate…I use it to prop my feet up. No calls? See, I told you it was easy! Betty, I'm gonna grab a copy of my Abuse Victim checklist so we can make some notes about your case. Hester, hand me that headset!"

Margaret slapped on the headset and pulled a clipboard from her extraordinarily large purse. The clipboard held a form that said ABUSE VICTIM CHECKLIST at the top. "Hester, you watch for the flashing light. I'm going to take Betty's info, ok?"

Hester nodded and stared at the red button until her eyes blurred. She listened as Margaret ran Betty through a list of routine questions.

"So, Betty. Any physical violence? Are you *sure*? Rape? Groping? Kissing? Fondling? Bruises or Cuts? Broken Bones? Abrasions? Use of Knives, Guns, Brass Knuckles, Pipes? How about verbal abuse…Swearing? Threats? Intimidation? Shouting? Hmm..ok, well, what about financial difficulty…Stolen Funds? Missing Personal Items, Jewelry? Purse-snatching? *Betty, look at me, why are you here?* What did Barney do?"

Betty opened her mouth in protest. "Oh, no, Margaret, this isn't between me and *Barney*, hell, he's still over at the Poe House with the camera crews and Cooler Jesus nuts. This is between me and another man…"

Betty eyed Hester, who continued to stare at the terminal's red button, then asked sheepishly, "Is this completely confidential?"

Margaret smiled, nodded at Hester and reassured Betty. "Yes, Betty, it is. Hester is here because she's a victim, too. Your secret's safe with us; we are sisters in the fight against the mistreatment of women and children at the hands of the sadistic animals we all know men to be…now, tell me the details. I can't help you without *details*, Betty."

Over the next half hour, between Dispatch calls, Margaret and Hester learned the ugly circumstances surrounding how the vile Roland Gastineau had lured Betty into his web of deceit, beginning with the Masked Ball dance party nearly two years prior. She'd endured months of stalking by Roland; he wooed her with an untamed vengeance. The lies rolled out of Betty's mouth in an intricate, slick tangle; she felt no remorse.

"Like a *fool*, I was ready to leave my own husband, my sweet son Billy," Betty sobbed. "I had my hair cut and permed because Roland asked me to.

I put on this dress, it's his favorite, and my best perfume. He told me to meet him at our secret rendezvous place, *tonight*, so we could leave town and be together forever…but on my way, I saw his car in front of Leigh-Lee & Sons. That *dogface* Danita Kay Leigh-Lee's had her eye on him for *months*…she forced him to be her date at the Masked Ball this year, you know, some kind of bribery, I think. Did ya'll see her picture in the paper?"

Hester and Margaret shook their heads. Betty stopped crying and her voice took an angry tone. "Well, Dogface went and had all kinds of plastic surgery! You won't even recognize her! She had her hair done and her make-up, bought some new clothes…all so she could steal away my one, true love, right out from under me!"

Betty sobbed once more at the memory of Roland and Danita Kay writhing on the Oriental rug. Margaret picked up her pen to make a note. "Exactly *where* was your secret rendezvous place, Betty? I need details!"

Betty looked up from her tears with a start. She didn't want to be too specific, in case Margaret decided to snoop around, verify her story.

"Margaret, I can't tell you *that*! It's a *secret*! So, anyhow, I saw his car out there and I just be-bopped inside that building…the door was wide open! It was almost like he wanted me to find him! I heard all these *sex sounds*, you know, gasping and moaning and well, you know, *sex noises*! So I followed 'em, they got louder and louder and there in Miss Boyfriend Stealer's office was my Roland and they were doin' the nasty on the floor! Naked as jaybirds! And Dogface says, *'Oh, hey, Betty,'* like it's no big deal!"

Margaret groaned in disgust and Hester gulped. It was very similar to her own discovery of Horry and Estéfan, with the exception of the homosexuality issue and the fact that Hester didn't own any purple mascara. Betty, pleased with the reaction of her audience, persevered.

"So, I screamed, and Roland gets up off Dogface and they don't even have any shame! Roland laughs and says, *'Hey, look, we can work this out, everybody can have a turn!'* but Dogface points at me, and says, *'No, it's her, or me!'* and so, right in front of me, he goes back over to Dogface and they start doin' it *again*, on her *desk*! I ran outta there fast and, well, here I am."

Margaret put down her pen; this was not among the truest and finest examples of Abuse she'd encountered and her caseload was very heavy at the moment. She detected the scent of alcohol on Betty's breath; it was her experience that liquor often encouraged the Victim to exaggerate. But she didn't want to upset Betty or lose a potential Abuse Victim Support Group member, so she decided to use an alternate approach.

"Betty, listen. This is a difficult case…very challenging. You see, if you willingly participated in any kind of activity with Roland, then you are not technically a *victim*…we don't need to go into the finer points right now, but

I can tell, just by what you've told me...your new hairdo, complying with Roland's wardrobe requests, you were going to leave town with him...this wasn't exactly one-sided, was it, Betty? You weren't taken from your home by force, or kidnapped, or anything..."

Betty inhaled and bit her lip. Margaret made a good point. "No, it wasn't like that. But he tricked me! He *cheated* on me! With *Dogface*!"

Margaret glanced at Hester, whose head dropped over onto her knees. Margaret shook her; she woke up and sleepily righted herself, and Margaret continued. "I understand your suffering, Betty, but it's not life-and-death, now, is it? I'll be glad to help you in any way I can, but your case is not at the top of my list in terms of verifiable life-and-death priority. There are about three cases ahead of you, in fact. Three cases where the victims *truly* were abused against their will, physically or mentally injured. Your abuse is more along the lines of what the experts describe as *'emotional jealousy,'* Betty. It's very *valid,* of course, but it's not the kind of case that demands immediate attention."

Betty pouted; she wanted Margaret to tell her that she'd slice Roland's balls off while he was sleeping and hang them in the town square for everybody to see. She wanted Margaret to arrest Dogface and put her in the pen for sexual misconduct, but apparently that was not an option.

"So why in the hell did I come here, then, Margaret McArdle-Graham, if you won't help me? I'm devastated! *Look at me*!"

Hester looked down and stifled a smile; Betty obviously had no clue as to the truly ridiculous nature of her appearance. The purple polka-dotted dress, matching shoes and bag and the frizzy, corkscrew curls screamed fashion fiasco. It was not polite to laugh at those experiencing emotional trauma, Hester observed, no matter how much they resembled a circus clown. Margaret stretched her long arms and stood to her full six-foot-plus height.

"Betty, I have an idea. Hester and I could really use your assistance with another case we're working. In fact, we could all work together on my biggest case...maybe we could wrap everything into one major effort and accomplish our goals with a few well-placed plans. What's today, Wednesday? Here's what we'll do...I need a few more days to set everything in motion, but in about a week, we'll be ready to strike. Can I count on you two?"

Betty nodded enthusiastically. Hester agreed as well, hoping that Margaret would soon release her to the comfort of her own home and hoping that Euladean and Henry wouldn't mind if she waived her right to pleasant conversation and went immediately to sleep.

The three new comrades took a solemn vow of silence and arranged to hook up the following afternoon in Margaret's apartment. For Betty and

Hester, the next few days were a whirlwind of mysterious activity, enacting the neatly typed list of to-do's Margaret provided. Some of the to-do's were executed from Margaret's apartment headquarters; some were assigned to the privacy of their own homes, on their own time. But it was understood that each comrade had a specific, vital role in what Margaret named, "Operation Flash." Phone calls were made, details were hashed out and money changed hands. It was an efficient, covert mission and it came together beautifully.

Eight days later, the evening of "Operation Flash," they reviewed every detail in minute scrutiny in Margaret's compact living room. They were each dressed in black from head to toe. As the hour of action loomed, Betty suddenly expressed her opposition.

"I don't like where this is goin'. It's all about *Margaret*, what *you* want. But what about *me*? When do we focus on *my* pain? When do you help me get Roland and Dogface?"

Margaret stopped loading a variety of items into a black duffel bag. She glanced at Hester, who stood reading the list of scheduled events planned for the evening.

"*Shit*, Betty, we've been through this a hundred times! *First*, we're gonna take care of an old debt and round up Gastineau and shoot him. *Then*, in a few weeks after everything dies down, we'll work on that love-slave of yours, and of course we'll figure out how to help Hester, too. These delicate campaigns take *time*, Betty...too many variables, it can all crumble like that! I am a trained professional, I know what I'm doing. You've got to trust me, trust Hester...we're good for it, I promise! Now, are you with us or *not*?"

Betty scowled and nodded reluctantly; she had no choice and she feared Margaret's wrath. Besides, this was a lot more fun than watching tv at home with Barney. Margaret shoved a few more items into the black duffel, then disappeared into her bedroom. She returned with three black stretch ski masks and handed one to each of her sisters in arms. Betty frowned. "I'm not gonna wear that, Margaret! It'll smear my makeup!"

Margaret's eyes blazed. "You'll wear this, Betty Gooch, if I have to put it on you myself! And you weren't supposed to wear any makeup until zero twenty-three hours! Now, put it on!"

The three women donned ski masks; Hester and Margaret, with their large frames, resembled lady wrestlers. Betty's new curls poofed the mask out around her head, such that she looked like an alien. Margaret gave the signal and they were off. Under cover of late-summer darkness, they piled into Margaret's van and drove out to the Peacock Inn.

Thirty minutes later, they crept through the service entrance of the Peacock. Hester had checked into a suite the day before to install the necessary "Operation Flash" paraphernalia. After midnight, when the security guard was asleep, Hester placed a large blob of epoxy on the latch to the service door so it wouldn't secure properly. Now, they crept up the fire exit stairs, inserted the key to their suite and stepped into their field command post. Margaret checked her military watch. "Betty, you sure Gastineau'll come…he agreed to meet you?"

Betty hollered "Yeah" from the bathroom. She had changed into a low-cut, powder blue evening gown and stiletto heels, and expertly applied the finishing touches to her makeup. But the most stunning feature of Betty Gooch was most definitely her long, black wig. The day before, masquerading at Gastineau & Gastineau, CPAs as Rowena Craven, ex-pin-up girl, she'd convinced Dan Gastineau that she was in dire straits. Not only was she in need of a good CPA, she was also longing for a man's attentions and in town for a brief stay. She'd carried a purse-sized whip, provided by Margaret, and after a quick, discreet flick of the whip across Dan's lap, he was snared, particularly since Dorothy Graham had abruptly halted their weekly trysts.

"Dan's s'posed to meet me in the lounge at nine. I told him if he was late there'd be no booty! Margaret…I'm scared…I've never done anything like this before…what if it gets *ugly*?"

Margaret fiddled with a huge camera, hidden inside the armoire across from the bed. She checked to make sure the trip cord worked properly; she literally had one shot for this mission to succeed. She cut an impressive figure in a State Trooper's uniform, ordered from a toll-free number found in the back of *No Victim Today*. Her personal .45 was loaded and ready in the holster on her hip. With her hair under the Trooper's hat and her mirrored sunglasses, Margaret could have passed for a man, except for the betrayal of her well-endowed bosom.

"Betty…excuse me, *Rowena*…it's gonna be fine. You forget I'm a black belt and that I'm packin'! If things go sour, we'll just take control…once Gastineau gets a load of me in this Trooper's uniform wavin' my gun around, he'll be putty in our hands. The only thing I'm worried about is him discovering who we really are …I've never been identified by a perp and I don't intend to be found out now!"

Hester wrung her black-gloved hands from her post near the door. She asked Margaret to run them through the order of events one more time. Margaret, satisfied that the camera was securely in place, focused and ready for action, agreed. She lit a cigarette, tipped back her Trooper's hat and leaned against the doorframe between the suite's living room and bedroom. This would be her finest hour, she observed. This was the absolute best-ever Abuse Victim Revenge Scenario in the history of the universe. Betty sat on the bed facing Margaret.

"Ok, ladies, *it's like this*. We're using slow film and a special night-vision camera. When Betty leads Gastineau in here, the lights will be very low, it'll be completely dark in the bedroom. Betty, that candle in the kitchen will help, so you don't bump into anything. Betty'll hand Gastineau a glass of champagne, challenge him to a drink-off, then start rubbin' him on his chest and get him to take off his shirt and pants. You gotta be *quick* and you gotta *do* what you gotta *do* for the sake of our mission ...if he touches you where you don't want to be *touched*, you grit your teeth and bear it. Your suffering *pales* in comparison to what *he's* gonna suffer! Then you gotta stand on that duct-tape 'X' over there so you'll be out of the camera's view."

Hester complained that perspiration stung her eyes beneath the black ski mask. Margaret sighed, took a drag on her cigarette and continued. "Then Betty's gonna tell Gastineau that her fantasy is to blindfold and spank him. We all *know* he's gonna say yes! So Betty, you get him in the bedroom, stand on that 'X' then blindfold him, spank him, take the photo, I flip on the lights, 'arrest' you, and he's outta here."

Betty nodded; pretending to be afraid of Margaret would not be a stretch. It was eight-fifty-five, time to dim the lights. Hester turned on the bedside radio to the jazz station. Betty reminded herself that this would be well worth it if Dogface and Scumbag Roland would be next. Betty/Rowena strode off towards the lounge and "Operation Flash" began.

Hester grinned with glee behind her ski mask and headed for her position at the elevator, cautiously holding the walkie-talkie that would link her to Betty/Rowena's hidden microphone and Margaret's radio. *Margaret is a genius, she realized, everything is happening just like she said!* She could hear Betty/Rowena entering the bar, toying with Dan Gastineau. But then she heard a familiar voice...it couldn't be...it was! *Uncle Hoot!* She had to make contact with Margaret! Hester pressed a button on the walkie-talkie and hissed into the microphone.

"Flash One this is Flash Two...*urgent*! We've gotta problem! Uncle Hoot's in the bar! He's pulled his chair over to the Perp's table! He's suggesting a threesome! Bait is trying to stall...what should she do? OVER!"

Margaret fiddled with the brass buttons on her State Trooper uniform and spoke into her walkie-talkie, trying to remain calm. *This is excllent! I couldn't have planned it any better myself!* "Flash Two...alert Bait she is to reel in both Perps! Don't worry, I'll handle it! Repeat, Bait is to reel in both Perps! Stay focused! OVER!"

Hester relayed Margaret's message through the walkie-talkie to the receiver tucked in Betty/Rowena's left ear. Betty/Rowena swallowed hard and nervously ran one hand down Dan Gastineau's arm. She hadn't counted on horrible Hoot Graham showing his face at the Peacock Lounge...*I thought he was over at the Poe House managing the photos...*

Hoot Graham took a swig of his bourbon and eyed Betty/Rowena up and down. "Well, now, ain't this a fine oppatunity! An' l'il ol' me jus' sittin' here all by my lonesome, thinkin' I was gonna be spendin' the night solo...so, whaddya say, Dan ol' boy? Think ya can handle a Hollywood Threesome? 'Course, I got *lotsa* experience an' all...I'll be glad ta walk y'all thew it..."

Hoot adjusted the ballcap he was wearing to hide his identity. *That bastard Gastineau's so drunk he ain't gonna remember if he saw me or not, and I gotta have me a piece a this cookie.* He stared hard at Betty/Rowena. *I'll be damned if she don't look just like Ready Betty Gooch. Fay, you oughtn'ta been out bowlin', hon! Shoulda been takin' care a yer man's needs.*

Dan Gastineau drained his Scotch and tugged at his silk ascot with a shaky hand. He was quite inebriated. "*Shih*, Hoo! Imf had me lossuf freesomes! HEY! You reahy, or whuh?"

Betty/Rowena flipped her long black locks and smiled suggestively. "Well, *sug*, I guess a threesome would be just fine with me! But I'm not in the mood to wait too long, you catch my drift? Ya'll ready for our little fantasy or what? Hurry up, now, let's go! I got champagne in the bedroom, and somethin' else ya'll really like!"

Hester listened, heart aflutter, as she heard bar stools scrape the floor and her Uncle Hoot whoop with enthusiasm. As they neared the elevator, Hester realized that Hoot was trying to lose the marinated Dan Gastineau in a hallway, the better to enjoy Betty/Rowena's womanly charms by himself. Then she heard Betty/Rowena scream and slap flesh.

"HEY! Gitcher hand outta my dress! Now I'm callin' the shots here, sug, an' if you can't play by the rules, then me and Danny-boy'll go it alone!"

Hoot snorted and chuckled to himself. When she could hear them coming down the hall to the suite, Hester gave Margaret the signal and hid behind a drink machine. Betty/Rowena giggled seductively and opened the door to the suite; she led a wobbly Dan by the hand across the room towards the champagne. Hoot immediately began to strip, taking no notice as Hester silently entered the suite and pulled the door closed without a sound. Both men dutifully drained glass after glass of champagne at Betty/Rowena's encouragement. Hester watched in naïve amazement as Betty/Rowena skillfully removed Dan Gastineau's clothes and teased both men with suggestive comments. Hester was shocked to see the enormous bulge in the front of her uncle's tight white underwear; Gastineau was nearly falling over on the floor and sported no such appendages. In the bedroom, Margaret perspired heavily and tried not to breathe out loud. Betty/Rowena went in for the kill.

"Now, have ya'll been good boys? I've been thinkin' about spankin' you, Danny, ever since I saw you yesterday! And oh, my, Hoot, aren't *you* the good soldier? You are ready, I must say! Now, ya'll hold still while I put these blindfolds on ya….ouch, HEY, I mean, *mmm,* that sure feels *GOOD*!"

Betty/Rowena expertly blindfolded the victims and led them by the hand towards the duct-tape 'X'. Hoot attempted to play grab-ass and kiss Betty/Rowena on the neck, but she carried out her mission undaunted, cautiously prodding Hoot and Dan close together to capture them both in the camera frame. Hester heard the slight click of the shutter, once, twice, *three times*! She flipped on the lights as a confused Hoot tore at his blindfold. Margaret/State Trooper aimed her .45 at her ex-husband's crotch and he screamed. Dan Gastineau promptly threw up, then fell over in a heap.

"HOLD IT RIGHT THERE, YOU'RE UNDER ARREST! YOU HAVE THE RIGHT TO REMAIN SILENT. YOU HAVE THE RIGHT TO AN ATTORNEY. IF…"

Betty/Rowena screamed effectively and feigned a punch to Margaret/State Trooper's stomach. Margaret/State Trooper doubled over and fell on the floor. Betty/Rowena yelled at her fantasy men,

"HURRY! GET OUT OF HERE BEFORE HE COMES TO!"

Hoot Graham fled for his life in a panic-stricken rush of underwear and bare skin; he scooped clothing and shoes off the floor and raced down the hall of the Peacock Inn in his skivvies. It took an entire pitcher of ice water to make Dan Gastineau come around; Hester and Margaret, through a combination of pulling and shoving, quickly loaded Dan and his clothing into the elevator and pushed "Ground." Hester and Margaret returned to the suite and breathed hard for several minutes.

The three comrades laughed uncontrollably on the bed; Hester closed the front door to the suite and opened a bottle of Dom Perignon. It was the last bottle from Chéz Horatio and she thought it a fitting toast to the evening's escapades. She took a swig from the bottle and passed it to Betty/Rowena, who removed her black wig to reveal a bird's nest tangle of damp frizz. Margaret shook out her hair, unbuckled her holster and grabbed the bottle. They spent the next twenty minutes recounting and reliving the most inventive and successful Abuse Victim Revenge Scenario ever enacted, period.

When the champagne worked its magic, the three women found a dance station on the radio and began to spin around the room. When the champagne was gone, they raided the mini-bar and between them drained several small bottles of whiskey, gin and vodka. The radio blared as they bumped and ground. At eleven-fifteen, the hotel manager called and asked the inhabitants of the Charles I Suite if they would mind lowering the volume. They turned off the radio and fell onto the bed in a giggling heap, then heard a sharp knock at the door. Hester timidly opened it as Betty and Margaret peeked out from the bedroom. A tall, striking blonde young woman in a white gauzy nightgown and bunny slippers smiled at Hester.

"Excuse me...I hate to bother you...you must be enjoying some kind of celebration, but it is quite late and I'm in the room next door. I wonder if you could keep it down just a bit...I'm very tired."

Hester stood mesmerized by the woman's face; it seemed to glow like a candle and her eyes and hair shimmered and twinkled. Hester's mouth gaped open; it was as if all of the heroines from her gothic romance novels were melded into one fantastically gorgeous princess. She stammered and nodded, "Uh...uh...uh...well...sure...we're sorry. We've just...it was so..."

Margaret intervened and gently pushed Hester aside. "Certainly, we're sorry for the noise. But we are celebrating. Are you alone? Would you like to join us? Single women in hotels should stick together, you know...there are male predators around every corner!"

The blonde woman smiled faintly and smoothed her hair. "No thanks, I've got to get some rest. Good night."

Margaret closed and chained the door and Hester followed her back into the bedroom, where they rolled onto the bed beside Betty/Rowena. Betty/Rowena's mascara was smeared, but this time it was from tears of joy. Hester leaned back against the headboard and sighed.

"Oh, man, this was so much fun! What a *rush*! Wait until those billboards get posted! The funny thing is, the perps think they got off scot-free! They think it's *over*!"

Betty giggled. "I can just see those two, struttin' all over town tomorrow, all puffed up like banty roosters! I've never seen a hard-on flatten so fast!"

Margaret ran a hand through her hair. "I couldn't have done it without you two, you know...utter perfection! No flaws, no mishaps...not even with a second Perp thrown in for good measure! But we were *ready*, weren't we, girls, we're *good*!"

Hester leaned up on one fleshy elbow, with a sad look on her face. "I hope Uncle Hoot doesn't find out I was involved in this...but I guess after what you've told me, Margaret, he deserves everything he gets. This was sure a lot of fun. I wish it didn't have to end..."

Margaret winked at Hester, and slapped the bed. "It doesn't end here, ladies, it doesn't end here! We're just getting *started*!"

After another hour of sharing their triumph, the three women changed their clothes and packed their gear. They crept down the hall towards the stairwell. Hester stopped. "I think I'm gonna go grab a Coke real quick...anybody need anything? Nope? Ok, I'll meet ya'll at the car."

Margaret and Betty hurried into the stairwell. Hester fished around in the pocket of her jeans for some change, but stopped dead in her tracks at the sound of her mother's voice. She glanced up, then found a familiar hiding place behind the Coke machine.

Down the hall was a sight Hester would never forget. Dorothy Graham, attired in a silky red negligee, fishnet tights and black garters, cradled a bucket of ice in one arm and Richard Leigh-Lee IV's bare-chested neck in another. Richard fumbled in his trousers for a room key while Dorothy nuzzled his back. When he successfully opened the door to his room, he turned around and Dorothy Graham encased his torso with her spa-pampered legs. Hester watched in horror as her mother prepared to kiss Richard Leigh-Lee IV full on the mouth, and she shouted helplessly, "MOTHER! WHAT ARE YOU DOING?"

Hester moved from the shadows of the Coke machine and walked closer to her mother. Dorothy Graham didn't miss a beat. "Oh, Hester! What in God's name are you *wearing*? Is it too much to ask to wear a little makeup and a clean shirt, if not for yourself, then do it for me!"

Dorothy removed her legs from Richard's mid-section and stood in front of the door, lightly touching her platinum hair. She glared at Hester as Richard backed into the room in a panic.

"What in hell are you doing here anyway, Hester? Whatever you think, this is none of your business! I'll trust you to keep it to yourself and..."

"MOM! What's going on? Are you *crazy*? You left us a *note*! You said you were in Canada, helping your cousin Cynthia! Does Dad know where you are? What's going to happen to *cousin Cynthia*?"

Dorothy rolled her eyes and threw a piece of ice at Hester's feet. "You moron! There is no cousin Cynthia! And I don't give a rat's ass if your father knows where I am or not, come to think of it. You can all go to hell...tell your father he can speak to my attorney...I'm leaving this town for good and joining real society, whether he likes it or not. Now get out of here, Hester, before somebody mistakes you for the maid!"

Dorothy Graham entered her hotel suite and slammed the door. Hester heard her mother's laughter float out into the hall. She tried to move her feet but they were frozen to the floor. After a few moments, she recognized Margaret's whispers from down the hall.

"HESTER! WHAT ARE YOU DOING? IT'S TIME TO GO!"

CHAPTER TWENTY-FOUR – NIGHT SHIFT

One A.M., Thursday September 2, 1999; Nell Graham's Hospital Suite

This has gone on long enough, Amelia! For over eight months you've known what you're supposed to do and all you've done is bought two lousy cars from the man. You've wasted too damned much time waiting for that high-and-mighty professor to get her ass down here and look where it's gotten you…nowhere! I'm surprised Granddaddy hasn't just struck you down dead where you stand! I've got to do something…got to tell Henry the truth, if nobody else. But with all that ridiculous shenanigans at the Poe House, nobody will give me the time of day because an old woman's confession pales in comparison to the face of Jesus on that stupid cooler door! What a ridiculous hoax Gooch has cooked up this time. Maybe if I just go over there and touch that Cooler Jesus, God will take me right then and there and be done with it! I'm sick of fretting about it…I'm tired and old and I just want to die!

Amelia Festrunk mumbled angrily to herself and paced back and forth between her bed and the hospital suite's bay window. Two hours ago she'd raised herself from the narrow cot at the far edge of the small living room in the suite's outer chamber. She'd fired up the coffee maker and downed the entire pot as anger at her situation coursed through her veins and boiled in her brain. Now she put down her cup and sat on the window seat cushion facing the Tuberculosis Garden. The soft moonlight illuminated the bright pink crape myrtles that hung heavy with blossoms despite the late summer drought. She could see lights flicking on and off in other Clinic rooms across the way…every patient in every room had a story and a family and an illness that was serious enough to prevent him from sleeping at home with his dignity. *That's what happens when you check into the hospital, 'Melie,* Granddaddy used to say…*you leave your dignity at the doorstep an' you'd best hope you can git well enough ta snatch it back!*

Loud rattles from the bedroom reminded her that Nell and Aunt Pearl were once again engaged in the Roommate Snoring Competition. She sighed quietly and stared up at the moon.

Dignity. Why is it that just because we get old we lose it? We don't even lose it…it's taken from us. Robbed! That snitty professor…promising to come up here and help me… 'wait until fall', she said. Now I can't even reach her by phone… 'she's on sabbatical' they said. Treated me like I'm a nobody just because I'm an old woman. She's got more important things to do. Well, my story's important…and by God I'll tell it, too. But Nell's right…without the dignity and respect of a professional standing up with me, they'll just shoot the messenger. They'll fill me full of meds and slap me in a home because I'm a threat to their status quo. Gave my life to this Clinic...now I'm stuck in that apartment and working as a glorified candy-striper for the Red Cross. Makes me sick how weak the people in this town are...lining up to stare at a freezer door, for God's sake but if I tried to tell them the truth about the Baileys and how the Grahams and the Leigh-Lees and even us Festrunks thieved and connived, and how every one of us owes Henry a debt, not a single person would give me an ear.

Amelia sighed and sat down on the edge of her lumpy cot. *Nell's doing so much better... Doc Kimball doesn't realize I'm throwing all her tranquilizers in the trash. Any day now she can be released and she can tell the whole danged world about Leonard and Hoot if she wants to. But nobody's gonna pay any attention to her, either, not with all this miracle business. Face it Nell, we screwed up. We wasted too many years keeping quiet when we should have just come clean and to hell with everybody.*

Amelia started; a cool hand caressed her cheek. It was Nell.

"Shit, Amelia, what are you so fired up about this time? Honey, you've lived your whole life in the past and you're still doin' it. You've gotta stop beatin' yourself over that hard head of yours...what's done or wasn't done...it's a moot point. 'Melie, you can't turn the clock back. I don't wanna hear it anymore...it's not like we're 'bout to fall into our graves, young lady!"

Amelia looked at her friend in disbelief. "Did you swipe your pills out of the trash? Have you taken a good look at yourself in the mirror lately? Nell Graham, we're *ancient*!"

Nell grinned. "Hell, 'Melie...we are not. We're just *wise*! And there's nothin' wrong with either of us that a good time in the sack or a nice hard toot of whiskey wouldn't cure! Honey, let me tell ya somethin'...you been worryin' and wastin' your whole life away...you got a few years left and you'd best enjoy 'em. I intend to! I wanna call Leonard over here and plant a big sloppy kiss on that looker right now!"

The two friends giggled quietly as Aunt Pearl shifted in her bed. They were suddenly silenced by a light tap at the main door to the suite. Amelia froze as her granddaddy's words raced through her brain. *Wait and watch. Listen and learn. Keep still and silent.* Amelia rose and cracked it an inch, peering out. It was none other than Leonard.

"Leonard! It's one o'clock in the morning! What are you doing here?"

Leonard smiled and when he saw Nell sitting on the cot his smile transformed his face. "Nell! Yer a vision, I tell ya! Couldn't sleep...here, I done picked these flowers fer ya!"

Leonard offered a huge bouquet of ragweed and Nell accepted it like it was nothing short of prize-winning roses. "Sugar bear, you'd best stop talkin' an' give me a kiss before I jump your scrawny ever-lovin' bones!"

Amelia stepped into the bedroom as Leonard and Nell embraced, melting decades of forbidden love. She tugged the door closed and sat in a chair at the foot of Nell's bed. Tears spilled down her cheeks. She folded her hands and prayed with the faintest of whispers.

"Oh, God in Heaven. Forgive me for being such an ungrateful, shameful excuse for a human. I've been proud, I've wronged my fellow man with my hatred, I don't deserve any of the wonderful things You've given me in this life. Thank You, God, for my sister and brother...for my parents and Granddaddy. And thank You for healing Nell and letting her have a few moments with Leonard tonight. I know what I need to do, Lord...please give me the strength, the courage...please show me the way."

Aunt Pearl Parker rolled over in her bed and propped her head up on one hand, staring at Amelia, clicking her tongue.

"Uh-uh, girl, the good Lord may be a lot of things, but he's no mapmaker! If you already know what to do, then get on with your bad self and *do* it! Quit wastin' time! What's that, Lord? Uh-huh, ok, I'll tell her."

Amelia Festrunk, startled by Aunt Pearl's outburst and embarrassed that she'd eavesdropped on her confession, huffed and sassily crossed her arms.

"How *dare* you spy on me! What is it *now*? St. Peter coming in his gold chariot again? You know I don't believe in your *messages*...it's just an act to get attention, like everything else you talk about. Nightly heart attacks and tuberculosis my *foot!* I'm sure you're a nice enough woman but I can see right through you and I know you're putting us all on, Pearl Parker."

Aunt Pearl leaned back against her pillow and dramatically flailed her arms in the air. "Fine, Miss Goody-Two-Shoes! But I'm tellin' you *right now*...the Lord said to me, he said, *'Pearl, you tell that uppity whitey nurse over there to put a stop to all that carryin' on at the grocery and see to it that she gets her skinny butt in gear after all these years like her grandpappy told her and tell the truth!'*"

Chills seized Amelia's body and raced up the back of her neck. Just then the door to the suite's living room opened and Nell and Leonard walked in, arms around each other's waists.

"Hey, we musta made a wrong turn and ended up at the funeral parlor, it's so morbid in here! Pearl, I know *you're* not dead 'cause all that snorin's shakin' the rafters! Hey! Snap out of it, now, Leonard brought us all a li'l nip...'Melie, honey be a sweetie and go get us some paper cups! Now, where's that guest of honor, Mister Jack Daniels?"

CHAPTER TWENTY-FIVE – THE TRUTH SHALL MAKE YOU FREE

Pre-dawn, Friday, September 3 1999; The Poe House Grocery

Ruby and Roy Quigley parked their yellow Lincoln behind the Poe House in the wee hours of a foggy morning. Ruby gently carried a blanketed bundle as they approached the back entrance near the grocery's loading dock. Corny Poe met them at the door and ushered them quickly inside. It was exactly ten days since the first appearance of the Cooler Jesus, yet the crowds, the media insanity and the prayers of the ardent remained at full tilt.

Ruby wept quietly and gripped the bundle; Corny glanced at Roy, who shook his head and said nothing. Corny offered a silent prayer for the Quigleys as he directed them inside the grocery, toward Aisle Five. He spoke in a low voice.

"Ruby, Roy, I want ya'll to know, we cleared out the crowds for ten minutes, so ya'll can have a private Cooler Jesus visit, ok? Ya'll ain't gonna be bothered by anybody, even me an' Daddy'll just stand at the end a the aisle. Now, we're prayin' for ya'll and for Miss Shu-Shu, so ya'll get on over there and ask the Cooler Jesus to hear you in this time of need."

Ruby Quigley sobbed openly; she tucked back a fold of the pink blanket to reveal a sickly Miss Shu-Shu whose eyes were closed, but who continued to breathe in shallow rattles. Corny stepped aside to let the Quigleys pass; they slowly and reverently approached the Cooler Jesus door. Ruby knelt down in front of the Cooler Jesus image, which was as vivid as the day of its premier. She offered up the bundle in her arms and hummed *Amazing Grace* as Roy spoke the prayer they'd discussed in the car.

"Dear Lord and Cooler Jesus…we know we got ever'thang in the world ta be thankful for…you done give us successful biznesses, like the Quik-Steak, the Beauty Box, the Realty, the car wash, the video store an' the Fun'ral Parlor…hell, ever'thang we've ever *touched* is turned ta gold! But it don't any of it mean nothin' 'out our li'l Miss Shu-Shu, Lord. Now ya knowed my wife Ruby is barren, but we learned ta deal with that and we brought Miss Shu-Shu inta our lives, raised her like our b'loved child."

Roy wept openly and held his head in his hands. "Lord, Cooler Jesus, it were all my fault! I didn't mean ta leave that doggie biscuit on toppa that glass table! How's I s'posed ta know Shu-Shu-Belle would give herself a concussion, tryin' ta git somethin' ta eat! Lord, she didn't know that was three-quarter inch tempered glass, she just knew she was *hungry*! Oh, Lord, *please* have mercy on Miss Shu-Shu…she's real sick an' doc says he cain't do nothin' more for her…Lord, if it please ya, take me instead! I cain't bear ta see my Ruby-love all tore up! She won't *never* forgive me if you take our Miss Shu-

Shu to Heaven! Please, oh, please, dear sweet Cooler Jesus, *please*!"

Ruby lowered her arms to check Miss Shu-Shu's breathing. *You're right about that, Roy Quigley! If my precious baby dies, you'll be sleepin' in the tool shed fer the resta yer born days!*

Miss Shu-Shu abruptly opened her eyes; she licked Ruby's hand and Ruby and Roy gasped for joy. But mere seconds after the little dog revived, she raised her tiny, dingy white head and the last breath rattled out of her body. She collapsed and Ruby Quigley collapsed on top of her, keening in anguish in Aisle Five of the Poe House Grocery. Corny checked his watch; there were only five minutes remaining in the Quigley's private audience. He did not wish to interrupt them in the midst of their grief, but there were throngs of willing-to-donate pilgrims outside who had patiently waited all night for a turn in front of the Cooler Jesus. Corny approached Roy and Ruby with soft steps and cleared his throat in warning.

"*Roy, Ruby...I'm real sorry.* I wish I could explain the God-given mysteries of the Cooler Jesus...why he healed Esperanza, but he won't heal your sweet doggie. But ain't none of us knows the ways of the Lord, 'ceptin' the Lord hisself. Now, look, why don't ya'll get along home an' I'll send Penni over later with her special Funeral casserole. Ya'll prob'ly ain't had a decent meal in days, I bet..."

Ruby Quigley stood up, shifted the blanketed body of Miss Shu-Shu to her left arm and beat Corny Poe squarely on the chest with her right fist. Roy sobbed uncontrollably. Ruby fumed.

"*You and yer damned Cooler Jesus*! It ain't nothin' 'but a *scam*, that's what it is! It ain't fer real, I *knowed* it! You an' Henry Bailey made this whole thing up fer profit, ta git yer pitcher on the front page a the paper! That ain't no real Cooler Jesus! The *real* Cooler Jesus woulda healed a *white* woman, not a Mex'can! The *real* Cooler Jesus woulda never let Miss Shu-Shu *die*! It ain't nothin' but a scam, I tell ya, a money-makin', two-bit *scam*!"

Corny blushed as Roy grabbed Ruby and wrapped his big arms around her. Raleigh Poe frowned at Corny from across Aisle Five. It was a good thing they'd cleared the store, this unfortunate episode could substantially impact Personal Cooler Jesus Tour revenue. Corny patted Roy on the shoulder and pointed toward the door that led to the loading dock.

"Ya'll better go on home, now, Roy. You an' Ruby've had a time of it, I know. I'm so sorry."

Roy nodded as tears streamed down his face and he held fast to Ruby as they walked in crooked fashion to the rear of the store. Corny helped them into their car and sustained another round of angry slaps from Ruby, but he took it in stride. It was almost daylight; Corny watched Roy's Lincoln pull into traffic, safely away from the Poe House crowds, but he recognized another vehicle as it entered the half-empty back parking lot. *Here comes that no-good stutterin' Culpepper, that alcohol-guzzlin', dance-attendin', social-climbin' preacher! He's gotta lotta nerve comin' 'round here again after what he said on tv last week! He's jus' jealous a the crowds we got over here an' the money we got comin' in.*

Brother Cameron Culpepper parked his Buick in a handicapped-zoned parking space and waved at Corny. He placed the "CLERGY" sign in his front windshield so he wouldn't get a parking ticket and walked over to Corny, who mumbled hello.

"*Mornin'*, Brother Poe! Another fog… I g-g-guess we're likely to have some ser-ser-serious snowfall come w-w-winter! How's the grocery business?"

Corny kicked the corner of the giant Poe House dumpster. "I reckon it's 'bout the same as the *last time* you were here, Brother Culpepper…right as rain and fulla the faithful! We're savin' souls at a record pace! Without alcohol or dancin', ta *boot*!"

Brother Culpepper ran a finger inside his clerical collar as he ignored the slur. "*Good, good*! I'm gl-gl-glad to see Stel-stel-stella Stanley is still at it! She was as big a sin-sin-sinner as the good Lord makes! She's a strong gal to c-c-carry that cross around all day!"

"Prob'ly not as strong as your *wife*, Brother C! I heard she's gallivantin' all over Europe at some nudie spa totin' suitcases for them Leigh-Lees! Now I ask you, Brother…what kind of a preacher turns his wife loose at a nudie place with a coupl'a hoity-toity *whiskeypalians*?"

Brother Culpepper again ignored Corny's comment. "Why, C-C-Corny, I was happy to s-s-send my wife on a trip to the Ho-Ho-Holy Land! The message of our Savior is avail-avail-available to any and all, don't you remember? Corny, you m-m-mind if w-w-we go inside and pray?"

Despite his opinion of Brother Culpepper, Corny was not a man to deny a preacher the opportunity for prayer. *Goodness knows we all need it, no matter who offers it up,* he figured. Corny led Brother Culpepper through the loading dock and into the store, where once again the ranks of the eager Cooler Jesus crusaders swelled up and down the aisles of the grocery. Corny scanned the exit area for his father; it was probably not a good idea to bring out the playground donation buckets just yet. But it was too late; the sound of clinking coins jangled Corny's ears as he and Brother Culpepper rounded the corner of Aisle Five.

Cameron Culpepper believed himself to be a true man of God; despite his seminary training and multiple degrees he was not pompous, and with the exception of the parking lot, he usually did not take advantage of his religious position. He believed it was his role to guide his parishioners toward their personal knowledge of the Lord instead of judging them, or assigning to them a roster of do's and don'ts. The Cooler Jesus Miracle was the proverbial line in the sand for Brother Cameron Culpepper, however.

Three days after the miracle, during a local television interview outside the First United Assembly of God's Children, Brother Culpepper politely but firmly insisted that the Cooler Jesus enigma was best left for God to explain rather than for man to interpret. *'I-I-I don't think we n-n-need an ap-ap-aparition on the side of a freezer d-d-door to be full of the Spirit; let us re-re-remember the Commandment: thou shalt n-n-not worship fal-fal-false images!'* His sermon that Sunday politely stressed to his flock that the Kingdom of God was open to all and that the Lord did not require good, decent, hard-working folks to spend an entire day waiting in line for an entrance pass.

Now as the frenzy surrounding the local miracle aggrandized, Brother Culpepper realized his parishioners had not taken the hint; they joined the hundreds and thousands of people who lined up daily to touch the cooler glass and who were asked to place their last shekels inside a dirty pickle bucket. It was not right and it was time to speak openly, and more specifically.

Corny led Brother Culpepper to the front of the pilgrim ranks. Several people grumbled *'no cutting,'* but were silenced when they noticed Brother Culpepper's clerical collar. He inspected the image of the Cooler Jesus with a nod, then surveyed the faithful as they trudged closer to receive their Personal Tour. As he turned back toward the Cooler Jesus, Cameron Culpepper spied a young girl and her mother; their clothes were tattered and dirty and they lovingly deposited what amounted to less than a dollar into the pickle bucket. He walked over to the woman and her child and spoke to them in a low voice.

Corny watched his preacher with a nervous eye; Brother Culpepper took out his wallet and handed the woman a card with the address of the homeless shelter and a hundred dollar bill. She thanked him profusely and pointed to Aisle Five, as if his action was a direct response from the Cooler Jesus. He patted her on the back and guided her and the child over near the cooler. He raised his hands and Corny's stomach knotted. The Official Cooler Jesus Camera Crew aimed its television camera at Brother Culpepper and a sound technician knelt beside him to catch his words in a long boom microphone.

"Brothers and Sis-sis-sisters! I am Reverend Cam-cam-cameron Culpepper, pastor of the First United Assembly of God's Children and I bring you a mes-mes-message from God!"

The crowd reverently hushed. Raleigh Poe flipped off the cassette player that continuously sent *Streets of Gold* over the grocery loudspeaker system. Brother Culpepper closed his eyes and raised his face to Heaven.

"God told me to come here to-to-to-day! He called me, in the middle of my-my-my cornflakes and He said, *'Cameron...go to the Poe-Poe-Poe House and see to my flock! Re-re-remind them of my Commandments, re-re-remind them of my love!'* And I said, *'Yes, Lord.'* And I say-say-say to you all... *again*...you don't n-n-need an ap-ap-aparition on the side of a freezer d-d-door to be full of the *Spirit*! Our G-G-God says, *'thou shalt n-n-not worship false images, but ev-ev-every word that uttereth out of the mouth of the L-L-Lord!'* I can't ex-ex-explain this, I don't know if it is a f-f-fluke of n-n-nature, or a Holy Vision, but I c-c-caution each and every one of y-y-you...the k-k-keys to the Kingdom of Heaven are within your s-s-soul, not on this c-c-cooler door! Now go home and r-r-read your Bibles, do a g-g-good deed for s-s-someone in need! That is tr-tr-truly the way to see the face of G-G-God!"

Murmurs of confusion raced through the Personal Tour line with a domino effect. Brother Culpepper smiled at the homeless woman and her child and led them toward the grocery exit, followed by twenty-odd Tour-seekers who stepped out of line. Corny motioned to Raleigh to lock the exit doors and he angrily blocked Brother Culpepper's way.

"Well, now, *ain't that great*! We got a preacher tellin' us that God spoke to him in the middle of his cornflakes this mornin', tellin' him to come over here an' ruin all these people's hopes of meetin' their Maker! Well, let me ask you somethin', preacher-man...you're tellin' us that this Cooler Jesus Miracle ain't for real...how do we know *you* really heard the voice of *God*? How do we know you were really eatin' *cornflakes* an' not *raisin bran*?"

Corny waved his arms through the air to drive home his point. He glared at Brother Culpepper. "How do we know you ain't drunk as *Cooter Brown*, seein' as how you told your own church members to have a glass a *wine* or go *dancin'*, or do *God knows what*? Ask this preacher where his *wife's at*! I tell ya...she's gallivantin' all over some nudie spa in Europe with a buncha Whiskeypalians, that's where she is! I don't know 'bout *ya'll*, but I find it hard to listen to a man's got a double standard, don't *you*?"

The Personal Cooler Jesus Tour crowd shuffled and mumbled comments. They looked to Brother Culpepper for a response. He released the hand of the homeless woman and shot Corny Poe a stern look. He pointed a finger toward the cooler.

"Corny, I never s-s-said this wasn't real! It's n-n-not for me to j-j-judge! It's not for me to j-j-judge anybody if they w-w-want to *drink*, or *smoke*, or *dance*, or ch-ch-cheat on their *spouses*, or ch-ch-cheat on their *taxes*! Only G-G-God can judge us and we've got to stop judging each other! B-b-but I am saying *this*...the point of G-G-God's love is to spread it around, h-h-help one another...not pur-pur-pursue selfish goals, like standing in line for a full day to s-s-see an image on a c-c-cooler door! The love of G-G-God is in our *hearts,* not at the Poe House Grocery! If w-w-we truly b-b-*believe,* w-w-we don't need to *see*!"

Someone in the middle of the Personal Tour line began to clap and many of the pilgrims followed suit. Corny turned beet red; he slapped the Official Miracle Cameraman on the arm.

"TURN THAT THING OFF! THIS IS MY STORE AND I'M TELLIN' YA, TURN IT OFF RIGHT NOW! *HOOT*! GET OVER HERE! GET THIS CAMERA CRAP OUT OF HERE, RIGHT NOW! YOU GUYS HAVE BEEN IN HERE, EVERY DAY, MAKIN' A FORTUNE OFF ME AN' YOU AIN'T PUT ONE THIN DIME IN THAT PICKLE BUCKET, YET! *HOOT*! WHERE ARE YOU? WE GOT US A NEW RULE! CAMERA CREWS GOTTA MAKE A PICKLE BUCKET DEPOSIT EVER' DAY, ER NO PHOTOS! *HOOT GRAHAM*!"

Hoot Graham, Official Cooler Jesus Miracle Event Manager, did not come forward, so the Official Cameraman stood his ground, but he did adjust his lens to wide angle, to fully capture the wrath of Corny Poe. Upon seeing Corny's fit, many of the prospective Personal Tour takers stepped aside and filtered toward the exit. Brother Culpepper stood in front of the doors and tried to pry them open with his bare hands.

"C-c-come, let us pray! Oh, dear Jesus, w-w-we humbly ask for your b-b-blessings on the poor, confused soul of Corny Poe. Open his mind, th-th-that he will o-o-open these doors, and..."

Cameron Culpepper's prayer was interrupted by the intrusion of Henry Bailey, who waved his arms and shouted, *"EMERGENCY!"* repeatedly until the Personal Tour crowd allowed him to cut to the front of the line. He led Amelia Festrunk by the hand; Amelia was dressed as ever in her starched nurse's uniform, cap and shoes. Henry's face was flushed and he gasped for air. He crouched, hands on his knees for several moments, trying to catch his breath, so he could speak. The Official Cameraman aimed his lens at Henry, to Corny's infuriated relief.

"*Hey,* Corny, *hey,* Rev'rend Culpepper...sorry 'bout carryin' on in the middle a yer prayin'...we came in the back door...ya'll ain't gonna b'lieve this...me an' Miz 'Melia jus' came from the hospital...see, me an' Euladean went ta see 'Melio, an' Miz 'Melia was in there too an' Miz Esperanza...well, she done woke up outta her comatose!"

Several Chestnut Ridge locals scattered among the crowd gasped; Esperanza Rodriguez had lain unconscious at the Festrunk Clinic since the Wart Removal Miracle, right here in the Poe House, ten days prior. Corny smiled at Henry, fully expecting him to relate Esperanza's exclusive Wart Removal Miracle experience for all to hear so they could forever silence the intruding preacher and get back to business. All eyes were on Henry as the

Official Cameraman flipped on a second camera; it was Cooler Jesus history in the making and he could take no chances with low batteries.

"Like I done said, ya'll ain't gonna *b'lieve* this! Miz Esperanza, she done come to, she blinked them big brown eyes at Miz 'Melia an' then she sets up an' asks fer a cuppa hot coffee, like twarn't nothin' unus'al! An' Miz 'Melia, she says, *'Esperanza, do you know what happened to ya?'"*

Henry gulped air as the crowd waited in suspense. "An' she says...or I *reckon* this is what she done said, 'cause I don't speak Mex'can English too good...anyhow, she says she had done tried out a new type a cleanin' fluid on them glass cooler doors at the Poe House last week! Ya'll know, she an' 'Melio got the contract ta clean up the Poe House ever' Mond'y. So she says, after usin' that new cleanin' fluid, all she 'members is that her hands was tinglin' an' itchin' sompin' fierce the nex' day. So she goes over ta the Poe House ta git her some calabash lotion, but she sees all the commotion, Stella Stanley tells her what's happ'nin' an' she beats it ta be first in line ta see the Cooler Jesus."

Henry gratefully gulped a Dixie cup of water handed to him by Corny, who'd noticed Henry's voice was a tad hoarse and he didn't want this Miracle Confirmation to be in any way diminished.

"*Thank ya, Corny.* So, anyhow, Miz Esperanza, she takes her a good gander at that door, but she realizes, *that ain't no image a the Lord*...it's nothin' but a *waxy build-up*, lef' over from that new cleanin' fluid, 'cause it lef' the same kinda goop on 'nother winda she done cleaned over ta Smyrna, the week *afore*! She had ta use a razor blade ta scrape it off! Now that waxy build-up it warn't no face a the Lord, Miz Esperanza said, it jus' sorta looked like Mickey Mouse, if ya held yer haid jus' right. So Miz Esperanza, she's gittin' all pissed off, *oh, 'scuse me, Rev'rend*...she's gittin' all riled up, thinkin' she done wasted money on a case a this here newfangled cleanin' fluid. But then, she gits a terr'ble pain in her hands like they was on far...it hurt so bad, she starts lookin' at her hands an' she sees that that new cleanin' fluid done made the warts fall right offa her *fingers* an' she was so happy she's a'praisin' God, but then the pain gits her agin, an' she passes out right there on the floor! Miz 'Melia Festrunk, she done looked at the label on that there cleanin' fluid bottle what 'Melio brought in an' then she looks at Miz Esperanza's blood work an' she says it warn't no Wart Removal Mir'cle after all...she says Miz Esperanza done had her a 'lergic reactionary to that new cleanin' fluid, an' she's lucky ta be *alive*!"

Corny Poe flushed scarlet; *no white-trash sloppy-ass used car salesman's gonna ruin my Miracle, my chance to take over the church, my chance to get my Senior Elder name plaque on the wall,* he fumed. He flipped Henry a bird.

"DEVIL! BE GONE! SATAN, YOU AIN'T WELCOME IN HERE!

YOU ARE BLASPHEMIN' HENRY BAILEY, LIKE THE POPE-WORSHIPIN' CATH'LICS YOU AN' YOUR FAMILY'S ALWAYS BEEN! FOLKS! HE'S LYIN! HE'S NOTHIN' BUT A THIEF AN' A LIAR AN' A CHEAT!"

Henry Bailey's eyes opened wide; the man who'd only last week told Henry he was wrong about him, that he was indeed worthy of respect, that he would indeed be on the right side of the Heavenly Fence one day accused him of lying. Henry stared at Corny in pain and defiance; Corny's greed for fame and fortune blinded him to the truth. He was the same Corny Poe, self-righteous to a fault, blaming others for his misfortune and his fate.

"Corny Poe, yer words ain't gonna hurt me, no more! An' none a the rest a ya'll is gonna hurt me with yer words, *neither*! Ya'll can call me what ya like, say what ya will, like ya been doin' alla my life, but here's the deal…no matter what ya'll say, I ain't no liar! This here's the truth an' if ya'll don't b'lieve me, then jus' listen up! Go 'head, Miz 'Melia, tell 'em!"

A woman called out from the Tour line, "But what about that Sweet Jesus Sweet Potato and that sign? Where'd it come from?"

Henry rubbed a hand over the meager strands of red hair on his scalp and motioned for Amelia to wait. "Well, sir, here's the Lord's gospel truth: Corny Poe was carryin' an' ol', moldy, stinkin' sweet potata 'roun' in a paper sack fer 'bout nigh on six months, thinkin' he done seen the face a Jesus on that veg'table. He toted that sack 'roun' ever'where an' it was stinkin' ta high Heaven! Ya'll don't b'lieve me, jus' ask Penni! So I figgered I'd have me a li'l fun…I tol' Corny that a Bathroom Angel done came ta my RV an' tol' me ta git that potata…well, sir, Corny b'lieved me, 'cause he was in a sorry state. But I done dropped that sweet potata an' it exploded, an' I had ta think fast, so's he warn't gittin' all upset er nuthin'. Well, it's all a big coincidental, but Miz Juliette, she done made a mess a sweet potata pies that very same day! An' she helt one fer me an' I carried Corny over there, but then, the joke's on me, 'cause some Pie Angel gal done tol' Miz Juliette ta give me that pie fer free. Well, sir, lemme tell ya'll, I was spooked good! But I figgered it twarn't nothin'. So, I tol' Corny my Bathroom Angel done tol' us ta put up a sign, jus' like that'n."

Henry pointed to the cooler door, where the yellow poster with red letters hung suspended over the nine-day old Sweet Jesus Sweet Potato Pie. He continued.

"Corny made that there sign, an' he tol' me he hung it up after the store closed. I figgered a coupl'a people'd git a kick outta it, give Corny a hard time an' that'd be it. But when me an' Euladean high-tailed it over here that mornin' an' seen that Cooler Jesus, I was scared ta death! I figgered the Lord my God was a'comin' with all his Angels an' Archangels, an' Bathroom

Angels an' prob'ly that Pie Angel, too, ta smite me hard fer playin' my joke! But then I heard 'bout Miz Esperanza an' I knew it was *fer real*, 'specially after Stella Stanley done run a hand thew that consolidation an' it twarn't movin'...'course, now I knowed, it's a waxy build-up is all. I been wantin' ta come clean an' tell the truth about that pie fer ten days, but Barney Gooch an' Hoot an' Raleigh an' all them coin-collectin' others, they tol' me ta shut up an' leave town or I'd be real sorry! I been hidin' out ever since't, waitin' ta be smited!"

Brother Culpepper smiled steadily at Henry and nodded. "Thank you, H-h-henry, for telling us the truth. Corny, w-w-why did you lie to the p-p-police about the sign?"

Corny gritted his teeth. "Don't you be harpin' on *me*, preacher-man! This is all Henry Bailey's fault! He started it! I had nothin' to do with it... Barney and Hoot, they took control of this whole store, right out from under me an' Daddy! *There* he is, there's that other Devil! Barney Gooch, your *Mayor*!"

The Official Cameraman swung wide and focused on Mayor Barney Gooch, who angrily stormed his way through the now less-devoted pilgrims.

"Thanks ta you, Henry Bailey, this whole town's a laughin' stock! They're broadcastin' this live, on the news, right now! And I'd jus' like ta say, people of America, that I, Barney Gooch, had absolutely nothin' ta do with this folderol an' that if I'm re-elected, I'll make sure this kinda thing ain't never gonna happen again!"

Suddenly the entrance doors to the Poe House Grocery Personal Cooler Jesus Tour opened and the frenzied, frustrated members of the international press corps swarmed inside. Hoot Graham was not around to keep them out any longer. Aisle Five of the Poe House Grocery turned into a full-fledged media circus; one reporter clawed his way to the front, held a mike to Barney's mouth.

"Mayor Gooch... I have just come from the town hospital, where the Cooler Jesus Miracle has been confirmed to be a hoax! We demand that you return the money we paid in good faith for photo rights! This is the most blatant corruption of public trust this reporter has ever seen! Rumor has it that you have also collected over twenty thousand dollars in those pickle buckets and there is no planned park for underprivileged children! How do you explain yourself, mister Mayor? And what are your exact plans for the return of the money?"

Barney wrung his hands and searched the crowd for Hoot Graham. "I ain't makin' no comment 'til Mr. Hoot Graham, Official Cooler Jesus Miracle Event Manager shows his face! Jus' like Corny Poe says, this here's all the work a Henry Bailey! Them Baileys has been crooks an' murderin' thieves in this town fer over a hunnerd years an' it's all Henry Bailey's fault!"

Henry raised his hands in protest, but suddenly the swarm of reporters parted and the crowd hushed. A tall blonde young woman in a long, white gauzy dress and sandals approached Henry and Amelia. She carried a tattered briefcase and her mouth creased in a peaceful smile. Her eyes shone at a nervous Henry as she walked toward him, her hands outstretched. Her voice was as soft as the fluff of a dandelion floating through spring air.

"*Henry Bailey*...I'd know that face anywhere! *It's really you*...my job is done...oh, thank God, I can lay down my burden! And you must be Amelia Festrunk! It's *me*...I'm your *savior*! It's time to tell the *truth*!"

A stunned Amelia looked over her trifocals at the blonde woman; a whisp of panic seized her. *I don't know this woman...do I? I've never seen her before in my life...* She turned to Henry, who had broken into a sweat and whose face was beet red, then glanced uncomfortably back at the crowd as the young woman stretched her arms around Henry and Amelia in a giant blonde embrace. She whispered into Amelia's ear.

"It's me, Ellen Gray! Professor Gray! I'm here just like I promised! Are you ready? It's time!"

Amelia nodded through tears. *This isn't how it's supposed to happen...I need to talk to her first...give me strength...I can do this...*Henry gulped gasps of air and wiped his brow with the back of one hand as the young woman released him.

"Uh, miss, was you over ta the Sweet Things bak'ry last week? Did ya off chaince buy an extry pie? Is you the Pie Angel?"

Doctor Gray nodded and smiled and whispered into Henry's ear, "Yes, I was and yes I did. Now you just take a deep breath and listen to Miss Amelia for a minute. She's got something very important to tell you that will change your life."

Henry fought back a wave of nausea; there were no less than a hundred cameras recording his every move for national television. Whatever Miss Amelia had to say, it probably wasn't good. Was she upset about the vehicles she'd purchased for MayBelle and Leonard? He'd tried to find her just the right car for herself but she was so danged picky...had he made her mad? He wanted to run, he wanted to crash right through the electric doors and keep on running far, far away from this place where they hated him, mocked him and blamed him and his family for everything bad that had ever happened in Chestnut Ridge, Tennessee.

Doctor Gray waved a slender arm to silence the crowd. "I am Professor Ellen A. Gray, from Richmond, Virginia. I am an expert in genealogy known for my specialty in Civil War-era families. I have been in your fair town now for about two weeks, silently observing you and your neighbors, because in the process of performing some critical genealogical research, I discovered an obscure fact related to this town's founding that has been cloaked in falsehood for over one hundred and thirty-six years and I'm here to set it straight. And yes, by the way, I'm the one who bought the sweet potato pie at the bakery, the very pie that sits rotting in that cooler right there! So I guess if there is a 'Pie Angel,' then it's me!"

Shouts of shock erupted from the crowd inside the Poe House. Cameras clicked and whirred. The local radio station's microphone hummed as it broadcasted this important event live over the air. All eyes were on Doctor Gray, but Barney Gooch and Corny Poe had heard enough. Their Miracle profits were quickly sliding down the drain and Henry Bailey was stealing their thunder.

"Ma'am, I hate to interrupt you, but I've just placed this here location under martial law. Ya'll all need ta git outta here an' say a prayer that we ain't offended the Almighty too much so's we can come back tomorra! Now, ever'body..."

The Mayor was interrupted by a cub reporter from the *Chestnut Ridge Tell-All.*

"Mayor, I've just come from the police station...what can you tell us about the obscene billboards that are on the outskirts of town? Do they have anything to do with this hoax? Don't they violate the federal laws against pornography? My sources says the billboards were rented by the City of Chestnut Ridge...your signature is on the purchase order...do you have any comment, Mayor?"

Barney Gooch's mouth fell open. "Son, I don't know what you're *accusin'* me of, but you'd best be *clarifyin'* yourself right quick! Now, look here, boy, I knew you when you was in diapers an' you'd best not *talk* ta me thataway!"

The cub reporter was undaunted. He retorted in a sarcastic voice, "I'm talking about the billboards at either end of town, Mayor...the ones that show two men in their underwear getting a good spanking by a scantily-clad female. Not only are the billboards *obscene,* Mayor, it seems they represent a conflict of interest, in that city funds were apparently used to advertise a private business enterprise. Any comment?"

Barney Gooch reached for the cub reporter's microphone and a brawl ensued. Doctor Gray grabbed Amelia Festrunk and led her to the back of the store where they exited at the loading dock and roared away in the professor's rental car. Henry Bailey and Corny Poe shoved each other and Aisle Five of the Poe House evolved into a crashing, frenzied mass of arms, legs, camera equipment and screaming women. A gunshot was fired into the air; Bull McArdle yelled through an orange police megaphone for all parties to be seated on the floor, *immediately,* or be taken to the city jail. All parties sat as requested.

"What in the hell-fire an' brimstone is goin' *on* over here? Has ever'body done lost their *minds*? Corny, Raleigh, ya'll open them doors an' let these here good people out…no, ma'am, you keep your money, there ain't gonna be no more donatin' here *today*! Go on, all of ya'll git outta here, go on back home. The 'ficial Cooler Jesus Mir'cle is *over*!"

Chief of Police Bull McArdle seized the Underprivileged Children's Park Pickle Buckets and watched his squad lead the citizens out of the grocery. Then he ordered all the reporters and media crews to Aisle Thirteen until he was ready to give a statement. He motioned Brother Culpepper aside and they whispered and nodded by the canned peaches for several minutes. Brother Culpepper led the homeless woman and her child out the door. Chief McArdle hitched up his sansa-belts and approached the remaining orchestrators of the Cooler Jesus Miracle.

"Now, then. Henry…Corny…Raleigh…Barney…Brother Culpepper filled me in on what's been happenin', so ya'll can jus' ferget about tryin' ta make up any more stories. Henry Bailey, stand up!"

Henry did as he was told and looked squarely up at Bull McArdle, who had at least a foot height gain on him.

"Henry, Brother Culpepper said you came clean 'bout the prank an' how this whole thing got started. He also told me you's the one that told all them people what Miz Amelia said 'bout Miz Esperanza's warts, an' how that Cooler Jesus ain't nothin' but a waxy build-up. Now, Henry…I gotta tell ya…I figgered this was all your fault since Barney had me run you off last Tuesday, 'cause you was threat'nin' folks an' stealin' money outta the pickle buckets…Henry, is that true?"

Tears of anger rimmed Henry's eyes. He clenched his fists. "No, Chief, it *ain't*! Barney Gooch and Hoot and Raleigh Poe, they was mad 'cause I was fixin' ta talk ta one a them mediators an' they was jealous! I tol' 'em it warn't right ta be chargin' folks ta see God an' nex' thing I knowed, here ya come, tellin' me ta git, else you'd put me in the pokey! I didn't steal no money outta no pickle buckets! Them Poes an' Barney wanted me outta the way, 'cause I was gonna come clean an' wreck their profits!"

"So, Henry, you didn't steal that money, or threaten nobody?"

"Chief, I swear onna stacka Bibles! You can ask Miz Hester Graham…she done foun' me last week settin' outside the bak'ry with nary a nickel in my pocket. She done give me a pack a breath mints, that was all I had fer breakfast! I been sleepin' in her house, livin' off her charity ever since!"

Chief McArdle nodded; Henry's tale concurred with Hester's. He sighed, "I b'lieve you, Henry, I do. Miz Hester tole me the same story. So you don't know nothin' 'bout them billboards, either?"

Henry shook his head, his eyes wide. "Look here, Chief, I ain't got nothin' 'gainst them people, but if it's one thing I *ain't*, it's a *pornography*! I don't know what ya'll are talkin' about! All I know is I'm wantin' ta go ta my own house an' sleep in my own bed, without them mediator-types pokin' at me."

Chief McArdle hitched up his sansa-belts and turned to see Will Graham enter the Poe House. Will looked tired and his clothes sagged on his body. "Hey, Will, I'm gonna have ta ask you ta step over ta Aisle Thirteen, ok? We got a three-twelve workin' here."

Will rubbed his neck in confusion but nodded his head. "Sure, Bull…I just came in to get some buttermilk for my ulcer…I'll come back later."

Chief McArdle raised a finger to his lips. "Will…on second thought…you gotta few minutes? You prob'ly better see this right now, get it over with. My men got their hands full an' I need an extra vee-hicle…can you take a ride with us for a sec? I'd sure 'preciate it…we'll be out there in a few…ALL YOU REPORTERS ON AISLE THIRTEEN…ya'll stay put an' keep quite or my men'll arrest ya, ya'll hear?"

Will waited by the newspaper stand outside. Chief McArdle pointed at each of the conspiracy suspects and shouted, "Now, we're gonna take us a ride an' have a look at them billboards! Barney, sure as shootin', I seen your signature's on the p.o. for them signs…you gotta heap a trouble, a heap a trouble. All right…I ain't gonna cuff nobody…ya'll stick tight. Barney, Corny, Raleigh, ya'll ride in the squad car with me…Henry, you ride with Will. We're headin' ta the edge a town, off I-24 West, 'bout two miles."

It was a textbook example of advertising perfection; the camera work was precise, the color magnificent and the identities of the two men plastered on the billboard unmistakable. It was the work of a true artist and as the two cars emptied of their passengers, hands were raised to faces, blocking the glare. Cars slowed considerably to review the message; it would indeed put Chestnut Ridge on the map.

The billboard displayed a photo of blindfolded yet easily recognizable Hoot Graham and Dan Gastineau in their underwear, kneeling down on the carpet of a tastefully appointed hotel room. Behind the men stood the torso of a woman in a powder blue evening gown and stiletto heels. The woman held a wooden paddle, and was in the process of spanking the men on their respective behinds. Bold black letters at the top of the billboard proclaimed, "COME TO THE SONS OF GLORY FESTIVAL FOR A SPANKING GOOD TIME!"

Chief McArdle's walkie-talkie buzzed and popped as he slowly pulled his hulking body out of the squad car; Barney Gooch and Henry Bailey stared at the billboard, mouths agape. Raleigh Poe was seized with laughter and rolled onto the ground in a hysterical fit. Corny Poe waved his arms and loudly quoted a passage from the Bible about Sodom and Gomorrah. Will

Graham swallowed hard, then ran thirty paces away from the group and vomited. Henry ran over to Will and offered his handkerchief. Chief McArdle surveyed the group of men; everyone was as stunned as he had been when he'd first driven out here shortly after daybreak, at the request of a State Trooper who was on his regular I-24 patrol.

"There's another one jus' like it on the other side a town. Fella at the sign comp'ny says they got put up early this mornin'. They was paid triple wages at the request a Mayor Gooch hisself. 'Par'ntly, the sign comp'ny didn't make the signs ...they was tol' ta pick 'em up at a warehouse 'cross county, yesterday. Says them signs was all wrapped up in brown paper when they got 'em. Fella tol' me his crews called in this mornin', gripin' 'bout the contents, but he tol' 'em, *'ya'll ain't paid ta be art critics...jus' put 'em up!'* I reckon they did, all right!"

Will Graham leaned against his car. He tried to breathe deeply, to avoid a second vomiting episode. *My own own brother! I knew that Rodriguez boy was bad news, I knew he was light in his loafers...but Hoot and Dan Gastineau, too? Wonder if Dorothy knows her boyfriend Dan swings both ways? What's this world coming to?*

Chief McArdle's walkie-talkie beeped and popped again, then he heard a familiar voice dispatch a request for assistance with a four-fifteen, *'Pomeroy, on your way back from that 311, take I-24...just out of town...you like art, don't ya? Well, take a look, you can't miss it!'*

Chief McArdle slammed his clipboard against his thigh as a wave of blood rose up his neck; *Margaret! This is her doin'! She coulda forged Barney's name, made all the 'rangements...she hates Gastineau...she's been waitin' ta trap Hoot for years.* Bull McArdle hitched up his pants, then let out a huge sigh as he noticed a swarm of network television camera trucks parking behind his squad car on the shoulder of the interstate.

Henry Bailey turned from the billboard and swallowed hard. *I knew Hoot warn't on the up and up! That's what them Best Boys is all about, I jus' knew it!*

"Ya'll git back in the car, now...I'll handle this...don't nobody, an' that means *you*, Barney Gooch, don't nobody say *nothin*! Henry, you git on that radio, punch two-three-seven an' give 'em the number on the dash...tell the state dispatcher we got us a thirty-forty-four an' ta send us a mess a boys with black paint and brushes, NOW!"

Henry's heart raced; a real police radio! He punched the buttons as Bull marched off to greet the reporters who ignored his waving arms and proceeded to set up their equipment in the tall weeds adjacent to the interstate. After about ten minutes, Bull returned.

"Will...you reckon you can git ever'body in that big Caddy an' take 'em back? I'm prob'ly gonna be out here a while...this ain't over, Barney, Corny,

Raleigh...I'll be comin' 'round later! Don't ya'll leave town! An' don't ya'll make no 'ficial statements er you'll be spendin' the night in jail, ya hear?"

Everybody nodded as Henry hollered, "SHOTGUN!" and ran to Will's Cadillac. Barney, Corny and Raleigh crammed into the backseat and they all endured a painfully silent ride back to town. Will dropped the backseat passengers off at the grocery and asked Henry if he would like to have lunch at the Graham residence. Henry's eyes popped wide at the invitation and he accepted. Minutes later, they were seated on the shady veranda, sipping iced tea and enjoying chicken salad sandwiches. Henry observed it was the best chicken salad sandwich he'd ever tasted, owing to the surroundings.

"Ya know, Mister Will, you always been real nice ta me, ya ain't never said nothin' bad 'bout me a't'all...I ain't a edjicated man like you, but I sure 'preciate yer kindness thew the years."

Will wiped his mouth with a napkin and nodded. "Why, Henry, there's no need to thank me. My mama always told me to treat people like I'd want to be treated; you seem to bear the brunt of everything bad that happens around here...that must be terrible. I'm not all that smart...I've had some unfair family advantages, I guess. Not like you."

Henry shrugged his shoulders and placed a giant potato chip in his mouth. "It ain't so bad...a fella gits used ta it, I reckon. Mister Will...ever'-body knows ya ta be an honest man...yer always he'pin somebody. But right now, ya ain't lookin' so good...ya look kinda sad...an' where's Miz Dorothy? She out shoppin' fer some a them fancy ballgowns I hear she's always a'wearin'?"

Will pushed his plate away, leaving a half-eaten sandwich that Henry eyed greedily. "Henry, I'm ok, I guess. I've had a couple of bad days, here lately. It seems the kids ran into some trouble...they've closed the restaurant. Horry's run off to Key West with that Rodriguez fellow. I sure didn't need to see what I saw up on that billboard, either... my own brother...but that's not the worst thing bothering me, Henry..."

Henry pointed at Will's uneaten sandwich and upon a nod from Will, stuffed half of it in his mouth. "Mphwhat's at, mphmister Will?"

"Hester stopped by early this morning. She was at some party at the Peacock Inn last night, and she saw Dorothy and Richard Leigh-Lee half-naked in the hall. Apparently they've been shacking up for several days. But Dorothy left me a note saying she had a pregnant, unwed cousin in Canada and she needed money to help her. Hester wouldn't give Dorothy the money, she never even asked me, she just disappeared. But now I find out that she's been sharing a room with Richard at the Peacock right under my nose...I'd never believe it except Hessie saw her with her own eyes... there's incontrovertible proof, all right."

Henry choked down the remainder of the sandwich. "I'm real sorry, Mister Will, truly, I am. I been in the same sitiation, my ex, Fay, she charged up alla my credit cards, moved alla my hard-earned money inta her own bank 'count, then took off with ever' fella that came ta town in a late-model car! Then she gits a divorce an' I gotta pay her alimony! Dang, she already done took ever'thing I owned! I says to her, I says, *'Fay, I cain't pay you no alimony! Whaddya want me ta do, give ya a hubcap a week fer the resta my life?'* Yeah, Mister Will...women is hard ta figger out, they ain't many worth a toot, that's fer sure. An' well, yeah, if you got *convertible* proof, then I reckon that's the clincher!"

Will drained his iced tea and leaned back in his chair. "The funny thing is, Henry, I've known for years about Dorothy's affairs...she's been sneaking off to the Peacock every week to meet Dan Gastineau for the last eighteen months. Hey, won't she be surprised when she finds out Dan's been two-timing her with her own brother-in-law! I kept noticing the grocery money was going to hell in a hand-basket and yet we didn't have a thing to eat in this house! And all the money I set aside to pay for a year's worth of Hoot's hotel and meals disappeared from the account a while back...I hired a detective from Nashville...cost me a fortune, but it was worth it. He found out that not only is Dorothy sleeping around, she's been moving money...my money, as well as money from the Festival, the whole nine yards and she's been forging checks. The irony of all this is, I was getting ready to ask Dorothy for a divorce anyway...see, Henry, no matter how straight a man's family tree may appear to be, it may have lots of crooks inside. I found out that my little social-climbing wife cheated on me with my very own father before we were married...and my ol' man paid for his good time by making Dorothy the beneficiary of our entire estate after Mama dies...cut me and Hoot out completely! Mama's been so out of it since Daddy passed, she didn't even know, I don't think she ever even read that will in the first place. But here lately she's been a lot better...Miss Amelia's been nursing her. And when I told Mama about what I'd discovered about Daddy and Dorothy...you know what, Henry? She already knew Daddy wasn't faithful, but she didn't know Dorothy was one of the flock. And she didn't know about her will, either. Madder than a wet hen when I told her about it...we've been working with Richard to get it re-drawn, cut Dorothy out for good. 'Course now my own lawyer's shacking up with my wife and I'm being made to look like a fool while they live in style at the Peacock. And of course, nobody ever believes the husband, do they, Henry?"

Henry shook his head and smiled. "Nope, Mister Will, they shore don't, but I keep tellin' myse'f...I say Henry, jus' 'member...ever' dog has its day! You mind if I's ta have me 'nother sandwich? That's shore good chicken salat!"

Will grinned, stood up and walked into the house. Henry surveyed the spacious white veranda of the Graham mansion and its blanket of green grass. A dozen huge oak trees framed the grounds; a tidy English boxwood garden lay to the left and to the right was a rose arbor that made Euladean's precious tree roses pale in comparison. A fountain off the veranda gurgled with sparkling water and a family of purple martens hummed in the tall marten house at the edge of the trees. Henry wondered what it would be like to live here, to walk in the maze of the boxwoods, sipping iced tea, your only concern would be what you should instruct the maid to cook for dinner, or which suit you should wear to the next Rotary function. The portable phone on the veranda rang and out of courtesy to his generous host, Henry answered it.

"This here's Will Graham's rezidents...who's a'callin', please?"

"*WHO IS THIS?*" a stern, uppity female voice demanded. "WHERE IS WILL...WHO ARE *YOU?*"

"This here's Mister Henry Bailey, ma'am, at yer service. Mister Will's in the kitchen, fixin' me one a them dee-licious chicken salat sandwiches...hey, holt on, here he comes now!"

Henry handed the phone to a surprised Will, who placed a fresh sandwich in front of a grateful Henry. "Will Graham here...*oh, Dorothy*...just a minute..."

Will pulled a small tape recorder out of his shirt pocket, clicked it on and held it to the phone. "How *nice* of you to call! How's Canada?"

"Are you *insane*, Will Graham? Allowing that white trash in our *home*? Feeding him a *sandwich*? My God, I won't be able to show my face in town for *months*! If the NDCA gets wind of this, I'll never be president! All my hard work, *ruined*! I'm surprised you're on the veranda...why not just take that filthy mongrel into our formal dining room where he could eat off the Haviland and the Baccarat! That would certainly make it easier for him to steal our silver, too, come to think of it! Why don't you just put everything in boxes for him? Will, you never cease to amaze me with your social graces and hospitality!"

"Dorothy, that's enough. What do you want... where have you *been*?"

"Don't be so *coy*, Will...I'm sure Hester spilled the beans on my whereabouts, you two have always been so *close*! The reason I'm calling is this: I innocently turned on the network news...what do I see, but your no-good *brother* and Dan Gastineau, disgracing themselves on a billboard for the entire world to see! It's all over, Will...I'm *devastated!* You must act fast...call whomever you must, pay whatever you must...it's time for damage control, my reputation is at stake! I will *not* lose the NDCA position or that year in West Palm all because your family has a history of *sexual deviancy!* Will...*do you hear me?* If you don't take care of this by tomorrow, I'll file for divorce, I *promise!* What do you think about *that?*"

Will hoisted his cowboy-booted feet and rested them on the table, across from Henry. He leaned back with a wide grin and a wink.

"Dorothy darling, let me tell you *exactly* what I think! Let me make it crys*tal clear! A*, I know you and Richard are sharing digs at the Peacock in the same suite where you've been screwing Dan Gastineau every week on our grocery money! And by the way, based on the nature of that billboard photograph, you might wanna be-bop over and get tested for AIDS, since it seems that your boyfriend Danny might swing both ways! Oh, and you can stop forging checks, too, dear, you're just giving us all more evidence. *B*, I know there *is* no pregnant cousin in Canada! *C*, I have no idea about the circumstances behind those billboards and I really don't care! I'm more concerned about the well-being of our children than your *reputation!* And *D*, I'll save you the trouble, because I've already *filed* for divorce, Dottie! I hope Richard has deep pockets because Mom just cut you out of your inheritance for good! Gotta go...you're spoiling my nice lunch with Henry! See you in court!"

Will hung up the phone and he and Henry whooped with laughter. Henry let out a loud whistle and a piece of lettuce flew from his mouth.

"Mister Will, ya shore gotta way with words! Nex' time I git in a fight with Euladean, I'm callin' ya ta help me *out*!"

Will rubbed his palms on the knees of his blue jeans. He felt as if thirty-year old chains had been unlocked from around his chest; he sucked in the first free air he'd breathed in a long time. "Henry...you're right, what goes around, comes around!"

Henry raised his iced tea glass in his host's honor. "Yep, Mister Will, it shore does. An' from where I'm a'sittin', if I's in yer shoes, I'd be thinkin' ta myse'f, *'this dog ain't fetchin', an' cowerin' an' playin' dead no more...yessir, this dog here, he has done had his day!*"

CHAPTER TWENTY-SIX – SOUL BENEFICIARY

Friday evening, September 3 1999; Quigley Funeral Parlor

The Quigley Funeral Parlor was filled to capacity on a balmy evening in downtown Chestnut Ridge. A steady stream of mourners filed through the white-columned entrance and into the grand foyer. MayBelle Festrunk took charge of the Guest Book; she was attired in a pink organza ball gown, a pink feather boa and a small tiara encrusted with pale pink amethysts. The Guest Book rested on a faux-marble pedestal traditionally reserved for the funerals of Chestnut Ridge's most upstanding citizens.

MayBelle and her Guest Book were conveniently located outside the door to the Peaceful Slumber Room. As the mourners filed in, they paused to sign their names in heartfelt, sympathetic script. Out of respect for the dead, a serene silence filled the funeral parlor foyer, broken only by occasional whispers. Indeed, anyone observing the scene would have surmised that the pomp, circumstance and grandeur must have been duly called for in tribute to a great and model citizen; a person of utmost character and sincerity, a person to whom the town owed a large debt for his or her devoted service.

That notion would be somewhat diminished, however, as one stepped inside the Peaceful Slumber Room and as one read the name written in gold chalk on the small blackboard, *'Miss Shu-Shu, Beloved Pet, Devoted Friend.'*

The Peaceful Slumber Room itself was the unlikely scene of an absurdly morbid carnival. Dozens of floral arrangements ringed its perimeter and rows of gold-vinyl cushioned chairs invited mourners to rest and contemplate their sorrow. At the head of the room, in front of a gold velvet curtain, a tiny, gleaming walnut casket with copper fittings rested on a pink satin bier. At the base of the casket, a giant floral wreath constructed of pink and white roses spelled the word, *'PAIN.'* A Hammond organ played *"How Great Thou Art"* in soft tones.

On either side of the casket, tables draped in pink satin displayed gilt-framed photographs showcasing the deceased in a variety of costumes. A collection of dog-show trophies, awards and ribbons fanned out around the photographs, and a tiny diamond tiara and a gold medal inscribed with *'Best of Show'* rested on a crystal tray, evidence of Miss Shu-Shu's win at the National Toy Dog Competition so many years before. In stark contrast to the glitter of Miss Shu-Shu's life as a canine debutante, a soiled, odiferous rag doll was exhibited at one end of the second table, next to a framed oil portrait of the white dog herself. The rag doll, lovingly referred to as *"Pretty Girl,"* initially sported a pink-checked gingham dress and pink yarn pigtails. Years of constant gnawing by Miss Shu-Shu, however, had turned the doll into a bald shadow of its former self; its dress was reduced to tiny epaulets and it could no longer, by any stretch of the imagination, be considered pretty.

Elspeth Kimball, in a ten-year old pink prom frock silently offered the Order of Service to each mourner who entered the Peaceful Slumber Room. Penni Poe stood by in her pink wool suit and pillbox hat and offered pink tissues to each mourner from a bejeweled box. Behind Elspeth and Penni, two pink-clothed tables groaned under a heavy assortment of refreshments that would be offered to guests at the close of the service. Juliette Kimball, attired in a light pink chiffon evening gown and matching jacket, supervised the food tables and arranged the dishes as they were delivered by her bakery staff. She was particularly proud of her new creation: pink bone-shaped cookies that were exact replicas of Miss Shu-Shu's favorite treat, Perky Poochies.

Juliette checked her watch; six-fifty, the service would begin promptly at seven and by seven-fifteen the grief-stricken mourners would be hungry. It was time to mix the punch. She whispered to one of her bakery assistants who placed a cherry-flavored ice ring into the massive glass punch bowl. Juliette carefully poured five gallons of pre-mixed pink lemonade into the bowl and added an entire gallon jar of maraschino cherries. Miss Shu-Shu, who absolutely loved cherries, would have been proud.

By six fifty-five, the Peaceful Slumber Room could hold no more and Reverend Cameron Culpepper took his place at the wooden podium to the right of the casket. Brother Culpepper was most uncomfortable; he did not believe that animals had souls and he was not at all pleased at the Quigleys' request that he perform this funeral service.

Ruby and Roy Quigley were charter members of the First United Assembly of God's Children's Top Tithers Club, however and Brother Culpepper did not wish to snub them in their time of great sorrow. At seven sharp, the organist ceased his hymn playing and substituted the mournful strains of *"One is the Loneliest Number"*, signifying the sad but dutiful journey unto death that everyone, including small animals, must make alone. As the chorus lilted over the mourners, Stella Stanley, sporting a hot pink satin pantsuit, marched down the center aisle of the Peaceful Slumber Room. She carried the wooden cross that she'd taken up at the Poe House and which had not left her side since. In the middle of the cross was pasted an 8x10 color photo of Miss Shu-Shu at the request of Ruby. As she approached the casket, Stella gingerly laid the cross, photo-side up, over the the pink satin-covered bier. Reverend Culpepper lowered his head and silently asked for strength in his time of need.

As the organist played the second verse of the anthem, a shattered Ruby and Roy Quigley braced each other as they walked slowly down the aisle. Ruby, dressed in a pink-sequined strapless gown and high heels, carried Miss Shu-Shu's pink rhinestone dog collar in one hand and a bouquet of pink miniature roses in the other. Roy wore a pink-checked sport coat that Ruby finished sewing mere moments before the service. *'You cain't wear black ta my precious baby's memorial service,'* Ruby'd tearfully said, *'you know pink was Miss Shu-Shu's favorite color!'*

Reverend Culpepper read several quotations from St. Francis of Assisi, Patron Saint of Animals. He praised Roy and Ruby for the years of excellent care they'd given so selflessly to one of God's creatures. Then he offered a prayer for Miss Shu-Shu, the Quigley family, and for all those whose lives Miss Shu-Shu had touched. The Reverend's son, Peter Paul, then read aloud a poem he'd written in the little dog's honor, a poem which he planned to submit to the American Young Poets Society in Miss Shu-Shu's memory. Many of the mourners shed silent tears at the dramatic, touching tribute presented by Peter Paul. As the organ played *"Nearer My God to Thee,"* Brother Culpepper also offered a silent prayer for Roy Quigley; it was not right for a woman to evict her husband from his own home just because her dog died. As the service ended, the organist abruptly switched gears and launched into a rousing version of *"Hound Dog."* Ruby stood, tugged at her strapless gown, and addressed those present.

"Me an' Roy'd like ta thank ya'll for comin' tonight. Our lives ain't never gonna be the same without our precious baby an' we know ya'll will fergive us over the nex' few, on account of our grief. Ya'll know how Miss Shu-Shu *loved* a party...so let's all try an' 'member the *good* times...ya'll help yerseves ta the eats, ok?"

The guests sipped pink lemonade and nibbled on the pink bone-shaped cookies while Roy and Ruby held court in front of the casket. The organ music stopped and a cassette of *"How Much is that Doggie in the Window,"* accompanied by none other than Miss Shu-Shu herself, barking in time, played repeatedly. A teary-eyed Ruby turned to Fay Bailey.

"Ya know, that was the smartest dog ever *lived*! How many other dogs do ya know could sing like that?"

Fay smiled and patted Ruby comfortingly on the shoulder. She didn't think much of Miss Shu-Shu, having been the victim of the ratty dog's constant ankle-biting over the past fifteen years, but Ruby was her boss and with Stella's exit from the Beauty Box, Fay intended to become head hairdresser.

At seven forty-five, the music ended altogether, to the great relief of the guests. Juliette and one of her assistants stepped to the casket area and gently tugged at the gold velvet curtain, pulling it in front of the casket and trophy display area. When the deceased and her earthly treasures were duly hidden from sight, Peter Paul Culpepper and Billy Gooch opened the vinyl folding partitions that divided the Peaceful Slumber Room from the Golden Memories Chapel to create one large, two-hundred seat capacity space. Billy dragged the wooden podium to the head of the room and the mourners joined the hundred-odd citizens already seated. A City Council meeting had been called to review the upsetting events of the past week and a half, and to determine the fate of the Sons of Glory Festival, in light of the negative publicity associated with the Cooler Jesus incident and the pornographic billboards.

MayBelle Festrunk, fresh from her Guest Book duty, wheeled Nell Graham into position safely at the back of the room, as Nell had enjoyed too many pink cookies and was now experiencing a deafening series of burps. A loud group of cackling Festival ladies took seats at the front. The members of the City Council took their places at a long table behind the podium and when everyone was seated, Barney Gooch banged his gavel. He'd quickly removed his suit coat and to reveal a bright white cotton t-shirt that read, "I SAW THE SWEET JESUS SWEET POTATO PIE MIRACLE."

"I call his here special meetin' a the Chestnut Ridge City Council ta *order*! Now, seein' as how this here's a *special meetin'* an' we ain't never had no special meetin's *before*, there ain't no minutes ta read, right Miss Gober? Right, so we're gonna dispense with that big waste a time an' get movin' on ta them issues at hand."

Barney glanced at a sheet of paper offered by Miss Gober. They conferred momentarily, then Barney banged his gavel again. "We got us some major issues ta discuss, tonight…*one*, is them billboard problems, I reckon ever'-body done already seen 'em afore they's covered up. An' *two*, on *accounta* them billboard problems, we gotta decide what we're gonna do 'bout this Festival. Now we've all been a might sidetracked with this Mir'cle bizness… *by the way*, I got two thousand a these here t-shirts in assorted sizes in my garage an' I'll be sellin' 'em after the meetin' if anybody's inter'sted, at low, low, gotta go prices."

A few murmurs of disapproval rang through the assembly. Leonard Festrunk waved his hand and when the Mayor reluctantly recognized him, spoke up,

"If the Mayor gits ta sell t-shirts at this here public meetin', then I git equal time! I got *me* some real nice shirts ta sell, too, 'specially if ya'll are gonna cancel the Fest'val, so ya'll come on over ta my house after, 'cause my prices are 'lot lower I bet an' my shirts is a heckuva lot more patriotic!"

Dr. Avery Parker, Jr. covered his face with his hands and sighed. Barney rolled his eyes and banged his gavel.

"Aw right. *First*…I wanna come clean on the fact that them nickels ever'-

body done put inta them pickle buckets over ta the Poe House is all been donated ta the Clinic...maybe git us one a them big cap scan machines. An' I ain't never wanna hear no more 'bout all that, neither...we's all caught up tagether and it's over an' done with. Now, *second,* Chief McArdle's investigatin' this billboard mess...as ya'll seen in the papers this mornin', me an' my staff's been cleared, somebody done forged my name on them purchase orders an' the Chief's purt' near figgered out who's respons'ble, right, Chief?"

Chief Bull McArdle nodded confidently from his official stance behind the City Council table. Barney smiled. "'Course, this here's a partic'lar *sens'tive* issue fer the Chief, *person'lly* an' as ya'll might expect, in this sitiation we gotta give him some time, not rush nothin'. Now what we..."

Barney ignored Leonard Festrunk who again requested permission to speak; after several seconds, Leonard decided he would no longer be ignored. He stood up from his chair in the middle section of the room. He was dressed in an aqua polyester leisure suit and white loafers. From the back of the room, Nell glowed with pride at the love of her life.

"Barney Gooch, Bull McArdle, ya'll *know'd* who done it! It's that *Marg'ret,* that's who done it an' ya'll are wastin' *taxpayer money* fartin' aroun' an' play-actin' like ya'll are some kinda F.B. an' I boys! We oughta jus' git on over ta that Dispatch Office an' put that gal in *jail!* Them billboards is the most outrageeous scandal's ever hit this town an' I feel sorry fer all the younguns that hafta look at that kinda stuff, it's the rueenation a America, 's what it is! An' we're wastin' *taxpayer money* sittin' here tonight *talkin'* 'bout it, too! It's ridicaluss, we got *proof!*"

Thunderous applause filled the air; Barney banged his gavel for control. Euladean Bailey, seated in the third row next to a wartless Esperanza Rodriguez, whispered, *"Henry says it ain't real proof unless it's convertible, ya know..."*

Bull McArdle crossed his arms and shot a sarcastic glance at Leonard Festrunk. Barney sighed and spoke again. "Thank ya, Leonard, fer yer *comments...*I ain't gonna say Marg'ret *is* a suspect an' I ain't gonna say she *ain't.* Bull McArdle an' his boys are workin' on this day an' night, I'm tellin' ya'll an' by Mond'y it'll all be over. Besides, Leonard them billboards is all been covered up now, so jus' pipe down."

Leonard turned to wink at Nell and reluctantly took his seat. Barney surveyed his voting public.

"Now, them billboards give us all kindsa bad publiss-ty an' on the heelsa the whole Mir'cle ordeal, the reputation a this town's at stake. We're in a bad way, folks, I ain't jus' whistlin' Dixie...monthsa work may be down the drain, here. *Hell...* heck, we had ta chase one a them tabaloid reporters outta the Peaceful Slumber Room jus' a few minutes ago...them people're vultures an' they're hell-bent on makin' us all look like a buncha redneck hicks who got hayseed fer brains! Ever'thing we done on this Festival is fer naught. Oh, we might get us a few folks in here ta see fer themselves if we're all a buncha crazies, but we ain't gonna get no serious Festival-goers, that's fer sure. An' another thing... Chéz Horatio's done closed! We cain't have no Festival without no food!"

Betty Gooch stood up behind Raleigh and pointed at her husband. "And that pervert Hoot Graham's not gonna direct me in that *play*, neither!"

As another wave of loud applause rocked the room, Betty blushed, smiled and sat down; as she did, she saw Roland Gastineau plant a wet kiss on the neck of Danita Kay Leigh-Lee. Betty turned away in defiance and disgust. Barney grasped the podium with both hands.

"Well, if it ain't *Pete an' Repeat*! You buncha ingrates! Thanks ta Hoot Graham an' his Hollywood photo negotiatin' skills, we was able ta donate thousands a dollars to the Clinic! Without Hoot them media folks'd eat us fer lunch! An' our new legal repasent'ive, Miss Danita Kay Leigh-Lee already done tol' them vultures they can't have that money back, neither, jus' 'cause that Cooler Jesus was all a big mix-up. Miss Danita tol' them boys we earned that money fair an' square, tol' 'em they took their chances an' it ain't our li'-bil'ty if it come up a bust! As fer Hoot, he ain't no *pervert*...now, I cain't speak ta Dan Gastineau, mind ya, but Hoot's as right as rain...them billboards is a *prank* an' ya'll ain't got no right ta be name-callin' an' bein' disrespectful! Now I reckon he'll be here any minute with some ideas, so ya'll settle down! Don't fergit, he's gotta contract ta film Miz Dorothy, too...by the way, where's our Madame Chairman *at,* anyhow?"

Some of the Festival Committee ladies eyed each other around the room; was this the day that Hoot's blackmail scheme would come to light? Was Dorothy in the back room with the FBI under great duress, preparing to testify? It wasn't like her to miss a meeting. Suddenly Will Graham strolled toward the podium to everyone's surprise. Will rarely attended City Council affairs. He loosened his tie, shook Barney's hand and smiled.

"Evening, Mayor, everyone. Ruby, Roy, I'm sorry about your loss...Miss MayBelle, thanks for bringing Mama over for me...I'm sorry I'm late...I was in a meeting with my new attorney, in Nashville..."

A web of suspicious whispers floated around the room; everyone in town knew that the Grahams' sole source of legal advice for over a hundred years was the firm of Leigh-Lee & Sons. It was unthinkable that the Graham family would ever solicit assistance from an attorney outside the county. Will cleared his throat and waved a hand in the air.

"Mister Mayor, I have some developments which you may find important to the context of tonight's meeting and if you don't mind, I'd like to bring everybody up to speed."

The Festival ladies braced themselves for the certain unveiling of the horrible Hoot Blackmail Scheme; it must be worse than they imagined, so terrible that Dorothy couldn't show her face and she'd sent Will to bear the news in her stead. Barney nodded and waved at Will to step up to the podium, which he did. He placed a pair of horn-rimmed reading glasses on his face and began.

"This has been a trying time for me, I must admit. But you should all know that as of today, I filed for divorce from my wife, Dorothy Chatwick Graham, uh, Festival Chairwoman."

Shocked gasps pierced the air; although Dorothy Graham's uppity behavior over the previous thirty years preceded her, no one believed Will to be the type of man who would ever seek a divorce. The Festival ladies gripped one another but maintained their composure; this must merely be part of the trap by the Feds, a method to lure Hoot out of his lair and secure the return of their Festival funds. Will cleared his throat and continued.

"This telegram I received from Dorothy will explain things much better than I can, 'cause ya'll know I'm a man of few words. *'Dear Will, at the advice of my attorney, I will comply with your request for a no-contest divorce, on the condition that you ship to me all of my clothing, shoes, handbags, jewelry and makeup, as well as any personal accessories yet to be determined. You cannot possibly expect me to live here after being publicly humiliated by your brother on those billboards. And you can tell everyone, including the Festival Committee and especially Mother Nell, to kiss my lily-white ass. I can't believe she cut me out of her will after all the years I've cared for her so lovingly, but she always was a real bitch. I am now headed for West Palm Beach with none other than Richard Leigh-Lee IV, who is coincidentally seeking a divorce from his wife and who has formally turned over his entire law practice to Danita Kay. We are very happy together and expect to carve quite a niche for ourselves in the West Palm social circuit.'"*

Will's face lit up like a firecracker. The assembled citizens had never seen the bank president so happy, with the possible exception of the birth of his twins. Will grinned.

"I hate to say this, folks, but it seems that not only had my lovely wife been cheating on me for a long time, she'd been playing games with our money...my money, Festival money...and there are some other things I won't go into, here, but suffice to say that Dorothy won't be Festival Chairwoman, she won't be inheriting anything from the Graham estate and she definitely won't ever come back to Chestnut Ridge, because if she does, we'll press charges!"

The Festival Ladies stared in gaping-mouthed shock. Leonard Festrunk stood up. "We're right sorry, Mister Will. Yer a good man an' ya don't deserve ta be treated thataway!"

The mourner-citizens honored Will Graham with a round of thunderous applause. He blushed and waved his hand for silence. "Thanks, thanks everybody. I'd like to apologize for anything my soon-to-be-ex-wife may have ever done to any of you good people. Now…next up, here goes. Bull, I'll get you a copy…you'll find it very interesting."

He pulled a second sheet of paper from his coat pocket and opened it, wistfully. "My daughter Hester left town this afternoon and left me this letter, which I share: *'Dear Daddy, I'm sorry if you're worried about me but Margaret McArdle-Graham and I are headed for Canada.'"*

Will paused and looked over his reading glasses at Bull McArdle; Bull and his deputies eyed one another in surprise, and one of them was immediately dispatched from the meeting to call headquarters. Bull nodded confidently at Barney. Will turned back to the letter.

" 'Margaret convinced me that Mom's cousin Cynthia may actually exist, and it's my duty to try and find her. Plus Margaret's allergies will be much better in cooler weather, and she's convinced me to help her open a shelter for Canadian Abuse Victims. I'm sorry I can't tell you exactly where we are…Margaret says there's a very active Female Violence faction around here and we must be secretive. But I'll write you and let you know how I'm doing, I promise. Go ahead and sell the restaurant, Daddy and my cottage… I've already packed up my things and cleared out, because Margaret pointed out to me that I may be gone for several months or longer. I miss and love you. I'm sorry about Mom, but you're better off if she's gone. Please say hi to everyone, especially Juliette and when I come home, we'll have a long talk. Love and kisses, Hessie.'"

Barney Gooch approached the podium to speak, but Will shook his head and pulled a third piece of paper from his pocket. He looked at Barney over his reading glasses. Barney reluctantly returned to his seat as Will prepared to deliver the next tidbit of information.

"Mayor…if you don't mind, I know this seems unbelievable, but I also received a letter from my son Horry today…nobody's seen him for almost two weeks and I know ya'll are concerned about his Festival catering contract. This ought to clear things up a bit: *'Dear Dad, Estéfan Rodriguez and I are living in a nice gay community in Key West. We are very happy together and plan to be married after the tourist season ends. I never wanted to hurt you or Hessie, but this isn't the kind of thing you can talk about in a town like Chestnut Ridge, is it, Dad? I think Mom's suspected all along, but she's too wrapped up in herself to care anyway.'"*

At this point, Will paused and said, "Key West's not too far from West Palm…maybe they'll run into Dorothy and Richard on the social circuit!"

The crowd laughed nervously; Esperanza Rodriguez wiped a tear from her face as Euladean Bailey patted her on the knee. Will resumed his reading.

"Back to the letter, now, where was I: *'Please thank all our customers for me, it was a great ride while it lasted and thanks for your confidence in me, Dad. I hope you're not too disappointed, but I am who I am. Love, Horry.'"*

Will removed his reading glasses and leaned on the podium. "Ladies and gentlemen, you can see that I've had quite a week! But I want to say right here, right now that I have never been happier in all my life. I endured a loveless marriage for nearly thirty years and getting a divorce is the best decision I've ever made. And although I will miss my children, I know they are doing what they want to do and I'm proud of their courage and their gumption. They will always be welcome in my home and I hope in this town. As to my brother, I'm sorry about the billboards, but I'm sure the authorities are hot on the trail of who we can all guess was the instigator. Thank you for allowing me to clear the air and thank you for the patronage you gave to my children's restaurant over the years...now, I would like to..."

Will looked down from the podium as he saw his mother steadily wheeling her chair toward him from the back of the room. "Mama...are you ok? What are you doing?"

Betty Gooch breathed a huge sigh of relief at the distraction caused by Mother Nell; although she was furious that Margaret and Hester had deserted her before enacting revenge on Roland and Danita, at least she was not named as accomplice to the billboard scandal. Nell Graham shook a finger at her son.

"Hush, puppy, I've got something to say and you just wait right there for me to say it! Where's your brother?"

Will shook his head. "We don't know *where* Hoot is, Mama."

She stood up from her wheelchair and slowly walked to the podium as the onlookers stared in surprise at the first steps she'd publicly taken by herself in years. Nell was shaky but determined and after a few wobbly efforts, leaned against the podium with Will's support. She pointed at Leonard and motioned him to come forward. Leonard stood and smoothed his aqua leisure suit, then strode up to stand beside Nell. She kissed him full on the mouth and then took his hand with a smile as she surveyed her scandalized neighbors.

"*Leonard*! You handsome devil! Look here, all of you... the last week this whole town's been turned inside out and ya'll aren't gonna leave me on the sidelines! I'm only gonna say this once...Will, you listen to me, now...Will, Hoot's only your half-brother. Leonard Festrunk is Hoot's real father...I've been in love with Leonard since near the end of the War when my no-good cheatin' husband, your daddy, was off lolly-gaggin' with his whores in

Memphis when he was supposed to be in the Pacific! Hoot's the dividend and I'm sorry I never told you, Will...I wanted to, but I never could seem to get up the nerve and because of that I always coddled that boy...well, I've been payin' for it ever since...that Hoot's acted a fool all his life just to spite me! But I don't regret loving Leonard one bit, because he is a fine and decent man... the only man I ever loved in my entire life. Can ya'll forgive me?"

Leonard kissed Nell Graham on her cheek and wiped away a stream of tears. Will frowned and shook his head. "Mama, what are you talking about? Did you take your medication today?"

Nell guffawed and slapped at her son's arm with unexpected strength. "HELL YES, now shut up! I'm *through* takin' medication...that bitch Dorothy was in cahoots with the doctors, tryin' to kill me so she could take my money...*your* money! But thanks to Amelia Festrunk for savin' my life, I feel better than I have in twenty years! Things are gonna be a helluva lot different around here, son...Leonard's movin' in with me and with the bitch gone I guess Hoot can move back home, too, if we can find him. Lord only knows what he's gone and gotten into. You ok, son? *Will?*"

Will Graham nodded slowly and ran a hand through his graying hair. He'd always accused Hoot of being unlike anyone else in the family and now he felt that his accusations had been validated, despite the circumstances.

"Yes, Mama, I'm ok. Ummm, Leonard...well...thank you for making Mama so happy."

Will stretched a firm hand to Leonard Festrunk who took it and pumped it proudly. Then Will, Nell and Leonard embraced tightly as the audience clapped once more. MayBelle Festrunk stood at the back of the room in a state of shock, comforted by Juliette Kimball. Will, Nell and Leonard turned toward MayBelle in a tumble of embraces and tears and Mayor Gooch stepped forth, banging his ever-present gavel.

"Land a goshen, if that ain't a saga fer them movie people, what is? Where's Hoot when we really need him? I guess he'll hear 'bout this later on. Thank ya, Will, fer enlight'nin' us. Folks, I reckon now we gotta make us some decisions 'bout the Festival an' how we're gonna 'dress all them setbacks we been havin'!"

Dr. Avery Parker, Jr. raised his hand to speak and the Mayor recognized him.

"Thank you, Mayor. It is my recommendation, as a *professional* and as a concerned property owner that we cancel the Festival completely! We stand absolutely no chance of retaining any credibility whatsoever after this Poe House fiasco and this horrible billboard embarrassment! In fact, Festival or no, I would like to inform you that I must withdraw my offer to deliver the Festival keynote address, as well as my offer to lecture the public on the true history of this town's founding. I, along with my wife, Diana, my son Rex and my dear Aunt Pearl will be moving back to Chicago where I have accepted a position as Director of the African-American Institute of America. Mrs. Gastineau, you may hereby remove me from your Festival Agenda!"

A lone clap of approval was offered by Corny Poe, who stood in the middle of the crowd and whistled. When it became apparent to Corny that he was celebrating Dr. Parker's announcement, he blushed and sat down. Izzy Gastineau approached the podium with a half-smile, to Barney's chagrin; time was wasting and they had work to do. Izzy extended a palm in the direction of Dr. Parker and his family.

"I'm sure I represent the feelings of this entire town when I say to the Parkers, good luck and godspeed. Although, Dr. Parker, none of us can ever take your place, do I have any volunteers to deliver the keynote address...so I can make the necessary changes to my agenda...oh, my....*I forgot*... I can't change the agenda without my computer...."

Izzy Gastineau raised her hands to her face and broke into tears. Roland rushed to her side. Barney snapped his fingers and clapped his fists together in a nervous display, waiting for Izzy to gain control; he didn't understand why she was so upset about the agenda, it was nothing a good bottle of cheap white-out couldn't fix. Izzy raised her head and tightly embraced her son. Then she daubed her eyes and addressed her fellow citizens.

"I'm sorry, everybody...I don't mean to break down in public...some of you may have already learned that Dan is in the federal penitentiary without bond. When those billboards appeared, he went crazy and got drunk at a bar in Smyrna. He started bragging about his financial prowess to a gentleman he met and after several hours, this gentleman revealed himself to be an agent with the Internal Revenue Service. Dan was arrested... oh, this is so hard to say...apparently, he's embezzled from half the families in the county. This afternoon my house was confiscated and all our possessions! Roland and I have been turned out into the street!"

Izzy bawled as Roland led her from the podium and into the hall. Eustacia Gober took a much-needed break from her shorthand. *These people are so morally depraved! I'm glad I paid for that Bible Bee trip in advance.* Mayor Gooch banged his gavel then reluctantly recognized Fay Bailey, whose red-nailed hand waved frantically in mid-air.

"Barney Gooch, if you cancel this here Festival, yer gonna rueen my future as a country sanger! I got me a Nashville agent comin' over here ta pers'nally witness my talent compa-tition in the Missus Chestnut Ridge Pageant an' it's costin' me a purty penny!"

Raleigh Poe piped up, "Fay Bailey, yer so ugly, we're all hopin' a strong wind don't come 'long by here an' blow yer clothes off! You ain't gonna never win no beauty contest, er be no country sanger, neither!"

Fay glared at Raleigh and she leaped over an empty chair and slapped him on the face. He was stunned but he chuckled loudly and swatted Fay on her curvaceous behind, to Corny's disgrace. Stella Stanley grabbed Fay by one arm and pulled her aside before she had the chance to scratch Raleigh's face with her four-inch red fingernails. Reverend Cameron Culpepper stood up from his honorary place at the City Council table and raised his hands.

"Brothers and s-s-sisters! It is ti-ti-time we said a prayer of thanksgiving to the L-L-Lord, to ask him to s-s-send peace and tran-tran-tranquility to us as we delib-delib-deliberate the future of our Festival. Let us pray...oh hear us, Heavenly Fa-fa-father, as we..."

The prayer was interrupted by a loud thud in the hall. The citizens looked up to see a grinning Hoot Graham saunter into the room. A large, bloody abrasion swelled on one side of Hoot's forehead; his hands were raised in the air, hostage-style and he was followed by a profusely sweating Henry Bailey who held a handgun to Hoot's back. Henry carried a dirty canvas bag. Several women screamed as Henry directed Hoot toward the front of the room. Barney Gooch banged his gavel repeatedly on the podium.

"Henry? Hoot? *What the hell...*"

Hoot, his hands in the air, nodded at Henry and stole Henry's thunder. *"Henry Bailey's stole our photo rights money an' he's tryin' ta leave town!"*

Raleigh Poe jumped up and yelled, "I knew it! He's a no-good bastard, Euladean, I been tellin' ya! All them Baileys are no-good bastards!"

Euladean Poe motioned to her father to hush, then she stood and looked at her husband from across the room. She could see he was nervous and upset. The gun wobbled in his shaking hand.

"Henry...what's goin' on? Henry...*look at me...*Henry Bailey, I believe in you, *remember*? Now you look me in the *eye* an' tell me what's goin' on!"

Henry nodded at his beloved wife, his rock of Gibraltar, without taking his eyes off Hoot.

"That twarn't it a't'all, Mayor! 'Bout haif-hour a go after closin' up the lot, I's walkin' past the bank, fixin' ta come over here...I'm mindin' my own bizness an' I see a man, comin' outta the bank an' ever'body knows the bank's done been closed fer 'coupla hours. So I hide myse'f behin' one a them big colyums an' I recanize it's *Hoot,* he's leavin' the bank an' lockin' the door behin' him! Hoot, he don't see me but I seen he's totin' this here sack...an' he's sayin', *'How you like them apples, Will Graham, how you like them apples, Barney Gooch? I'll be haif-way ta Tahiti afore they figger out their money's all gone!'"*

Hoot shook his head and grinned wth mock amazement in response to Henry's words; he rolled his eyes and glared at Barney. "You gonna b'lieve this peckerwood? Ya'll know he's nothin' but a big, fat, Bailey liar!"

Henry gulped and continued. "I done figgered out, Hoot's robbed the bank a that photo money an' he's fixin' ta leave town. *'Ya gotta do sompin', Henry Bailey, I says,'* so I looked down on the groun' an' I seen this big rock...I whacked Hoot on the head, not *too* hard, but I had ta make my point...an' this here gun fell outta Hoot's pants leg when he fell. I fetched the gun, Hoot was out cold an' I looked in that sack...an' it's fulla money an' jew'ry an' all kindsa papers!"

Barney banged his gavel and motioned to Bull McArdle. "We ain't got time fer no more a yer lyin, Henry Bailey! Arrest him, Chief! It's obvious Henry robbed the bank an's tryin' ta blame it on Hoot! Henry Bailey, I'm sicka yer connivin'! Yer nothin' but a common crim'nal an' this time yer goin' ta jail where you b'long! Bull, git over there an' do it, now!"

Bull McArdle lowered his head and reluctantly put a hand on Henry's shoulder. A deputy pulled Henry's hands behind his back; he struggled in protest as Bull slowly unhooked a pair of handcuffs from his police belt.

"*It ain't true*! He's *lyin'*, I tell ya, how in the hell'd I git inta that bank, huh, Hoot? I was yer Best Boy an' ya done turned me in fer yer own crime! Ya'll gotta b'lieve me, it ain't *true*!"

Before he cuffed Henry, Bull instructed the deputy to open the cloth sack. The deputy pulled out thirty stacks of currency, several dozen stock certificates and a metal chest that opened to reveal the Graham family jewels, in particular, the pearl brooch given to Major Jebediah Horatio Graham's wife one hundred and thirty years before. Bull stared at Henry, then looked at a grinning Hoot.

"That's a lotta money, boys...somebody come clean, now...come on...ain't no need fer all this."

Miss Gober put down her City Council Secretary pen in exasperation. The events of the past thirty minutes far surpassed the standard City meeting secretarial challenge and her hand cramped into a useless claw. Euladean Bailey rushed to her husband's side and tears cascaded down her face as she begged Bull McArdle for leniency. Hoot grinned at Barney, then pulled a gold vinyl-cushioned chair to the side of the podium and took a seat, proud that his innocence had not been questioned by the good people of Chestnut Ridge. In his glee, Hoot did not notice that his brother Will stared at him, hard. The crowd buzzed; suddenly, the door opened again and in ran a tall, strikingly beautiful blonde woman in a long white gauzy dress and sandals, followed by a breathless Amelia Festrunk. They stood next to Barney, who frowned at the women and waved his gavel at them to stand down, but in a matter of seconds, Barney did a double-take and realized that the blonde was none other than the Pie Angel. Despite the stern look on the blonde woman's face, Bull McArdle thought he'd never seen a more glorious vision. He stopped fiddling with the handcuffs he'd placed on Henry; a wave of peace fell over the prisoner and he caught Euladean's eye and nodded in the direction of the blonde.

Euladean whispered, *"Is that her?"* Henry nodded. The Pie Angel set down her briefcase and walked over to him as Barney as Bull gawked at her in awe. She placed a loving hand on Henry's face.

"Hello, Henry, are you all right? Chief McArdle, those cuffs won't be necessary. I suggest you remove them at once."

Bull McArdle obediently pulled a key from his shirt pocket and popped the handcuffs off of Henry's wrists. Barney Gooch banged his gavel in frustration.

"*Hey, Pie Angel!* Whaddya think yer doin'? We got us an arrest ta make, an' if yer not careful, yer gonna spend the night in the pokey too! Bull, put them cuffs back on Henry, *right now!*"

The Pie Angel pressed soft, delicate fingers across Bull McArdle's rough hands. "You don't want to do that, Chief. I promise you I can be trusted...do you believe me?"

Bull nodded enthusiastically; he'd never seen eyes that shade of blue, not in thirty years of policing or romancing. He stood hypnotized as Barney banged the gavel once more. Betty Gooch gritted her teeth, instantly jealous that this dazzling Pie Angel had spent time with her own husband in his office supply store right under her nose. The Pie Angel turned to the podium and pointed a finger at Hoot, who shrugged in defiance.

"We saw everything, Miss Festrunk and I. We were running late to this meeting because my rental car blew a tire and we were right across the street from the bank waiting for a tow truck. That man, *there*, used a key to gain entrance into the bank building, I saw it all with my night-vision binoculars...I'll explain that in a minute. But he disconnected the alarm and smashed the security camera. He carried a small yellow flashlight and he held a very old, very quaint key in one hand. After about twenty minutes, he left the bank carrying that bag. If you look in his left shirt pocket you will find the key and what I suspect, as well as I could see with my binoculars, is a bus ticket."

Hoot Graham sank back in the gold vinyl-cushioned chair; he broke out in a sweat. "Who the hell are *you*, bitch? You can't come in here an' start accusin' me of stealin' from my own family's bank! I ain't never seen you around here before...Bull, you'd best be callin' for reinforcements! You're gonna hafta arrest Miss High-falutin' here, too!"

Barney aimed his gavel at The Pie Angel. "Henry Bailey is a known thief! His fam'ly's been stealin' from folks in this county fer a hunnerd years an' he's fin'lly got caught! It's time fer him ta pay!"

The voters of Chestnut Ridge buzzed, although no one could quote specific details as to the exact nature of the Bailey family's misdeeds; it was just the thing to do, to blame Henry Bailey. The Pie Angel stood her ground. Her ice-blue eyes flashed at Barney and her ivory cheeks flushed rose. She stomped a foot on the floor in anger.

"I will ask you *again* Barney Gooch, what proof do you have of Henry Bailey's thievery? Have you forgotten the passage, *'Let he who is without sin cast the first stone?'* I saw that man rob the bank with my own eyes...Chief McArdle, would you care to take my statement?"

Chief McArdle nodded and motioned for Miss Gober to take down the witness' testimony. Miss Gober's hand flew across the page in a flurry as the Pie Angel relayed her tale.

"About a half-hour after that man went into the bank, Henry Bailey was walking on the sidewalk in front. I saw Henry look at that man, then at his watch, and hide behind a column. Then he hit the man on the head with a large rock. When the man fell down, Henry grabbed the gun that fell out of the man's pants leg. When the man woke up, Henry forced him to walk over here, so he could inform you of the theft. We would have been here sooner, but there's a *severe* shortage of parking spaces in this town."

Barney rolled his eyes at the Pie Angel's last comment; parking was a sensitive issue and he did not want to go there at this particular moment. Henry waited eagerly for Bull to release him. Bull hitched up his sansa-belts.

"Excuse me, ma'am, but you mind tellin' us who you *are*?"

The Pie Angel handed Bull McArdle a business card. "My name is Ellen Armistead Gray, Ph.D., of Richmond, Virginia. I am a Civil War historian, named in honor of my great-great grandfather on my father's side...Colonel Eletius Armistead Gray, leader of the band of Confederate soldiers known as the 44th Regiment of the Tennessee Riders; the band of soldiers from which the founders of this town *deserted*, I might add."

Corny Poe's face reddened in anger at the reference to Confederate deserters in his family tree. Dr. Avery Parker, Jr. imperiously strode to the front of the room and extended a hand to a bewildered Dr. Gray.

"Thank the stars for a voice of reason in the wilderness! *Doctor E. A. Gray*, the noted historical genealogist? Welcome to my little corner of the world, Doctor! I am Avery Parker, Junior, historian and African-American scholar...I'm sure you've heard of my work?"

Dr. Gray shook Dr. Parker's hand slowly and pursed her lips in quizzical fashion. Barney Gooch leaned on the podium. Amelia Festrunk wrung her hands nervously. The evening was getting ridiculous and totally out of control. Barney grabbed the Pie Angel's business card.

"Lemme see that card, Bull..."

Barney surveyed it skeptically; *how come she's been masqueradin' as the Pie Angel,* he wondered. Juliette Kimball returned from the restroom, stared at Dr. Gray and yelled,

"That's *her*! That's the *Pie Angel*! That's the woman who bought the sweet potato pie for Henry Bailey!"

Bull McArdle, like the true investigator that he was, anxiously eyed the Pie Angel/Historian, then Henry Bailey, then Hoot Graham. His instincts told him there was heinous mischief afoot. He ordered the doors to be closed and told everyone to be seated.

"Miz Eustacia…your hand ok, can you be helpin' me with all this?" Bull asked.

Miss Gober nodded tersely and flipped a page on her legal pad. Bull offered a chair to Dr. Gray and invited her to sit down. He firmly instructed a scowling Barney Gooch to hand over the gavel and sit with the City Council members while he questioned Dr. Gray. Then he crouched next to the chair upon which sat the world's most beautiful historical genealogist and he said in a low, steady voice,

"*Doc Gray*…I really wanna b'lieve ya, I swear, but I don't know you from Adam. I'm a man a the law an' I don't like ta see innocent people accused. Henry Bailey's always gettin' blamed for stuff around here, like it or not, but ain't nobody ever brung me no proof an' the law says we gotta have *proof*!"

Henry piped up, "Yeah, Bull's right, an' it's gotta be *convertible* proof, right, Mister Will?"

Will Graham stopped staring at his brother and chuckled. "You're right, Henry! Incontrovertible!"

Dr. Gray looked the Chief in the eye and bit her lip. Bull stood to his full, massive height and slowly stepped in the direction of Hoot.

"Now, Hoot Graham, the man you saw robbin' the bank…he stole some money from his own fam'ly some years back but the Grahams never did charge him, on accounta he'd come back from Nam an' he was all tore up. Doc, I heard your story, but I ain't never laid eyes on you before…so you can unnerstand how I gotta reason ta be *curious* 'bout what you're doin' *stalkin'* us folks with a pair a night-vision, high-powered bi-noc'lars!"

Dr. Gray shrugged her shoulders and smiled. "I'm only too happy to fill you in, Chief. But first, I suggest you check that man's pockets!"

Bull sighed in exasperation; she was right, he forgot to check Hoot's pockets. He completed his journey toward Hoot, who looked up from his chair and saluted Bull sarcastically.

"Hoot, I'm gonna have ta ask you ta empty your pockets…"

Hoot laughed skittishly, rared back and crossed his legs at the ankles. He shot his aw-shucks grin at the Chief.

"Bull McArdle, I've known you ever' since we played on the high schoo' state championship team together, an' hell, I's married ta your sister Marg'ret! You know I didn't take nothin' outta that bank!"

Bull said nothing, but waited for Hoot to comply with his request. Hoot sat up in the chair and rubbed the palms of his hands on his knees, anxiously searching for an out.

"Mama...where are ya... *Will!* You tell him! You tell him there ain't no way I'd rob my own fam'ly! I'm a successful L.A. filmmaker! I don't need your stupid money!"

Will slowly rose from his chair and moved toward his brother. "Hoot...I'd like to believe you, but I'm afraid I have my doubts. I guess anybody could rob that bank if they wanted to. But Hoot, the money's not what concerns me...it's Mama's antique pearl brooch...when the Major built that vault, he knew it might get robbed from time to time. But he devised a secret compartment inside the vault door to hide that pearl brooch from the Yankees. That's where generations of Grahams have been hiding their treasures ever since. That pearl pin's been locked inside that vault for at least twenty-five years because Dorothy hated it and refused to wear it. See, Bull, the thing is, in order to get to that brooch and the other jewelry, you've got to have a special key...a skeleton key...like *this.*"

Will dangled a dainty brass skeleton key from a chain. He handed it to Bull, who examined the key closely. Intricate carvings decorated the face. Will raised a finger to make his point.

"And, see, there were only *two* keys made to fit that vault. When Hoot left for Vietnam, Daddy gave one to Hoot and the other one to me when I graduated college. Now, here's my key, I've been *here* for the last half-hour. But Hoot...where have *you* been? Is your key in your shirt pocket? Let's have a look, Hoot...come on. If you needed money so badly all you had to do was ask. But to steal the Major's pearl brooch, the family jewelry...that's *unforgivable*, Hoot, unforgivable."

Hoot lowered his head in shame as Will reached a finger into his brother's shirt pocket. He withdrew the matching skeleton key as the spectators gasped. Then Will pulled a bus ticket out of the pocket and handed both items to the Chief. Hoot reddened in rage and yelled at his older brother.

"You've always gotta be the *big man*, don'tcha, brother! Mister Big College Boy! Mister Big Bank President! *Mama!* Wake up! Will's framin' me, Mama!"

Nell Graham stood up from her parked wheelchair and pointed a wrinkled finger at her sons. "HOOT! Shut up, you shit-for-brains! Shut up and sit down!"

Leonard Festrunk stood beside Nell. "Son, you listen to yer Mama! Reckon you ain't heard yet but I'm yer real daddy an' if ya don't behave I'm gonna tan yer hide with my belt! An' whilst I'm at it, what does a grown man like yersef need ta parade 'round in his underpants, gittin' a spankin' with another man? You one a them 'happy' fellas? You a fairy, boy?"

Hoot stood up in a fury and started toward Leonard but Bull motioned him back into his chair and raised a hand into the air. "Aw right, ever'body jus' sit down an' hush up."

At Bull's signal, the deputy handcuffed Hoot and prepared to remove him from the premises, but Dr. Gray intervened.

"Chief McArdle, would it be possible for the suspect to remain here for a few more minutes? He has a vested interest in what I'm about to say...it's quite a long story, actually, so I recommend that you all find a chair."

Barney banged his gavel in protest. "Look here, miss, we's in the middle of a town meetin' an' we ain't got no more time fer hysterics right now!"

Amelia Festrunk had heard enough. She stomped an orthopedic-shoed foot onto the floor and waved a bony finger at Barney. "Gooch, shut your trap! Ellen, it's time to spill the beans."

Bull motioned for Hoot to sit on the floor in front of a deputy and warned him not to try anything. He leaned against the podium as Amelia continued.

"Every person in town knows the story about how my Granddaddy was murdered by Hardy Bailey at the quarry. Not a day goes by that I don't think about it...I was seven years old and to witness that death...the death of a man I worshiped and loved with all my heart...I'll never forget it. *Never.*"

A hush fell over the audience. There was an ethereal quality to Amelia's voice they had never before heard. She slowly walked to a chair and sat on the edge, facing her fellow town folk. She ran a hand through her white hair.

"But I never told the truth about that day...and before my Granddaddy got pulled over the edge of that quarry he made me promise to do something and I never did it...until now. What I'm about to say will disrupt the lives of many people in this town so I hope you can forgive me and not ascribe it to the failed memory of an old woman...when I'm finished, Dr. Gray will confirm everything I've said, so please listen and be silent...this is very difficult for me to do."

Amelia took a deep breath and recounted her tale of her childhood encounter with Hardy Bailey and his story about being the long-lost son of a wealthy Confederate officer from Virginia. She relayed in a low, tired voice how the old drunk said he'd been repeatedly victimized by his own regiment officers; how they'd set him up for murdering his quarry foreman when in fact they murdered Hardy's wife and children. The shame of the Bailey family was nothing compared to the seventy-seven years of humiliation that spilled out of Amelia's soul and into the ears of her neighbors. As she finished her story, she rose and approached Henry through a veil of tears.

"Henry Bailey, if I'd spoken up years ago…I have no right to ask for your forgiveness. I want you to know that my entire life has been a sham…I made no sacrifices, I did nothing valiant with the Clinic…you're the one who had to sacrifice your dignity and childhood and everything you've ever owned and I'm sorry. I'm so, so sorry, Henry. You have every right to hate me."

A bewildered Henry Bailey gulped in air as he stared at Amelia Festrunk. For the first time in his miserable life, he was speechless. He offered a hand to Amelia and she grasped it firmly. They embraced and Euladean wrapped her arms around both of them as they cried. Barney Gooch rapped his gavel on the podium in disbelief.

"Well, now, ain't that sweet! An' next week is Christmas an' alla us li'l good boys an' girls is gonna git somethin' from Santy Claus!"

The crowd murmured and shuffled. Barney slammed the gavel on the podium with a loud bang. "Miz Amelia…you have gone plumb off yer rocker…you an' Mother Nell've been nippin' the whiskey agin…aw right, lets us git on ta the nex' order a bizness an'…"

Dr. Gray grabbed the gavel from the surprised Mayor's hand. "Mayor, I suggest you take your seat and apologize to Miss Festrunk this instant, or I'll file charges on you right here and now! Didn't you listen to what she said? Now, as a certified professional who also happens to have a vested interest in this matter, I'll thank you to sit down and listen to me!"

Barney obediently sat and slumped in his chair, arms crossed, as Dr. Gray adjusted the microphone on the podium.

"When I was a doctoral candidate, it dawned on me that my own family lineage could provide the perfect material for my thesis. There has always been a bit of mystery surrounding the death of my ancestor, Colonel Gray; the official statement, taken from a Mrs. Aleta Jameson, in Mississippi, said that Colonel Gray went to the well in the middle of the night to retrieve some fresh water and provide his ill cousin, that's Mrs. Jameson, with a cool drink. Mrs. Jameson claimed that the Colonel fell into the well and drowned. A separate Union investigation into the Colonel's death ten years later noted the interesting testimony of one of Mrs. Jameson's slaves, a girl named Daisy. Daisy, it seems, was Mrs. Jameson's personal maid and she reported that the Colonel died after a sexual liaison with Mrs. Jameson. It seems he was murdered, thrown from Mrs. Jameson's bedroom by a Major Jebediah Graham and a Lieutenant Richard Leigh."

Gasps of shock pierced the Peaceful Slumber Room; the town founders... murderers?

Bull McArdle blushed and coughed. "Go 'head, Doc, but you can leave out all the sex-yal stuff, ok? We done had us enough a *that* 'round here lately."

Dr. Gray shrugged and continued. "The Colonel's death would not have been such a puzzle to my family except for several strange facts that did not compute. *First,* the Colonel was in poor health and had not served in the field for many years; yet he made a sudden request of General Lee for assignment as commander of the 44th Regiment of Tennessee Riders. It's curious, you see, because the Colonel was a proud *Virginian* and yet he refused the General's offer of a Virginia command, in favor of a command in *Tennessee.*"

Dr. Gray paused to allow Chief McArdle to digest her first point. "*Second,* the Colonel made a sudden, mysterious withdrawal from his personal Federal bank account of exactly five thousand dollars in gold; he had to travel secretly across the Mason-Dixon line to accomplish this, by the way, which placed him in great peril as an officer of the Confederacy. I don't know if you realize it, Chief, but in those days, five thousand dollars in gold was an enormous amount of money! And why would a Confederate commander, whose every need and want was securely provided by the army he served, require five thousand dollars in gold for a journey into Tennessee and beyond?"

Bull McArdle shook his head, he could not presume to second-guess the financial dealings of a man who'd been dead for one hundred and thirty-six years. Dr. Gray ran a hand through her silken hair.

"In the process of completing my thesis, I researched every minute detail related to my ancestor's untimely death. I pored over Confederate records, I traveled his combat route and searched the historical texts of every city along the trail in an effort to locate some morsel of untold truth. And then, as I was nearly ready to abandon my search, my father died and the Colonel's house passed to me. I decided to renovate the crumbling antebellum structure, to make it my own home and restore it to its former glory. On the very day I arrived to meet the contractor and give him my ideas for the house, one of the workmen discovered a cache of papers hidden in a small chest behind a loose brick in the Colonel's office. You can imagine my excitement. It was *indescribable!*"

Dr. Gray clapped her hands together in glee. She noticed Dr. Parker nodded, his arms crossed, as if he knew exactly what she was going to say next.

"There were several fairly routine letters, mostly from the Colonel's two sisters. The original deed to the home was intact. That was *very* interesting. But the real prize..."

Dr. Gray closed her eyes and lifted them to the ceiling in some kind of enveloping rapture.

"...the *real* prize was the discovery of the Colonel's journal. I would like to read to you the critical passage in that journal…it is most enlightening and everyone in this town deserves the right to hear it."

Chatter bantered around the room as Dr. E.A. Gray removed a sheaf of papers from her tattered briefcase. She unfolded it and smoothed the pages.

"This is a Xerox copy of the original text; I keep it with me at all times and when you listen to the Colonel's words, you will understand why I am here…it begins:

'May fifth, eighteen sixty-two…I write this humble account, knowing I may never make another entry in this journal, knowing I may never again sit in this chair or gaze out this window at the green valleys of my home. What I must commit to paper is now the story of what sustains me each and every day. It is my duty and my responsibility and although I cannot divulge to my wife or to my children the real nature of my desire to leave Virginia and return to Tennessee, I know in my heart they will forgive me, should they ever discover these pages and learn the truth.

In the lush Spring of my twenty-eighth year, while I was a lieutenant stationed in Nashville I by chance met a young woman named Maureen, an immigrant from Ireland. She worked as a maid in Mrs. Henderson's boarding house where I, as a military officer of the United States, resided in plain and simple comfort. There were yet no military dormitories to house me between my missions, that of safeguarding delivery of the Federal military payroll from Nashville to Louisville by rail. From the first enchanting moment of our initial encounter, wherein this young woman served me a most delicious supper, her beauty was seared into every chamber of my beating heart. Tall, fair and freckled, Maureen wore her dark red hair bundled at the nape of her graceful neck and the flash of her green eyes could reduce a mere mortal to tears.

I, a lonely soldier, far from home, did not relish participation in what I considered to be a rather droll Nashville social circuit; true Virginia blood flows in my veins and I did not wish to pass the few solitary hours afforded me each evening in the company of transparent young women who viewed me merely as a marriage ticket into Richmond society. Thus, having made my excuses under the duress of a lieutenant's paperwork, I readily spent each evening happily in Mrs. Henderson's study, reading by the fire until that magical moment when my young Irish lass would pass by quietly with an offer of sherry or tea.

As the days progressed we engaged each other in a manner of conversation most polite and most appropriate; as the weeks progressed, we delighted in the sight of each other and as the spring twilights lengthened and marched toward summer's fury, my Irish rose arranged to meet me in secret every Sunday for long walks together along the banks of the Cumberland River.

It was a summer of untold splendor, of pungent flowers and delectable Sunday picnics, spread like Earth's bounty across a thin blanket woven of good Irish muslin. Ours was a love like no other and we dreamed the dreams that countless young lovers concoct, those of happy lives together in a place where a Virginia blueblood lieutenant may be free to marry his honest, fresh-faced Irish love without fear of familial retribution or discharge from his chosen profession.

Alas, as September's sunny fire began to smolder, I was informed of my imminent transfer back to Richmond. Any other man might have been overjoyed at the promotion, or at the opportunity to rejoin his family and friends, but not I. With the determination of a young man in love, I resolved to resign my post, marry Maureen and set out for the prairies of the West where, though we might be poor and without many resources, we would at least be together. On that last Sunday picnic, as my cherub-cheeked love lay in my arms, I relayed my decision and asked for her hand. As I had no resources readily available with which to purchase a suitable engagement ring, I offered her my mother's filigreed pearl brooch and pinned it to her breast. With the tears of a thousand angels, she granted me the reply I had so desired and informed me that she carried my child in her womb. My happiness was beyond compare and we agreed to meet a week hence, at which time I would present to her the draft of my resignation letter as proof of my sincerity and as a token of our future life. 'My duties take me tomorrow to Louisville,' I informed her, 'but I shall return on Saturday, for our joyful reunion picnic.'

Alas, it was not to be. On the day of our tryst, I arrived at the edge of the Cumberland, fresh from my room, where my hand had penned what I considered to be the perfect letter of resignation for my commanding officer; my lass is merely late, I mused, perhaps Mrs. Henderson is attending to the needs of a demanding traveler and requires the assistance of her most dependable maid. After an hour, I returned to the boarding house, sought Mrs. Henderson and inquired as to the whereabouts of the young woman with the sherry. 'Oh, she'll not trouble you any more, sir, as she left me early this week. A strange girl, that one, nay, she'll bother you no more.'

My heart nearly burst in agony and disbelief and I violently shook poor Mrs. Henderson, demanding to know the girl's destination. Mrs. Henderson rebuked me strongly for my behavior until I convinced her, by way of a contrived tale, that I suspected the girl had stolen an important object from my room and that I intended to find it and her, as well. Mrs. Henderson readily replied that the girl supposedly had a distant relation in Chattanooga, and she suggested politely that I check there. I immediately requested a short leave of absence from my commanding officer, who graciously conferred it based upon my excellent service, and I traveled to Chattanooga, where I did indeed locate my betrothed's relative.

The woman, a haunting wretch with a houseful of small children, offered to me a letter, penned on stiff parchment, written in my beloved Maureen's own hand, informing her aunt that she had departed Nashville and that she intended to make for herself a new life among the Irish who had settled in the East Tennessee mountains. 'They will accept me for what I am,' she wrote, 'and not judge me ill by my actions.'

I wrote my name and the address of my father's home in Richmond on a scrap of paper and told the woman that if she ever learned of Maureen's whereabouts, she should write to me immediately and I would wire her fifty dollars in gold upon verifying the discovery. With a weary body and a ragged soul, I trudged back to Nashville and then made my way slowly through the East Tennessee mountains, with my unit, back toward Richmond. It was difficult, but I managed to make several vague inquiries among the Irish mountain folk along my journey, but none had either seen or heard of my red-headed lass who was with child.

In Richmond, I soon became a wealthy man upon the death of my father and some years later, I married a woman in an arranged match that guaranteed my financial security. She bore my children and she remains steadfast in her love for me, but I regret, I cannot afford her the same emotion. The sun has not yet risen on a day that I don't think of my lost Irish love and our child, or mourn the life I might have lived.

Last month, as my youngest son was nigh on fifteen and I a fat, forty-four year old balding Colonel in service to the great Confederate General Lee, I received a letter that to this day brings me the greatest of joys. It bore a Chattanooga postmark, as well as the family name of my Irish lass; the eldest child of the wretched woman I spoke with so many years before had indeed made good the promise.

'I cannot apologize enough for the lack of contact between us over the years,' it began, 'but my mother made a solemn vow to her niece that she would never reveal her place of residence. I, however, made no such promise, yet out of respect to my own dear mother, I remained silent these many years. Upon the death of my mother, God rest her soul, last week, I feel no further obligation to hold my tongue. I regret to inform you of the death of Maureen some months ago after a lengthy illness,' the letter read, 'but happily, I can inform you that your son yet lives and is seeking entrance in service to the Great Confederacy. He departs in a fortnight to join with the 44th Regiment of the Tennessee Riders and perhaps you may yet meet him, face to face.'

I immediately wired my young informant his fifty dollars in gold and dispatched my sergeant to verify that my son was indeed a new member of the Tennessee regiment. Upon his confirmation, I then approached the General and begged him to restore me to active field duty as commander of the 44th Regiment of the Tennessee Riders; a request which he reluctantly but steadfastly granted, to the great confusion of my family and friends. In the days before my departure, I resolved to make right the misdoings of my past and I traveled in secret, across

Virginia lines into the vile Union, where I withdrew five thousand dollars in gold coin from my ample Federal bank account. Upon my safe return home, I placed the coins in a simple, rusty black tin box and devised a plan; I forged a Union payroll document, a simple writ I had seen on many occasion during my own days of Federal service and placed it inside the box.

Should I encounter any difficulty, I reason now, as I prepare to depart tomorrow, the forged document may serve as explanation to my Confederate brethren for my heavy load. But should the good Lord provide me with the opportunity to gaze upon the visage of my own son, the child of my one true love, I will shower upon him not only my affection, but also a small fortune in coins, in an effort to afford him the start to a respectable life. Oh, how bittersweet the taste of this cup! This miserable war brings me the occasion to perhaps meet my son and experience the joy and peace that I have longed for since my return to Richmond. I cannot wait to hold him in my arms and tell him of the love I yet feel for his mother; I cannot wait to invite him into my tent and listen as he tells me the tales of his youth and his mother's ways.

Therefore let the record stand, that I, Colonel Eletius Armistead Gray, being of sound mind and body, do hereby confer upon my eldest son, born to my true love Maureen in the State of Tennessee in 1847, the right of sole inheritance of all my earthly possessions. It is my intent, upon locating this son, to bring him back to Richmond and to welcome him wholeheartedly into the family fold, with all rights and privileges due him as a member of the Gray ancestry. Should I never return from my sworn duty, I hereby instruct my executors to take every step necessary to carry out this, my last request, this request which I now sign to take precedence over and above any other will, agreement or codicil, that I might honor the memory of my beloved Irish rose and sustain the life of my firstborn son in due fashion.

Should my executors fail in their task, upon exercising every method known to them to locate my son, I instruct my subsequent heirs to take up my search and do right by my memory. If it takes a hundred, or a thousand years, it is my full intent to remand full financial and social honors upon those descendants of my happy summer picnics with my simple Irish maiden, for there is no truer joy than that of the love of a good woman and I experienced no greater love than my love for Maureen and for our son.

—Colonel Eletius Armistead Gray, Richmond, Virginia, Confederate States of America.

Dr. Ellen Armistead Gray silently folded the copy of the journal entry and blinked at the audience that sat frozen in the still air of the Golden Memories Chapel/Peaceful Slumber Room. Bull McArdle gripped the podium. Dr. Parker raised his hand.

"I *knew* it! That gold was stolen from the Colonel's personal effects after his death and the money was used to repair the grist mill and build this town!"

Dr. Gray smiled, and nodded. "Yes, that is exactly what happened, Dr. Parker. We can verify the gold's existence from the Colonel's war diaries; he records on a daily basis an entry which reads, *'G.C. still intact,'* which I believe is a reference to the gold coins. In fact, that was his last entry, made on the evening of his death. What remained unclear to me was why Colonel Gray, after a full seven months in the presence of his son, did not relinquish the gold to the young man, or make any notations regarding what must have been his joy at meeting and conversing with his offspring firsthand. I suppose he was very careful to keep his secret until the war was over and he and his son could take their leave in safety."

Dr. Parker could barely contain his excitement. "And *you*, Dr. Gray, you can verify the identity of the Colonel's son and you say that person was not one of the three men accredited as the town's founding fathers?"

Dr. Gray nodded once more. "You are correct, Dr. Parker. The three men historically credited as the financial heroes of Chestnut Ridge: Major Jebediah Horatio Graham, Captain Homer Festrunk and Lieutenant Richard Napoleon Leigh are *not* related to the Colonel and they most definitely did not share their five thousand dollar bounty with the Colonel's true heir. For years I believed that perhaps, in fairness to the Major, the Captain and the Lieutenant, that they probably didn't know anything about the Colonel's real mission, his gold, or that his own son was right under their noses, a simple soldier of Irish descent."

Bull McArdle stiffened. Will Graham coughed nervously. MayBelle Festrunk walked up and stood next to her sister and they gripped each other tightly. Dr. Gray sighed and searched her briefcase for another file.

"But you have heard only *part* of my story! After finding this journal, of course, I became obligated to make good the Colonel's wish, his wish to find his one true heir. And against all odds I have done just that. It has taken me the better part of five years, but I have finally, without a doubt, authenticated my research. The Colonel's descendant yet lives among you, and according to my family's attorneys and this document, signed by a federal judge in Washington, the heir has a legal claim to the proceeds engendered from every act of commerce that has been undertaken in this town since its rebirth in January of eighteen sixty-three."

Will Graham's head began to spin; the Festrunk sisters swallowed hard and Roy Quigley raised his hand. "You mean ta tell me, that fella's got a right ta ever' dollar that's run thew this town? Or jus' a right ta the money the Grahams, Festrunks and Leigh-Lees done earned?"

Dr. Gray responded, "*Every commercial dollar generated in this town*; you have all benefited from the initial five thousand dollar investment, you see, in some form or fashion. The judge's initial calculations total somewhere in the neighborhood of over a hundred million dollars."

Barney Gooch shoved Bull McArdle from the podium and pounded it with his fist. "Pie Angel, you mean I gotta spend hours cipherin' in my office jus' so's I can fork over a portion a the proceeds a *my* business, the business my great-great granddaddy started a hunnerd years ago, ta somebody that ain't even *knowed* he was deservin' in the first place?"

Dr. Gray ran a hand through her long blonde hair and smiled. "Yes, Mayor, I'm afraid so. And I have the paperwork to enforce it. That is, if the descendant chooses to exercise that particular option. The judge has written an alternate recommendation and knowing that the descendant has honorable Gray blood flowing through his veins, it is hoped that he will act in fairness. You see, tracking and itemizing every business transaction for one hundred and thirty-six years would prove quite a formidable task and risks the ruination of this community. The judge strongly suggests the descendant elect the second option: if the heir would have received that money as intended and deposited it in a bank, if you allow a modest four percent interest, compounded over one hundred and thirty-six years, the heir would have the right to a little over one million dollars. The current business owners in town could thus pool their resources to pay this fine and then commerce would continue as usual."

A stunned silence gripped the air. Several people turned to stare at Amelia Festrunk. Every citizen in the room was seized with the unspoken realization that murdering Hardy Bailey claimed to be the son of a Confederate officer who was in possession of five thousand dollars in Yankee gold. If Miss Amelia's story was true, then consequentially Henry Bailey would reap the proposed financial benefits that could completely shut down the town. But no one dared to speak. Finally, the Mayor waved his hands into the air.

"Well, then, you gonna name names, or what? An' if that's why you're here, why all the playactin' like you was the Pie Angel?"

"*You* said I was the Pie Angel, Barney Gooch, not me! I never claimed to be anything but a casual observer. I wanted to note exactly how my distant relative behaved, what his or her life was like, watch how he or she was treated by others. The type of revelation that I'm delivering could be quite a disturbing blow, a major disruption of one's life and I wanted to make sure I was doing the right thing, obligation or no. After making my observations, I am convinced I am doing exactly what Colonel Gray would have wanted me to do."

Barney rared back and grinned. "Well, Pie Angel, go ahead, lay it on me! I *knew* I liked ya that day ya come inta the Office S'ply! Ya'll are lookin' at the newest member a the millionaires club, boys an' girls! Come on, don't be shy, Pie Angel! *Hit me*!"

Dr. Gray tilted her head sarcastically in Barney's direction. "Certainly, Mayor Gooch, I'd be happy to identify you as Colonel Gray's heir...but your name's not Henry Bailey! You see, your insults to Miss Amelia were completely uncalled for...she is *correct*...Henry Bailey is the descendant of one Hardy Bailey, illegitimate son of Colonel Gray and Maureen Bailey."

Screams and shouts erupted from the crowd; Henry Bailey's eyes widened until he could no longer focus. He turned to Euladean, who kissed him on the head, then he fell to the floor in a heap. As Euladean ran to fetch a cup of water, Fay Bailey dashed to Henry's side, sat on top of his stomach and wrapped her spandex-encased legs tightly around her ex-husband.

"Oh, Henry, Henry, baby, it's Fay, wake up, honey, it's your Fay, *darlin*! Why'd you ever leave me, Henry, you knowed I love you so!"

Fay planted red-lined kisses on Henry's face and arms until she was smacked full on the ear by a raging Euladean.

"GET OFFA MY HUSBAND, YOU MONEY-LOVIN' HUSSY!"

Euladean poured a full cup of water on top of Fay's lacquered hairdo. As the water splashed over Fay and dripped onto Henry, Henry revived and blinked in confusion. Euladean shoved Fay onto the floor as Dr. Gray knelt beside Henry and helped him sit up. She hugged him and clasped his hand.

"Welcome to the Gray family, Henry Bailey! Your great-great grandfather, Hardy Bailey, was the son of Colonel Gray and his Irish fianceé, Maureen Bailey. We have a great deal to talk about and I hope your newfound financial freedom will in some way repay you for all the years of tragedy and humiliation you and your relatives have suffered. But Henry, this is about much more than money...it's about respect, *generations* of respect. The Grays of Virginia are an honorable people. We take great pride in our dedication to truth and justice and valor and service to the needy. Oh, sure, we've had our share of bad apples, don't get me wrong. But you, Henry...you and your family for some strange, unknown reason, never enjoyed the respect in this town that all men deserve and thus you were never given a fair chance. Now that may change, but there is one undeniable fact we've learned here tonight, ladies and gentlemen, outside of ancestral claims..."

The stunned citizens of Chestnut Ridge gaped in awe at Dr. Gray...*now* what was she going to tell them? Dr. Gray pointed at a now-handcuffed Hoot Graham, who flicked his tongue and thrust his pelvis at her before the deputy threatened him with a nightstick.

"Henry Bailey single-handedly foiled a bank robbery and was honest enough to collar the thief *and* bring back the money! Not many men today would do that, Henry, so you see, you didn't really need *me* to come here and inform you of your Gray ancestry, just to earn a little respect. You've *always* behaved in accordance with your Gray heritage, but now, you have incontrovertible *proof* that you're a hero!"

The citizens applauded and shouted at the Pie Angel's words. Henry blushed to the roots of his scalp. He stood up, hugged and kissed his wife, then shook Dr. Gray's hand once more.

"Yep, it's like I always been a-sayin, there ain't no proof like a convertible one! I shore do 'preciate ya comin' all the way here ta tell me 'bout this, Doc! Hey, did ya git yer feces done, after all that investigatin'?"

Dr. Gray laughed. "Yes, Henry, I did, that's why I've earned the right to use 'doctor' in front of my name. It's pretty silly, though...I'd much prefer to be known as Ellie!"

Avery Parker, Jr. scoffed. He had no time for second-rate academics that did not insist on using their proper titles. He ushered his wife and son from the room; they had a lot of packing to do. Barney Gooch and Corny Poe sat on the floor and cried like babies. They shared the misery of the realization that Henry Bailey was now one of the wealthiest and most successful men in town, by a fluke of nature. And Henry a no-good Catholic, to boot.

Henry Bailey rubbed his head. "So, not ta be greedy, er nothin', Ellie, but tell me agin how much I'm due?"

Ellie Gray inhaled slowly. "Henry, that all depends on what you decide to do. If you choose to pursue the full extent of the claim, it would take years and years of research and you would probably spend between three and five million dollars on legal fees, but you could stand to collect over a hundred million dollars, compounded in today's figures. Then, however, you would be required to pay approximately half of that to the government, in tax, and you'd have to press legal charges against all the business owners in town. Or, you could receive an immediate, one-time assessment of a little over a million dollars from the said business owners, tax-free and spend nothing in legal fees."

Henry pursed his lips in thought. "Sorta like playin' the lot'ry, ain't it? Like if a man was ta buy hisse'f a ticket, which a course I ain't sayin' *I* ever done, ya can either scratch off the Lifetime Jackpot, payin' over fifty years, or the Instant Jackpot where ya walk off with a lot less but all in a big lump at one time. Man, that money'd buy me a heckuva car lot, fer sure!"

As Ellie nodded, MayBelle Festrunk screamed, *"It's Nell, she's having a heart attack!"*

Will raced to his mother's side as she fell to the floor of the Golden Memories Chapel. Leonard Festrunk leaned close to Nell's face and she planted a sloppy kiss on his mouth, then keeled over, clutching her chest. Leonard held her hand and stroked her cheek; Will leaned over his mother's face.

"It's ok, Mama, you're gonna be ok. We've just called for an ambulance, so you just rest easy here..."

Nell Graham gripped her son's shoulder tightly and pulled him close. She spoke in a whisper, which was most unusual.

"Will...do you forgive me? Please say you do...I know I don't have the right to ask this, because you've always taken care of Hoot no matter what kind of tangle he's gotten himself into... please keep on? He's in a melluvahess and I'm asking you to look after him for me. Please, son? And 'Melie...you promise to take good care of my man, here, ok? Leonard Festrunk, I got it bad for you, looker!"

Will nodded and shot a worried glance at his mother, as Juliette Kimball flitted around the room, yelling for an ambulance. Amelia Festrunk blinked back tears to no avail and gripped Nell's hand like a vise. No one in the entire city of Chestnut Ridge had ever seen her cry. "I promise, Nellie, I promise...Nell...Nell...NELL!"

Nell Graham breathed her last, holding the weathered hands of her lifelong friends, Amelia and Leonard Festrunk. Will bowed his head and offered a prayer in his mother's name. Doc Kimball shoved his way in, examined Nell's body and sadly pronounced her dead. Despite Roy Quigley's generous offer to place Mother Nell immediately in the Peaceful Slumber Room, Will declined; his mother would haunt him forever if he placed her in there with a dead dog and a floral wreath that spelled out "PAIN."

"Thanks, Roy, but the ambulance can take her. I think Doc's gotta do some official paperwork and then we can bring her back here for the service. But I do appreciate your kindness."

A bleary-eyed Barney Gooch retrieved his faithful gavel and banged it on the podium. "I don't know 'bout ya'll, but I'm ready fer this night ta be *over*! All in favor a cancelin' the Chestnut Ridge Sons a Glory Festival until next year, say, *'aye*!"

A loud chorus of 'ayes' bounded off the walls. "All against, say *'nay*!"

A single *'nay'* uttered forth, from the mouth of Elspeth Kimball. Barney rolled his eyes.

"Miz Elspeth, you ain't said a word at these meetin's in six months! What's it *now*?"

Elspeth wrung her hands nervously and took a deep breath. She looked around at the disarray of the Golden Memories Chapel/Peaceful Slumber Room. The residents of Chestnut Ridge were mentally exhausted and ready to leave.

"Mister Mayor, it is my humble opinion that we should at least *try* to heavily promote the Festival this year, instead of just giving up! I'd be happy to break the Federal Rules Against Post Office Impropriety and deliver the fliers on regular carrier routes!"

Barney threw his hands into the air and banged the gavel repeatedly. "*MEETIN' ADJOURNED*!"

The good citizens of Chestnut Ridge filed out of the Quigley Funeral Parlor in a daze; Bull McArdle led a handcuffed Hoot Graham to the foyer and prepared to cart him off to jail, but he was interrupted by Leonard Festrunk.

"Chief, you mind if I's ta have a word with my son?"

Bull nodded and stepped back. Leonard rubbed a hand over his mouth; he was no good in these situations.

"Son, now, I'm right sorry you gotta go off ta jail! An' I'm right sorry I done missed alla yer PTA meetin's an' such...but when you git outta the pokey, I promise ya, if I'm still kickin', we'll go do us some fishin', ok, although I reckon I gotta punish ya fer showin' yer ass in public. But I love you, son, I ain't never tol' ya before, but I'll be thinkin' 'bout ya ever' day! Me an' your Mama, we's us a pair! Now, son, this is gonna hurt me more than it's a gonna hurt you, but I promised Nell, an' son, I'm a man a my word...you done a bad, bad thing over ta that bank!"

Leonard Festrunk rared back a hand and laid Hoot Graham's lip wide open. Hoot growled and then broke into tears. Leonard rubbed his knuckles and waved as Bull McArdle led Hoot away.

"*Bye*, son, you behave, now, like a good boy! I'll come see ya, on yer visitin' days! An' son...you make yer daddy proud! Don't ya be wastin' my taxpayer dollars over there at that penitent'ry now, *ya hear*?"

CHAPTER TWENTY-SEVEN – TURN OF THE CENTURY

Friday, September 7, 1999; Nashville International Airport

AnnElise Leigh-Lee stomped through the Nashville International Airport in an effort to beat Forrestine Culpepper to the baggage claim. Fourteen hours on a series of planes with Forrestine and her incessant chatter on proper airplane hygiene had given her a massive headache, and she intended to point out her bags to a porter and sneak a cigarette before Danita Kay arrived to take them home. She flagged down a feeble man with a cart and instructed him to collect her bags and wait for her on the curb near the "ARRIVALS" level. Then she stepped through the electric doors, walked to the far corner of the building and lit a cigarette with shaking hands.

The events of the previous weeks replayed in her frazzled mind. For the first five days, the trip to the Greek spa had been an enormous, luxurious success. In a brilliant stroke of luck upon their arrival, they learned that the Greek telephone workers decided to take a two-week strike. AnnElise sent a simple telegram conveying that fact to Richard, informing him that she was much too much engrossed in follicle care to be bothered with messages and phone conversations, and would he do her a favor and relay the same message to the Reverend Culpepper on Forrestine's behalf. Everything tripped along fantastically until Monday. On Monday, the strike ended, and during her therapeutic massage session with Ari, one of the salon maids delivered a fax to her from Richard; he was filing for divorce and living in sin with none other than her sworn rival Dorothy Graham, in a brand new condo in West Palm Beach. He intended to take her to the cleaners in retribution for blocking him from her bed five years prior and he had retained one of the best shark lawyers in the country to do it.

The confounding thing to AnnElise was Richard's mention of some kind of lewd videotape she'd supposedly starred in…as hard as she racked her brain, that one just didn't compute; the only tape that came to mind was the one that *bitch* Dorothy'd referred to, the secret blackmail video that supposedly featured prominent citizens boinking in the bathroom during the Masked Ball… then it dawned on her… she'd innocently toyed with the janitor as he came in to clean the restrooms, as the Masked Ball crowd filed out. *Surely they don't have that on…surely they don't think that I…no, it's not possible…I only flirted with him! Maybe I flipped him a little cleavage, or kissed his neck, but I was drunk! I only pretended to want him! Oh, this can't be happening*…AnnElise threw the fax in the trash as Ari informed her that he could not be expected to work massage miracles if she remained so tense.

On Tuesday, as she awoke to the realization that she might have to actually find a job, or at the very least, a new rich husband to support her, she'd called Danita Kay, to persuade her daughter to be sensible and approach Richard with some kind of mediation plan. Danita, however, informed her mother that she should from this moment forth refer to her as *'Pooky,'* and that she was not allowed to discuss the pending divorce case or her parents' legal affairs, as she had been unanimously elected Chairman of Leigh-Lee & Sons following Richard's resignation and his subsequent recommendation of Pooky to the Board. It was simply now a conflict of interest.

Danita Kay did, however, bring her mother up to speed with respect to the crazy happenings in the burg of Chestnut Ridge during the weeks her mother, sister and Forrestine spent traipsing in and out of the Greek health spa. When Pooky expressed surprise that her mother had not seen anything about either the Cooler Jesus Miracle or the pornographic billboards on any of CNN's international newscasts, AnnElise replied that she was way too involved in Ari's plan for restoring her natural skin elasticity to take a break and do something so mundane as watch the news or look at a paper. When Danita Kay inquired as to the reason why AnnElise had not made use of her cell phone to call home, she replied weakly that Forrestine had borrowed the phone and lost it at some silly, weather-beaten ruin called the Acropolis.

On Wednesday, after a mutually satisfying midday romp in the hay with Ari, in her private suite at the spa, AnnElise showered, and dressed in her spa robe, padded down the hall to the room shared by Tiffany Noel and Forrestine. She intended to personally inspect Tiffany's pores for signs of pigment impediments, as Ari had advised her to do; they had arrived at a critical juncture in Tiffany Noel's tanning program, and the condition of her pigment cells were now at a make or break point.

Despite AnnElise's repeated knocks for her daughter, however, no one answered the door to Tiffany and Forrestine's room. She rang the maid for a spare key and remembered that Forrestine had taken a day trip to Athens to purchase more cheek mud. Upon entering the room, AnnElise noticed that Tiffany's closet was bare; her shoes, jewelry, everything she owned was gone. She screamed and stormed down to the front desk where she found Ari fondling the silken backside of a young spa patron in a thong bikini.

Ari laughed at AnnElise's fury and told her that she was merely experiencing what it was like to love a Greek man for the first time, and that all Greek men expected their women to be obedient and share their bounty with other lovers. He retrieved a note from Tiffany that had been stuffed into AnnElise's mailbox and AnnElise promptly slapped him on the face and returned to her room. She poured a glass of scotch, took a tranquilizer, sat down on the bed and read her daughter's note, which was scratched in Tiffany's sloppy handwriting on a piece of spa stationery.

'Dear Mama, You know that guy we met, Dmitri, the good-looking hunk in the navy sportcoat and white slacks? He has a gigantic diamond pinky ring and his daddy owns all those tankers we saw in the harbor? Well, we have been meeting every night after dinner, when you think I've been swimming laps in the spa pool. He's amazing, Mama and he's asked me to go to someplace called Lickinstine with him...his family owns a castle there and a grape farm, I think...he wants to buy a movie studio, and he says that with my face, I have a real future as a film goddess (don't tell Miss F., she'll think that I'm changing religions and give you a lecture). Don't worry, I'll call you in a couple of weeks. Please tell Miss Forrestine I'm sorry, but Dmitri says the Miss American Beauty pageant organization cannot fully appreciate my sensuality, or something like that. Say hey to Daddy and Danita Kay and Delilah, too. Love, T.N. XXOO'

Upon Forrestine Culpepper's return from her Athens mud-buying shopping spree, she insisted that a maid open the door to AnnElise's suite, after fifteen minutes of unanswered knocking and telephoning; she discovered Tiffany's note, as well as AnnElise who was passed out on the bed. Forrestine read the note and then slumped in a brocade-covered chair and wept for an hour, ignoring her own advice with respect to running mascara. *Twice, that little bitch has dumped me for a man,* she cried, *twice she has robbed me of my right to see my best contender win the Miss American Beauty pageant!* Forrestine stepped out onto AnnElise's spacious balcony.

I certainly don't have a view like this from my room, she mused. She angrily shook her fists at God. *You've let me down for the last time, I tell you! If this is one of your little tests, well, you can just forget it! I quit! No more missions to beauty-deprived countries! No more monuments in your honor! Cameron can just find another Sunday School superintendent, that does it! How can I ever show my face in public again?*

On Thursday, as AnnElise nursed a hangover and screamed at Ari, Forrestine spent the entire day on the phone, trying to track down the errant Tiffany Noel. Near eight in the evening, she finally located the young woman with the paid assistance of one of the spa workers who was fluent in both Greek and English.

"*You listen to me, young lady*! Your father's filed for divorce! Your mother's a *wreck*! She's using *chemicals* to console herself! Now, you get yourself on a *plane* and get back here by tomorrow afternoon so we can pack up and leave this godforsaken place and go *home*! You will not do this to me! Think how hard I worked to bring the Miss American Beauty Pageant to Chestnut Ridge! You're practically a shoe-in, missy! You can ruin your life *after* you win that crown!"

Tiffany Noel held the phone away from her ear and ran a naked, tanned leg seductively up the equally naked, tanned leg of Dmitri as they lounged in his father's castle-top hot tub.

"Miss Forrestine, let's be realistic, *ok*? *Let's review*...a castle and Dmitri, or you...*NOT!* Now that you have my phone number and you know I'm safe, you and Mom can go back home and live your boring little lives, *ok*? But I've discovered a new way to have fun and I'm *never* going to give it up...don't you want to know what it is, Miss F.? It's *S-E-X,* that's what it is and I don't care if it ruins my pores, or my skin tone, or rots my teeth! I never knew I could feel so good and have such a great time doing it! Look, Miss Forrestine, you'll just have to work your skin tone magic on somebody else...why don't you give Chastity Weatherford a call? She'll look a lot better in that Miss American Beauty tiara than I will...it's so big, it'll balance her fat ass! I'm sure *she* could use your help! Gotta go, now, *bye*!"

With that, AnnElise and Forrestine packed their bags; in actuality, Forrestine packed all the bags while AnnElise drank Scotch straight from the bottle. Forrestine then insisted on being taxied to the Athens airport in the middle of the night to demand the next flight home. They were informed, however, by their driver, upon their arrival at the airport and upon finding it closed, that in Greece, the airport closes at ten p.m. and there are no flights to America until three o'clock the following afternoon. Their driver refused their offers of cash and credit cards in exchange for depositing them at a decent hotel; his girlfriend was waiting and he was already late. And because the citizens of Greece *knew* the airport was closed, no other taxis or vehicles dropped by to offer them a ride. Forrestine located a payphone, but neither savvy world traveler had any Greek coins and AnnElise's cell phone was long since lost in the ancient dust of the Acropolis.

AnnElise and Forrestine spent the next eight hours sitting on their luggage in front of the Athens International Airport. When Forrestine unlocked her suitcase to find her makeup remover in an effort to preserve her skin tone, AnnElise screamed insults at her and kicked the makeup bag down an open, stinking sewer. Forrestine discovered a half-eaten package of peanut butter crackers in the bottom of her purse; it was the last of the two-dozen packages she brought from home, because one simply could not trust foreign cuisine. She did not offer so much as a cracker crumb to AnnElise, but openly ate her snack, and then, in violation of all Forrestine Culpepper Beauty Principle Basics, loudly smacked her lips.

AnnElise smoked fourteen cigarettes in succession and promptly developed a sick headache. At six in the morning the doors to the airport opened and the two women changed their tickets, checked their luggage and dashed to a restroom to freshen up as best they could. AnnElise was tempted to purchase a new *lingerie ensemble* in Duty Free, but suddenly remembered that she would soon be involved in divorce proceedings and that she might be required to somehow borrow money to pay for everything she purchased, subsequent to Richard's faxed intentions.

AnnElise placed a collect call to Danita Kay, informing her of their imminent departure and relaying the fact that her sister was cavorting recklessly across half of Europe with a gentleman named Dmitri. She'd then boarded the first in a tedious series of airplanes and now, AnnElise and Forrestine were only minutes away from being rescued by Danita Kay; in an hour, they would be home. AnnElise snubbed out her cigarette as she saw Danita Kay's white Volvo station wagon round the corner of the "ARRIVALS" port. She flagged down her daughter and was surprised to see Roland Gastineau driving Danita 's car. She hugged Danita Kay tightly, ignored Roland, then the three of them watched as the porter attempted to deposit the luggage next to the car, despite Forrestine's insistence on showing him the photos from her recent trip to the fringe of the Holy Land. Forrestine climbed into the backseat as did Roland, who noticed that both Forrestine and AnnElise smelled ripe with perspiration, smoke and olive oil. In roughly ten minutes' time, Forrestine fell soundly asleep. AnnElise would have liked to nap as well; however, 'Pooky' and Roland wanted to personally deliver some very exciting news. Danita Kay tapped the steering wheel in excitement.

"Mom, I told you about the Poe House Cooler and all that billboard business...well, as a result, but in a separate incident, Roland's father was arrested for embezzlement and he's in jail in Nashville, waiting for trial. Gastineau & Sons is no longer operational, but thankfully, Roland has been cleared of any associated charges. In fact, Roland's coming to work with me, Mom...he'll be heading the tax law division and next Spring, he's received permission from the Dean at UVA to complete his coursework by correspondence, isn't that great? We'll be renaming the firm...Leigh-Lee & Gastineau, what do you think?"

AnnElise rubbed her forehead. "That's simply fascinating, *ma cher*. Now, if you don't mind..."

"But that's not the *biggest* news, is it, Roland, sweetie?"

Roland grinned and patted Pooky on the back. AnnElise didn't like where this was headed; she didn't like this at all. She could not be expected to concentrate on her daughter's personal life when her own world was threatening to end in serious, money-grabbing litigation.

"The *big* news is that Roland and I are *engaged*, Mom! See my ring...isn't it *gorgeous*? Roland got a *great* deal on it! You always said you wanted a June bride in the family...what do you think? You and Izzy can talk about all the details...oh, did I mention Izzy and Roland are staying in the guest house for awhile until the IRS releases the lien on their home?"

AnnElise's head pounded; she needed a drink, a smoke and a tranquilizer, fast. "*Mais non*, dear, it must have slipped your mind...Danita ...excuse me, *Pooky*, would you mind stepping up the pace a bit? I...*what is that ridiculous sign*? Welcome to *Baileyville*? Danita Kay, did you take a wrong turn? *No*, there's the town square...is this some kind of *joke*?"

Forrestine stirred and opened one eye as Roland chuckled.

"Oh, didn't Pooky tell you? Henry Bailey is a certified millionaire! He was discovered to be the long-lost ancestor of some Colonel E. A. Gray, from Richmond, Virginia. I won't go into all the details, but Henry's got a new bank account full of settlement money and we found out he's the proud descendant of a respectable, Virginia blue-blood family, one that came over on the Mayflower, as a matter of fact! Turns out, his great-great-granddaddy was the one whose money bankrolled the rebuilding of the town, you know, when they repaired the grist mill and he should have been credited as the rightful founder of Chestnut Ridge, not the Festrunks, the Grahams, or the Leigh-Lees... oh, sorry, I guess I thought Pooky would have explained everything to you both by now..."

AnnElise's mouth gaped open; not only was her husband divorcing her, using some kind of scandalous bathroom episode as allowable courtroom evidence, her social position as the wife of a founding-father descendant was apparently now being challenged. Roland droned on.

"Well, according to a federal judge, Henry *could* have dragged Chestnut Ridge into a hundred million dollar lawsuit, since the town survived on money stolen from his great-great-granddaddy by the Major, the Captain and the Lieutenant. But he'd have pretty much closed us all down, so Henry opted for a single million dollar lump sum, tax-free and everybody was so ecstatic, they voted to rename the town for him! Besides, we haven't had any chestnut trees around here for over seventy-five years, so I guess it was time for a new name."

AnnElise and Forrestine sighed. They could not, in their wildest imaginings, picture Henry Bailey as a wealthy, respectable citizen, with Virginia blue blood racing in his veins. Neither could AnnElise imagine that she was now living in a place referred to as *'Baileyville.'* She would surely be dropped from the Charleston social register after word got out. AnnElise decided she was having either a bad Twilight Zone-esque dream or hallucinations from smoking too many cigarettes in one fell swoop. As Pooky turned the Volvo into town, they passed the Festrunk Clinic and Forrestine read aloud from a construction sign, parked in front of a trailer.

"NELL GRAHAM MEMORIAL OBSTETRICS WING...what in the *world?* Did poor Mother Nell finally pass?"

Danita Kay nodded, "Yes, Miss Forrestine, I'm afraid so. But she amended her will and gave a ton of money to the Clinic and to Leonard Festrunk. Oh, that's another thing...*Hoot* Graham is only *Will* Graham's half-brother...it seems Leonard Festrunk was his *father* and he and Aunt Nell had a wild fling during the War...isn't that a *kick*?"

AnnElise inhaled sharply and pressed a cheek against the cool glass of the front window. "Oh, it's a *kick*, all right, that's exactly what it is...*mon Dieu*, Danita Kay! I don't think I can take any more surprises...we've only been away four weeks...this is *preposterous*! I feel as though I've been written into an extremely bad Dickens novel!"

Forrestine clicked her tongue and rolled her eyes at her former travel companion. "I *told* you, AnnElise, that strange things would start to happen as we count down to the new Millennium! We must all straighten our affairs, put our houses in order as the Good Book says, or we will be smited by the Angels of the Lord and made to suffer intolerable pain...I know I intend to have *my* little personal affairs tidied up *well* before the Pageant begins! I can't afford to take any chances! I only hope Chastity Weatherford's family adheres to my same philosophy...I suppose I'll have to discuss that upfront, when I call to inform them my services are now available..."

Pooky shook her head. "Uh, Miss Forrestine...didn't you hear? With everything that's happened in the last few weeks, city council voted to cancel the Festival completely...that means there won't *be* a Festival Queen Pageant."

Forrestine raised an eyebrow. "Oh, dear, no! Well, I'm not surprised, based on everything that has apparently taken place in our absence! No matter, Chastity Weatherford already has the requisite titles to enter the Miss American Beauty Pageant; have you two purchased your tickets yet? Oh, won't it be great, all that Pageant pomp and finery in our own home town!"

And all the associated credit inscribed in the annals of Pageant history in my name, thank-you-very-much, Forrestine silently mused. Pooky glanced at Roland in the rearview mirror.

"Miss Forrestine...I don't know how to break this to you, but when word got out about those obscene billboards and the Cooler Jesus Miracle fiasco and then the Sons of Glory Festival was cancelled, well, the Miss American Beauty Pageant Grand Marshal came to town and informed us that they would be relocating the Pageant to Lansing, Michigan. He said it was more representative of Middle America and traditional family values ...I'm really sorry!"

Forrestine Culpepper leaned back against the headrest in the backseat of the Volvo. She forced herself to silently repeat her motto, *'Public tears are the chinks in the mortar of self-control.'* This absolutely could *not* be happening; she could not be expected to steer Chastity Weatherford to a winning crown in a place as totally devoid of Southern grace and manners as Lansing, Michigan! That was it! She would tell Cameron tonight; she planned to convert to Hinduism…it was obvious to Forrestine Culpepper that her one, true Christian God was out to lunch, *permanently* and in her profession, she required twenty-four-hour a day backup, the backup that only a whole *host* of gods could provide! *I wonder if you can still be a Hindu without one of those stupid red dots on your forehead…red is just not my color…*

AnnElise stared out the window as they waited for the Main Street traffic light to change. In place of the former Henry Bailey Used Car Lot, there was now a sparkling expanse of macadam, covered in shining late-model Cadillacs. A sign on the front of a small metal building with a glass front proclaimed, *"MILLIONAIRE MOTORS."* She spied Henry Bailey, in a surprisingly well-tailored navy suit and a tie, tapping the fender of a red DeVille as he handed the keys to a happy new customer. As Pooky drove past the car lot, Henry and his customer, Miss Amelia Festrunk, looked up and waved. Henry chuckled as Amelia got into the shiny vehicle.

"Well, Miz Amelia, ya sure are one lucky gal! This here's the besta the best! An' red's yer color, I do b'lieve!"

Amelia smiled and placed her bony hands on the white leather-wrapped steering wheel. She inhaled the intoxicating scent of new car and turned to Henry.

"I ought to be ashamed of myself, paying this much for basic transportation! I don't even get out much anymore…just to the Red Cross a few times a week. But it sure is fun, Henry and I thank you for all your efforts. I would have preferred *green,* though, but I guess at my age it's time for a touch of wildness."

Henry rocked on his heels and nodded. "Yep, Miz Amelia…I'd say ya done had more'n yer fair share a serious stuff, carryin' alla that mis'ry 'round all them years."

Amelia raised her hand to speak but Henry cut her off. "Nope. I ain't a gonna hear it no more. You was nothin' but a li'l gal back then an' there's no hard feelin's, 'k? Water unner the bridge as they say. I got me more money than I'll ever need an' I'm happy as a clam on this here new car lot. Bizness is boomin' an' I jus' picked out the sweetest li'l vacation home fer Euladean in PCB…that's all we want outta life, Miz A…each other'n ta be happy. I'm proud I can holt my head up high, ain't no need ta be 'shamed a bein' a Bailey no more. Miz A…I shore hope you can be happy, too."

Amelia nodded and smiled. "Well, let me figure out how to start this thing so I can go show Leonard! He's moving into Will's big house today…Will insisted. They're gonna go fishing and then visit Hoot at the prison, I think, and I'm due at the Red Cross…big blood drive today, you know. You take care, Henry Bailey…you take care!"

Henry waved at his satisfied customer and trotted into the new office of MILLIONAIRE MOTORS. Euladean smiled at her husband from the dealership switchboard. Fastened to her light blue dress was Maureen Bailey's filigreed pearl engagement brooch, restored and polished to its antebellum glory. Henry greeted the ten-odd customers inside the showroom, then pointed to an idle salesman with a stern gesture that suggested he should get off his lazy duff and approach the browsers. He crossed to Euladean and gently lifted her operator's headset.

"Hey, honeybunny! The Carsons just took d'livery! I ain't never seen a gal so pleased! An' guess what? I jus' seen Miss Pooky in her big Volvo… *'at reminds me, I gotta talk ta her 'bout the extravaglances of a Cadillac*…she's drivin' her mama an' Miz Forrestine home from the airport, I reckon."

Euladean smiled, answered a call and waved a finger at Henry to hold on.

"*'GoodDayMillionaireMotorsHowMayIHep-You? Just a moment, please, I'll transfer'*… Hon, is fish sticks ok for supper? I hadn't had a chance ta thaw nothin' else out, I keep forgettin' we got that big ol' new deep freeze!"

Henry nodded blankly, as if distracted. "Ya know, babe, I was jus' *thinkin'*…now that Miz Leigh-Lee's back, we gotta have her over ta the new double-wide…she'd prob'ly'd like ta catch up on ever'thang's been happ'nin', ya know, shake the dust off her skivvies…I mean, she's s'posed ta be one a them *Charleston* bluebloods, ain't she? I betcha ten bucks we's *r'lated*, somehow, you reckon? Ya know, alla them bluebloods done intramarried back in them days…yep, won't she be su'prised ta hear we prob'ly got fam'ly ties?"

Henry slapped a hand on top of the marble receptionist counter. The idea sounded better every second.

"Yep, hon, whyn't ya give her a call in a few…we can stop by the Poe House on the way home an' pick up a coupla more packs a fish sticks…I mean, jus' 'cause we got *money*, don't mean we cain't hob-nob with our friends over a few fish sticks! An' besides, I reckon Miz L-L's all by her lonesome now that her man's done filed fer divorce. She's prob'ly got a powerful hankerin' fer a good, home-cooked meal…served in the comp'ny of a fine, upstandin' Virgin-yan like myse'f, 'cause, *ya know*, us bluebloods, we gotta stick *tagether*! Like *glue*!"

-finis-

About the Author

Bunkie Lynn was born in Tucson, Arizona, raised in the American South, earned a B.S. in Radio-TV-Film from the University of Texas at Austin, and now resides near Nashville, Tennessee. Although the lazy, pj'd life of an author is her preferred calling, she dutifully avoided a serious writing career through forays into advertising, public relations, international business management and motherhood. When she's not spending time with her husband, son and two Labradors, Bunkie is presently working on her next novel…unless something lazier and more lucrative comes along.

About the Artist

Klair Kimmey was born, a good while ago, in Atlanta, Georgia – a true southern city in a very southern state. After completing her tour of the SEC, Klair received her B.S. in Fine Art from the University of Tennessee. In the following years she has worked in the field of graphic design, married a Knoxville boy, and brought another Knoxville boy into the world. Working on this book has been a fun journey – like revisiting her roots. "I talk the way this book is written… what's so funny?"

To order copies of ***A Comedy of Heirs,*** you may visit the author's website at www.bunkielynn.com for wholesaler and bookseller links.

LadyBug Publishing LLC is a member of the Publisher's Marketing Association. Contact the publisher at ladybugpublishing@aol.com.

For author appearance and event information, and previews of Bunkie Lynn's next comedy fiction novel, visit www.bunkielynn.com.